all the Angels were Jewish

Other Books by Kevin E. Ready:

—

The Big One (1997)

Gaia Weeps - The Crisis of Global Warming (1998)

The Holy Koran - Modern English Translation (editor) (2014)

—

<u>and with **Cap Parlier:**</u>

TWA 800 - Accident or Incident? (1998)

all the  Angels

were  Jewish

by

Kevin E. Ready

SAINT GAUDENS PRESS
Wichita, Kansas & Santa Barbara, California

See other great books available from Saint Gaudens Press
http://www.SaintGaudensPress.com

Saint Gaudens Press
Post Office Box 405
Santa Barbara, CA 93464-0405

Cover Art and Concept by Alicia Tauty
with contribution by Michel Mota Da Cruz via http://www.123RF.com

**Saint Gaudens, Saint Gaudens Press
and the Winged Liberty colophon
are trademarks of Saint Gaudens Press**

**This edition originally published in hardcover in 2014,
entitled The Disambiguation of Susan
This edition Copyright © 2016 Kevin E. Ready
All rights reserved.**

**Print edition ISBN: 978-0-943039-20-6
eBook ISBN: 978-0-943039-31-2
Library of Congress Catalog Number - 2016908074**

Printed in the United States of America

This is a work of fiction. No character is intended to depict any real person, living or dead. Certain entities, including business, charitable, religious and educational institutions and even some famous families, are depicted for purposes of providing a proper setting for the reader to understand, enjoy and relate to the fictional story. The policies, activities and people associated with these entities, as depicted in this story, are also fictionalized. Other names, characters and incidents are the products of the author's imagination and bear no relationship to real events, or persons living or deceased.

—

In accordance with the Copyright Act of 1976 [PL 94-553; 90 Stat. 2541] and the Digital Millennium Copyright Act of 1998 (DMCA) [PL 105-304; 112 Stat. 2860], the scanning, uploading, or electronic sharing of any part of this book without the permission of the publisher constitutes unlawful piracy and theft of the author's intellectual property. If you wish to use material from this book (other than for review purposes), prior written permission must be obtained by contacting the publisher at: editorial@saintgaudenspress.com. Thank you for your support of the author's rights.

"I wanted a perfect ending. Now I've learned, the hard way, that some poems don't rhyme, and some stories don't have a clear beginning, middle, and end. Life is about not knowing, having to change, taking the moment and making the best of it, without knowing what's going to happen next. Delicious Ambiguity."

Gilda Radner (1946-1989)

Chapter One

Susan startled when the rarely used desk phone rang to life at her elbow. Her constant companion iPhone made the old land line a relic. She had tried to disconnect the land line, but discovered it was part of the cable TV, phone and internet package her father had signed up for, so it remained. The old phone number had been the same as long as Susan could remember. One of her earliest memories was learning to recite that phone number and their address in Moline before starting kindergarten.

Her voice conveyed her curiosity about who would be calling on that line when she answered, "Hello?"

"Yes, hello. Is this Miss Fisher?" The deep baritone voice had some faint accent, but it was not the common Mid-West accent one usually heard in Moline, Illinois.

"Yes, and who is calling?" Susan replied.

"Miss Fisher, my name is David Tannenbaum. I am an attorney with the law firm of Wassermann, Ephraim and Moore, in New York."

Susan closed the Facebook page and the browser window she had open on the Macbook on the desk in front of her to pay attention to the call. She replied, "I see, and …?"

The man's voice said, "Before I explain the reason for my call, could you confirm you are Susannah Rachel Fisher, the niece of Mrs. Rachel Metzger?"

Susan ignored the slight misstatement of her first name and answered, "Yes, Rachel Metzger is my aunt."

Susan heard the man quickly clear his throat before saying, "Miss Fisher, it is my unfortunate duty to inform you that your Aunt has passed away."

Susan did not say anything. Her reaction was both due to astonishment at hearing a sentence like that, as well as the fact that she had no idea what to say in response.

Susan's delay in answering caused the attorney to ask, "Miss Fisher? I know getting news like this is a shock, but there is really no other way to tell you."

Susan struggled with words, "Yes, uh, well … How did it happen?"

"Mrs. Metzger passed away this morning at Columbia Presbyterian Hospital. She had been ill for some time."

"But, I just saw her a couple months ago," Susan fumbled for words, "… she seemed fine."

"Yes, she mentioned that she had not told you of her illness. She was concerned about you having lost your parents quite recently and she did not want to burden you with her illness. It has been clear for some time that she was in her last days and she wanted to save you from all that."

Susan again fumbled for words, "But, I … she … I just …."

"Miss Fisher, I understand. You have my condolences at your loss." The attorney said. "I am sorry to have to surprise you with news like this. However, I needed to let you know. And, we need to get you here to New York as soon as possible."

Susan paused again, and then said, "Pardon…, to New York?"

"Yes, Miss Fisher, you realize there are arrangements that must be made. They cannot wait. And, our firm needs to talk to you about the estate."

"Estate?"

"Yes, Miss Fisher. You are Mrs. Metzger's next of kin and our firm is handling the estate. There are many things we need to talk to you about and it is our policy to do so in person, not over the phone. And, as you know, the funeral arrangements cannot wait." He paused for a moment. "To assist you in this time of sorrow, our firm has taken to liberty of arranging a pre-paid ticket first thing tomorrow for you to come to New York."

"Tomorrow?" Susan questioned.

"Yes, your flight leaves Chicago O'Hare airport at 6:40 tomorrow morning. We will arrange to have you met at the airport here in New York. All you need to do is take down the reservation number and get your ticket from the desk at the airport byshowing your ID. Everything will be ready for you."

"Well, I guess…." Susan paused. She was vaguely aware that her end of this conversation was entirely one-word answers or disjointed questions.

The attorney continued, "Do you have something to copy the reservation number with?"

"Uh, yes, just a minute." Susan found a pen on the desk and an old utility bill envelope to write on.

Susan copied down the airline reservation number and the name, office and cell phone numbers of the attorney. Then, the attorney ended the call with a promise to see her the next morning and the assurance that if she needed anything, anything at all, she should call him.

She had barely put the old phone handset into its answering machine cradle when Susan realized a problem with the reservations. The New York attorney had assumed that a flight from Chicago was satisfactory, but Illinois was a big state and Moline was at least a three-hour drive to Chicago. To get to a 6:40 flight she would have to drive in the wee hours of the morning, if she drove. Also, she did not like the idea of leaving her car at the Chicago airport.

Susan reopened the laptop browser window she had been using when the phone rang to see if she could find a connecting flight from the nearby Quad City Airport in Moline to Chicago. As she checked the travel websites, her thoughts flitted between her memories of Aunt Rachel and the other thoughts that Rachel's death brought to mind.

Rachel Metzger had been her mother's sister. As the attorney had mentioned, both of Susan's parent had passed away in the past year. Her father had been an only child and this Aunt Rachel was the only sibling of her mother. All of her grandparents had long since passed away. Bluntly put, this dead aunt was the last living relative Susan had ever met, and now, she, too, was gone.

She had no idea how such things were handled, but the prepaid ticket seemed unusual to her, but then she had little experience with what was the usual in the ways of New York lawyers.

Susan had checked her iPhone for the time. The lifeless clock on the wall had dead batteries, since her mother had last changed them before her death and Susan always used her cell phone for checking the time anyway. She never used a watch. Nobody her age did, not with their smartphones at hand. She saw she had time to call her work, at the Macy's in the shopping mall across the Mississippi in Davenport, Iowa and tell her boss who worked the day shift that she would be going to New York.

There was no problem with Susan taking off work; the Macy's store manager liked his best cosmetic counter salesgirl. He gave his apparently concerned condolences at Susan's loss and told her to take whatever time she needed. June was not a very busy month for the department store anyway. She knew the manager remembered the two previous funeral leaves she had taken in the last year and she assumed he was honestly concerned for her. He was a good man and not bad to work for. The spring term at Augustana College, in neighboring Rock Island, Illinois, had ended in late May and now, in early June, she had not registered for any summer term classes, so her college schedule was not a factor. Susan was free to travel to New York.

The web browser now showed a regional feeder airline had an evening flight out of the Quad Cities, but nothing the next morning that would make her connection to the flight the law firm had scheduled. She would have to overnight in Chicago, but that was better than driving to Chicago. Susan had to hurry though.

After reserving her connecting ticket and a cheap room at a Super 8 motel in Elk Grove, close in to O'Hare, Susan went to the garage and pulled her father's old, black American Tourister suitcase from the top of a pile of boxes and his stored possessions that had not been touched since his death. A similar pile of her mother's things was next to it. The entire garage floor was a morass of piles of storage boxes. Susan's old mental note that she 'had to go through all this stuff' reoccurred to her, and she suppressed it yet again. Her father's old suitcase was bigger than hers was, and had wheels, and she could get by on the trip to New York with only one checked bag. She wondered if her ticket to New York required a checked bag fee, some of the airlines did and some, like the feeder airline she had booked to Chicago, did not.

—

Susan could have used her Illinois driver's license for ID, but instead used her old passport. The TSA officer's fingers quickly thumbed the two pages to where a photo was in a US passport and turned the passport sideways and up to compare to the young woman who stood before his lectern. While the photo in the passport was of a wide-eyed teenager with her dark hair pulled tightly back, the woman before him had waves of golden-brown hair falling to her shoulders. The teenager had copious freckles and a few blemishes, and the woman had a flawless complexion and perfect, if understated, make-up. But, the oval face, wide chin, full lips and high, expressively angled brow above dark brown eyes were the same in both the pictured teenager and the adult beauty before him. He quickly checked the issue date of the passport, then her birthdate. He compared the name on the passport to the boarding pass.

"Miss Fisher, you only have a short time left on this passport. Your five years is almost up. It expires on your 21st birthday in October," he said as he folded the passport and quickly scribbled an illegible scrawl next to the flight number on the boarding pass. "And the passport has 'Susan', but your boarding pass says 'Susannah' you should try to keep them the same, no nicknames."

"Thank you for the reminder. I haven't had much use of this passport recently. And, somebody else purchased the ticket for me. I guess they thought it was Susannah. The passport is right, Susan," she said with a sincere smile as she took her papers back.

"Have a nice trip," he said, his eyes doing an up and down view of her as she turned away.

Ahead of her, groggy business people reformed for yet another long line. Many were carefully draining the last drops of Starbucks before disposing of their cups in the trash and flipping their carry-on bags on the conveyor belt that fed into the X-ray machine. Loose change, car keys, eyeglasses, shoes and wristwatches were noisily dumped into the nylon trays that followed the black bags into the maw of the scanner machine. The early, red-eye flights from Chicago's O'Hare airport to New York's JFK were primarily the domain of these Midwestern salesmen and corporate employees making an obligatory early morning pilgrimage to clients, home offices or trade shows in New York.

Susan smiled at the TSA officer behind the conveyor belt and went to get in line to walk through the body scanners. She was oblivious of the interest shown her by her fellow travelers and the TSA body scanner operator. The operator seemed a bit disappointed that she went quickly through the first scanner archway without a beep, preempting his ability to pass his flat, gray scanning wand near her trim body. He was disappointed that the sweater dress had not budged when she was asked to raise her arms over her head and spin around for his 3D scanner, not once but twice. The only metal that highlighted on his 3D scanner screen were the dual crescents of her under-wire bra and her earring posts, she did not even have metal dental fillings.

—

From: Peter Ephraim <pephraim@wassermannephraim.com>
To: David Tannenbaum <dtannenbaum@wassermannephraim.com>
Subj: Metzger, Rachel
CONFIDENTIAL Attorney Work Product
DO NOT FILE IN CLIENT FILES

Dave,

Before our new client gets to town, double check any files she might have access to and make sure any personal notes or requests from Rachel that could embarrass our new client are removed and put in attorney eyes only files, things like the request for a P.I. report and credit check on the niece.

Peter

—

Susan Fisher gathered her backpack, shoes and purse from the exit landing of the X-ray. As she walked down the concourse, she double checked the gate number on the boarding pass and found her seat assignment.

She had actually slept well at the motel near the airport and she would probably be awake for the whole trip east. She tucked the passport into her purse and, in turn, zipped the purse in the front backpack pouch. All she needed to board was the boarding pass. Her backpack would fit easily in the overhead bin.

Susan had gotten that passport for a trip to Paris, when she was sixteen. The thought of the passport brought her back to the nagging thoughts of her parents and their deaths. Her father had been lost to a massive stroke that had defied his lifelong healthy lifestyle and love of sport and adventure. Her mother, lost to a vicious onset of something called wheat cell carcinoma that hearkened back to a youthful penchant for Winston filters. Susan suspected that the quick death of her mother also had something to do with the loss of her mother's soul mate and love of her life. Her mother was gone only six months after her father's death. Heartbreak and cancer were a deadly combination.

Now, the New York attorney had told her she must deal with this next death.

Susan's mind went through the few memories of her aunt she had. In her memory, Susan could only trace a recollection of a few meetings with Aunt Rachel. There may have been more in early childhood, but not in her conscious memory. She remembered a couple trips with her mother to New York. She had vague memories of a trip when she was very little, just a blur of disconnected memories. The next trip, when she was eight or nine, stood out. Her aunt had shown them the town in great style and Susan had fond memories of the good times and the joy her mother had in talking for hours with her older sister. There was another trip through New York in her tweener years where the whole family had laid over in New York on a trip to some place and both her mother and father stayed up late into the night comparing notes and life stories with Aunt Rachel. Susan had been bored stiff as she knew none of the people or events that seemed to so intrigue her parents and her aunt. However, Susan did recall falling asleep while fooling around with the laptop computer her aunt had carried to the hotel room with her. At the time, nearly ten years before, a laptop computer that could get the internet in a hotel room had been a unique treat. Back in Moline, the home computer that her father used for work was not to be played with by little girls. Times had changed since then.

Her last and most vivid recollections of Aunt Rachel was when she appeared for both her father's and her mother's funeral. On the first occasion, her mother and Aunt Rachel had spent hours talking and commiserating, and Susan had been only peripherally involved in those conversations. But, the next time, after the funeral ceremony for Susan's mother, a seemingly frailer Aunt Rachel had reminisced with Susan about her life with her sister Rebecca, Susan's mother. Stories of moderately risqué conduct in late '60's New York and the dreams, adventures and loves of the young women.

Rachel Metzger was a good storyteller and did a better job telling of the childhood and young adulthood of her mother than her mother had done in twenty years. She heard more about her dead grandparents from Rachel than she ever had from her mother. In retrospect, Susan now realized that her aunt's frailness on the second occasion probably foretold the death that had now taken her, but she had done everything possible to be upbeat with Susan, in spite of the funeral that had taken place that day. Susan was further intrigued that this aunt she barely knew had done graduate study in art and art history, the same field of study Susan was now pursuing at Augustana College. But, this aunt had a postgraduate degree from an Ivy League school. On the other hand, Susan was studying art at a modestly good, but tiny, Midwestern liberal arts college. A college where her father had taught history before his death and which gave the now orphaned daughter of a well-loved professor a big break on tuition.

After many hours, over two days, of esoteric yet meaningful talk with this lonely, but brilliant and cultured old woman, Aunt Rachel had left with Susan promising to come visit her in New York when she had a chance, maybe after the school year. Aunt Rachel had said that would be nice and she hoped it would be possible. Susan had never heard back from Rachel after the visit and in her busy life of school and work, she had forgotten the mention of a visit to New York in the summer. Susan now realized that her aunt's hesitancy to promise a meet-up in New York probably foretold her impending death as it had come only a few months later.

—

As Susan sat in the Chicago airport waiting area, she thought about this being her first plane trip on her own. Every other plane trip had been with one or both of her parents, usually the family's summer vacations. She had also gone with her mother the few times to New York and once with her father to check out colleges in Minneapolis and Boston, before she relented to the inevitable and accepted her fate of attending the college her father had spent most of his life teaching at. Even though her high school grades had made the possibility of a scholarship to someplace else a reality, and the fact that a consortium of small colleges gave mutual aid to children of faculty from the other member schools, she realized that the saved expenses of living at home were a key factor in her college choice. The fact that this college her father taught at had a good reputation in her chosen field of art and art history clenched the decision.

This thought that it was her first trip by plane alone set in motion a chain of thoughts that had perplexed her for many months. Susan's self-image and personal identity had always revolved around her being the daughter of these two people, her parents. Throughout her life she had thought of herself in relation to these parents; those ever-present parents who had rudely taken leave of her this last year. As a teenager, her closeness with both parents had been a blessing in helping her through the pangs and mysteries of puberty. Susan's world-view radiated out from the small Fisher family home in Moline she had known her whole life. Even with her parent's successful attempt to give her a broad range of travel exposure and interests, which range was always grounded in the family unit and her identity as the daughter, the only child, within it. Susan had a nagging feeling that with the rapid deaths of both parents she had become unstuck from her own identity. Without her parents presence the little house was a mere possession, not the central anchor it had once been. Without her parents, Susan's anchor of identity was missing or frayed.

Susan had thought of this emptiness before and had struggled to quantify her own place in things. Sure, she had made a start with her own persona, 'look' and intellectual pursuits. The refined apparel and grooming she had picked up in her two years of part-time work at the Macy's clothing and, then, cosmetics departments were a change for the moderately geeky bookworm she had been in high school. She also had many friends at college and having grown up in the same area for twenty years, not to mention the new contacts one made these days online. None of this really seemed that important anymore, but, then, she had no idea what was important.

The maturity and grounding her relationship with her intelligent and sophisticated parents had given her made her aware that she was not the sort of young girl for whom looks and the blessings good looks could bring were a defining point in her life. The Augustana campus had its share of that sort of girls. She and her best friend Heidi had nicknamed them 'bimbos and jockettes.' However, even in the conversation in which they had named the campus females' cliques "bimbos and jockettes' Susan had realized that while Susan had meant the term to be derogatory, that Heidi did not fully share Susan's disdain for that group and seemed a bit jealous of them.

While she was, indeed, quite attractive, Susan had trouble viewing herself via a self-image of how she looked. Her looks, her face, her body, were mere accouterments, not a part of her own self-definition. Unfortunately, this nagging emptiness left her yearning for that self-definition. Her parents had been born Jewish, but her parents' intellectual secularism had left no place for much, if any, religion in Susan's life and upbringing. In fact, she and her parents had found themselves in an odd position as non-Christians in an overwhelmingly Christian hometown and her father teaching in a small-town college with Lutheran roots. Even her mother's job as a schoolteacher in public schools had been entangled with Christmas plays and Easter vacation that a Jewish teacher found awkward.

Susan herself had never really questioned the religious, or rather the non-religious, aspect of her life, her parents' full gamut of literature and art and history had left her with no need for any of that. That is, until the loss of those parents who had taught her to love the literature and art and history had left her with a vacancy at her core. She had spent her whole life defined as "that Jewish girl on 4ᵗʰ Street," but she realized now that Jewishness played no real part in her life, her beliefs and anything else she viewed as important. Now, recently, she even found herself questioning whether she really wanted to continue studying her college major, art, or whether something else might be more useful and beneficial to study.

The question of religion had come up when the pastor of the Augustana College chapel had asked Susan's mother what sort of service she wanted for the funeral of Susan's father. The grief stricken widow had been unable to give him any guidance. The pastor had known her father for many years and managed to have a friend who was a rabbi at the Jewish temple in Davenport share the duties for the funeral, giving a Hebrew blessing along with a eulogy that was decidedly religiously neutral. Susan could remember her mother sobbing after the Hebrew prayer, but she had never discussed it with her. Then, a short six months later, her mother had joined her father in death and Susan asked the pastor and rabbi to do the same for her. Susan's aunt had been there for both and seemed to be pleased with that. However, all of that still left Susan with little substance to fill her own emptiness of identity and core beliefs. Again, she had always been known as a Jewish girl but she had little Jewishness in her identity or experience. Of course, her knowledge of history and culture made her fully aware of the Jews and things Jewish, but that had simply never been much of a part of her own identity. She could count on one hand the number of times she had been to a Jewish religious service. Her Jewish experience consisted of random cultural icons, a menorah and celebrating Hanukkah instead of Christmas and a few rare stories and family activities that were uniquely Jewish, but which had little impact on her life or self-image. Now, she struggled with what, exactly, that identity was. She still had no answers for herself. She was almost perturbed at her dear, dead parents for sticking her with an ethnic identifier that had no real substance for her.

Susan looked around the airport waiting area. She played the observation game her father had taught her, trying to surmise who a person was and where they were going by just looking at them. Most of her fellow passengers were no challenge. The putty faced businessmen gave off such a disinteresting aura that it was easy to make up a boring tale of sales trips and product conventions for them. On this mid-week day in early June, the mix of students on summer break and families heading out on summer trips were also unchallenging to prognosticate. Only one man was of any real interest to Susan or her imagination. On a row of seats, facing hers across the other side of the boarding gate aisle was a man in a tan sport coat and an open collared white shirt who held only a New York Times in his hand, no carry-on, and his boarding pass showing in a shirt pocket. Susan's interest in him was partly based on his interest in her. He had been staring at Susan much of the time she had been sitting there philosophizing. She had seen that as she flitted her eyes across the room, careful not to lock eye contact with him. She had already done that once, locking eyes with him, and had been forced to return his flirtatious leer with her less enthusiastic smile.

Now, she could feel his gaze. Her identity game guess about him was that he was a dot-com executive heading to New York to close some deal. He was about that age, mid-thirties, and wore well-polished, expensive dress loafers, not Doc Martins or that ilk. In one of her quick views of him, Susan saw that the left hand holding the Times had no ring on the ring finger. So, he may be unmarried, or he might be the type to refuse the male wedding ring, or he could be a cad on a trip without his spouse, having hidden his ring and making eyes at the pretty girl on the plane to New York. That thought made Susan think about what he must be thinking about her if he were playing the guess the identity game.

Many people had told Susan that she looked older than she was, not in a negative sense, but just that nobody would guess that she was only just finishing her sophomore year at college and not yet even 21. Susan's above average height, pretty face, well-endowed, but slim, figure and precise grooming could pass for a woman anywhere in her '20's. The make-up skills that Mrs. Prince, her supervisor at Macy's, had taught her easily camouflaged her youth and had confounded many potential suitors as well as adult Macy's customers who never knew the salesperson giving them a makeover and grooming advice had actually been a teenager at the time. So, what was this dot-com executive guessing about Susan? Besides his being totally wrong about her age, Susan decided he might be guessing she was an advertising rep returning to New York after a trip to sell an ad campaign to her Midwestern clients. Susan was considering this view of herself from his perspective, when she realized his view of her must be confounded by the silly purple backpack at her feet that she carried to protect her laptop. The 20-something advertising agency rep from New York would never carry such a bizarre carry-on, the purple backpack was out of place.

"Good" Susan smiled and thought to herself, "I've got him confused." She made a mental note to consider buying a regular laptop case, maybe one with a handle and wheels. But, then, that would not fit her needs as a student on a college campus. Her introspective view of herself and her admirer's viewing of Susan was interrupted by the boarding call. The admirer stood with her when first-class and mileage-plus members were called first to board. Standing behind him in line, Susan tried to finish her evaluation of him and struggled to see if he had a tan line on his ring finger. Not that she was interested, just curious.

—

Chapter Two

Twitter by @SusyFisher: #airlines I wud really like 2 know whats sposed to happen if some1 leaves their cell on when stewy tells them to turn off in flt. R airliners that sensitive?

—

Twitter by @SusyFisher: #NewYork In Big Apple 4 an adventure.

—

Even with the hour time loss on the flight to New York, it was not quite mid-morning when Susan pulled her suitcase from the huge oval baggage carousel at JFK and headed into the crowd leaving through the imposing stainless steel doors labeled "To Ground Transportation." The flight had been uneventful and unusual for Susan being in 1st Class. Her boarding gate admirer had turned his attention to one of the flight attendants. Outside the baggage claim area, she saw the usual mix of rental car counters, courtesy phones, doors leading outside and a crush of people. To one side she saw a throng of people, mostly in chauffeur's uniforms or wearing taxi drivers' hats, holding up placards with the names of various customers, tour companies or groups they were waiting to pick up. She assumed that was where she would make contact with her ride, but she did not recognize her name on any of the placards. As she watched, the drivers and their passenger clients connected, including one particularly large cluster of oriental tourists, and they filed out the automatic doors to the curb and taxi stand outside, thinning out the waiting crowd a bit. To one side she saw a lanky young man in an ill-fitting pinstripe suit holding a hand-printed sign that read "METZGER, Susannah." She walked over to him.

"I'm Susan Fisher, Rachel Metzger was my aunt. I think you may be looking for me?" She said to the young man. Up close, she could see he wore his sideburns in curly Orthodox Jewish side-locks and had a skullcap on his head.

She had surprised the young man a bit. "Ah, yes, I guess so. I was told to pick up Susannah for the Metzger Estate. For The Wassermann, Ephraim & Moore law firm?"

"Yes, that's me." Susan dropped the suitcase and extended her right hand to the young man. "As I said, I'm Susan Fisher, it is not Susannah?"

The young man took an awkward second before he accepted her handshake, as though uncertain as to whether he should take her hand. Then he grasped her hand in an overly strong and somewhat sweaty handshake and said, "Pleased to meet you, I'm Jeremiah Berg. I'm an intern for Wassermann Ephraim. We have a car waiting for you outside."

As Susan bent down to pick up her bag, Jeremiah nervously said, "Oh no, I can get that. Here." He almost bumped her head with his as he reached to pull the black suitcase out of her hand, rather clumsily. She let go of the bag and let him take it.

When he motioned to the backpack on her shoulder, she smiled and said, "No, that is Okay, I've got it."

The obviously nervous young intern nodded and mumbled, "Okay, this way," and he turned toward the doors. Susan followed, keeping to herself her amusement at the awkward nervousness of the young man in her presence.

Outside in the loading area, Jeremiah walked toward a stretched Lincoln limousine where a tall, muscular black man in a long sleeved blue shirt with epaulets and a chauffeur's cap waited with open passenger door and trunk. The chauffeur met them, took the suitcase from Jeremiah, and reached for Susan's backpack. Susan hesitated a moment and unzipped the front pouch on the pack, retrieving her small black purse. She re-zipped and handed the pack to the driver. Jeremiah motioned for her to get in first. He again showed his unease when he took overly long to decide whether he should sit in the rear facing seat across from where Susan sat or next to her, facing front. He chose the latter, but all of the way over next to the far window from her. He jumped a bit when the chauffeur slammed the trunk behind them.

When they had settled and the driver pulled into traffic, Susan asked, "So how long will the drive be… into the city?"

"Ah, well," Jeremiah again seemed alarmed at having to speak to her. "I don't drive much, myself, but you hit the morning rush hour in-bound to Manhattan pretty much right on, it is probably going to be an hour or more, I think it was a little under an hour coming out here." Then, holding up a finger as though he had thought of an idea. He reached across the facing seat and slid the partition glass open to the driver's seat. "Uh. How long will the drive to Midtown be?"

The driver answered in a deep, firm tone, quite different from the intern's nervous tenor voice. "Probably an hour, but less depending on what it is like on Queen's Boulevard. I'm gonna cut over and take the north route, straight into mid-town on 60th. Williamsburg Bridge is crappy this time of morning and Long Island Expressway has lots of construction this summer. Best way will be the Queen Bee. But, hopefully an hour, maybe less. Could be more, if there is trouble."

Jeremiah made a curious open-handed gesture, as though saying 'there, you have it' to Susan and sat back in his seat. Then, recognizing the noise of the radio blaring R&B from the driver's compartment, he reached across and slid the window closed again, overly hard. He sat back down and stared ahead, in silence.

An electronic click sounded and the driver's voice came to them over speakers by the back window, "By the way, there is an intercom, the silver box, next to each door, you don't have to open the window to talk to me." The speaker clicked off. Jeremiah shrugged, but continued to stare straight ahead.

Susan, like Jeremiah, rode in silence for some time, grabbing the door's armrest occasionally as the huge limousine swayed through heavy traffic like a sports car. Susan watched the view outside, thousands of cars, far more business signage than she was used to along streets and highways in Illinois, many really grubby looking older buildings, an odd mix of crowded together commercial and residential properties and driving that was nothing less than chaotic; everyone tailgating, weaving across lanes, and punctuated by far too frequent horn honking.

As she looked from one side to the other, she had a chance to study the young legal intern closer. He still stared straight ahead, without any movement or speech. He was a few inches taller than Susan, which put him a bit over six feet and he was thin to the point of being emaciated. His hair was quite black, and the side-locks seemed to be oiled to curl like that. His skullcap, she finally remembered its name, a yarmulke, was black with thin gold piping on the rim. His facial features were harshly square and gaunt, his cheeks were sunken and he seemed to have the start of a five o'clock shadow even though this was early morning. He was certainly not handsome, but there was something very interesting in his appearance, he was a true 'character.' With that, Susan had an embarrassed thought that his nose was a caricature of a Jewish nose, or, she thought, maybe it was Lincoln-esque. He sat with hands folded benignly in his lap, one on top of another, not with fingers intertwined, in an ethnic mannerism that seemed to match the odd open-handed gesture he had made earlier. This young man's unique mannerisms gave him a slightly foreign aura, or, at least, foreign to the young men Susan knew back in the Mid-West.

At last, after many minutes of total silence, Susan decided she had to say something to him. "So, you said you were an intern at the law firm. Does that mean that you are in law school? Or what?"

He again seemed startled when she spoke. "Ah, yes, a student at Cardozo Law School. My work-study grant has me working full-time in summers and part-time during the year to help pay tuition." And, more silence.

She noted he started everything he said to her with an "Ah" and there was the barest hint of a stutter, as though the 'ah' let him get his thoughts together to avoid the stutter. She continued her attempt at conversation, "Cardoza? I'm not familiar with that school, it is in New York?"

"Yes, ah, part of Yeshiva University. It is fairly new, as law schools go, but fairly large also, about 1000 students, near Greenwich Village."

"Oh, I'm not quite sure where that is."

To her surprise he continued, "Are you familiar with New York? Have you been here before?"

"Couple times, when I was much younger. I just know about the major landmarks, Central Park, Wall Street. And, I guess the old World Trade Center; everyone knows about that now. But, not the neighborhoods."

"Ah, well, then I guess you could say Greenwich Village and Cardozo Law School are about half way from Wall Street, or the WTC, up to Central Park, they're right in the middle of things, heart of Manhattan, but down to the south a bit."

"And where will we be going now?"

"Oh, quite a ways from there. Right in Midtown, which is just on the south side of Central Park. Both the law offices and your hotel are in Mid-town."

"So, you've got a hotel arranged for me? I had wondered."

"Ah. Yes. The firm always puts the out of town clients up at the Hilton. It is pretty easy to get to from the office. Only a few blocks away."

"So, do you work on my Aunt's estate matters?" she asked.

"Oh, no, not really. I am just a first year law student, second year this September. I am pretty much just a gopher, and I just started at that. I did meet your aunt the week before last, when the partner handling her case asked me to take … ah …something to her. She was at Presbyterian Hospital, you know, where she… ah..." He drifted into silence.

"Where she died?"

"Yes, my condolences on your loss." He said softly, finally looking directly at her.

"Thank you," she said, giving him a meek smile. She was going to say something else, but Jeremiah saw something outside the car that made him quickly reach into his suit pocket and pull out a cell phone. She looked out and saw they were going over a bridge.

Jeremiah pushed a single number key to call someone on his speed dial and waited. "Hello, this is Jerry Berg. I have Miss Fisher in the car and we are just coming into Manhattan. We should be in the office in ten to fifteen. Please tell Mr. Tannenbaum." He paused to listen. "Okay, thank you."

He turned to Susan. "The plan is for us to go to the office where you can meet with the attorneys. The driver will take your bags on to the hotel and check them, where they will be delivered to your room when it is ready. The check in time is noon, I think. That will all be done for you. After you are done today, you can just go to the hotel and everything will be ready for you, all checked in and bags in your room. Sound OK?"

"I guess." Susan did not really relish the idea of losing contact with her stuff, but she assumed everything would be all right. She felt somewhat like a visiting princess, with everything being done for her. It was a big change from life back in Moline.

Susan pulled her iPhone from her purse to check messages and friends' Tweets and Facebook posts. Nothing of interest.

—

Chapter Three

They drove from the bridge into Manhattan on a busy street through a canyon of buildings. Susan saw a street sign saying 60th Street, which the driver had mentioned. They shortly thereafter turned left on another much broader street which they traveled on for some time. This was followed by a series of turns and jogs she lost track of. Then, they switched lanes rapidly and then took several turns around a block until the limo pulled up with the passenger side door facing the entrance of a huge high-rise building of gold-mirrored glass. The chauffeur got out and raced around to open the rear passenger door for his passengers. Jeremiah had another moment of indecision as to whether he should get out first or wait for his charge, Susan. He finally seemed to realize he was closer and she would have to climb over his long legs, even in the large limo, so he went first.

Susan got out and felt thick humidity and the temperature envelop her; the angora sweater dress would soon become oppressively hot in this weather. The chauffeur offered her his hand to stand up. Then he told her, "I'll get your bags to the Hilton, if you won't be needing anything in them here?" He paused for a second while Susan shook her head and then he finished, "And you can get the receptionist to arrange a ride for you. Then, all you'll have to do is show some ID to the hotel desk."

The chauffeur touched the brim of his hat and trotted back to the driver's seat. Susan followed Jeremiah, who was already heading to the door.

Susan caught up and asked Jeremiah, "Did we need to tip him? I never know those things."

"Ah, no. He works for the firm, a contractor. He probably wouldn't have taken your money."

Susan nodded.

The lobby of the building was a mausoleum of polished brass and brown/gray marble, decidedly cooler than outside, but still muggy. Two somber guards behind a counter watched them pass; actually, they watched Susan pass. Several people were moving through the lobby, all at a hurried pace; several men and a few women, but both mostly carried briefcases and wore business suits. The elevator cluster in the middle of the lobby had at least a dozen elevators, most had numeric groups of floors each elevator serviced. Some had additional brass signage listing the bank, brokerage or other tenant who either occupied the whole floor or had clout enough for its own sign. 'The Law Firm of Wassermann, Ephraim & Moore, P.C.' was one of these, and its brass sign listed the four floors it occupied, 14-17 with a note the Reception was on 17. Susan wondered momentarily how many lawyers it took to fill four floors of a building this size. She had no idea.

On the 17th floor, the elevator opened directly onto a spacious lobby of dark brown carved mahogany paneling and deep green carpet. Gone was the mugginess of the lobby, the atmosphere here was perfection. The firm's name was emblazoned in gold metal letters on the wood panel directly in front of the elevator highlighted by two small spotlights suspended from the ceiling. A U.S. flag and a blue flag Susan assumed was New York State's stood on poles to either side of the sign. Another somber guard was seated motionless on a wooden stool by the U.S. flag and a young woman was seated at a mahogany desk to the right, by the blue flag. Jeremiah Berg nodded to the guard, gave the receptionist a cheerful wave and gave Susan a tour guide's arm motion for her to follow him down a cavernous mahogany hallway to the right.

A few paces down the hall Jeremiah turned from the hallway and opened a wide door into a waiting room that could have been a ballroom in a palace. The ceiling was half again the height of the ceiling in the hallway. The carpeting changed color to a dark powder blue at the doorway and the entire blue and gray room was decorated in matching furniture that Susan's study of design history recognized as Empire Style. However, the paintings on the walls were not the French emperors and courtesans nor American founding fathers Susan might expect in Empire or Nouveau Empire style artwork, instead they were dour old men in suits. Susan saw one of the paintings was of a young Army officer in a World War II era Eisenhower jacket.

"Ah. Please make yourself comfortable. Can I get you a drink? Or perhaps you need to, ah, use the … facilities?" Jeremiah said.

Susan declined.

"Well, I'll let them know you are here. It was nice to meet you and maybe I will see you again during your stay." And with that, Jeremiah Berg nodded to Susan with a near bow and walked out of the room.

—

Twitter by @SusyFisher: Oh Susannah, don't you cry for me! I have come to #NewYorkCity an attorney for to see.

—

Susan put her cell phone back in her purse and sat on the edge of a blue brocade salon chair, waiting for 'them' to arrive. The art historian in her could not resist getting up to inspect the paintings of what she assumed were the firm's partners. She went around the room carefully studying the paintings. The paintings were all oil on canvas and very well done, in classic, highly detailed portrait styling. Most of the older men, and the soldier, had brass plaques listing their birth and death years beneath the picture, the others just listed their name. The soldier had died in 1945. Almost all had recognizably Jewish names. A couple had side-locks like Jeremiah. She recognized several with the names of the law firm, Wassermann, Ephraim and Moore, but there were other names also. There were no women pictured.

After a few minutes, the door opened to reveal another man in a pinstripe suit. However, this one was worlds apart from Jeremiah. He was just as tall, but his build was that of a well-fed and well-exercised athlete. The cut and cloth of the suit on his trim, broad-shouldered frame was clearly an expensive private tailor's work. His handsome facial features defied any ethnic typecasting. Only the tight curls of the close-cropped black hair gave any hint that he was affiliated with what Susan now realized was a predominantly Jewish law firm.

"Hello, Miss Fisher, I am David Tannenbaum, we spoke on the phone." He walked over to Susan who shifted her purse to her left hand and offered her hand to him, which he shook with a gentle tugging squeeze that lingered to the point of being borderline sensual. "Can I call you Susan? I understand from Mr. Berg we screwed up on your first name." He spoke with a clear, deep voice with only the barest hint of what Susan now recognized as a New York accent.

Susan saw him giving her the up and down look as she stood by him. She was glad she had worn the angora dress now. "Yes, it is Susan. Call me Susy."

He only said, "Well, let's get you in to see Mr. Ephraim. We have a lot to cover."

The next office that David Tannenbaum escorted her to was back into the same color scheme and style as the lobby and hallways. The occupant of this office probably had a say in the office's main decor, it was the same dark wood and somber, deep green. This office was also quite colossal. The entire right side of the room held a large conference table and chairs with landscape paintings on the wall, flanking a large TV monitor, which was off. The far wall was entirely floor to ceiling windows interspersed by folds of dark green velvet draperies and gold-corded sashes. Through the windows, she could see green parkland in the far distance, behind rows of tall buildings. On the left was an oversize dark desk faced by a half dozen black leather armchairs. A huge oil painting of some biblical scene in an ornate frame hung behind the big desk. As Susan entered, she saw a young woman in a business suit rise from an armchair near the far end and a man stood up behind the desk, rising from a huge padded leather chair. He came around the desk to meet her.

David spoke, "Miss Fisher, may I present Peter Ephraim, our managing partner. Peter, may I present Susan Fisher." He emphasized the 'Susan.'

Peter Ephraim took Susan's outstretched hand, but he did not do as well with his shake as David had. "Pleased to meet you Miss Fisher, sorry that it has to be in these circumstances."

Susan nodded and said, "Pleased to meet you."

Susan noted that Peter Ephraim was considerably shorter than she was, and had exactly the same physique and features as the majority of the old men in the paintings in the waiting room. She guessed his age in his fifties.

Ephraim spoke again, "And, Susan, this is Devorah Feldshuh, one of our associates. She will be working with us, uh … on these matters."

The young woman in the black business suit skirted the intervening armchairs and quickly shook Susan's hand without saying anything, but nodding her greeting. She was medium height and wore her dark brunette hair in a pageboy helmet of touch-the-collar length. Susan decided this woman would be considered very pretty in the right circumstances, but her overly serious expression and apparent lack of make-up hindered that conclusion now. The dark gray silk blouse with a black silk scarf knotted under the man-collared business suit added to the dark demeanor of the young female legal counsel. In the dim light of the dark office, the entire color scheme of this woman was in shades of gray and black, why, even her earrings were simple black balls, not silver or gold or jewels.

Peter Ephraim with an upturned palm pointed Susan to a seat in front of his desk. David sat immediately to her left. Not to be left out of the seating plan, Devorah Feldshuh rushed over to the far armchair she had been sitting in before and retrieved a black leather portfolio and came to sit on Susan's right side.

Peter cleared his throat and began. "Susan, I hope your trip was all right. I understand you came directly here from JFK. Can we get you anything?"

Seeing Susan's slight shake of her head he continued, "First, let me give you my condolences. I knew your Aunt for many years and her passing has left a void in the hearts of anyone who knew her."

Susan nodded, but before she could say anything Peter Ephraim continued.

"If you don't mind, we have a lot to do today, so I'll get right to business. Our purpose this morning is to give you an overview of the situation and explain what you can expect. This will just be that, an overview. There will be details to take care of later, I think David will have a longer meeting with you, perhaps tomorrow, and your Aunt was pretty specific on some things she wanted to take place. She left instructions for that. However, that can be handled later.

"For now, Susan, can I ask how much you knew of your Aunt's legal and business affairs and her family here in New York?"

"Actually, I know very little about my Aunt's life. We met on many occasions; last time was when she came out for my mother's funeral late last February. We had a long talk then, but … She and my mother were quite close. But, not … me."

"Yes, we talked when she came back from that Illinois trip. It was then she had us replace your mother's name with yours as the beneficiary."

"On her will?" Susan asked, incredulously. She naturally understood that they wanted to let her know she had some interest in her aunt's estate, but was not ready to be called "the" beneficiary.

"Actually not only her will, but also her trust. She does have a will with a codicil, but it is the same joint will she signed with her late husband, Isaac Metzger, back in the '70's. It has some charitable bequests he wanted to make and his will passed the building they lived in to Rachel, directly. However, both his will and hers have a trust carve-out to cover the assets that were put into his and her *inter-vivos* trusts. Actually, we still manage some assets from the trust of her late husband's father, which he left to his sons and their heirs. In addition, your aunt's husband, technically your uncle by her marriage, added to those original trust assets with his somewhat legendary real estate deals in the '60's and '70's. He left much of that in a trust for his wife, your aunt, which now comes to you, as her sole remaining heir and the last beneficiary of that side of the family's trusts."

"What's a codicil?" Susan asked. Susan recognized that she was rapidly losing track of what this attorney was saying.

"That is kind of an addendum a person adds to their will, to keep it up to date, but without changing the original, much." The attorney explained.

Susan just sat blinking at Peter Ephraim, so he continued.

"It is a rather complicated situation and set of assets, the management of which is our firm's duty. I am the trustee of your aunt's trust, I was co-trustee with her until her death, but our firm managed everything and I made the management decisions. She kept out of the trustee side, except for an occasional item she wanted to do. And we are still handling the trust now, and you will become a co-trustee along with our firm, as the adult beneficiary under the terms of Isaac's and Rachel's trusts, when you reach 21 years old, which I understand will be this fall. Right?"

Susan could only nod her head.

He continued, "The trust actually makes things really simple, something you will rarely get one of us trust and estate attorneys to admit. On the complicated side, for the will, we will have to file a probate case in court and get the court's approval of a settling of the assets that pass under Isaac and Rachel's old will; like charitable bequests to a synagogue and university bequests. But, for the trusts, we only have to manage the assets, make financial reports to the beneficiaries, and file those financials for the record and the taxes need filing too, state and federal, but in the name of the trust. There will be some tax consequences personal to you, estate and income, but we will handle those tax filings, of course, at your direction and any taxes due are paid from trust assets."

Ephraim paused and Susan took the opportunity to ask, "So what do these trust assets consist of?"

Peter Ephraim sighed and smiled at her, "Ah yes, and the smart, young lady cuts to the chase. The trust assets are not that simple to explain. In fact, Mr. Tannenbaum here spends a good deal of his time keeping track of just that. David?"

David Tannenbaum moved forward in his chair so he could turn to face Susan, their knees almost touching. "As Peter, Mr. Ephraim, said, the oldest assets involved are those still held in the name of the trust set up by Isaac's father, Morris Metzger. Those were split between Morris's widow, Isaac and his named beneficiaries, and his brother Aaron and Aaron's beneficiaries. Isaac's beneficial interest upon his death was split between his wife, Rachel, and Isaac's son and daughter from his first marriage, Joseph Metzger and Sarah Metzger Birney. That half that passed to Rachel now comes to you. Aaron is still alive, you will meet him this afternoon and Sarah, and Joseph, too. I am assuming Joseph got back from Antigua. All of them have set up *inter vivos* trusts, that means 'during life,' in which they designate their spouses and children as heirs, or rather beneficiaries. And Morris' old trust still has three pieces of real property in it, but they are doozies. One covers a fee interest in a sizable chuck of Brooklyn coastline that is covered by long term 99 year leases from the '50's which provide good cash flow, but which really are not depreciated yet, so there is no reason for us to sell them.

"So, anyway, Morris' trust has three gold standard real property assets that produce cash income, considerable cash income. When the cash income exceeds the expense covering needs of that trust, which is usually, we move half of the excess cash his widow's trust, half of the remaining half to Isaac's trusts, and pay the last portion to Aaron, or rather to the trust set up for him.

"Then, we have Isaac himself, who was actually a better deal maker than his father. In the late '60's and '70's Isaac Metzger was one of the first people to realize that the dilapidated old industrial properties in Chelsea, and the nearby Meatpacking District and the Garment District were the next candidates for New York residential gentrification. He saw the Avant Garde influx into The Village in the late fifties, you know, the Beat generation and the associated literati, and Isaac figured the neighborhoods to the north and west were the next place for the urban elite to buy lofts and converted condominiums in former factories and warehouses. Chelsea is now the highest priced property in New York. In addition, Isaac was one of the first of the new wave of developers there. Either he bought up the whole building and parceled the pieces out as condos, or he bought the dirt and charged developers hefty rents to build or refurbish the building sitting on the dirt with long-term leases like those that he learned from his father. In some cases, he just bought the whole shebang, built or refurbished and set up a property management company to manage the rentals. He also did financing for other developers who cut him in on the equity of the development company or the tenant business. And, if their company failed, he was there with a mortgage to foreclose and profit on. He made money on those either way.

"Of course, with the nature of tax treatment of income properties, many of those pure income situations have been fully depreciated, we are talking forty years ago, or more, now, and converted to cash assets or reinvested by now. However, there are quite a few remaining fee-owned properties, coupled with a sizable portfolio of unregistered equity assets, and then totally liquid investments, a sizable stock portfolio. Those assets of Isaac's, he followed his father's example, he placed in trust, half to go to his children from his first wife, Joseph and Sarah, and half to his second wife and any children he might have with her. Rachel survived him, but without surviving children and got her half and now that goes to you, as her only close blood relative. At our advice, she also set up an *inter vivos* trust of her own, to hold the cash assets and income that came to her from the other sources, that trust, fairly sizable itself, is now exclusively yours."

Susan blinked at him and asked again, "But, what exactly are you talking about? In actual value?"

David nodded, "The real property is hard to put a value on because the acquisition value is from so long ago and we wouldn't bother to appraise unless we wanted to sell. They are transferred to you, the beneficiary, at acquisition cost given the way the trust is set up. It was good estate planning, there is no significant tax until you sell …"

"David, Susan wants a dollar figure!" Peter Ephraim interrupted, giving voice to Susan's frustration at David's confusing lawyerese.

David nodded, "Of course, the liquid assets and marketable equities and securities, after the taxes we do have to pay, is somewhere in the mid eight figure range. The real estate, if you actually sold, after taxes would be considerably more than that. Way more. However, if we sold that real estate, the capital gains taxes and estate taxes would be significant. Because the main estate vested into the trust, the estate tax was paid on vesting to the trust and is avoided in large part at this stage."

Susan slumped back in the big leather chair. The three attorneys could see her counting to eight digits on her fingers, calculating what that actually meant. "I don't suppose you are counting the decimal places on that?"

David shook his head, "No. All eight are left of the decimal."

"Mid?" Susan asked, meekly.

David waggled his outstretched hand as a gesture of approximation, "Mid to upper," he explained. "We are working on those calcs now; there will be some estate tax. Figuring the realized and base values of real property held this long is quite a task."

Susan just closed her eyes for a long time. They waited.

"Are you okay?" Devorah reached over and touched Susan's right hand as she asked. Devorah's voice was a deep, but feminine, contralto without any accent.

Susan opened her eyes, reached her left hand over and put it on top of where Devorah touched her other hand, saying in gently mocking sarcasm, "Do you really think I should be anything like 'Okay?' Yesterday I had to beg my boss at Macy's for time off from my make-up salesgirl job to come talk to you people and today you are telling me I am a millionaire … multi-millionaire, I guess."

Before any of them could respond they heard a click of the office door and they turned to see an old man, using an aluminum cane with a four, rubber tipped feet to keep balance, come across the room toward them. The old man walked as rapidly as his infirmity would allow, carefully placing the cane before each step. He wore a black suit with a black tie. And he had small rimless, circular glasses worn low on his nose. He had a short fringe of white hair above his ears, but his large head was completely bald other than that. Peter Ephraim stood up and came around the desk. Susan followed the lead of the two younger attorneys as they immediately stood, almost like a bailiff had announced, 'All rise,' when a judge came into court.

"Susan, may I present my father, Benjamin Ephraim, our firm's partner emeritus. Father, this is Susan Rachel Fisher, Rachel's niece."

Susan thought she remembered him from the portrait gallery, but he seemed older than the portrait.

"Yes, yes, I know. Why do you think I am here?" The old man tottered toward Susan, causing David to back quickly out of the way behind his chair. Benjamin Ephraim spoke with a much more distinctive New York accent, or could it would be called New York Jewish, than the other attorneys.

"My, let me see you, young lady." Benjamin Ephraim faced Susan, set his walker/cane to the side and reached up to lightly grasp Susan's upper arms, ignoring her outstretched hand. He was nearly a foot shorter than Susan. She could smell the old man was wearing the same cologne as her father had. Old Spice? He looked her up and down, then pushed his glasses up on his nose and stared into Susan's eyes. "Yes, you are the spitting image of your aunt when I first met her. She told me so when we last talked. Maybe you're even a little prettier, though. But, in her youth, Rachel was a real beauty. All of us envied Isaac for his prize catch." The distinct word emphasis of the old man's accent got even stronger when he reminisced. "And your uncle Isaac, he was something of a prize himself, best negotiator and salesman I ever met. He could have been a bigger thing than Tishman if he had only been a little more ruthless, less charitable, and wee bit greedier."

Peter spoke up, "My father was the original attorney who handled Isaac Metzger's real estate transactions. They went way back."

Benjamin continued, "And Isaac's father, too, don't forget, and I was a witness at Isaac and Rachel's wedding. I remember your mother, young lady; she was the bridesmaid. Another beautiful girl, that she was. Your father was a lucky man, too. I don't recall that I ever met him."

Before anyone could say anything else Benjamin gently pushed Rachel out to arm's length and looked at her clothes. He looked up at her and asked. "That is very nice, indeed, but you aren't going to the funeral like that, are you?"

"Funeral…?" Rachel left the question hanging and looked to Peter and then David.

Peter spoke. "Yes the funeral is this afternoon. Didn't you know?"

"No, that is the first I've heard of it. I had no idea about the funeral and I have nothing to wear any better than this. Is that a big problem?"

Peter and Devorah both looked at David, who rolled his eyes to the ceiling and shook his head. "I'm sorry. I told her she needed to be here today. And made sure she got here. I just assumed she understood it was for the funeral. I am very sorry."

Peter scowled and scolded the younger attorney. "Mr. Tannenbaum, an attorney never assumes his client knows something that it is the attorney's duty to tell them. You cannot assume that Miss Fisher out in Illinois with no contact with the family here, understood that a traditional Jewish funeral taking place in New York is going to take place at the earliest possible moment it can, usually the day after. We, all of us, knew Mrs. Metzger's death was imminent, and we could make plans. But, Rachel only knew about this when you called her yesterday and she only knew what you told her."

Peter moved to his father's side, handed him the walker cane, and with an arm on his shoulder he moved the old man toward the door. "Father, thanks for stopping in. I'll come get you when we leave for the funeral. You can see that we have some things to do."

The old man turned toward Susan, pointed a finger at her, made a clicking sound, gave a broad smile and a wink, then took his son's hint and waddled to the door and out. As Benjamin walked out, Susan noticed he had been wearing a yarmulke way back of his head, as Jeremiah Berg had. Neither David nor Peter wore one. She wondered how he kept the yarmulke from slipping off his shiny, bald head.

David tried to say something, but Peter shushed him with an abrupt wave of his hand. Peter turned to Devorah, "Miss Feldshuh, you're up. I need you to make sure Susan is ready for the funeral and out to Mount Zion Cemetery in Queens by 2 o'clock. David, you can go now. Make sure you talk to both rabbis and they have things straight between them. Check to be sure that all of the other arrangements are set. … Doubly sure." Peter added the last with an ominous tone.

As David Tannenbaum retreated quietly from the room, Peter turned to Susan. "Miss Fisher, I apologize for our mistake. We did not give you the information you needed."

Susan replied, "It's Okay, it's really not that big a deal…."

Peter cut her off, "From your perspective, perhaps not a big deal. However, for the Metzger family, our very important clients, it is a very big thing. And for me, and my father, who have spent much of our life making sure the entire Metzger family was treated fairly and was well-represented, I just can't …." He did not finish that thought. He continued. "Susan, this is important, I think you will understand later. But, for now, I have to ask you to listen to Devorah and do what she says. She knows about these things, her grandfather and uncle are, or were, rabbis. And she is pretty sharp in her own right. That is why we bring her in for these kind of situations. As you can guess, a law firm with a sizable probate and trust practice deals with this type of situation often.

"I can't emphasize this enough. You do what she says and everything will be fine. Okay?"

Susan blinked at Peter Ephraim. She really did not understand and she had no idea what was so important, but still said, "Okay."

Peter went back around his desk and sat. Susan realized that when he sat, he was almost as tall as when standing, his chair must be elevated behind the oversized desk.

Devorah turned to Susan, "And you really don't have anything, at all, proper to wear to a Jewish funeral? At the hotel?"

"I don't know exactly what is required, other than for any funeral, but I was rushed to leave home, I only had a couple hours before the flight into Chicago, I didn't even think of it, I guess I should have. I had a black dress I used for my parent's funerals, but not here."

Devorah nodded and pulled a big-screened smart phone from inside her portfolio on her chair, she sat tentatively on her chair's front edge. Susan sat back down and tried to digest all that had happened and was happening. She saw Devorah scroll with a flip of her finger through a contact list and choose one entry. Susan looked at Peter, he gave her a little nod, a half smile and motion with his head that Susan should pay attention to Devorah.

The phone beeped and Devorah listened, "Hi, Ginger, this is Devorah Feldshuh. … Yeh, it has been while. I'm calling because I have a semi-emergency. I have a young woman who needs to be ready for a traditional Jewish funeral, fashionable but conservative, and we need to be ready and out your door by not long after noon. … Yeh, the same situation as last time. What? Okay… ."

She cupped the phone in her hand and asked Susan, "What dress size are you? 8? 10?"

Susan blinked at the question, then said, "This is a 10, but I usually wear 8, I needed a 10 in this because 8 was too short and this stretched fine, you know, the knit."

Devorah nodded and pursed her lips, "Yeh." She turned back to the phone. "She is an 8, but *really* tall and for the funeral she can't show too much leg, you know."

Devorah listened and spoke, "Okay, that would be great, cost is not an issue, bill the firm, like last time, we have a corporate account with BG, that's Wassermann Ephraim. We will be at the 5th Avenue entrance in, say, fifteen or twenty minutes. … Just a sec."

Devorah turned again to Susan and looked down at her feet, eying the gray heels and suntan toned nylons. Then she asked, "Shoe size?"

Susan answered, "Nine and a half."

Devorah spoke into the phone again, "And Ginger, have someone bring a couple styles of low heels, black patent, *not leather*, plain, no decoration, size 9, 9½ and 10. And some black or dark panty hose, tall length. Have them in the fitting suite with the dresses. … Fine, thanks. Oh, and make sure the dress choices you have for her all have cloth collars with seams. … Yeh, for that."

Susan pursed her brow at Devorah, having no idea what she was talking about or why she gave the rather peculiar and firmly worded instructions.

Devorah finished the conversation with, "And can you get us reservations at Goodman's, the one on the Beauty level. We are not going to have time to stop and eat anywhere else. Thanks, Ginger. See ya soon."

Devorah beeped the phone connection off and immediately poked and held a speed dial number on the phone and waited. "Willie, Devorah, we need you and the car by the elevators on level P1, now, and it will be until late afternoon. … NO! Doesn't matter, tell them that Mr. Ephraim is bumping them, hav'em get a taxi. This effort is number one priority now. And call in somebody else from the service, also, the two Mr. Ephraims and Mr. Tannenbaum will need a formal limo with a uniformed driver to Queens for a funeral at quarter 'til one this afternoon for several hours and you will still be with us. … Yeh, the gal from the airport. … OK."

Susan noticed that Devorah Feldshuh's New York accent came out of hiding when she got excited and hurried. Her use of 'gal' to describe Susan seemed out of place for her and 'airport' came out more like 'aapaht.'

Devorah popped her phone into the portfolio and turned to Peter, who was watching from his desk. As she talked to her boss, all trace of accent disappeared, "I'll have everything set. Don't worry. We'll see you in Queens by 2:00."

Grabbing her portfolio in one hand, Devorah took Susan's elbow and urged her up. "We have to be going. Lots to do."

Peter Ephraim got up to walk the two young women to his office door. To Susan he said, "Sorry, again about this. But, listen to Devorah; she has you covered. I'll see you at the burial."

Susan was still in shock from the "millionaire" talk and did not quite understand what was happening, but she smiled at Peter and hurriedly followed the quickly moving young attorney out the door. She finally understood why Devorah was entirely in black today. She was amazed at herself for not even thinking about the funeral for Aunt Rachel, it was not as if she had not already done this twice in the last year.

Devorah walked rapidly through the law firm's halls, checking behind her to make sure Susan was keeping up. She opened a heavy metal door and Susan followed her down a wide stairway to the floor below and through another set of heavy fire doors. The decor changed in the stairwell, changing from posh elegance to utilitarian office.

The office hallways they now raced through on the floor below had the same green carpet but not padded so heavily, and the carved wood moldings and panels on the floor above was replaced with patterned wallpaper and simple wainscoting. Secretaries worked at desks, rows of filing cabinets and copy machines spaced along the hall. Jeremiah Berg was moving a large stack of document storage boxes on a two-wheeled dolly. He nodded to Susan as he moved to the side of the hallway out of the way of the charging Miss Feldshuh.

Susan could see through some of the open doors that the offices beyond the secretaries' desks on the right had window views of the skyline. Devorah turned left, passing an unoccupied secretary's desk and into an office with her name on the door with a title of Senior Associate showing.

This office was perhaps a quarter of the size of Peter Ephraim's, windowless and its main furniture consisted of a large white and gray desk with glass and chrome accents and a white leather desk chair. Behind the chair was a matching credenza with a two large computer monitors and a single keyboard. Desk, credenza, chair and the visitors' chairs in front of the desk were all stylish modern design, matching the white geometric pattern of the wallpaper and generally light decor of the office.

"Please have a seat, if you want, while I get my things," the attorney said, pointing to the two white leather armchairs before her desk, as she picked up a leather shoulder bag from the corner behind a silver coat tree where a single black vinyl raincoat hung.

Susan did not sit; rather she stood and looked around her. One wall had diplomas and bar admission certificates. She saw Barnard College and New York University on the diplomas. On the opposite wall was a four paneled painting. The white background landscape on the four panels was offset by brilliant colors in the fruit-bearing trees, birds and a brilliant funky sun. Susan recognized the artist. "I like Megan Duncanson's work. What does she call it, Counterpoint style?"

Devorah looked up from where she was slipping a computer tablet into her shoulder bag and followed Susan's eyes to the artwork. "Yes, I have another of hers in my apartment. I think it helps brighten this place up and helps make up for the lack of windows. They offered me a window office down on the fifteenth floor when I finished my second year as associate, but I opted for location closer to the power elite…" she pointed up, "rather than amenities."

Susan did not know how to respond to that so she just nodded. Devorah took her small black purse from a desk drawer and added it and her portfolio to the shoulder bag. She had taken her smart phone out of the portfolio and now slipped it into a zipper pouch on the shoulder bag.

She then went through a finger-counting motion to confirm she had everything she needed. She seemed satisfied and started to shoulder the bag when she put the bag back down and wiggled one finger in the air to indicate she had remembered something. She opened the top drawer of her desk, rifled around and pulled out a small pair of manicure scissors. "Can't forget those," Devorah said, apparently to herself, as she put them in her purse.

Susan wondered why manicure scissors were a 'can't forget' item.

With that, Devorah slipped her arm into the bag strap, motioning Susan to the door. "We're off."

—

Chapter Four

Willie had the limousine door open waiting for them when the elevator door opened on the parking level. Susan had no idea why they had gotten out in front of the building before if you could get into the car a few feet from the elevator by just driving down to the basement parking garage.

"Did Sylvester give you a hassle about having to take a taxi?" Devorah asked the driver.

With a wry smile Willie answered, "Debbie, you know Mr. Sylvester better than me. He started to call Mr. Ephraim to complain, but I guess he thought better of it. I am not exactly sure where he sits in the pecking order."

As she followed Susan into the car, Devorah answered, "Sylvester sits considerably higher than me, but nowhere near the level of anybody named Ephraim. First thing, get us to Bergdorf's 58th and 5th."

Devorah put her bag on the opposite seat and settled into the seat with a relieved sigh.

"This will be a quick trip, you know, just at 58th and 5th." Devorah repeated.

Susan nodded as though that had meaning to her. Then Susan asked, "He …Willie, called you Debbie, but I saw your name on your office door, with a 'V' like I thought I heard when Mr. Ephraim said your name. You go by Debbie?"

"Willie and most acquaintances naturally think of the gentile version Deborah, instead of the moniker with Hebrew "V" out of the Torah that my father, the rabbi, gave me. And then they assume I use the nickname that goes with Deborah. Growing up in public schools on Long Island, I finally gave up trying to correct everybody and let them call me Debbie. To friends and family, I have always been Devorah." She held the seat tightly as Willie negotiated a spiral ramp drive out of the parking basement.

"You see, my father hated Debbie; he used to correct my teachers when they called me 'Debbie' at parent-teacher conferences. Then, when I was in 10th grade, I was selected for the JV squad of cheerleaders. I was so proud when I came home with my cheerleading outfit. I felt I had arrived in society, for sure. The rabbi's daughter makes the squad. Big moment! Then my father saw the little 'Debbie' nickname embroidered in script letters on the pleated skirt, like all the cheerleaders have. He blew his top, came unglued like I never saw before. He wasn't going to have his daughter traipsing around in front of people with a *shiksa* name on her dress. He forbade me to wear the outfit and when I mouthed off to him, he even took the skirt away from me. I wound up in tears. That was the Shabbat and I had to go to over to the synagogue with red eyes.

"Anyway, on Monday, after school, I went in to the teacher who coached the cheerleaders. I was almost in tears again, trying to figure out how to tell her what my father had done and said. Before I could say anything, she told me my package had arrived by courier. I didn't know what she was talking about. It seems my father had taken the skirt to a garment company owner who was a member of the synagogue, who had his people work on the dress over the weekend and replace the Debbie with a matching Devorah." She smiled at the memory.

"So, the gangly Jewish girl with braces got to be a cheerleader. Thank God, we had enough Jewish athletes in the school district that they didn't have games on Friday evenings. I wouldn't have wanted to tell my father I had to cheer a football game on Shabbat."

Devorah sat up in the seat and looked out. "That was quick." Then she keyed the intercom, "Willie, go to the 5th Avenue entrance. We can let ourselves out. We'll be there maybe an hour and a half. Get yourself something to eat and meet us right back where you drop us. I'll call you if something changes. Actually, I'll call you, one way or another, when we finish up."

"10-4," was his answer. Susan saw Devorah furl her brow and then smile at this response.

Turning to Susan she explained, "Fifth is one-way headed south so we'll get out on this side," as she gathered up her bag. Susan looked out her side and saw a huge tiered fountain surrounded by trees and lots of people.

Willie turned right and pulled to the curb. Susan followed Devorah out into the hot, humid air and cacophony of sound that was New York's Fifth Avenue in late morning. The bright sunlight was an abrupt change after the dark tinted windows of the limo. They hurried across the sidewalk, through the revolving bronze doors labeled Bergdorf Goodman.

"Debbie!" they heard, just inside the door. A tall, titian-haired woman maybe in her late 20's came toward them.

Devorah turned to Susan with an expression that said, 'See what I mean.'

The redhead met them and then gave Devorah a hug, not the formal cheek touching one might expect, but a full embrace and squeeze of old friends. Devorah returned the hug.

Devorah turned to Susan and explained, "Ginger and I go way back. Her kid sister was in my grade at school. I called them my adopted sisters. Ginger, this is my client, Susan Fisher. Susan, my old friend, Virginia Fonseca. Ginger to her friends."

"Byrd, now. Not Fonseca anymore. Mrs. Byrd, now." Rebecca corrected.

Devorah smiled and nodded, "Yeh, I forgot, Ginger Byrd."

Susan and Virginia Byrd shook hands.

"I'm the Personal Shopping manager for BG. I have everything ready to show you in a private viewing room off the designer floor on Three. I understand you are in a hurry, so let's go. Elevators this way." They followed.

In the elevator, Ginger turned to Susan. "Have you ever been to Bergdorf Goodman before?"

"I think I remember my aunt taking my mom and me to lunch on the top floor when we came to visit when I was like eight years old. But, I don't remember it much."

"So you are from out of town?"

"Quad Cities." Susan saw from her expression that the woman did not know what the Quad Cities was. She added, "Western Illinois."

"And you are here for a funeral, I understand?"

"Yes, the aunt I mentioned."

"I'm sorry for your loss."

Devorah cut in, "Susan got into town this morning, not knowing that the burial is this afternoon. Traditional Jewish ceremony, large extended family, lots of well-to-do people whose first impression of Susan will be how she looks and handles some pretty rigid expectations that Susan might not be aware if. Your job is to get the costume right. Mine, on the ride out to Queens will be to coach her on what to expect."

"So, you're not Jewish?" Ginger asked Susan.

"My mother was, and my father's family was, like, you know, when he grew up. But, I grew up in a household that really wasn't that religious. My father taught at a Lutheran college, after all. So I …."

Ginger nodded. The elevator door opened. They walked out into a lavishly decorated array of clothing racks, mannequins and designer logos everywhere. A few women seemed to be earnestly shopping, but many people seemed to be tourists, agog at the opulence of this big city fashion icon. Ginger directed them around mannequins and racks and across the main floor to a door on the far wall.

"We use these rooms for private showings; designer's limited release shows or when we have a celebrity or dignitary who doesn't want to have to brave the sales floor. It will work for us today."

The room's decor was neutral colors, beige, ecru and gray. There was a low runway flanked by chairs leading from a curtain on the far wall and several slated saloon doors that were obviously dressing rooms. In the middle at the head of the runway, there were seven silver pole racks with black clothing hanging from them and a rolling rack behind that with what appeared to be the same outfits, probably other sizes. A Hispanic salesgirl stood waiting near three chairs moved over to face the clothing racks. A young man with a mullet was just finishing stacking shoe boxes on a folding table to the left. He stacked three stacks of three boxes and set one shoe of each stack out in front of the stack.

Ginger spoke to him, "If you are done, you can go. You can pick up what is left when we are done."

The young man checked the larger box he had unpacked the shoes from and tossed three plastic wrapped packs of panty hose on the table near the shoes before picking up his box and leaving. Ginger followed him to the door and flipped a brass lever like a hotel room had to keep anyone else from coming in.

Devorah headed over to the clothes. Susan followed behind her. Devorah checked first garment, a wool jacket and skirt with a dark gray blouse.

"This is nice, but it will never work today. It is upper 80's out there and Susan will have to stand in the sun for a long time. It is bad enough they have to be black. Too hot." Devorah checked each of the six other dresses. At the second to the last dress, she shook her head. "Won't work, wrong collar."

Devorah turned to the salesgirl, "Can you take this and this away, so we can focus on the others?"

The girl obeyed.

Devorah turned to Susan, "Miss Fisher?" She waved her arm out in a Vanna White imitation towards the dresses.

Susan moved to the dresses, still wondering why Devorah seemed fixated on collars. She felt the cloth, read the labels and, out of habit, she checked the price tags. She went back and forth.

Ginger spoke up, "You can try them on in the dressing room. Or if you want, right here, if you don't mind us …."

Susan walked over to Devorah and spoke in a low voice. "These are really nice. Especially the Donna Karan. But, the blouse alone for the Donna Karan is, like, thirteen hundred dollars!"

Devorah blinked at Susan, twice, then spoke softly but firmly, turning so that only Susan could hear, "I understand you are having trouble taking all of this in, but you need to realize what David was talking about. You are inheriting your aunt's estate. And she, when she was alive, had no trouble with the price tag on any Donna Karan. She bought many, I'm sure. She knew how to look like Isaac Metzger's widow. Now, you get to look like Isaac and Rachel Metzger's heir. You are a wealthy heiress now; you are not a Macy's salesgirl anymore. You like the Donna Karan?"

Susan stared at Devorah, thinking for a long moment, and then nodding, finally she put up a finger indicating she was considering something. After that pause, she turned to Ginger with a question. "I see that each piece is separately priced. Is it too gauche to mix and match designer wear?"

Ginger seemed surprised at the question, "Oh no, not at all. You want to create your own outfit; we can mix whatever you say."

Susan nodded and thought again. "Then let's try the Donna Karan blouse and cummerbund, but I don't like that gray and black weave dress as well as this. This seems better for a funeral, sedate." She fingered the knee length Jersey skirt on the last outfit, a Burberry. "And, I'd like to try the silk jacket from this other Donna Karan outfit, here, on top."

Ginger Fonseca Byrd snapped her fingers at the salesgirl, who started gathering Susan's choices.

—

They emerged from Bergdorf Goodman and saw that Willie was, indeed, waiting for them, blocking curb lane traffic and drawing honks. Seeing them, he got out and Devorah handed him the BG bag with Susan's old clothes in it to put in the trunk. Susan was not used to the below the knee length skirt and felt the need to tug the hem up as she ducked to step into the limousine. However, she immediately realized the long slit in the back allowed good movement.

"Wait," Devorah said.

Susan stopped and turned to Devorah.

"Take off the jacket first. I'll need it in the car." Devorah reached to help Susan out of the black silk jacket with the wide decorative lapels.

As Devorah folded the jacket over her arm and motioned Susan into the car, Susan gave the attorney a quizzical look. She had not said much about what Susan could expect while they ate lunch at the crowded café in the basement "Beauty Level." When Susan had asked something about the Metzger family Devorah had shushed her with a finger to her lips, then indicated the people all around them. The attorney did not want to talk Metzger family business in a crowded public place. Instead, they had talked about Susan's studies at Augustana. Then Susan heard of Devorah's time at Barnard College and in law school. When talk infringed on personal family information, Devorah changed subjects.

The clothing purchase had gone well. Susan had tried on her choices and everyone agreed that the outfit worked. They had to send the salesgirl running for a different Donna Karan cummerbund, though. Susan's thin waist actually fit best in a size 6, whereas the size 8 or 10 items Ginger had brought in were fine for skirt, blouse and jacket.

They settled back in their seats. Devorah keyed the intercom, "You've got the address in Queens, right?"

"Yup," came back from the speaker. "The cemetery, Long Island Expressway, exit at Maurice, been there many times."

Devorah mouthed a quiet "Duh!" under her breath, making a palms up hand sign to Susan that her question and Willie's answer should have been obvious to her.

Devorah next pulled her shoulder bag from the opposite seat and extracted her manicure scissors and a pair of reading glasses from her purse. Donning the glasses, she then turned Susan's silk jacket over on her lap and laid it out with the collar folded out. She clicked on the little overhead light above the passenger seat. As Susan watched in wonderment, Devorah carefully snipped the underside seam running in from the notch in the lapel, the entire width of the collar, to the edge of the neck.

"Okay, Devorah," Susan said, "You need to start explaining things. I just watched you rip a seam out of a Donna Karan jacket we just paid, like, a thousand dollars for."

"I didn't rip it out, I just snipped every other back stitch. It won't actually rip until you pull it apart. Should come easy." Devorah refolded the jacket on her lap, before handing it to Susan. "Sit forward and slip this on. You'll need it on when we get out of the car. And, put on your new earrings."

Then, taking off her glasses and flicking off the light, she turned to Susan, "Okay, time for your Jewish Funerals and Mourning 101 class. We'll start with *Kriah*, since you obviously have no idea what that is. Pay attention because there will be an exam." She looked at her watch. "A final exam in fifty-five minutes."

Devorah let that sink in before continuing. "Your aunt had mentioned to Peter that she was concerned about how you would react to what you are getting hit with today. She apparently realized from speaking with you how little contact with Jewish rituals and religious practice you have had. So… the funeral today involves the extended Metzger family, my clients, Rachel's in-laws and stepchildren, your cousins or, rather, cousins in law. They are Jewish."

Susan cut in with a "Duh!" Devorah shushed her with a stern hand gesture and continued. "There are many kinds of Jews. Orthodox, Ultra-Orthodox, Conservative, Reform, Reconstructionist, Humanist, yadda yadda yadda …. The ones we care about today are the Reform, Conservative and the Orthodox. That's because the Metzger family were Conservative, Isaac's father and his mother, et cetera. Isaac was raised in a very Conservative Jewish tradition, but joined a Reform temple after he married Rachel, apparently at her request. But, the Metzger family burial plot is at a Jewish cemetery affiliated with a Conservative congregation. Isaac and Isaac's first wife were buried there and his ancestors, too. We had a bit of a standoff yesterday when we started to make funeral arrangements with the surviving Metzger family members and the cemetery being Conservative and Rachel being Reform. Apparently, the Metzger's rabbi is *very* Conservative, almost Orthodox. Rachel's rabbi is very liberal Reform. It was not certain where the funeral service would be or who would officiate. They decided to simply do a burial site ceremony, avoiding the decision on a synagogue and both rabbis would handle it together. I guess they have a protocol for that kind of thing. That was what Peter was talking about when he told David to check on both rabbis. On top of that, the Metzgers have many close friends, associates and some intermarried family who are Reform, Conservative and Orthodox. Many of the attorneys at our firm are Conservative. Some are Reform. Some like Jeremiah Berg, you met him, the intern, are Orthodox.

"It doesn't take too much thought to guess the difference. Orthodox has set rigid rules, customs, laws and social norms that cannot be changed. Conservative is close, but less strict, not much different in some things, like ceremony. Reform, less so, but built on the same traditions. But, in reality, the big differences between them are theological, stuff we don't need to get into today. They have a slightly different view of where religion comes from. But, many of the social and ceremonial things aren't that different. For today, we are talking family, life, death, and mourning. If you follow the strict rules, for these things, it really works for both or all three, rather. The Reform Jew likes to keep in touch with his ancestors and origins by going through the motions on the traditions that the Orthodox thinks are absolutely necessary, commandments from God himself. So since most of the close family is Conservative, you will do well to follow the strict rules."

Susan asked, "Which one are you?"

"My father is a Conservative rabbi, and my uncle was." Devorah answered, but Susan recognized it was a non-answer, about her father, not about her. Devorah then turned her knees toward Susan, tugged on Susan's jacket collar to get it straightened and then, grasped Susan's hand, "Susan, also, your Aunt married into the Metzger family as the daughter of a Conservative Jew, a rather strict one, and her father was a rabbi to boot, like mine. I know your mother rebelled from that and made a different choice. But, your Aunt Rachel married into a practicing Jewish family and at least as long as Isaac was alive, that was her life. And as far as her relation to this family went, even long after Isaac's death,

Rachel was his widow. In addition, from what I understand she played that role very well, even if she did have her dalliances in later years with a lifestyle that strayed from that. You will find out about that after we honor her life with the Metzger family today.

"So, for today you need to realize that the Metzgers are burying Isaac Metzger's widow, a wonderful, generous lady who remembered every grandchild's birthday, and cousin's wedding and bar mitzvah every year for what? Forty years? However, this is also about Jewish 'family.' Rachel married into the Metzger family, but your mother and you were her blood relatives. You are her only living blood relative and, in fact, you are therefore inheriting her estate. But, it is not only her estate, it is part of Isaac's estate, and to some extent even Grandfather Morris Metzger's estate. That is why Peter Ephraim wanted to let you know the background before the funeral. You are stepping into this traditional Jewish family as, essentially, to them, the equivalent of Rachel Metzger's daughter , her next of kin. However, in another sense you are an interloper. Here is where the important part comes. You are going to have to go through the motions that her next of kin, her daughter, would. In addition, don't you think for a minute that word about you hasn't spread like wildfire around the family and friends. If they Twittered these things, which, thankfully, most of them do not, you would be 'trending big.' However, some of them are probably already 'following' you."

Susan frowned, but nodded. She wondered where that tidbit came from.

Devorah continued, "Every busybody in the family has been rumormongering about you and your mother ever since they heard about Rachel's illness and certainly since her death. They are going to be watching to see if this girl from Illinois is worthy of stepping into Rachel Metzger's shoes …and property. Everything you do is going to be noted. And it is going to be noted from the eyes of traditional Jews whose way of life still cares about customs and clothing and prayers and the Torah and …."

Devorah stopped to balance herself after a particularly abrupt sway of the limo on the highway. "I need to give you enough information so that you melt into the image these people hope that you will fill. These are good people, but their expectations of what they want to see from you are rigid. Rachel spoke to Peter about just this before her death. That is why she told us as much about you as she could. We are going to these lengths to fulfill her directions. She thought about telling you this herself, but she got too sick, too fast, to do so.

"So, I am going to tell you a few things you need to remember. But, I probably cannot remember to tell you all the minutiae about customs and relationships, so I am going to try and keep by your elbow this afternoon and evening to …"

"Evening?" Susan asked.

"Yes, by the time the funeral is over, and they travel back from Queens to Manhattan to have the dinner and Kaddish at the house and everyone visits and reminisces, *ad nauseum*, my guess it is going to be well into evening."

Susan bit her lip and then said, "So, what is a Kriah, and … Kaddish?" as she sat back and folded her arms, waiting for Devorah's lesson.

—

Everyone was arriving at the burial when Willie pulled the limousine into the cemetery. Devorah had been nervously checking the time as they encountered heavy traffic in Queens. Several dozen cars and a couple taxis stood alongside the narrow lane in the cemetery. Gravestones encroached on all sides, right up to the road's edge.

"Go around all these parked cars and drop us up ahead, you can see the gravesite over there to the left, all those people. Tell the guards we're next of kin." Devorah instructed over the intercom.

Two uniformed security guards were attempting to control the cars. Susan heard the whirr of an electric window and saw Willie stick his head out the driver's window and say something to one of them, who waved them on. After getting as close as he could, Willie pulled up alongside several other cars near a flatbed utility cart that had a pile of soil on it. He got out and raced to open the door closest to Susan, but Devorah got out the far side by herself and was already waving to Peter Ephraim, who stood nearby talking with his father, David Tannenbaum, and three other men. Peter pointed their arrival out to what Susan could now see were two men wearing rabbi's garb with fringed prayer shawls and black hats.

Before the men got to them, Devorah came up beside Susan, "Ready for this?"

Susan shrugged and asked, wrinkling her nose, "What's that smell?"

Devorah motioned towards two smokestacks on the horizon beyond where the cars were parked, saying, "New York City utility and sewer plant next door. Most of the full time residents in the cemetery don't complain about the smell."

Devorah left Susan's side to walk over and report to Peter. The rabbis and the other man who was carrying a stack of white cards passed Devorah on the stone path and came over to Susan. The rabbis briefly introduced themselves and the man who was the funeral director and gave their condolences. Susan lost track of their names in the jumble of introductions, so she just thought of them as the fat old rabbi and the younger tall rabbi. The tall rabbi had said he was Rachel's rabbi, the fat one had said he was the Metzger family rabbi, thus declaring their jurisdictions, as though Susan cared or understood the difference. Tall rabbi offered his hand to Rachel to shake, but fat rabbi did not. They indicated Susan should follow them. Walking between rows of headstones, they went up a small rise to where a crowd had gathered. There were three rows of folding chairs, most already filled and a crowd of several dozen people milling around behind and to the side of the chairs. There was actually a gravestone with a granite Star of David atop it sticking up between rows two and three, so close were the gravesites to each other. In front of the chairs was a simple wooden coffin resting on a tubular silver frame above an open grave surrounded by green carpeting. The open grave was a few feet to the right of a large headstone that Susan could see read "ISAAC METZGER."

The funeral director had offered Susan his arm, gently leading her to the front row, right hand seat. There was a distinct murmur from the people gathered behind when Susan was escorted by the funeral director and rabbis to sit in the front row. A tall, white-haired man rose from the seat next to hers and bent toward Susan to whisper in her ear, "I'm glad you could make it here. Just in time. I trust you had a good trip from Chicago. I am your Uncle Aaron. Last time I saw you, you were in pig tails"

Susan nodded, gave a slight smile and tried to hide the bewilderment of not knowing what the man was talking about. Pig tails?

As she and Aaron sat down, the funeral director gave Susan an engraved, folded card from his stack, the cover of which read:

In Loving Memory

Susannah Rachel Metzger

שושנה רחל מצגר

Inside the card, Susan quickly read the following:

Susannah Rachel Metzger (nee Rothmann)

Rachel, as she is known by friends and family, was born in New London, Connecticut, April 20, 1949 to CDR Solomon H. Rothmann, Chaplain Corps (✡), US Navy, and Tova Elspeth Rothmann (née Katz). She was married on June 6, 1972 to Isaac "Ike" Metzger. Rachel is preceded in death by her beloved husband, Ike, by a daughter who died in infancy, her sister Rebecca Sariah Rothmann Fisher and by her parents. She is survived by a niece, Susannah Rachel Fisher, a stepson, Joseph Metzger, and stepdaughter, Sarah Metzger Birney.

Susannah Rachel Metzger received a baccalaureate degree with dual majors in Art History and Romance languages from Columbia University in 1972. Following her marriage, she made her home with her husband in Manhattan and supported him in his successful real estate and investment business. Following the death of her husband in 1979, Rachel returned to Columbia University where she obtained a Master's Degree and Ph.D. (ABD) in Art. She died on June 3rd, after a lengthy illness.

Susannah Rachel Metzger has been an active supporter of and fundraiser for many worthy causes. For many years, she was a board member of the New York Civil Liberties Union and served on an advisory board of the Museum of Modern Art. Memorial contributions can be donated to memorial funds at the Park Avenue Synagogue or to the Temple Emanu-El, New York City.

Shiva will be for close family and invitees, only, at the Aaron Metzger residence in Manhattan.

The back of the card had something called a Mourner's Kaddish with several rows of Hebrew lettering interspaced with rows of English character phonetic syllables from the Hebrew.

Susan had little time to contemplate the information on the card. Not only did she share the same middle name with her aunt, she had always known that, but she had always thought the 'named after' was only the middle name. She had only ever heard of 'Aunt Rachel.' She now found out that her mother had really named her after her older sister, as Susannah Rachel was obviously the full Hebrew form of Susan Rachel. Everyone here in New York had even assumed that the niece's name was Susannah, and not just Susan. That explained the name on her airline ticket and the other times when 'Susannah' had been used. Then there were more surprises, a daughter who died in infancy, Susan had never heard that before. There was a lot of information on the small white card to think about, not to mention the man who said he was her uncle. And, she had always known her long dead maternal grandfather had been a US Navy officer, but seeing him described as being a rabbi in the Chaplains Corps brought memories of snippets of family history her mother and aunt had told her. She realized how little she knew of her mother's family. However, Susan had no time to think of that now, the fat rabbi raised his hands to hush everyone and began the graveside service.

The fat rabbi stood to face Susan and the family members in the front row. Her uncle stood and took hold of Susan's arm, urging her to stand. The rabbi kept looking toward Susan as though expecting something from Susan. After a brief pause, Susan realized the rabbi was waiting for her to perform the *Kriah* as Devorah had taught her on the car ride from Manhattan. Susan reached up with fingers under her right collar and felt the thread ends of the snips Devorah had made in her collar seam. With a feeling of dread, she grabbed each side of the collar seam on the lovely new silk jacket and pulled hard. Devorah had more than prepared the seam for the *Kriah*, as the collar ripped easily, and noisily, all the way to the neck seam.

Susan thought about the words Devorah had made her recite dozens of times in the limo and she spoke out in a firm voice that was the only sound in the now-silent graveyard, *"Barukh atah Adonai Eloheinu melekh ha'olam dayan ha'emet."* Susan was surprised at how well she had done, or at least she thought so, her foreign language study in high school and college and her foreign travels with her folks had allowed her to mimic Devorah's phonetic syllables quite well. As she spoke, she saw the fat rabbi nod his head and say an Amen. The tall rabbi also nodded to Susan and gave a gentle almost-smile, as though he knew her secret.

Susan had barely finished when Aaron Metzger also reached up and ripped his suit's right lapel flap, repeating the same words. Then, a very old lady to his left a few seats did likewise. Susan heard another rip and then another woman say the prayer in the row of seats behind her. Susan wondered about the identity of the two women; Devorah had said only close family did the Kriah. She had more family members, or at least her aunt did. Following the four people and the Kriah there was a murmur of indecipherable chants and prayers and amens from the assembled crowd behind Susan.

The funeral service was short, but quickly blurred into the incomprehensible for Susan, being totally unfamiliar with both the tradition and the prayers. The fat rabbi and tall rabbi traded off doing the Hebrew prayers. At times, the people around her would mutter "Amen" as one of the rabbis finished a prayer for the departed and for the mourning family. Susan followed Devorah's instructions to mimic what everyone else did, but it was hard to see that from the front row. The words spoken were partly in English and several prayers were in Hebrew. The 'Amens' seemed to come after the Hebrew. Finally, the funeral director read the information inside the card to the mourners.

After a moment's pause, the fat rabbi walked over right next to where the wooden casket sat on the silver interment frame. The tall rabbi and funeral director followed him. As they stood graveside, two workers in shabby sport coats and ties, but wearing muddy work boots came forward and released the pulley mechanism on the interment frame, causing a roller mechanism to release and the casket slowly dropped into the hole beneath it. When it was on the bottom of the grave, the workers pulled the three canvas straps up from under the coffin, quickly rolled the straps back onto the silver frame and then walked out of Susan's sight.

The fat rabbi then stepped forward to the foot of the grave. There was a pile of sand on a large piece of green Astroturf at the foot of the now empty silver frame. The rabbi bent and grasped a shiny brass shovel that was stuck into the sand. The rabbi reverently took a small shovelful of sand and poured it slowly into the open grave. He said something in Hebrew as he did, followed by another "Amen." The rabbi stuck the shovel back into the pile. Then the tall rabbi and then the funeral director did likewise, again repeating the words in Hebrew, to which the fat rabbi said, "Amen." The shovel was again shoved into the pile of sand and the three men backed away, behind the grave. The funeral director caught Susan's eye and nodded his head slightly, indicating it was her turn. Susan had not been forewarned of this duty, but seeing their example, it was near enough to her own parents' funerals at the Moline Cemetery back in Illinois that she knew what to do.

Susan stepped forward and bent at her knees, as primly as she could manage in heels and knee length dress. She carefully stood sideways so the Burberry skirt's back slit opened out of the audience's direct view. She took a shovel of sand and stepped toward the grave. She heard the sand hit to wooden casket. She did not know the Hebrew but she was pretty sure of the right words in English. "From ashes to ashes, dust to dust." The fat rabbi nodded and said "Amen" again. Susan had gotten it right. The funeral director moved over to show Susan where to stand, off to the side at the foot of Isaac Metzger's grave. As she walked over, Susan could see another grave with a smaller headstone immediately to the left of Isaac's near where she now stood, it said Elizabeth Metzger and had a date of death in 1967. Old Isaac now had his first and second wives on either side on him.

Aaron Metzger followed Susan to the grave and picked up the shovel. He knew the Hebrew, of course. When finished he came to stand on the far side of Susan. A very old, chubby woman, clearly the one who had also ripped her clothing in the Kriah came forward, but had trouble bending to get the shovel, a teenage boy in a black suit rushed forward from his seat to help her. The old woman's hand shook as she poured the sand into the grave. She handed the shovel to the boy who returned it to the sand pile and then she came over and surprised Susan with an unexpected hug before moving on to the far side of Aaron. She was followed at the sand pile by an attractive, well-dressed woman, who came to stand on the other side of Aaron, between Aaron and the old woman. It was obviously his wife. Several more people from the rows of seats got up to take their turns with the shovel, putting the shovel back in the pile each time. Then, each one filed past Susan and Aaron silently. One man and one woman, surprisingly, gave the sign of the cross after the shovel was put down. Others followed, including the law partner, Peter Ephraim and his father. Susan saw that Peter Ephraim was now wearing a yarmulke like his father; in fact almost every man at the funeral had either a yarmulke or a fedora-type hat on, even one man who had crossed himself.

Following the act of emptying the shovel of sand by the close family members who grouped themselves off to Susan's right, Susan saw that the people who had been standing and some of the family members had now formed two rows, forming a path back away from the grave toward the lines of parked cars. Aaron whispered to Susan, "You go first" and gestured for her to walk through the aisle of people. Looking to her side, Susan saw that this time Aaron took his wife's arm and they followed her down to path in the crowd. Looking down the path of people, Susan saw that the twin utility towers on the horizon acted as a slightly bizarre marker of her path away from the graveside. As she passed, Susan could hear most of the people whispering *"Ha-Makom yenahem etkhem b'tokh sha ar aveilei tzion vyerushalayim"* Behind her, she heard Aaron Metzger reply with a short Hebrew phrase. However, Susan could only nod her head in acknowledgement the obvious words of condolence.

Susan saw Devorah waiting for her at the far end of the aisle of mourners. As Susan approached, Devorah put her hands on her shoulder and whispered, "You were great!"

Susan gave a demonstrative sigh and asked, "What's next?"

Before Devorah could answer, Aaron came up behind them, having left his wife behind with the other family members who congregated behind them. He heard Susan's question and Devorah's answer, "The Shiva will be at your Uncle Aaron's townhouse on the Upper East Side."

Susan nodded, but said, "Yes, I saw that in the card, but Shiva…? Is that the dinner?"

Before Devorah could answer, Aaron cut her off. "I didn't know you were non-observant, but I guess I should have guessed knowing your mother. The Shiva is a period of mourning, supposedly seven days, but for our purposes today, it will be the *seudat havra'ah* a meal prepared for the grieving family, kind of like an Irish wake, but more sedate. For you, it will also be your chance to meet your relatives, Rachel's relatives, from our side of your family. Although it has been a long time since my brother's death, there are a many people who thought a lot of your aunt, and through her, my brother."

Susan quickly asked, "Wait, you said 'knowing my mother.' You knew my mother, too?"

Aaron chuckled and said in an ironic tone, "Yeh, I guess you could say I knew your mother."

Susan had a confused expression for a brief instant, and then his tone of voice led to the realization of whom this man was; it flashed into Susan's mind. She brought her hand up to her mouth to mask her astonishment. "Oh, my gosh. That was you? Mom and Aunt Rachel told me about it, but I didn't connect that it ... I mean you, were Rachel's brother-in-law."

"Yes, that 'it' is me. The other guy. And it was I who introduced your mother's big sister to my older brother, and they were the ones to get married. Your mother and I parted company, she married your father, and the rest is history. Your history."

Aaron saw his wife approaching and quickly said, in a hushed voice, "We can discuss that later."

He reached out to bring his wife into the group. "Myra, let me introduce you to Susannah Rachel Fisher, Rachel's niece ... our niece. Susannah, my wife, Myra."

Myra Metzger said, "It is nice to meet you," with no emotion. She pulled Susan to her in a barely-touching cheek-to-cheek embrace, as though they were celebrities meeting on the red carpet, and just as emotionless.

Susan looked into the chiseled face of Myra Metzger. She was obviously many years younger than her husband, who Susan realized had to be in his 60's given his relationship with Susan's mother. Whatever Myra's age she was well preserved and carefully packaged. Her double-breasted bluish black suit obviously had a pedigree that would compete easily with Susan's new designer wardrobe. Blue-gray eyes and dark blonde hair in a fashionable bun were offset by alabaster skin and perfect make-up. She had the same black spheres for earrings that Devorah had made Susan buy on their way out of Bergdorf's. Aunt Myra's face showed little emotion and gave no hint as to her thoughts.

"Will you be riding home with us?" Myra asked.

Before Aaron could speak, Devorah spoke up, "I have our limo here, I thought we could drive her to your home and Susan could have a chance to, ah, recover, from this service and all that has been going on for her."

"And you are?" Myra asked, somewhat haughtily.

Aaron cut in, "This is Devorah Feldshuh, one of the attorneys who manage the Trusts, I thought you knew her."

"No, we haven't met." Myra made no effort to shake hands with the attorney. Devorah was clearly hired help to Myra, who continued, "But, I was thinking, Susannah is going to be faced by lots of family members, and acquaintances, at our house. And I am sure that Miss Feldshuh cannot help her know what to expect, who's who, you know. Susannah should be with someone from the family on the ride uptown."

Before Aaron could respond, Susan said," By the way, my name is just Susan, not Susannah. Or you can call me Susy, my family and friends do." No sooner that she said the word 'family' Susan realized that these strangers she was just meeting were all the 'family' she had.

Aaron raised his eyebrows and said, "Sorry about that, we got that from one of your aunt's emails after she went to your mother's funeral. She must have thought you were Susannah, like her." He turned to Myra, "I think Devorah and Myra are both right, it would be good for… Susan, to relax on the trip uptown, but one of us could ride with them."

Myra nodded, a bit sarcastically, "Well, obviously, you should be the one to fill her in on the family, since you knew your brother's wife and Susan's mother. You ride with Susan and Miss Feldshuh and I will get your mother and the children home. It is getting late; we should get this cortege moving."

Myra turned once again to Susan, "Susan … Susy, it has been nice meeting you, too bad it is such circumstances. We can talk more at home." With that, Myra Metzger turned abruptly and headed for a nearby Mercedes sedan.

—

Chapter Five

Devorah chose to sit on the rear-facing seat across from where Aaron Metzger sat next to Susan. She canted her legs toward Susan's side of the car. There was silence when they first sat down, with Aaron and Susan smiling, but saying nothing.

"Well, I can't ... you know ... well, I can believe ...." Aaron had trouble starting, finally stopping and restarting his sentence over. "You certainly do look like you belong with the Rothmann girls."

Susan looked at him curiously and then smiled when she figured out what he meant. "You mean Mom and Aunt Rachel. Yeh, I've been getting that a lot since I got here."

"It's true though. You are probably the same age as your mother was when I first met her. At a party in the Village. She came down with a group of her fellow Columbia co-eds, slumming it with us NYU students downtown. We had a reputation for throwing good parties, for sure.

"Your mother had curly brown hair halfway down her back and these huge brown eyes that a guy could lose his soul in. I spent most of the party trying to impress her enough to get her phone number."

Susan smiled, "My father used to say I looked like her, too."

Aaron paused before speaking, as though he were unsure of whether he should say something. "I only met your father once. After your mother and I broke up I saw him and your mother at Ike and Rachel's wedding. Seemed like a fine man, but my ego and I suppose, broken heart, made me hate him immensely. It was somewhat awkward. I was best man and your mother was bridesmaid. I bit my lip and did my duty as kid brother."

Susan asked, "You mentioned the last time you saw me, I was in pigtails?"

Aaron smiled, "Well, actually I guess it was a pony tail. You and your mother were in New York, visiting Rachel and one of Joseph's children had a birthday. Your aunt usually came to things like that and she brought you and your mother there. I brought my daughter, to her cousin's party and met up with you and your mother with Rachel."

"Oh, I remember the birthday party, vaguely, but I'm sorry, I didn't remember meeting you. I was really little, but was totally intrigued by the party. The idea of real clowns for a kid's party was not something I had experienced before."

"Yes, that was after Hannah died, Joseph's first wife, and Joseph tried his best to make up for it with his kids, as best as he could ….”

“So that Joseph, he’s Isaac’s son?”

“Yes, from the first wife, I mean, Isaac’s first wife, Elizabeth. Both Joseph’s first wife and his mother died before they were thirty. Elizabeth died in a car accident on the way out to Southampton in the late ‘60’s and Hannah had breast cancer. Pretty tragic, both of the main women in his life, and some in our family blame it for Joe’s cavorting around since Hannah’s death.”

“Pardon?”

“My nephew Joseph, Joe, is our family’s candidate for black sheep. No secret that. Let us just say he is doing his best to spend his father’s money on fast cars, Caribbean beach houses, Riviera villas and a stream of women half his age. In fact he was in where, Antigua …?” Aaron paused to look at Devorah, who nodded. “…When Peter got hold of him to come home for Rachel’s funeral. He had trouble with the flight connection and I got word he should be in now, and will meet us at the house.”

Rachel was touching her fingers, counting people, “So you and Isaac were Morris’ only children?”

“Yes, he, Isaac or Ike, was quite a bit older than me, what, twelve years? Our father was away during the war, Army, Isaac was pre-War, and I was a post-War baby boomer. He was already married and widowed by the time I was in college. That is when I met your mother, and then she invited her older sister to a party at my apartment while we were dating. And that is when Rachel met Ike and hit it off.”

“But, Aunt Rachel was only like a year older than my Mom, so she had to be a lot younger than Isaac, Ike, when they married?” Susan asked.

“Yes, she was early twenties and he was well into his thirties and already pretty firmly established as a real estate mogul. They had less than ten years together when he died, suddenly, heart attack. And Rachel found herself a widow at age thirty with a trust fund that Ike split between his young wife and his son and daughter, her step kids?”

Susan asked softly, “Uh, the funeral card mentioned a daughter who died in infancy. I never heard about that.”

Aaron nodded, sadly, “Yes, a couple years after they married, Rachel got pregnant. Baby was born premature, with complications, heart defect. The baby died after a few months and shortly thereafter Rachel found out she could not conceive again. Hit her hard. She and Ike were thinking of adopting when Ike died. Jewish orphans from Russia, as I recall. She certainly did not have it easy. One can hardly blame her for letting loose after his death.”

"Again, I don't …." Susan sputtered.

Aaron, grimacing, raised his hand to cut her off, "No, it is my mistake; I should never have mentioned anything about that. Today is our day to remember Rachel for the good … no great woman she was. I don't think any member of our family ever missed getting a birthday card, a bar mitzvah or bat mitzvah gift from her or couldn't expect Rachel at every wedding and funeral and most birthdays. Aunt Rachel's gifts were legendary, even for a fairly well-to-do family. She did her best to be the wife that Isaac Metzger thought she would be, even as his widow. Most of us heard rumors of her private life after Ike, but her good works, her charity and her kindness endeared her to everyone and that is what everyone is remembering today."

Susan nodded, and then said, "I know about the gifts first hand. When I graduated from high school, she gave me an Apple laptop with every bell and whistle possible. That Apple is still my constant companion. I was in shock; it was so cool for a high school grad to get a gift like that. … Who else, family, should I know about?"

"Well, first and foremost is Bubbe Hannah -- my mother, Isaac's mother, the old woman who surprised you with a hug at the funeral. Hannah Metzger, the matriarch, not to be confused with Hannah Metzger, the Younger, her deceased granddaughter in law, Joseph's first wife. We keep track of them by calling her Bubbe, that is, Grandmother, Hannah, and the other one was just Joseph's Hannah.

"Anyway, Bubbe Hannah is in her nineties, still going strong. My mother is the bulwark of the family, keeper of traditions, teller of stories, and matchmaker for whoever comes within her reach. She probably has someone ready to introduce to you already. No, seriously. She has married off her children and grandchildren. And now her last granddaughter is getting hitched. You are new *shidduch* material for her to work on, along with her great grandchildren." He smiled wide.

Susan sat back and listened to Aaron's detailed family portrait and as many stories as he could tell her for the hour ride back into Manhattan.

—

Willie pulled up to the curb in front of the gray limestone townhouse, but he did not have to get out as there was a black-suited footman flanked by two uniformed police officers at the curb. The footman opened doors for the cars arriving at the curb marked by orange traffic cones and 'No Parking – Funeral Only' signs. The limos and taxis bringing people in from the burial dropped passengers off and moved away, making room for others. Seeing this arrangement, Susan wondered at what kind of influence was needed to make a no parking zone on a busy New York street in mid-afternoon, not to mention your own police officers. She did not have much time to wonder as Aaron exited quickly and the footman held his hand to Susan to help her out of the car door. As she got out, Susan heard Devorah giving Willie instructions over the limo intercom.

Standing up and making sure the long black skirt was hanging right, Susan looked up at the four-story edifice with craved limestone cornices and balustrades with wrought iron bars on the lower windows, the larger of which were stained glass. "It's beautiful. This is where you live?"

Aaron said, "Yes, for most of the year. It is one of the few original townhomes in the East '70's that isn't turned into apartments, condos or totally converted to offices. Or just torn down and turned into high rises. Fifty years ago, or more, this area was the home of the real gentry of the Upper East Side, everybody who was anybody had one of these. Now, the area is mostly commercialized and the classic townhomes as single-family residences are mostly gone. But, we love it, the best location in New York, by far. Your Aunt Rachel's place in Chelsea is a close second."

Susan heard Devorah come up behind her as Aaron motioned them to go up the steps first. At the top of steps to the side of the doorway a young woman in what seemed to be an all-black, long-skirted maid's uniform poured water in a silver bowl on a small wooden table and offered a white towel hung over her arm. Devorah put her hand on Susan's shoulder and whispered in Susan's ear, "Another tradition, ceremonial cleansing before entering the house after a burial. Just wash with water quickly, use the cup to pour on your hands." Susan saw a porcelain cup sitting by the bowl and she followed instructions.

Wiping her hands dry and handing the little towel back to the maid, Susan stepped toward the door, it immediately opened from the inside, by another footman dressed like the one at the curb. She entered, followed by Devorah and Aaron. As she entered, Susan saw a small TV monitor on the entry wall to the left, showing a view of the front porch and stairway, explaining how the door had opened so promptly for them.

"There they are!" came the announcement from the next room before Susan's eyes had not yet adjusted from the sunlight outside when she saw a form rushing her and giving her another hug. Bubbe Hannah quickly ushered Susan in.

"Welcome to my home," Susan heard the old woman say. Her eyes had adjusted just enough to see Myra's eyes roll ever so slightly up when she heard her mother-in- law announcing this was her home. Susan smiled at Hannah and said thank you.

"Come in here and meet everyone." Hannah said as she pushed Susan toward an adjoining room.

"Whoa," Myra raised her voice as she stepped in front of them. "They just came in the door and Susan has had quite a day. Let's give her a chance to collect herself before running the Metzger family gauntlet. Susan, let's have you and Miss Feldshuh come upstairs for now, there will be plenty of time to meet everyone."

Myra stuck her arm between the old woman and Susan, leading Susan toward a majestic stairway of marble and oak.

The old woman relented, "Yes, I guess that's best."

Myra and Susan went up the stairway with Devorah following them.

"Here, the master suite has two restrooms." Myra opened a wide carved oak door. They entered a bedroom furnished in a manner that would befit Versailles. Everything was gold with red accents on satin, brocade and a huge matching Persian carpet in front of a huge canopy bed. "Can I get you anything?"

Susan smiled, "No, just show me the door to that restroom."

"Me, too," chimed Devorah.

"That door there opens into two side doors. Mine is to the left, Aaron's right." Myra pointed to the door on the far wall. "I heard you started this morning in Chicago and haven't had a moment to rest since."

"Yes, it has been quite a day."

Myra and Devorah were waiting when Susan came out.

Myra asked, "Do you want to rest up here for a while before I turn you back over to Bubbe Hannah? She considers introductions her bailiwick. And, most everyone down there is her children, grandchildren, great grandchildren or cousin. I guess she's earned her right to lead you through the 'gauntlet.'"

"No, I rested I the car, while Aaron told me who is who." Susan straightened her jacket and shifted the cummerbund left and right to make sure it was in place. Myra reached forward to touch her collar.

"That's a clean rip, if you need to know a good tailor, mine mends Kriah quite well. Lots of practice. That's a Karan, right?"

"Yes," Susan answered meekly. She had to respect Myra's eye for designers.

"Miss Feldsh… Devorah tells me you have a room at the Hilton. That's fine, but I wanted to let you know we kept one guest room here open in case you wanted to stay here."

"I guess they already have my suitcase and things at the room there."

"I assumed as much, but wanted to offer. My guess is that after an afternoon and evening with that crowd downstairs, I'll envy you your room away from here." Myra smiled and led them to the door and down the stairs.

Hannah Metzger saw them descending the stairs and waited at the bottom.

"There, Mother, she's all yours." Myra stood back as Hannah took Susan's arm.

"You go ahead, I'll be over here." Devorah headed for a gold velvet loveseat near the stairs. Susan was all alone, following the old woman's lead.

The living room was spacious, a large marble fireplace on the far wall and two bay windows with the stained glass she had seen from the street to the right. On the other side, there was a wide archway of carved wood heading to another room, which appeared to be a dining room. The living room decorated was elegant, but low-key light gold and beige colors with hints of light green in the furniture and window draperies.

There were several people standing or sitting around the room, most of whom stopped and turned to see Susan and the old woman enter. Hannah Metzger headed for the big, light green couch that was near the fireplace. Two young boys sitting on the couch reading comic books were already moving when their grandmother made a shooing motion to get them to move for her and Susan.

"Here, let's sit and you can tell me all about yourself. The mystery girl from Chicago." Hannah Metzger sat and patted the sofa to show Susan where the old woman wanted her to sit.

Rachel sat and situated herself on the sofa, but before she could say anything, the old woman spoke again. "We all loved your Aunt Rachel. Rachel, that is funny, we all just called her Rachel or Isaac's Rachel, and I had even forgot her full name was Susannah Rachel Rothmann Metzger. That's you, too, Susannah Rachel?"

Susan started to repeat her explanation that she was just Susan, but the old woman cut her off and continued in a loud voice. "Yes, Rachel was a good woman. I was not too sure about her when Isaac decided she was woman enough to replace his Elizabeth… that was Isaac's first you know, but Rachel was a good woman. I knew she would be OK when I heard she was a rabbi's daughter." The old woman paused for a second as though in thought, but maybe to catch her breath. "And your mother too, Rebecca, she was a good girl. You know when she was seeing Aaron and Rachel was engaged to Isaac, we went to the rabbinical council to make sure that was not a problem. You know brothers marrying sisters, but they said it was fine, they did it in the Torah and I guess it happens all the time in Israel, on the kibbutzim. But, he did not have to worry, your mother and Aaron …. So, tell me about your mother, I have not seen her since the wedding, Isaac and Rachel's. I know she passed away recently?" The old woman ended the question about Rachel's mother with a whispered prayer in Hebrew.

When Hannah stopped whispering and Susan was sure it was her turn to speak, she said, "Yes, Mom passed away in February. And Father last September."

The old woman nodded her condolences and patted Susan's knee. "It has been a rough year for you. And your parents, tell me about them. You father was a scholar, eh?"

As Susan answered, she noticed that the people sitting and standing in the room had quieted and turned to focus on her conversation with Bubbe Hannah. "Yes, Dad was a professor of history at Augustana College and Mom was a teacher, in East Moline, at the high school. She retired two years ago. Dad still taught though, he said he would never fully retire. He was at his podium giving a lecture when he had his stroke. . . ." Susan paused trying to keep tears from flowing.

"And now your Aunt Rachel, too. Oy..." Hannah patted Susan's knee again. "But, your parent's they had a good life?"

Susan realized the old woman's words were meant as much as a statement than as a question, but she confirmed it by saying, "Yes, they gave me everything I ever needed, or wanted. We had a nice home in Moline, right near where Dad taught in Rock Island. He was a good provider and Mom worked hard, too. And, almost every summer we went somewhere nice. That was the advantage of having teachers as parents; they had the whole summer free most years. One summer we would go to Europe, maybe France and the next summer we would go to Israel. . . ."

"You've been to Israel?" Hannah and a couple other family members listening perked up at the mention of Israel.

"Yes, in fact twice. My father got grant funding and spent two whole summers working on an archaeological dig in northern Israel. My mother and I got to go along. We stayed in a hotel in a city near the dig site and got to travel the whole summer. It was great!"

"So, your father was an expert on ancient Israel." Bubbe Hannah beamed her approval of this.

However, Susan had to tell the truth and admitted, "Well, actually it was an old Crusader fortress on the Israeli coastline. Father was an expert in Medieval History."

Hannah thought about this for a minute and decided to switch topics. "So, do you know about our family? The Metzgers? My Morris?"

"Yes, a bit. My aunt talked about the family and Morris." Susan lied a little bit before adding, "And, the attorneys filled me in this morning."

"Ah, the attorneys, don't talk to me about attorneys. My life has been nothing but attorneys since my Morris died, what, fifty years ago now, forty-five? Attorneys say you have to do this, attorneys say you need to buy that. Acch!" Bubbe Hannah swung her arm in gesture toward a man and woman standing nearby, listening, "The attorneys, they have even taken over my own flesh and blood."

With that introduction, the man stepped up to the sofa and introduced himself, "Susannah, I'm Jack Birney, Jacob to Bubbe Hannah. And this is my wife, Marjorie."

"Hello," Susan said. She decided to stop correcting the "Susannah' thing.

When he saw that she did not recognize the name, Jack added, "My mother, Sarah, was Rachel's step-daughter, Isaac's daughter."

"He's the district attorney," Hannah added.

Jack smiled, "I'm an assistant district attorney for Manhattan. So is Marjorie."

Marjorie offered her hand to Susan, who stood and shook it.

Jack Metzger's introduction to Susan signaled the end of Bubbe Hannah's private audience and everyone in the room now came over and introduced himself or herself. Jack and Marjorie introduced their sons, the two boys Hannah had shooed from the sofa. By ones and twos nearly a dozen people quickly introduced themselves. Among the family were several people who were just family friends or friends of Rachel. Their names were spoken, but the glut of information was rejected by Susan's brain. Susan was on identity overload.

One particularly attractive young woman in her 20's came through the archway from the dining room. She had a white towel she was wiping her hands with as she came up to Susan. "Excuse this, I've been playing hostess for Mom," she indicated her wet hands as she extended her hand to Susan. "I'm Ariel; my father says we met before at Amee's birthday party years ago."

Ariel Metzger was clearly Myra's daughter. She had her mother's beauty, broad even features and dark golden hair. But, she had her father's charm. "Gramma, can I have Susannah now, I'll show her around and get her fed?"

Hannah Metzger smiled back at the granddaughter and waived her arm toward the dining room. Susan turned to the old woman and reached down to clasp her hand. "It was great meeting you, I'll come back in a bit and you can tell me more about Morris and Isaac and the rest of your family." The old woman beamed at this. Susan followed Ariel into the dining room.

The entire dining table, sideboard and two other tables were filled with food. Stacks of little, round powdered cookies, sliced fruit, breads, candies, cookies, the variety was bordering on outrageous. One table was totally covered with fruit juices, sodas in a tray of ice and several bottles of wine.

One of the smaller tables had a selection of beef, chicken and cold cuts. Ariel saw Susan staring at the meat and announced, "Yeh, I wondered about the meat table, too. I guess since a meal like this, with people bringing *shiva* food gifts, that might not be totally kosher, you know, using milk as an ingredient when meat is served, they put all the meat on one table so people who follow strict kosher can decide for themselves, you know, what to eat. We do have separate plates on that table. "

Susan nodded as though she understood. A maid brought Susan and plate with lentils, stewed greens and a poached egg on top. Susan looked at Ariel and blinked an unspoken question.

Ariel shrugged and flipped her long hair back behind her shoulders, "Yeh, I didn't get it either, apparently it's tradition, the rabbi's wife explained it to me when Aunt Myrtle died. You get the eggs and lentils first, and then you get the goodies." Ariel indicated the spread before them. "The idea is that this is a meal for the mourners, celebrating the life of the deceased, but starting out with serious Jewish food. I guess there is nothing quite as Jewish as boiled eggs and lentils. Real old country, I guess, not like I'd know."

"So, Ariel, you're Aaron and Myra's daughter. You have a brother, too?"

"Yes, Adrian. He is here somewhere, with his wife Cindy and the twins."

"And your father said you arc engaged?"

Ariel lit up at Susan's words, "Yes, later this month Eddie and I get married and I become Ariel Rothschild. I wish Aunt Rachel could have been here. We'd like to have you come, if you can."

"Rothschild, as in the Rothschilds?" Susan could not keep the awe out of her question; she hated her tone even as she said it.

"Well, sort of …the American branch. The actually go back in America to the Revolution. Not the super-rich Europeans. It is a big family, even compared to the Metzgers. Daddy joked that Eddie is my ticket into the Daughters of the American Revolution. ... Here's Amee."

Another young woman rushed across the dining room and hugged Ariel, spinning the two around. As they stopped Ariel said, "You made it. Been a long time."

Amee Metzger was considerably shorter than Susan and Ariel. She wore her dark hair short in a long, almost masculine haircut. However, her large brown eyes and full lips gave her an almost doll-like quality.

"Yes, took the train down from Boston. Felt kind of weird on the Amtrak wearing this." She indicated her black blouse and skirt. "I'm sorry I missed the funeral. Is my Dad here yet?"

Ariel shook her head, "Haven't seen him. Amee, let me introduce you to Susannah, Rachel's niece."

Amee smiled and took Susan's offered hand, "Oh, I saw on Adrian's Facebook page they were expecting you. Sorry it had to be at a funeral we meet. We haven't met have we?"

Before Susan could answer, Ariel cut in, "Actually, she was at your birthday party, remember, the one with the clowns?"

"Oh, God, the clowns. Who can forget, scared the living crap out of me. Dad never asked me about them, just surprised me. And they scared me to death. You were there?" Amee asked.

"Yes, one of my first memories, I was like, a toddler, all I remember was the clowns. My mother and I were visiting Aunt Rachel and she brought us."

"Yeh, the clowns are burned into all of our memories…."

Amee was interrupted by Bubbe Hannah raising her voice from the living room, "Joseph!"

Amee smirked, "Sounds like Father Dearest has arrived."

Susan did not understand Amee's reaction to her father's arrival. She followed her to the entranceway.

The house was filling up with people. The most recent arrivals, around whom a crowd was congregating, were a tall, well-tanned man in a sport coat with a loosened tie and a woman in a red business suit. The man had balding gray blonde hair and the woman was a platinum blonde in her thirties. Aaron had briefed Susan in the car about Joseph Metzger and his girlfriend, Sandra. Aaron and Myra were greeting them when Susan entered with Ariel and Amee. Susan also saw that Peter Ephraim had arrived and was standing to one side, speaking with Devorah.

Hannah Metzger elbowed through the crowd and hugged her grandson Joseph. Another couple followed by two young boys stepped forward and caught Joseph's eye. Joseph escaped his grandmother's grasp and reached to hug the young man and then the woman, and finally picked the two boys up in each arm, hugging them. Then, Joseph saw Amee standing across the room and rushed to her, handing the arm full of little boys to their father. "Amee," Joseph said as he came to hug her. "And Ariel too." Joseph ended the hug of his daughter and reached to touch Ariel's shoulder starting to draw her into a group hug. He saw Susan standing to Ariel's side. "And there is no doubt who this would be. Susannah?"

Susan nodded. Joseph pursed his lips and nodded, eyes growing wet, "I am sorry to meet you like this. Rachel was a wonderful lady. More than a stepmother, she was my best friend at a time when I really needed someone. I suppose you have already heard how much you look like her."

"Yeh, so I've heard."

"Well, let's make sure and talk later. Right now I need to ask my Harvard scholar, Amee, a thousand questions." Joseph put his arm around his daughter and moved her toward the living room. Cousin Ariel followed them.

The rest of the crowd that had gathered at Joseph's entry now moved to other rooms. Devorah and Peter were still talking. Left alone near the entrance was Sandra, the girlfriend, standing uncomfortably. In her red dress, she was totally out of place in the house full of mourners in black and somber colored clothes. As Susan watched, tears swelled up in Sandra's eyes and she rolled her eyes to the ceiling, jaw clenched, grimacing. Sandra looked around the room and over to the living room where Joseph had left with his daughter. As tears started, Sandra almost ran up the stairway. Susan looked around the room and saw that nobody had paid any attention to Sandra's abrupt exit, nor did anybody have any idea she was in distress. Susan sat her lentil plate on a side table and followed Sandra up the stairs.

Susan saw Sandra at the far end of the second floor hallway, standing with her back to Susan, head slightly bowed, shoulders slumped and fists clenched. Susan thought she saw the movement of a sob. The heavy carpeting masked Susan approach and Sandra jumped when Susan said, "Hello."

"Oh, gosh, you scared me." Sandra turned to face Susan. Her mascara was streaking.

"Can I help?" Susan asked.

"Joe said we were coming for a funeral, not that we were arriving at the funeral. Until we were almost here, I thought we were going to the hotel. Not … this. Then he disappears, leaving me standing there in the lobby looking like a neon sign saying 'this woman doesn't belong.' I'm sure I look like the floozy they all think I am anyway." She fingered the bright red dress.

"Well, let's get out of the hallway." Susan motioned Sandra toward the only room she knew upstairs, Aaron and Myra's bedroom.

"Is this Myra's?" Sandra asked.

"Yes."

"Oh God, the inner sanctum."

In the bedroom, Susan went to the make-up table she had seen earlier, took a Kleenex from a box, and handed it to Sandra.

"You have anything to change into? In the car?"

"No, we were in a rush to get here; the baggage didn't keep up with our flight change. This is New York; I assumed I would have time to get something here. I had no idea the funeral was today."

"You weren't the only one." Susan put her hands on her hips and looked at Sandra. She nodded her head, having made a decision.

"You wait here. Bathroom is in there." Susan pointed. "Get your raccoon eyes off and I'll be back with help. OK?"

"OK. Who … are you?"

Susan smiled at her oversight, and offered her hand, "I'm Susan Fisher. My aunt was Rachel, the one who died."

Sandra took her hand and gave a weak smile, "I'm Sandra Will. Joe and I …."

"Yes, I understand. I'll be right back." Susan turned and left.

—

Devorah was still standing with Peter; they were both holding their eggs and lentils plates in the downstairs entryway. Devorah saw Susan march down the stairs with a stern expression, like a woman on a mission. Devorah took a few steps forward to ask her what was wrong, but Susan held out her hand in a 'stop' signal, shaking her head and mouthing 'no' then she turned in the living room. Devorah saw Susan tap Myra on the shoulder and then whisper something in her ear. Myra thought for a moment and then nodded her head. Susan turned and walked back to the entry and up the stairs, with Myra at her side matching her determined pace. Devorah looked at Peter, raising her eyebrows in a question. Peter shrugged.

—

Sandra was leaving the bathroom when Susan and Myra entered. Myra walked up to her and took both her arms, judging her size and then saying, "Sorry you had a problem. Sometimes Joseph can be a real *schnook*. He should have made better arrangements and at least told you what was happening."

"Yes, *schnook* is a good word for Joe, sometimes, other times he is a real mensch."

"They all are, aren't they? That is why we love them."

Myra turned and headed for another door on the far wall, motioning with crooked finger over her shoulder for Sandra to follow. Myra opened the door and flipped a light switch on in a massive walk-in closet. Sandra looked sideways at Susan and exchanged glances, expressing each woman's surprise at the immense wardrobe before them. Myra did not notice and walked to the far wall purposefully.

"You are a bit thinner than I am, but some of my old stuff will fit." Myra pushed clothes hangers to one side, selecting one hanger and then another. "Here, how's this work?"

She handed Sandra a dark gray blouse and a black wrap skirt. Sandra held them in front of her. She nodded, and said, "These will work great. But…"

Sandra held the clothes away and looked down at her feet, at the bright red faux alligator heels.

"Yeh, that won't do. What size are you?" Myra asked.

"10?"

"Uuh, I'm only seven and a half. Same with Ariel."

"Wait," said Susan. "My turn. Get dressed and I'll be right back." Susan turned and left.

—

Devorah was sitting in the dining room, still with Peter, when Susan came up to her.

"Is Willie parked outside?" Susan asked.

"Yes, across the street. Why?" Devorah asked.

Susan spoke softly, "Call Willie and tell him to bring my shoes from the bag in the trunk to the front door. Hurry, I'll be waiting for him there."

"Why? Wha…?"

"No big deal, just helping correct a wardrobe malfunction. Do it." Susan turned and went to the front door. Peter listened to Devorah giving the instructions to the driver on her cellphone.

In a few moments, the two lawyers watched from the dining room door as their newest client rushed back up the stairs with a pair of gray heels in her hands.

—

Upstairs, Susan found Sandra already dressed and waiting for her. Sandra was just giving a Visine bottle back to Myra and taking another Kleenex. Susan handed the shoes to Sandra, who sat down on the upholstered bench chest at the foot of the bed. She pulled the shoes on. "A little tight, but they'll do. Yours?"

Susan nodded, "I had my own wardrobe change earlier today. Luckily, I had these in the car."

Sandra stood and Myra motioned with her hand for Sandra too spin around so they could check her. Myra held her finger up and motioned for Sandra to follow her to the vanity table, saying, "One more thing."

Myra grabbed yet another Kleenex and made the motion of squeezing her lips together as though blotting her lipstick. Sandra nodded agreement; the bright red lipstick was too much. She did as Myra told her.

When Sandra was done, Myra signaled her approval. "I declare you to be in proper attire. Now let's go downstairs and give that *schnook* of yours a hard time."

As Sandra turned and left the room, Myra caught Susan's eye and smiled. Susan smiled back.

Devorah was waiting near the dining room archway when the three women appeared at the top of the stairs. Peter stood talking to one of the family members nearby. Sandra Will came down first, Devorah recognized that the bright red dress was gone and the platinum haired siren was now clothed like a platinum haired mourner. Myra and Susan followed Sandra down the stairs and into the living room. Devorah saw that Myra's hand was on Susan's shoulder in a decidedly motherly gesture. The Illinois girl seemed to have been accepted by the queen bee of the Metzger clan. Devorah let out a little sigh. She looked to Peter who gave her a thumbs up sign; a successful day for the firm of Wassermann, Ephraim & Moore.

—

Twitter by @SusyFisher: Long day in #NewYork, we laid my Aunt Rachel Metzger to rest in Queens and I met wonderful Metzger kinfolk. Nice room in #Hilton NY. Zzzzzzzzzzzzzzzz

—

Facebook: Susy Fisher likes Bergdorf Goodman and NY Hilton

—

Chapter Six

Willie pulled up to the stanchions near the elevator in the parking garage and quickly ran around to open the door for Susan.

"Have a nice day." Willie said as she started to walk to the elevators.

Susan started to thank him, but stopped short and turned to the chauffeur. "Willie, could you tell me something?"

"Sure?" He answered with a questioning tone.

"When you first brought me here you dropped Jeremiah and me off upstairs at the front entrance to the building, but, yesterday and again today, it seems you usually use this entrance, and it is much handier. Why'd you drop me up there first time?"

Willie smiled wryly, "You know, I wondered that myself, but they told me that first time visitors were supposed to go through the front door. It is some tradition, you know, this firm, they have lots of customs and rules. I don't question it, they make the rules and send the paycheck, and I drive the car. Maybe Debbie … Miss Feldshuh can explain it."

"Yes, I've noticed all the rules. Thanks. You have a nice day, too."

"I called up so they are expecting you," Willie gave her a hat brim salute.

Susan chose the elevator with the right floors indicated and followed the telephoned instructions to go to the 16th floor, this time, for her second morning with the lawyers.

—

"Good morning, Miss Fisher. I'm Joyce Bertram, Mr. Tannenbaum's secretary. Please follow me."

The thirty-something woman who met Susan at the 16th floor elevator wore a conservative brown jacket and skirt and her black hair in a bun. Joyce's visage was almost as stern as her atonal, no nonsense greeting.

In the labyrinth of hallways, Susan recognized where she had come down the stairs the day before on the way to Devorah's office, but Joyce turned to the right, away from Devorah's office and then turned into a secretary's nook to open an office door that she held for Susan to enter. Joyce said nothing else.

Susan walked into the office and looked around to get her orientation. Straight ahead, the windows opened on a vista of city skyline with a waterway and another city on the far shore. This was different from the view of Central Park from Peter Ephraim's office. The office itself was larger than Devorah's, but still less than half the size of Peter Ephraim's. This office was decorated in standard modern office furniture, substantial, but real wood and conservative. A tan leather couch was on the left, a small conference table near the windows and a desk on the right. Susan was getting an idea that the pecking order in the law firm could be calculated based upon office size. She wondered what old Benjamin Ephraim's office was like.

David Tannenbaum rose from his desk as Susan walked in. "Good Morning, Susan." He gave her a big smile and came around the desk to meet her. Susan offered him her hand and they shook. He held onto her hand for a moment as he motioned her with the other to one of the tan chairs before his desk.

"I hope everyone was all right with your accommodations? And that you have recovered from the matzo balls and poached eggs from last night." He returned to his seat as Susan sat down.

"Oh, yes. It was an interesting day. My head is swimming with people's names and snippets of life stories."

"There are a lot of people to remember." David sorted through some stacked papers on his desk. "I see you are wearing your Kriah still?"

Susan looked at him for a moment, then nodded and fingered her jacket collar. "Yes, Devorah explained it pretty well, but I Googled it last night when I got back to the hotel and it seems I am expected to wear the rip for seven days. I kept the jacket that was ripped, but changed my skirt and blouse. That cummerbund and long skirt seemed a bit much."

David nodded agreement, "Well, you can do what you want, and yes, the Kriah is usually for seven days. Some Orthodox rabbis even say thirty. However, once the funeral is over and unless there is some additional mourning event like another family dinner or meeting, you are probably OK to relax the wearing of the Kriah, whenever you feel all right with it. Especially since, it was mostly for the benefit of your Aunt's in-laws and guests. Everyone expects something like that at a burial."

"That's good to hear. All of that is new to me."

"Yes, Susan, I understand now," David locked his eyes on hers. "And I want to give you my sincerest apology for not letting you know what to expect. I should have …."

Susan interrupted him, "You don't need to apologize, and I should have known better myself. It is not as if I haven't had plenty of funerals this year. My mother and my father. I just wasn't thinking about the funeral being so soon."

"And that is what I should have told you about. And didn't."

"I hope it didn't cause trouble with Mr. Ephraim, uh, Peter."

"Oh, no. That should not concern you. He and I have talked. His bluster was mostly for his father's benefit and to let you know how serious we are about taking the best care of you we can."

"I appreciate that. All of this lawyering stuff is pretty new to me, too. An old friend of my father handled everything for his death and then my Mom's and there wasn't anything about trusts and certainly nothing like what you described yesterday. My parent's only assets were a tract house and a small pension fund. Plus a small life insurance policy. Nothing like this trust and complicated probate stuff."

"And that process is what we are going to get a handle on today. I'll be explaining what will happen and the details of how things work. OK?"

Susan nodded.

"First, we have some paperwork to get out of the way. Would you happen to have your Social Security number and a couple forms of identification we can copy for the records? We will have to be filing affidavits with the court, the bank and tax people and need to be able to assert that you have been properly identified. As well as for the bank signature cards and stuff we will file for you."

"Let me see here," Susan opened her purse. "I have my passport and Illinois driver's license for ID. And I don't have my Social Security card in my purse, but this is one of my pay stubs from Macy's and it has my SSN number on it? Sorry it is kind of folded up." She started unfolding a tiny strip of paper.

"That's perfect. Let me give you this to fill out." David picked up a paper and a pen from his desk and walked around to her. He pulled a piece of molding out of the front edge of his desk and a wooden leaf pulled out so that she had a place to write. He took the IDs and pay stub she had offered and returned to his chair.

"That's handy," Susan said, indicating the hidden leaf, as she read the form, a blue 5 x7 card, he had given her to fill out, 'Client Information – Attorney Client Privilege.'

"Yes, those hidden writing table things are standard equipment in probate attorneys' desks; we sign lots of wills, documents and the like around here."

"You want my main address back in Moline on this?"

"Whatever you intend to use, so we have a permanent contact point. I suspect that there will be some changes coming into your life. But, for now, use your old address. We know the New York addresses."

David keyed an intercom on his desk. "Joyce, could you come in?" And to Susan he said, "Don't worry about the SSN or ID blanks; we will fill those in from these ID for you."

Joyce entered and David handed her the ID's and pay stub, "Make a couple sets of copies, put one in the financial folder and one in the client information folder. She will have the card ready for you when you come back. Each bank will need a driver's license copy, too."

Joyce left without a word.

David started to say something, but Susan cut him off with another question, "This says 'Home phone, Work phone, Cell phone' and I really don't use that home phone you used to call my on, you were lucky I was actually there to reach me. Is my cell phone OK for home phone?"

"Yes, certainly, and I guess the work phone doesn't make much sense either."

"Why?" Susan asked, looking at him with furrowed brow.

David answered her with his own expression of confusion, "Well, I really can't see you keeping your job clerking at Macy's anymore, do you?"

Susan took a breath and let it out, "Well, no, I guess not, I just hadn't thought it through. I've worked at Macy's all through college. I guess if your asset estimates are correct, I should be able to quit Macy's, huh?" Susan was smiling as though she had just figured out a puzzle or learned a secret.

"One would hope so. And my estimates are pretty close, if not a bit conservative. We'll get to that." He stood to take the blue card she handed him across the desk.

Joyce was back. She handed the ID to Susan and David handed the card to her. She again left without speaking.

"And this," David handed her a sheaf of paper labeled Retention Agreement. "Although our firm is already designated your attorney since we are Trustee, there are many other things we need to do for you as legal counsel that go farther than just Trustee work. So, we need you to sign this authorization."

Susan thumbed quickly through the four pages of small print. "You want me to read this?"

David laughed, "My duty as an attorney is to tell you that you should always read every contract you sign, but ... no client has ever really read one of those and you would need a law degree to understand why it says most of what it says. Translation is: you are hiring this firm as your attorney and if we screw up you can sue us."

Susan signed the last page and handed it back to David, who co-signed.

Slipping the papers into a folder, David rocked back in his desk chair and said, "Okay, let's explain how this works.

"As you heard yesterday, your aunt's estate, her trust and the other trusts that feed it, have properties that are extensive. There is a business, a company, the Metzger Companies, Inc., that goes back to Morris Metzger himself, which handles all of the real property management, for all of the trusts and related family members. The Metzger Companies is actually a management company for a conglomeration of many limited partnerships and other business entities that each have a purpose and different owners. That company and its various parts are owned by the trusts and reports to the Trustees. For your purposes, assume that Peter Ephraim is your trustee. It varies for the other trusts. I am designated by him as Assistant Trustee.

"So, we have the real estate company handling the property management, but there are lots of financial assets, stocks, cash accounts, and all that kind of stuff that needs to be kept straight. We have a team of attorneys, business managers, bookkeepers and the like who act on behalf of the Trustee to keep track of things. They are on the floors below this. And they work closely with a related CPA firm in this building that we are associated with that handles the accounting, audits, tax returns, etc. Actually, most of the CPAs who run the accounting firm are also attorneys with this law firm. They are trained in law, business, and tax accounting. Like me, I am a CPA and attorney, both.

"But, for our clients, the beneficiaries of these trusts, there is more than just running a business, these trusts and their funds are a key aspect of these clients' life. Our Trustees and the support staff play a key role in the lifestyle of our clients. Not only paying the bills, but personal management, problem solving, even down to the kind of thing Devorah did for you yesterday. It is a rather unique relationship that a law firm that is acting as a Trustee has with its clients, the trust beneficiaries. And that is what I need to explain to you, so you are comfortable with that relationship."

David sat up and asked, "Can I get you anything, something to drink? I need a Perrier or something."

"That would be good. I had a Denver omelet for breakfast and the red peppers are kind of sticking around with me."

David smiled and went to a piece of furniture that looked like a bureau, but concealed a refrigerator in one side. He took two Perrier bottles and then got glasses from the other end of the bureau. Susan guessed that the middle section of the bureau was a hidden bar for stronger refreshments, as she had seen in movies. David sat Susan's on the desk leaf, breaking the seal of the Perrier cap for her and went back to his seat.

He continued, "For your Aunt, we managed her personal affairs rather completely. She had her own bank accounts and all, but the funds were forwarded to those accounts by our staff and they reconciled the account and so on. Of course, as an adult, she was Co-Trustee with Peter, so she had full authority to direct the staff on those things that arose out of her trust. We kept track of her investment account with her stockbroker, which by the way has already been put in your trust's name. She gave our Client Services PO Box as the address for her bills to be sent and our bookkeepers paid them. We also handled all tax filings and the like. So, you get the idea of what we mean by personal management. Not to mention the usual services you can get from a law firm, good advice, warnings of what to watch out for, going to court when needed, lending a shoulder to cry on ...."

"Hmm, do you have a team to do that, too, or is that a one on one service."

"Whatever is necessary." He matched Susan's smile.

"We are assuming you will want pretty much the same services from us as your Aunt. Actually, you don't have a say in that until your 21st birthday. But, we are pretty good at what we do and the whole Metzger family has been our clients for decades. Well, with one exception.

"So, with that said, I think it will be easier to do this at the table over here." He set the folder with retainer contract aside, picked up a large pocket folder and a binder from his desk, and motioned Susan to follow him to the small conference table by the window. He sat down in the chair next to her.

Their seats at the table faced the bank of windows. "That is quite a view you have here. Is that the river or the harbor or what? And what is over there?" Susan pointed to the far shore across the water in the view out of the windows.

"Both. That is the Hudson River and it widens out to be New York Harbor. And that is Union City, New Jersey, straight west from us."

"West, huh? I've been all turned around here. But, that isn't unusual for me. I grew up in Moline, Illinois and the Mississippi River runs east and west through Moline and the Quad Cities. When I was little I couldn't handle the fact that the rest of the country thought the Mississippi ran from north to south." Susan explained.

"I never had that problem. I grew up on the East side of Manhattan, and the sun came up over the East River in the East and went down over Jersey in the West. Of course, the East River really isn't a river, but that didn't bother us."

David stacked the folders and the binder he had brought to the table, and lifted some others things out of a box near the table and began. "It has been pretty clear for several weeks that the end was near for your Aunt and so we were able to make some arrangements already." He stopped as Susan waved her finger and opened her mouth to speak.

"Yeah, just a second on that. Yesterday Peter said, when he was chewing you out, that you have all known what was coming, but I was not told. Now, you have confirmed that everyone knew she was dying, but I was not told. Why not? It would have been nice to see Rachel one last time. Why was I kept in the dark?" Susan's frustration, bordering on anger, was clear.

"Susan, I understand completely. However, rest assured we were following your Aunt's instructions, to the letter. Until she passed away, she was our client and it was our duty to carry out her wishes. You are going to get the chance later on to hear from her directly, but for now, please bear with me on this."

"Directly? From her?"

"Yes, she recorded a video for you. Actually, several of them. And we will get to that in good time." He looked her in the eyes and waited for her acknowledgement. Seeing her angst had not abated, he decided he needed to say more, "Okay. To explain a bit more fully, I think I can say that her reason for not telling you was her not wanting to burden you with her death and final illness, she thought you had gone through enough of that with both of your parents already this last year. Especially, your mother, I guess you told her how hard it was for you to watch her waste away in the hospice bed from the cancer. Your Aunt Rachel's death was not much different, and she wanted to spare you that. However, she did her best to make up for it. For now, let's finish the paperwork and other practical details."

"What exactly did she die of? Nobody was talked much about that."

"I understand it started out as pancreatic cancer, and it spread throughout her organs. She knew she had a problem for the better part of the year. Last winter, just after her visit for your mother's funeral the doctors at Presbyterian gave her the final prognosis, a few months, maybe six to eight at the outside. But, she didn't get that much time."

"Now, I wish I had lightened up talking about Mom with her. She might have let me be with her."

David just raised his palms up in an unspoken question. Maybe? He opened the largest folder and took out the contents; papers, brochures, credit cards, some manila envelopes and several sets of keys. And a stack of several DVD disks in paper jackets.

"We also have another folder besides this, with her last possessions, the things she had at the hospital, like her purse and wallet, personal stuff, a snapshot of you and your mother, your high school graduation photo, I think. And her laptop, she had that at the hospital to record one last video for you," he kicked the box at the end of the table at this point. "We will give that to you, too, the laptop that is. These things here need some explanation, though." He sorted the pile from the folder.

"As I mentioned, the trusts simplify transfer upon death. At 10:07 AM the day before yesterday, upon Rachel's death, you became the beneficiary, the beneficial owner, of her personal trust, a new living trust that she had us set up in your name and the other trust interests that she had assigned to you. Trusts are a different way to own property, the beneficiary has the right to the benefits of the property, but a person called the trustee has the legal right to control the trust, sometimes they are the same person. You also became the heir under her will, but the main thing in that was the building she lived in, now and when Isaac was alive. I am not totally sure why he did that, it has always been in her name as surviving spouse. We will handle the transfer of that to you in probate court. But, all the personal property in her home, and elsewhere, were named in the trust and became your property. Those include ..." he picked up the keys, "A 2012 Mercedes S420, and ... a 2010 Toyota Prius." He pushed the keys over in front of Susan. "Interesting mix of automobiles your Aunt had. ..."

"Well, I now have two of them ... Priuses, I mean. That was what Mom drove, too."

"Hmm, sisters to the end." David realized the alternate meaning to his words and hurried on. "The cars are parked in the back of the Chelsea building; she has free parking, since she owns the building. Parking in New York is a precious commodity. And.... These are the keys to the personal residence, they are yours, even though title to the building won't be complete until after probate orders. Rachel's trust actually rented the residential apartments from her personal estate; there are some business expense write-off advantages to handling it that way. So, you are the tenant and owner of everything in the apartment immediately. She occupied the top floor, of this sizable building in Chelsea, originally a factory building, but converted by her late husband Isaac to commercial on the lower floor and residential apartments higher up. I have visited the main apartment, very nice, elegant but somewhat dated decor, but I am told that she was quite a pack rat, actually, she said so herself, and over the years she filled the two apartments on that floor of the building with possessions, records, artwork, you name it. That is all yours. We will make arrangements for the building manager, who works for the Metzger Companies, to get you in to use these keys and help out in whatever way you need." He passed a large oval ring of keys to her.

David stretched his fingers dramatically, and said, "Now comes the fun part, I assume, for a young woman. Well, I guess for anybody." He pushed a silver and black colored Visa card to her. "This is your cash management account card that is linked to the beneficiary's operating account at the brokerage we use for cash management. With it, you will have access to the cash funds assigned to the beneficiary by the Trustee. Of course, until you are 21 next fall, Peter still has say-so as to disbursements, but for all practical purposes, unless you go crazy, you will have almost any level of funding you need. Just call me or Peter and clear anything big you want to purchase."

"What does 'big' mean?"

David thought for a moment. "Don't buy any cars or sailboats without talking it over first, but definitely go have a good time buying clothes and such. You will probably need to upgrade some things if you decide to live in Rachel's place. Of course, most of that will not come off this card; you can just ask the guys at Metzger Companies to do what you want done. Just remember that Isaac, and Rachel, and even old Morris, spent their lives making sure this was around for your generation to partake of."

Susan sat back in her chair a bit, "Wow!"

David continued, "Oh, and there is a regular checkbook in your name that draws on the cash management account for when you need to do a paper transaction … less and less these days, huh? And this is important, the silver Visa, they call it Platinum, is the cash management access card, so it is really just like an ATM card, linked to real money in your brokerage account. Safeguard this card. There are different rules from the banks about how that is covered in case of theft or fraud. So, do not use the cash management card for things like internet purchases or anywhere you are not totally sure of, security wise. For that, use one of these credit cards," he passed her two, one red from Bank of America, one blue from Bank Leumi, "They are regular credit cards with set use limits, pretty high though, and better fraud protection. They are issued by banks our firm uses based on the credit of the Trust. The bills for these go to our bookkeepers and they pay the bills from your trust account. Oh, and the cash management card and both credit cards are set up with the last four digits of your Moline home phone number as the passcode for ATMs. You can change that online or at a branch. Instructions are …"

"Why two?" Susan asked.

"Good question. We have arrangements with both banks as to spreading our clients business around, and many clients want to separate the credit bills, maybe one for business and one for personal, or one for husband and one for wife. In your case, it does seem to be extraneous, but it is standard procedure. You know, maybe if you reach your daily limit on one card you can switch to the other. Oh, and if you need something else, like an American Express, you can ask us to arrange it."

Susan snickered, "You know, I am still waiting for a little announcer guy in a plaid sport coat and bow tie to pop out and tell me this is all a set up they are taping for a TV practical jokes show."

David smiled with her and said, "'Fraid not. Come to think of it, though, you are having your own pretty cool reality show. Aren't you?"

Susan grinned, "You have no idea. But, too bad it had to …." She did not finish that thought.

He set a stack of forms in front of her and opened a fountain pen from his suit pocket. Susan could feel the heat of his body from the pen as she accepted it. David continued, "Here, sign each of these at the red plastic 'X' tab. They are signature cards and account agreements with the brokerage and banks for the accounts. In addition, an insurance policy for the cars, we use an insurance company we like to work with for all our beneficiaries. That, too, is paid by the bookkeeping people, as is the property insurance, maintenance, security and utilities for the residence."

He pushed other brochures and printed materials in front of her. "These are instructions, like for changing your passcode and legal notices for the cards, locations of ATMs in New York, all the stuff they give you when you open the accounts. Probably a lot of stuff you really don't need to worry about, since we handled the details."

Susan showed one of the credit cards to David. "The Platinum Visa says Susan Fisher, but the credit cards both say Susannah Rachel Fisher."

David said, "Yes, when we learned yesterday that your Aunt had given us the wrong name, we got the brokerage company to issue a new card, their headquarters is here in Manhattan a couple blocks over, but the banks take longer. We have already ordered new ones, both accounts. If you need to use them, like for internet purchases or ATMs, they will work. But, we will get the new ones in the right name to you ASAP. And, we have corrected all the other paperwork, like insurance and car title. Everybody knows you are really 'Susan.'"

David shifted the remaining DVDs and envelopes. "Okay, a few more things.

"Your aunt made a series of videos. I understand they started out as her memoirs, I think she explains that on one of these. Then when she knew she did not have long to live, she started supplementing the life history with details for you to know about her, her possessions and things she thought important for you to know. This last one, the bronze colored DVD with our firm's label, was made by Rachel at the hospital just a week or so ago. Sort of her last testament to you. We had to look at that, for legal reasons, to make sure she had not … well you do not need to know the legal details, just know that we did view the last one, but she left the others for you to look at. And, she had apparently, when she made the videos these last few months, assembled letters, pictures and other things from her life to supplement the individual videos, they are marked with roman numerals as to what DVD matches what envelope. She said that some of the DVDs point you to more materials in her apartment and gives you hints at what you might want to go through in detail in her home and what is junk. Or so she told us."

He put the DVDs and envelopes back into the pocket folder and pushed it to the pile that was building in front of her. A dark green ring binder followed this with the law firm name embossed in gold on the cover. "Now, one more thing. Since our personal management and trust management amounts to the main business of many of our clients, a lot of them spend a lot of time working with us. Over the years, it became clear that we could better serve them if we had some office space for them to use to meet with people, negotiate deals, answer correspondence that comes in to them through us. So, down on the 14th floor we have several offices, with computers, secretarial services, copiers, faxes, Internet access, all that, for our clients to use. They usually have openings on a walk-in basis, but if you need to schedule an appointment with someone and want to use our client's offices, you should call ahead and reserve one of them. A few of our clients, like real estate investors, actually have their own full time office down there. And, we can have a service answer a dedicated line in your name, if you ever have need of that. However, short of that, we have a phone number that you can use for messages, that gives a generic answer and finds out who the caller wants, and then they take a message. Lastly, you can use the 14th floor address or a PO Box we give you, in this information binder, as an address for deliveries, applications and correspondence, for privacy and security purposes. We will have someone show you around. Read this Client Information notebook and if you have any questions, any of us will be happy to answer. There is even a couple little info guides of these services from our firm and contact numbers and addresses that you can put in your purse.

"The reason I mention all that in terms of the DVDs is that you can watch them on one of the big screen computers in the client office space. Or, we have your aunt's laptop that is yours now."

"If they are regular DVDs I can use my own laptop, in the hotel."

"Whatever you want, we will have the laptop and the other personal items your aunt left here in the office when you want to get them or you can take them with you now. And, since you mentioned the hotel… you are free to stay in the hotel as long as you want. The trust is paying for it. Or if it works for you, you can stay in your aunt's apartment, or, you can make other arrangements. We really do not know your plans, as far as how long you will stay in New York. I guess, that all considered, you may not know your plans yourself yet."

Susan shook her head, "You're right, I have no idea what I am going to do. This has all descended on me rather quickly."

"I understand, and if you need help or someone to talk things over with, we intend to be there for you. And, specifically, you can call Peter Ephraim, or me day or night, our numbers are in the binder, put them on your cell. And, since things seemed to work out well yesterday with you and Miss Feldshuh, Peter has assigned her as your client liaison. Her info is in the binder, too, and several business cards for her, Peter and me. She will be available to run interference for you if there are problems, or if you have a question. She is a sharp attorney and a really well connected New Yorker, if you need anything, ask her. OK?"

Susan nodded.

David said, "You know, that is quite a pile of stuff I gave you. I'll have Joyce get you a tote bag to carry it in. If you have no more questions for me, Peter wants to talk to you briefly before Devorah shows you around downstairs. Joyce will take you to Peter and she will call Devorah to take over and show you around downstairs and introduce you to the staff who will be handling everything for you. So, we are going to triple team you today. Any questions of me?"

David waited for an answer. Susan raised her hands, showing she was perplexed. "You know, I have the beginnings of a hundred questions in me, but reality has not jelled enough for me yet to be able to finish any of those questions." She paused for a second and then added, "You know there is one thing… I have all my existing debts, you know, credit card and student loans. Can I handle those through the trust, too?"

David smiled, "Of course. You know… you can probably just tell Mary down in Bookkeeping to run a credit check on you and then she can send change of address letters to any listed account and we can get them forwarded here so she can handle that without any bother from you."

Susan just blinked at him and said, "Wow."

—

Peter Ephraim was waiting for her at his office door when Joyce dropped Susan off. Susan entered the office and started toward the desk.

"No, let's sit over here," Peter said. "Talking over that big desk isn't the best for a heart to heart talk." He motioned her toward several green velvet wingback chairs sitting in the corner that Susan had not noticed the day before. Such was the size of the attorney's office.

"Heart to heart talk, huh? You're going to tell me there has been a big mistake and all of this isn't true?" She sat in the middle chair.

Peter laughed, sitting in a chair next to her, "No, nothing like that. We just need to get serious for a moment."

"Whoa, that's ominous, the last talk I had in this room wasn't exactly light hearted banter."

Peter did not respond to that, he just adjusted his chair a bit so he faced her directly. "There are lots of names for people in my profession; attorney, lawyer, litigator, barrister, shyster, ambulance chaser, and so on. But, one of our titles that is often overlooked is 'counselor.' I am going to try to fulfill my duties as counselor for you.

"Susan, we have hit you with a lot, in a short period of time. We started off with bad news, a death in the family. Then we have informed you that events and documents and rules you had no idea about are going to totally change the rest of your life. And, we introduced you to family members you never knew before and who came from a sub-culture of Americana that apparently was totally unfamiliar to you. You have become the heiress of a fortune that you couldn't have dreamed of a few days ago."

He paused a moment before continuing, "That is where the counseling comes in.

"There are plenty of pop culture stories about people who won the state lottery, became a celebrity, or some such, and the money did not improve their lives but ruined them. That is true too often. And the situation you are facing is similar, in many ways. Not only have you come into a truly staggering amount of money, but also you have done so in circumstances that have also stripped you of every family member you have ever known.

"You don't have any family members who can take you aside and offer advice on how to deal with this. Actually, you do, but you just met them yesterday. Moreover, you do not have any friends who have any frame of reference to help you either. More on friends in a moment.

"On the other side of things, the world is full of people who thrive on taking advantage of people. A young woman in your situation is a perfect mark for the unscrupulous. You are going to need to know how to deal with the people trying to take advantage of you, but more importantly, you are going to need to know how to handle yourself.

"And the problems will come not only from strangers trying to take advantage of you, but also friends and acquaintances who see your newfound wealth as the answer to their problems. People who come into large sums of money, whether inheritance or lottery winnings or pop culture instant celebrity, routinely have problems with those people on the periphery of their life putting pressure on them to share the good fortune and use your wealth to solve their personal problems. Too often, that really amounts to those friends sharing their problem with you instead. You may have to retreat from some former friendships if that happens. You may have come into a lot of money, but it is not enough to satisfy every hard luck story that the world presents to you. You need to learn to take control of your life and your wealth to do whatever bigger purpose you have in your own dreams and not simply write a check for a former buddy's bad debts or hard luck.

"For every problem you might have in dealing with the changes this wealth will bring, your old friends and the people you run into hereafter will have those same problems magnified by their own self-interest and no interest in what is best for you, Susan Fisher.

"Instead of a college girl who struggled to make ends meet with a night job at a department store and who had to be frugal enough to pay bills and tuition, you were just given a piece of plastic that can pay for all sorts of dreams to come true. On the other hand, it can pay the entrance fee to chaos, if not used wisely. Susan, helping people manage different levels of wealth and cope with the pressures that entails is my job. We have dozens, tens of dozens of clients, not just the Metzgers, although their family has some aspects of both the good and the bad experiences of wealth in it. For my various clients, other families, I have had to counsel people whose wealth has purchased drug problems, serial divorces, nervous breakdowns, gambling habits, a breakdown of moral codes and many more ills. While not having enough money may be a problem, having money is not a panacea. Wealthy people can buy problems that the poor or average working people could never imagine."

Peter Ephraim paused again, thinking of the right words to continue. "Susan, as you find out more about your Aunt's life, you will find out that even she had a period for some time after her husband's death when the wealth she had inherited and the freedom she had after Isaac's death started to lead her into a life with that chaos I mentioned. It is my personal opinion that few special things allowed her to get back onto the life track that made her the great woman she became. Those things, the things that saved her, in my opinion, were her connections to her dead husband's family, her heritage as the daughter of a good Jewish couple and her relationship with her sister Rebecca, your mother. Those things helped as did the counsel of a wise old man that you met in this room yesterday, my father, who was her counselor in those years when she struggled to make sure that girl, that woman, Susannah Rachel Metzger, did not get lost in the chaos that Isaac Metzger's wealth brought her.

"It is now my duty to make sure that Susan Rachel Fisher has everything she needs to insure that Isaac and Rachel's wealth is a blessing and not a curse. I will be full Trustee for a few more months and then you will join me when you turn 21 as a trustee of a truly stupendous repertoire of wealth. You are a beautiful young woman. You have a good intellect and, I perceive, a good soul. But, the bad guys and the vices and the con artists and the would-be lovers and all the rest are waiting to do you wrong. That is the way things are. And I want to help protect you from them, while allowing you to live what most people could only describe as a fairy tale.

"As you proceed, keep in touch with me; keep in touch with David and Devorah. If it works for you, build a relationship with the Metzgers. They really are good people and they probably understand what faces you better than you can imagine. As I understand it, they are the only family you have. Do not be afraid to ask for help, ask for advice. Ok? Understand?"

Susan blinked and nodded.

"Okay, then I will proceed with my first bit of specific advice." Peter stopped and pulled a large yellow Post-It note from his suit pocket and unfolded it. "You understand that our job is to protect you, and knowledge of things that could cause you harm is a tool we have to keep you safe?"

Susan shrugged and semi-nodded and Peter continued, reading from the Post-It, "You have a friend who goes by @PoodyTat on Twitter?"

Susan's jaw dropped down in surprise, "Yes, Heidi, we go to college together, been BFFs since junior high. Why?"

Peter took a breath and let it out slowly, "Well it seems you spoke with her and gave her the news about your inheritance sometime after we spoke yesterday. Your @PoodyTat friend, Heidi Whats-her-name, apparently thought it was OK to broadcast a couple of Tweets about her best bud, @SusyFisher, who had inherited 'millions' and she joked that she hoped it wouldn't go to your head, but she couldn't wait to go shopping with you."

Susan blinked again, "Wow, I hadn't seen that. But, you guys track my friends' Tweets?"

Peter shook his head, "No, we don't, not exactly. But, we do subscribe to a service that spiders, that is, searches, the Internet for our clients names and finds any news reports, web pages, blogs, Facebook postings, Twitter posts, and the like involving them so we can track potential problems, opportunities, reputation dangers, security issues and whatever other information we need to protect our clients' interests. Your friend @PoodyTat used your own Twitter name, @SusyFisher, in her post that told every one of her 767 followers that my client, you, had newfound wealth and was a ripe target for those bad people who hunt for opportunities to take advantage of a 20-year-old woman with roughly $60 Million dollars in the bank. And then, three other people, Augustana College students, I guess, re-Tweeted her post to God knows how many other people."

"Gosh."

"Yes, and it is worse than that. The inheritance of the Metzger estate is big news in some circles, New York society and New York real estate circles for example. In addition, there are members of the media who do the same Internet searches our firm does. I have no doubt that a little thing like @PoodyTat's tweets could set off stalkers, paparazzi hunters, con artists, would-be dealmakers and who knows what else. This beautiful young woman who overnight became incredibly wealthy now has a target on her." He made the sign of crosshairs with his index fingers, aiming at Susan. "And, I have a duty to warn you to prevent this type of thing from happening.

"You need to get hold of your friend and ask her to delete those tweets and the other students, too. Then you need to limit your own use of social media and how much you tell people about your personal affairs, until you get a handle on how this is going to affect your life. You should not let your GIS in your cellphone Tweet your location when you go out to eat, nor do you post your plans or requests for recommendations for the theatre or dinner out on Facebook, Pinterest or whatever. You should not post your vacation or entertainment plans on Facebook or blog about them. You should not list your class schedule at college or your favorite haunts online either. You need to realize that every email you send can and, possibly will be forwarded and is totally out of your control after you hit Send. You should not give personal information like your address to anyone you cannot trust to safeguard it. That is why we give you a secure delivery address at the firm offices downstairs.

"And, Susan it is not just PoodyTat. By now you will be very lucky if there aren't paparazzi waiting for you at the Hilton, given that you informed your own Twitter followers late last night that you were, indeed, the surviving niece of Rachel Metzger, and putting two and two together, therefore the Metzger fortune heiress and that you were pushing zzz's at the New York Hilton. I can't really blame @ PoodyTat too much, you did as bad yourself." He paused for effect, "Be prepared for your Facebook profile picture, which your Twitter profile links with, to be on society blogs and columns by this weekend. You will be lucky if your name and its relationship with the Metzgers doesn't start 'trending.'"

Susan shook her head, "Gosh, I'm sorry. Devorah told me that a Tweet I did about coming to New York for an adventure might be looked at by the Metzgers in the wrong light, so I thought I would say something nice about them." Susan winced as she spoke, remembering something else. "And, I'd better clear out my Facebook photo gallery, I have some college party pictures you, we, really don't want out there."

"Do that and delete your own Tweet that mentioned the Hilton and maybe the adventure Tweet, too. And, let us call this a lesson. Just because social media gives you the means to spill your guts to the cyber-verse, does not mean you have a duty to talk about your private business online. You are no longer just a pretty Macy's salesgirl nor a simple college student, you are wealthy heiress who will be a real magnet for hangers-on, story hounds, and con artists and, God forbid, kidnappers and assorted perverts."

He stood, "Now, with my counseling out of the way, let's get Devorah to show you the operation we have downstairs to keep you safe, happy and perpetually wealthy."

—

SMS text: Heidi, no answer on your cell. I gotta talk to you ASAP. Call me, Susy

—

The room, one of Wassermann Ephraim's Client Services loaner offices, was half to two-thirds the size of Devorah's office. It had maple wainscoting and a blue-green hued leafy print wallpaper. Reprints of Monet paintings graced each wall. It was neither Spartan nor lavish, but its maple desk, matching credenza with computer and the visitor chairs made for a good work center, the type an accountant or mid-level manager might have. Susan sat with her back to the door, typing on the computer.

Devorah could see Susan was typing on a blue and white Facebook page when she entered. Devorah stood behind Susan as she finished clicking the mouse multiple times followed by an Enter key hit; she was deleting the Facebook photos.

"How ya doin'?" Devorah asked.

"I deleted all of my Facebook entries and Twitter posts mentioning New York or anything Metzger-ish. I sent Heidi both an email and Twitter private message asking her to delete any of her Tweets mentioning me. I still have not had a callback for my call to her. I also asked the other Augustana people who re-Tweeted Heidi to delete the re-Tweets, two of the three were mutual friends and one was a sort of nerdy guy who keeps trying to impress Heidi enough for her to go out with him. I hope that that will work. I feel kind of like a schoolgirl writing sentences fifty times on the blackboard for violating a school rule." Susan closed the Facebook page.

"Peter and the rest of us are just trying to protect you."

"Yeh, but I should have known better." Susan clicked the mouse again to log off Facebook. "But, there is an attitude, a complete way of life, almost, that revolves around your 'Friends,' your Tweets, your Reddit posts, how many followers you have and how cutesy and pseudo-intelligent you can be in posts, Tweets, Tumblr and mini-blogs. Like me and Heidi, in our years at high school and maybe the first year at Augustana, we were inseparable, shared everything over a Coke and couldn't wait to meet at lunch to compare notes. Now, we are face to face a lot less and our conversations are shared with who knows how many other people. It is weird. I just never had cause to question how much I posted and the impact it can have."

Devorah smiled knowingly and leaned back on the desk edge, "Let me tell you a story. You are not the first client who had trouble, or could have had trouble, with social media. I cannot identify our clients, but I can tell you Peter has good reason to warn about it. One of our clients was a very well known person; you would instantly recognize his name, and his wife. It was this couple's anniversary and his daughter wanted to take them out to eat. She Tweeted her followers, she had lots of followers, for recommendations of a good seafood restaurant near … well, near her parents' home. And she got dozens of replies, she decided to respond, thanking her friends and telling them which restaurant sounded best to her. Then, when she made the reservation she hit the Facebook logo on their web page and posted that, too, as a Facebook Like…

"The daughter took her mother and father out to eat at this out of the way restaurant that was 'simply marvelous' according to her Tweet at the table. They had a wonderful dinner and this man had a heart to heart conversation with his wife and daughter, explaining the details of the 'legal problems' he was facing and how he and his lawyers planned on dealing with his opponents, his legal enemies. Then, after dinner as they started to get up to leave their table the nice couple at the neighboring table got up quickly and the man dropped legal papers on the Mr. X's lap. That man was a private investigator sent by Mr. X's opponents' law firm. Not only did they personally serve him with a complaint and subpoena Mr. X had been avoiding by living at a secret rental house for months, but they had also sat through the whole meal and heard Mr. X's heart to heart talk with the women in his life about what his lawyers had said. The information the P.I. had heard was devastating to our work to solve the situation the man was in and it took us months to overcome it. We eventually got the other side into a situation where, in order to use the information in court, they had to explain in a deposition how they came by it and we found out they had a complete transcript of the dinner conversation and had sent their crew, the law firm's paralegal and the P.I., posing as a couple to the restaurant by keeping track of the daughter's Tweets and Facebook posts. We were able to get the use of the transcript limited because it violated attorney client privilege, since the wife was our client and the transcript made clear the husband was communicating his attorneys instructions to a co-client and the investigators were hired by opposing counsel which should have respected attorney client privileged information. But, the next week our firm subscribed to the service that lets us track every public Internet mention by or about our clients who have any kind of public persona or have anyone who might be trying to harm them. You will see that from mid-March onward, right after your Aunt gave us your name as her new beneficiary, you had new Friends on Facebook, new followers of Twitter, and the equivalent on any other social media, blogosphere and the like that you participated in or which had your name. Those contacts allowed us to protect our client, your Aunt, and now you."

"Is that legal?"

"As long as the service did not use false information to trick their way into the cyber lists, there is no violation of any law. Your Twitter follower list will have a true name of an internet security service worker and you, yourself, accepted Roberta Self, I think that is the name they use, as a friend without the least idea of who she was. Check your Facebook Friends List. If you friend me or probably any of the Metzgers, she will be a mutual friend with all of us."

"Jeez."

"I have always found it interesting for Jews to use 'Jeez' or 'Jesus' as an expletive."

"That's assuming that I really am a Jew."

"I'm giving you the benefit of the doubt. But, you did pretty well on your exam yesterday. At least, according to the Metzger clan." Devorah said with a sincere smile. "Let's get something to eat."

"Okay, but after that story and your shushing me yesterday at Bergdorf Goodman's cafe, don't get your feelings hurt if I don't talk to you at lunch."

"There are lots of places in this city that cater to a clientele that want to have private conversations." Devorah pulled out her smart phone and scrolled her contacts. She poked a contact and waited, phone to ear. "Yes, I need a reservation for, say, Noon, straight up, but I need it at one of your private tables, maybe the ones in the wall alcoves, by the pool tables in the cellar… Great! Last name is Feldshuh. … Thanks, see you soon."

—

The taxi ride was short. Susan still marveled at the ferocity of New York drivers. She smiled as their taxi driver used his horn frequently as a means of communicating his frustration with other drivers. Back home in the Quad Cities the car horn was used only as an emergency warning device. Not so here in New York.

The restaurant's façade was deceptively small. At the sidewalk, it was merely a door with two windows on each side below a neon marquee, surrounded by other businesses. As soon as they entered, Susan saw that after an entrance hallway and coat checkroom the place expanded, deeper in the building, into a wide open bar area with deep red rust colored walls and chrome light fixtures and other glittery appointments. The scantily clad hostess checked their reservation and led them down a chrome and glass stairwell to an even larger basement area, proclaimed as 'the Cellar' in muted red neon lights at the bottom of the stairs. Another bar area serviced the basement which had the same color scheme with several pool tables mixed with large group banquet tables in the middle and a myriad of small two and four person serving tables ringing the main floor, each in its own walled alcove. Both the main floor and the lower level were filling with young professional lunch goers, Devorah's peers.

Each alcove had an antique New York City street sign on the wall above, identifying it. The alcove they were led to was Barclay St. The lighting for their table was a miniature street lamp extending out from the wall. It even had the orange-ish glow of a regular street lamp.

"Wow, for all the people in this room, it is remarkably quiet," Susan said as she put her purse against the back edge of the table.

"Yeh, told you so." Devorah reached back over her head and rapped her knuckles against the blood colored wall behind her head. A very dull thump was all that could be heard. "Cork walls, pretty private."

A waitress, Marny, per her nametag, came to take their drink order. She wore the same outfit as the hostess had, a rust colored, almost maroon, satin pirate girl shirt, falling off one shoulder with a big scooped neckline clinging precariously above ample cleavage. She wore pedal pusher pants of matching color to the shirt with black patent platform heels. The costume of slutty street girl was obviously the restaurant's intent, but Marny played the part overly well with her big hair and huge wad of chewing gum.

"Okay, two Perriers comin atcha. Be back for yuah fud orduh," Marny said as she turned and left.

After Marny was safely out of hearing range, Devorah raised her eyebrows and said to Susan, "Really? Perrierrrs," emphasizing the trilled 'R' Marny had used.

Susan smiled and she wisely declined to comment on other New York accent foibles she had recognized since arriving in town.

"So, how do you like our fine city so far?" Devorah asked as she unbuttoned her celadon green suit jacket. She had a matching silk blouse and jade earrings. Susan also noticed her makeup was an improvement over the sedate funeral day look she had worn yesterday. The black eyebrows that had been overly dark and brooding yesterday were now dark and sultry when the brows were paired with dark eye makeup. Devorah Feldshuh could be a real babe when she wanted to.

Susan answered, "I really haven't seen much of it yet. You guys have kept a pretty tight rein on me, you know."

"Yeh. ... If you're into salads, I recommend the Salad Bar, it is awesome here."

"That sounds good to me."

The waitress was walking nearby and Devorah mouthed 'Salad Bar' and pointed up to the waitress who nodded. Marny's work had been made easier.

Devorah stood up and Susan followed. Susan had no sooner turned from the table than Devorah "tsk-tsked" and patted her own purse under her arm. "Susan, you never leave your purse or anything you don't want pilfered alone in New York. It will be gone in a New York minute."

Susan grabbed her purse from the back edge of the table and followed Devorah up the stairs to the main floor salad bar. On the way up the stairs Susan asked, "So what's a New York minute?"

Devorah stopped momentarily and turned to face down toward Susan on the step below her. "You know, I really have no idea. That is just the term I have always heard, it denotes a time that is shorter than you'd expect, really short. Funny, I had never questioned 'New York Minute,' have no idea where it comes from."

They filled their plates at the huge glass-encased salad bar and returned downstairs. Little green bottles and glasses filled with little ice spools were waiting for them at their table. As they settled down to eat, Susan heard and felt Devorah kick her heels off under the table. This beautiful and highly educated lawyer who used 'it denotes' in a sentence instead of simply 'it means' got pretty laid back fairly easily. Susan would never think of taking her shoes off in a restaurant, no matter how dimly lit and private.

Susan spoke first, "So, after my talk with Peter Ephraim, is this a bonding dinner so I trust you enough to come to you with problems before I get myself in trouble?"

Devorah finished chewing her first mouthful of sprouts and sunflower seeds and answered, "It could be that if you want, but if its firm business I have to bill you for my time. It will cost you several hundred dollars less if we just make it a lunch between two friends."

"Good point. I am new to this stuff. Friend designation acknowledged."

Devorah spoke next, "So, Susy, since I leveled with you about my Debbie nickname war story and since we so screwed up on your correct name, tell me how you wound up with Susy, with an "S" and 'Y' instead of just Susan, or Susie, with I-E or Sue or with a final "I" or whatever?"

"Well, truth is I went through that exact thought process not once but twice. When I was in junior high and 'searching for my identity' I actually wrote it as S-u-s-i with a little flower over the 'I.' Then when I was going into high school, when I 'matured' enough to realize how *positively Valley Girlish* that was, I did an Internet search for all the possible variants. I Googled Susan, Susie, Sue, Sus-e-y, Susy and every other possible variant, even with a 'Z' and double oh's, like Swoosie Kurtz, to see what famous people had used what.

"I wasn't sure until I switched to a Google image search for 'susy' and I found a painting by a fairly well-known American painter, Frank Mason. He had done a painting he called 'Susy in a Straw Hat' with 's' and 'y' in Susy. The painting was kind of hokey or informal compared to the neo-classical works he was fairly famous for, but in my mind it looked like he had done a portrait of me. Never mind that he painted it fifteen years before I was born, in my mind this famous painter had named his painting for the real me. So, I adopted the name and I guess somehow the artist also infected me, because by the time I was out of high school I wanted nothing more than to study art in college. I was no great artist myself, but I loved art. Although, I am really not sure, at this point, that art is the end-all pursuit for me. I've had some thoughts of switching majors. Anyway, when I chose my name I even went so far as to reserve a dot-com domain for myself, SusyFisher.com."

"So you have your own website, not sure that was reported to us."

"Probably wasn't reported since it only consists of the domain name and my picture. I have thoughts of, when I get out of college, using it for posting my resume, maybe grad theses and/or a blog. But, for now, the site is just a cover page."

Susan saw Devorah was smiling at her and asked her, "What's so funny?"

Devorah shook her head, "Nothing, I guess you and I are kindred spirits in some ways. I have my own website too. I got it when I was in my last year of law school and was fearing I wouldn't be picked up by a firm and would have to hang out my own shingle, scrounging clients and chasing ambulances, so to speak. And I reserved a domain name to use for that business, you know, the Law offices of Devorah Feldshuh. I guess it was a rarity these days, especially since there is a fairly famous actress with the same last name, but I was able to reserve just my last name, FELDSHUH.com."

"Cool, almost all the single name sites are taken, at least for dot coms. I guess Feldshuh isn't that common."

"You think?" Devorah asked sarcastically.

"So you use it for anything?"

"Nope. Just one page, like you, and an email address I use for private stuff."

"Let me guess. Devorah@Feldshuh.com?"

"Of, course."

"Mind if I contact list that?"

"Sure. What's your private email?" Both young women pulled their smart phones from their purses in unison.

"Duh! Susy@SusyFisher.com, what else? Let's call each other so we can assign it directly to the contact list." They did.

After they put their phones away Susan ate a few bites before speaking, "So, if we are going to be friends, I'm going to need a lot more info from you, significant other preferences, vices, secret ambitions, favorite romantic conquest story, emotional Achilles Heel, the works."

"Umm, Okay," Devorah struggled to finish another mouth of sprouts before continuing. "All right, in reverse order. Emotional Achilles Heel, actually more of an emotional quandary, my ovaries and my parents, are screaming 'make babies,' but my ego and my condo mortgage are saying 'make partner.' And, in our firm I doubt a baby-making female is going to make partner unless she is married to a Wassermann or Ephraim. The Moores won't work since all of the current crop of marriage-age Moores are gay. And I have seen no real prospects I want to make babies with amongst to eligible Wassermanns and Ephraims, although Peter has a real cute son who'll be good baby generating material once he finishes high school and if I want to do a Mrs. Robinson thing." She gave a lusty smile after this.

"What's next?" Devorah asked while taking another bite.

"Umm, favorite romantic conquest story."

"I've got a great one, but this isn't a good time to tell it. I'd tell it better after a few glasses of cheap wine some evening. Suffice it to say that it involves part of the New York Mets infield, a couple Barnard College gals and a physical act that is illegal most places south of Ohio. Next?"

"Secret ambitions?"

"Mixture of the first two answers - make babies with a sweaty athlete with rock hard abs and other stuff. Next."

Susan counted back on her fingers, "Vices."

Devorah smiled, "Lots. Anything with rum in it. And, since I am a daughter of a Conservative Rabbi who grew up Kosher, I should probably admit to Five Guys' cheeseburgers, especially with fried onions. I see you don't keep kosher, with your bacon bits on the salad."

Susy looked surprised at this, "Uh, no. As I'm sure you realize, my upbringing was decidedly, uh, 'non-observant,' I think was the word Aaron used. About the only mention of Kosher in the Fisher kitchen was my mother telling me how different things were for her when she was growing up or my father cracking a joke once about eating pork chops. And I really didn't get his joke. I really don't know much about what kosher entails at all, other than the very basics."

"You're not alone; keeping kosher is not a growth industry amongst Jews these days. It is tough to keep kosher in a world with McDonalds, Taco Bell and Pizza Huts tempting you. I sometimes think the whole Vegan thing is a conspiracy between the Orthodox rabbis and the New Age gurus."

Susan had to think about that one a moment. "Okay, and I guess we've already covered your significant other preferences, that being cute underage boys and sweaty infielders. Right?"

The attorney nodded, "Yeh, that about covers it. And you."

Susan dipped some celery in ranch dressing while she thought. "Emotional Achilles Heel? I'm pretty stable, but this year I guess I'd have to say 'people dying on me.' It's been a bad year. And next, sad to say for my worldliness, my best romantic conquest story probably IS a cute high school boy. I seem to have a knack for attracting cute jocks who can't seem to find their way from the fieldhouse to the library. Details later, over that cheap wine."

Devorah considered this and asked, "Secret ambition?"

"I once told my best friend Heidi, of @PoodyTat fame, that I wanted to meet a rich guy who could buy me an apartment in Paris, or Rome, where I could spend all day going to art galleries and museums. I guess I'll have to revise that since I can buy my own apartment now."

"And, actually, you already own an apartment in New York, which probably has more galleries and museums than Paris and Rome combined."

Susan smirked, mockingly, "See, you New York attorneys have totally screwed with my secret ambition with all this inheritance stuff."

"Poor girl. ... Vices."

"Well, no preferred alcohol. I've had a pretty sheltered existence as to vices. College frat parties in the Quad Cities are pretty well supplied. But, booze hasn't really struck my fancy."

Devorah added, "And, I forgot you aren't even legal drinking age until this fall."

"Yeh, but nobody cards you at frat parties or keggers. All you need is boobs to get as much alcohol as you want. As to vices or addictions, my only real weakness is an addiction to those little perfume samples. I love them. Putting me to work at a Macy's cosmetics counter was my downfall."

"Preferences?"

"Mm mm. Your sweaty short stop sounds cool, but I would gravitate toward a silent, creative type who could intrigue me. Worldly, urbane... a younger version of the Dos Equis beer commercial dude. Exciting, witty and intelligent."

"Like Daddy?"

Susan stared at Devorah for a long moment, expressionless, "Mom could have done a lot worse."

The two ate in silence for a moment. Devorah clinked her empty Perrier bottle at Marny, who smiled and nodded.

Devorah started to eat a carrot, but mid-bite reconsidered and asked Susan, "I realize all of this inheritance stuff has come as a surprise, but ...you had to realize something was up when we called you to come to New York."

Susan shook her head, and with her tongue pushed a seed from her teeth under her lip before she spoke, "Not really. David talked to me about the same thing. You have to realize that my entire experience in all this is my two parents' deaths. An attorney, an old friend, who was actually a bowling team buddy of my Dad, handled everything for both deaths. I don't need to go into the gory details, but there was a small insurance policy on both of them, and they each had an employee pension plan that had some cash-out value upon death, but their only real asset was the little tract home that they had owned since before I was born. Insurance and pension fund paid what was left on their mortgage and car loans and what was left over was a good little nest egg, very little, but it still had me needing a part time job to make sure I could pay expenses for finishing college. All this trust fund talk and the rest is a total surprise to me. I had little knowledge of Aunt Rachel's lifestyle or family situation in New York. And, I had no idea whatsoever that she considered me her heir. When David called I had visions of that scene you see in that video service's commercial on TV where the family is at a reading of the will and the dead guy leaves some little piece of property to each family member. The gold-digger blonde gets the fortune and one nerdy nephew is thrilled when he inherits rights to the video service movies. For all I knew, I was the nerdy niece. My expectations would have been far exceeded if I had gone home with just Rachel's used Prius."

Devorah laughed, "Guess we showed you, huh? I have actually been to will readings that weren't too far from that commercial. Not so funny, just sad. … Changing subjects, you're just twenty, and you're gonna be what, a junior in college this fall," she saw Susan nod, "But, you seem fairly mature and sophisticated, pardon my New York big city prejudice, but my guess is your maturity and intellect are not exactly the norm for twenty year olds from, what do you call it, the Quad Cities?"

Susan looked at her for a moment, pursing her lips, "Congratulations on a work of art sentence, you managed to give me a wonderful compliment while totally trashing my home town and all my friends."

"That's why I apologized in the middle of the sentence." Devorah finished off the carrot.

"As for any sophistication or intellect, it is all my parents. I was the only child of a college history professor and a high school English teacher and I was born late in their life. They talked book reviews and philosophy at the dinner table, took me to places like Versailles and Venice instead of to Disneyland, and made sure I loved reading as much as they did."

"I guess my parents had the same general goal, it is just that I got Hebrew School in Great Neck instead of going to Versailles."

"You didn't turn out too bad."

"The conservative rabbinical jury is still out on that."

"Hey, they can't be too upset about Barnard College graduate and lawyer from NYU."

"Don't get me started on the story about having gotten my acceptance letter from Barnard the first day of Hanukkah, and they cou... I said don't get me started." Susan heard Devorah lapse into her thicker accent when she turned storyteller. "It's just that, at age 28, I would be a good daughter if I married a dentist or a rabbi or some such and gave my parents a grandkid. Being a successful attorney, even for a Kosher law firm, is a far distant second place... for a daughter."

"Do you have any siblings to give them grandkids?" The instant Susan asked this she saw Devorah's expression darken.

"I did."

Susan waited after Devorah's short past tense sentence. Devorah stared down at her salad plate with a menacing fork as though looking for a victim to eat. Instead, she reached over and stabbed a small clump of blue cheese-dipped broccoli that Susan had pushed to the rear of her own plate.

After chewing and washing the broccoli down with a swig of Perrier, Devorah finally looked up at Susan and explained, "I had a brother who was four years older than me. He died just before he started his second year at NYU." Devorah stopped as though thinking whether to continue, then added, "My brother, Daniel, died on 9/11. He was down at the Trade Center picking up his summer internship check to pay tuition for the fall semester. Bad timing." She said nothing more and Susan could think of nothing to say either.

Devorah clinked her fork down on her plate and flopped back into her chair, locking eyes on Susan. "His death is how I had the money to finish both college and law school. My father had a 529 account with matching contributions from his congregation for both kids. When Daniel died, the 529, that's a tax free student savings plan, had a provision were you can roll it over to another surviving child in a family and keep it tax free. I think my parents rather view my going to law school as being the legacy of their dead son, not the success of their living daughter. On top of that, I am also stuck with Daniel's allotment of grandkid production and that production is four years in arrears. Plus, my mother once suggested that I could, maybe, name my firstborn after Daniel. God!"

Devorah pushed the salad plate over to the edge of the table. "As a protection against having to name my son after my dead brother I even dated a couple of Daniels."

"You mean that would make him named after the father, not the dead uncle, like Daniel, Junior?"

"No, if I married a Daniel my son wouldn't be named Daniel. Jews don't do that. You rarely see any Jews named Jr. or the III. There is an old Yiddish folk tradition that the angel of death might get confused if they come to get the guy whose number is up and there is a younger family member of the same name. You often see some Jewish kid named after an already dead relative, but not a living one."

"But, I have the same names as Aunt Rachel?"

"Blame your secular parents for that one. I'm sure half the people at the funeral were wondering why this girl had the same name as her recently deceased aunt. We just don't do that. Actually, some Jews do, the Sephardic Jews do have Juniors and such, but not the Ashkenazi."

"The wha…?" Susan asked.

"Oh, yeh. The Ashkenazi are the Jews who came from Eastern and Central

Europe. The Sephardic Jews are the ones from Spain and Portugal, the ones that Queen Isabella, of Columbus fame, kicked out of there. Most American Jews are Ashkenazi. Some Sephardi. We Ashkenazis call any Jew who doesn't have roots in the Yiddish type culture 'Sephardi,' but that isn't really correct.

"Anyway, the people at Rachel's funeral were mostly Ashkenazi, except for a couple Italian friends, and the Ashkenazi probably thought your being named after her was a bit odd."

Susan shrugged. "I guess I should know that. I recall Dad saying something about the kinds of Jews."

Marny walked by the table and Devorah held up two fingers to her, "Bring us two of your cheesecakes, no syrup."

"Oh, n…" Susan protested.

"Ssshhhhh!" Devorah interrupted, with mock anger. "You got me talking about dead brothers and angels of death, and now I need cheesecake therapy. Wouldn't hurt you any, either." Devorah reaffirmed her order with an emphatic two fingers to the waiting Marny, who turned to comply.

Susan set her salad plate on top of Devorah's and asked, "So, what is the schedule for this afternoon?"

"Well, we are about done with you for now, unless you have something else. You need to look at the stuff Rachel left for you at the office and we need to get you connected with the property manager, Laszlo Kiss, to help get you into Rachel's place. That will be quite a job over there. Remember we can get you help with whatever you need, or you can ask Laszlo. Remember, he works for you now. You can look at Rachel's stuff, the video, at the office, or at your hotel. Unless, you are anxious to get into the apartment, you might want to wait and start that bright and early in the morning. Or you can take a couple days off. Your choice."

"I think I'll do that, tomorrow. Watch her video at the hotel today and go over there in the morning. And, I am going to have to call home and make some arrangements. I planned this for a three day trip and it is obvious I'm not going home tomorrow. I need to tell work I am not coming back and get somebody to water the grass at the house and stuff."

Devorah raised a finger to mention, "One more thing, tomorrow evening is Shabbat and Rachel's synagogue called to leave a message that they are mentioning her at the service, she donated money for a new children's library or something and they want to recognize her. They want to know if you can be there." Devorah raised her eyebrows questioningly.

"Oh…" Susan said softly, "What do you think?"

"I think it would be good for you to see that. Temple Emanu-El is a pretty cool place as synagogues go. Nice people, good atmosphere. I believe it is like the largest synagogue on earth, really impressive. It would let you see another piece of the Jewish puzzle. I guess I can go with you, if you want. That way I could tell my father I went to synagogue and not be lying to him, for once." Devorah smiled deviously.

"That would be cool. Her rabbi was the tall one, right?"

"Yeh, that's right, the tall one." Devorah smiled.

Marny brought the cheesecake. She sat Devorah's plate in front of her saying, "Yuah therapy, Ma'am. And, if there is nuttin' else, I have yuah check."

Devorah started to reach for the check, but Susan quickly, but gently, slapped her hand. "My tab. I have a brand new piece of plastic that needs breaking in."

—

Chapter Seven

From: Susy@SusyFisher.com

To: dmorton@dav.macys.net

Subj: Changes

Derrick,

I tried to call you but your phone was on messages and I wanted to get this to you ASAP.

I hate to give this to you by email, but there have been some changes in my life with this trip to NY and my Aunt's death. I won't be returning to the store. Sorry about the lack of notice, I really did not have much choice. I want to thank you for being a great boss, it has been great working for you.

Oh, and if you are wondering who to put in my spot, I'd recommend Jessica. She is being wasted in Sportswear and she says she can use more hours. She did great when she filled in at Cosmetics over the holidays. Please give my best to everyone, especially Mrs. Prince. I'll try to stop by the store when I am back in the QC. Thanks for everything.

Susy Fisher

———

Susan's room at the Hilton was a two-room suite. The desk in the living room had the wired Internet connection, so that is where Susan sorted out the pile of documents, envelopes and DVDs David Tannenbaum had given her. It was still mid-afternoon so she pulled the golden tapestry print curtain to get the glare off the computer screen. Her Aunt's MacBook had a bigger screen, so she booted it up to watch the first video, the one on the law firm logoed disk. Her aunt had left the system password on a sticky note by the keyboard. She pulled the fleece pants and a velour t-shirt outfit she usually wore as pajamas out of her suitcase, and she got comfortable. After two days in formal dress and the hectic schedule, it was good to have an afternoon by herself when she could kick back. She pulled her hair back and tied it with a ruffled black scrunchie.

Susan had no idea what to expect from the DVD except David's remark that it was made by her Aunt in the week before her death, at the hospital. She closed the DVD drive door and waited. A box appeared giving her choices of what to do with the DVD. She selected Play Video. Then, she selected the 'full screen' icon and clicked on the Play triangle that appeared in the video window.

The video opened with a view of a man's striped tie and his hands on the keyboard of a laptop computer from the view of the internal web cam above the screen. She heard a weak woman's voice asking "It is running?" Then she heard Jeremiah Berg say, "Yes, yes, just a minute, here." His tie disappeared and the view shifted to where Susan could see her Aunt propped up in a hospital bed with several pillows behind her. The perspective changed as the computer was moved on what must be the rolling hospital bed table that was moved until Susan could see a full view of her aunt.

Rachel Metzger had a cloth around her head, peasant style, not quite hiding her bald head. Her face was thin and boney, vastly different from the attractive older woman Susan remembered from last February when she had last seen her. Susan was shocked to see that Rachel closely resembled Susan's mother in her last days, the resemblance between the Rothmann sisters followed them to the very last. The old woman had no make-up this time and Susan could see large splotches of dark stains in the paper-thin skin of her Aunt's face.

"Closer!" Rachel said, reaching toward the web cam.

"I'll get it," Jeremiah's voice, off-camera, responded. The camera rolled sideways and closer, and was re-positioned to point at Rachel again. A new light came on in the hospital room, making it easier for Susan to see the video.

"It's recording?" Rachel asked.

"Yes," was Jeremiah's answer.

Susan could see Rachel's hand appear and put half-round reading glasses on her nose, then a sheaf of papers popped up from below the picture, held shakily by Rachel's thin hands. Rachel looked down at the papers, and then tried to smile into the camera.

Rachel took a deep, labored breath and began to speak, in a breathy, weak voice, "My dear Susy. As I sat here this week and tried to write a script for this, I tried desperately to think of something other than 'if you are watching this, I'll be dead' but alas, there really is nothing else that one can say to start out a message like this, is there?

"I suppose I should start out with an apology and an explanation. I know you are wondering why I chose to make my last words to you this impersonal recording, instead of asking you to be here in person. I know you would have come if I had asked. This is just how I wanted to do this. I have had some very bad days in the last few weeks; last night was particularly bad. They say it was a warning of the end. My fine doctors say that my organs are shutting down and I only have a short time left. Apparently, my kidney is not playing nice with my liver, or some such. I didn't want you to be burdened with this, since there is nothing that you could do, except for listen to my ravings when I am conscious, like today. But, you can do that with this video and not have to partake the gory details. I know how hard it was for you to go through this with you mother. And, when you finally get around to going through my biography notes, you will learn that I had my time dealing with the prolonged final illness of a dear friend of mine, years ago. A death from AIDS is much like a death from cancer. So, I know what it is like to watch someone waste away, and I did not want that to be your final view of me."

Rachel smacked her lips together and said, "Mr. Berg, could you pour some water?" After a few off-camera sounds, a man's hand with a blue plastic cup entered the view and it was passed to Rachel. She took a sip and sat it out of view, near the computer.

She continued, "I knew about this for some time, but I got the doctor's estimate of how much time I had left just after we talked in Moline last March, or was it February, I can't remember. They said they thought I had six to eight months. I knew that I wanted to make you my beneficiary and I started putting together some things, papers, instructions, video explanations like this, that I hoped to be able to give you when you came to visit this summer, like we had talked about. Several years ago, in my vanity, I thought that my life and adventures might be of interest to others and I had actually started to make a collection of video memoirs, that I hoped to hire someone to put together into a ghost written autobiography. But, I eventually, and wisely, chose to keep my sordid details private. But now, you will have those old videos, along with the recordings I made this spring, to be able to know a bit about this old woman. When I first started this video process earlier this spring, I had a grandiose idea of giving you a detailed recounting of my life which tied into the earlier biographical videos I made. But, the realities of the shorter time I have actually had interfered and I now leave you with only a few videos, talking about my family and yours and a couple about the property I have left you. After our wonderful talk after your mother's funeral, I am pretty certain that much of what I have done and collected over the years will be of interest and value to you. I recommend you look at the recent videos I made to understand what needs to be done with my property. You can look at the old biography videos sometime down the road. No rush on watching the postscripts of an old woman's life. I do want you to know that the old biography videos are only for your viewing; please don't invite anyone else to partake of that."

Rachel took several wheezy breaths and then sipped more water. She read from her papers and set one sheet aside, "So, I had a couple months of reasonably good health in which to review some of my things, my artwork, my valuables, and my collections of memorabilia for the last sixty years. But, when things started to get bad for me in early May, I still had not sorted out the important things from the collected garbage of my lifetime. You are going to be faced with quite a mess. I was a packrat, albeit a discerning packrat. But, as I am sure you have heard, I am leaving you with the means to hire people to help you out with the mess.

"It makes me very happy that I am able to leave you with an inheritance that will allow a very brilliant and wonderful young woman to make dreams come true. Use the wealth that my Isaac left to make the world a better, more beautiful place. I have done my damnedest to do just that during my life and now I think you are a wonderful person to carry on with that. I was so proud when your father and mother told me they had named you after me. You know that I was never able to raise my own children." Rachel's voice cracked, and she waited to continue. "And when I got to know you as a little girl, I had this fantasy that this lovely daughter of my little sister was somehow my daughter, too. You were the new generation of Rothmann girl. Now, with my death, I am able to give you a chance to partake of the things that Isaac would have wanted to go to my… our… daughter."

Susan felt her own eyes grow wet as she waited.

Rachel sat another page of paper aside. "Susy, you will be given several of the recordings I made this spring. They also have envelopes of notes, lists and instructions for each one to help you sort out my mess. It would be best if you watch those other videos in the rooms I talk about in the video; it will make more sense to you. As you may know, and will certainly find out, I had the luxury of conducting my packrat habit on a large stage. I had the original apartment where Ike and I made our home, and then I used a neighboring apartment when I went back to school and needed an artist's studio. Not that I ever did justice to it as an artist in my own right, but I did use it as a home base for some very artistic friends and once upon a time to house an illicit paramour or sidekick, in my years of widowhood."

After another sip of water and change of page, Rachel continued, "Anyway, in the envelopes and videos I made this spring you will get my recollections of some of these memories of my life and you can go through things in the rooms to see what value you can wring from them. Also, in a large stack of banker's boxes sitting in the corner of my dining room, you will find the recordings of my memoirs, letters, diaries, photos and the like. There is a big collection of things from your mother; I saved every letter she sent me. There are probably some surprises in there, maybe some embarrassments. I debated whether I should go through all of that myself, but now that I think about it, I am actually glad I did not have time to edit her letters and my diaries. I think you will get a precious view of our life, in a manner that would be impossible any other way."

Rachel stopped, clearing her throat. The throat clearing turned into a cough, rasping and then deeper. She reached for a Kleenex and wiped something from her mouth.

"Susannah, also in those boxes you will have photos and things from my parents and their life. The primary difference between your mother and I was our relationship with our parents and our connection with all things Jewish. For reasons I never agreed with, but understood, your mother chose to turn away from our parent's religion and way of life. I married myself into it. Your mother even left her photo album of our childhood with me when she moved West with your father. I have that there. You have probably already met Aaron, who came very close to being your father. You can see a bit of that aspect of your mother's life, she left that behind in New York, too, and in my packrat best, I have saved all of it."

The coughing racked Rachel once again. She again reached for a Kleenex and this time Rachel could see she was coughing up blood. As the coughing stopped, Rachel took another sip of water, waited, put aside the last page of paper and then continued.

"Susannah, I have come to the end of what I wanted to tell you today. Please realize that I have come to terms with what is happening to me. And, any sadness I have with my predicament is more than overcome by my excitement and happiness I have for what is in store for you. I have had the blessing of a life of plenty and experiences I can never regret. I am thrilled to be able to give you a chance to use the blessings I am able to pass on to you to carry out your heart's desires. Please learn whatever you can from my musings, memories, and trinkets. Get to know your mother in a new way. Have fun with the bank accounts, but be cautious that you don't lose your way because of the bounty of it all. I almost did that once. Most importantly, find yourself a good man, build a family, realize that those you love are the most important and valuable thing you will ever have.

"I have to go now; I can feel things getting bad again. This is the end of my recordings and soon, my life, but I know it is the first recording you will see and you will soon be going through all the other bits and pieces of my life after this. I hope that I have chosen the right way to do this and that you will appreciate my hopes and good intentions. I ask God to bless you and everything you do in your life. Your mother, your father and I, and even my Isaac, will be watching you from heaven, our little girl, as she lives the life of the wonderful woman we know she is and will be. Goodbye."

Rachel stared into the camera with watery eyes for a long moment with one last half smile, half grimace, as Susan could see she was stifling another cough and in pain. Jeremiah's arm reached across, blocking the web cam's view of Rachel and hitting a key to stop the video. Susan's computer video window went to black and a sideways triangle appeared, offering to replay the video.

Susan had watched the whole video with rising emotion. With misty eyes. She had nevertheless pretty much kept her composure until the last sentence. Susan's tears let loose at the thought of her aunt and mother in Heaven watching over her. Susan realized she had responded in exactly the way her Aunt had expected her to. Susan was not really sure she believed in heaven, but there was a primordial sort of sense that caught her off guard with that image.

Susan's reaction to these last words of Rachel Metzger was complex. Sadness, curiosity, regret, love, consternation, pity, thankfulness and many more mixed thoughts and emotions crowded for Susan's attention.

Susan had heard that Rachel had intentionally kept word of her illness and death from Susan, to spare her. But, Susan, nevertheless, had a feeling that she, herself, had somehow failed her Aunt by not being there. When her mother had died, Susan had not arrived at the hospice in time to be there for the moment of death, but the hospice staff had actually waited for Susan to get there before taking her mother's body from the bed. They even asked Susan to help them move her to the gurney, by holding her nightgown in place while the orderlies picked her up. They had said it was the hospice policy to do so, in order to help the bereavement process take root with the reality of the death. Susan had not understood that then, but now with only a memory of the closed casket at the graveyard and now this video, however heartfelt, Susan understood what the experts in death at the cancer hospice in Illinois had been trying to do. Susan felt she had missed something by not being with her aunt at the end.

And, Susan had heard Rachel call her Susy and then Susannah, but not Susan. The old woman had clearly thought that Susannah was Susan's name, like hers. Susan had no idea why her parents had made the decision to shorten her name, since they obviously intended the namesake connection. And, Susan had no idea why Rachel always went by her middle name but not her first. Before she saw Rachel's first name, Susannah, in the funeral card, Susan had always thought the two sisters had just been given alliterative names, Rachel and Rebecca, by their parents.

And the curiosity about the names, extended to the intriguing mention of letters and photos from her own mother's life. Now, as she sat and thought about it, Susan could only recall ever having seen one old portrait of her grandparents on her mother's side. She had never questioned this; it was just the way it was. But, now, she wondered what had prompted her mother to leave her childhood photos in New York when she moved to the Midwest with her new husband. Aunt

Rachel had left more tempting morsels for the curious, her talk of a 'thespian' period, an illicit paramour and "a hoard" of artwork left in the apartments. This, when added to the hints from Aaron and Peter of a secret, unspoken lifestyle for Rachel after Isaac's death intrigued Susan. Rachel had said that the 'sordid details' of her life she had decided to keep private would made clear to Susan in the collected boxes in the apartment. Susan checked her iPhone, but it was too late to go to Rachel's place. It would have to wait for tomorrow, as they had planned at lunch. But, she still had much of the afternoon available and all evening with nothing hanging over her for the first time on this trip.

The video had been intensely emotional. Her earlier idea of relaxing by herself in the hotel room did not seem a good idea anymore. Susan realized she needed to get out of the hotel room and not brood on the video she had just watched. There would be time enough to appease her curiosity. She closed the video window on the computer and opened a browser.

Ever since she went to work at Macy's after high school, she had heard of the flagship Macy's on Herald's Square in New York. Even before that as a young girl she had watched the holiday parades in front of New York Macy's. Google Maps showed the flagship Macy's store to be straight down the street, Avenue of the Americas, from the Hilton, but a long way. She had no idea how much taxis cost and she was not sure she had enough cash, probably not. She pulled the bank ATM brochures from the big folder David Tannenbaum had given her, and then she entered the bank addresses and compared those to the Google Map on the screen. Both of the banks for the new credit cards she had in her purse had branches in the same block a short distance from the Hilton and almost on the way to Macy's, but over one long block east on 5th Avenue. So, she could get some cash and then head to Macy's. Susan had no printer for the map, so she emailed herself the map link so that she could get it easily on her iPhone. She compared the maps on phone and computer. The first leg of the trip was only one big block east to 5th and four or five short blocks south to the banks.

Susan sat the cell phone next to the computer and stood up to prepare for her first New York trip. She stripped out of the fleece pants and t-shirt, laying out on the bed the brown pantsuit and comfy flats she had brought with her. She removed the scrunchie and flipped her hair back and forth to fluff it up. Her 'adventure' in New York was finally underway. She hoped Aunt Rachel would approve. Shopping was better therapy than cheesecake.

—

Chapter Eight

Susan crossed the street and was only a few hundred feet from the Hilton, crossing on the side street over to 5th Avenue, when she was surprised to find herself staring at the entrance to the Museum of Modern Art, the place mentioned in her Aunt's obituary card. She had no idea this icon to every art student has literally across the street from her hotel. She gave a moment's thought of foregoing the shopping and entering MoMA instead. But, it was already mid-afternoon and there was not time to do justice to the massive museum. Susan would remain loyal to her 'shop at Macy's' urge.

Turning right on 5th Avenue Susan saw a Salvatore Ferragamo store across the street. She was again tempted to stray, but resisted. Then, everywhere she looked for blocks she faced another marquee brand name on a store front, H&M, Versace, a huge fortress-like Banana Republic, and then Saks, *the* Saks, here on 5th Avenue. And then Michael Kors, and finally Esprit and Ann Taylor. She could take no more and decided that Ann Taylor would work as well as Macy's for her needs that afternoon. She was a big fan of the simple beauty of Ann Taylor designs. But, she saw the Bank of America she sought was directly across the street. She would get the banking out of the way and then decide on shopping.

The ATM inside the Bank of America took the credit card and her partial Moline phone number as passcode like she had been a lifelong customer. She clicked the bottom choice on the ATM screen, $300.00, and the ATM obediently whirred out fifteen crisp twenties. She held the bills in her hand for a moment. The fact that the ATM gave her cold cash without any question seemed to be mute confirmation that all that the attorneys had told her these last two days was not just some bizarre fantasy. It was real.

Susan put the cash and card in her purse and left the bank. Outside on the corner, she surveyed the Ann Taylor store on the corner to the left with Esprit occupying the same entrance. There were dozens of taxis on the streets ready to take her the few dozen blocks to Herald Square and the big Macy's as she had planned. Then she saw the Sephora cosmetics store on the far corner and she knew the Macy's trip was unnecessary. Ann Taylor, Esprit and Sephora, all on the same corner, were all the therapy she would need.

But, what first?

After considering her options, Susan decided she would start the afternoon with a busman's holiday to the huge cosmetics store on the far corner. She had spent almost three years kowtowing to farmer's wives and teenyboppers at the make-up counter at the Davenport, Iowa Macy's. She had, at times, enjoyed helping someone do a makeover or suggesting a new look for someone who really needed it, but it got old. Now, Susan Fisher would reverse the process and have these big city cosmetics girls patronize her cosmetic needs.

The Sephora store had a large facade of antique black and gold. She entered the gilt doors and looked around the cavernous store. She walked a bit further in and saw a display of make-up cases, large and small. Her eye was caught by the bottom stack of two styles of shiny silver and black faux crocodile cases. She opened one, the coal black croc version, and saw that it was laid out much like the old fishing tackle box she used back home for artist's oil paints and brushes. This make-up case had two tiers of trays for cosmetics, pencils and the like and a large storage area for perfumes, bottles and brushes below. The sign on the stack said, "Sephora Traincases, silver or black, $110.00."

Susan fully realized that she had no real need for a huge make-up case that would do a supermodel proud, but this was not a time for practicality. This was time for an ex-makeup girl to get therapy, serious therapy.

 An attractive saleswoman in her early thirties with an ash blonde bob and a bit too intense a mix of her store's product on her face came over to Susan. The blonde smiled and asked, "May I help you?

Susan smiled back and she handed the black traincase to the blonde, "Certainly. Fill 'er up!"

The woman laughed and said, "Yeh, right."

Susan gave her best faux serious look to the woman and replied, "No, I'm serious. We are going to fill this baby up. Lipstick first."

The saleswoman had no choice but to follow Susan to the nearby lipstick counter with the open traincase.

—

When Susan finally exited the Ann Taylor store, she was glad she had not gone all the way down to Macy's. She had several Sephora, Ann Taylor and Esprit shopping bags in one hand and the larger Ann Taylor hanging garment bag and another smaller bag over her shoulder on the other side. She was afraid the traincase was too heavy for the Sephora bag. She needed a taxi, even though it was only a few blocks back to the Hilton.

Susan did not have any problem hailing a taxi. In fact, she almost caused an accident when two taxis converged from different angles across the heavy 5th Avenue rush hour traffic. The winner popped out of his car and opened his trunk for the bags. He seemed curiously disappointed that it was only a six block fare, but opened the rear door for the brunette beauty in the blue silk pantsuit and striking make-up. When the Sephora manager had figured out how much she was planning on spending she had given the saleswoman orders to invite Susan to the big chrome high chair and give her a 'the works' makeover. Then, Susan had done an 'I'll wear this home' at Ann Taylor for the suit, blouse and matching wedges.

Due to the one-way streets, the taxi driver had to do a wide circuit around the Hilton and come in from 7th Avenue on 54th Street, exchanging honks with another taxi that objected to his radical, abrupt turn into the Hilton entrance. The covered drive-through in front of the Hilton was crowded with the early evening rush hour of people leaving trade shows and heading for dinner engagements and Broadway shows. They had a queue of hotel guests waiting for taxis. The taxi driver would have no trouble getting another fare here.

When the Hilton bell captain saw the huge selection of shopping bags coming out of the taxi trunk he motioned to a bellboy who rushed forward to offer assistance. Susan's first reaction was to refuse and say she could handle it, but after a short pause, she reconsidered. She smiled, batted the false eyelashes that had been added to her look at Sephora and gave him her room number. Susan wondered if they still called them bellboys, it seemed a demeaning term, but then, so was 'cosmetics girl.' He piled her several shopping bags on the brass baggage cart and hung her overstuffed garment bag on the top rail. The bellboy led the way to the elevator. Things were changing for Susy Fisher.

Since she only had the ATM's 20's in her wallet, the bellboy got a great tip for the simple trip with the shopping bags to Susan's room. Magnanimity fit Susan's mood. He had piled the shopping bags on the armchair as she directed, but hung the garment bag on a hidden hook that popped out of the wall near the closet. Susan had not noticed the hook before, like the secret string doodad that unreeled above a hotel bath tub to hang wet clothes on. She wondered what other secret assets a hotel room might have that were not obvious.

As Susan kicked her shoes off by the armchair, she heard her iPhone vibrate its missed call pattern on the desk. She had loaded the map to Macy's and then forgotten to take it when she went shopping. That was rare, the iPhone had become like a part of her anatomy. It was good she had not needed it during her foreshortened trip. The cellphone was indicating the contact she had entered earlier for Devorah's cell phone had called her.

Susan unhooked her left earring and punched the callback on the phone.

She listened, and heard, "Hello, Susy."

"Hi, sorry I missed your call. I went shopping and actually forgot my cell."

"Shopping, huh, where'dja go?"

"I walked over to Ann Taylor and Sephora. Sort of a trial run to make sure you guys weren't pulling some elaborate practical joke on me with the credit cards and all."

"How'd that work for you?"

"Fine, except after the makeover at Sephora I look sorta like somebody going to a fancy society event or photo shoot at Vogue. But, I got some nice clothes and shoes to wear here in New York."

"Good, clothes were one of the things I needed to talk about. But, first, I wanted to let you know that we contacted Laszlo Kiss, the property manager for your Aunt's building. Instead of having you try to take a cab down to Chelsea and find him and the building, we arranged for him to pick you up at the Hilton at 8:30. That's earlier than we talked about at lunch, which is my cool segue between why it is earlier and the clothes topic.

"You said you wanted to go to Temple Emanu-El tomorrow for your Aunt's recognition thingy, and I called the rabbi's assistant to confirm. The Friday evening service is at 6:00PM. But, Shabbat service is supposed to be a celebratory event, so, change of rules, especially at a Reform synagogue, you don't wear your Kriah clothes there, if you are even wearing them at all anymore. And, I assumed you'd be wearing something casual for starting to go through your Aunt's stuff and it will be a long day, but you need to get back to the hotel and change to something nice in order to go the Temple, but not the Kriah outfit. Got it?"

"Yup. How we going to the Temple?"

"It is just over to 5th and left about twice the distance you walked to Ann Taylor. Across from Central Park. Probably don't want to walk though. It is a short cab ride. You have anything planned for tonight?"

"Nope. Just hang around here. Maybe go through all the stuff David gave me. You?"

"Actually, I'm still at work. I have some clients who actually require some lawyering out of me, not just fashion advice like you. I'll be here a while yet."

"Say, you know anyplace around the Hilton I can get carry out supper, maybe a deli? I don't feel like going out to a restaurant by myself, but I'm not spoiled enough yet to try room service."

"If you're really dolled up like a Vogue girl, you can probably get company for dinner by standing around the lobby and waiting for offers."

"Huh uh."

"There's a nice little deli just across 53rd, middle of the block south of you, and there is a ritzy upscale deli to the left, up 6th, that's Avenue of the Americas to you out-of-towners, maybe two blocks on the other side of the street from the Hilton. And, it is not a deli, but there's a really great pizza place, by the slice, on the other end of the block the Hilton is on."

"Do you have this whole city memorized?"

"No, just the restaurants and delicatessens."

"You know, you can probably get counseling for that."

"Nope, memorizing the restaurants was therapy for another condition my shrink says I shouldn't talk about."

"Oh. … See ya tomorrow at five? Here?"

"Yup.

—

Chapter Nine

Breakfast for Susan had been in the Hilton lobby café, again. They had a good breakfast buffet, but it had a confusing set of options for pricing the breakfast fare, with pricey add-ons for different, more desirable choices. She did not bother to understand them; instead she just chose her food and charged the meal to her room without checking the bill.

Susan was back in the brown pantsuit and flats; her new stuff was not exactly casual. She had no idea what to expect at Rachel's apartment, but the talk of stacks of boxes and decades of packratting made her think she might have to do some serious work at the apartment.

Susan was waiting at the Hilton entrance, waiving off an offer from a taxi driver, when she saw a dark blue crew cab pickup with 'The Metzger Companies' on its door pull up at 8:30 sharp. She waived to the driver of the pickup. He pulled to the curb in front of the taxi line and backed up to her. He started to get out, but Susan waived her hand back and forth, indicating she would get in by herself.

As Susan stepped to the truck, she saw a photographer standing near the jewelry shop at the far end of the crowd waiting for taxis. The photographer was focusing a camera with a long lens on Susan. She had not noticed the photographer before; she wondered how long he had been taking pictures of her.

Susan got in and put her backpack with Rachel's computer inside on the floor. She offered her hand to the driver, "Hi, I'm Susan Fisher."

"Pleased to meet you. I'm Laszlo Kiss." He put the truck in gear and pulled away, taking a right onto 53rd, before turning left again.

As he settled into the southbound morning traffic, he said, "Sorry about the truck, not very elegant transportation. I didn't have a chance to get anything else."

Susan looked over at the man. He was a round faced, jocular sort, in a khaki shirt with a Metzger patch over the pocket. "Don't apologize. Where I come from a crew cab GMC is considered a luxury ride."

"Where is that, where you come from?"

"The Quad Cities."

"Ah, on the Mississippi." He was the first person in New York that had any idea what or where the Quad Cities was.

"So how far is this, to where we're going?"

"Quite a ways, as things go in Manhattan. I'll cut over to 11th it will be faster than 7th or 9th this time of day, and go down, what, maybe thirty blocks."

"I have no idea where anything is here. All very confusing? Is this home for you?"

"Yes, lived almost my whole life here in Manhattan. Actually, I've worked all that time for Metzger. My dad got me a job after my Air Force enlistment; he worked for Metzger, too, ever since he came over from Hungary in '56.'"

"Wow, that's loyalty."

"Loyalty is a two-way street; Metzger family has been good to us. I knew your Aunt for a long time; her building has been one of mine for many years."

"So, you manage several buildings?"

"Oh. Yes. It varies, I've had anywhere from eight to twelve. No, make that fourteen, And most of the time I have other people who do the resident managering for me. I've got nine properties I manage now, plus I show rentals to new tenants for other Metzger rentals. Mine are mostly on the west side, Midtown. A couple of apartment buildings, big ones, those are the ones I need a resident manager for, a few straight commercial props and the hybrid ones, like your Aunt's and that mess across the street."

"Mess?"

"Yeh, the place right across the street from your Aunt's place, I guess the mess is your place now or partly yours, anyway, the place across the street is owned by the trusts, that is, split between your trust, Joseph's and, I think, your Uncle Aaron's trust. It has been owned since the '70's, forty years come next year. And the long term leases have all been subleased over the years, splitting up the tenancy, and those long term leases are running out. The good tenants have left or subleased to the riffraff and they know we are probably gonna sell when the main leases expire within the next year or so."

Laszlo turned left and immediately honked at a delivery truck that chose to park in the traffic lane. He went around it and continued.

"Anyway, that place across the street, on 10th, is an old factory, your Uncle Isaac bought it and put commercial on the bottom two floors and residential on the top three. Fine for a long time, but with the uncertainty about the leases the good commercial tenants have moved out leaving dollar stores and Iranian fast food places and the like. The residential people don't like the character of the businesses below them and so they are not renewing and the vacancies and problem tenants are killing us. With the problems there, there isn't enough revenue to fix anything up and that just adds to the cycle of decay."

"I can't believe the Metzger Companies can't come up with money to fix a property up." Susan said.

"It isn't that easy, just throwing money at the problem. It is something about the fact that it is split between the two, or three, trusts and the tax issue, it is fully depreciated and doesn't pan out to put more money in unless there is a good long term tenant. I can't explain it any better than that, I don't do taxes, ask the attorneys."

Laszlo continued, "Bottom line, that property has become a headache and without some new infusion, say a long term tenant whose revenues justify a fix up, or a deal to have the long term tenant do the improvements it needs, we are going to have to get rid of it, sell it and pass the headache to a new developer who is willing and able to be throwing in cash. We had one in similar shape last year that the new owners tore down and built a high-rise. The bare dirt in Manhattan was more valuable than a rundown building."

Susan thought a moment and then asked, "So how is that different from Aunt Rachel's, pardon me, my building?"

"Different set up. Your building is owned by an individual, not multiple trusts. And it has six floors with five of them residential, now. The big bucks in Chelsea are in residential, high-end stuff. Since your Aunt lived there she had us really keep the place up over the years, you know, like custom refurb of the historic design stuff, and when she found a tenant who was a good person to have in the building she had us offer them a long residential lease with guaranteed rent cap. The long-term leases make the tenants able to sublease to other people who have the resources to buy the sublease for cash or finance it from the original tenant, say, if the original guy needs to move. That did two things – made the tenants good people with a vested interest in having a nice building and because of the property tax rules on rent controlled apartments; it kept the property taxes down. Even your Aunt's floor is rent controlled; her trust rents the apartments she has lived in from her personally. She rents to herself, or rather; you rent to yourself, now. So, the attorneys have figured out how to have a privately owned apartment as a tax break. Again, I don't know taxes, but I do know your building is working fine and the other corner is shi…uh, not working."

Laszlo thought and then added, "Also, since your Aunt owned the building outright, not in different family trusts that needed to show a profit to the beneficiaries, she could eat a little vacancy on the commercial floor, until she got a good tenant. Your building has an art gallery, a gourmet restaurant and night club and a Bank of America branch as fairly long term tenants; she could let me wait for good tenants, not the weirdoes I have to rent to just across the street to generate a continual cash flow."

Laszlo turned left onto a side street lined with a mix of buildings. Susan noticed a few mothers walking toddlers and with strollers.

Susan asked, "So, if you could find a good long term tenant for the building across the street, it would still make money?"

"Yeh, sure, this is New York, property is money, but the deal would have to be right, all planned out for taxes and depreciation of what you put back into it, and with a good anchor. Don't hold your breath in this economy. Here we are."

Laszlo turned again, onto a larger street and crossed to the far right side.

They pulled up to a stop light on what Susan now saw as 10th Avenue, from the sign. She was going to ask which building was hers, when she saw the red Bank of America sign on the red brick building on the right corner. Closer to them on 10th she could see silver and black 'bistro' marquee.

Susan did ask, "Which one is the headache building?"

Laszlo pointed to the building to their right on the far corner. From her passenger seat Susan could see a vacancy sign and a shabby sign identifying a budget furniture rental shop. A dark skinned man in a muscle shirt stood with arms crossed outside of the rental place, staring at the traffic.

Laszlo pointed to her building as he slowed to turn into the alley, waiting for a truck to leave and get out of their way, "The building is just a big cube shape, six floors; the top floor is your private apartments. The four floors of residential below that have between four and eight apartments each floor, all high end residential tenants. If you could cut down on the two apartments your aunt held for herself, you could make quite a bit more money, say rent the other big apartment out, and as far as I know she is just storing stuff there. That other apartment is huge, not as big as the main one, but big. And, in a building this nice and well located it would bring thousands of income. But, I guess your aunt really didn't need the income, though. Anyway, … there is a sort of courtyard cut out of the bottom floor off the alley from 10th, here. It used to be loading docks when this was a factory, now we use it for parking."

"Factory? What kind of factory?" Susan asked.

"There were still a couple old panel signs and miscellaneous junk in one of the subbasements; it was a paper goods manufacturer. Once upon a time, I saw some old photos of the building in its heyday. They made and sold boxes, shopping bags and the like. And, bulk card and paper stock to send to printers to print. All the floors have high ceilings to handle the paper machines and warehouse stacks, sixteen to twenty feet tall. Some of the residential units on the second floor where it is twenty feet per floor have even gotten permits to split the floors into two ten foot living areas, or have interior balconies. Really nice. Their leases allow them to do interior remodeling, with our OK and the city building department permit. Those are the units with the highest rent." The truck moved and Laszlo pulled forward into the alley behind the building. He had to wait a minute more while restaurant workers cleared boxes they had just unloaded out of the way. Laszlo waved to the guy who looked like he was directing things.

Laszlo had described the set-up correctly. Fifty feet into the alley was the start of a cutout courtyard that had enough room for four columns of three cars to park facing a raised loading dock area. Several dumpsters sat in a chain link fenced area to the left. Above, the second through sixth floors were built over the courtyard. The overhang above and the solid brick wall on the building across the alley made the parking area fairly dark, even though the sun was shining out on the street. Two orange mercury vapor lights were on, in daylight, illuminating the parking area.

Laszlo pulled into the far parking column where the column only had two cars, a white Mercedes and a white Prius.

"Those are mine?" Susan asked.

"Oh, yes. I forgot, yeh, those are yours. Carlos, my assistant who works this building has an additional duty from your Aunt to take care of the cars. Makes sure they are maintained and washed. She hasn't used them much recently though. Carlos sometimes drove her. And, she let him borrow the Mercedes for his wedding."

"Cool."

"Carlos should meet us here this morning, not sure when, he had an eviction to do."

"Eviction?"

"Yeh, one of our tenants in the Village got busted for drugs, and was in lock-up and hasn't paid rent for months. We finally had to evict his girlfriend this morning. Getting eviction paperwork signed and executed is a real pain. Everybody, the marshals, the courts, the law itself, takes the side of the tenant. Even a scuzzbag like him."

Susan got out of the car with Laszlo. It was a tight fit on her side.

"You can get into the main lobby through here," he pointed at the loading dock area. "That big brown door with the Metzger logo. That's how you'd get in, normally, from the parking area. You should have a key. But, first time, we ought to go around and come in the main door."

Susan wondered vaguely about the law firm and, now, the property manager both insisting first time visitors had to come in the front door.

Now out of the truck, Susan could see that Laszlo was about her height, fiftyish and had a good beer belly. He put a Yankees hat on his balding head. The Yankee blue of the hat matched the truck and his Metzger patch on the shirt. The fact that he had no foreign accent at all confirmed he was probably born after his father's arrival from Hungary in 1956. He stood at the front of his truck looking at the Mercedes. "Damn, they did it again."

"What?"

"The hooligans, they come in here and snip the hood ornament off the Mercedes for souvenirs. I told Mrs. Metzger she should give up and stop putting it back on. We even started putting plastic ones on, because the dealer told us it was less pilferable. No chance. This parking here without round the clock security is a problem in the city. Fortunately, Chelsea is a better area than most."

"Who do the other cars belong to?"

"Bank manager, gallery owner, and some of the other private tenants. Reserved parking in Manhattan is worth its weight in gold. They pay extra for the parking."

Susan followed Laszlo down the alley and around the building, passing the bistro, the bank and the gallery around the corner. She made note that Bank of America was one of the banks she had her new accounts at, which was handy. Susan paused for a second in front of the gallery. They seemed to be changing exhibits on the multi-angled white partitions within the gallery. She could see some plein air paintings being taken down. She could not see what was replacing them.

Laszlo turned into an entrance vestibule with ornate windows and brass doorbell panel. Beyond the vestibule down the street there was another commercial entrance in this building that she could not quite see.

"You got the keys?" he asked.

"Yes, got em," she patted her backpack. "You need them?"

"No, not for this, just checking for upstairs. I have master keys for the entrance, elevators and common areas, so does Carlos. But, Mrs. Metzger kept her apartment keys to herself. We had to get her to let us in. She mislaid her keys once and we had to call a locksmith. Not like the other residential tenants, we have spare, emergency keys for them, in a lock box at the office."

In the lobby, Susan saw the decor was refurbished to match the original 1920's era style; the walls were painted plaster with detailed Art Deco moldings. The floor was marble. The lobby was old, but well kept, like entering a time machine. A frosted glass in the oak door facing the elevators was labeled as the 'stairway' in gilded lettering. They had done a good job to do a restoration of the original Art Deco decor. Above the double elevators there was still a decorative wrought iron panel that was emblazoned 'Chelsea Paper & Box Company.'

Susan put her free hand to her chin, in thought, as she turned to survey the lobby. Looking around she had a *deja vu* feeling in the lobby here. She shook it off. It could just be a scene from an old movie.

"These two elevators would normally serve all six floors, but we have them turned off for access to the top floor. You can use a key to turn it back on if you want," Laszlo explained.

"Then how …?" Susan started to ask before Laszlo motioned toward another door to the right of the elevators. He opened it with a key.

"Those other two were the passenger elevators from the old days. This," he waived his arm beyond the next door, "was the freight elevator. It is now the private elevator to the Metzger floor. Not as elegant as the others, but all yours, private entrance." They entered a room with a large elevator with a horizontal gate and the room had another, wider door in the rear. "That door goes to the parking area, remember the brown door? And there is the hallway to the other ground floor tenants to get to the loading dock. "

He lifted the elevator door from the floor and it flew upward, counterweighted to lift easily. There was a separate, matching lift door in the elevator car. Susan followed him into the elevator. Despite the utilitarian purpose, the antique freight elevator had its charm, with brass control column and an intricate Moorish screen pattern on the drop-down gate. The walls of the elevator were refinished tongue and groove, varnished to a light oak color. Laszlo dropped the gates back down and showed Susan the levered control column in the corner. It reminded her of the old steamship speed control you see in movies.

"Here, you just push this all the way over, to here.' Laszlo pointed to the lever. "The elevator guys refurbished it and have set it to go to the sixth floor, at this notch all the way over here. The other floors are remodeled to have a separate freight elevator entrance room just like the ground floor, but they are locked to the other residents unless they need them to bring up heavy or large furniture that they have to call us for. So you use this to go to your floor, the ground floor and the basements. Those are marked on the dial, here. The two passenger elevators don't go to the basements."

He moved the control lever to the far side and the elevator jerked skyward. Machinery churned somewhere below them.

At the top, the Moorish doors slid up to reveal an entirely different view. Whereas the bottom floor had been antique and commercial in nature, this floor was designed and decorated purely as a residential apartment hallway, the same as you might see in any upscale building, although a bit outdated. Or so Susan assumed, not having any actual experience going into New York luxury apartments. The floor's lobby was large and went to the front of the building with the two other elevators doors there near a window. There were taupe walls, white ceiling and blue carpeting, ringed with ring of carpet matching the wall color around the walls, which had the sole apparent purpose of showing the carpeting installation was custom to the room. There was also a stairwell door across from the other elevators. Two decorative fluorescent fixtures lighted this hallway. One of the bulbs was flickering very slightly. There was an old, musty smell to the air inthis lobby area.

"The sixth floor. Isaac Metzger originally remodeled this as two large residential apartments. Really large, if you consider the size of the building and only two apartments on this whole floor. Word is he originally intended to sell them as luxury condominiums, that is why he did the freight elevator thing, but when he got married Rachel liked this front one and they moved in as their home. In the '70's Chelsea was just becoming the residential gem of Manhattan, the place for the rich and famous to buy or rent a home. Then sometime after Isaac's death, the other apartment that had been rented out went vacant and she took over that, too, used it as an art studio. She did let some friends stay in the other apartment from time to time, and one of her stepkids once. The last time I was in this extra apartment on the sixth she was using it for, like, storage and had some artsy stuff there. She had lots of stuff, Mrs. Metzger. That's for sure"

"Those are the out of service passenger elevator doors." He pointed to the end of the hallway near the front window. "Like I said, you could use them if you want, you should have a round, cylinder shaped key that will turn the controls on for this floor."

Laszlo scuffed his foot against the carpet. "We recarpeted last year, it was pretty dirty and worn, forty years old. Mrs. Metzger asked that we put the same carpet in that it originally had. Supposedly this looks just like it did when Isaac Metzger built it out. This custom border pattern wasn't cheap." Laszlo went over to one of the two massive entrance doors on opposite sides of the hallway, this one labeled '6-B.' Next to the door was an alarm panel. He poked four numbers and turned to Susan. "Entry code is 1972. Just enter the code and push "Off" or "On" when you leave. There is a duplicate panel inside this door and in the master bedroom where you can set it from there, and the inside panels have a red panic button. Push it and the security service will respond, verbally through the speaker and if they can't reach you, then with a patrol car. Oh, and they patrol the building at night, you'll see them several times every night, they get out of the car and check the doors and stuff. Can I see your keys?"

Susan zipped open her backpack pouch and separated the car keys from the tangle of the larger oval key ring. She handed it to Laszlo.

"Wow, that is a pile of keys. If you have trouble figuring out what is what, Carlos can help you. He was usually the one Mrs. Metzger had in here to do stuff for her. That's probably all the keys for everything. You probably want to separate out the ones you'll use, to carry with you. We can get you copies. See here, that is the elevator key, for the passenger elevators." He showed her a round key.

Laszlo inspected the brand on the door's deadbolt and guessed at a key. He had to change his choice twice before a key turned in the deadbolt. The solid oak door swung inward. As she followed Laszlo in, Susan pushed the door bell to test it. From within the apartment came a deep donging chime, like a grandfather clock. This bell worked. She wondered what the bell from the doorbell panel at the lobby's front entrance sounded like.

Crossing the threshold into the apartment, Susan saw the twinkle of a golden mezuzah attached at a tilt on the door jam. Susan smiled in remembrance of the heated discussion her mother and father had a few years back when her father had decided they needed to put a mezuzah up on the door of their home in Moline. Her father wanted to show solidarity with Jews who were fighting a court battle in Illinois for the civil right to put mezuzahs on the doorframes of condos in Chicago. Her mother had said it was silly of her father to put up a religious symbol as a political statement when he did not practice the religion. In the end, her mother relented and the mezuzah went up, but her mother made her father buy another one for the kitchen door. She had said that if they had to have a mezuzah they should do it right and put it on all outside doors. Her father had explained the significance of the mezuzah at the time, but Susan could not remember the whole story behind the mezuzahs on Jewish doorways.

The moment Laszlo entered the foyer an automatic switch turned the light on. In the high ceilinged foyer, she stopped still and looked around her. There was an efficient air conditioner working. The large mirror above the overly elegant Louis XV table and the other similar furnishings were a similar style to Aaron and Myra's house, but not as well maintained. The light was a crystal chandelier hung from the high ceiling. A few of the faux flame bulbs were out in the chandelier. A Persian carpet filled the room, with a small trim of oak parquet flooring at the edge. As she looked around, she slowly nodded her head up and down.

"What?" Laszlo asked. "It's a bit dirty, huh? She discontinued the maid service when she started to go to the clinic for treatment so often in the spring. She didn't want them in here unless she was home. "

"I've been here. I didn't remember until now." She looked around and then walked slowly into the next room, a cavernous dining room. Laszlo followed her.

"Yeh, the window. I sat here looking at it." Susan stared at the geometric stained glass pattern above the wide bay window.

"Yes, each of the front apartments have this, it fits in the architecture of the brick columns, half hexagons, on the front of the building. The side windows on the western side have stained glass bay windows, too. The outside wall on the east and the alley is flat with fewer windows." Laszlo explained not quite sure what she was saying. "You like?"

"Yes, of course. But, what I mean is that I came here once when I was a little girl. I didn't recall it until I walked in here. My mother and I visited when I was small. I remembered a birthday party from that trip before, but now I can barely remember coming in here. I guess it makes sense. Why wouldn't we have come here to her house when we visited. That's funny."

Laszlo smiled, "Childhood memories are funny sometimes. I can remember my father taking me around his work when I was little. I can't remember where we went or what we did, but I can remember this bright red hard hat he gave me to wear in the construction sites. I can remember him pulling hard to tighten the strap inside to make the big, red hard hat stay on my little head." He shifted his Yankee hat at the memory, then remembering he was inside, took the hat off and tucked the brim into his belt at his back.

Susan was smiling and looking around the dining room.

"We had other visits to New York, later, but I don't remember coming here then, just the first time when I was really little." Susan finally broke out of her daze and turned to Laszlo, "So, what's our plan? Go through all the rooms. You need to do that with me?"

Laszlo shrugged, "Your house. You tell me. We can help you get in the other apartment and you can take stock of things. I'm here to help. You want to be alone and go through things? Or if you need someone here, I can come back after an appointment I have or Carlos should be here soon. Or if you need help with something you can call us."

"Show me around and then I'll call you if I need you." Susan's words were interrupted by a double clang of an alarm bell from the outer hallway.

"That'll be Carlos. We left the elevator gate up and he needs it down to call the elevator down to the first floor. You look around, I'll get him."

"Okay." Susan circled the large carved oak inlaid dining table, streaking her forefinger through the dust that covered everything. The cream-colored candles in the centerpiece candelabra were warped from having sat, unused, for so long. The dining room was also Louis XV and the golden wood china cabinet was full of equally elegant china and glassware. In the corner, by the bay window, Susan saw the pile of maybe ten banker's boxes of which Rachel had spoken. There was a writing tablet and pen on the table, near a pile of mail. A dust speckled spider web draped between the golden light fixture on the wall and the red and gold tapestry patterned curtains on the bay windows. She heard the freight elevator head down.

On the left wall, beyond an archway and across a hallway that ran to the right, was a closed carved wood double swinging door with a round glass portal in each door. Susan sat her back pack on the floor by the dining room archway. She pushed one side of the swinging door open and found the kitchen beyond. The kitchen had a motion sensor light switch that turned on with her entrance, but the room was already bright from a skylight inset in the ceiling. The kitchen was massive; to Susan it seemed to be half the size of her parents' home in Moline. She saw two separate granite food prep islands in the middle with racks of pots, utensils and glassware hanging above and drawers below. There were a myriad of cabinets on every wall. There was an old-fashioned white wall telephone on the wall by a pair of doors on the rear wall. A large stainless steel dishwasher sat below cabinets on the back wall. A large double door stainless steel refrigerator filled the far right corner. A metal double deep sink and cutting board counter were next followed by a huge over-under oven like you would expect in a pizza parlor. A commercial size combination grill and six burner stove with a vent hood finished that wall.

On Susan's immediate right was built-in wall unit of ultra-modern appliances, each with a Míele logo crest. First, next to the door, a French door refrigerator and another smaller sink and small counter area next to ceramic stovetop above a large stainless steel dishwasher and a convection microwave unit was at eyelevel toward the far end of the built-in cluster with cupboard doors above and below it. The built-in unit was obviously a recent addition; it still glistened in its newness. It was the kind of glitzy thing you would see in an architectural design or gourmet cooking magazine. This modern, custom wall unit seemed to have a duplicate of all the larger appliances in the kitchen. Everything was duplicated.

Susan opened the French door refrigerator. On the upper shelves were milk and orange juice jugs and things like cheeses, pickles and vitamin water bottles. There were several plastic refrigerator dishes, a couple open bottles of wine with rubber stoppers and miscellaneous products on the lower shelves. Then, the smell hit her. The refrigerator was on, but the milk jug had long ago spoiled and popped its red plastic lid off. On the bottom she saw green goo in the clear glass vegetable drawers. She slammed the door. She did not try the bottom freezer drawer. At the end of the wall unit beyond the microwave Susan found more wine in glass-fronted specialized wine-cooler. The wine cooler was filled with a large selection of wines and champagne bottles. The wine cooler was as tall as Susan and many shelves were loaded two deep and six across with bottles. There had to be a hundred bottles of wine in the high tech cooler.

"Miss Fisher?" Laszlo came in through a different door to the left directly from the foyer. "Let me introduce you to Carlos Ramirez, my assistant. Carlos, Miss Susan Fisher, our new, uh … boss."

Susan was uneasy with this man who was old enough to be her father calling her his boss. But, she could learn to live with that.

Carlos shook hands with Susan. He was a stoutly built Hispanic, probably in his mid 20's. He wore the same khaki Metzger Companies shirt as Laszlo. However, he wore a Mets cap. His muscular, calloused hand enveloped Susan's in the shake.

"Nice to meet you." Carlos said. Susan nodded and smiled.

"This is quite a kitchen, huh?" Susan said, looking around.

"Yeh, some of our buildings have entire apartments this size." Carlos commented.

Susan turned to Laszlo, "You mentioned that maid service that Rachel discontinued in the spring. What would it take to get that back on? I just opened this frig and it is really gross. I'm going to need some help getting this place together."

"Then you've decided to move in?" Laszlo sounded excited at that prospect. He opened the refrigerator and quickly closed it.

"Well, I haven't really decided that much yet. But, whatever, we need to get this place spruced up." Susan moved toward the far wall. Even as she said it, Susan noted her use of the word 'spruced.' Since coming to New York, she seemed to have noticed differences in language more. Where did 'spruced up' come from?

"We can get the maid service back on again. But, they are maintainers, not fixer-uppers. From the looks of this place you need to do a full deep cleaning and rehab. There is a service we use to prepare apartments for rent and properties for sale, that service will handle everything and we can get everything you want done in one fell swoop. They are bonded and reliable."

Again, Susan found the 'one fell swoop' term curious. She, of course, understood it meant 'everything at once,' but she had no idea where such a term came from. Like 'spruced up' or, Devorah and the 'New York Minute.'

"Yes. Get someone in here to do a deep cleaning in this apartment. Just clean it all, like the frig. Everything. But, leave the champagne where it is." She smiled. "I guess I will probably stay here instead of the hotel, once we get it livable, of course."

Susan's path through the kitchen found her in front of the big stainless steel refrigerator. She pulled the large metal lever and opened it, one door at a time. The left door was the freezer, it was barely used, with a big bin of cylinder-shaped ice cubes from an icemaker and two packages of meat with a couple bags of what looked like frozen vegetables. The right side, the refrigerator, was the same, it only had a few items, shriveled fruits and what looked like leftovers of cooked sausages. The smell was not as bad as the other, but things were not fresh inside. She pushed the door wider for the two men to look in.

"Yeh, we'll get the cleaning crew in here. Monday OK? Today's Friday, I'll call them and set something up, first thing Monday? Hope they are available."

"Yes, that will be fine." Susan said, gingerly poking a finger at something on a platter in the refrigerator, an unidentifiable puffy, speckled mass, under plastic wrap on the middle shelf of the big refrigerator. It collapsed inward at her touch with a soft hiss of released air. She shivered and closed the door. She ran some water on her hand from the big sink. She found it curious that the kitchen seemed to have two of everything.

Laszlo spoke, "If it is all right with you, I'll leave you with Carlos, now. Like I said, he knows your Aunts' place better than me. He can get you in everywhere so you can look around. I need to meet some people for a commercial rental walk-through that we previously scheduled. One belonging to your trust."

Susan smiled at the thought of being a landlord. "That's fine. It has been nice meeting you. I look forward to working with you … with both of you." She shook Laszlo's hand as he left.

As Laszlo left, Susan turned to Carlos, "Where's the bedroom?"

"Which one? It has four. Master bedroom out on the front corner." He pointed out beyond the big refrigerator. "Three more off the back hallway. Not counting the maid's quarters, there." He pointed to one of doors on the back wall of the kitchen.

"Master bedroom," Susan decided. She wondered if Rachel and Isaac had ever had a live-in maid for the maid's quarters. They probably had.

Carlos led her out the swinging doors toward the dining room and turned left into a wide hallway. It was dark and Carlos hit a light switch, turning on several small crystal chandeliers that ran the length of the hallway. Two very long fringed oriental rugs, end to end, ran the length of the hall. Susan could see a room with another stained glass window at the far end of the hallway. The high ceiling with intricate crown molding in the hallway and its rich furnishings, gold and ruby filigree wallpaper with original oil paintings spaced on each wall, made the modern hall to her suite at the Hilton seem totally drab by comparison. Carlos walked quickly and Susan had barely enough time to note the paintings appeared to be quite old, she would check them out later, on her own. However, their passage down this hallway frightened a mouse couple from their hiding place behind the leg of another Louis XV wall table with a dusty Chinese vase on it. The two very fast mice disappeared into a darkened doorway on the left. This was a beautiful place, but there was a lot of work to do.

—

Chapter Ten

Susan was in her hotel room, trying to decide on which outfit to wear to the synagogue when there was a knock on the door. She had her white silk blouse, underwear and hose on with a blue silk Ann Taylor suit on a hanger in her left hand and a dark plum tweed Esprit outfit in her right. She went to the door and checked the peephole. She put both hangers in one hand and flipped the brass door catch over with her other hand, opening the door for Devorah while moving out of sight behind the door.

"Hi, you're right on time." Susan said, as she kicked the door closed behind Devorah, "Help me decide what to wear." She held the blue suit in front of her as Devorah turned to look. Susan saw that Devorah was in a dark burgundy business suit.

"Either one will work for a Reform temple. They are pretty cool about people's dress as long as it is respectful." Devorah watched as Susan switched the tweed in front of her body. "But, the blue is prettier. Are these from your little shopping trip?"

"Yup, my first New Yorker clothes." Susan hung the tweed in the closet and started putting the blue suit on.

"How was your New Yorker apartment?" Devorah moved an Esprit bag on the chair over to the TV table and sat in the armchair.

"Gawd!" Susan said as she was fastening the skirt button and spinning the skirt into place. "Don't get me wrong, the main apartment is beautiful, and huge; really nicely decorated. Kinda like Aaron and Myra's place, as to decor. But, I guess cuz she's been sick, it hasn't been taken care of recently. Thick dust everywhere, mice, bugs. They're calling in a cleaning service Monday. Rachel wanted me to go through things, but we need to do a bit before I can really start. There are some gross mystery lumps in the refrigerator that are right out of a B-movie sci-fi flick."

"So, what are your plans? Any idea yet?"

"Well, I really need to stay here at the hotel until they get that place livable. Then I'll probably go there while I go through the sorting process. Rachel wasn't kidding when she said she was a packrat. She wasn't, you know, like a hoarder or anything. She has really cool stuff, but just a lot of it. She didn't seem to like to throw stuff away when she replaced it. The other apartment has enough old paintings and artwork to start a reasonable sized gallery. A couple of the extra bedrooms have closets filled with old clothes. Some of it, no, a lot of it, designer stuff. In one of the back bedrooms in the main apartment, a red gown still in plastic caught my eye. I pulled it out of the closet and checked, it was a Balenciaga evening gown, maybe forty years old, but it still had the Saks tags on it. And it was Size 8, too. Then, I checked the rest of the closet. That whole closet was new or almost new designer stuff, like a time machine had sent the costume department from the '78 or '79 Oscar or Tony awards forward to the present. And there seemed to be more recent haute couture stuff, too. And furs and shoes to go with."

"Wow."

Susan finished dressing with a pair of blue heels.

"Yeh, and one of the bedrooms in the other apartments she has on that floor was like it had been closed up in 1990 and never touched again. It even had a 1989 TV Guide on the bed stand. Thick dust. I checked the closets there and it was totally different. I found a leather jumpsuit that would do Catwoman proud. And some bangle dresses right out of Dirty Dancing. Some of the shoes were positively kinky, you know, disco era, some almost fetishlike. It was getting late by then, so I just peeked into the other rooms. One of them was the art storage place. Another was kind of a warehouse for old furniture. There was an old white IBM PC computer on the desk that was so big it almost covered the desk, maybe 1980's era. I have my work cut out for me."

There was a knock on the hotel door. Susan looked at Devorah and mouthed the question 'Who could that be?' She went to the door and after peeking in the hole, she opened the door. It was the same bell boy as helped her before.

"Miss Fisher?"

"Yes."

"This was delivered for you." And he handed her a large oblong box and a receipt to sign.

Susan took the box, signed and said, "Thank you." Susan shut the door on him. Susan explained to Devorah her lack of a tip for the bellboy with, "I already tipped him really big last time."

The box was wrapped in brown paper and had a white envelope taped to the front. Susan sat the box on the bed and opened the card, reading it to Devorah, "Thanks for being there when you were needed. Much appreciated. Let's get together next time we are in town. Sandra Will [and Joe Metzger.]" There was a phone number and an email address on the card.

Susan ripped the paper from the box. When Susan had partially ripped the paper, Devorah spied the logo and bright red box and announced, "Ferragamo."

Inside the box, Susan found her old gray heels she had lent to Sandra as well as a new pair of black knee high Ferragamo stiletto boots. She checked the size on the box, it was the same 9 ½ as the shoes she had loaned Sandra. She handed one to Devorah.

"Ferragamo calfskin boots. That's a cool thousand dollar Thank You gift!" Devorah said, fingering the soft leather. "Looks like another branch of the Metzger family gives you a thumbs up."

"Wow, well ….." Susan did not say anything else, and she put the boots on the desk. Susan went into the bathroom. She shouted out to Devorah, "So what is our schedule for this, tonight?"

Devorah raised her voice to be heard in the bathroom, "Well, we are right on time to get there for the 6 PM service. You are lucky Rachel was Reform and not Conservative or Orthodox, because Reform has lots shorter Shabbat services. This should be an hour, not more. And they'll have an Oneg Shabbat afterward, so we can decide if we will still want to go get something to eat after that."

"A what?" Susan yelled out.

"Huh?" Devorah responded.

Susan came to the door of the bathroom, brushing her hair. "You said they are having something afterward, a Hebrew word? What was that?"

Devorah nodded, "Oh, Oneg Shabbat. That is like a big buffet they have after the Friday evening service. In law school, I dated a guy that went to Temple Emanu-El and he took me to Shabbat service once. He was one of the Daniel's I mentioned to you. Emanu-El has a pretty good spread of food for Oneg Shabbat. Catered, not BYO like little synagogues."

"Oneg Shabbat, huh? Another thing to add to my 'To Google' list. Last night I Googled your Ashkenazi and Sephardic stuff. Interesting."

Susan came out and started gathering her iPhone and things into a purse.

"New purse?" Devorah asked.

"Yeh, got it on my shopping trip yesterday. Shoulder bag so I can have my hands free for my next shopping trip."

"So, you've got more shopping trips in your sights. And, you are going to live at your Aunt's apartment while you go through her stuff. Are you getting converted to the New York life? Maybe permanently?" Devorah raised her eyebrows as Susan pondered her answer.

"God knows. I have lived my entire life in Moline. My entire identity and world view radiates out from the Quad Cities. It would be a big move. But, there are obviously good reasons to consider a move here. I don't know. Whether I move here or not, I really need to go back to the Quad Cities soon to tie up loose ends. Gosh, I got a call on my cell last night from a guy I had given a tentative okay to go out with tomorrow night. I had totally forgotten about it and I'm sure my story about 'Oh, I'm in New York' sounded a little strange to him."

"Anybody serious?"

"No, not really, hence my totally forgetting about his date. First date actually, we were in class together last term, Modern European History, and he asked if we could go out after he got back from his National Guard Summer camp these last two weeks. He was going to Augustana on his GI Bill after a tour in Afghanistan and he stayed in the Iowa National Guard to help on expenses. They have to do two weeks of summer camp training each year. So, he was a bit older than the other students and I thought he might be interesting to get to know."

Devorah put her hands to her temples and made circular motions with her fingers as though she were a fortune teller or clairvoyant, "And let the Great Madame Devorah make a reading, did your father also attend college on the GI Bill?"

"Stop that!" Susan ordered, then softly added, "Yes, he did."

———

"Well, what did you think?" Devorah asked as they stood up from the pew, waiting to exit the synagogue.

"This was quite different from the other times I went to a synagogue." Susan said putting her purse strap on her shoulder.

"I didn't know you had been before. It didn't sound like you had been."

"Oh, it was just a couple times, in Israel and later in Davenport, Iowa. Dad wanted to placate the Israeli professors who had invited him back to the archaeological dig that summer. They went to a synagogue in the little city near the dig. I went, too, but Mom went very grudgingly, only because Dad said it was important to our hosts. But, it was a lot different than here, all the music was just one guy who chanted without the organ they had here and they had the men and women in different sides of the room, separated by a wooden screen-like thingy. And, of course, it was totally Hebrew. Then, I think Dad wanted to take me to a regular Sabbath service in the Quad Cities to show me it wasn't as spooky as in Israel, Mom wasn't too keen on going, either place. The temple, I think they called it, in Davenport was more like this, but lots smaller, that whole temple would fit in the lobby here."

"Oh, in Israel that would have been an Orthodox synagogue. Orthodox is more like the standard in Israel. It is the exception here. That's totally different."

"And your father's …?" Susan asked as they turned toward the rear of the chapel.

"He is Conservative. More like this, but still a bit different."

"I was surprised that they had two women running the service. And the one was fairly young."

"She was probably an intern in training from the seminary. The other older woman was the assistant rabbi; I talked to her on the phone. The main rabbi is your 'tall rabbi' as you called him, from the burial."

"Music was fantastic. I didn't recognize anything, tune wise, but the soloists' voices were amazing, especially that woman with the soprano voice, she was awesome. It was nice of them to mention Aunt Rachel like that, in the service. This room is pretty awesome, too. The stained glass, this ceiling!" Rachel indicated the towering stained glass and arched stonework on all sides of them. The setting sun was now shining through the big, colorful windows above the main door. "And I did recognize the words you taught me for the Kriah, the guy with the deep voice kept singing '*Barukh atah Adonai Eloheinu* …'" And then it changed to something else."

"Yes, most Jewish prayers start out like that. That 'guy' was the Cantor."

They were approaching the back door of the chapel and Susan recognized the tall rabbi from the burial was shaking hands with people as they left. The female rabbi was handling the other side of the line of people exiting.

"Miss Fisher, I'm so glad you were able to join us tonight." The tall rabbi said, not reintroducing himself and grasping her hand. Turning to Devorah, "And it is Miss Feldshuh, correct?"

"Yes." Devorah answered.

"You wouldn't be any relation to Rabbi Abraham Feldshuh, by any chance."

Devorah smiled. "Yes, he is my father."

"Ah ha! I thought as much. Give him my regards."

"I'll do that."

"Will you ladies be joining us for Oneg Shabbat this evening?" Seeing their nods, he added, "Good, I hope to be able to talk to you more."

As the rabbi turned to the next couple behind them, Devorah pointed Susan to the right, "They have Oneg Shabbat over there."

Susan followed Devorah and when they were away from the line in the lobby she said, "I was a bit surprised at how few people there were in that huge chapel."

Devorah nodded, "It really varies. Right now, on a warm Friday evening in June, that is probably a good turnout, considering. But, come back at Yom Kippur and you'll probably have to get here a half hour early to find a seat, they open up the other little chapel too, then, and have speakers piping in the service from the main chapel."

As the entered the next room Susan said under her breath to Devorah, "This is quite a spread, like the Shiva at Aaron's."

"Yeh, same concept. Celebrate a life with food, celebrate the Sabbath with food. Oneg Shabbat means Sabbath Delights, a party after the service. A time for everyone to gossip, munch and rub elbows."

They got in the short line for plates and proceeded around the table gathering various items. They took their plates and a small glass cup of juice and stood near a flower arrangement on a wall table. Susan had just taken a bite of a little stuffed pastry when the female rabbi came up to them.

"Miss Fisher?" she looked between Susan and Devorah.

Susan nodded and indicated her mouth was full. She swallowed quickly and said, "Yes, Susan Fisher." She put the last bit of pastry on her plate, brushed her fingers on the back of her other hand and offered her hand to the rabbi.

The female rabbi was shorter than both Susan and Devorah and had dark sandy blonde hair with streaks of gray, cut mid-neck length. She wore a blue satin vestment and a white and blue prayer shawl. She was about forty and average build, no make-up, "I'm Kim Seltzer, the assistant rabbi here. And then you would be Devorah, we spoke." She shook Devorah's hand.

"Thank you for your kind words about my Aunt." Susan said.

"Oh, those words were not enough, by far." Rabbi Seltzer said. "She was quite a lady. She was the heart and soul of the Books for Kids program and an important member of our congregation for decades."

Susan asked, "Yes, the Books for Kids program, what exactly was that, books for kids here in the temple?"

"Oh no, much more than that. It was a multi-church program for any school, public or private, that was interested in getting the books in their school. In the 1990's there was a push to keep public schools from purchasing religious oriented or even religious-tinged books for children in public school districts, you know, separation of church and state. Your Aunt and many others thought it was ridiculous. They got together, from many corners, Jewish, Christian, Buddhist, and even Muslim, and made up a book list of award winning books, some about religion, some about ethical conduct and some they just thought ought to be in a school library but probably wouldn't be on an official book list. They created a charity that collected donations and presented an impressive package of children's literature to any school that would accept it. It got to be pretty well known. Your aunt was one of the guiding figures in the group. You know, there is somebody

I would like you to meet. Just a sec ….."

Kim Seltzer headed across the room to gently elbow into a group of woman standing together. She said something to one of them. Separating her from the group, continuing at length about something she wanted the woman to understand. Susan quickly finished her little pastry. The rabbi escorted a woman toward them. The woman was as tall as Susan, fairly stocky and dressed in an expensive, turquoise silk suit with matching pumps and purse. She had short, gray hair and one of those older female faces that can best be described as handsome, rather than pretty, which she would have been forty years before. Susan guessed she was a well maintained 60-plus.

"Miss Fisher, let me introduce you to Betty Mueller, Mrs. Mueller, Susan… Fisher." Susan thought the rabbi had started to say Susannah, but shortened it to Susan. Somehow, word was getting around about her correct name. As an afterthought, the rabbi added, "And this is Susan's friend, Devorah Feldshuh."

Betty Mueller ignored Devorah and took Susan's hand and shook, cradling it with her other hand as she did. "Miss Fisher, it is nice to meet you. I wanted to tell you how much your aunt will be missed, by everyone who knew her."

"Thank you." Susan did not know what else to add.

The rabbi cut in, "I was just telling Susan about her aunt's work on the Books for Kids program." The rabbi turned to Susan to explain. "Mrs. Mueller was a member of the group that coordinated the program for Temple Emanu-El, along with your aunt."

Mrs. Mueller finally let loose of Susan's hand and said, "Really, the whole program, for the whole metro area was an outgrowth of your aunt's original idea. We now have branches in Jersey and on Long Island. But, your aunt was its soul, I was proud to work with her these many years."

Mrs. Mueller paused and glanced quickly at the rabbi, who gave the barest nod of her head, urging Mrs. Mueller to continue, which she did, "You know, I understand your aunt's funeral was just this week. But, since I have the opportunity to speak with you, some of us have thought that you aunt's work on the Books for Kids program would be best honored if she could have someone to carry on her work. We thought she might be honored to have you step into her shoes on the coordinating committee. We know things must be hectic for you, but we wanted to give you our suggestion and let you mull it over. Maybe we could call you after things have settled down, maybe have you see the kind of work the program does for a school. It is really a great thrill to deliver a load of books to a grade school and see the anxious paws rummaging through a pile of new books."

Susan was taken aback and searched for a response, "Well, uh, it is an honor to be asked to try and fill the shoes of my aunt. I …"

The rabbi butted in, "I think it is a great idea. Your aunt would love to have someone like you to continue her good works; that was one of her true mitzvahs."

Susan did not know what she meant by a mitzvah, but got the message, this was obviously not a chance encounter and Mrs. Mueller's invitation was obviously rehearsed. She answered, "You know, I think you are right about what my aunt would want, but right now I have a lot to consider. As you know, I live out of town and am only now considering moving back here to take charge of my aunt's affairs. Let me do like you suggested, consider it. Once I get a handle on which direction things are going I would certainly consider something like that. But, not yet."

Betty Mueller took Susan's hand in her again, "That is all we could hope for. Please accept our sincerest condolences and when you get a chance please give me a call." She palmed Susan a business card, "Or you can reach us through the Temple."

"I'll do that." Susan said with a smile.

Mrs. Mueller finally acknowledged Devorah's presence as she offered her hand to say, "Nice to meet you."

Betty Mueller walked back to her group. Kim Seltzer also shook hands with Devorah and then Susan, "I hope you will consider that, I think it is a great idea. And if you are considering a place to worship, we would love to talk to you about joining Temple Emanu-El. Actually since we have membership fees by family and you are taking over your aunt's affairs, I guess you could consider yourself already a part of the Temple."

Letting go of Susan's hand, "And now, if you will excuse me, I need to tend the flock."   She smiled and walked away.

Devorah and Susan looked at each other. Devorah smirked slightly, "Well, I guess we know the reason behind our invite tonight."

"Recruitment, you think?" Susan stated, more than asked. "Her request didn't seem to be off the cuff. Pretty well rehearsed."

Devorah edged closer to Susan and spoke in a softer voice, "Yes, and I am sure you will find if you look at the trust accounts' charitable records, that your aunt was a major contributor to the 'program.' And, they hope that whoever takes her place at the committee table also has access to her checkbook. Don't get me wrong, I'm sure there are a lot worse places you could spend your aunt's money, I've heard of the Books for Kids program, they do good work, but I just wanted you to know that the offer to fill you aunt's shoes was not just honorary, it has financial strings attached. Or so they hope."

Susan smiled, "Yeh, I got that drift on my own. Who knows, maybe it would be a good place to stretch my legs, doing something worthwhile. But, right now, I don't know answers to basic questions about where I am going to live, or anything. I just can't …."

"Well, welcome to the rarified air of your aunt's social circle. I think Mrs. Mueller's is just the first of many entreaties you are going to get to join the upper crust. You have been offered an entrance into 'Our Crowd' or what is left of it today."

"Our Crowd?" Susan asked.

Devorah smiled and continued to speak softly, right next to Susan's ear, "I am going to have to get you a book on American Judiaca. 'Our Crowd' is a famous term used by, and about, the great Jewish families of the 19th and 20th centuries in New York, the Lehmans, the Guggenheims, the Goldmans, the Sachs, the rich Jews of the East Side of New York whose wealth was legendary in New York, in America even. Their money built this place," Devorah flipped her wrist toward the main chapel of the Temple. "… and Wall Street for that matter. These rich Jewish families called themselves 'Our Crowd' because they were totally exclusive and you couldn't join without having 'old money' or a hell of a lot of new money. You've heard the expression, 'she's just not one of Our Crowd.'" Devorah said this last with a fakely pretentious, haughty tone. "The term comes from that."

Devorah finished with, "Glendon Mueller, her husband, is one of the wealthiest investment bankers in America. Mrs. Mueller is the 21st Century equivalent of 'Our Crowd' and you just got your invite." Devorah thought for a minute and added, "Really, that is not quite right…not an invite. The Metzger family are dues paying members of 'Our Crowd' and that was Mrs. Mueller acknowledging your pedigree via your Aunt Rachel."

'Hmmm-mmf," was Susan's answer, she had taken another bite of food, a gooey honey-flavored potsticker-like dumpling with nut filling that stuck to the roof of her mouth.

They ate in silence, watching the milling people in the room. Devorah saw Susan staring at one group of people, apparently lost in thought. She asked Susan, "Where are you?"

"Huh?" Susan asked, looking quickly over to Devorah.

"I said 'Where are you?' You were staring at those people, obviously totally spaced out. I wondered what universe you were in."

Susan nodded and brushed her fingers together over her plate to get rid of pastry crumbs. "I was looking at that gray haired guy in the camel hair jacket talking to the teenage girl. I'm guessing father and daughter. It reminded me of my father and me. And here in a synagogue I was thinking back about some talks we had about religion. We had had some pretty serious talks about philosophy at times, but not usually about pure religion. He was pretty straightforward secular or humanist, not openly religious at all, although he was raised in a mainstream Jewish family. He never talked much about that. And I know my Mom was raised in a strict Jewish family, but she was openly hostile to the Jewish religion. Again, she never really talked about it and neither did my Dad. But, on this one occasion, the one I was just thinking about, my Dad was kind of saying that things that are the outgrowth of religion become part of a culture for a people or a nation and vice versa, things that are part of a culture get adopted by a religion. He gave the example of the Christmas tree that has become a symbol of Christmas, but really is a pagan pre-Christian icon that has absolutely nothing to do with the Christian religion, except by tradition. And, Americans have pretty much adopted Christmas, and its tree, as a universal holiday tradition with very little recognition of any religious connection. Then he mentioned how we always had a menorah in the front window for December, just to make a showing about the Holidays. It was one of the very few Jewish traditions we kept. In Moline, we were known as 'that Jewish family on 4th Street,' but the Jewish religion and most of the traditions were rarely in our lives.

"With all of the Jewish stuff I've encountered at the burial and at Aaron's and now here tonight, I was just taking stock of where I fit in here. I was wondering how many of the people here tonight, like that father and daughter, are coming because it is just part of their culture and identity, and not because of any strong religious need or belief."

Devorah shrugged, "Good question. I can only answer for myself. I was raised in a total emersion Jewish religious way of life, but somewhere over the years, between late childhood and college girl, I came to realize that I really had no deep belief in the religious part, but the traditions and culture was so much of what I know and feel that I have kept it as part of my life, even to the point that I work for a law firm that is pretty much one hundred percent Jewish. And, I have a mezuzah on the doorframe of my condo and virtually every guy I have ever gone on a second date with has been Jewish. But, I can see how you might be experiencing some culture shock with all this."

Susan added, "Yeh, culture shock, but also sort of a guilty feeling that as a 'Jew' I ought to know more about who I am, or should be, or that I shouldn't feel like so much like a tourist in a place like this."

Devorah smiled, "Well, that guilt is a good sign you may be a better Jew than you think. We Jews are masters at giving ourselves guilt trips."

Susan poked the remains on her plate with the little silver plastic fork.

"These tidbits and hors d'oeuvres are exquisite, but not really what I need. I had a long day and could use some real food. Maybe meat and potatoes?"

"Sounds like a plan. I think your work here is done, for now." Devorah smiled. "There is a great steak house just off Park, straight south of here, I think on 54th. Rothmann's."

"Rothmann's? Like my grandparents?"

"Was that their name? Maybe you have cousins in the restaurant business. Friday night though, gonna need to see if we can get a reservation spot this late. "Devorah pulled out her smart phone and started keying in a search for the restaurant.

—

Chapter Eleven

Who would have thought her first Saturday in New York would require work clothes? Susan had not packed any jeans for the trip to New York and all her purchases the evening before last had been fancy clothes. She now knew the apartment and sorting through Rachel's stuff would be dirty, dusty work, even with the help coming on Monday to clean things. So, on the way to the apartment on Saturday morning Susan, using her new bus pass, stopped at the big Macy's on 34th Street. But, instead of dressy fashion she would have thought she would be shopping for, she had purchased a couple styles of jeans, a colorful Madras blouse and a pastel print peasant blouse, plus a pair of white leather cross-training shoes and white socks. Those sat in her Macy's bag as she finished the trip on the cross-town bus to Chelsea.

Susan's guess that the bus on Saturday morning would not be busy had been wrong. The westbound bus was nearly full, with many of the riders carrying shopping bags like her. There were two young mothers with small children who carried empty fold-up wire carts as though they were intending to shop.

Several riders got off with Susan at the 10th Avenue stop, including both of the mothers. This bus stop was two blocks or so north of Susan's building, she headed for the corner to cross. She saw both of the mothers turn into the entrance to a supermarket on the corner. Susan thought for a minute and decided to go into the supermarket, too. She could use some drinks and fresh snacks for her day at Rachel's apartment.

Susan was surprised at how small the store seemed, and crowded. There were four checkout counters with long lines at each. Beyond that were many rows of narrow aisles and to make their way through the aisles the only carts the store had were tiny two foot square bi-level rolling baskets, not the large handy shopping carts Susan knew from her hometown supermarkets. Susan walked through the entrance aisle that channeled incoming shoppers around that checkout stands. Now able to look down the aisles, she saw the back of the store, only a few dozen feet away. This supposed 'supermarket' in New York was only a third or a quarter the size of a normal supermarket back in the Quad Cities. It was more like the old mom and pop grocery on the street corner in the oldest section of Moline.

Susan wanted to get something to drink and eat at the apartment that would not need to be prepared in that disgusting kitchen. She decided on iced tea, some yogurt and maybe some bags of snacks.

On the canned drinks aisle she found two or three types of zero calorie iced tea, but only one of the national brands she expected and the iced tea they sold was in four can clusters, not the twelve packs she was used to. Susan checked the price for a four pack and saw it was nearly the same as you would pay in a machine. The cans of the unfamiliar brands boldly announced they were entirely organic and came from fair trade sources in apparent hope of explaining their high price. She frowned and picked two four-packs, sampling these new East Coast organic tea brands.

Her trip to the yogurt case was even worse. There was a crowd at the neighboring milk jug rack that made it hard to get to the yogurt. They had some familiar brands, but the space was so small they only had a limited number of flavors. Her favorites, Kiwi and Cherry Vanilla, were not there.

The snack aisle was better, but all bags were small sized and she was poked in the butt by another shopper's cart in the crowded aisle when she reached high to get her choice of seasoned pretzels. The woman who bumped her blamed the position of Susan's cart for the problem and did not try to apologize. It was clear that shopping cart drivers in New York used the same courtesy handbook as cab drivers.

On her way to the checkout, Susan also picked up some spray cleaner, paper towels, rubber gloves and a few other things. Again, the selection was limited and the good brands of paper towels only came in single rolls. At the checkout there was one 'express' lane that Susan would have qualified for, but a quick check of the carts in that line told her the express line limit of twelve items or less was a fiction. She chose the shortest line; three people were ahead of her.

Her checker was a young, olive skinned woman with dyed yellow hair. The woman gave no greeting, just proceeded to scan Susan's purchases. When she finished, Susan handed her two twenty dollar bills.

"Ya got nuthin' smalluh then a twenty?" the checker asked in a nasal voice and annoyed tone.

"No, I got these from an ATM. They're all I have."

"Ah need wunz!" the checker bellowed to nobody in particular. The nasal twang was even worse when she got loud.

A fat man chewing a red licorice rope appeared and held out his hand to the checker who gave him one of Susan's twenties. He handed her a stack of one dollar bills held together with a paper clip. Neither said a word. The checker counted the ones slowly and intentionally dropped the paper clip to the floor.

The checker gave Susan her change without a word and turned to start with the next customer. Susan turned to the bag boy. He had fiery red hair and scores of freckles. He smiled at Susan, handed her the bag and said, in a clear, friendly voice, "I double bagged that for you. Have a nice day!"

Susan returned the smile and said, "You, too." The bag boy obviously had not worked here long enough to be synched with the surly attitude of his co-workers.

Susan walked south with her Macy's bag and purse in one hand and grocery bag in the other. Traffic was heavy and there were many people walking. She saw one of the mothers with kids from the bus push her now-full wire basket; wheeling it to the east bound bus stop on the next cross street corner south. Susan was getting a feel for the grid of one way streets in Manhattan.

Farther south Susan passed the problem building Laszlo had told her about. She stopped to look in the window of the furniture rental place. The merchandise was cheap stuff, living room sets, TVs and beds. The guy in the muscle shirt came outside to ask her, "Need some furniture?"

Susan shook her head, "No, actually I have plenty of furniture right now."

Muscle shirt guy shrugged and said, "We buy stuff, too. If it's in good condition."

Susan nodded and turned to walk away; smiling to herself about the thought of what this place would do with some of Rachel's Louis XV pieces. Rent-an-Antique, low weekly rates?

The rest of the problem building's storefront facing 10th was vacant, with windows painted from the inside and Metzger Companies' 'For Rent" signs. At the corner, she saw the building had several more for rent signs, then a garish 99¢ store and beyond the large, front entrance stairs, a seedy looking restaurant and market with a folding sign on the sidewalk advertising "Chelow Kebab!" in fluorescent hand-painted lettering.

Across the street Susan saw her building. She liked that thought. From this vantage point, she could see the Bank of America on the corner, the art gallery and beyond the front entrance to the apartments, she could now see was a walk-in medical clinic that occupied the eastern third of the building's storefront. The clinic had a large red and blue medical cross logo on its marquee, bright, bold graphics in the windows advertising it was 'open 9 to 9', and 'We take all insurance.' The traffic light changed and Susan crossed to her building. She definitely liked the thought of it being 'her' building.

Yesterday, Carlos had sorted the keys for her, making a ring with just the main keys she would need to get into the main apartment, the lobby and the door back to the parking. He had also given her his cell phone number in case she needed any help, but she wanted to avoid that. Her plan was to do another walk-through by herself, snooping around and then play Rachel's next DVD, to get an idea of what to expect from those DVDs that supposedly discussed the apartments and what she would find.

At the front door, she sat the Macy's bag on the ground to fish the key ring out of her purse. But, before she could get the key in the lock, it opened from the inside. A man was trying to get his bicycle through the door and out of the lobby. Susan pushed the Macy's bag out of the way with her foot and grabbed the door to hold it open for him.

"Oh, Hi, thanks!" the man said pushing the bike past her. He had short sandy blonde hair, was about her height, maybe slightly taller, and seemed to be wearing a royal blue soccer uniform with a bicycle helmet and goggle-type sunglasses. "Oh, you're going in? With groceries? You new in the building?"

Susan looked at him, wondering what she should answer of this stranger's questions. He did not look dangerous and he was coming out of her building, so she said, "Yes, second day here."

"Well, hello. I'm Paul Waldman, 2-C." He backed up his bicycle enough to reach her and offered her his hand, while balancing the bike on his leg and pulling his sunglasses off with his left hand. He had piercing blue eyes with even, square-ish features and a good tan. Susan noted this man lived on the second floor, which Laszlo had said was the nicer bi-level residential floor, the high-rent one.

Susan took his hand and shifted her weight to balance against the door she was holding open, saying, "Susan Fisher, Uh ... 6-B, I guess."

"6-B? I didn't know they had apartments up there, the elevator doesn't seem to go up there."

Susan shrugged, "Well, they do, if you will look at the mailboxes and call box you can see our numbers. I use the other elevator, back there." She pointed to the rear of the lobby. "I'm just getting things cleaned up and sorted out.,"

He looked back inside at the call box buttons and said, "6th floor, huh? Oh, learn something new every day. If you need help with anything let me know. Remember Paul Waldman, 2-C, or you can reach me through the clinic reception."

"Clinic?" Susan asked.

"Yeh, the clinic. I'm a doctor; I'm one of the partners who started the walk-in clinic here." He pointed over his shoulder toward the walk-in clinic.

"Oh, Yeh, I noticed that, seems like a nice place. So, you work in the same building you live in. That's convenient."

"Well, not quite. My real job is as an ER surgeon at Presbyterian. The clinic is an investment, several of us doctors pooled our money to buy the franchise. We thought we saw the need in this area and put our money on it. We all fill in there, but we hired other doctors to cover the main schedule. You know, like retirees that don't want the hassle of their own practice or a hospital schedule, but want to keep practicing part time. I only work there once or twice a month, and usually not that often, to fill in."

Susan nodded. Before she could come up with something else to say, he added, "What do you do?"

Susan paused, knowing that the true answer would lead to more questions, but she had no choice, "I'm a student."

"Where? NYU? CCNY?"

Susan hoped he did not see her internal sigh at having to answer, "No, Augustana College. It is a small college in Illinois."

"Wow, that is going to be a monster commute. Huh?" He smiled.

Susan decided to play along. "Yes, the subway connection is a real bitch."

Paul stumbled on his next words, not having another handy come back ready, so Susan added. "I went to Augustana this last year. The jury is still out on what I do next, other than get this apartment livable."

He nodded, "Well, it has been nice to meet you, as I said, let me know if I can help out with anything."

Susan's mind quickly flittered past things this handsome guy could help her out with. But, Susan nodded, smiled and started to turn inside, but stopped and said, "Wait, I have to ask. You are in a soccer uniform and riding a bike. Where do they have playing fields around here and how can you ride a bike in this awful traffic?"

Paul Waldman nodded and said, "Good questions. They have a decent bike path over on the waterfront and a few dedicated bike paths in the neighborhoods, like down old unused alleys between buildings that have been converted to residential. And there is a really nice elevated deck called the High Line, that's an old un-used elevated train track. where you can go for dozens of blocks north and south, walking or biking, without any car traffic. The bike path by the waterfront goes up and down the harbor and you can take it all the way down to Pier 40, where they have soccer fields, and other athletic fields, on filled in waterfront land, actually a big building on the pier. Nice set-up. There is also a soccer field at Chelsea Park on 10th. But, that is mostly for kids." He pointed in the direction of each location as he explained to Susan. "By the way, you don't play soccer by any chance?"

"I have. Why?"

"Well, the Sunday morning soccer league is co-ed and we are always getting dinged a point because the women we signed up with never show up. If you don't have two women on a side, you have to spot the other co-ed team a point. We are always looking for female soccer players. We'd love to have you come over."

Susan gestured with her hands and a shrug that she might consider it and said, with a bit of mock contempt, "Well, I'm glad to hear that the handicap of having two women is worth one man's team point. Really? … You know, maybe, sometime, but not right now. I have to get my life in order now. I only just bought a pair of tennies to wear," she wiggled her Macy's bag, "until I get my other stuff here, and certainly couldn't come up with soccer cleats. I'll consider it, sometime."

"Well, it doesn't hurt to ask. Nice meeting you."

"You, too." She smiled and watched as he walked to the curb, turning his toe basket on the bike pedals up to put his toe in. From behind Susan saw that he had very broad shoulders and muscular, tanned and very hairy legs above his soccer socks. Lots of shiny golden hair on those strong legs. Before hopping on his bicycle, Paul turned to look back at Susan, and he caught her watching him. She gave an embarrassed smile and quickly turned inside.

Susan could not believe the handsome doctor had caught her ogling him. She hoped it was not too obvious. But, it had been. God!

She wondered how old he was. He seemed to be young, for a doctor. She did a quick calculation of eighteen, maybe seventeen, plus four years for college and three for med school. She had no idea how long a trauma surgery specialty took. He could be within seven to ten years of Susan's age. That could work. It was closer than Rachel and Isaac had been. She made a mental note to run a Google on Paul Waldman, M.D. at New York Presbyterian Hospital. That was where Rachel had died, Susan reminded herself. She needed to find out where Presbyterian was.

As she calculated the number of years for medical school and their probable age difference, Susan sat the grocery bag and Macy's bag on the marble floor of the lobby and looked to figure out which key Carlos had said was for the brass mailbox panel on the wall. The choice was easy, it had 'mail box 6b' in black marker pen on it. Duh! She took the key and opened the box on the far right labeled 6-B. She noted that there were boxes for the other 6th floor apartment Rachel had occupied; she wondered what was in that mailbox. 6-B's box was so full that it was hard to open. The last thing in the back of the box was a bright pink card notifying her that the carrier had been unable to put all the mail in the box and directing her to pick it up by presenting this card at the Post Office will call window at 421 8th Avenue, weekdays 9-5, Saturday 9-2. An errand to run, but not today. She stuffed the pile of crumpled letters and magazines in the Macy's bag and tried to figure out which key was next, to open the doorway back to the freight elevator room.

—

Susan stood under the big chandelier looking around the room. She still had a funny feeling about the deep childhood memory she had of this place. She kicked the front door closed behind her. It latched with a solid click and thud. She sat the bags on the floor and closed the deadbolt on the door. See saw her backpack was still on the floor where she had left it yesterday.

She looked at the grocery bag and wondered where to put it, she did not want any food in the kitchen until it was cleaned. Well, maybe the yogurt in the big frig; it was cleaner. She remembered the mice in the hallway and decided to get the groceries up off the floor, the dining room table would be better.

Next, she needed to change into the jeans. She could do it here, but she opted for the main bedroom. It would give her a chance to look around there. She had not done so with Carlos yesterday, looking into Rachel's personal bedroom stuff while Carlos was there seemed somehow rude.

The master bedroom was as over-sized as each of the other rooms in the place. It was on the front corner of the building, overlooking the intersection. It had two large windows on the west, one of them the stained glass you could see from the hallway. She could hear the sounds of the traffic and an occasional honk below. On the right, or north, side of the room there was another double set of windows that gave a full view of the Midtown skyline beyond the 'problem' building. On this bright morning, the windows gave the room plenty of light. The bedroom was not as dusty as the rest of the house; apparently, Rachel had spent most of her last days before the hospital here. There was a bag of medical supplies labeled with an in-home nursing service logo on the nightstand. Susan absent mindedly went through the nightstand drawer. There was a TV remote, a pad of paper and pens, and, amazingly, an open, but little used box of Trojans. Out of curiosity, Susan checked the package date, a knowledge pointer she had picked up in high school health class. The condoms were fresh-dated. Susan wondered who had used the Trojans with Rachel. At Rachel's age, the issue was obviously not fertility, but rather safe sex. Rachel was an interesting old woman.

The decor of the bedroom was more of the ornate antique style that Rachel seemed to prefer. Kind of a French Provincial theme. Susan discovered when she opened the big armoire between the windows that the antiqueness of some of the furniture was a well-made sham, as the armoire was actually a well-designed home theatre set-up with a huge flat screen television, DVR, and the works inside. The cable box was still on, showing a channel number, so it was connected. The big screen TV faced the large king-sized bed. The bed was unmade; Rachel had slept in it before going to the hospital. There were two tall multi-drawer clothing dressers sitting against to wall in the left and right corners of the room and a vanity with three-section mirror near the bathroom door. In the far corner was a writing table with an all-in-one personal computer and a printer. The computer did not seem to have been used often with a thin layer of dust on the screen and the table seemed to be a gathering place for miscellaneous junk. There was an old-style desk phone next to the computer. It had a dial tone.

Rachel pulled the covers up on the bed and put the Macy's bag and her purse on it. Taking the clothes out she saw that each piece and the shoes had Macy's new, hard to remove tag loops that were almost impossible to remove without scissors. She chose the stretchy Levi's and madras shirt for today. She turned to hunt for something to cut the tags with. The mirrored vanity seemed the best choice.

On top of the vanity were perfume bottles, many of them and cosmetics, lotions and various stuff, but nothing to cut with. The upper drawer in the middle had a locking key in the keyhole which when turned revealed a collection of jewelry boxes. She made a note to check it later. The right hand drawer was more cosmetics, but she saw a red leather zippered bag, which turned out to be a manicure and grooming kit, with two kinds of scissors.

With the clothing tags removed, Susan started to strip out of her brown pantsuit. She stopped, self-conscious about disrobing in a room with three huge windows and open curtains. However, looking at each window, she realized that this building was higher than anything nearby. The privacy of a top floor city apartment was different from the tract house bedroom window where she had grown up. She stripped and pulled the jeans on - perfect fit, and tucked the blouse in, and then she decided to keep it out for working. The white socks and new shoes were next.

She had no hanger for the pantsuit and the other pair of jeans and blouse, so she went to the closer of the two walk-in closet doors on the left of the bed. This large closet had a musty smell about it, as though it was used for storage, rather than everyday use. It had many winter coats and garment bags on hangers, multiple boxes stacked in the rear and old hats and more boxes on the shelving. In the far back corner there even seemed to be several hangers of men's clothing. She found empty shirt and pants hangers and hung the unused clothing on a hook on the back of the closet door.

Since she had opened this closet, Susan decided to check out the other one. The other closet was much larger, actually a room in itself with its own window. This was obviously Rachel's main clothes closet. It was well organized, by clothing type -- dresses, skirts, pants, tops, all hung in their own area, very orderly. Several dozen shoes of every type were arranged on a multi-shelved shoe rack, floor to ceiling. There was a very light, distinctive woody smell in the closet and Susan saw that entire room was lined with cedar panels, this was a custom designed closet meant to store expensive clothes. Susan picked up a pair of white leather tennis shoes and checked under the tongue for a size. It was 9 1/2, the same as her size. She was uncertain whether she wanted wear any hand-me-down shoes, or clothes, from her aunt, but if she wanted to there were virtually every type and color of shoe she could imagine. She put the tennis shoe back and picked up a deep maroon patent pump with three inch heels. It was Prada and the bottom was shiny and unblemished. It had never been worn. Hmmm. As she put the Prada pump back the shelf shifted a bit. She discovered the two shoe shelving panels were hinged on each side. She swiveled the panels out to the sides and discovered another gallery of items behind, some on hooks and some shelves. There were many purses, umbrellas, scarves, belts and the bottom was lined with boots of every kind. The back sides of the shoe panels were mirrored.

Closing the shoe rack, Susan quickly checked a few of the dresses for sizes and maker. They were mostly 8 and a few size 10. The size 10 dresses were on one end and appeared to be more frequently worn. The labels were a mix of every designer and fashion house.

Susan clicked off the closet light and instead, a different set of lights came on. Susan checked the switch plate closer and discovered that the closet had two sets of lighting, both fluorescent and incandescent. You could choose your clothing and match colors depending on what lighting conditions you were dressing for. Susan turned off both sets of lights and went out into the bedroom.

Susan looked around the room, wondering what she should do first. She remembered the jewelry boxes. She turned the key, opened the large top middle drawer of the vanity and lifted out a large, heavy lacquered jewelry box, sitting it on the vanity. The inlaid lacquered lid in a Middle-Eastern geometric pattern was a work of art in itself. It had a flip up lid with a cut glass mirror on the inside and the next layer was split in the middle to cantilever double tiers of velvet-lined trays to each side. She opened it out fully. There were rings, broaches, earrings, necklaces, chains, hair pins, hair clips, and several watches, including two Rolexes rimmed in diamonds, one gold and one silver. Moreover, all of the jewelry appeared to be gold, silver and real gems, nothing looked the least bit like costume jewelry.

One of the compartments was exclusively earrings and on top was a set of diamond stud earrings whose stones were nearly the width of Susan's little finger nail. Next to the diamond studs were gold bangle earrings in the shape of a Star of David with each of the six points of the star being another peppercorn sized diamond. There were many other earrings, smaller diamonds studs and every other sort of gem and style.

Susan was astounded at the wealth of jewelry in this one jewel box. She guessed it had to be worth what … tens of thousands of dollars? Then, considering the diamonds studs alone, that guess was surely low. And her aunt had left it sitting in this semi-abandoned apartment. This one jewel box was worth more than her parents' entire estates when they died. She wondered if this kind of thing needed to be reported for estate taxes. Surely the lawyers were aware, but they seemed satisfied to let her go through everything and deal with it all herself. Susan did not have words for her wonderment at this trove. And, this was just the first drawer she had opened.

She looked into the drawer below where she had pulled out the big box and saw numerous smaller jewel cases. She picked one soft blue leather box about six inches across and slightly longer. It had "Tiffany & Co, New York" embossed in silver into the leather. The rectangular box flipped open the long way with a tiny silver pushbutton catch. She found a large sapphire necklace in a tear drop shape trimmed in small diamonds, it had matching earrings and ring. The ring's sapphire was half the size of the thumbnail sized necklace stone and the earrings half the size of the ring, with earrings and ring each having their own circle of diamonds surrounding the sapphires. It was the kind of thing you might see in a museum or on the red carpet at the Oscars. Susan thought of trying the necklace on, but it seemed wrong to wear such a gem on a madras work shirt. Instead, she put the ring on. Of course, it fit her. It sparkled and felt heavy on her finger as she wiggled it to catch the light. The ring fought her efforts to take it off as though it was magically anxious to be worn. Susan laughed to herself about this as she put the ring back and then closed the box back in its place. She closed the lacquer box, too, putting it back in the drawer. She had seen enough for now. This drawer would need more careful study sometime when she was not wearing work clothes.

Susan stood there, staring into the open drawer and tried to take stock of how she felt about what she had found. Her wonderment at the wealth of this trove led her to the insecurity of what it meant to have this much treasure in the apartment. This was the kind of thing that a burglar would kill someone for. Why, a robber might slit your throat to steal any single item in that drawer. This find was unsettling and wonderful at the same time. She gently closed the drawer. After thinking a moment she locked the drawer and took out the key, adding the key to her keychain on the bed. Instead of going through any more drawers now, she decided to explore the apartment.

On the way out of the bedroom, Susan flipped on the light in the master bath briefly. It was large and nice, totally walled in dark silvery gray ceramic tiles. The shower was a modern glass encased unit with multiple shower heads, probably eight feet on each side. It had a matching tub with Jacuzzi jets. Susan noticed the bathroom had a European style toilet with matching bidet. Susan smiled at the memory of her father once telling her that the hotel bidet in Venice was for washing your feet and her mother had shushed him and later explained the real use to Susan in private.

Carlos had walked her quickly through the apartment, but she had not gone into every room. The apartment was a large square, with most rooms along the outer walls. There were hallways connecting these rooms in another square and the kitchen, study and utility rooms filled the middle. The entrance foyer was on the eastern side, near the elevators. There was a sitting room off of the side of the foyer, followed by the dining room she had gone into first. Susan slid open a double sliding door on the street side of the hallway between the dining room and the master bedroom and found a large living room with a fireplace, a couple of couches and armchairs. A baby grand piano sat in the left corner. The living room had the same antique decor style as the rest of the house. It was done in a blue color scheme with floor to ceiling velvet draperies on two large windows. At one end of the living room was a formal oil painting of Rachel, but when she was probably in her mid-twenties. It was stunningly beautiful. Susan now understood why so many people had commented on how she looked like Rachel. Susan recognized the resemblance, but her self-image rejected the idea that she had that level of beauty.

Aunt Rachel's portrait wore a gown of shimmering blue satin, cut low and the painting was done in a classical style as though she were royalty. Looking closely at the painting, Susan realized that Rachel was wearing the sapphire necklace from the Tiffany box in the drawer. On the opposite wall, over the fireplace was a matching portrait of Isaac Metzger. Susan could see a resemblance with Aaron, although the Aaron she had met was now twenty-five years older than the Isaac in this painting. In the painting, Isaac stood in a dark suit and dark blue tie with his hands on the back of a brocade chair. He was handsome and regal, his temples just barely going silver and his expression direly serious. Susan noticed the same dark blue chair still sat in the far corner of the room by the window. With the paintings, the Metzger's still faced each other across this lovely room. Susan left the door open when she left. This place needed to be opened up more.

On the other, interior, side of the hallway, Susan opened a partially ajar door to a room with another of the skylights like the kitchen, but the skylight seemed to be covered with a dark film coating, blocking most of the light. She reached around inside the doorway and found a dimmer switch, turning on the lights and discovered that the room where the two mice had escaped the day before was a study and library. The lights that had turned on were two matching Tiffany-style ceiling lights of green, gold and brown stained glass. They hung from a ceiling that was slightly higher than the other rooms on the apartment, maybe to accommodate the tall shelves along the wall. The walls were lined with rows of books in mahogany shelves; each side was so high it had a rolling wall ladder to access the upper rows of books. Any wall spaces that did not have books were covered in dark forest green wallpaper. A small fireplace nestled amongst the bookcases on the left wall flanked by two square leather hassocks to sit by the fire on. A large desk of carved dark wood filled the far end of the room with a black leather high-backed desk chair. Two other leather wingback chairs flanked the desk. Susan understood the reason for the dark film over the skylight, even in daytime this room had a dark stateliness about it. High above her, Susan saw the ceiling was a plaster arch up to the skylights, with little scenes painted on the arched panels. She could not make out what exactly the scenes were. The two Tiffany lamps hung down on chains from the ceiling. This high-ceilinged room had a palatial quality about it.

A large painting of a vintage New York street scene hung over the desk. Susan walked over to view the painting closer. It was an original, but Susan did not recognize the artist, Guy C. Wiggins, adding it to her mental list of things to look up. The ornate frame was gilded and very intricate. Two black leather couches faced each other over a low table in the middle. Reading lights on floor stands that matched the Tiffany shades above stood near each couch. Susan noticed the desk lamp was also matching Tiffany style. The right side had a glass-cased cabinet with a large selection of liquor bottles and glasses. Susan made a mental note to check out the book titles when she had a chance. She turned the light off on what was clearly a man's sanctuary -- a wealthy, intelligent man's sanctuary and someone who did not mind spending the money to have custom paintings done on the apartment room's ceiling, reminiscent of the Sistine Chapel. Susan suspected the room had not been used much in the thirty plus years since Isaac Metzger's death.

Turning left just before the entrance to the master bedroom, Susan entered the side hallway. There were no doors in this hallway until she got down to the door of the second bedroom where she had found the closet full of designer gowns the day before. On further inspection, this appeared to be a guest bedroom with more modern, but still elegant furniture. Susan resisted the urge to look again at the closet of designer dresses. There would be time for that.

There was a smaller bathroom with tub and shower to serve the other bedrooms on the interior side of the hallway. This bathroom had white ceramic tile and floral wallpaper, dating the bathroom decor as many decades old. Rachel had obviously updated the master bath recently, but not this one.

Just before the hallway again turned to the left in the far southwest corner of the apartment there was another door that Susan had not entered the day before. The door opened with a slight squeak. This was another bedroom, with rose colored wallpaper and it had another of the matching stained glass windows, like the dining room and the master bedroom. Entering, Susan saw the room definitely had a feminine flair, with floral print wallpaper and a pink satin chair at a small vanity. The bedclothes and curtains had the same rose coloring as the wallpaper. As she stood admiring the room, Susan realized that her *deja vu* while looking at the beautiful window in the dining room had really been a memory of sleeping in this room as a little girl. This was where she had slept on that long ago trip to New York. The small twin four-poster bed was where she had lain, looking at the colors of the stained glass. After having read about the little daughter that Rachel had lost as a baby, Susan wondered if this room had been meant for that little girl. Thinking of that, Susan remembered the Metzger stepchildren had been teenagers when this apartment was remodeled, so this might have been Sarah Metzger Birney's bedroom.

Next in the back hallway was another less interesting bedroom without a window, but with its own bath, then a laundry, a sewing room with a Bernina sewing machine and tailor's mannequin, a large linen closet and a utility room with cleaning supplies, vacuum, a pegboard with a few tools and the like. The back wall of the apartment did not appear to have windows; the wall was against the alley. At the far corner, opposite corner from the master bedroom, was another large room that appeared to be used for mostly storage. She saw an old couch, miscellaneous furniture and a large console TV stereo set that looked decades old, sitting with various cartons and boxes. This might once have been a family room, circa 1975 given the sports team posters in frames on the walls. The big poster of a Los Angeles Dodger player seemed out of place here in New York and Susan vaguely recognized the name on the poster, Sandy Koufax.

The linen closet had shelves full of towels, sheets, pillow cases and table clothes. She noticed there was a large chute labeled 'Trash' in the utility room, a stainless steel drop-down door you could drop your trash bags into to fall who-knows-where below.

She opened the first door on the inside of the hallway and saw it opened into the maid's quarters Carlos had mentioned. The door on the far end of this spartan sleeping room with bath opened onto the kitchen. Another door at the end of the hallway was the rear door of a pantry that had another door on the far end that would open on the kitchen. The pantry seemed to be well stocked with canned goods, boxes of mixes, spices and powders, as well as culinary equipment, but it, too, had a musty, rotting smell from something that was decomposing. A broken rice bag that had fallen to the floor and spilled made Susan suspect the mice had been at work here.

Back in the hallway beyond the family room, a final left turn brought Susan to another hallway back up to the foyer. There was a nice guest bathroom, albeit dated, with monogrammed "M" towels on the left, and, on the right side, a large coat closet in the final length of hallway before the foyer. There was also a door to a small square room that was apparently designed for storage, it was full of miscellaneous boxes, a set of red luggage and a large golden Hanukah menorah was poking out of a large Tide detergent box. At first, Susan wondered why you would put a storage room out front instead of back by the utility room, and then she realized that this storeroom allowed deliveries to be made to the apartment nearly at the front door without the deliveryman entering the living areas. A luxury apartment with no service entrance had to make accommodations.

Susan saw that the storage room had an angled wall at the back left side like a stairway was behind the wall angle. Coming back into the foyer, Susan noticed one narrower door that she had not noticed before as it had been behind the entrance door when it opened. It had a deadbolt with the knob on this side as though it were locking someone out from entering the apartment. Susan opened the deadbolt. It was, indeed, a stairway up. The air in the stairwell was stale and hot.

Susan could see a light switch that she flipped on and a bare bulb hanging from the ceiling illuminated a bare-walled stairway. She decided to go up, brushing away cobwebs as she went up. The air temperature increased with each creaking step up. At the top of the stairs she found another door, this one locked with a heavy hook and eye latch, to keep someone from coming in. She unlatched it and was hit with a blast of hot outside air and blazing sunlight. She was on the roof.

It took her a moment to get her eyes to adjust to the sunlight, but she stepped outside. She was standing next to a wedge-shaped structure that was the stairway she had come up. There were two other similar wedges on the roof. One wedge, nearby, mirrored this one and seemed to come up from the other apartment across the hall, the one Rachel had used as an art studio. The other wedge was toward the front of the building, above where the stairway was labeled in the lobby below, Susan could see a large brass padlock on that door down to the common stairway. There were also waist-high platforms roughly where the elevators were below. These had access ports, probably to get to elevator machinery. Aunt Rachel's apartment had its own private rooftop. Susan looked around.

Susan shared the rooftop with numerous pigeons. There was an area where a collection of really old looking nylon-webbed lawn furniture, folding chairs and loungers, was sitting. A closed black and white striped beach umbrella stood in the middle of a round white table with many rust spots showing. There was a rusty, cylinder-like barbeque cart off to the side of the lawn furniture. There was also a green metal frame with a frayed canvas hammock. The pigeons seemed to like the barbeque and hammock for a perch. In the far left corner, there was an area of six low wooden boxes that appeared to have dirt in them. A tin water sprinkling can and a shovel and hand hoe sat nearby. Just beyond that was a single five-gallon paint bucket with a long dead sapling tree trunk in it. Someone had tried to do rooftop gardening, a long time ago. Everything about the roof told her it had been a long time since anyone had used the rooftop area. At the back of the building, there was a large cube structure with doors and metal grates. Susan could hear air conditioners whirring in the cube. There were also three elongated pyramids of multiple panes of glass spaced across the roof representing the skylights in the kitchen and study and another for the other apartment. The glass panels of the skylights were covered with pigeon droppings and she could see the dark, green lacquer on the study' skylight. There were also clusters of smokestacks and vent pipes from fireplaces and kitchen vents on the floors below.

Looking around her, Susan saw that she had an unrestricted view of the entire New York skyline. There were no nearby buildings tall enough to block the view. She could see from the Statue of Liberty to Midtown Manhattan. She had as good a view of the Jersey shore from here as David Tannenbaum did from his office, just not as high. Until now, she had not fully realized how close this building was to the harbor, it seemed farther on Google Maps. To the East she had a wide panorama of the skyline of the City. Susan Fisher stood and slowly turned to take in the view around 'her' rooftop.

Going back down to her apartment and locking the roof entrance back up, Susan next opened the paper towels and spray bottle of multi-purpose cleaner she had purchased and gathered a dust rag she found in the utility room. She finished cleaning the dining room table and swung the rag to catch the big cobweb between lamp and curtain in the corner. She would let the people Monday clean the house, but she needed someplace to watch Rachel's video and the dining room table near the pile of banker's boxes with the records and photographs was as good as any.

The laptop was still in the backpack by the door were she had left it yesterday, along with the envelopes and DVDs. She looked around for a plug, but decided the walls were too far from the table. Batteries would work, but she wanted a plug-in. As she checked to see if she could move the table, she saw that there was a brass panel inlaid into the parquet floor directly under the table. It had the round caps of an electrical box. She was able to open one of the caps with a silver butter knife from the china cabinet and plug the laptop in. She turned it on.

While the computer booted, Susan looked at the pile of boxes. There were ten. The top two were labeled 'Metzger Photos and Memories.' Another was "Rothmann." Several were labeled "diaries' or 'journals/bio.' A couple more were "Correspondence" and "Research." One was "Rebecca." And the one on the bottom was "Vital Records and Documents.' She also saw that there was a large Canon video camera on a folded tripod with cables lying down behind the boxes near the big window. A video light on a metal stand was next to it on the floor. The large video camera was elaborate, professional looking and obviously quite expensive, not what you would expect for an old woman making videos for a family member.

Susan heard the MacBook's orchestral start-up sound. She turned the chandelier off to reduce the glare on the screen. Before she got the DVDs, Susan loaded the browser and spent several minutes browsing the list of things she could remember she wanted to Google – 'Our Crowd,' supermarkets in the Chelsea section of Manhattan, the painter Guy C. Wiggins, mezuzahs, and, most importantly, one Paul Waldman, M.D.

Finally satisfied with her internet searches, she went to get the DVDs. The DVD with the Roman numeral I and the matching envelope were at the front of the stack she took from the backpack, right after the deathbed DVD she had already watched. The envelope, like all the others, was marked "Do not open until you watch my final video, for Susy's eyes only." She loaded the DVD and then selected play.

She increased the video frame to full screen and sat back. The video started with a view of the dining room wall behind her head. The room was brightly lit and the figure of Aunt Rachel walked into view and sat in the dining chair.

This was the same Rachel Metzger that Susan had seen at her mother's funeral, vital and very attractive for her age. Rachel's dark hair was styled in a pageboy cut and she wore a pink silk blouse. Susan shifted her chair and sat back to watch.

"My dearest Susy, I don't know yet how I am going to show this to you, so I apologize in advance if this is awkward or confusing. I am making this video the second week of March, no, I guess third week now. I was just out to see you at Rebecca's funeral and I cannot tell you how saddened I was that her last days were so hard for her, and you. Unfortunately, a week ago I got a similar prognosis myself. A different kind of cancer, but in the end I fear I will meet my end much like my dear sister. And so, right now, I don't know how I am going to tell you of my fate. I am drawn between having the opportunity to tell you personally about the life I have led and that life your mother and family had, or just using these taped messages and sparing you the trauma of watching me dissolve away like your mother did. But, if I decide to do the former, these will still be a valuable record for you. If not, these will be my personal legacy to you. Since I don't know which I will do yet and since I have no clear idea of how long I have, I will simply tell you all the things I think you might want to know. And, maybe some things you would rather not know, but which you need to understand. Enough preamble, let me begin.

"I had a wonderful time talking to you in Rock Island, or I guess your house is really in Moline. Even with our hearts heavy with your mother's passing I think we had a real synergy between us. Or maybe that was just the imagination of a crazy old woman. I hope not, and I really doubt that. You seem in every way to be the embodiment of the best things I knew of your mother. Her beauty, her wit, her curiosity, her compassion. All that was good about her I saw in you. My ego also says that I saw much of me in you also. I am still amazed that you have chosen art as a course of study; as I did. Where did that come from, I ask you? Where did my love of art come from? Maybe from the same gene, or kindred spirit. I was truly excited when you showed me your provenance study files on the computer I got you. Your eyes sparkled when you talked of artistic genre, and styles and art history. I seem to remember that same sparkle once upon a time in me. I was sadden to hear that you questioned whether studying art was practical for you and that you were thinking of studying something more practical, with better job potential. It was then that I decided I needed to do what I could to give you the opportunity to carry on and enjoy the fruits and blessings of my life. I have told my attorneys to make that happen, but you will already know that when you hear this.

"I was surprised at one thing when we talked after Rebecca's funeral, which was, how little you knew of your mother's life before your father entered the picture and how little you knew of your grandparents, the Rothmanns, my mother and father. I guess it might not be surprising considering the traumatic break your mother had with our parents, but then you know nothing of that either and there was no way I could talk about that so close to your mother's death, so I will try to do that now.

"If I do this the way I want to now, there will be an envelope there with you numbered the same as this disk, number 1, so please take that envelope out now and open it up. Don't skip ahead and spoil my fun, I have this all planned out."

Susan opened the envelope, there was a stack of papers with a bright pink cover sheet marked 'Top.'

"Okay, Susy, go to the first picture."

It was a black & white photo of a tall, handsome middle-aged man in a Navy uniform, a pretty woman with tightly permed brown hair in a sweater and skirt and two pretty, young girls standing on either side of the couple in matching sailor dresses. Susan had never seen the photo before.

"If we have done this right, you are looking at this," she held up the same photo, on the video, "a photo of the Rothmann family, taken a few months before my father's retirement from the Navy. This was at his final duty station in Jacksonville, Florida. He retired as a Navy Chaplain, a Commander, and they had purchased a home in Jacksonville and decided to make that their home. That was a big decision for them. They had both come from the New York area, but neither of them had close family left there and they had spent twenty-five years in the Navy, and Jacksonville, with its perfect weather and a sizable Navy community seemed to be a good place to raise their two young daughters. There was even a new Conservative synagogue that wanted Father's services as an associate rabbi after he retired. It seemed perfect to them.

"And it was perfect in many ways, but there were frictions. Both Rebecca and I were good students, but we were pretty, young girls going through our teen years in suburban Florida in the 1960's. You know, the Beach Boys, the Beatles, miniskirts, the sexual revolution, and so on. However, we were also daughters of a Conservative rabbi who also had spent his entire adult life in a strict military lifestyle. Talk about a bad combination. To say that he was a strict father is an understatement. He was strict, expected absolute discipline and was absolutely determined that his daughters would be perfect students and ladies; not just good… perfect. Turn to the next two pictures."

Susan found two yearbook-style portraits of the Rothmann sisters, Rebecca and Rachel. They seemed to have been scanned on a computer and printed enlarged. Each had '60's era 'big' hair and Susan could see how very much the two pretty brunettes looked alike back then. Again, Susan had never seen either photo.

Rachel flashed the two photos for the video camera. "These are us in our senior class pictures from Andrew Jackson High School in Jacksonville; mine was a year before Rebecca's. Remember, this was back when such schools were segregated, the blacks had another school, and Andrew Jackson High was all white. The few Jewish students were tolerated, but really an anomaly in '60's Florida. All that changed later.

"Anyway, we turned out to be pretty good students. But, I was the older one and I gave Father the first problems. My date for my junior year Homecoming, Buddy Jeffers, was pulled over by a trooper for having an open container in his car, and Rabbi, ex-USN Commander, Solomon Rothmann had to pick his daughter Rachel up from the Duval County Sheriff's office at midnight, on the Sabbath, no less. I remember waiting on that wooden bench outside the drunk tank in my coral pink formal, knowing …fearing … well, you get the picture. I was put on a much shorter leash, and unfortunately, that also meant that most of Rebecca's last three years of high school were tainted by my misdeed, or rather Buddy's misdeed, but who is quibbling. However, we continued to do well in school and I was soon ready to go to college. I anticipated another problem with that, but I was wrong.

"Solomon Rothmann wanted the best education for his daughters. I was actually surprised when the time came for college applications, that Father rejected the local colleges in Florida and said he expected me to go to the best university I could. He had saved for years for our education and he wanted us to have the best. He had gone to college and rabbinical school in New York and he seemed pleased when I was accepted to Columbia. Amazingly, he trusted me enough to go to New York and live in a dorm. I guess he thought his strict upbringing had done its trick. Next picture!"

Susan found a snapshot of Rebecca and Rachel, as older teenagers, on either side of their mother standing in front of a train car. A Post-It note on the picture said "Tova, Rachel and Rebecca Rothmann." A large suitcase sat by Rachel's foot. In the video, Rachel fingered the snapshot.

"I have not said much in this video so far about our mother. I guess that tells a lot about the way she was. She was the perfect rabbi's wife. Always there, supporting him, urging him on, but quietly. Her views were, if anything, probably even stricter than father's, but she was softer about it. She had married quite young; she met Father when he came home on leave from the War. Her only advanced education was what she got as a very young Navy wife, standing at Father's side. Being a Jewish rabbi's wife in a very Gentile community of Navy officers had not been easy. If you aren't familiar with the kind of anti-Jewish sentiment that was in vogue in some parts of society back in the 1940's, I have a DVD of the movie *Gentlemen's Agreement* with Cary Grant in my collection in my bedroom video cabinet. You should watch it, even if you have seen it before. I try to think of my mother trying to survive as an officer's wife in an age when being Jewish did not fit in, in some places. And, the totally white, mostly Protestant, U.S. Navy officer corps was one of those places that Jews fit in poorly. I have a whole bunch more recollections about Father's Navy days in the journals and notes I prepared when I thought I wanted to write my life's story. They're in one of those boxes over yonder." Rachel pointed toward the dining room corner.

"Anyway, Mother was soft spoken and deferred to Father, at least in public. I often suspected that she had him wrapped around her finger in private and I questioned how much of his strictness, and high expectations, was just Father trying to meet Mother's own expectations of him. He worshipped her; I can never remember a harsh word between them. So, this picture is of Rebecca and me, with Mother, on the day they put me on the train north to Columbia University, in 1968. They had arranged for me to check in with a family friend who lived in Washington Heights, not far from Columbia, frequently, and I was under orders to write Mother every week. That was the deal to allow me to go to school in New York. And also, I had to put up with one or the other of them coming up frequently to check on me. There was a passenger train called the Silver Meteor from Florida to New York that got a lot of business from the Rothmann family in those years. Next!"

The next photo was another computer enlarged black and white snapshot, this time it was just Rebecca and Rachel, standing together on a New York street, in very short skirts.

"Rebecca also got admitted to Columbia and joined me the next year. Father actually said once that he considered moving back home to New York in those days, since both of his girls were up here. I think Mother nipped that in the bud, she had learned to love Florida. She was thriving in the Jewish community that was building up there in the late '60's.

"Rachel and I roomed together. There was a sorority, actually there were several, for Jewish women. They had a fairly nice sorority house and we roomed together, which brought us closer, if that is possible, than we had been before. It was, however, not as conservative a place as our parents expected. Young, educated, Jewish woman in the late '60's were on the forefront of most of the social movements of the day and our sorority sisters' behavior at Columbia University was no exception. And, we partied quite well, and taught those Ivy Leaguers some new tricks. Imagine a group of rabbi's and bankers' daughters turned loose in 1969 New York City in the days of Woodstock, drugs, sex, civil rights movement, protests and so on. Use your imagination. Next photo, please."

This was a photo of a young brunette beauty holding hands with a tall, handsome, blond haired young man. He was in a suit and she was in a fancy, silk dress, like they were going to church or out on the town. Susan looked closely and mouthed "Oh. My God!" Not only did Susan recognize the young Aaron Metzger, but she also saw her mother, the 19 year old Rebecca Rothmann, as Susan's virtual clone, or vice versa, albeit with a bouffant hairstyle and more pronounced '60's make-up.

Rachel continued, "I assume that you have met this gentleman, if not, you will soon. In the fall of her second year at Columbia, that would be 1970, Rebecca went with some friends to a party in Greenwich Village. I missed it; I was studying for once, being a junior by then. She went to a party at this young gentleman's apartment. Aaron Metzger was a student at NYU, business major, Finance, I believe. He was introduced to Rebecca at that party and was quite smitten by her. She was quite a babe, as you can see. He, as you can also see, was a Jewish Troy Donahue. I assume you know who Troy Donahue was, I may have dated myself there."

Susan made another mental note to Google Troy Donahue.

Rachel continued, "Aaron called her at the sorority house almost daily for a week or so until she agreed to go on a date with him. In those days we had one phone for the whole sorority, no private lines or cell phones back then. I got one of his calls myself when he called and asked to speak to 'Miss Fisher' and he said 'This is Aaron Metzger again' and he asked me if I wouldn't please go to *Fiddler on the Roof* on Broadway with him. He had good tickets for that weekend, he said. I really wanted to see *Fiddler,* it was "the" big thing right then, but I was a good big sister and explained to him that there were two Miss Fisher's and he probably wanted my sister Rebecca. To shorten the story, she went to *Fiddler* and they became a frequent couple. Several weeks later, he had another party at his Village pad and Rebecca asked me to come. Aaron had his older brother there. Isaac was considerably older than us college kids, he was kind of a duck out of water, I mean fish out of water, at this party of young undergrads. I mixed my metaphors there, huh? He was well into his thirties, and I found out, he was already a widower. But, I found him charming, urbane, witty, and, as an aside, incredibly wealthy. He apparently was as taken by me as his brother was by Rebecca. When I finally got to see *Fiddler,* we were dropped off at the Broadway theatre in a limo Isaac hired. And, within a few weeks there were two different Rothmann-Metzger couples keeping the #1 Line subway busy between Greenwich Village and our sorority house in Morningside Heights. I used the subway less than Rebecca did, because Isaac had this black Jaguar XKE that he loved to pick me up at the sorority house in. Next picture!"

Susan's next picture was of four people, two couples posing for the camera, the Rothmann Sisters and two young men wearing fedoras, Isaac and Aaron. All were in long winter coats and they were standing in front of what was obviously a large synagogue with elaborate stone carving around the doorway, but not the Temple Emanu-El that Susan had seen.

"This picture was taken in December 1970 out front of the Park Avenue Synagogue, the Conservative synagogue on the Upper East side. This is my Isaac and me and your mother with Aaron. Things were getting serious for both couples by then. So much so, that when the holiday break came, Hanukkah came the same week as Christmas that year, we told our parents some lame excuse for why neither of us could come home to Florida on break and the Metzger sons took the Rothmann daughters to the Metzger house on the Upper East Side for Hanukkah dinner. Everyone had a wonderful time and old Hannah Metzger, their mother, approved of the Rothmann girls for her boys. The story is that Hannah and her older sister Myrtle even went to the rabbi to make sure there was not a problem with two brothers marrying a pair of sisters. There was not, apparently.

"By New Year's 1971 it looked like there were two marriages on the horizon. Our parents got wind of this and they both took a plane, not the usual train, up to New York and met the Metzger boys. They thought they were great, but Mother took me aside and asked if I didn't think Isaac was a bit old for me. I told her emphatically 'No' and pointed out how her age difference from Dad was almost the same. Isaac's age seemed to be their only concern. We had their blessing, too.

"But, around then things started to unravel, mostly for Rebecca, but to a lesser extent for me. You see, we had both been free, young college women living in the fashion, culture and entertainment capital of the world for a couple of years by then. Life was good and a damned sight better than life back home under a domineering Conservative Jewish father and his docile wife. Both Metzger men were wealthy men about town while we were dating them, but as things started to get serious, we both started to see that they were truly sons of old Morris and Hannah Metzger, Jewish sons, and they had visions of building a traditional Jewish family, like they had come from.

"Rebecca and I talked about this and she was clearly having second thoughts about getting married. Both Aaron and Isaac were on a full court press by that time to make a commitment as to when. Aaron even talked Rebecca to go for an extended weekend away with him that February to talk it out. It was Valentine's Day weekend. Things did not work out well and Rebecca was back in our room on Sunday night with tear streaked mascara. They had broken up. They had gotten serious about discussing the future, he had told her how he wanted things to be, she had explained her concerns, things got heated, she ran scared from the commitment. "

Susan saw Rachel throw her hands up in the video. "But, a couple weeks later, Rebecca came to me, again in tears, and she told me she was pregnant. There had apparently been more than just talking on their long weekend away together. We both knew that Aaron would take her back and marry her in an instant, but by that time she was totally sure she did not want the life our mother had led for herself and her children. Aaron had, apparently, confirmed her worst fears when he had confided in her his hopes for them.

"Remember, this was 1971 and it was a rough time for a girl who was barely twenty years old to deal with an unwanted pregnancy, even in New York City. There were a lot of good reasons to just go with the inevitable and marry Aaron, but your mother was determined. She asked me to help her get rid of the baby. This was a radical concept, even for enlightened me. I stewed over what to do. I am not quite sure how it came about, but our mother got wind of the pregnancy and told my father, but that was the same time as his first heart attack and neither of them could come up to New York. Maybe the heart attack was because of that news, we had our suspicions and later Mother would voice her own accusation of that to Rebecca. At first, I think they naturally assumed Rebecca and Aaron would do the right thing and get hitched, you see, they had not been told about the breakup yet. But, Aaron knew nothing about it and I didn't let Isaac know either, at least not then. It was the Rothmann girls' secret.

"Rebecca made her decision to have an abortion. It all happened rather quickly, it had to. One of our sorority sisters, who also found out about it, told us about a Reform rabbi that had set up a network to help girls in a spot like Rebecca. And, on a blisteringly cold day in early March, a full-fledged blizzard was blowing; I took Rebecca to a medical office on Park Avenue in New York to have her abortion. You see, the popular myth about the 'back alley abortionists' was not true in our case. The New York abortion rights network people had top doctors on their side and helping them out. But, it was not cheap. We pooled our money and got a loan from the sorority sister who had told us about where to go. The deed was done and they even had a sleeping room at the clinic where we stayed overnight, to make sure there wasn't any bleeding. That was a miserable night, for both of us."

There was a funny ringing sound on the video, like an old fashioned alarm clock. Rachel looked off camera and then said, "And on that high note, let me take a break. Somebody is ringing from downstairs."

Rachel walked off camera and the screen blinked black and gray static before Rachel's face appeared again as she turned the camera back on. Susan took the opportunity to move the cursor to the Pause button and click it, freezing Rachel's face on the screen.

Susan sat back in the chair and rubbed her eyes from the strain of watching the laptop screen video. She stared at the screen as she tried to digest what Rachel had said. Her own mother, who had given Susan her own lessons about the 'birds and bees' had, at about the same age as Susan right now, gotten knocked up by a blond hunk of a Jewish millionaire and had decided to get an abortion rather than lock herself into a life in a Conservative Jewish family. Susan was slightly numb at this revelation. But, she had little time to think about it before the loud ringing that had terminated Rachel's video caused her to jump in her chair. Her eyes shot to the computer screen, which had not changed. She quickly realized that the sound was not from the computer, but from the foyer and the ringing occurred again. Someone was ringing her from downstairs, just as Rachel had been interrupted on the video.

Susan went to the foyer and saw a tan plastic square on the wall by the front door. She went to it, but before she got there it rang at her again. She saw a button on the box labeled 'Intercom – Push to talk and listen.' She pushed it and said, "Yes?"

"Welcome Wagon!" a man's voice said.

"Uh, what?" she answered.

"This is Paul Waldman, the guy on the bike, apartment 2-C. You said you were just getting your apartment livable, so I figured it might be tough to get lunch prepared up there. It is almost lunchtime, so I brought you a Welcome Wagon lunch."

Susan tried to think of what to say, "Uh, well, I'd invite you up, but I wasn't lying, my apartment is crappy right now. No visitors allowed until cleaning crew comes on Monday."

"Well, we could eat at my place."

"My Momma taught me not to go to the apartments of men I just met when they promise me candy … or food."

"And your Momma was probably right. What do you suggest? I bought a great lunch spread at the Kosher Deli over on 9th for you. We could sit here in the lobby and eat it if you want, or in the park."

Susan thought about options, and delayed a bit, thinking, "Kosher Deli, huh?"

"Yeh, Kosher Deli. And all the trimmings for a great lunch."

Susan smiled to herself, "Well, in that case. Stay there. I'll be right down to get you."

"Yes, Ma'am!"

She thought quickly. She went to the large gilded mirror on the foyer wall to check herself out. She shook her hair to fluff it out, decided her make-up couldn't be helped in the time available and then unzipped the Levi's to tuck the madras shirt in. She carefully gathered and folded the tucked material on her back side to make sure it was not bulging out, leaving a clean, trim waistline. The stretchy Levi's had been a good choice for her figure. She looked at herself and decided she looked fine, all considered. It was the best she could do.

She headed for the door and then quickly went to the dining room table to pick up the key ring.

In the elevator, she shifted the control lever to the ground floor notch and it lurched down. At the bottom she lifted the gates and went to the door to the main lobby. Paul Waldman was standing there with his arms full of delicatessen bags. He came over to the door.

"Hello, again. Should I call you Paul or Doctor Waldman?" Susan asked with a smile.

"Paul will do."

"Since you are trying to feed me, you can call me Susy. Three bags, did I look especially hungry to you when we met?"

"Perhaps a twinge of hunger showed through." He smiled at this, Susy could feel a blush. "But, I knew very little about you and I had this vision of buying a pastrami on rye for a vegetarian, or for that matter a veggie burger for a carnivore. So, I bought options. Then I saw the cheesecake, salads and dill pickles and the purchase quickly got complicated."

"I understand. Follow me!" Susan held the door wide for him to come through. She walked to the elevator and waited for him to follow.

"I thought you said we couldn't eat in your apartment."

"We're not." Susan said as she pulled the gate down and moved the lever to the sixth floor.

As the elevator whirred upward, Paul said, "An antique Art Deco freight elevator, to this is how the *ubermenschen* on the sixth floor live."

"Is it your usual tactics to try to bribe people you declare to be *ubermenschen* with *Kosher* food. Besides, don't knock it. Do you have your own private elevator?"

"No, can't say that I do."

They arrived and Susan lifted the gate. Paul walked out into the sixth floor lobby and turned around to inspect the lobby.

"Two apartments? There are only two apartments on the sixth floor. What else is up here?" Paul asked.

"Nothing, just two apartments." Susan went over and opened her apartment door.

"Again, I thought you said we aren't eating in your apartment," Paul followed her into the foyer.

"We aren't. Wait here. By the way, do you have drinks?" She asked as she went to pick up the cleaning rag and bottle of spray cleaner in the dining room and leave her keys on the table.

"No, I figured we could get something, water if nothing else. … Truthfully, I forgot." He looked down at the cleaning clothe and sprayer in her hand quizzically.

"Okay, then I can contribute to this. Do you prefer warm no-calorie organic iced tea or chilled champagne? Those are your only choices." She asked with a slight smile.

He smiled back, "Is that a trick question?"

"No, not a trick question. Just part of a psychological battery you are taking part in."

"In that case, definitely the champagne."

"Good choice. Hold these. Wait here." She piled the cleaning clothe and spray on top of the deli bags he was holding in his arms. She went into the kitchen.

First, Susan chose two long-stemmed goblets from the glassware racks above the food prep tables. They were dusty, but sparkled under the dust. She quickly ran water over them from the little sink and shook them briskly to remove the water. She held them with the bases in her hand and the glass stems sticking out through her fingers. She went to big wine cooler unit. She noticed all of the champagne seemed to be in its own section at the top. She picked a champagne bottle out of the top row and looked at it. It was French. Okay. She shut the cooler.

As she entered the foyer, Paul gave a restrained sneeze.

He sniffed and said, "The ammonia made me sneeze."

Susan looked and saw that she had stuffed the damp cleaning rag on the deli bag right below Paul's nose.

"Sorry about that. But, it clears the sinuses." She took the rag with her fingers that held the glasses and laid it over her arm with the champagne. She then hooked the trigger of the spray bottle with her last free finger of the hand holding the glasses.

"Okay, I'll remember that treatment. I can use it in the clinic, if all else fails." He grinned.

Susan went to the corner and sat the champagne on the floor by the narrow door with the deadbolt. She twisted the deadbolt open.

"I thought you said your apartment was crappy. This is nothing short of majestic. And it covers half the building?" Paul said as he looked around in the foyer.

"Actually, over half. But, it is just a façade. There are evil, rotting entities living in the refrigerator and monster dust bunnies in the back hallway that could eat you for lunch. Watch your step up here." She flipped on the stairwell light and went up.

Paul was halfway up the stairs when Susan unlatched the upper door and noontime sun flooded straight down the south facing stairwell. Susan went out and waited for Paul to emerge blinking into the sunshine. After a moment's wait for their vision to adjust, Susan headed for the old patio furniture.

Susan heard Paul mutter an awestruck "Wow!" as he took in the skyline, turning to look around him. When she approached the table with the umbrella, Susan sat the sprayer, champagne and glasses carefully on the pebble and tar roofing material, well back from the table.

"Stand back!" She warned. She took the cleaning rag and started to snap the rag to swat dust off the umbrellas and table.

When Paul saw what she was doing, he put the bags down and said, "Wait. Let me help."

He tilted the table and umbrella on one leg and shook it firmly. Dust cascaded in a cloud from the umbrella and tabletop. As he shook, the umbrella slipped out of the floor stand and deeper into its hole in the table and he had to wrestle to maintain control of the table and put the umbrella down into place in the umbrella stand. He finally sat the table back down and fiddled with the umbrella until it opened fully. Susan moved in with the spray bottle and cleaned the table while Paul got the bags. When Susan was done, she picked out the two most reliable looking chairs, banging them together to dislodge the dust and debris covering them.

"Don't be concerned about the pigeon poop on the chairs. They only allow very hygienic pigeons to roost on this building," Susan said. She sprayed the chairs with the spray cleaner and cleaned them as best she could with the rag.

"Right." Paul took the chairs and sat them on the north side of the table facing south so the noonday summer sun would be shaded by the umbrella. Then he opened the bags and started laying out the food.

Susan got the glasses and champagne. She saw the food he laid out and said, "You said you bought options, this is a feast."

She handed him the champagne and said, "Here, you open." She sat in the left hand chair.

Paul looked at the champagne and exclaimed, "Oh, No!"

"Something wrong?" Susan looked concerned.

Paul just looked from the champagne to Susan, expressionless, and then said slowly, "Susy, you just handed me a bottle of Bollinger '97." He paused.

"Is that bad?" she asked, meekly.

He smiled at her, "Susy, I am by no means a connoisseur of fine wines. But, I do read on occasion and have a fairly keen memory. Bollinger is like one of the premier vintners on Earth, of the likes of Dom Perignon. And, I think I recall 1997 being the best of the best years. This bottle you want me to uncork here amongst the pigeon droppings is like two weeks wages for the gal who made our sandwiches."

"I didn't know. I just picked the one with the prettiest foil on top."

He laughed at her, "You have more like this?"

"Yeh, I guess, actually lots, maybe a hundred. But, most are just wine, not champagne."

"A hundred bottles of wine in your refrigerator?"

"It is not a refrigerator. It is like a custom wine cooler."

"So, you have a hundred bottles of vintage wines in your custom wine cooler. And, you sit there innocently blinking those big, brown eyes at me when I say Bollinger and Dom Perignon. Where did you come by this vintner's treasure?"

"My aunt gave them to me."

"I suppose there is a good story beyond those simple words."

"Yes, and I'll need more than a pastrami sandwich as a bribe to divulge it."

Paul nodded, "OK. So, do I open this or not?"

Susan said firmly, "By all means. And after your lecture it better be damned good champagne."

"I didn't mean to lecture you."

"You most certainly did. Really … big brown eyes?"

"Is this our first argument?"

"You should be so lucky, if you think this is an argument."

"They are big and brown, though."

"Open!"

Paul shrugged and slit the foil with his thumbnail, untwisted the wire cage and carefully popped the cork. It popped up against the umbrella and nearly hit Susan on the rebound, the sound unsettling the nearby pigeons. Susan moved the glasses closer to Paul. He poured two glasses and handed her one.

"Aren't you supposed to smell it first?"

"That's for regular wine not champagne. I think with champagne you taste a little bit in the glass before you pour for your guests."

"You didn't do that either."

"You do that for unknown vintages you aren't sure are going to be palatable. I'm going to give Bollinger '97 the benefit of the doubt. Cheers!" He lifted the glass to her.

"L'chaim!" She clinked his glass.

"You are Jewish!"

"Uh, yeh, long story. It is part of the 'aunt' story you haven't earned yet."

"But, you knew I was?"

"The Kosher lunch was a good hint, but have you ever Googled yourself? There is a lot out there about you, your physicians' group and your parents in Connecticut. And your sister Julie and brother Ed. Ed and Betsy's wedding at the synagogue in Boston. And you were pretty sharp in your Speedos at Princeton." She drank some more champagne.

"So, we just met three hours ago and already you have Googled my life story?"

"So, we only met three hours ago and already you have decided I need feeding?"

"Touché!"

"Whatcha got to eat?"

"The aforementioned pastrami sandwiches, a semi-cold veggie burger and a choice of walnut salad or a cucumber couscous salad. Some miscellaneous stuff I picked up while waiting for the pastrami and veggie burger. And after that cheesecake or fruit salad." He took his sandwich.

"Pastrami and couscous."

He sat the sandwich box, a plastic dish of salad and a plastic fork in front of her, balancing the fork on top of the salad to keep it off the table.

After finishing a bite of his sandwich Paul asked, "So what did you think of the Bollinger '97? Was it good enough to be like a thousand dollars a bottle?"

"I have no idea," Susan said between a bite and a sip.

"What? Why no idea?" Paul stopped eating for her answer.

"I have no idea, because I have never had champagne before and I have nothing to compare this to. It seems quite nice. Really bubbly."

Paul raised his eyebrows and huffed, "Quite nice? Never had champagne before? Next you'll be telling me the reason you have never had champagne before is that you are underage."

Susan said nothing, but fluttered her eyelashes at Paul.

"You're kidding!"

"Nope. I debated telling you, but figured you would find out. I turn twenty-one next October."

"So, I just committed a crime by serving you alcohol."

"Oh, no. I saw it on the internet. A person under 21 can consume alcohol in New York at their private residence, but not in public."

"So, you think that out here on the rooftop in front of the entire city of New York is in a private residence?" He swung his arm around to indicate the skyline.

"Yeh, it is my rooftop."

"No, you rent the apartment downstairs. But, unless you've some kind of funny lease that includes this roof, it is not a private residence."

"No, Paul, I actually own this roof. And, I don't rent my apartment, I own it. And, in fact, I am the owner of your apartment, too, and your clinic. You are the renter, I own them?"

Paul sat staring at Susan, not sure whether she was crazy or fooling with him.

"Paul, do you have any idea how precious that look on your face is?" Susan asked.

"Would you mind explaining? I don't like to have a 'precious look' on my face."

"Well, I really should not have said that much. My attorneys warned me about telling people. I just couldn't help myself."

"Attorneys? Civil or criminal?"

Switching to a very straight and mock serious face, Rachel answered with a slow nod, "Criminal. You see the rest of the story is that I am a deranged psychopath. They have me hidden here until they can plea bargain the mutilation killings over in Jersey."

"Seriously."

Susan took a deep breath after finishing another gulp of champagne, trying not to burp again and said, "Okay, since I started, I guess it is easy to explain. Pay attention now. … My aunt died, she was really rich, she was nice and smart, and she was Jewish. Her husband died before her, and he was really, really rich and he was really smart and he was really, really Jewish. His father died long before that, and he was really, really rich and really, really, really Jewish. My father died, he was not rich, but he was really smart, and he was once upon a time Jewish, but tried hard to ignore it. Then, my mother died, she was not rich at all, but she was really, really nice and she used to be really, really Jewish, but not much anymore. Then there was me, I was not rich, I was sort-of smart, like my father, I was sort of Jewish. But, then, all of the really rich, really Jewish people died, and so did my parents, and I was the last one left, so I became really rich and all of the really Jewish stuff kind of snuck up on me and that is why I sit around in pigeon shit on rooftops with really nice, really smart, Jewish doctors, drinking really, really expensive champagne and saying really, really stupid things. My nice, rich, Jewish and now dead aunt owned this building and that big pile of vintage wine and now I do. Is that clear?"

After she finished speaking, Susan drained her champagne glass, giving a very tiny burp at the end.

Paul looked into her eyes, not quite smiling, "I understand perfectly, but do you know what, Susy? After hearing that explanation, I have no idea whether to cry with you, or laugh with you."

Susan jerked forward quickly to stare directly in Paul's eyes, poked Paul's arm with her finger, saying in a comical, accented voice, "There you go, Doc. You do understand the situation perfectly. That is exactly how I feel. Don't know whether to laugh or cry."

They looked at each other a moment and then Susan sat back in her chair and said, "Wow!"

"What wow?"

"Wow, as in that there wasn't me. That was Bollinger '97. I don't act like that, or talk like that."

"Maybe you've had enough for the first time."

"No. I now understand the concept of a Champagne Buzz. I like it. More Bollinger and the fruit salad."

"No cheesecake?"

"Eh, no."

Paul handed her the plastic dish of fruit salad. She handed him her glass. He filled hers, but less than before and took a drink of his.

They both ate and she spoke next, "Now, let's change the subject to something a little more cheerful. Let's talk about you. Tell me, what is it like to sew up mangled, broken bodies in the ER?"

She caught him off guard and he laughed, but his mouth was full of champagne, which he managed to spray on his hand, his arm and her pant leg.

He reached for the cleaning rag.

Susan quickly moved the rag out of his reach. "Wait. Leave it alone. That is very expensive champagne. It is a sin to waste great champagne." With that, she reached for his hand and, locking eyes on Paul, slowly stroked her finger across his champagne-soaked hand. Then she licked her finger. Then, at the same time, they both laughed.

"Now I know you've had enough." Paul pretended to reach for her glass.

She countered by pulling it away. "Hey, I'm not the one spitting champagne. Do you have a clean fork for the fruit salad?"

She finally gave him the rag.

He gave her a new fork.

Before she took her bite, she said, "Now, I really do want to know what your day is like as a doctor. Not the gory details, just the heart-warming, inspiring stuff that I am sure your day must be filled with. Impress me." Then Susan ate a piece of pineapple and waited to be impressed.

—

From: Jesse.Morgenthau@MorgenthauMolineRealty.com

To:Susy@SusyFisher.com

Re: Your Moline Property

Ms. Fisher,

Thank you for contacting us regarding the possible listing of your property in Moline for sale. We would be happy to help. First, a more detailed answer for your question -- in almost all cases a residential property like yours sells best when emptied of the clutter of furniture. There are several reasons for this. I am familiar with the homes in that area of town, that tract, and the small size of many of the rooms, especially bedrooms. They look best to a potential client when furniture is removed and the walls are repainted the lightest color possible, if not all white. Unless you have really unique and eye-catching furnishings most customers prefer to picture the home with their minds eye of how their things will look in it. Second, few home purchasers these days want to buy a furnished place. And lastly, if you can clear everything out and put a few thousand dollars into a thorough cleaning, painting and refurbishing, for a house the age of your Moline property it will easily pay you back in increased traffic on the listing and final purchase price.

So, yes, we would recommend retaining a service to go through the house, taking those things that are saleable to an estate auction and disposing of anything left over. In this area, there is an excellent auction firm across the river in Muscatine that handles everything; they sort, cart off and sell what's valuable and haul away the rest. After the personal property is removed, as I mentioned above, we highly recommend painting and carpet cleaning.

Once we can get access to the property to do a walk-through we can firm up the recommended listing price. Please realize the $190K price I mentioned on the phone is merely the prevailing price in that area and will change depending on condition, market conditions and whether you need a quick sale or can wait for the right offer. As you know, the market is still pretty soft. Please let us know how you wish to proceed and how we can get in to do the walk-through.

Sincerely, Jesse Morgenthau

Managing Broker

Morgenthau Moline Realty

After their conversation and Susan's questions about his career and life in New York, Paul Waldman waggled the Bollinger bottle to indicate it was finally empty. Susan shook her head, mimicking despair, "You know, the bad part of this is that if that was the best champagne money can buy, then I am cursed to spend the rest of my life drinking second rate champagne."

"How sad for you." Paul straightened in his chair and looked at his watch. Their talk and lunch had lasted the better part of an hour.

Susan said, "We really need to do this again sometime. But, maybe in moonlight next time, 'cause, whew, it is really getting hot up here.

Paul nodded, "Yes, it has been great getting to know you, but I have to get some sleep."

"Sleep-p?" Susan sputtered. "You didn't have that much champagne. It's not even the middle of the afternoon yet."

"If you had paid attention to me, I said the ER docs work a rotating shift. I'm on the late night shift this cycle. When we met this morning, I was going out after work for soccer practice. Right now is like close to midnight, or after, according to my internal clock. I have to get some sleep before getting up around eight, eight-thirty tonight and starting to work at ten. Then, after work tomorrow morning I have my soccer game at 9 AM sharp." Paul started to gather the used plastic plates, forks and salad boxes and put them in a bag.

Susan started to help pick up, "Okay, it just seems really weird to be going to sleep at two in the afternoon."

"One gets used to it. The hard part is eating breakfast at normal bedtime and lunch in the hospital cafeteria at one in the morning, if I am lucky enough to get time to eat. Saturday night at a New York ER is hellish. That pastrami was my supper."

Susan stood up and said, "Put the stuff we didn't eat in this bag." Then she gave another tiny, quick burp.

"Gosh, 'scuse me" Susan said, Paul just laughed.

Paul threw the remains of the half-eaten bun from Susan's sandwich and the remains of his salad toward the pigeons watching them from the barbecue. A raucous pigeon fight ensued. Paul and Susan picked everything up, loading the three bags. Paul lowered the umbrella. Susan and Paul walked toward the stairway door.

"Thank you, that was nice." Susan said.

"Yes, best supper I've had in a long time."

They came to the door and Susan said, "You go first, your hands are full and I have to latch the door."

"And you watch your step. Champagne and dark stairways don't mix well."

"You, too."

In the apartment foyer, as Susan latched the deadbolt to the stairway, and she told him, "I'll need to take you down, so the elevator is up here for me afterwards."

Paul set the bags on the floor. "How will I get in touch with you, other than ringing the buzzer downstairs? Let me give you my card and cell phone number."

"Just a sec!" Susan ran into the dining room, setting the used glasses on the dining room table and came back with her iPhone. She did something on the phone and handed it to Paul. "Here, dial your number."

He did and handed it back to her. She pushed Call and his pocket gave a musical tone, the Bee Gee's *Tragedy* theme.

"There, we're linked up."

Paul nodded and said, "OK. Can't I just take the stairs down, so you don't have to go all the way down in the elevator?"

"I have no idea. I've never been in the stairs. Let's just do the elevator."

"No, that's fine. I'll do the stairs. Just show me where they are."

"You think I'm too tipsy to run the freight elevator, don't you?"

"The thought had crossed my mind. I thought you were going to trip on the carpet when you ran back with the cell phone."

"I'm not that drunk."

"Whatever, I'll take the stairs. You want this extra food?"

"No, I don't want to put anything in the frig for the evil, smelly thing to mess with. Besides most of what's left is the veggie burger and pickles, and I am carnivore at heart" She smiled.

"I'll remember that."

Susan then said, "You know, if you don't mind. I will take the cheesecake, neither of us touched it. I can save it for my supper tonight."

"Ok." Paul checked the bags and gave Susan the one with the cheesecake, taking out his veggie burger.

Susan opened the apartment door and Paul followed her across the lobby to the door with the frosted 'Stairway' window across from the unused passenger elevators.

"Those don't work for this floor?" He moved his head to indicate the two elevator doors.

"They're turned off; I have a key though, somewhere." Susan tried the stairway door and discovered it opened. There were dim lights in the stairs. She tried the knob inside the stairwell and it was locked. "One way, you can exit, but not enter. Hopefully you can get in on your floor and don't have to go down to the lobby."

Susan opened the door for Paul to go down. He walked over and turned and stopped next to her.

Paul said, "It has been a wonderful lunch. I'm glad we did it."

"Me, too."

After a moment's pause Paul moved forward and gave Susan a quick kiss on the lips.

Susan blinked at him, and after a short pause, asked, "Is that your best?"

"That was just right for a slightly tipsy young beauty who I just met four hours ago. It's a good starting point."

"Yeh, I guess it was a good start."

"You are definitely the nicest landlady I could hope for."

They looked in each other's eyes and smiled. Paul turned and headed down the stairs. Susan watched until he disappeared, shut the door and turned back to her apartment.

In the foyer, Susan pushed the door closed with her heel, and stood and looked around. She definitely was not ready for a continuation of the abortion story from Rachel, as interesting as it had been. She did not want to think about that now and spoil the good mood the impromptu lunch had given her. She realized she was not in any shape to do any work, rummaging or sorting right now. She decided a short nap would be good, or at least a little while for her to lie down and take stock of events.

She walked back down the long, main hallway. The new treads on her tennis shoes scuffed against the thick carpet and she nearly tripped. She did not want to lie on the big bed that had not had new bedding since Rachel left for the hospital. The couches in the living room or den might work, but there were three other bedrooms that would be more comfortable for her nap. The main guest bedroom was the obvious choice, but the linens there were used, instead, Susan chose the little rose colored bedroom on the far corner of the apartment.

The bright afternoon sun lit the west-facing room and the direct sunlight shown in a square on the floor near the far wall, but split itself in the big window's stained glass crystals to bathe the remainder of the room in thousands of tiny glinting rainbows. The cool air from the air conditioning vent fought with the warmth of the sunlight. Susan thought of closing the heavy drapes to darken the room for her nap, but instead she just curled up on the luxuriously soft mattress that she had not lain on for fifteen years. The murmur of traffic on 10th Avenue was audible, but not intrusive. She fluffed the pillows behind her head and lay there contemplating the fleeting bits of her girlhood memories the colors, feel, sounds and smell of the bedroom gave her. She went over the afternoon's events, the conversation with the intriguing, young doctor. In spite of the sparkling lights and traffic sounds, Susan was fast asleep in a few minutes.

—

Susan awoke with the late afternoon sun directly on her face. She had slept for several hours. As she lifted her head to avoid the light, she had a throb of pain in both temples and a stiff neck. The champagne! She sat on the edge of the bed, rotating her neck and rubbing her temples to get rid of the slight hangover headache. Her mouth was pasty dry and she wondered if Rachel had some aspirin in her bathroom. She got up from the bed and stretched.

Aunt Rachel had an amazingly well-stocked medicine cabinet in the master bath with every sort of consumer medicine product represented, as well as many prescription bottles that Rachel made a mental note to get rid of. Susan chose a green Excedrin bottle that claimed to be extra strength for headaches.

The warm iced tea worked to swallow the pills, but it also made her realize that she really had not eaten that much at the rooftop tête-à-tête with Paul, considering the amount of champagne she had drunk. She was hungry again and the pretzels, yogurt and even the leftover cheesecake would not do. While she thought of it, she took the yogurt out of the bag and put it and the cheesecake in the larger, less smelly refrigerator in the kitchen.

Coming back from the kitchen, Susan stood trying to decide what to do next. The afternoon nap in the little rose colored bedroom had been nice. Nice enough for Susan to consider whether she was ready to make the move from the Hilton to the apartment. She had not planned on moving in before this place was completely clean, but the cleaning crew would be here Monday morning. Susan considered the options.

Finally, Susan decided that, since the check-out time for the Hilton had already passed there was no good reason not to spend one last night in the hotel. It was already late afternoon and by the time she collected her things from the hotel it would be getting dark. It would be best to just stick with her plans and stay at the Hilton tonight. But, thinking about the task of moving all of her things from the hotel, Susan had an idea.

Susan opened the door to the storage room under the stairway to the roof and flipped the lights on. The three pieces of red luggage sat in front of the big pile of boxes and assembled junk. Looking closely at the bags, Susan saw that they were all matching with a Louis Vuitton logo pattern and bright red embossed patent leather covering. There were two identical extra-large bags with wheels and an extending handle and a smaller rectangular jewelry box that fit on top of large bags coupling with the handle. She tested them for weight and found that they were empty. She took one of the larger bags, which was easily big enough to carry all of the extra clothes that she had purchased on her shopping trip and the items of Rachel's that she had been given by the attorneys which were still at the hotel.

Susan gathered up her purse, shut down the computer and turned off the lights. She locked the apartment and entered the code to set the alarm system. She would get something to eat on her way to the hotel.

—

18:15 CDT

From:Heidi@Heidi.ws

To:Susy@SusyFisher.com

Subj: Tweets

Susy,

Sorry I dint get back 2 u quickr. Went 2 WI Dells 4 while w/ folks & kid brat & 4got my cell @home. Sure, deleted Tweets. Not sure Y ur so bent. Call me, tell me whazzup. Sounds 2 exciting in NY. Don't get 2 spoiled w/$$$.

Heidi

Sent from my iPhone 6

—

Chapter Twelve

Facebook: Susy Fisher Likes Home Depot at 28 W 23rd St Front 1 New York, NY 10010

—

The taxi driver spoke with a thick Irish accent, or maybe it was Scottish or Welsh, Susan had no idea how to distinguish between them. She had found an address for a Home Depot on 23rd Street and the Irish/Scots/Welshman had waited at the curb while she ran in and bought two bundles of packing boxes, tape and trash bags. The driver was pleasant mannered and helped her carry the luggage and her purchases to the door of her building. He waited while she opened the entryway door. Susan paid him with a healthy tip added.

Packing her bags, getting breakfast and checking out of the Hilton had taken longer than she thought, so it was well past 9:00 AM and Paul would already be at his soccer game. She wondered if he might stop in again today, after the game. She was wearing the stretchy jeans again, but this time with the low cut peasant blouse. And she had taken extra time prepping before she left the hotel in case she did meet him again. She was probably overly primped, considering her plans called for a full Sunday in the apartment, with more DVD watching and some work to get the apartment livable, since this was move-in day. Maybe her looks this Sunday morning could explain the polite attentiveness of the Celtic taxi driver.

Susan managed to get all the luggage and purchases into the freight elevator. In the apartment, she took the luggage directly to the master bedroom. Susan had planned out her day, noting the housekeeping, sorting, cleaning and DVD watching she hoped to accomplish. Rather than unpacking immediately, she left the luggage in the bedroom and started to strip the linens from Rachel's bed. She took the bedspread, sheets and pillow cases to the laundry room.

She had not paid much attention to the laundry yesterday, but now saw that Rachel had an extra-large front loading washer and matching dryer. They were high tech steam cleaning models and they were in the latest fire engine red color, setting on matching storage pedestals. Susan wondered why anyone would bother to give laundry machines a paint job like a sports car.

Susan again noted how some things in Rachel's apartment had not been updated in decades, but other things, like the laundry, the master bath, video camera and the new built-in counter in the kitchen were the latest, most expensive items available. Thinking about this, Susan also reminded herself to stop thinking about this as Aunt Rachel's apartment, Rachel's bed and Aunt Rachel's washer. As of today, it was Susan's intention to start to make this Susan's apartment and make sure that whatever remained would be Susan's stuff. That was why, after contemplating this at the Hilton last night, she had bought all of the boxes and trash bags this morning. Aunt Rachel had forty years' worth of things stuffed in every corner of the two apartments and Susan had to take control and make this place hers. Aunt Rachel had been generous in giving everything to Susan, but Susan realized that the enormous task ahead of her would be done best if Susan had the right mindset. A big part of that would be figuring out what from Rachel's life was valuable and would fit into Susan's life and what needed to be donated to charity or trashed.

However, as Susan stood in the laundry watching through the big round window at the water filling on the sheets, she realized that the commitment she had made to herself to get Rachel's things straight had never been done for her own parents. Back in Moline, after her mother's death, the only real change she had made was moving into the big bedroom and putting her mother's clothes in a box in the garage. And, when she did that she found her mother had never cleared much of her father's things out either. She understood why and it was not just because her mother's final illness had followed her father's death so quickly. It was a difficult, emotional transition to make; throwing out a deceased loved one's personal possessions was tantamount to passing judgment on the things they valued, if not on their life itself. If you threw away their cherished stuff, you had to admit they were really gone and what they had thought important in life really did not matter anymore. Susan had never really gone through that with her mother's or her father's things. Susan thought back on the items from their Las Vegas outing she had found in the suitcase when she packed for this trip to New York. There were piles of boxes, mementoes, and property in the old house in Moline that Susan had told herself she needed to go through, but never had.

Susan thought of the questions the lawyers, David Tannenbaum and Devorah, had asked about her intentions of moving to New York or staying in Illinois. She now admitted to herself that she had already made that choice, given her email inquiry about selling the house in Moline. And, with that realization, she also knew that, first things first, she needed to get her old life in order, back in Moline, and sort through the remains of the first twenty years of her life and her parents' lives, before she could realistically get this new life in New York put together.

Susan ended the philosophizing in the laundry and went to the linen closet, where Susan found the shelves were labeled for which rooms the linens went in, master bedroom, guest #1, etc. She picked out clean sheets, pillowcases and a different bedspread for the big bed, careful not to think of it as Rachel's bed.

As she went to get her new bedroom in order, Susan thought of how she could schedule a trip back home and what details she needed to take care of.

—

Susan finally sat in the dining room chair after a couple of hours working in the bedroom and bathrooms. She had used the trash bin door in the utility room and dumped a full trash bag of Rachel's old cosmetics, underthings and everything else Susan was sure had no value to her or any charity group. She had been stumped by the myriad of expensive perfumes she had found. The fragrances were not exactly to her taste, for the most part, but she was not sure if they needed to be trashed as they represented hundreds, if not thousands of dollars in purchases. So, she deferred the decision by packing them in a box, maybe she could decide what to do with them. Everything she was sure she could donate to charity she had in several other boxes.

She remembered a public service commercial warning you against putting old prescription medicines in the trash or down the drain, so she had those in another separate box. Now, with this first sorting task done, she would go back to the DVD where she had left off yesterday before Paul Waldman's lunch visit. She wondered how he was doing at his 9 o'clock soccer game; it was probably over by now. She was still hoping he would stop by again.

She had both Apple laptops here now, hers and Rachel's, but she booted Rachel's, as it still had the DVD she was watching in its drive and was already plugged in under the table.

Susan did a quick search for round trip air connections between New York and Quad Cities airport. The airfare booking website had a wide range of connections and prices, plus a confusing set of New York connections, at three different airports, La Guardia, Newark, as well as JFK, where she had arrived on Wednesday. She figured she would need at least three days for the trip, but was not sure, so she purchased a more expensive upgrade ticket that could be exchanged for a different date. Most connections were through Chicago with a second commuter flight to the Quad Cities. Her mother's old Prius was parked in the long-term parking lot at the Moline/Quad Cities airport. Susan wondered what the parking bill would be.

Susan chose La Guardia since it seemed to have the most connections to Chicago and was closer to Manhattan. She reserved flights for Wednesday morning and returning late Saturday afternoon. She went to her purse and chose the Bank Leumi credit card, which she had not used yet. It worked fine to pay for the airfare. The reservations site said it had sent a QR code graphic to her cellphone email, which she could use to pick up the ticket at La Guardia.

Susan had finished the reservations back home. However, with her thought of that, she realized that might be the last time she used the term 'home' for Moline. Next, Susan thought of searching for places she could turn in Aunt Rachel's old prescription drugs in Manhattan, but after she typed the search in, she had a better idea, one that would serve an ulterior purpose for her. Susan grabbed her iPhone and found the contact she had entered for Dr. Paul Waldman. She sent him a text message to his phone number:

SMS Text: Paul, A little medical advice needed. I have large quantity of old prescriptions from my deceased Aunt. Where can I turn in old meds for destruction around here? Susy Fisher

Good! That would get her an answer and keep up a contact with Paul. She wondered what he had thought of her. Susan was anxious to see what might develop with him.

Before she set the iPhone aside, she entered another text message to Devorah's phone:

SMS Text: Devorah, I have lots of Rachel's property that would be good to recycle/reuse by donating to charity. Do you know a good charity that does donation pick-ups in Manhattan? Susy

After sending that to Devorah, Susan thought of one last message to send that was probably best done by email, although she would probably follow up with a phone call before she left for Moline. She opened the law firm's client info handbook to get the email addresses and opened the MacBook email client. She realized this was her Aunt's MacBook, not hers, and she had to enter her own email account into the software. Susan also saw that there were dozens of messages waiting in the email program for her Aunt to read. It was a disquieting thought that she probably had to go through Rachel's final email messages for her. Later.

Immediately upon entering her personal email info, she got the incoming mail that had accumulated. There were three new Facebook friend requests, Ariel Metzger, Amee Metzger and Adrian Metzger. She clicked and accepted the friendships on her Facebook page, sending each a Facebook message giving them her direct email address. The new generation of Metzgers were synched with online social media.

Then, she typed her new email message:

From: Susy@SusyFisher.com

To: Peter Ephraim <pephraim@wassermannephraim.com>;

David Tannenbaum <dtannenbaum@wassermannephraim.com>;

Devorah Feldshuh <dfeldshuh@wassermannephraim.com>

Subj: Moline Trip

Dear Attorney persons,

Things are going well at Chelsea apartment, cleaning crew is scheduled tomorrow. Checked out of Hilton. I have made reservation to travel back to Moline on Wednesday. I'll be back here over weekend. I intend to list the old homestead for sale and contract to auction off old personal property. According to your client handbook, it seems I should prepare the documents/contracts as Me c/o David @ your firm address. If you have any advice on that process or donating Rachel's unwanted things to charity, please let me know.

Do I pay inheritance tax on Rachel's personal property? We should probably talk before I leave. Some questions.

Anybody have any connections at a good college with late admissions in NYC? It is a little late to get admitted this year.

Regards,

Susy Fisher

—

Finally done with her routine chores, Susan fast forwarded the DVD to the place she had stopped watching yesterday. She popped open one of her iced tea cans and sat back to watch Aunt Rachel again. But, before it started she heard a text message tone from the iPhone. The message read:

SMS Text: Susy, NY City program lets you turn in old scripts at any police precinct, fire station and many hospitals and clinics. You can give a closed bag/box of old meds, sharps, etc. to our receptionist at the clinic downstairs.

BTW, any interest in getting together for dinner without pigeons this Friday. I have evening off, for once.

We won. Paul

—

Susan realized her heart was actually beating faster as she read the BTW sentence. That kind of feeling was different for her!

—

SMS Text: Paul, I would love to have dinner, but [drats!] just made reservations to fly back to Illinois Wednesday thru late Saturday. Rain check, please. What other options?

Is your game next Sunday also at 9 AM?

Susy

—

Susan went to get a new yogurt she had stored in the big refrigerator. By the time she got back there was another text:

Susy, Need to check sched for other dinner option. Friday was my only clear opening, may have Sunday eve, too... Will get back 2U.

Yes, next Sunday game at 9AM. ??? Paul

—

Susan smiled to herself at this message. Right now, she did not want to answer his "???." She was happy to know something of his intentions. She hit the play icon on the DVD player.

On the video, Rachel had just hit record on the video camera and sat back to continue speaking.

"Sorry for the interruption. A late afternoon delivery. A stock of my new cancer meds to try to stretch my longevity envelope out a bit. Where was I?

"Of course, plot point one, the abortion. I know that is probably a shock to you. It was clear to me that after speaking with you about your mother, you probably had no idea about it. However, I thought you really needed to know about it to understand what came next for your mother. But, please keep it to yourself, you are now the only living person who knows, as Aaron never found out, I don't think even your father knew. If you were surprised to hear about it, imagine what our parents, Solomon and Tova Rothmann, had thought -- first hearing about the pregnancy and how their daughter was NOT going to get married to the father and then discovering that their supposedly angelic, younger daughter had gotten an abortion rather than marry a Conservative Jewish millionaire. You see, our attempt to tell mother and father that Rebecca had a miscarriage didn't pass the parental interrogation test. Father was recovering from his first heart attack, a bad one, the first health problem he had in his life. Mother was on the verge of a mental breakdown over both heart attack and then the pregnancy slash abortion. There was a huge blow up between Rebecca and our parents, first by phone and then in person. I was in the dog house with them, too, for letting it go this far.

"The fight got to the point where father said something about 'no daughter of mine would ever have an abortion – no good Jewish girl would ever do that' and threatened to withdraw all financial support from Rebecca. Of course, that wasn't strictly Jewish doctrine, but it was the reaction of our conservative parents. Then, Rebecca responded 'Fine, then I am not your daughter and I am not a Jew.' That cut our parents to the heart. You can understand the emotions involved and can probably picture the mess we had to deal with. That was probably in early spring of that year, maybe April. Of course, we were family and the parties backed off of that a bit. Our parents backed off more than Rebecca. She had already made a big split with her Jewish roots in deciding not to marry Aaron. This was the last straw for her. It was traumatic and she never really got over it.

"All the while this was going on, I was still with Isaac. He and I had talked over the split between Aaron and Rebecca. He, of course, did not know about the abortion, but I explained that Rebecca had rebelled from being married into a Conservative Jewish lifestyle. In my explaining this and family background to Isaac, he saw that I had some of the same feelings and concerns as Rebecca. He did not want things to go the same between him and me, and he was a bit more mature and worldly than Aaron was at the time, so Isaac agreed that we would make our life whatever I needed to be happy, even if that meant not being strictly Conservative. Anyway, our relationship hung on and we kept seeing each other.

"All the while, that spring, Rebecca was an emotional wreck, almost dropped out of school. Then, right at the end of the school year, in early June, Father had another heart attack, from which he never recovered. We buried him that June. Rebecca made the flight to Florida with me for the funeral, but Rebecca and Mother barely spoke. Mother made the mistake of hinting that the stress of the pregnancy and abortion had strained Father's health and Rebecca figured Mother blamed her for Father's death. It was the end of the line for any relationship between Mother and Rebecca. She kept sending Rebecca the tuition money that Father had saved for her, though. Father's Kriah was the last Jewish prayer Rebecca said for a long time. At one point, I was unsure if she would even say the Kriah for him. She did, but she was never the same. It took her months to really smile again, and she wanted no part of anything Jewish. We both worked in New York that summer and went back to Columbia again in the fall.

"That was my senior year and I was still seeing Isaac and getting to know his two children from his first marriage. They were, like, eleven and twelve then, Joseph and Sarah. I got along quite well with them, Sarah in particular, but also Joseph, who was quite a handful for Isaac. I think the way I got along with the step kids was part of what sealed the deal between me and Isaac. He and I were getting quite close and pretty intimate. It was a formality that we set the date to get married the next June, right after my graduation.

"Susan and I were renting a two bedroom apartment by then. Small place on Upper West Side. I was seeing Isaac quite often. He actually tried to get me to try and get Rebecca back together with Aaron again. We had not told him any of what happened. I was thankful when your mother started seeing another guy, as it gave me a good excuse to tell Isaac about Rebecca no longer being an option for Aaron.

"Next picture."

Susan pulled the next picture from the pile. It was her parents as a young couple, with her father in a winter parka and her mother in a rabbit fur jacket and a long skirt and high heels. They appeared to be on a railing of a building's balcony cuddling in a winter wind. Susan remembered this picture from a family album in Moline.

Rachel continued, "Yes, Jeffrey Fisher was a teaching assistant in the History Department at Columbia with another year left to get his Ph.D. He taught your mother a Renaissance History seminar in fall of her junior year, which was the first semester after the events I just told you about. Meeting this erudite, charming soon-to-be-professor was the cure your mother needed for her emotional state. He was Jewish, but not religious. He was a mature veteran; he served a tour as an Army officer in West Berlin, an ROTC grad, before returning to Columbia for graduate study. He was paying for grad school with his GI Bill. Compared to Aaron Metzger's money, Jeff Fisher didn't have a pot to piss in, to use the vernacular, but your mother fell head over heels in love with him, and he with her. So, he asked her to marry him and she agreed, almost beating me to the altar. Next Picture."

Susan pulled a wedding photo from the pile. It was Rachel and Isaac as bride and groom, standing under a flower encrusted, square-roofed arbor/archway. Rachel's white lace dress was strikingly beautiful, as were she and her bridesmaid. Both the groom and best man were in light blue tuxedos. The groom at Isaac's side was Aaron Metzger and the bridesmaid at Rachel's left was Rebecca Rothmann.

Rachel said with a chuckle, "You see, our family situation led to a very ticklish situation when Isaac and I chose our best man and bridesmaid for our wedding in June of 1972. But, Aaron Metzger was a perfect best man, even when he had to shake hands with the bridesmaid's fiancé, your father, the victor in the battle for Rebecca Rothmann' s heart. For your mother's part, she was so happy about her scheduled wedding the next month she played the part of the bride's younger sister perfectly. Even my mother, who came up from Florida for the wedding, didn't let on to the Metzger clan anything about the problems that had occurred the year before. But, alas, when Rebecca and Jeffrey got married in a civil ceremony the next month, in July, Isaac and I were there, but Rebecca did not invite our mother, the ultimate insult in a mother-daughter relationship. Oh, next picture, I forgot."

It was a picture of Susan's mother in a simple white wedding dress with a nice lace bodice and flowers around a modest neckline and her father in a dark suit and bow tie, standing in front of what looked like a New York State seal emblem on a courtroom wall. Susan had seen this photo also.

In the video, Rachel interlocked her fingers and stretched her arms as though cracking her knuckles. She continued, "So, that takes us to July 1972. Isaac and I were married, and I had my degree and a ready-made family with a multi-millionaire husband and two teenaged stepchildren. Your mother and father were married with both of them having one more year to graduate from Columbia with her B.A. in English and his Ph.D. in History. My husband and I had an agreement that we would live our lives in a Jewish tradition, but with an open mind and liberal dose of worldliness. Your mother and father were two peas in a pod in their secular view of life with their Jewish roots rarely intruding on their Middle American, but quasi-intellectual lifestyle and perspective. It took Aaron another fourteen years to find a beautiful blonde of his liking who had no problem with his wish to have a traditional Jewish family, kosher kitchen and all the rest that your mother had rejected so vehemently. However, he had no lack of sample candidates for that position in those fourteen years, he became quite a Lothario. I often wondered how much of that was fall out from his broken heart and how much would have occurred anyway and maybe your mother made a wise choice. I do know that Aaron's eventual wife kept him on a short leash, successfully. You've probably met her by now; Myra?"

Rachel straightened up, sat forward in her chair and looked directly into the camera. "That brings us back to you and me, Susy. I have just skimmed the surface of my stories and only the first years of what I want you to know about. I plan on following this with other videos. After we spoke and I realized that you knew little about any of this, I thought this was a good idea. If you want to know more, there are whole boxes of other papers, letters and pictures of your grandparents, the Metzgers, and your parents.

"Once upon a time, several years ago I thought, very egotistically, that my life had been interesting enough that I needed to write about it for others to read. I actually put to words the parts you will find out about later of my years after Isaac's death, several chapters, but when I tried to put this story I have told today to paper, I couldn't bring myself to do so, not for the world at large. Aaron turned out to be a fine man, he needn't hear of his aborted child. Your mother's decision and her lost relationship with her parents need not be known by anyone, except you. After talking to you, I thought you needed to know why your parents had not involved you in that aspect of your heritage and culture that your mother rebelled against and your father ignored for his own intellectual reasons. My decision to stay within the fold of Jewish heritage with Isaac Metzger and his family has given me a wealth of experience that I saw was missing in your life. You can decide what you want in your life, but I thought you had the right to know where you came from and what shaped the world you grew up in and who you have become. When I decided a few weeks ago that I wanted you to be the recipient of the wealth I have enjoyed in life, I also thought you needed to know everything about it; why I cherished this or that; what I thought was important in life, and why.

"Now, that is enough of this for now. Put this thing away for a while and when you come back I will start to give you the tour of my life's hoard. Oh, have you ever heard George Carlin's comedy routine about people's 'stuff?' It is hilarious, he rants about how people are focused on their 'stuff' and why none of their 'stuff' is really as important as people think it is. Thinking about what I have to say about my 'stuff' made me think of that. Go, now, have a good meal and maybe a nice glass of Chianti. Do that for me. Ponder about what will make you happy and then, go do it."

Susan got a kick out of Rachel's comment about a glass of Chianti. In Susan's world, it was barely noontime on a Sunday. And, Susan was not a wine drinker, but Susan would follow the advice to get something to eat. It was time for a walking tour of Susan's new neighborhood. It was a beautiful Sunday afternoon and it seemed like a good time. Too bad it was a Sunday; she could have picked up the undelivered mail at the post office. Susan thought of what she needed to take with her, not much, iPhone, purse and the new cross-trainers, for comfy walking. She had already checked the locations for restaurants and grocery markets in Chelsea, most were farther east. Her goal for the afternoon walk was to find a good restaurant and locate some food stores that were a bit nicer than the disappointing first supermarket she had found. She could only find two national chain groceries, Trader Joe's and Whole Foods. She was familiar with neither of those, as they had no stores in the Quad Cities, but their websites seemed promising, so she would give them a try. They were several blocks away, the long east-west New York blocks, over on 6th and 7th Avenues, but she had nothing better to do.

—

Chapter Thirteen

It was a scene that Abe Hemming, her college painting instructor would have called a Cecil B. DeMille sunset. The waning sun cast crimson, pink, violet and deepest purple through turbulent clouds stretching back from the setting sun. The landscape beneath this cliff top viewpoint was equally dramatic. Forests covered the hills with majestic outcroppings of rock and red cliffs framed a valley floor filled with the twinkling lights of the village in early evening. Towards a distant seashore ran a river which split the valley and the town. The river and far-off sea took on the colors of the sky.

"If I tried to paint that they would call me a liar," Susan thought, or did she speak it out loud.

She had no sooner said, or thought, the words when she had another momentary sense of unease and questioning of where she was, but this thought also passed with the realization and comfort that this was her home. This was where she was meant to be. Then the thought occurred that this was not a cliff top, but a roof top.

All thoughts of scenery, locale and sunsets ceased with the touch of her lover's lips. He knew just the right spot on the nape of her neck to make her half-squirm, half-stretch in a way that only a woman being kissed on the neck does. As kisses drifted up behind her ear and then out and down the line of her chin, she felt his strong hands from behind her gently moving over her silken nightgown, around her waist and then up. His hands stopped momentarily to mold her breasts and then he grasped her firmly beneath her arms and lifted her as he would a child, pulling her back onto the bedding and pillows.

Susan's fleeting thoughts realized she had little understanding of what was happening. Mellow doubts and questions crossed her mind and left before she had a chance to consider them or their answers.

The questioning thoughts lost meaning as she was already fully engaged in a love wrestle with her lover. Legs and arms intertwined as they kissed long and deep. His lips moved down and as his hands again cupped her breasts he kissed the soft, rounded vale formed between them. She locked her fingers through the curly hair of her lover's head and he continued down. His tongue played for a moment in the downy-soft, near imperceptible mist of hair that stripes the centerline of a woman's belly.

He was now kneeling between her legs and as his tongue tickled her navel she locked her feet behind his knees. Keeping her fingers coiled in his hair she allowed his head to move lower on her.

His nose was near Susan's navel when she heard a disquieting sound; either a truck horn or an alarm clock.

It did not matter. Neither sound belonged in this cliff top or roof top love nest. It was at precisely the moment when Susan realized that the interruption was both a truck horn and an iPhone alarm app that her lover turned into a pillow. The curly hair she had grasped in her hands was the embroidery on the pillow case seam. She threw him/it aside and gave a swat to the iPhone on the side table by the bed.

It only took a moment for the hum of traffic on 10th Avenue and the memories to flood back into her mind. She had slept well the first night in the apartment. It was always nice to awaken directly out of a dream that you still had enough memory of to contemplate again as you lay half asleep. The cleaning crew would be here soon. But, that dream needed to be logged in a diary, or somewhere.

Susan reluctantly crawled out of bed.

—

8:10 AM EDT

From: David Tannenbaum <dtannenbaum@wassermannephraim.com>;

To: Susy@SusyFisher.com
Cc: Peter Ephraim <pephraim@wassermannephraim.com>;
Devorah Feldshuh <dfeldshuh@wassermannephraim.com>

Subj: Personal Property Estate Tax WAS: Moline Trip
Dear Susy:

Yes, the Trust will pay both federal and New York estate taxes on both real and personal property to the extent necessary. We have nine months to file the returns, but in anticipation of her death, Rachel had us prepare estimates of personal property that are being used to prepare filings. Much of personal property was transferred into your trust using Rachel's gift exemption. Values for real property are not so easy, as we discussed. Entire trust and estate was planned to minimize tax consequences. We will handle everything on that, but if you have specific questions, please call me.

Have a good trip to the hinterlands.

David

—

Carlos arrived shortly after 8 AM and the cleaning crew came shortly thereafter. Carlos assured Susan that he would take care of everything. As she watched from the dining room, the cleaning crew, consisting of an older woman who introduced herself as Brenda Kelcher with four female and two male assistants spread out with almost military precision. Several large machines -- an industrial vacuum, carpet cleaner, a utility cart and a canister-like steam cleaner --came up the freight elevator. Within minutes the crew was working in the kitchen and throughout the apartment.

Brenda Kelcher asked Susan to come to the kitchen to direct what she wanted thrown out and what saved. Susan told her that most everything that was not in unopened bottles, cans or packages should be thrown, thus saving the bottled wines, but otherwise clearing the refrigerators, except for the new yogurt and sealed frozen foods which Susan pointed out. In the pantry, Susan told them to take extra care and throw out anything that the bugs or mice could have gotten into. The man with the hissing steam-cleaning machine was already scalding the main kitchen appliances while Susan and the supervisor watched. One of the women was loading glassware into the smaller dishwasher and pots and pans into the large one.

Brenda shouted to Susan over the hiss of the steam, "I noticed this is all kosher here. Our steam cleaning qualifies to make everything totally 'kasher' after the 24 hour waiting period. So, if you want the 'kasher' to be certified by a rabbi, we have a retired rabbi from Brooklyn we contract with who can be here tomorrow and give the rabbinical certification. You want that?"

Despite the noise Susan could tell Brenda was obviously saying 'kasher' and not 'kosher' and it did not seem eot ba trick of New York accent. So, Susan really had no idea what she was talking about. Susan would have to Google 'kasher' next chance she got; it was obviously something like 'kosher'. Since Brenda had indicated that whatever she was talking about was an option, Susan just told her, "The rabbi won't be necessary, your steam cleaning is just fine."

Susan answer seemed to make sense to Brenda. The woman nodded and went to tell the steam-cleaning guy something. He stopped for a moment to spread a tarp under the air vent hood above the big stove and grill unit. Susan decided to wander around and see what the others were doing in her apartment.

In the back hallway, a young dark-skinned girl with intricately braided dreadlocks was throwing bed sheets and blankets from the bedrooms onto the hall floor near the laundry. In a thick Caribbean accent, she asked Susan, "Do you want all of the stored linens re-washed?" indicating the linen closet.

Susan answered, "No, just change the stuff that is on the beds now. Of course, if you find anything stacked that is obviously dusty or dirty, clean that, too."

The woman nodded. Susan saw someone had stacked the storage boxes and smaller furniture pieces that had been sitting in the family room in the hallway, probably to clean the carpet in there.

Continuing clockwise around the hallway, Susan found the other man in the crew using the exhaust end of his vacuum canister to blow dust from the shelves of library books in the study. The dust cloud from the study clouded the hallway air, but he had a large fan unit labeled 'Red Devil' running in the study doorway that had an air filter bag on the exhaust end of it. In the master bath, one woman was mopping and another polishing the mirror and shower glass. The bed Susan had just changed yesterday was already stripped, too. Oh well. Susan double checked that the jewelry drawer was still locked and her own bags were out of the way in the corner of the bedroom.

Coming full circle back to the dining room, Susan saw Carlos had his back to her, standing in the foyer. He had a clipboard in one hand and was talking on his cellphone with the other. Susan decided she was extraneous to the cleaning effort for now, so she sat at the laptop on the dining table. A quick search showed 'kasher' was the cleaning and inspection process to insure that an item, tool or food qualified for use in a kosher kitchen. There were emails.

—

08:47 CDT

From: registrar@augustana.edu

To: susy@susyfisher.com

Subj: Transcripts

Ms. Fisher,

This will confirm that we have received your request for seven academic transcripts to various institutions and CommonApp.Org. They should go out today, all but one of those recipients accept electronic submission of transcripts. Your credit card you gave us will be billed for the transcript fees. Please be aware that the instructors may not have completed reporting grades for the Spring semester. If the transcripts sent are incomplete, the receiving institutions may require supplemental transcripts at a later date. We will send one courtesy hard copy to you at your home of record, so you can check for complete grades. Please let us know if you have any questions.

Joanne

—

07:36 CDT

From:Heidi@Heidi.ws
To:Susy@SusyFisher.com

Subj: Thursday
Susy,
Sure, Thursday lunch it is. Can't wait for an update. Noonish, right?
Can you pick me up at our house? My old Ford crapped out again, this time the tranny. Dad says we may have to disconnect life support.
Heidi

—

Susan sent a return email to the college registrar, changing her home of record from her Moline home address to the client service address at the New York law firm. She reminded herself to collect the old bills from the house in Moline to check that all her creditors and business contacts around the Quad Cities had been on the list to whom the law firm bookkeeper had sent change of address letters.

Susan felt uncomfortable with her back turned to all that was going on in the apartment; she turned the laptop around, moved to the end chair at the dining room table facing toward the foyer and kitchen doors. Carlos walked by the dining room, now accompanied by a man with a small spotlight mounted on his white hardhat and wearing an orange jumpsuit advertising his exterminating service. As Susan sat back in the dining chair, she marveled at how totally her life had been rearranged in just six days. Here she was in a strange city, in a strange apartment, watching people work for her in a pursuit she could never have imagined this time last week. Her old friends and life had been rendered mere relics. She was contemplating, or rather undertaking, a total overhaul of everything that had been until now important in her plans and dreams. Susan's most cherished possessions in her life were now totally overshadowed. Even that formerly ever-present companion, her old laptop, was sitting unused on the other end of the dining table while she used Rachel's slightly bigger, newer Apple laptop.

Susan realized the changes were not just to the outer accouterments of her life, like residence, school, wealth, property and such, but also to how she was behaving and the people in her life. Gone were her employer and workplace friends of the past several years. Soon to be gone was the college she planned on graduating from and which had been the center of her father's entire life, and her life for the past two years. All the communicatio ns she had this past week with her closest friend were two short emails, and that old friend would clearly have little place in her new life. She had barely posted a thing on Facebook, Tumblr and Twitter, and that had been a major pastime and preoccupation for her prior to this week. Her newest Facebook 'friends' were three, young relatives from a family tree she had known nothing about six days before. Her new confidants and trusted advisers, who were intent on molding a new lifestyle for her, were a trio of attorneys belonging to a culture, profession, city and society that was fairly alien to Susan's past experience.

Susan could not help the feeling that she had become unhinged in every aspect of her life. The fact that she had questioned her own identity even before this, with the death of her parents and how that affected her self-image did not help things at all. Now even those few things that had remained in her life a week before would be uprooted, never to be the same again.

All of this presented quite a quandary for Susan. She really could not complain about the good fortune that had come her way this week. Anyone would have to admit that this was a dream come true. But, with the flood of wealth, changes and new opportunities came a feeling of emptiness and loss of the values she had held to as her anchors. Everything that had once been of value was now rendered irrelevant. Everything and everyone that would henceforth surround her -- people, culture, locale, family, property, opportunities, hopes, and dreams-- was totally new or utterly unknown.

Not having anyone she could really talk to about this perverse identity crisis, Susan decided to throw herself back in the pursuit of understanding her Aunt Rachel's messages to her. Rachel was the immediate cause of this quandary, perhaps her words and viewpoint in the DVDs would help find the answers Susan doubted were there.

But, before she turned to the next DVD, Susan decided to go through one of the boxes stacked in the corner. The 'Rothmann' box was near the top, seemed to fit into the earlier DVD Susan had seen and was her choice for this first venture into the boxed archives.

The Rothmann box was perhaps two-thirds full. On top were three glassed frames. One large frame was an ornate certificate in hand lettered Hebrew script. This was a beautiful, important looking document, but Susan could read nothing on it other than two signatures, a man's and a woman's name that she did not recognize, on signature lines at the bottom. Another less ornate frame had a diploma for Solomon Rothmann as a graduate of the Jewish Theological Seminary in New York, in June 1940. In a matching frame, but turned long ways up and down was a certificate with an engraved eagle and an anchor at the top that read:

"The President of the United States – To all who shall see these presents greetings – Know Ye, that reposing special Trust and Confidence in the Patriotism, Valor, Fidelity and Abilities of ___Solomon H. Rothmann___ I do appoint him __Lieutenant__ in the Naval Reserve of the United States Navy to rank from the Sixteenth day of January 1942. ..." This Navy officer's commission continued on and at the bottom it was signed "By the President --Frank Knox, Secretary of the Navy."

The box was filled with a myriad of photos, old letters and documents. The Rothmanns' marriage certificate from 1946 was near the top. There were small stacks of black and white photos, showing the Rothmanns as a young couple, an old fading photo of Solomon standing in a cap and gown with a middle aged couple in 1930's clothing and then a matte sepia-colored high school graduation photo marked on the back as Tova Elspeth Katz, May 1945, showing that her wedding to Solomon was not very much later than her high school picture. There was blue folder with Tova' s high school diploma from Samuel J. Tilden High School, in Brooklyn, NY also dated in May 1945. There was an old fashioned real estate brochure advertising tract homes in Jacksonville "Starting from $9,750.00, VA & FHA Financing available." There was an envelope with two Florida death certificates from the '70's and various deeds, insurance policies and bank and insurance company correspondence. The box had smaller versions of the Rothmann girls' Florida high school pictures Susan had seen with Rachel's video and other photos of the various Rothmann and Katz family members and some unknown people. There was a picture of a young teenaged Tova and a man in a prayer shawl, apparently her father, smiling at the camera. From what Susan knew of such things, she guessed it was a Bat Mitzvah photo with Tova at age 13. At the very bottom of the box were four stacks of letters tied with strings, ribbons and one had rubber bands that crumbled from age as Susan's fingers touched them. A quick look at a few letters showed they were addressed to Rabbi & Mrs. Rothmann from their daughters in New York. Another stack showed they were addressed in a woman's handwriting to Mrs. Tova Rothmann at the Jacksonville address and an earlier address in Newport News, Virginia, with a return address of V. Teitelbaum, c/o Merksamer Drug Co., 1475 Amsterdam Avenue, New York 27, NY, and yet another stack showed that same return address except it had a Zip code of 10027 and the postmarks were from the same dates as the Rothmann daughters first days at Columbia. Susan smiled at how all of the Rothmann girls' letters had six cent stamps and a couple postcards were five cents. The older New York 27, NY envelopes were four and five cents postage. Susan guessed the later Teitelbaum letters were reports from the family friend who Rachel had said was their 'chaperone' at Columbia. Susan sorted through the box, learning about her grandparents that she had only ever seen one photo of. There were many items and packets of letters in the box that Susan did not examine in detail; military papers and the like.

While Susan was sorting through the box the exterminator came into the dining room, excused himself for interrupting Susan and did an inspection on hands and knees, shining his helmet light around the floorboards of the dining room and under the china cabinet, apparently finding nothing of interest to an exterminator.

Although the Rothmann box had a lot to discover and snoop in, Susan was anxious to get to the next video. She replaced the items in the box and sat the box in a new pile in the far corner of the dining room, a pile for boxes she had looked at. Susan put the next DVD, Roman numeral II, in the laptop and clicked play. She pulled her earphones from her backpack, so she could hear with the houseful of vacuuming and steam cleaning sounds and keep the videos private.

"Dear Susy. My guess is that you are watching these videos in fairly rapid succession, but for me there has been a two-week delay since the earlier one. My doctors decided it was worth a try to see if chemotherapy could fight the cancer, or perhaps delay the inevitable. They have me going to the oncology clinic every other day. And, the first week's treatment really knocked me on my keister. It was much the same as you told me your mother went through, so I needn't go into detail for you. I have not felt like doing anything for much of the last week, but they have the treatment balanced now, or perhaps I have just gotten used to it. They say I'll start losing hair in a week or so. Not really relishing that experience. Anyway, let's continue."

Susan could see Rachel straighten a pile of papers to read from them. Rachel was wearing what looked like a fleece warm-up jacket and her face was tired and a bit gaunt. Gone was the silk blouse and good-looking matron of the first video. "So, in the first session we got through the two marriages, so I'll pick up from there and that will let me segue into talking about the apartment. Go ahead and open the next envelope."

Susan opened the next envelope and Rachel's video guided her through a stack of Metzger family photos. There was a family photo of Morris, Hannah, with Isaac as a teenager with Aaron as a young boy. Next came Isaac and Rachel on honeymoon in Paris. Then, Rachel, Isaac and the two teenagers, Sarah and Joseph, standing on the beach in the Hamptons and finally some society photos and newspaper clippings of an elegant Rachel and tuxedoed Isaac at a few charity balls and business related dinners in the '70's. Rachel's recounting of her life with Isaac during their decade together was informative, but tame in comparison with the jarring emotion of the previous video with its abortion and engagement breakup. The only discordant note was Rachel's very brief description of losing the baby early in their marriage, but she seemed to pass quickly through that and move on. There was no picture for that part of the story and Rachel's voice cracked when she recounted the news that she could not have any more children. But, Rachel immediately switched topics and launched into a description of their new apartment in Chelsea, explaining to Susan how they had come to design the apartment for their family and lifestyle. Rachel said she would leave details of the apartment for later, when she would give Susan a tour.

Rachel proudly showed a clipping from a business magazine in the '70's that mentioned Isaac Metzger as an important player in the New York business scene. Rachel was particularly proud that the article compared Isaac to Robert Tishman. Susan had no idea who that was, but remembered that the old attorney Benjamin Ephraim had also mentioned Tishman. Susan had something else to Google.

Susan looked at the photos of Joseph and Sarah graduating from high school and then heading off to college. Rachel continued, "Life seemed perfect. Isaac had developed the connections and business formula that seemed to lead to success after success in his real estate deals. And I had become quite adept at being Isaac's Metzger's better half, hostess and cheerleader. I was truly enjoying a life of entertaining and socializing. I really became a clothes horse with the designer fashions for this event or that. A wealthy real estate mogul and his twenty-something trophy wife had no lack of awards ceremonies, Broadway openings, movie premiers, political parties and the like to go to. Isaac loved to spend money on me and I was quite obliging to accept. It was a real fairy tale.

"With the step-kids away at college, Isaac and I were totally in synch and so much in love. Things were going so well that Isaac got up the nerve to suggest that maybe we were ready to adopt. I was taken aback at first. We had talked about that earlier, when I lost the baby, but I always assumed it was Isaac's attempt at taking my mind off of losing the baby and not being able to have more. Now, he brought it up several years later and after a few weeks of cogitating on it, adoption seemed like the most wonderful idea I could imagine. I told Isaac my decision and he and I quickly became enthralled with the idea. Isaac had a business associate who indicated he had contacts that could arrange an adoption of a couple of orphaned Jewish children from inside the Soviet Union. Remember this was not the modern era, it was the height of the Cold War, but Isaac's attorney found a law firm with the proper overseas contacts and it seemed possible. That is, for the right price, and Isaac had the finances to pull it off.

"We had gone so far as to get word there were a brother and sister available at an orphanage in the White Russian province or republic, whatever, of the USSR, but the process would take as much as six months and probably a couple trips to the Soviet Union. The lawyers with their agents in the USSR even explained to us how this would probably require well-placed bribes, which they would handle, to get the proper approvals. Their euphemism for the bribes was "lubrication of the Soviet bureaucracy." We gave the go-ahead to proceed."

"Then, one bright sunny day in 1979 I came home from a shopping trip. I had purchased some things to send to the orphanage in Minsk where the children we hoped to adopt lived. The light was blinking on the answering machine. The message was from the secretary at the Metzger Companies management office. She said Isaac had had some kind of health problem and an ambulance had taken him to Mount Sinai Hospital. That is all the way up on the Upper East Side. She said I needed to go there, immediately. No real word other than that. I tried to call the office back, but only got through to the answering service.

"That trip by taxi through Manhattan traffic and all the way up the length of Madison Avenue seemed like it took hours. This was before cell phones and I spent to entire trip wavering between fearing the worst and believing that there was probably nothing to worry about. I was going crazy.

"The taxi finally let me out at the emergency entrance of the Mount Sinai complex. I ran inside and got the gal at the desk to tell me where I could find Isaac Metzger. She told me Cardiac Intensive Care. My heart dropped since I had lost my father to a heart attack and I ran to the elevator. As I exited the elevator, I saw Aaron standing in the hallway talking to a doctor. I ran to him and he took me into a room.

"We went into the room, just in time to see a doctor with his back to the door take his stethoscope out of his ears and say to a nurse with a clipboard 'Time of death 11:47 AM.' Then he looked around and saw me. The doctor's expression was an apology to me for those words. I looked at the bed and saw my Isaac with tubes coming out of him and a machine next to him making a steady tone, no heartbeat. I don't remember anything further. I woke up in a bed myself. I had passed out and they gave me a shot of something to calm me down. I got off of the bed and cried on Aaron's shoulder. I had been out for quite a while, and they had already taken Isaac away, I never got to say goodbye. Then Aaron took me down to Bubba Hannah's house where she and I had another good cry. My entire world seemed to end on that morning. I went from having a joyous world at my finger tips to utter, total despair in about an hour."

Susan could see in the video that Rachel was wiping a tear from her eyes. "I'm sorry. You would think I would be over this by now. Over thirty years now. I think I will end this for now. I guess these videos are turning into some real maudlin downers, huh? Well, I promise the next one will be happy. I'll give you a detailed tour of your new apartment and the goodies I have left for you. And then, I will tell you everything I know about your parents and the wonderful life they had. You know, I'm really hoping you decide to live here. I think that would be really wonderful. Bye for now."

Susan searched the DVD directory to make sure there was nothing more on this disk. There was not. She closed the program, stood and stretched. The video had taken quite a while; Susan thought she would check on how the cleaning was going. From the dining room archway, she could hear the whooshing whine of the steam cleaner was no longer coming from the kitchen. Swinging open the kitchen door, she could hear the two dishwashers running as well as the vent fan over the big grill, but nobody was in the kitchen, everything sparkled and the room smelled of pine scented cleaner. Quite a difference!

Susan turned to look down toward the master bedroom. She could hear the vacuum running, maybe in the living room, and the big fan unit was now sitting silent in the hallway. Susan started down the hallway when she heard someone come in the entrance across the foyer behind her. Susan stepped toward the foyer and saw it was the Caribbean girl with the dreadlocks carrying in a plastic jug of some pink liquid. The girl motioned to someone behind her, pointing to Susan.

Ariel Metzger appeared in the doorway. Susan blinked at her appearance and Ariel smiled and gave a little wave, saying, "Hi, hope you don't mind me bargin' in. Dad said the attorney told him you would be here today with a cleaning crew. He kinda wanted me to check on how things were going for you."

"No, of course not, come on in." Susan said, walking into the foyer. "Excuse the mess, just getting things cleaned up. You are kind of my first guest." Susan lied a little, considering Paul's visit.

Ariel looked around, "Nice place, I don't think I have ever been here before." Ariel was carrying several shopping bags and wore a light blue long sleeve t-shirt and blue jeans, with high-heeled wedge sandals. "I saw Aunt Rachel quite often, but she was usually visiting us, or at a wedding or party somewhere."

Susan indicated the shopping bags and said, "So, you've been out shopping?"

"Oh yeh, getting stuff ready for the wedding and honeymoon. Trousseau stuff, I guess is the right word for it. My college girl wardrobe doesn't quite fit a honeymoon cruise on the Mediterranean." Ariel smiled. "Which brings me to why I'm really here. I mentioned my upcoming wedding when we met, but we did not get to talk much. I wanted to make sure you got an invite. Dad and Mom say it would be a good chance for you to meet the family in little more cheerful surroundings than at Aunt Rachel's ... a... funeral." Ariel handed Susan an envelope from her purse.

Susan took the invitation, "Thanks, I actually saw an invite in Rachel's mail pile. Your wedding is in Southampton, that's out on Long Island, right. The end of the month."

"Yes, the last Sunday in June at the summer house, right overlooking the beach. Then there will be a catered dinner that night in a tent they are putting up on the lawn. It is going to be quite a wedding. Mom and Dad are giving away their only daughter and are literally sparing no expense. I'd love to have you come. I know it is short notice. And, I realize you are new in town and probably don't have any date to bring."

"Is it going to be the kind of thing where a date is expected?"

"Not necessarily, you can come without a date; it is going to be a full blown Jewish wedding, all the regalia, customs and a fancy dress occasion. You know?"

Susan did not really know, but said, "But, if I wanted to bring a date, it would be OK?"

"Yeh, a date would be best, we put most invitee's down for two seats at the dinner, unless we know they are coming alone or with kids. And it is quite a drive out there, or train ride, a lot of people reserve a hotel room for after the wedding dinner. There are several good hotels in the Hamptons, but they get booked up in summer." Ariel looked behind Susan down the main hallway, obviously curious.

Susan answered, "I'll see what I can do about the date? Consider this my RSVP, hopefully with a date. Would you like to see around the place here?"

"Sure, that would be great. Mom has always talked about Rachel's huge apartment."

"Put your bags on the dining table and follow me." Susan waited for Ariel to follow her down the hallway, then changed her mind and followed Ariel into the dining room.

"Ariel, would you like to see something Rachel left for me? I thought it was really interesting and I think you will, too. But, you have to promise not to tell your mother I showed you." Susan walked to her stack of manila envelopes.

"Not tell Mom? Sure, I guess." Ariel gave a quizzical look.

Susan opened envelope number one and thumbed through the stack, pulling out two pictures. Susan said to Ariel as she showed her the first picture, "I'm guessing you have never seen this photo. It is my mother and your father. They were like engaged, way back."

"Ohmigosh!" Ariel covered her mouth as she looked at the photo.

Then Susan handed her the next photo, "And this is your father and his brother Isaac, and their fiancées, my mother and her sister, our Aunt Rachel."

Ariel shook her head, "And so, your mother and my Dad broke up, huh?"

"Yeh, my mother broke it off with your father. He told me in the car from Rachel's burial that she broke his heart. And then my Mom married my father the next year. He was one of her instructors at Columbia. And, Isaac and Rachel got married."

Ariel handed the picture back to Susan, "You know, I may have heard something from Bubba Hannah about that, once upon a time, but 'No,' I had never seen a photo and didn't know any details. That's cool. And you are right; Mother would not appreciate mentioning this."

"And, now, let's show you around and tell me more about your wedding plans. And, your fiancé… Eddie, right?" Ariel beamed at the mention of Eddie. Susan motioned for Ariel to follow her down the hall.

—

The two men from the cleaning crew moved the furniture from the foyer to the sitting room next to the dining room. They folded the big Persian carpet into a floppy loose roll, and then folded it over lengthwise while Susan watched. They struggled to lift the large, unwieldy rectangle of folded carpet.

"Why didn't you just roll it up?" Susan asked, from her vantage point in the hallway by the storage room.

One of the men turned to her and said, "It is a 16 by 20 rug. If we just rolled it there is no way we would get a sixteen foot long roll into the elevator or down the stairwell."

Susan nodded at the obvious and felt stupid for asking the question and sticking her nose in these men's business.

Three of the women on the crew followed the men down to the freight elevator. Each of them had piles of draperies over their shoulders from three of the bedrooms, the living room, dining room and sitting room. Each bundle of draperies was tied with cords and had a label noting the location of the draperies. Susan had not realized the cleaning service would include taking the carpets and draperies for a deep in-plant cleaning. But, it made sense.

The crew had been there for six or seven hours. They had eaten their lunches together in the kitchen from their lunchboxes. True to Susan's first impression of them, they had gone through the apartment like a military operation with Brenda as their commander. Nothing had been missed. They even did a cleaning of the flues in the two fireplaces and the kitchen vent.

Brenda and Carlos followed the three women. Carlos still had his clipboard, checking off something. In the foyer Brenda handed Carlos what looked like an invoice and stepped toward Susan handing her another paper.

"Here is your receipt for seven rugs and six rooms of draperies. Will tomorrow at 1:00 in the afternoon be Okay to return the rugs and drapes," Brenda asked Susan.

"Why, ah yes, sure. That would be fine." Susan shook hands with Brenda as she turned to leave.

When Brenda was gone, Carlos came over to Susan and asked, "Can you handle tomorrow without me? I have a remodel project I have to shepherd all day tomorrow."

"Yeh, sure, they are just returning the stuff. I can handle that. I wasn't sure what to expect today. What they got accomplished was impressive."

"Yeh, they are good. But, this was nothing. You have a pretty nice luxury apartment that had a few problems. I have seen them hit a building that was previously a flop house and drug den, and get it clean as a whistle in two days." Carlos continued, "I made notes of some things I see you needed for fix-up, you know, repainting, plaster, minor electrical or plumbing work. You need some upgrades. I will call to work out a day for us to handle that after you get back from your trip. Nothing big, our Metzger guys can handle it so we don't have to bring anybody in. Oh, and the exterminator finished his work. He set some of those plastic mouse traps where they can get inside, but can't escape, around in the pantry, kitchen and utility room. You can throw those away in a week or so, or if you hear anybody scratching inside 'em. He'll call to come back monthly to make sure their guarantee holds true. Oh, and he recommends you do his service in the place across the hall, too. The critters can travel around pretty easily."

"Okay, thanks. I appreciate all your work to get me settled in here." Susan smiled.

"No problem." Carlos smiled back as he headed out the door. "Have a nice trip to Chicago."

Susan thought it was funny how all of the New Yorkers spoke of Susan coming from Chicago, as though the big city was the only thing of importance in Illinois.

The day had gone well for Susan. Ariel had toured the apartment and quickly left to get to a dress fitting appointment uptown. As they talked, Susan had gotten some suggestions on what was proper to wear as a guest at the wedding. Susan had a little over two weeks to get something. It did not sound like Susan had anything appropriate in her current wardrobe.

After Ariel left, Susan watched Rachel's next installment, the description of the apartment.

Rachel's video on the apartment was accompanied with only a few photos, primarily from a few parties with noteworthy visitors decades before and a couple snapshots of Rachel and Isaac or the teenaged stepchildren in their rooms. Rachel seemed particularly proud of a mid-1970's visit by an Israeli foreign minister whose name Susan did not recognize and a couple of supposed show business celebrities whose identities were equally murky to Susan. The oversize rooms of the apartment did seem to be conducive to entertaining.

Rachel had also described how she had decorated the apartment, and how Isaac had taken charge of the design and decor of his study himself. That had been obvious to Susan. Rachel had recorded the video as though she were informing someone who had not seen the apartment before. Since Susan had already gone through the apartment several times herself, Rachel's video was mostly anticlimactic.

One part of the video Susan had really appreciated was when Rachel described the paintings Rachel had left behind for Susan in the main apartment. Rachel hinted at how the stored paintings in the next apartment were even more impressive. Susan paused the video to copy down the names of artists Rachel spewed as she described the paintings. Susan recognized many of the artists, but not all of them. Susan was embarrassed she had not recognized the work of a couple of the modern masters that Rachel said were on the walls of the sitting room and the main hallway. Susan had noted them as she passed them on her quick tours around the apartment and told herself she would inspect them later. She should have paid more attention. Susan mentally chastised herself for not paying better attention to her supposed "field of study."

Next Rachel spoke of the old designer fashions and jewelry she had left behind. Rachel was careful not to presume that Susan would want to wear any of the old designer dresses, but Rachel knew the contents of the closet in the second bedroom would be of interest. Rachel carefully dropped names of Balenciaga, Versace, Prada and Furstenberg. She fully understood the value of the jewelry she had left for Susan in the dresser, and she assumed it would be worn by her. She had also explained there was a safe with other jewelry and a coin collection of Isaac's in the back of the smaller walk-in closet in the master bedroom. The smaller walk-in closet had been Isaac's, according to Rachel. Susan had finished watching that video in the early afternoon, wishing that the cleaning crew and Carlos would leave so she could try the combination Rachel had recited for the safe.

Now, with Carlos finally gone Susan had to choose between heading for the walk-in closet or going out and getting something to eat. She had not left the apartment and the last yogurt and Melba toast she had for lunch was long gone. But, she might be able to find something in what was left in the pantry.

However, Susan locked the front door and headed for the master bedroom, picking up the slip of paper with the safe combination from the dining room table. Two turns right stop at 1, left to 9, right to 7, left to 2. The safe combination was the same number as the alarm system code, the year Rachel had married Isaac.

Food could wait. Susan had an old wall safe to explore

—

Chapter Fourteen

Susan dumped the two overstuffed satchels of Rachel's old mail from the Post Office on the dining room table. She added to it the rest of the original mail pile she had found on the dining room table when she first arrived, but had not finished going through. The walk over to the Post Office, a stop at Starbuck's and a trip to the Trader Joe's to start restocking the now clean kitchen had been a good way to start Tuesday morning. She was surprised at the quantity of mail. At the post office, the two bundles were contained with a single rubber band each and threatened to come apart as Susan carried them the several blocks back to the apartment. Susan had asked the postal clerk if he had something she could carry it in. The postal clerk joked, tongue in cheek, that they were not supposed to give out the oversized Mylar envelopes used for Express Mail unless the patron was going to actually use them for sending Express Mail. Susan obediently promised to send her college applications in by Express Mail in return for the big envelopes.

Just sorting through this pile would take quite a while. But, Susan had nothing to do today other than this and watching another of Rachel's video disks, and, of course, to be at the apartment when the Persian rugs, the hallway runners and the apartment's draperies got returned by the cleaning crew at 1:00 PM. She already had everything ready for tomorrow's trip back to the Quad Cities.

A lot of the mail looked like obvious junk mail, but she knew so little about Rachel's life and affairs that she could not be sure without opening the envelopes. Rachel had an eclectic penchant for magazine subscriptions, *New Yorker, Town & Country, Time, American Art Collector, McSweeney's, Reform Judaism, Columbia Magazine* and few others added to the bulk of the mail pile. Susan set the magazines in a separate pile.

Susan had been told that most of Rachel's important financial mail went to the law firm client service address, but there were a couple things that would have slipped by if she had not decided to open everything. An envelope that had been in the stack already on the table that looked like an appliance advertisement was actually a sizable rebate check from Miele International for Rachel's purchase of the wine cooler for her kitchen wall unit. Another letter was an agenda packet for Rachel as a member of an advisory committee for the Museum of Modern Art. Susan found an email address on the documents she could email to notify MOMA of Rachel's death.

Susan went to get a trash bag to put the reject mail in. She thought briefly of the little paper shredder her father had told her to use for mail trash, to prevent idenitty theft. She had nothign like that here. She also had to finish putting away the stuff from Trader Joe's. This would be a morning of household chores and re-exploring the apartment now that it was clean.

—

0913 AM EDT

From:Reservations@southamptoninn.com

To:Susy@SusyFisher.com

Subj: Reservation for June 29th

Ms. Fisher,

This will confirm your prepaid reservation at the Southampton Inn in Southampton, NY for two adjoining rooms for one night checking on Sunday evening, June 29th. Due to the tight booking situation for summer weekends, your credit card has already been charged and refunds cannot be guaranteed. Our normal minimum stay policy for summer weekends was been waived, since, as we mentioned, we had a partial cancellation and we can accommodate your requested date.

Check in time is 4:00PM, but with your prepaid reservation you can check in any time thereafter and your room will be available. We understand from your phone call that you and your party may be arriving late from a wedding event. If your wedding event starts before 4:00PM, you can park at the Inn and we will be happy to give you a ride in our courtesy van in the local area. Many of our wedding patrons like that service.

Thank you for giving us the opportunity to serve you. We hope your stay with us will be pleasant.

Southampton Inn

91 Hill Street

Southampton, NY 11968

631.283.6500

Reservations@SouthamptonInn.com

—

Scrounging through the utility room, Susan had found a stack of replacement faux-flame bulbs that matched the burned out bulbs in the foyer chandelier. The stepladder behind the door in the utility room was just high enough to replace the bulbs. Susan could still smell the ammonia on the now sparkling chandelier crystals. The cleaning crew had not missed anything, except the burnt-out bulbs.

Last night, Susan had made a point of checking out the artwork in the hallway and sitting room that she had ignored until Rachel's latest video had described them. Although the sitting room was the first room inside the front door, to the right of the dining room archway, Susan had pretty much ignored it so far. The room's drapes had been closed, the sliding door partially closed and the room dark. However, today, without the draperies, the room was bright and Susan could appreciate it.

The sitting room had two red brocade couches facing each other on either wall with two matching side chairs nearby with lamp tables and ornate lamps between couches and chairs. Then, the *pièce de résistance* of the room was the long chaise lounge at the far end, under the window. Most people would call the lavishly upholstered red chaise lounge a casting couch or recognize its style from the famous painting of Empress Josephine lounging on one. Susan could not resist sitting on it and then lounging to the side with her long hair flipped over the round pillow on the right end. She had a quick daydream about posing for a formal portrait on this romantic piece of furniture.

Above each of the couches and chairs on the side walls were paintings, four in all. Susan was particularly impressed with a George Stimmel original, a Hudson River Valley scene. On the same wall was an Edward Cucuel painting of a young girl picking an apple, or perhaps it was a rosy peach. It, too, was original. Susan recognized that these two paintings by well-known painters must be very valuable. She wondered what they had been listed at in the personal property appraisal Rachel had the attorneys do for estate taxes. Then, thinking about it a moment and recalling the diamond tiara and Rolex and Tag Heuer wristwatches she had found in the wall safe the previous evening, she realized that it was probably better not to ask again about personal property appraisals. How could the estate tax authorities know what was on the sitting room wall of an old lady's apartment or in a safe in a bedroom closet? David Tannenbaum had been rather evasive when Susan had asked him about paying inheritance tax on personal property. Susan had a feeling that some things were better left unmentioned and unquestioned.

The opposite wall had two paintings similar in style and era, but by artists Susan was not as familiar with as Cucuel and Stimmel. They would be another topic to Google when she got a chance.

As she was sitting on the chaise lounge, Susan noticed a small secretary desk and chair hidden in the corner of the sitting room near the sliding entrance door with cordless desk phone and separate answering machine. So, there was another other land line phone that went with the desk phones in the master bedroom and study and the wall phone in the kitchen. The telephone worked, but the answering machine was unplugged. Susan plugged it in and pushed 'replay messages.' It responded, "No – New – Messages." Aunt Rachel had wiped the messages and turned the answering machine off at some point. Susan suspected it was much the same as had occurred with her mother. Toward the end, last January, Rebecca Fisher had grown frustrated at the number of well-wishers calling her, asking how she was and she had asked Susan to cover for her and answer the calls or ignore them. There was only so many times a person who knew they were dying wanted to hear old friends give heartfelt, but totally wrong prognostications that 'everything will be all right' soon. Susan left the answering machine on now.

Susan vowed to keep the drapes open in the sitting room from now on. She really liked the elegance of this room.

—

"You like?" Rachel said as she fingered the bangs of a brunette bob wig that came down mid-neck. "The chemo has kicked in and I am now relegated to this wig. But, I do feel a bit better than before. I am not sure what that really means."

Susan noticed that Rachel, in this DVD seemed a bit more chipper than in the previous one about the apartment. Rachel was wearing the fleece outfit again, but looked like she was wearing some make-up this time.

"I guess this video is supposed to be about the Fisher family. It may be a bit shorter than the previous ones, since I realize you already know a lot of this. Envelope IV is a bit thicker as I have gone through all of the pictures Rebecca sent me over the years and put the best in the envelope. Oh, there is still a lot of correspondence in the 'Fisher' box over in the corner. And I won't bother you with describing each picture, you can figure most out. What I want to do is talk about what I know of you parents in between their marriage and your childhood years. Again, when we talked last month you didn't seem to know a lot about that."

Rachel wiggled in her seat trying to get comfortable. "Sorry about my gyrations. I've lost quite a bit of weight in the last month and my boney butt doesn't sit as comfy as it used to.

"I left off telling you about your parents' wedding. Rebecca was in the apartment on the Upper West Side that we had rented together when they got married. Jeff was rooming with two other graduate students. So, after the wedding he moved into our old apartment with your mother. They both had one year to go at Columbia. He had a teaching assistant job. Your mother didn't work much the fall semester, just some retail clerking for the holiday shopping season, and had her student teaching in the second semester."

Susan remembered how her mother had told her when Susan got her job at Macy's, how Rebecca had once clerked in New York City.

Rachel continued, "I did not have a lot of contact with Rebecca that year.

I was busy getting settled in with Isaac and his two kids. He had a four bedroom townhouse on the East side, where he had been living with them. I got together with your mother for lunch, once in a while.

"It seemed to be a good time for them. Jeff defended his dissertation and would be getting his Ph.D. and was applying across the country for university teaching jobs. I am not sure when Rebecca decided to get the teaching credential. Prior to that last year she had an idea of using her English degree in publishing. But, since she had to follow Jeff wherever he got his history professor job, I guess she decided she needed something portable, since there is not a lot of publishing outside of New York, or wasn't back then. Anyway, your Mom did her student teaching and took the teaching credential classes, I think through Barnard College, that last semester to be able to get a teaching license with her Columbia English degree. For some strange reason Columbia does not have a teaching program itself.

"Our mother came up to visit that spring. Remember, Mother was still a fairly young woman, only in her mid-40's then. She spent two weeks staying with Isaac and me and during that two weeks Rebecca only saw her twice, once when we invited her and Jeff over for dinner and once when I invited her out to lunch with Mother and she couldn't come up with an excuse to refuse. Rebecca's relationship with Mother could, at best, be described as 'polite' and the feeling seemed to be mutual. I was amazed that these two people who I was so close to were so disconnected with each other. The emotional turmoil of the abortion and Father's death had just ripped them apart. And, they never got over it.

"Your mother was a happy, loving person to everyone, but to her mother she was a different person, and vice versa. I didn't understand it. Oh, I knew the events and the causes, but I just didn't understand why Rebecca and Mother acted like that. Maybe there was something else that had gone on between them that I was unaware of. I don't know. I don't think so.

"And, since Mother, and Father, had been her link to all things Jewish, Rebecca turned her back on most everything Jewish. She never went to synagogue. She didn't keep Kosher any more. And, because of his own personal philosophy, that seemed to be just fine with your Father.

"Your Father. I don't think there is much I can add about your Father that you don't know. He grew up in Philly, uh, Philadelphia, and went to Penn State for undergraduate and he took ROTC, getting a commission in the Army when he graduated in the mid-60's. He was lucky to know German from his parents and they sent him to Germany for his two year active duty tour. His parents were older folks, they had been in the States since way before the War. His father died when he was in college. His mother died in his first year back at Columbia. Your father was an only child, so by the time he married your mother, she was his whole family. With her attitude about Jewish lifestyle, your father's own personal philosophy about religion and the realities of his employment at two different Christian chartered colleges out West, I guess they just naturally gravitated away from having anything much Jewish in their lives."

Rachel straightened up in her chair and said, "Oh, wait, I have forgotten to do the pictures." She sorted through a stack of pictures on the dining room table, as did Susan.

Rachel continued, "Well, you can look as easy as I can describe. You know the players well enough. All of these pictures are what your mother sent me after they left for Denver."

Rachel set the pictures aside. "Of course, right about the time when your parents were getting ready for their next move to Illinois, my Isaac passed away. Your mother and father came for the funeral, they flew in. And so did my mother. Rebecca and Mother buried the hatchet for my sake at the funeral and after. They stayed on and helped me get put back together for a couple weeks. Rebecca was really good with Sarah and Joe. And Bubba Hannah and my mother were good together. But, when Mom left after the funeral, that was the last time Rebecca saw her mother. Mother was fifty or so by then and the diabetes was getting to her, she didn't walk as well as she had before. She died a few years later, complications of the diabetes."

Rachel showed a picture to the video camera, "These were good years for your parents. Here's a photo they sent me of them in front of their new house in Moline. Well, it wasn't new, but it was new to them. All their own. Your father got his appointment as an associate professor in the History Department at Augustana. I guess that was a promotion and pay raise from being an assistant professor at University of Denver.

"Your mother and father were trying hard to have a baby now that they had their own home. I think your mother had three miscarriages in all, one of them pretty far along. I got a letter from her where she questioned whether this was her punishment for what she had done to her first baby in New York. She obviously had a lot of Jew still in her, because she was laying a monster guilt trip on herself. I didn't know what to say to her.

"I wasn't a very good advisor to a young woman who wanted to have a baby, but couldn't." Rachel paused for a moment. "By that time the gynecological problems that had kept me from having more children had progressed to the point where I had to have a hysterectomy; I was not even forty then."

Rachel stopped and shook her head with the wig hair swinging side to side. "Wait, didn't I promise this was going to be a happy video, for once. Well, it got happy, for Rebecca. She gave up trying so hard to have a baby, and her and Jeff took to travelling each summer – Germany or Aix en Provence, building their life in Illinois and they were happy for what? Ten years or more. Then, she invited me to come out and visit them for Yom Kippur in the early '90's, which I thought was kind of funny because, as far as I knew, they didn't celebrate Yom Kippur.

"I flew in to your little airport out there, and my sister Rebecca met me with the biggest belly you ever saw. She was eight months pregnant and had not told me for fear of jinxing the new baby. We had a wonderful time that week. So joyous, Rebecca knew how to cook. Jeff said that was the first time they had really celebrated Yom Kippur.

"We went out to this really dinky little Jewish Temple across the river in Iowa for the Yom Kippur service. I had to leave, my stepson Joe's wife Hannah was ill back in New York, but about three weeks later, your mother gave birth to a ten pound baby girl, Susannah Rachel Fisher. I was so happy when I heard they named her after me."

Rachel smiled at the video camera, "Those were good years. I had resolved some of my personal problems, which I, hopefully, will talk about later. And, Rebecca and Jeff were so happy with their bouncing baby girl. I came out twice to visit when you were a tiny baby, and then you and your mother came to New York to see me when you were, what, in Kindergarten? Pre-school? I remember taking you to a birthday party for Joe's daughter. I got to see you off and on every few years after that, always with your family visiting me in New York, on your way to your summer adventures. I never made it back to Moline again until your father's funeral… Again with the downers, huh?"

Rachel pursed her lips, "I guess the downers are an important part of our life story, right?"

Rachel straightened the stack of photos. "You can look through this last pile of photos. Most of them are you, mugging for the camera, or doing something to make your parents proud. I don't think my words can add much to them. And there are other letters and stuff in the big 'Fisher" box by the wall. Take your time going through that. I think seeing your mother's letters to me, in good times and bad, will give you a better picture of who she was and how your life came to be.

"I'll break this off for now. My intention is to back up to cover the 1980's from my perspective next. That will cover a dark time in my life, followed by a highlight and, then, another dark time that helped me grow and find out what matters in life. Auspicious goal, huh? Actually, I lived a pinball game in the '80's, up, down, up, down, up. And it will also explain and show you around my hoarding areas in the other apartment. I trust you are watching these in my apartment, aren't you. If you aren't, you ought to arrange to do so and have access to the places I talk about.

"So, now, go have some fun. If it is a Thursday in your world, I can recommend going down to the Bistro in my building, or rather, in your building now, and sitting in for a session of the nice little jazz quintet they have playing there on many Thursday nights. There is a little ginger-haired chanteuse that sings blues classics with them sometimes who is amazing. Bye for now."

—

It took the two guys from D'Angelo Carpet and Drapes several trips to get the rugs and draperies up from the lobby to the apartment. Susan was beginning to dislike the freight elevator system that required her to go down to the lobby to let visitors come up. It would be much handier to just buzz them into the lobby when they rang and let them use the regular elevator to come up. The added security and privacy of the exclusive elevator might have been important to Aunt Rachel, but Susan saw the inconvenience as a problem. She would discuss it with Laszlo or Carlos when she had a chance.

As the two men were rehanging the draperies in the dining room, Susan said to them, "I expected the people from the cleaning crew would have come to return this stuff."

The older of the two replied, "No, they contract with us on the draperies and rugs. We have a plant up in the Bronx that has dry cleaning machines and huge, flat-bed dryers for the big rugs and we also do draperies for many of the storefront places in the city where you drop off drapes for cleaning. It is a big, pretty efficient operation. And our installation crews specialize in the rehanging, so if customers are missing hooks or have bad rods and pulls we can fix them and get everything shipshape when we rehang."

"Ah, I see," was all Susan could think of to say. Susan followed them as they laid rugs and hung drapes throughout the apartment. As they left she received an invoice from them marked "Prepaid –Metzger Companies Account." She thanked them and took them down to the lobby.

Back up in the foyer she noted how the huge Persian carpet's colors had brightened with the cleaning and realizing that 'Susan's Apartment in New York' was clean, reassembled and ready for whatever life she could make in it. She thought for a moment and headed to the study to finally check out what books filled the many shelves there.

—

Chapter Fifteen

Arrival at the Quad Cities International Airport was a stark contrast from her experiences at La Guardia earlier in the morning or at either JFK or O'Hare airports the week before. First, Susan exited the little commuter plane down an old-fashioned rolling stairway and walked across the tarmac in a cluster with her fellow passengers to an open doorway in the single story terminal, not through a telescoping jet way one would expect from a place christened an international airport. And, even though it was approaching midday, their United Express flight from Chicago appeared to be the only commercial airplane at the terminal. The twelve people who got off the flight with her more than doubled the visible population of the terminal building. She had gotten spoiled by the hectic pace and bustle of activity in New York. She now saw her hometown airport as a Podunk oddity. Of course, she had started every trip for her entire life from this same little airport, but this time through Susan Fisher seemed to be looking at her hometown through different eyes. The moniker of International Airport seemed to Susan to be a cruel joke her hometown was playing on itself. As a final proof of this, Susan counted the total of departures on the arrival-departure monitor in the airport. There were a grand total of thirteen daily flight departures and none of them showed a destination that justified the name 'International.'

The baggage arrived via a handcart with bags loaded on a small sloped rack by a single baggage handler, no need for an automated luggage carousel like JFK's when only six people had bags and only Susan had more than one. She felt kind of silly as she lifted her two red bags from the luggage rack. One of her red Louis Vuittons was totally empty and the other only had her laptop and backpack inside. She had brought them empty to pack her clothes from the house. On her trip back to New York the bags would be full and she planned on shipping a lot of stuff in boxes via UPS.

Outside the terminal was further reminder of the small town nature of this place. Only two taxis waited for this flight and only one of those got a fare to pick up. Both taxis seemed to be recycled, repainted police cars, judging from their twin spotlights on the doorposts. Everyone else, like Susan, proceeded across the traffic-free street to the sunbaked, open air parking lot, no parking structure was needed here. The upside of the small town airport was that the parking fee for eight days of long term parking was less than the taxi trip to La Guardia had been. Her mother's old white Prius seemed like a long lost friend, comfortable and familiar, but a friend she would soon be saying goodbye to.

There was little traffic, even when Susan reached Interstate 74 for the brief, one exit ride into Moline proper. She had a comfortable feeling of knowing exactly where she was going here though. Her subconscious and the Prius got her off the interstate and onto John Deere Road in southern Moline. There were quite a few things she would need for this housekeeping, sorting and archiving task ahead of her. First, boxes and packing supplies from Lowe's, then some grocery store supplies and miscellaneous items for her last stay in the old house.

The big bag of Styrofoam packing peanuts filled the Prius hatchback. She had to put the backseat down for bundle of boxes and peanuts to all fit. Susan made an unplanned stop on the way from Lowe's to the big Jewel-Osco grocery and drug store. The road between them passed the Moline city cemetery, and Susan felt obliged to stop. Her parents' graves were easy to find, side by side in the newest section near the access road. The gravestones were identical dark gray schist with their names, years of birth and death and a Star of David inlaid in lighter stone. Her father's gravestone also had 1LT, US Army 1963-66 on it. She had never spoken about such things with her mother and after Rachel's story she wondered how her mother would feel about the symbol. But, then, the star was the same as her mother ordered for her father, so it did not seem to have been inappropriate for Rabbi Rothmann' s daughter. Of course it wasn't, and Susan would never even have questioned it, but for the story about her mother Aunt Rachel had told her on the video. Susan spent several minutes at the graveside with her thoughts about her parents and the fact that this might be her last time here for some time. When Susan sold the house there would not be much in Moline to draw her back here. That thought was sad in itself.

The grocery store stop led her to the last errand before she went to the house. At the Illinois Secretary of State automobile registration office over in the nearby town of Silvis where she had taken her first driver's exam they answered Susan's questions about car titles and gave her the forms and duplicate car titles she needed. It seemed that her father's bowling buddy who handled her parents' estates had gotten both cars put in Susan's name correctly. Then, Susan headed for the only home she had ever known.

The trip across Avenue of the Cities from Silvis through the heart of East Moline and then Moline to her house took Susan past both Moline High School and, after the jog up to 19th, past John Deere Middle School. She had fond memories of both. School was out of session for the summer and so both schools looked sadly empty. Finally, she took the last turn down the side street that she had walked, roller skated and bicycled down ten thousand times in her life. Nothing much changed in this neighborhood, ever. The Morton's lot on the last corner was still vacant; they had never rebuilt after the fire several Christmases ago. Susan guessed it did not make sense to rebuild on a small lot in an old neighborhood, when you could put the same money in the same house design on a larger lot on the outskirts of the city.

Then, the little white, vinyl sided tract home that had always been the center of Susan's universe appeared.

It was, of course, the same as she had left it eight days before, for what she presumed would be a non-eventful three day trip. But now, the cottage seemed somehow tinier, the need for the trim to be painted more obvious and everything about it seemed a bit remote and detached, compared to how it had felt a short while back. Looking at it was like viewing the old photos in a family album, with fond but almost dimming memories. She realized it was the loving parents who had lived here that she would miss, not this simple, unassuming structure. This old house was of no further value to her, not any more than the old high school was. Both had served their purpose. She parked the Prius behind her father's metallic green Explorer in the driveway.

The key for the house was on the Prius key ring. She had another house key in her purse, which she would give to the real estate broker tomorrow morning. The air inside the closed house was hot in mid-June, and she had forgotten to take the kitchen garbage out before she left last week. Old food scraps stank in the garbage. She left the kitchen door open as she took several trips to unload the supplies and bags from the car. There was no air-conditioning in the old house. She stood in the kitchen and thought of what she should do first. Susan felt she had well planned what she needed to do this long-delayed chore in an organized manner; she just was not sure how long the sorting would take. Some rooms, like the kitchen, would have little that needed to be saved; pots, pans and dishes from here would be of little use in New York. Most kitchen items would go to the estate auction company. Maybe there were some keepsakes in the kitchen, but not many. This would be a good place to start on and get crossed off the list of to-dos.

As she expected, the kitchen was fairly easy to rummage through. There were, of course, memories associated with many items, but Susan was sticking to her yardstick for keeping things that must have some intrinsic value in her new life or something that she could show to someone else, say perhaps, her own children someday, and they would understand its value, or its message. With this measurement, Susan was able to go through the kitchen and only felt the need to save a few pieces of antique carnival glass she found in one cabinet and a fairly nice set of carving knives she had given her parents as a gift. At the same time, Susan intended to learn from her mother's error and not let this break from her past keep her from showing her own future children who their grandparents were and how their mother had grown up. But, there was little in that category in the old kitchen. She started to fill a trash bag with foodstuffs that she couldn't use and could not be auctioned. She doubted whether sending the closed canned goods to New York via UPS was cost effective. She was not sure what to do with the food, so she boxed the canned goods and pre-packaged food and set them to the side. Throwing away perfectly good food seemed silly. She would decide later what to do.

Then, in the dining room, she had been stymied. The silver service and good china had been cherished possessions of her mother, gifts in their early days of marriage. From Rachel and Isaac? She knew her mother would have wanted her to take them with her, but Susan knew Aunt Rachel's china cabinet had far better and there was only need for one set of good silver in one's life. Then, Susan played a mind trick on herself, imagining that she had two daughters in the future and having this set of grandmother's silver and china would help spread the family heirlooms around a bit. Susan packed the silver and china in a box to ship to New York.

The living room was more of a problem. The furniture and TV were old and as bourgeois and outmoded as you could get, so they would obviously get auctioned. She unplugged the cable box and made a call to get cable service turned off. They told her they needed her to bring the cable box and remote in to terminate the account. Another errand to do. Next, the wall of shelves held numerous childhood soccer trophies, snapshots in frames, favorite books, souvenirs of foreign adventures and photo albums. In the end, much of the shelves' contents got packed.

The Fisher home's single bathroom in the hall was much the same as the kitchen. Even Susan's personal items were of questionable value when compared to Susan's present buying power to replace them with new in Manhattan. Shipping a two-thirds empty bottle of hair conditioner to New York did not make sense. The linen closet was much the same, except it did supply plenty of towels to pack the carnival glass, china, photo frames and souvenirs from the other rooms. Susan did find a storage box of many miscellaneous photos on the top linen closet shelf that she packed. And, she packed several blankets and patchwork quilts that had memories attached.

Slowly, Susan worked her way through the main bedroom, then the small third bedroom her father had used as a study/office. Each presented its own sorting challenges. It was only Susan's knowledge that she would have to find a place to store anything she took amongst Rachel's even larger horde in New York that helped her reject knickknacks, binders of old schoolwork and even some of her own clothing stash that had no place in a Manhattan lifestyle. Susan had Gucci pumps to wear in New York; she need not save the well-worn black heels she had saved her Macy's wages to buy off of the 'last year's clearance' bargain rack.

After discovering that the closet in her father's office was stacked with a dozen or more boxes of historical research, Susan put in a call to the head of the history department at Augustana. The boxes were her father's files and research, which Susan would have no use for, but which were certainly of some value academically. She left a message on his machine for the professor to call her back. Susan also decided her father's old computer CPU would get shipped to New York; it might have useful information or photos on it. But, the old-fashioned boxy monitor and printer would be auctioned. Her father's camera bag with the new digital SLR his mother had bought him the Christmas before his death would go to New York also. Plastic bins of CDs and old floppy disks also got sent east. In one binder labeled 'Archibald Project,' Susan found papers from her family's trips to Israel, including an invitation letter and grant award from the Israeli Antiquities Authority. Susan assumed 'Archibald' was nobleman associated with the old Crusaders' castle near Acre her father had worked on those summers. She packed that binder. She also found a file cabinet drawer with dozens of folders of family information, New York marriage license, tax returns, her parents' old college transcripts, her report cards, etc. Those got packed, too.

Susan was still at work in the afternoon when she felt the woozy sensation in her lower abdomen that sent her to the bathroom. She found she was missing one thing that would require another errand trip to the nearby drugstore. She had chosen a bad few days of the month for this trip. What timing! The sorting of her old bedroom and the garage could wait for tomorrow. Besides the drugstore, Susan would hit the cable TV office and the Hardee's on 16th and get her favorite cheeseburger and fries. She had not seen a Hardee's in New York.

—

Jesse Morgenthau was a sweaty, little man in a too small sport coat and stained tie who smelled of musk cologne. But, he seemed to know about real estate, or, at least, he had a quick answer for every question Susan had for him. He had brought with him a stack of printouts showing recent sales in the Moline and Rock Island area comparable to her house. He brought his digital camera with him, but when he saw Susan's stacks of boxes he said he would come back for the interior listing pictures when the house was cleared out. After a quick walk-thru Jesse dropped his $190,000 estimate down to a suggested price of $184,900 for the sales contract. He said the old carpet and lack of recent decor updates, especially the tiny, old-fashioned bathroom, did not justify more than that. He seemed pleasantly surprised when Susan did not contest the drop of five thousand dollars. His mood brightened more when Susan told him she owned the place outright, no mortgage, and did not mind accepting a seller's second mortgage for down payment, so long as her New York attorney agreed to the terms. She turned over the extra house key.

Forewarned by Susan's email that she wanted the estate auction company to handle the personal property, Morgenthau had a contract and bill of sale ready from that auction service, as well as the sales listing with his real estate brokerage. The auction firm took a healthy 25% commission, but the fee included the work of sorting everything left by Susan and carting away the junk, while selling the valuables, or rather, the salables. After signing the 25% commission contract with the auction company, the 6% for the real estate sales commission seemed minimal. Susan suspected that is why Jesse presented them to her in that order.

After the auction company finished carting off the trash, the broker would send in a prep crew to clean and paint the place. The old house would be stripped clean and ready for buyers and open house showings within the week or so. Susan gave Jesse the New York law firm's address to send the bill for the work and the other paperwork. As Jesse Morgenthau left, he gave Susan a couple of his cards. Since all further contract approvals and deal decisions would come through her attorney, Susan gave Morgenthau one of David Tannenbaum's cards. At the last minute, Susan remembered to give Jesse the key to the garage, which was different from the house key, and reminded him to have the auction company remember about the garage.

Susan was watching the broker drive off in his new Buick sedan when she heard her iPhone ring. She answered.

"Susan! Pete Moresby, how are you doing?" a voice said.

"Just fine, Doctor Moresby, and you?"

"Fine, fine. I'm glad you caught me. I got your phone message before I headed out for my summer project trip in Iroquois country next week. I saw you around the building last term for a class, but I don't think we talked since your mother's funeral. What brings me the pleasure of your call?"

"Well, Professor, I finally got around to clearing out the house and when I got to Dad's office I found maybe ten of those, what do you call them, bankers' boxes, of his project materials. They look like a several manuscripts and all of the supporting photos and maps, etc. You know, he was working on the Carolingian book and the French Castle photo book and some other miscellaneous stuff." Susan hoped he remembered, she thought she had the subjects right.

"Yes, I recall him talking about both of those projects. And…?" the history department chair left the question hanging.

"Well, since I'm clearing out the house, and I have no use myself for his papers, I have heard of scholars or their heirs donating papers and research materials to their institutions, and I wondered if you could tell me how that works."

"Oh, well, yes. That is frequently done. And your father's work is precisely the kind of thing that could be of value to someone following up on his work. Our department has archives of several former staff members' and alumnus' papers. You were thinking of an outright donation to Augustana?"

"Yes, he spent almost his whole career there, he would be proud to have his work be of some lasting value."

"Of course, we can arrange to have the donation made. But, tell me, you say you are clearing out the house. Are you moving?"

"Yes, actually, I am. My aunt, on my mother's side, passed away in New York and left her estate to me. I've decided to move there."

"But, Susan, you are what, a junior? What do you intend to do about school?"

"This decision is pretty new to me. It looks like I am going to have to find someplace in New York to transfer to. If you have any suggestions, I'm open to…ideas."

Moresby paused, "Well, as I recall, both your father and mother were Columbia grads, you might want to network that alumni connection, and we at Augustana will provide whatever you need for references. In fact, I'll put a refderence letter in your Augustana student file before I leave for the summer. That is quite sudden, you sure it is the best?"

"Yes, it is sudden, but it gives me a really good opportunity, financially and … uh… it just seems right."

"Okay, what is the time frame for getting these papers?"

"I am cleaning right now. The house should be empty by next week for the real estate people to take over. I'm here through Saturday. I can bring them by the campus tomorrow."

"Oh, no, that isn't necessary. Ten boxes, let me see if I can get one of the summer interns out there to pick them up. Can I have someone call you?"

"Yes, this number is good, anytime today or tomorrow."

"Well, okay Susan. I will do that. I hope this move is good for you. Augustana is losing a gem; you've grown up at Augustana. I remember little Susy playing jacks on the floor of her Daddy's office. I wish you well."

"Thanks, give my regards to everybody."

"I will do that. Stay safe."

"Bye. I'll miss all of you. And Augustana."

Susan had forgotten about playing jacks while she waited for her father in his office as a child. It was amazing how a conversation can ripen long forgotten memories. The conversation with Moresby made Susan wonder who else at Augustana she needed to call. Art instructors, financial aid office, soccer coach; she had already contacted the transcript people, who else? And, it was summer and some people would be away. Plus, she had said she would stop in at the Davenport Macy's when she was back in town. She was beginning to doubt she could get everything done in the next two days.

Before the real estate broker had arrived on Thursday morning, Susan had started on going through her old bedroom. After her mother's death Susan had moved her clothes and currently needed items to the larger bedroom, but she had left all of her girlhood treasures; the collection of old toys, scrapbooks, souvenirs that she had collected throughout her childhood in the old bedroom. Now it fell upon her to make the decisions needed to sort through her own memories and 'stuff' to decide what could be packed for New York.

But, finishing that sorting of her old bedroom would have to wait for the afternoon. As she put the iPhone down from the call from Moresby, Susan saw it was nearly noon and she had set an appointment for lunch with Heidi. She had to get ready. Her work clothes needed to be changed, and she needed to check and see if her father's Explorer would still start. She had not driven it in some time, usually driving the handier Prius. The only time she had ever driven the Explorer much was between her father's death and her mother's. Now, she planned on driving it to deliver all of the boxes to the UPS shipping place, and it would be her only transportation after she got rid of the Prius.

Heidi Hapsburg still lived with her parents in a house virtually identical to the Fisher's house. The two houses were one block over and three blocks up from each other, so Heidi and Susan had gone to school together most of their life, but they had not become close friends until middle school. Susan still remembered the first afternoon she had brought Heidi over to the house and her father had asked the blonde middle-schooler about her last name. He said Hapsburg was a famous name of a royal family in Europe although with a slightly different spelling, but Heidi knew nothing of any family connections like that, her father was a supervisor on the John Deere tractor assembly line. Heidi had liked the idea that Susan's father, the history professor, had thought this machinist's daughter might be descended from royalty.

—

Susan did not have to go in or honk her horn; Heidi was waiting in their porch swing and ran out to the car. She was wearing blue jeans and a t-shirt. Susan should have stayed in her jeans she had been wearing to sort this morning, instead of changing to skirt and blouse.

Susan leaned across the console and gave Heidi a quick hug when she got in. Susan noted that Heidi was wearing a too-sweet smelling perfume. Susan guessed it was the new Taylor Swift label, a syrupy, girlish fragrance Susan would not be caught dead wearing. As always, Heidi had her blonde hair hanging straight almost down to her shoulder blades. Heidi was chewing a wad of gum. Heidi was not wearing any make-up and her freckles made her look much younger than her twenty years. Heidi was probably going to get carded at bars for most of her twenties. Heidi would beat Susan to her twenty-first birthday, Heidi's coming in August, two months from now.

"So, how ya been? I wanna hear everything." Heidi said, flopping back in the seat and buckling up.

"Okay, where you want to eat? Is Café Fresh all right?" Susan asked.

"Sure, if you want to do sit-down. Give us a chance to talk." Heidi waited while Susan drove to the corner and turned, then continued, "So, tell me all about New York. You were all excited that first night you called. Then nothing since, except chewing me out for Tweeting."

Susan had thought long about what to tell her best friend. There was a time when Susan would have spilled her guts to Heidi about anything and everything. However, she remembered Peter Ephraim's lecture on the way her life would be changing and how to deal with people. Susan carefully phrased what she needed and wanted to tell Heidi about the changes in her life since she had left for the trip to New York.

"Well, it is like I said. Aunt Rachel left me her estate. I get her apartment in New York and she had a trust fund that will be mine too, but not right away, at least not all of it. And there's this attorney who is the Trustee who controls the trust and all the money." This was the first half truth Susan had formulated to keep her friend somewhat in the dark about the extent of her inheritance. She had tried to remember what she had said that first night and wanted to keep her story straight. Susan waited to say more as she pulled up to the stop sign and waited to turn toward downtown Moline on 5th Avenue.

Susan continued, "And… I guess there is no way to put this gently… I decide to move to New York."

"What? No way… when?" Heidi was, as Susan expected, flabbergasted.

"Right away. I signed a contract to sell the house this morning. I am going through everything, sorting what I need to keep and all. I expect to be out by Saturday. A company is going to sell everything else in an auction over in Muscatine."

"Wow, I can't believe it. You're quitting school?"

"Well, Augustana, at least. I ordered transcripts to transfer to someplace in New York, not sure where yet. And, …" Susan paused as she opened the storage bin in the console and handed Heidi an envelope.

Heidi opened the envelope and read the papers within it. Heidi got quiet as she read.

"This is a bill of sale for zero dollars and registration for this car. You put it in my name?"

"Well, not yet, until you file the title docs with a proof of insurance over at the Secretary of State's office in Silvis. You have to get your own insurance for it, but I wanted you to have Mom's car. You need something to replace that old beater of a Ford. And, I didn't feel like selling this to some stranger for next to nothing. It is a good car and I thought it was a good idea for you to have it."

"But, I can't take it for free." Heidi protested.

"Why not? Aunt Rachel had a Prius, too. I get that and can't use two cars." Susan intentionally did not mention Rachel's Mercedes. "I want you to have this. My Mom would like the idea, too."

"Susy, I don't know what to say."

"Heidi, you don't have to say anything. I can see how round your eyes are right now. That is all the thanks I need."

Susan pulled into a curb parking space near the restaurant. Susan could not get over how different downtown 5th Avenue in Moline at lunchtime was from 5th Avenue in New York. You could actually find a parking space on the street in the heart of Moline at noon and traffic was very light. She turned off the car, unsnapped the catch on the key ring and took her house key off the key ring, handing the Toyota key to Heidi along with the extra key ring from the console. "There, HeidiHo, it is all yours. When we are done you can drive me home in your new car. Now, let's eat."

———

After the trip back from lunch, Heidi got out to give Susan a hug in front of the house, before driving off in the Prius. They resolved to maybe get together again Friday evening, if things were going well with Susan's packing. Heidi volunteered to help, but Susan declined, saying that most of the work was the really personal choice of what to keep or pack.

Lunch had gone fairly well, with Susan telling a series of half-truths about the extent of her inheritance and Heidi asking lots of questions. Life seemed to be going as normal for Heidi, working a part-time summer job three days a week as a temp worker at the Rock Island Arsenal, apparently an offshoot of her business class internship at Augustana the previous semester. Heidi had broken up with a guy she had been dating who had only a few credits left to finish in the fall semester to graduate in business. Heidi confessed that she had not been sure this guy was right for her and he had started talking about commitment as he approached the end of his college days, whereas Heidi had two years left, like Susan. And, the guy had said that he was going to use his business degree to modernize and expand his family's farming business up in northern Illinois, and Heidi had no wish to be a farm wife, even a wealthy one. But, such was Heidi's usual story with guys. Guys threw themselves at the pretty blonde, but she really did not know what she wanted and she rarely stayed with any beau for more than a few months, if that.

Susan watched Heidi drive off and could not help but think how she and her bosom buddy had diverged from each other. Heidi was a simple college girl, smart, certainly not an airhead, but focused on dating and what classes to take next semester. Susan had a difficult time engaging her in any meaningful conversation about the issues Susan really needed a friend to confide in. That is, her concerns about the direction her life was going, her identity 'crisis' if you could call it that, the stress of the way things had changed in just a few days. Of course, much of the problem with that was that Susan was not fully honest with Heidi, keeping the extent of the inheritance from her and all. And, Susan knew from experience that Heidi had no idea anything of the issues Susan faced regarding her struggle with Jewish family and identity or the feelings of emptiness and loss Susan was struggling with. Heidi came from a big Lutheran family and had both parents and two younger siblings, and a large extended family of aunts, uncles and cousins who lived locally. Susan fully realized that this close friend from her childhood was really out of touch with the person Susan had become. Susan hated to admit it, but her old friend Heidi had really grown apart from her. Susan felt more at home talking with someone like Devorah than she did Heidi. That was not Heidi's fault; it was Susan who had changed. Heidi was still the pretty blonde college student from Moline; Susan was the one who was out of synch.

During lunch Susan had gotten a phone call from Professor Moresby's secretary saying she would have an intern over to the house at 2:30 or 3:00 to pick up the boxes of her father's research papers. She said the intern would have a donation form to sign.

Susan fished the Explorer keys from her purse and opened the hatchback. She would take a load of boxes to UPS before finishing her room and tackling the garage and its mess of boxes, piles and whatnot. She could easily make it back by 2:30.

—

Susan was dragging two heavy double-bagged trash bags from the garage to the curb when she saw a red Ford pickup pull to the curb. It was a nice 4x4 truck and had large custom wheels and was lifted, extra high. She dumped the trash near the ever growing pile of trash bags at the end of the driveway and watched a man get out of the truck.

She recognized the man. It was Greg Harkness, the guy she had stood up for the date last Saturday night, giving him the excuse that she was away in New York. He was in blue jeans and a short sleeved Minnesota Vikings jersey.

"Greg?" Susan wiped her hands on her jeans.

Greg walked toward her with a paper in his hand. "I thought you were supposed to be in New York or something like that."

"I was, I flew in yesterday morning. What are you doing here?"

"I'm working." Greg said, letting Susan wait for more explanation.

"Working?" Susan waited for a better answer, as Greg walked up next to her. Susan looked up into Greg's face. It was a rare person who was this much taller than Susan. He had to be at least six-four with his brown hair cut very short in a clearly military haircut. His handsome face had a darker tan than she remembered from class last term.

Greg waved the paper in his hand and said, "Yeh, the secretary in the History Department office says I am supposed to get Professor Fisher's daughter to sign this donation and copyright consent form and pick up some valuable research files for the Department."

"Oh, they sent you. I didn't know you worked for the History Department."

"Just started this week after I got back from summer camp with the Guard. This is my Work-Study Grant job to help pay for next year's tuition." Greg turned to look at the large pile of trash bags Susan had set out.

"Well, good, I guess. Just wasn't expecting you."

Greg pointed to the trash bag pile. "What's all this? You moving or something?"

Susan nodded, "Yeh, moving out of the old place. I decided to move to New York."

"What? Wow! That was quick. You didn't mention that last week when I called." Greg seemed shocked and sad.

"Yeh, I guess it was pretty quick, huh?" Susan said. "I think I told you about my aunt dying. I told you she had left me some stuff, and that included her apartment in New York and a sort of trust fund. It kind of makes sense for me to live there and try to get into a school in New York."

"When you leaving?"

"Saturday. I listed the house this morning. And this pile is the reject pile; I'm sending the good stuff to New York."

"Gosh, Saturday, huh? I guess I better call in that IOU for a date quickly. How's tonight work for you."

Susan raised her eyebrows, "You want to go out tonight? On a date?"

"Of course, I spent two weeks over in Fort Dodge, Iowa, playing National Guard fun and games thinking about the beautiful girl I was going to go out with when I got back. And all I had to show for it was a phone call from New York. I'd love to go out, tonight."

"That would be fine with me. But, with my move to New York, there is not much chance of our relationship… going someplace," Susan answered hesitantly, choosing her words carefully.

Greg smiled, "Susy, as much as I would love a relationship with you that 'goes someplace,' I don't need that as a sole incentive to want to spend one enjoyable evening conversing with a beautiful young woman who actually knows who Metternich, Dreyfus and Disraeli are and who knows that the Emperor overthrowing the Second Republic is not a Star Wars episode."

"Wow, with a compliment like that it is pretty hard to say no." Susan noted that as the daughter of a history professor she had apparently made an impression on Greg in their European History class last term.

"I certainly hope not." Greg smiled confidently.

"Okay, what time and what should I wear?"

"Sevenish. And, since the Quad Cities has a definite paucity of four star dining places, let's say wear something for a typical family restaurant and maybe jacket or sweater for the air conditioning in case I can talk you into a movie after dinner."

"Seven it is." Susan smiled. "Let's go get the boxes turned over to you."

Susan turned toward the house, but Greg did not follow. He was still looking at the huge pile of trash bags.

"Susy? You need some help hauling this off? The city trash guys are never gonna take all of this. You have to have it in the normal gray trash carts they can pick up with the automated trucks or order a roll-off box."

"I was thinking about that." Susan put her hands on her hips.

"After I load the boxes, I'll load this up too. I can put it in the dumpster when I unload your boxes at the Sorensen Hall."

Susan nodded, "Thanks that would be a big help."

Chapter Sixteen

After Susan helped Greg load the boxes and all of the trash bags, he left, but only after reconfirming he would be back at 7 o'clock. Actually, she had only carried a couple of the boxes to the truck and he loaded everything. With the big wheels and lifted 4x4 frame the truck bed was too high for her to do much to help loading it.

Susan headed back toward the garage. But, she stopped short, remembering one last loose end she needed to handle.

She had knocked on the Johnsons' door the previous evening, but there had been no answer. An inside light was on and the radio she heard playing was probably camouflage for an empty house. Then, she had heard her neighbors and their kids return late last night, and she now saw their old Toyota Corolla parked in the driveway. She crossed the grass to her neighbors' front door.

Phil and Valerie Johnson had lived next to the Fisher's for most of Susan's life. She knew that they had moved in when she was a small child, but she could never remember them not living there. They had moved into the house as a young couple when Phil got work with the Moline Public Works Department as an operator at the sewer plant, now he was some kind of utility manager. Valerie had taken care of Susan when she was in kindergarten and the half day kindergarten schedule did not mesh with her mother's full day schedule teaching at the high school. Valerie had been home with a newborn Phil, Jr. back then. Phil, Jr. would be going to high school now, but Susan had lost track of what grade Jennifer Johnson was in, somewhere in middle school. The Fishers and the Johnsons had developed a close relationship over the years, as neighbors often do, even though the two families came from different stations in life, one academic, and one blue collar. One family's kids had been cared for by the other and the neighbors could be counted on to cover for each other. It had been the Johnsons who Susan had called to come over and water the grass when she was in New York last week, so the lawn would not shrivel in the hot summer sun. It had also been Valerie who had closely supported Susan's mother after her father's death last fall and again being beside Susan when things got really bad for her mother last February.

Susan knocked on the screen door. The partially open screen door banged shut with a sound much louder than Susan's knock should have caused. Valerie came to the door drying her hands on a dish towel.

"Susy! You're home." Valerie said, "Saw your car when we drove in last night."

"Yeh, I came over earlier yesterday and you were gone."

"Phil took a couple days off; we went down to Galesburg to check on his folks. They are getting on in years." Valerie opened the screen door. "You wanna come in?"

Phil appeared behind Valerie.

"Not now. I gotta get back to work."

Phil spoke up, "Yeh, what's up with all the trash you were putting out? I see it's gone now."

"Well," Susan hesitated, "That's what I wanted to talk about. I wanted to let you know that I'm moving."

Both Phil and Valerie came out onto the front steps upon hearing this. Susan had to back up, stepping down to the sidewalk. Phil asked, "Moving? Where? When did this come about?"

Susan shrugged, "Well, I told you my aunt died in New York. She left me her place there and enough money to get by there pretty well." Susan was getting pretty good at this little white lie. "So, after talking to the attorney for her estate back in New York, I decided it would be best for me to move there."

Valerie stepped next to Susan, reached out and put her arm around Susan, "Ah, honey…"

Both Phil and Valerie fumbled for words. Phil spoke first, "Wow, that's a shocker. When you moving."

"Right now. That's why the pile of trash."

Valerie spoke next, "Susy, that's pretty sudden. You sure about this? Sometimes decisions you make in haste, you regret later."

Susan nodded, "I realize it seems pretty sudden, but for lots of reasons I can't really go into, it really seems like the right choice. With both Mom and Dad dead, I don't have any family left here at all. And back in New York there is at least my aunt and uncle and a few cousins. That's something as far as family goes." Susan knew the Johnsons did not know enough about the Fisher family to know that those relatives were all in-laws of her aunt.

Susan continued, "And, like I said, my aunt arranged for me to have a good bit of her estate, so I'm actually better off there, financially, than here at home. And I'm working on transferring to a college there."

Valerie hugged Susan and said, "Well, it is a shock, and we will miss you. When will you be going and is there anything we can do to help?"

"I fly out Saturday, early afternoon. And yes, you could help me by dropping me off at the airport, just after noon, Saturday?"

"Of course, I'd be glad too." Phil volunteered. "Anything else you need? Around the house? Or, with the move?"

"I think I've got most everything covered. But, you know…." As she spoke Susan realized she had not thought of something obvious as she made her packing decisions. "I've been going through the house, throwing out the trash, packing what I think I can use in New York, and the real estate agent has set it up so everything else either gets sold at an auction over in Muscatine or thrown out by the auction company. But, I'm moving into my aunt's place in New York, and it has got most everything I need to live. So, there is a lot of useful stuff I am leaving behind. I'm not going to get more than a few pennies on the dollar for the stuff they sell at an auction. So, what I'd like to do is have you two, and maybe the kids, come over with me on Saturday morning after I finish packing and see if there is anything you folks can use, before I turn it over to the scalpers from the auction." Susan waited a second and added, "And, I've already got two boxes of food stuff, like canned goods and cake mix, that I am bringing over to you, whether you like it or not. It doesn't make sense to pay shipping charges to New York for food you can easily use right here."

Phil and Valerie looked at each other and back at Susan. Valerie spoke first, "Well, I don't know, I guess we could look, if you're sure that is what you want. It would be hard going through your folks' stuff like that."

Susan said, "Don't be silly. That is exactly what I have to do now. And you know that Mom and Dad would want you to have whatever you can use. Better that than some 'dealer' buying it at an auction for next to nothing."

Both Phil and Valerie still hesitated. Susan added, "And, it just makes sense for you to see if there is anything you can use. Dad left all of his tools in the garage and what use am I going to have for an almost new weed whacker or electric chain saw in an apartment in New York. And, Val, I have my aunt's food processor in New York, you know Mom would rather you have her Cuisinart than give it away to some stranger."

Susan saw Phil's look when she mentioned the tools, so she ended the discussion with, "Enough talk, I'll call you Saturday morning, and you can come over. Right now, I have to go finish my sorting. Going through my parent's life and property, deciding what is worth keeping is no easy task. See you guys Saturday morning."

Susan stepped up and gave Phil a hug and kiss on the cheek, then a longer hug for Valerie. Then she turned a walked toward the garage. She could almost feel their stares as she walked away.

—

Even with the garage door open, it was oppressively hot in the garage with the afternoon sun beating down on the uninsulated shingle roof. The first two trash bags Susan had carried out when Greg arrived were the easy pickings in sorting out the garage. That had been the useless junk even her parents had relegated to the garage years earlier; a leaky air mattress, used painting tarps, and miscellaneous useless items that should have been thrown out when her parents first brought it to the garage. But, for a family living in a tiny cottage like the Fishers, the garage served as the primary storage area for family valuable and keepsakes. This was where you put those things that could not fit in the three bedroom 1950's-designed tract house that only had one narrow hall closet and a small clothes closet in each bedroom. There was not even a basement like in the newer housing tracts in Moline, farther south.

So, with the garage being the primary long term storage for the Fisher family, Susan was faced with a huge task of going through the garage. She had known that ahead of time. She decided to tackle it in reverse, she decided to separate out what she knew she would not want or need in New York, or for the rest of her life. Or, things she would have trouble shipping.

First and foremost was her bicycle. It was a nice adult bicycle, but not a great road bike. Her father had given it to her in high school and she had even used it to go the dozen or so blocks to Augustana the first year. She had thought about keeping it, especially after hearing Paul tell of the bicycle routes he used in Chelsea, but she really doubted she become a frequent biker in crowded Manhattan. If she did, a bicycle was one of those things her newfound wealth would get her, in the form of a state-of-the-art road bike with the latest equipment, not this Taiwanese refugee from Sears. Even if she wanted the bike, she did not think she had a handy way to ship it. Besides this bicycle she had used recently, she could also see that her earlier bicycle from middle school days with pink and purple streamers coming from the handle bar grips was hanging upside down from a garage rafter. The bikes would go to the auction, unless the Johnsons had a need.

Susan started on the left, at her father's old tool bench. Contrary to his status in academia, Jeff Fisher had reveled in his do-it-yourself skills and puttering around the house and yard. And, he had the tools to show for it. She knew everything there would have been near and dear to her father's heart, but having looked through Rachel's utility room when she was looking for the light bulbs, Susan knew she had most every tool she would need in the apartment, already there. Here, there were power tools, garden tools, hand tools, various flashlights, partially opened paint cans, battery chargers, *ad infinitum*. There was even a dark green toolbox, just like the one Susan used for art supplies, but this one was full of fishing gear and Susan could not remember her father ever going fishing. She would make a point of showing that to Phil Johnson, he might be interested.

Susan poked around over and under the tool bench for several minutes, but found nothing that met her criteria for shipment to New York. She felt bad she had not found some token of her father's tool horde to take with her.

So, finding little on the bench covering the left wall of the garage, Susan would use that as the reject pile. There she stacked and piled rakes, shovels, coils of garden hose, fishing pole and long rolls of power cord for the electric lawn mower. That lawn mower and its companion leaf blower went next, along with the weed whacker and chain saw that seemed to have tempted Phil.

Next, Susan came to the stack of boxes that had a sign on each box in her mother's handwriting that said, 'Send to Goodwill.' Susan peeked in the top box and found a nice, pink winter parka that Susan had not worn since middle school. Susan resisted the urge to inquire further and put her trust in her mother's judgment that there was nothing in this stack that any member of the Fisher family needed. She briefly considered driving the stack down to the charity drop box in the shopping center parking lot, but chose not to. Susan had enough to do without errands to donate to Goodwill. This stack went, unsearched, into the left side of the garage. She would ask Jennifer Johnson about the parka.

Next, she came to the suitcase pile where she had found the black suitcase to take to New York. She shook her head. Why had she dragged the two Louis Vuitton's all the way from New York when she had four more suitcases here? That had not been good planning on her part. Remembering the forgotten Las Vegas trip items in the black suitcase, Susan checked each of these for things inside. The only one with anything inside was the bottom suitcase, a monster old-fashioned squarish case with multiple stickers and decals from foreign trips. That bag had sets of her father's khaki pants and shirts and some suede work boots, like he had worn in Israel at the dig. She took the clothing out and sat it on the Goodwill stack and slid the big suitcase outside. She would use it if she needed more luggage for the airplane trip.... Susan smiled and shook her head; in her mind she had thought the words 'the airplane trip *home*.' It was disconcerting to think of the trip from Moline to New York as a trip 'home,' but that is what she had done. Her unconscious had declared New York home and Moline away. The remaining suitcases were stacked on the left.

Susan opened, inspected and rejected the next stack of boxes. The old clothing, long ago replaced dishes and old magazines were not needed back east. That left her with a half dozen more stacks of boxes. She pulled her iPhone from her jeans pocket to check the time. She had maybe another hour to work before she needed to get ready for Greg.

The remaining boxes were of various sizes and ages. Most had no markings and just had the top flaps folded in, but some had tape on them. But, on the very bottom of the stack just to her right, the base of the stack was not a box, but an old trunk, covered in glossy red sheet metal. It was small; maybe two feet square on the end and three feet long. It piqued her interest. She did not recall ever having seen it before. Susan stacked the four boxes on top of the trunk to one side, two and two, and used the two short stacks as a platform to place this trunk.

Susan guessed the little trunk was forty or fifty years old, maybe more, from its style and condition. The tinny red sides were scraped and the riveted, cheaply plated edges and round corner caps were dented. There was a metal handle on the side, by the hasp, and another handle on one end, to carry it upright, or load it up high. The end of the hasp was a two inch chrome circle which had a thin keyhole slot in the center. This locking chrome circle was inset into a round flange on the trunk body. And, it seemed to be locked. She could not find a release for the locking hasp. And, she had no idea where a key might be.

Susan went to the tool bench to see if she could find something to open the trunk with. She chose a set of pliers and a thin flat-head screwdriver. She tried the pliers to see if she could just pull or pry the hasp out of its flange, but no luck. She considered trying to leverage the hasp open with something big and long, but first she tried sticking the little screwdriver head into the key hole. It spun around without effect. Then she angled the screwdriver 45 degrees and spun the end of the screwdriver in a circle clockwise and then counterclockwise. On the second circle there was a click and the end of the hasp popped out of its round hole. Either the little red trunk had worthless security, or Susan was a natural lock picker. She was sort of proud of herself for this feat.

Susan sat the tools aside and released the wire loop levered latches on either side of the lock. She opened the trunk and immediately smelled that the contents were old. It smelled just like the insides of the Rothmann box she had opened in Rachel's dining room. Correction: in Susan's dining room. There was a McGovern:Shriver '72 bumper sticker stuck to the underside of the trunk lid.

There was a shallow, cloth-covered paperboard tray with two divisions that sat inside the trunk. On the upper right side was a large, soft bundle wrapped in what was once white tissue paper, but had now yellowed. Even before she opened the bundle Susan guessed what the bundle was, since she caught sight of the picture below it. Her guessed was confirmed when she saw the lacy bodice and flowered neckline of the wedding dress. Along with the wedding dress was a black silk clip-on bow tie. Beneath the dress was that picture of her parents as bride and groom in front of the New York State seal that she had seen with the video. There were also other memorabilia of the wedding. They had apparently gone to Newport, Rhode Island for their honeymoon.

The left side of the trunk's tray was a pile of things about Denver and the

University of Denver. There were a couple of color Polaroid snapshots of the Fishers in front of an old house and one in front of a '70's car on a mountain road. There were a couple of letters addressed to Dr. & Mrs. Jeffrey Fisher at an address on South Franklin Street in Denver and various other papers. One envelope to Mrs. Rebecca Fisher at the Denver address had a return address of Mrs. Rachel Metzger at a Marriott Hotel in Paris, France. This was a great addition to the box and video on her parents that Rachel had given her. The years after her father had been hired as an assistant professor by the University of Denver right after graduation from Columbia and before he was hired at Augustana were an era Susan did not know much about. This trunk was obviously going to New York and needed more study, but she sat the tray up on the lid and looked underneath.

The bottom of the trunk was a morass of papers, folders, bundles of envelopes, an old Augustana course catalog and a stack of maybe twenty journals of various colors. The bound journals were all about the same size, but some of the journals were labeled 'Journal,' others were 'Diary," some had blank, decorative covers, one said "Mein Tagebuch" and one was titled "Addresses." The latter had tabs on the edge for letters of the alphabet. Susan opened this first, but found it was not addresses, but a diary in her mother's handwriting from 1974. Flipping randomly through the diary, an entry in bright, magenta ink caught Susan's eye. Susan read her mother's words, "Tuesday February 18th -- It is too fucking cold in Denver!!! But, another substitute call today from the suburbs, out in Lakewood. At least this godforsaken cold weather makes the regular teachers get sick & stay home, leaving the scraps for us subs. Jeff should try for his full professorship in Texas or California. I am even feeling homesick for Florida. Enough cold weather! Last week Jeff was saying that it didn't look like he would ever get his promotion from D.U. and inside I was screaming "Good, Yes!" while on the outside I had to look sad and lament with him like a loving wife should. This old place we are renting leaks cold air like a damn sieve. Jeff says he likes sleeping in a cold bedroom, he says it gives him a good excuse to spoon me. But, I did have a nice President's Day off yesterday when Jeff took me ice skating at the rink down on 16th Street, near the big May/D&F department store. It reminded me of ice skating in New York. He bought me some fluffy mittens. At least there was something good about this fucking cold weather."

Susan was a bit shocked seeing the wording her mother used; it did not match her mind's picture of her mother. She counted years and guessed that her mother was 23 when she did the coarsely worded diary entry. This young wife and substitute teacher who was complaining about the cold was barely older than Susan was now. It was kind of funny to hear her mother complain about cold weather in Denver, when Moline was not what you could call tropical. In fact, the Quad Cities in winter had to be worse than Denver. She closed the journal.

Susan moved the contents around to see if anything different appeared, then she quickly checked some random dates in the journals. They seemed to start at her parents' marriage and the last year at Columbia and go through the year before Susan's birth. Susan had already found her mother's 'Baby Book' journal for baby Susan on a shelf in the living room. She replaced the 1974 diary and sat the tray back in the trunk. She closed the trunk. She would study it in New York. She would have to splice two of her larger shipping boxes together with tape to ship the trunk. Susan had never seen and never knew anything about these journals and letters of her mother's and now she had this trove to compare to what Rachel had provided.

It was time to get ready for the date. As a last thought, Susan stuck the screwdriver in her back jeans pocket, to unlock the trunk next time. So, one of her father's tools was going to New York with her. Susan closed the garage door and lugged the heavy trunk and big, empty suitcase to the house.

—

The doorbell rang precisely on time. Susan was in the bathroom checking make-up and hair. She wished she had brought some of the nice clothes she bought in New York, but she had a thing or two here in the closet, bought with her Macy's employee discount, that were perfectly good to impress a one-time-only date. This turquoise organza dress would do fine. And, since Greg was so tall, she could actually, for once, wear real heels without feeling self-conscious.

Susan opened the front door and got an appreciation for exactly how tall Greg Harkness was. His head was almost even with the top of the door jam. He was wearing a dark blue suit, white shirt and a red power tie. He looked like a young politician, running for office.

Greg looked at Susan and blinked, "Wow, Susan, you look awesome. Err, nice, really nice."

"You look pretty good yourself, too. I'm glad I didn't follow your 'family restaurant' dress advice. You would have really outmatched me." Susan smiled at him.

He fingered his suit and said, "Ahh, this. You can blame my stepmother for this. I called home to let her know I would be home this weekend and mentioned I was going out. She asked about you, and then what I was wearing. Then she literally demanded I wear this. She said she raised me as a gentleman and a gentleman should always assume a lady will dress nicer than she assumes the gentleman will dress, so he should up his wardrobe to exceed her expectations."

"Hmm, your stepmother sounds like a wise woman. Your stepmother raised you?"

"Since I was a toddler, but we can do life stories on the way to Davenport." Greg held the screen door and stepped to the side, so Susan could come out.

Susan shifted her purse in her hands and locked the door behind her. They walked out toward his truck at the curb.

"Excuse the big step up into the truck. It's all I have to drive. Not very elegant," Greg apologized.

When he heard Susan laugh, Greg added, "It's that funny?"

Susan shook her head. "No, that is not what's funny. Last week in New York, an apartment manager had to give me a ride in his truck, and he apologized that it was not very fancy. I told him that back where I came from a GMC crew cab like his was a luxury ride. Now, I get back here, and you are apologizing for taking me out in a perfectly fine truck."

"But, not a crew cab nor a GMC."

"Nevertheless, it is a nice Ford 4x4. And, how many seats do you think I need?" Susan reached up and grasped the chrome boarding handle, putting the toe of her high heel on the nerf bar, and as she climbed aboard she asked, "Davenport, huh? Where we going?"

"Cracker Barrel. It supposed to be fairly good. And, if the truth be known, I have a gift certificate to use." Greg shut her door and hurried around the truck.

Greg climbed and started to buckle up. He saw Susan was having trouble finding the seat belt buckle.

"Here let me get it. The buckle tucks into the seat cushion; you have to pull it out. Let me get it for you. Pardon my reach."

"No problem. That would be a pretty good line for copping a feel though," Susan said.

Greg started to say something, but stopped. They buckled up and he started the truck.

After he turned the corner, Susan said, "Okay, we are on the road to Davenport. Time for life stories, you get to start."

Greg took a deep breath, "Okay, Gregory Milton Harkness, son of Milton Harkness and Debra Kay Greene, of Waverly, Iowa. My father owns a farm machinery dealership and garage in Waverly. My mother was his childhood sweetheart. When I was three years old, my mother gave birth to my little sister, Marjorie. During the birthing process something happened that gave my mother a condition called sepsis. When Marjorie was three days old, they airlifted our mother to the hospital at the University of Iowa in Iowa City to try and control the sepsis and that is the last any of us ever saw of her. She died shortly after she was admitted in Iowa City."

Greg turned onto the Interstate, headed north and continued, "The good ladies of Waverly, Iowa, decided it was necessary to help widower Milton out with his newborn daughter and toddler son, and they proceeded to get organized in their lend-a-hand efforts. My father had no lack of baby-sitters, baby clothes, ready-made Sunday dinners, offers to do anything a grieving father could need to care for two young children. One of the organizers of this charitable effort was a young assistant pastor at the local Lutheran Church in Waverly, a young female pastor by the name of Ingrid Stenholdt, formerly of Minneapolis, Minnesota. It doesn't take too much imagination to see where this story is going, huh?

"By the time I was in kindergarten, Marjie and I had a new stepmother who wore a funny little black and white collar on her work clothes, and was as different as night and day from my father. She was as refined, intellectual and as staunch a Democrat as you could get. He worships Reagan, belongs to the NRA and thinks Larry McMurtry and Louis L 'Amour are literary giants. She has a Master of Divinity degree from Luther Seminary; he has taken every mechanical course for farm implements taught by International Harvester and New Holland corporations. Worse yet, she is a Vikings fan and he is a Packers fan. But, she is devoted to him and his kids; she has given him two more daughters of her own after Marjie and I. And he worships the ground she walks on. They are as different as night and day, but they love each other. That is where I come from."

Susan commented, "I noticed you had a Vikings shirt on today. You picking sides there."

"I had no choice there. Last week I took my clothes home to wash on the way back from Fort Dodge, and my Packer shirt mysteriously disappeared. Honest." He laughed.

"Continue, that only gets you up through kindergarten," Susan chided.

Greg was making a transition to the east-west Interstate. He waited and continued, "I grew up in Waverly. Great childhood. All-American corn-fed boyhood. Obviously raised in the Lutheran Church. Despite my size, I managed to disappoint everyone in high school as not being very good at football. But, I was decent at hoops, reasonably. And I was a really good student. I started at University of Northern Iowa and spent two years there. Then, I decided I wasn't sure what I wanted to do, what to study, what was important in life, so on and so forth… general indecision. I think everybody goes through something like that. But, I did something about it. I saw a TV show about Pat Tillman and went down to Cedar Rapids and enlisted in the Army. Shocked everybody."

"Pat Tillman, he's that football guy?" Susan asked.

"Yeh, pro football player, gave up everything, enlisted in the Rangers and died in Afghanistan." Greg said. "At least I had some sanity left in me. If you sign up for four years they will let you pick your job in the Army. They had like two and a half pages of stuff, jobs to choose from. You know, machine gun operator, medic, helicopter crew, light infantryman, that stuff. But, then at the end of the list there were some really off the wall stuff, like linguists and journalists. One of them popped out at me. As the step-son of a Lutheran pastor, I thought it would be cool to go into the Army and be a Chaplain's Assistant. I could be a macho volunteer, join the Army, but at the same time I could do something my clergywoman stepmother, really the only mother I ever knew, would appreciate. I enlisted. They gave me two grades of advanced enlisted rank for my two years at U.N.I. and sent me to Fort Jackson, South Carolina, to learn to help military chaplains do their job."

"Wow, interesting connection, my grandfather was a military chaplain," Susan added.

"Really? Army?"

"No, Navy."

"What denomination?"

Susan took a breath, and said, "Conservative Jewish."

"I guess that explains your mezuzah."

"You noticed that? Very observant." She smiled at him.

"Part of my training at Fort Jackson. They trained us in all the religions; their requirements, rules, ceremonies, foibles, faux pas to avoid, whatever you might need to know to help a chaplain of whatever denomination minister to every other denomination in the field. When I got sent to Afghanistan, I was assigned to assist a Catholic Chaplain and then a Unitarian. Well, here we are."

Greg had exited the freeway in far northern Davenport and pulled into a turn lane leading to the Cracker Barrel sign on the other side of the boulevard.

Greg parked the truck. The parking lot was nearly full.

"Pretty busy for a Thursday night," Susan commented.

"It's a national chain. They've got like 600 places. They have lots of network TV advertising. It works," Greg explained.

He got out and raced around the truck to open Susan's door. Susan hesitated a bit as she contemplated getting down from the truck cab in her heels. There was no way to safely step down on a rounded chrome nerf bar with three inch heels. Greg saw her dilemma and said, "See, that's why I apologized in advance for the truck."

Greg reached up and spread his fingers on each side of Susan's waist, his big hands almost encircling her. He lifted her to the ground and sat her gently down.

Susan smiled, "It has been a long time since I was lifted out of a car. You're pretty good at that ballet lift."

"I have little sisters that I have to do that with every time I take them to school or church. Besides, you're deceptively light."

Susan squinted at him, "Deceptively, huh? Since I think that was meant as a compliment, thank you."

Greg had phoned in a reservation and was right on time, so they avoided the standby waiting line in the lobby. Susan and Greg were seated in a corner booth separated from most of the other tables by a latticework room divider covered in the Americana antique whatsits and paraphernalia that served as decoration in Cracker Barrel. It was fairly private.

A young waitress wearing an untucked man's dress shirt, Dockers and an apron brought them menus and asked for their drink choices.

As Susan looked through the menu, she asked Greg, "You've got a gift certificate for this place?"

Greg nodded, "Yeh, the National Guard company commander at my summer camp has some connection with the Cracker Barrel restaurant over in Clive, Iowa, that's outside of Des Moines. He had a bunch of gift certificates good for any Cracker Barrel that he gave out as prizes for the best performances in various things during summer camp. You know marksmanship, PT test events."

"So what did you win for?"

Greg laughed, "I field stripped and reassembled an M4 sniper rifle in the quickest time."

"Sniper rifle? That doesn't sound like a chaplain's assistant."

"Oh, that was my job on active duty. When you join the National Guard back home you have to take whatever openings they have in the local units to get a spot. I'm assigned to an infantry support battalion in Cedar Rapids, in a clerical job, and I take officer training school classes as my weekend duties. And I didn't even go to summer camp with my own unit. I needed to get summer camp out of the way between spring term at Augustana and summer term, so I could do my Work-Study and take summer classes. So the Iowa Guard let me do my officer training internship with a unit who did their summer camp over in Fort Dodge, the guys with the sniper rifles, the last week in May and first of June. Worked out well for me."

"National Guard, Army, all that military stuff. Not something I know much about or have ever had much contact with. Although my father was a

First Lieutenant in the Army, over in Germany, and like I said, my grandfather was a Navy Chaplain."

"Tell me about them. Your family." Greg set his menu aside.

"I'm still waiting to hear about Afghanistan," Susan protested.

Greg shook his head, "Later, I gave you all my basics. My turn to hear about Susy Fisher, your family, what makes you tick. Why you are abandoning us at Augustana and moving to New York."

"Okay," Susan said before she took a drink of her ice water.

The waitress chose that moment to return for their orders. They ordered, and then Greg grabbed a piece of bread from the basket and gave a rolling hands signal to Susan indicating she needed to continue telling her story. So, she started to give Greg her life story, much as he did for her. She told about her parents, spending her whole childhood in one house in Moline, and travelling widely with her parents. She described her childhood and her best friend, Heidi, she explained her interest in art, art history and general history itself, and her doubts about whether she wanted to continue her college major in art. And she ended with a recounting of the events of the past year that had taken her parents, and now her last living relative, her aunt, from her. She explained the events in New York and information she had received from Aunt Rachel, even her mother's break with her parents, but carefully withholding the real reason for that and the full extent of her inheritance.

"Well, Susy, you've sure had an unsettling last year, but I am not understanding why with all you have been hit with, all the loss, why you would add to the loss by removing everything else you have left. You know, all your connections to this area, Augustana, your old friend Heidi, and just about every connection you have ever had by pulling up roots and moving to New York." Greg shook his head slightly as he finished speaking.

"I got exactly the same reaction from my neighbors, from Heidi and from Doctor Moresby, when we talked. To each of them I said the same thing, that it just seems right," Susan paused a moment, thinking. Then she continued, "But, it is more than that. And it is not just a result of my aunt dying and leaving me with a very attractive option of stepping into a cushy lifestyle in New York. Even before this last string of events, I was having real problems with a whole panoply of life questions. I always identified myself in terms of being the daughter of Jeffrey Fisher and Rebecca Fisher. Their approval was what I used to judge my success. My own philosophy and worldview was totally a result of what they had taught me. I was going to a college where my father had taught for, what, thirty years. When I got on the plane for New York, I realized I had never gone anywhere in my life before except with my parents. The only thing that was exclusively my own was my study of art, and this last year I started questioning whether the study of art was enough to satisfy my personal need to do something important with my life. Knowing the names of all the pre-Raphaelite painters, or the like, was no longer something worthy of the effort. My earlier love of art was still there, but I questioned whether I wanted to dedicate my life to just that anymore.

"And, most importantly, I had this deep nagging feeling of being unstuck… disconnected to the parents who had always been my anchor and had now been ripped from me. One of them taken quickly and unexpectedly, and the other in a most tortured, grueling and heartbreaking way."

The food came. Susan said, "Let's eat. Good time for a break."

Greg touched her hand as she picked up her fork, "No, not yet, you were on a roll. Food can wait. You need to finish this through. Okay? You were telling me you felt disconnected and your parents, your anchors, were ripped away from you. What was the deep, nagging feeling that you were left with?"

"Well, all right," Susan paused, thinking and continued. "It had me thinking that I really had no idea who I was. I had always been known as that Jewish girl who lived on 4th Street in Moline, or the Jewish daughter of that Jewish professor, but I really had nothing Jewish about me, especially after my parents, the real Jews who themselves stopped acting Jewish, left me. I had only ever been to a synagogue three times in my life."

"Three? Just three times? That's hard for a son of a pastor to fathom," Greg commented. "Sorry, continue, didn't mean to break your train."

Susan shrugged, "Yeh, never been part of a Jewish church. Only had a mezuzah on our door because my father wanted to make a political statement. Only had a menorah in the window for the holidays because I think my parents felt the need to give me something since they didn't do Christmas trees."

Susan paused to catch her breath and Greg said, "Can I add one to your list?"

Susan shrugged.

"You are that Jewish girl who orders totally non-Kosher food when you go to a restaurant," Greg pointed to her plate. "Cream gravy on country fried steak is about as un-kosher as you can get."

Susan looked down at her plate and nodded, "See, yeh! You probably know more about kosher from your chaplain assistant class than my parents taught me in twenty years. And, then, I go to New York and I am immersed in a world of my cousins, my aunt's in-laws, where they live strict Kosher, expect me to do proper prayers in Hebrew over my aunt's casket. I get an insight into my mother's life as the daughter of a Jewish rabbi, that I never knew anything about. This aunt who was my last blood relative told me more about my Jewishness than I knew existed."

Susan pointed to Greg's plate, "You really need to eat your steak, it's getting cold."

"Okay, I will," Greg agreed. "But, do you understand what is going on inside your head? You've given up some really potent clues."

Susan furrowed her brow at Greg, and she said, in mock sarcasm, "No, *Doctor*, I don't. That's my problem. I suppose you do know exactly what is going on inside my head?"

Greg took his first bite of steak, and nodded his head as he quickly chewed it. Then he spoke, "Yes, I think I know exactly what is going on. I learned it at the side of a really wise Catholic priest while he counseled lonely, depressed young soldiers in the barren hills of southern Afghanistan."

Susan ate her first bite and motioned with her hand that Gregg should continue. He nodded and used his fork to mush the butter and chives into his baked potato.

"My analysis is that Susy Fisher has come up against two very basic human truths. One is a mix of psychology or spirituality and the other is pure sociology." Greg took a quick forkful of potato, washed it down with Diet Coke, and continued. "The psychology or spirituality thing is most famously stated by French philosopher Jean Paul Sartre, but he was just parroting a concept known by every religious leader since the world began. He said, 'The human soul has a deep, dark hole in it that is exactly the shape of God,' or words to that effect. Of course, he meant just that, that we in our inner most intellect, our soul, have an innate need to explain things we cannot explain ourselves by attributing them to some higher power or understanding. We need God to fill that hole in our soul, whether we believe in a God or not. A modern science-oriented mind may try to explain everything in terms of science, but there is still that hole in their psyche or soul that causes people like Einstein to acknowledge the need to attribute some things to a higher power. You, Susy, had wonderful parents who did their best to give you their philosophy, their understanding, their intellect, but they forgot to give you anything to fill that deep dark hole in your soul. They gave you a tempting smidgeon of the kind of thing that can fill that hole with the bits and pieces of Jewishness they kept in their lives, but they never gave you the opportunity to fill the deep, dark chasm. They probably still had their deep, dark hole filled with the vestigial Jewish substance of their birth and heritage, but for both good and bad reasons they kept that substance from you."

Hearing that Gregg appeared done with that thought, Susan wiped a smudge of gravy from her lip and said, "Okay, I get it. I have a deep, dark hole in my soul that needs filling. What is my sociological problem?"

"That is actually a much easier concept. It goes to the core concept of sociology. Human beings are, in essence, social creatures. We have a core need to belong to a group, a society. Almost everything we hold dear in our lives is given its merit based upon how our societal group views it, or how we think our societal group should view it. Humans need to belong to a group. That is why we have criminal gangs, political parties, fan clubs, families, sports teams, armies, cities, nations, religions. Anything important in human endeavor is either done in a group, or by an individual to impress or help a group. Gang members, soldiers, martyrs and family members will give their life to protect their particular group. People like Pat Tillman are willing to sacrifice everything for their nation. And, otherwise intelligent people will 'drink the Kool-Aid' if their group mentality tells them to. We yearn to belong, and if we lose touch with our group, it hurts us. If humans don't have any group they identify with they lose their moral compass. We call their behavior 'anti-social,' and it can devolve into really bad results, from suicide to mass murder. Being part of a group keeps us focused with the needs of our group, without it we become unhinged."

Susan asked, "So, I'm going sociopath?"

Greg smiled and shook his head, "Heavens no, just the opposite. You have a strong moral compass, good values and all of the other positive things good socialization gives you. Your problem is that the group that you most strongly identify with, the one that formed your values has disappeared on you. Your primary group only had three main members and two of them died. Now, you quite clearly recognize the impact of the loss of that group, and you are struggling to find a replacement group to attach to. Augustana with your father's peers and your childhood friend didn't meet your standards for a worthy replacement group upon which you can dedicate your life. You are hoping that the wealth and newfound opportunities presented by the New York move will fill your need to belong and at the same time give you something to fill your deep dark hole."

Susan put her fork down on the plate while Greg took the opportunity to eat. "Wow, that is some pretty heavy analysis. Do you really think my problems are so deep seated?"

"I think you are doing yourself a disservice by labeling it as 'deep-seated problems.' But, you yourself used the words 'become unstuck' and explained that your former favorite pursuit of art no longer seemed 'worth the effort.' That sounds pretty serious to me. My analysis is open to your criticism." Greg buttered his cornbread and ate.

"Okay, so how does my questioning of the study of art fit into your tidy little analysis, either spiritually or sociologically?" It was Susan's turn to butter cornbread.

Greg chewed cornbread, washing it down and thought. Then, he raised his forefinger, while catching a last bit of cornbread with his tongue and said, "Got it." He took one more drink, "Your core group, your family, prided itself in intellectual pursuits, knowledge and enlightenment. Your mother was the English teacher, she focused on the literary. Your father was the historian and political scientist. They strived throughout your life to excite you in intellectual pursuits and to follow their lead. They eschewed personal wealth and lived by modest means in a small, parochial Ivory Tower called Augustana, but made sure to instill in you their love of art, travel, literature, history and learning. But, young Susy had to find some area of intellectual pursuit in which she could stand out personally and which was her own bailiwick. Art was not only a key part of their teaching of you and travels to Versailles and the Louvre and Venice, but it was an area where Susy could specialize and show her own personal expertise that transcended her parents' fortés. But…," Greg raised his finger again to make his point, "… when your close, intellectually oriented family began to die off and leave you all alone, you had to question whether art, in and of itself, remained of any transcendental worth to you personally absent the input of your group, your family. The study of art became an intellectual orphan, like you. Unless you can find a replacement sociological group where the study of art is as worthy a pursuit as it was to your family, you are going to have to find something else worthy of your life's pursuit. You worry that that is not going to happen, so you question whether you should be studying art."

Susan sat staring into Greg's eyes for a long moment. At last, she nodded her head and pointed her fork at Greg, "You are a real piece of work, Mister Greg Harkness. On the outside there is the façade of the handsome, corn-fed Iowa farm boy who has adopted the various disguises of a mild-mannered chaplain's assistant, historian and National Guardsman. But, on the inside you are some kind of spiritual Van Helsing searching for and rooting out deep, dark holes in the souls of unsuspecting potential sociopaths."

Greg smiled, "Ahh, we all have our secrets. You have discovered my secret fetish for probing the souls of beautiful women."

"I'm gonna pretend I didn't hear that," said the young waitress who had appeared around the room divider. "Are you folks ready for some dessert yet?"

—

Phil Johnson came back from delivering the chainsaw and box of tools to his house. Valerie was still standing and talking to Susan in the Fisher driveway. A pony-tailed Jennifer Johnson passed her father as she wheeled her new bicycle back to her house. There was a box with a food processor and various items by Valerie's feet. Susan had her two red suitcases behind her, by the Explorer.

"This is a lot of things. Are you sure we can't give you something? This Cuisinart, by itself …?" Valeria asked.

"Absolutely not!" Susan protested. "My mother would never allow me to take anything from you, after all you folks have done for us over the years, and especially this last year."

Valerie nodded, "Yeh, it has been a tough one for you, hasn't it, Hon?"

"Yes, it has." Susan accepted another quick hug from Val.

"And, Phil," Susan turned to Phil Johnson. "I'm all done in the house. All packed. Everything that is left goes to the auction. And I'm ready to go to the airport. But, I have one last favor for you to do. I need you to drop this off over in Silvis. Maybe on Monday?"

Susan took two papers out of a manila envelope she had under her arm. She handed them to Phil. Phil obviously recognized what the pink and blue certificate with the decorative border was. But, he started to protest when he read the Bill of Sale form that went with the car title.

"No, absolutely not. We can't let you give us your Dad's car." Phil tried to give the papers back to Susan, who refused to take them back, keeping her hands behind her back.

Susan realized that after their protest about her gift of the other property that the Johnsons would be tough to convince to accept the Explorer, so she decided to try some dramatics. Susan stomped her foot and raised her arms out, hands signaling Phil should stop, "Phil, just quit it. Don't make this any harder on me than it is. I think I am doing what my father would have wanted me to do, so don't give me a rough time about what I think my Dad would be telling me. You know that since I am not buying a new car a dealer would not give me anywhere near what Dad's car is worth. So, I am sure my father would want his Explorer in the hands of someone who will appreciate it and can use it. You just have the Toyota, and Val is trying to get a fulltime job again, you know you can use the Explorer."

Valerie said, "We really…."

Susan cut her off in a strident voice, "No more, don't say anything else. I made my decision. That's it. I want you to have my father's car. Shhhh!"

Susan was rather proud of her dramatic performance. It was totally out of character for her, but she hoped neither Val nor Phil knew that. Neither of the Johnsons could think of anything to say. Susan reached into the pocket of her denim jumpsuit and handed Phil the two Ford key fobs and one other key.

He took them, silently.

"I need to lock the house, and you can drive me to the airport. I'll take one last ride in Dad's car. I gave you the extra house key. The real estate guy already has two. You can give this one to the new owners when they move in. But, you can watch the place for me 'til it sells. The auction crew and painters will be here next week. Oh, and one more thing, all you need to do is file those papers in Silvis, but you need to show a proof of your new insurance to transfer title." Susan finished up with, "There is one last thing I need to do."

Susan took her father's little flat-headed screwdriver from her pocket. She went to the front door of the house and then the back door. At each place, she closed and checked that the door was locked. And then, with the screwdriver, she removed her father's mezuzahs from the former Fisher home.

—

Chapter Seventeen

It was a strange feeling to arrive back at the apartment in Manhattan with a thought of it being a return home, when Susan had so recently dislodged as her 'home' Moline and the Quad cities. Maybe this unsettled feeling would go away as she got back in the mode of making Rachel's home truly Susan's home. Susan wheeled the two red suitcases down the main hallway to her bedroom and thought of what her plans were for tomorrow, Sunday. She noticed that the apartment actually smelled different from her first trip down this hall with Carlos. Gone was the musty, dusty smell.

She could unpack later. After dropping the suitcases by her bed, Susan went to the dining room, sat at Rachel's MacBook, still on the dining room table, opened the browser and went to Google.

First, she signed in to her Google user account and set the intersection outside the apartment on 10th Avenue in New York as her new 'Home' for Google Maps so her location searches would no longer start in Moline, Illinois. Then, after a few false starts and refinements, she got a map that showed her goal, a large Sports Authority sporting goods store that was open until 9 PM on Saturdays, almost exactly at the intersection of the crosstown bus that ran east and west just south of her apartment. But, this time, Susan decided a taxi would be best, although she had enjoyed the bus trips in New York. She still did not fully trust the driving of the taxi drivers, but it would be dark by the time she got back, and she was not ready to try driving herself in town. Susan decided the stretch denim pantsuit she had worn for the flight would work for the shopping trip and possible dinner out.

—

Her iPhone alarm rang, and Susan reached for it. But, she was not yet used to the different location of the nightstand in the New York apartment. The last few days in the old bedroom in Moline had set her acclimatization to New York back a bit. She found the iPhone on the second swat. The iPhone face showed, "6:30 AM EDT" and was flashing to show one alert, which she knew about already.

There were no dreams this morning, unfortunately; she had enjoyed the cliff-top dream her first night in the apartment.

Her sleepy mind struggled to re-decide whether she was correct in how much time she would need to get ready. She had no reason to change her mind, so she swung her legs out of bed.

The large windows let the bluish morning light into the bedroom. Susan immediately noticed a strange smell. Looking around she saw that it was the remains of the gyro with Tsatsiki sauce she had picked up last night from the Halal Guys food cart, rather than go by herself to a sit down restaurant. Tsatsiki sauce did not age well sitting out overnight. Her bedroom stunk of cucumbers and garlic. When she got home from her Saturday evening shopping trip, Susan had changed into a black silk nightgown she had found, still in its Saks wrapper and tags, in Rachel's wardrobe and had eaten the Gyro while trying on jewelry from the jewel box drawer, and then watching Saturday late night TV on the bedroom home theatre set-up. She checked on the Internet what wine went with a Gyro and found several Rosé bottles in the wine cooler. She picked a California vintage. She had never had a glass of wine like that before, by herself and alone at home. It had been a good evening alone in her new home. The jewelry try-on worked well with the mood set by the silk negligee and the Rosé. The negligee was the first item of Rachel's clothing Susan had tried, and she found did not mind the hand-me-down, especially since this was unworn.

To wake herself up Susan took a long hot shower. She learned to appreciate the huge shower area and built-in bench seat as she shaved her legs well. Then, she trimmed her pubic region, just in case. Then Susan brushed her teeth twice to make sure no trace of Tsatsiki or wine remained on her breath. She dried her hair, brushed it back tightly, and found a strong scrunchie amongst her things in the suitcases to tie the hair back. She looked at her face in the harsh fluorescent light of the bathroom. She would have to go with very little makeup this morning. She went to the vanity and took a dark red all-day lipstick from the Sephora traincase and put it on. Then, with a Kleenex she blotted it mostly away before it set. Good, that left just a deep red hint of color that would not rub or sweat off. Instead of eye shadow, Susan used a waterproof eyebrow pencil and rubbed it against her forefinger. Then she buffed that smudge from her finger to the lower edge of her eyelids. That made her eyes dark, but again, run-free and virtually smudge-proof. Two tricks learned in a college sports women's locker room. She noticed that without any other make-up her remaining freckles would show. Good! She went back in to the sink and washed the eyebrow pencil off her fingers. She looked at herself again, and decided she looked good, even without her new clothes, perhaps especially without. Back at the vanity she put on a healthy dose of antiperspirant and her usual perfume, brought from Illinois. Her period had hit the first day in Moline, so she was done with that.

Susan set the bag with the gyro remains outside the door in the hallway, an offering to the mice, if they had survived the exterminator. She recorked the Rosé bottle on the vanity. Then, she set the two bags from the previous evening's purchases on the bed. She got her scissors from the manicure kit and started removing tags. From the Sports Authority bag, the new black backpack emerged first. She had decided the old purple bag was a bit garish and would clash with the blue items that came next -- royal blue T-shirt, blue soccer shorts and knee length royal blue soccer socks. They were as close as she could remember to what Paul wore the previous Saturday morning. Sports Authority had not had any blue soccer cleats for women, but she had found some Adidas chrome cleats with blue stripe accents. She had packed her old white college uniform cleats in Moline, but that was in the shipment in transit, and she chose to buy totally new stuff for this outing. The chrome was a bit gaudy, but they were good looking shoes, too bad if they were better suited to a Rave than a soccer match. Next came the shin guards, and a good blue sports bra. Lastly, a plain blue women's exercise suit, to go over the soccer outfit.

From the other bag, she took the white summer dress with red piping and the matching low heels she had found in the TJ Maxx store across the street from Sports Authority. She also had new pure white underwear, bra and panties, which would work with the white dress.

Susan dressed in the soccer outfit, except for the cleats that she could not wear on the trip across the city. She put the new exercise suit on over the soccer outfit. She finished with her white cross-training shoes. Then the summer dress, new white shoes, hose and cleats went in to the back pack in case there was an opportunity to change after the game. Finally, she added some make-up, for later, from the train case to her purse and put her clutch purse into the back pack. She rethought that and took three twenties and her iPhone from the purse and put them in her track suit pocket. She took stock of herself in the full length mirror on the closet door.

Time for a bit of breakfast, she needed to be light on her feet. She would get a bagel and juice at the Metro Café she had found on 9th Avenue.

—

The taxi driver drove from Hudson Street across the triple intersection of cross streets and stopped in front of a huge blue sign announcing 'Pier 40 Hudson River Park.' The Asian taxi driver said "Ate doe leh foe reh tee pull eez."

Susan had to think for a minute what the driver was saying. He was obviously asking for money and she finally figured it out by sneaking a peak at the meter, giving him a ten left over from her change at breakfast and saying to him, "Keep the change."

He did not say anything, but turned to face her nodding his head repeatedly as he smiled broadly with really bad teeth. She nodded back and got out.

Susan looked around. The building was huge. She walked to the entranceway, where cars could drive in through a truck-sized tunnel in the building. Signs advertised monthly parking available. She could see green grass inside the building in an open air courtyard. She walked back through the dark tunnel toward the fields.

The turf area inside the courtyard was surrounded by what appeared to be parking structure all around. The fields were busy with several baseball and softball games this early Sunday morning, no soccer there. She saw a parking attendant at a booth and walked over to ask him where the soccer field was.

After listening to her question, the parking attendant directed her back into the tunnel and up some stairs to the roof. Just as she entered the tunnel, she saw three people in soccer uniforms coming the opposite way, two men in maroon and a tall, lanky woman in royal blue. The men disappeared into a doorway. Susan tried to shout to the woman, but the woman turned sidewise into the door and disappeared. Susan ran to catch her.

Susan saw the woman's feet disappear upstairs as she turned, ascending a concrete stairway to the floor above. Susan finally caught up with the woman as she exited the stairway into the sun on the roof level.

"Excuse me, Miss!" Susan shouted ahead, short of breath from the run up the stairs.

The woman turned to Susan and raised her eyebrows in question, "Yes?" The woman was as tall as Susan with thin legs and body. Her dark dishwater blonde hair was pulled back in a ponytail like Susan's. She had a broad jaw and wore no makeup, such that Susan could see, since the woman wore wrap-around sports goggles. She wore royal blue soccer gear, and carried a red and black bag.

"I, uh, saw your soccer colors, are you by any chance on the team with Paul Waldman?" Susan asked, out of breath from running after her.

"Paul? Ych, he's on our team."

"He said you needed women for the team?"

"Women? Yes, sure do. I'm the only one who shows up usually. You gonna play with us? You seem to have the outfit," the woman turned and indicated Susan should follow her.

"Yes, I thought I might try."

The woman stopped and turned toward Susan, looking Susan up and down quickly. She held out her hand to Susan, "Glad to have you. I'm Andrea Greene. Call me Andi."

Susan took the woman's strong handshake and said, "Susan Fisher, call me Susy."

Andi walked on, Susan followed. Andi said "Yeh, Eric got these two women to sign up, since we needed at least two women on the field for this co-ed league. They both came to the first game or two, in May, but haven't seen them since. I think they were nurses who work with Paul and Eric and they came just to get an in with Eric, but backed out when they saw he had invited two of them. Too much competition; and they weren't very good at soccer. How about you? You any good at this?"

"I've played my share. And you." Susan said as she looked around, they seemed to be passing an aerial gymnastic apparatus on their left. She could see a soccer field on the corner of the building ahead of her.

"Yes, quite a bit," Andi said, patting her athletic bag which Susan could now see a logo on. "University of Maryland, I was the Lady Terps MVP at the ACC tourney three years ago."

"Ah, a fellow collegian. I was All-conference striker for Augustana College last year," Susan told her.

"What conference?"

"Nothing like the ACC, Augustana is in CCIW."

"CCIW?"

"College Conference of Illinois and Wisconsin. Think of it as a tiny ACC with lots of corn-fed farm girls who play soccer because they won't let women play tackle football."

"Ah, I get the picture. But, at least you know what you're doing." Andi followed the two men in maroon through a chain link fence gate, and they entered onto a turf soccer field.

It was not a full size field. Susan guessed it was maybe three quarters or two-thirds the size of a college soccer pitch. She said to Andi, "Kinda small field."

"Yeh, they put the summer co-ed adult soccer and the afternoon kids leagues up here. The baseball and softball have first dibs on the main fields downstairs for summer. In late fall and winter, they have full size soccer fields down in the middle area. They have both men's and women's leagues in fall, plus all the kiddies. This co-ed crap is just to tide everybody over." Andi waved to somebody ahead of her.

Susan could see the Maroon players congregating on the far left side of the field and several royal blue uniforms were on the right. She peered ahead to see if she could see Paul. There were six or seven men in blue, getting cleats tied and pulling on their jerseys. Susan saw Paul tying his shoes with his back to her on the far end of the team area.

Andi walked Susan over to a bald guy with a clipboard. "Steve, this is Susy

Fisher. You got one of the extra jerseys for her? She's gonna play for us."

Steve walked over to Susy, shaking her hand, "Glad to have you. Andi recruited you?"

"No, actually it was Paul. Do I need to sign up with someone?" Susan asked.

"No, the adult leagues are pretty free form. If you're over 18 and human, you can play. If you're female, we'll even cut you some slack on the human part. I'll just need to add you to the line-up card. F-I-S-H-E-R, right?" Steve pulled a blue jersey labeled '00' out of his equipment bag and wrote it on the line-up card. "This is the only one that will fit you at all. Our other two women, some nurses who never show up, kept their jerseys at home."

Susan saw Paul stand up on the end of the bench. She walked toward him. Several of the other players introduced themselves on the way.

"You decided to come." Paul said.

"Duh!" was Susan's response. She unzipped her track suit top and pulled the sweatpants down to her knees, before sitting on the bench to finish disrobing. She pulled the Blue jersey down over her head and stuffed the track suit in her backpack as she pulled out her shoes.

"Whoa! Where'd you get those shoes?" Paul asked.

In the bright sunlight the chrome Adidas cleats glistened in her hands. "These are my flash. My plan is to get the other team to watch my feet and not the ball."

A player who had introduced himself to Susan as Boris interrupted, "Hey this little lady has some shoes here. Them's mighty fine shoes, Susy."

Susy smirked at Paul, "See, Boris likes my shoes."

Paul smiled.

Steve shouted to everyone, "All right, everybody gather up." When they came over, he continued, "We've only got nine, so everybody plays, no subs. Lee texted me and NYPD called a mandatory overtime today for his precinct, so he can't play. Same slots as usual, plus Susan. Eric, Paul and Raph on offense. Me, Susy and Andi at midfield. Boris 'n Salud on defense. Jenkins goalie. I'll fall back on defense when we need it. Susy if I go back to defend, you come over to my side in the middle. And Susy, until you get the hang of this, don't try anything fancy, if you get the ball, pass to me or back to the defenders to set up the play, don't try to move it up yourself and lose it."

"I ca…," Susy started to say something to Steve, but he ignored her and ran to the middle of the field for the coin toss.

The Blue team walked onto the field, as did Maroon. Andi moved over to walk beside Susy, and said, "Don't let him get to you. That's how they are. Even though I've finally got some respect as a player, I'm still stuck on mids. But, tell you what, if we get a chance let's show them. I assume you know how to do a wall pass?"

"Of course," Susan sounded a bit insulted at the question.

"Well, that's probably the easiest, and snazziest, play we can pull off together without practice. So, if you or I get the ball with enough room to do a wall pass, let's run it and show these Neanderthals some moves. OK?" Andi gave a thumbs up fist to Susan. Susan bumped Andi's fist with her own thumbs up. Steve was coming back from the center indicating they would receive on the right half of the field.

Maroon lined up across from them. Susan saw that the Maroon women, two Hispanic girls, were in the midfield position, too, on the outsides. It looked like a center midfielder who would be coupled with Susan was a gawky young guy with a crew-cut and a bad complexion. She saw her opponent was wearing Converse All-stars high tops, instead of soccer cleats.

Paul, as center striker, was just outside the center circle, a few yards ahead of Susan for the kick-off. He looked back at Susan and smiled, "By the way, thanks for coming. You ready for this?"

"Are you ready for this? Look!" Susan shouted and pointed behind him.

Paul turned back to the ball just in time to see the kick off lateraled sideways from the kicker to his teammate on the left. Paul ran up to meet the player, who kicked it sideways to the Maroon player who had moved in front of Steve. The Maroon and Blue players moved into their normal field positions as the Maroon strikers passed the ball between themselves pushing it farther into the Blue end of the field. The Maroon back and forth ended with a sloppy shot on goal that was easily defended and grabbed by Rob Jenkins, the Blue goalie.

Jenkins kicked it far over midfield to where Paul skirmished with the African American Maroon defender who was covering him. Eric and Paul passed between themselves trying to move the ball to the Maroon goal, but the black guy stole it from Paul and kicked it quickly to the Blue half. Salud got the ball for Blue and both Andi and Susan cleared away from their Maroon cover to take a pass from Salud, but, instead, he passed cross field over to Steve, who was far less open than either Andi or Susan. It was obvious that passing to Andi or Susan was a last resort for Blue. The female Maroon covering Steve made an excellent tackle on Steve, slicing the ball away from him without fouling. Before Steve could respond, the little Hispanic woman passed the ball to the pimply guy in the center of the field with Susan. He passed before Susan could get to him. The ball went toward the Blue goal and Salud moved to intercept it with his Maroon striker on his heels. The Maroon player got there first and tried a quick shot on goal, but Jenkins cleanly blocked the kick with his body. The ball bounced hard toward Andi's position.

Just after Andi got to the ball, her Maroon opponent tried to do a take-away tackle like her teammate had done to Steve. But, she was not as good at tackling and her foot hooked Andi's ankle, sending Andi flying to the grass. The yellow-shirted referee whistled the foul and spotted the ball right where Andi had fallen.

Steve yelled, "Boris, take the kick!"

But, before Boris could run from his defense position, Andi popped to her feet, gave a thumbs up sign to Susan and kicked the free kick before her Maroon player had turned around to face her and before Boris could move forward to take the kick.

Seeing the thumbs up, Susan had cleared back away from the pimply guy into the open field in the center. Everybody except Susan was expecting a long, hard kick from Andi and were surprised when she kicked a firm, direct pass somewhat sideways to Susan in the middle of the field. Susan took the pass and dribbled directly toward the pimple faced Maroon.

This Maroon player charged Susan and saw her take a triple stutter step toward him. She dribbled weakly right, and then did a move not unlike an Irish jig with her feet, as though she were dribbling left. Then as the Maroon player went left to meet her, she immediately stopped the dribble and gave an easy kick to the right, while Maroon moved to her left losing his footing in the quick turn. That was why you wear cleats for soccer. Clear of the pimply guy, Susan kicked the ball hard to the right sideline. The Blue women's wall pass was underway.

As soon as Andi had done the free kick, she had raced up the sideline. The Maroon girl who had tripped her was not yet turned around and watched Andi's pass go to Susan causing her to move that direction in reaction, while Andi herself ran quickly along the sideline behind this Maroon midfielder, who eventually spun around to follow, but behind Andi.

With her head start Andi was well ahead of her Maroon cover when she got Susan's pass near the sideline. She dribbled quickly up the sideline toward the far corner. In that corner, Raph and his Maroon defender jockeyed for position, certain that Andi would pass the ball in to Raph.

After passing to Andi, Susan was running at full speed directly toward Paul and the black guy defending him. These two men were almost stationary, not knowing which way Susan would head or why she was charging toward them. Just before she reached them, Susan did another short stutter step and passed to the right of the black defender. Having passed Paul's defender in the center Susan abruptly stopped short of the position where the Maroon defender covering Raph was standing. Susan did not want to be off side when Andi kicked the ball.

Now at full speed up the sideline, Andi faked a dribble kick to Raph and then kicked the ball very hard directly toward, not the goal, but the open Maroon penalty circle. The Maroon goalie had been on the far right side of the goal to defend an attack from Raph when he saw the sideways kick from Andi. Too late he saw Susan was now at full run again after awaiting Andi's kick. The goalie stretched out to try a block Susan's kick. Susan's path intersected the ball's path in the left side of the Maroon penalty circle and the ball hit Susan's kicking leg shin guard. The ball caromed off Susan's leg directly into the left side of the Maroon goal net.

Susan had to bank hard to avoid going into the net herself. She jumped high over the now supine Maroon goalie and spun to a stop in a spinning hug from Andi. Paul and Raph joined in at the end of the hug.

As they broke the group hug apart and headed back for the kick off, Steve came up to Andi, and started to say, "I said Boris …."

Andi spun toward him and held up one finger, "Steve, you have shitty timing. Just look at the score and can it. And … next time, I take my own free kick." She turned her back on Steve and walked to her spot on the far sideline.

As they walked back to receive the kickoff, Susan moved next to Paul and asked, "How do you like my silver shoes now? All that my guy saw was these shoes. That is what we call flash!"

"Pretty good. You have some surprises in you, Susan Rachel Fisher."

Susan looked at Paul, "I don't recall that I gave you my middle name."

"The computer at the ER desk has Google, too."

———

The Blue team members were congratulating each other on their win and were pulling off their cleats. Another team, in gold jerseys, was already moving in to use the field next.

"Do they have showers around here?" Susan asked nobody in particular.

Andi answered first, "They have men's and women's shower rooms downstairs, if you can call them that."

Paul added, "And they have as pretty bad reputation. Thefts from both locker rooms, and streakers running through the women's shower. They promised to fix it up, but it is not what you'd want to use."

Susan finished tying her white sneakers and tucked her T-shirt into the track suit pants. She wiggled the blue team jersey at Steve. "You want me to keep this, or give it back."

Steve smiled, "Your choice. You coming back again?"

"I'd like to. I think I can fit it into the schedule." Susan said as she zipped the track suit jacket up halfway.

"Well, then take it. It doesn't get washed in the equipment bag. Eric, can you check with those gals you brought. Are they going to come or not? If not, get our jerseys back."

Eric nodded. He sat next to Paul. Susan had learned Eric Schwartz was a surgeon who worked the ER with Paul and was one of the partners in the walk-in clinic. He was taller than Paul and rather thin, but athletic. He had longish brown hair, a handsome face and strong New York accent.

Paul asked Susan, "What's your plan after this?"

"I dunno, any suggestions." Susan looked at Paul.

"We usually like to go to the Cornelia Street Cafe for brunch." Paul pointed east into the City. "They don't seem to object to the aroma of a soccer team that hasn't showered."

"Sounds good to me."

The five members of the team who decided to go to eat caught a mini-van taxi out front of Pier 40 and rode to the café. Eric, Susan, Paul and Raph rode in back. Andrea climbed in front by the driver.

As they rode through the narrow, often one-way streets, Paul asked Susan, "Have you been to the Village before?"

"Greenwich Village? Is that where we are? No, first time."

Andrea looked back and joined the conversation, "Never been to the Village? You new to New York?"

Susan answered, "Yeh, second week here."

"Wow, a real newb. Where'd you pick her up Paul?" Eric asked.

"She's my landlady." Paul answered with a smile. Then, poking Eric in the shoulder, he added, "Actually, she's our landlady, for our clinic. It is a long story."

Before they could ask any more questions, the taxi pulled over on a narrow street in front of the sidewalk café. When they got out, Eric paid the taxi, it was apparently his turn. The waitress with 'Maggie' on her name tag seemed to recognize the soccer players, without speaking she showed them to a table in the far corner by the open French doors. She took a chair from a nearby table for the fifth person. Maggie handed out menus and left to get coffee.

Andrea spoke to Susan, "If you are real hungry the *Prix Fixe* is a good deal, if not, I'd recommend the French Toast and Fruit. Really done well." Andrea finally took her sports glasses off. She had brilliant blue cat-like eyes, wide set.

And, she wore no make-up.

Susan nodded. She noted that the other four did not consult the menu, they apparently had their favorites. Maggie was already back, pouring coffee and taking orders.

After the others chose, Susan picked the recommended French toast with strawberries.

After the waitress left, Eric turned to Paul and Susan and said, "I need to hear more about this 'landlady' stuff."

Susan gave Paul a palm up hand gesture indicating he could take the answer, "Paul, you brought it up, you explain it."

Paul finished a sip of coffee, added a second sugar, and started, "Well, it starts out as many stories do, with me seeing a pretty girl. She was trying to get in the door to our building with an armload of groceries. I was strategically blocking her way with my bicycle. I managed to introduce myself, and then ask her to play soccer with us and she refused. Later that day, totally for the sake of our team, I gave her my best full court press in hopes she would change her mind about playing soccer. I assure you I had no ulterior motives. She countered my full court press with a rooftop champagne lunch, during which she disclosed she was, indeed, the new owner of our building. She still gave no indication she would play, but my efforts were rewarded today when she did show up, a week later. That's the long and short of it."

"Paul, your explanation sucks as to details. Susan?" Eric said.

Susan shrugged, "Well, he actually got everything right. The missing details are that my aunt just died and left me the building, I'm from Illinois and I'm working on moving into the building."

Raph finally spoke up, "What do you do, Susan? For a living?"

Susan laughed lightly, "I guess as to profession, my best answer is I am a recently unemployed Macy's salesgirl. I was a student last year. Just moved from Moline, Illinois. No further plans for now."

"Wait!" Andrea blurted out, "I saw something in the *About Town* blog on our Realtor Board's web site. You aren't the Metzger heiress are you?"

Susan's eyes rolled up briefly, before staring silently at Andrea. After a moment, Susan asked, "Metzger Heiress? That's what they are calling me?"

Andrea nodded, "Yeh, and if what was in the blog is correct that isn't an understatement."

Susan looked sheepishly at Paul, who said, "I take it there is more involved than just the building."

Susan pursed her lips and said, "Yeh, a bit."

Andrea snickered, "Yeh, like numerous chunks of Manhattan and a not so small fortune."

Susan finally broke the staring contest with Paul and took a deep breath, while stirring her coffee. She shifted in her seat and turned to Raph. "So, enough about me. Since you started this, Raph, what do you do for a living? Details. And give me your full name again, so I can remember it."

Raph took her plea for relief and said, "Raphael Dipalo. I'm a programmer for Deutsche Bank. I write and certify custom interfaces for clients to connect with bank systems. Graduated from Carnegie Mellon. Been in New York since moving from Philly five years ago. Divorced, but not looking, too soon. Andrea, your turn."

Andrea put down her coffee cup, "Andrea Colton, I'm a real estate broker, but currently focusing on appraisal. Specialty is commercial finance appraisal. In a relationship with my partner Vicky. Lifelong Manhattan resident, 'cept for four years at U. of Maryland. Eric?"

Susan hoped she had hidden her surprise that Andrea was in a same sex relationship. She turned to Eric.

"Eric Schwartz. Chest cutter. Went to NYU all the way through med school. Grew up in Queens. Single and doing my best to garner a reputation as a scoundrel and lady killer. I work with Paul at Presbyterian and we are partners in a storefront clinic, apparently in your building."

Paul started to say something, but Susan cut him off, "I got your story Paul …."

"Apparently better than I got your story," Paul said.

"Ooohhh, awkward silence permeates!" Andrea said under her breath.

The food arrived.

———

Paul and Susan watched as Andrea gave a last wave and she, Raph and Eric headed east together.

"This way," Paul said, picking up his bag and heading west.

Susan shouldered her backpack and followed him. "So, why no bike today?"

"On game day I come straight from the hospital if I am on duty, eating on the way. Riding the bike down would tire me too much before the game." Paul turned at the corner, right.

Susan saw the street sign and said, "Hey, Bleecker Street, like the Simon and Garfunkel song."

Paul just nodded.

"So where exactly are we going? I need to get a better handle on where I am in this city."

"Well, I usually hit the subway up at Sheridan Square. Unless the 'heiress' wants to take a taxi."

"Paul, that's enough with the hard time about that. What did you expect me to say? Hi, I'm Susy, I'm an orphan, but I just inherited a fortune of sixty million dollars." Paul raised his eyebrows at this figure. "I did say I was 'really rich,' my exact words. This has been a hell of a couple weeks for me. It is now Sunday at noon, if my life had not become unstuck the Wednesday before last, my plans for today would have been to man the perfume counter at Macy's selling lots of men's cologne in a last minute gift rush for Father's Day today. And now I …."

"Damn!" Paul interrupted, shaking his head.

"What?" Susan asked, looking over at Paul. Then, as she saw the consternation on his face she figured it out and said, "Ahhh, somebody forgot Father's Day, did he?"

"Yeh, totally. Today is Father's Day. And I promised Mom and Ed I would join them for dinner at the folks. Julie will be there, too. They were going to use Father's Day as a family get-together. Julie coming down from Dartmouth and Ed and his family from Boston for a big dinner with the folks."

"Do you still have time? I have no idea how far Connecticut is. Connecticut, right?"

Paul shook his head, "There are only four trains on Sundays that go all the way up to where my folks live and I've already missed the mid-day run. The only way to get there on time on a Sunday would be to drive."

"And?"

"I'd have to rent something. That would be a lot of trouble and not much time."

"You don't have a car?"

Paul huffed as though it was a silly question. "No, never need one living here. And my landlady charges too much for parking." He smirked at Susan. "Well, I had one, a 300 Z I drove to Princeton, but I sold when I saw how little it got used here in town. Most Manhattanites don't have their own cars."

"You could borrow mine." Susan struggled to keep up with Paul's stride.

"You have a car?"

"Yeh, two of 'em. But, wait, don't you have to sleep for work tonight."

"No, I got the next two nights off, I was going to call you and make good on your raincheck, maybe tomorrow . Then I work the afternoon and evening shift starting Tuesday. But, you are right, I haven't slept since eight o'clock last night. I'm bushed, which partly responsible for forgetting about this. It would be tough to stay awake for the drive to Connecticut."

"I could drive you," Susan offered.

Paul looked at Susan, half smiling, "Kind of you to offer, but it would be kind of awkward, taking you to meet the family before a first date."

"Yeh, but that is a lame excuse for missing a family dinner and your Father's special day. You should go."

"Maybe, but why do you seem to care so much about this?"

Susan thought for moment and answered, "I think it is probably because this is the first year I haven't had Mom and Dad around for Mother's and Father's Day, and my heartstrings get strummed at the thought of somebody … anybody… missing a chance to hug their folks." Susan's voice broke in the middle of the sentence.

Paul walked in silence for a few steps before speaking, "Okay, offer accepted. But, we are going to have to hurry. I need a shower, I'm pretty ripe."

"Me, too." Susan said as she started waving her arms wildly over her head, trying to signal a passing taxi with a roof light showing it was available.

—

Chapter Eighteen

Susan was at the dining room table separating the Mercedes key ring from the master ring of other keys in her old backpack pouch when her iPhone sounded. She answered.

"Are you coming down?" Paul asked.

"Yeh, it takes me a bit longer, more to do. Where are you?"

"Waiting at the cars. We're taking the Mercedes? It's behind the Prius."

"Yup, I am getting the keys, I'll be right down."

"OK."

Susan had decided to stick with the new white summer dress, even though it had been scrunched in the backpack for the trip to the soccer game. It was lightweight cotton and shook out nicely, and it really was a cute dress. She changed her shoes to low white heels she had bought the night before. She checked herself one last time in the big gilded mirror in the foyer. She had done a quick make-up application, fairly mellow, considering it was for a Sunday family dinner, but just enough to switch her from a freckle-faced soccer player to a pretty woman who a New York doctor would not mind meeting his parents. Her hair was what it was, no time to do anything special, she had washed it in the shower and did a quick blow dry. For this once she appreciated her trouble free hair. She had chosen one of the wide silver and diamond barrettes from Rachel's jewel case in the vanity to keep her unstyled waves back off of her face. She had also added a couple matching stud earrings, small ones, not the big diamonds. The barrette was an old art deco piece that Susan decided was not too pretentious for afternoon wear, but enough to be noticed. Aunt Rachel definitely had good taste. Susan gathered purse and keys and locked the apartment, remembering to set the alarm code as she left.

At the ground floor, she took the back door from the freight elevator room. Laszlo had said this was the shortcut to the parking area. She emerged on the old loading dock and saw Paul waiting by the cars. Before the door closed she turned to check that she had the key to the loading dock door on the key ring. After a couple tries, she found she did.

"Wow, you clean up pretty nice!" Paul said as Susan walked up to where he leaned on the front bumper of the white Mercedes.

Susan said nothing, but smiled and blinked at Paul to acknowledge the compliment. She noticed that with the low heels she was exactly his height. He was wearing a dark blue sports jacket, khaki pants and a tie-less white Oxford shirt.

"I noticed it is pretty close to the wall, I'll have to get in on this side. You want me to back it out?"

Susan checked around the car and back to the alley, "No, I can handle it."

She opened the car door with the electronic key fob and stood back for him to crawl over the console to the passenger seat. As he passed close to her, Susan could smell his cologne, Blue de Chanel. Her days at Macy's had given her a unique skill set for such recognition. And, his close passage caused his shoulder to rub against her sleeve and breast. He did not seem to notice the touch.

As Susan settled in the driver's seat, Paul said, "Nice car, same as my father's, but his is dark silver gray. Somebody stole your Mercedes hood emblem."

"Yeh, I'm told they do it regularly." Susan turned the ignition and the big engine roared to life and dash displays flashed on. She had a momentary qualm about her ability to pilot this big car, it was a lot more car than the Prius she was used to or even the Ford Explorer. She put the car in gear and checked her mirrors. Rachel's mirror positions seemed to work for her. Paul stifled a yawn.

"Tank is full. You point me in the direction of the highway to Connecticut and put your seat back and sleep." Susan said.

"I can do better than that. Hold on a sec." Paul sat forward in the seat and poked the big display panel on the dashboard. Susan put the car back in park.

Paul used a large silver knob on the console and a soft female voice with a distinctive British accent spoke from the panel, "Syncing current location" and the same message flashed across the screen along with a map of the street grid in Manhattan.

Paul moved the silver knob again and the voice said, "Enter desired destination."

Susan watched as Paul scrolled through menu entries for Connecticut, Westport, Bayberry Lane and then a house number. A map of streets appeared on the screen. Paul moved the silver joystick knob and a message appeared with the voice saying, "Destination set and saved."

Paul poked the joystick again and the map was back to Manhattan and the message panel and the voice said, "Follow marked route. You are off marked street."

Paul explained, "There, you are all set with the navigation, all the way to our driveway. Pull out on the street, and she will tell you when to make turns."

"You aren't going to be able to sleep much with the Brit lady talking, can you turn off the voice, and just let me use the map and instructions?" Susan asked.

"I don't think that will bother me. I'm a pretty sound sleeper, comes from having to catch catnaps on a gurney in the ER hallway as a resident; but yes, we can try that." Paul poked the knob again. The voice started to speak. He quickly hit Mute. The voice stopped and a crossed out speaker icon appeared on the screen. "If you need to hear it again, just use the control knob and un-mute it."

Susan carefully backed car out of the narrow parking space. Negotiating the backing turn in the alley took several tries, back and forth. When she pulled up in the alley across the 10th Avenue sidewalk, by the Bistro, a blue line appeared on the screen. It showed that she should turn north on 10th and then go left two blocks north and over to follow the Lincoln Highway north.

Once Susan was heading north along the harbor, Paul followed her instructions and put his seat back in order to sleep. He was snoring before they went by the 79th Street interchange.

—

Susan quickly got into the driving groove. She really enjoyed driving this Mercedes. It was comfortable, quiet and she felt safe. She had a lot of time to think and contemplate the situation she was in. She liked it.

Susan made mental plans of what she would do the following morning and decided she would investigate closer the possibility of getting into a college in New York. She daydreamed different scenarios of how her life might change in the months ahead.

True to his word, Paul slept soundly, alternating between snoring, heavy breathing and fitful fidgeting. He actually mumbled in his sleep a couple of times, Susan could not understand the mumbling, though she tried. He was still asleep over an hour later when the map directed her to exit the Merritt Parkway into Westport, Connecticut and follow the side streets to Bayberry Lane.

As she approached Bayberry Lane, she pulled up behind a black Cadillac SUV at the stop sign with its turn signal on, turning the way the map was telling her to go. The window shading on the Cadillac was too dark to see who was driving. The map was showing the blue line ending just ahead. Bayberry Lane was a narrow, tree-lined route with expensive homes on both sides.

As she neared the destination marker, the Cadillac slowed, put on its turn signal and turned into a driveway. Next to the driveway was a cast iron pillar holding the mailbox and above that, was a metal flag with 'Waldman' printed on it. The Cadillac SUV was going to Paul's parents' house.

Paul was still snoring beside her. Susan thought of waking him, but reconsidered, he had been so tired, she would let him sleep as long as she could. She waited a moment so she was not directly tailing the Cadillac, and then turned up the drive.

The Waldman house was a large white, two story Colonial house with multiple gables in the roof, actually a third story, and a three car garage. 'Mansion' was really a more correct description than 'house.' Bisecting the large, lush, green lawn, the driveway was cobblestone, flanked by privet trees, The driveway ended in a circular drive centered with a large fountain in front of the double-doored entrance. The black Cadillac was pulled up to the front door and a woman was opening the rear hatchback. Susan pulled up behind the Cadillac, partially in the early afternoon shade of the house.

The woman turned to them and walked over. She was a middle-aged woman, medium height, with her golden blonde hair pulled back in a bun. She was wearing what appeared to be a white tennis outfit.

Paul was still snoring, a bit louder than before. Susan decided to leave him alone and try to get out without waking him. She quietly unbuckled the seat belt and started to open the door. The woman was now in front of the car, shielding her eyes from the bright sky to try and see who was inside the car which was in the shade of the house. She did a double take when she saw who was in the passenger seat, asleep.

Susan removed the keys, to prevent the donging when she opened the door, and got out, getting her purse hanging behind her seat's headrest. She gently pushed the door almost closed. She knew the Mercedes door would thunk hard if she actually shut the door. Susan put a finger to her lips, urging the woman to be quiet and the woman followed her a few steps from the car.

"Hi, I'm Susy Fisher." Susan said, offering her hand to the woman. "Paul hadn't slept since last evening, and he fell asleep on the trip up here. I thought I'd let him sleep a bit more."

"Uh, Okay. I'm Greta Waldman, his mother," She spoke with the barest hint of a foreign accent Susan could not recognize. She looked toward Paul. "Paul was always a deep sleeper, especially on long car trips. He can sleep anywhere. Let's just let him sleep a bit. He'll be fine there, in the shade."

Greta Waldman turned back to the Cadillac, Susan followed.

"Paul didn't mention he was bringing anyone, when we talked, what, two weeks ago?" Great said over her shoulder, leaving a question hanging.

"It was a last minute thing. He was so tired, he had the midnight shift and then a soccer game this morning. I was afraid he would fall asleep at the wheel, so I offered to drive him." Susan followed Greta, who picked up two paper grocery bags. Susan picked up the other two bags, "Let me help with that."

"This is certainly a beautiful house," Susan said as she followed Greta across the front entranceway. The foyer ceiling was two stories high and had a large winding staircase up to the upper floor and a huge chandelier above them. They passed through a dining room with a long formal dining table with many brocade chairs, under another chandelier.

"Yes, beautiful indeed, but really too large, too much trouble, now that it is an empty nest." Greta sounded sad at these words.

"I heard it won't be an empty nest this evening. Paul said all three children are coming?"

"Yes, and the two grandchildren from Boston, too. I'm still working on getting into the grandmother mindset."

"You certainly don't look like a grandmother," Susan complimented, following Greta into a large kitchen. They sat the bags on the counter.

The Waldman's kitchen was huge, with lots of stainless steel, white ceramic tile and white marble counters.

"Thank you for that. Oh, put the plastic bag over on the other counter, I always have the dairy stuff in a plastic bag," Greta directed.

Susan did not understand why Greta had said that. But, she put the plastic grocery bag on the second kitchen island counter. Susan could smell something already cooking in the oven, beef. A roast?

Greta put her purse next to the sink, slipped a short apron over the tennis outfit and started unpacking groceries. Susan saw that Greta had a perfect athletic figure given her age and the short tennis outfit showed it off, especially the tanned, muscular legs. Her golden blonde hair was probably dyed, but it and her entire look denoted polished beauty, well preserved. She was perfectly manicured and wore a huge diamond on her wedding ring finger. She had sedate, but distinctive make-up, even in the casual tennis outfit.

"Can I help with anything?" Susan asked.

"Oh, sure, I guess. You want to put the stuff in the plastic bag into the dairy fridge. It is the one in the corner," Greta pointed towards a large double door refrigerator behind Susan.

With mention of the 'dairy' refrigerator, Susan now noticed that there were two refrigerators, two stoves, two sinks and she had already noticed the two islands in the middle of the large kitchen. Like Rachel's kitchen, the Waldman's kitchen had two of everything.

Susan had Googled 'kosher' after the Shiva dinner at Aaron's, and between the new internet information and her prior knowledge she understood the reason for the two refrigerators in this kitchen and Rachel's (or hers now, she reminded herself) and the matching food preparation tables, stoves and sinks. The Waldman's magnificent kitchen was designed as a full kosher kitchen with duplicate, separate storage and prep areas for meats and dairy products. She assumed that Myra and Aaron's was the same. Susan only had a basic understanding of things kosher, but it seemed to be a big part of several people's lives. Even Devorah had joked about her addiction to cheeseburgers being a problem for a rabbi's daughter. Once again Susan felt like a tourist viewing a Jewish lifestyle.

Finishing with the grocery bags, Greta put numerous large Russet potatoes on a cutting board and started to peel them. Susan walked over and started to reach for a knife.

Greta said, "Wait, if you are going to help peel get the other apron over on the hook. The iodine in the potato skins will really stain your white cotton dress. Nice outfit, by the way."

Susan retrieved the apron, but had more trouble tying it than Greta had. Tying an apron behind her back was not in her repertoire.

"Here, let me help you with that," Greta said, wiping her hands and reaching over to tie Susan's apron.

Greta and Susan started peeling the potatoes with knives from a wooden knife rack by the cutting board. Greta watched Susan for a minute, and then opened a drawer and pushed a regular potato peeler over to Susan.

"It might be handier for you to use the peeler. Peeling vegetables and potatoes quickly with a knife is a skill I got as a recruit in the Army."

"You were in the Army?" Susan sounded incredulous.

"Oh, yes. Israeli IDF. That is where I met Paul's father." Greta answered, the source of her slight accent now apparent to Susan.

"He was in the Israeli Army, too?"

"Oh, no, not Ted. He was doing a semester abroad program from UConn at a kibbutz near Nahariya. My Army post was nearby. We met, courted, got married, I got a discharge, and Ted brought a new bride home from Israel to meet his parents after an eventful semester abroad. They were pretty shocked."

"I bet."

"Yes, that was thirty years ago, next December." Greta smiled at the memory.

Susan realized Greta had given her a good hint on Paul's age, given their anniversary information. He was less than thirty. Susan searched her memory for something to keep the conversation going.

"Nahariya, that is near Acre, right?" Susan asked.

"Yes, just north. You are familiar with Acre and Nahariya?" Greta stopped peeling a moment to look at Susan. Susan noticed that Greta said the Israeli place names in a totally Hebrew accent.

Susan nodded, "A bit, my father was invited by the Israeli Antiquities Authority to help on an archaeological site near Acre, and I got to go with him for two summer trips. Nahariya was near the site, if I remember correctly." Susan was glad she had skimmed through the 'Archibald' binder she had found in her father's filing cabinet.

"Your father is an archaeologist?"

"Actually, he was a history professor. He had published a paper on the historical people, the European Crusaders, they thought might be involved in the site during the Crusades. He helped tie the ruins into the historical context."

"Interesting. You said he 'was' a history professor?" She emphasized the 'was.'

"Yes, he passed away last September."

"I am sorry to hear that, my condolences. And your mother?"

"She was an English teacher, and she passed away in February."

Greta set her knife down on the counter and turned toward Susan, "My, this has been a tough year for you."

"Yes, quite a lot to deal with." Susan said this with a deep breath. She was saved from having to say more by her cell phone ringing from her purse on the counter. She pulled it out and checked the caller. "I need to get this."

Susan stepped back from the counter. She answered, "Hello, Devorah."

"How was your trip back home? You're back in New York right?" Devorah asked.

"I'm back from Illinois, but not in New York. Right now I'm actually in Connecticut."

"Connecticut, what'cha doing there? If I might ask."

"Right now, I'm peeling potatoes. It is a long story. I'll fill you in later." Susan smiled over to Greta as she said this. "Everything went fine in Illinois; the real estate broker is sending David a copy of the listing agreement. I think I got all the loose ends tied up. You are going to get a huge pile of shipping boxes addressed to your client service address. Estate auction for personal property is set for a couple weeks out, they'll send your office the proceeds check."

Devorah continued, "Okay, we'll get someone to send those boxes on down to your apartment, if that is what you want, or they could be stored."

"Send them down; I have plenty of storage room."

"All right, what I called about is that Peter wanted me to call you. Can you be in his office Tuesday at 10:00?"

"Tuesday at 10? Sure, what is up?"

"Peter said to have you come, dressed to meet someone important. He didn't give me details. Some kind of surprise for you. Wear the same dress you came to the synagogue in, maybe. It was nice."

"Huh, mystery meeting at 10 Tuesday in Peter Ephraim's office. Sure, not a whole lot on my calendar to conflict with that."

Devorah ended with, "Okay, that is all I had, but I will be expecting a report on peeling potatoes in Connecticut."

"Will do, see you then. Bye." Susan put the phone back in her purse.

Since Greta had only heard half the conversation, Susan explained, "That was my attorney, some meeting to go to on Tuesday."

"Attorney? You're a pediatrician. Right?" Greta asked.

Susan looked at Greta with her eyebrows furled, "No, not a pediatrician. Why did you think that?"

"I'm sorry; I jumped to a wrong conclusion. The only female friend Paul had mentioned recently was some pediatrician he knew from med school. I wrongly assumed that was you."

"Nope, not me. And the attorney is nothing really about my profession. They are the attorneys for my aunt's estate." Susan smiled to herself that Paul's mother thought she was old enough to have finished med school with Paul.

"You aunt died, too?" Greta asked cautiously.

"Yes, last week." Susan picked the peeler back up.

Greta shook her head, "Gosh, your family is having a bad streak."

Susan nodded.

"What is your profession?" Greta asked, finishing up on the loose end of the conversation.

Susan raised her eyebrows as though the question was hard, "Until recently I could have said it was full time student. But, that is in flux. Right now, I guess the best answer to my profession is real estate investor. That is what is paying the bills." Susan thought this was a cute answer, evasive, but true in its essence. And, it fit in with what Greta had heard on the phone call.

Susan decided to add, "That is how I met Paul. I'm his landlady."

"You own that big building he lives in, or maybe just the sublease for his apartment?" Greta stopped peeling again.

Susan answered, "The building."

Greta continued her questions as she started to quarter the peeled potatoes, "And how well do you know Paul?" The hidden meaning behind a man's mother asking that question was obvious.

Susan did not answer immediately. Then she put her closed fist to her mouth, stifling a giggle. Her giggle soon burst into a laugh.

"So, my question was funny?" Greta asked. Her Israeli accent came out in the way she worded the question and her rising intonation.

Susan stopped laughing and smiled at Greta. She knew she needed to explain her slightly rude laugh, "No, your question was fine. It is just that when you said it, I thought of an idea for a set up for one of those chick flick romantic comedies, or the dreadful Hallmark Channel made for TV movies. You know, young woman meets the mother of a handsome eligible bachelor. The mother asks the woman about what her relationship with the son is. The young woman knows the mother doesn't know anything about her, so she makes up a great story about how she and the son are in a big romance and all. And the son, for whatever reason, doesn't want to call the young woman a liar, and the characters all spend the rest of the chick flick undoing the mischief the young woman's story about the romance causes. When in reality, the young woman had only just met the eligible bachelor, and her meeting with the mother was almost by accident. That was the mental movie plot I laughed at."

Greta thought for a moment and said, "So that latter part, that is the real story."

Susan shrugged, "Yeh, unfortunately. I *am* his landlady. We played a co-ed soccer game together this morning. We haven't actually been out on a real date yet, although he has tried. I took pity on him, not wanting him to fall asleep at the wheel driving up here, so I drove him up for his Father's Day dinner with his family. Whole story!"

Greta again thought for a minute, and then smiled, shaking her head, "No, I think I like the first story better. Because, my almost thirty year old son has never brought a girl home for me to meet before. He should be married. And, he could do a lot worse than a beautiful, apparently well-to-do young woman, and one who isn't afraid to peel a potato. I vote we stick with the Hallmark Channel plot. We need to work on that."

Greta and Susan laughed together as Greta put the potatoes in a pressure cooker and onto the stove.

Both of them were startled at a loud voice coming from the kitchen door, "Anybody know why my eldest son is sleeping one off in a car in the driveway?"

"Oh, Ted!" Greta turned and went to give a quick kiss to a man who entered the kitchen. He was fiftyish, fairly trim, slightly balding and wore khaki pants with a white polo shirt. Susan surmised Paul favored his mother's looks. Greta answered Ted's question, "Paul hadn't slept since last evening. He fell asleep in the car and we two decided to just let him keep sleeping."

"And this is?" Ted indicated Susan.

"Oh, yes, Susy meet Theodore Waldman, Paul's father; Ted, meet Susy Fisher… Paul's … fiancée." She could not keep a straight face though, as both she and Susan laughed.

Susan stopped laughing and offered her hand to Ted Waldman, "Hi, I'm Susan Fisher, a *friend* of Paul's" She emphasized 'friend' as a contradiction to 'fiancée.'

Ted took her hand, "Hello, uh … friend… not fiancée?"

Greta answered for Susan still with a smile, "No, not fiancée, just friend, but Susy and I were here in the kitchen conspiring for Paul's eventual downfall. I was testing one of our tactics out on you there."

Ted furrowed his forehead and said to Greta, "I'm not sure I understand."

Greta gave a pretend serious face and said, "Ted, you aren't supposed to understand. It's a woman thing. Besides, if you understood, you might tell Paul and ruin the movie plot."

Before they could say anything else, a woman's voice came from the dining room, "Anybody home?"

"Julie's here," Greta announced, quickly undoing her apron and rushing out of the kitchen, followed by Ted. Susan decided to follow, too, taking her apron off and leaving it on the counter

Greta was hugging a young woman in the dining room. A young man stood behind them. Next, Julie Waldman got a big hug from her father, one that lifted her off the floor. Greta also hugged the young man, a polite hug, but nowhere as exuberant as the hug for Julie. Ted gave the young man a very abbreviated handshake, no hug.

Julie was the same medium height as her mother and had long, kinky hair the same dark blonde color of Paul's. She had a nice, cute face, but was not a real beauty, with many freckles. She wore a white culotte and a gray and white striped V-neck top. The young man with her was very handsome, dark, maybe Italian or Spanish descent, and had slightly shaggy black hair. He was dressed in Kelly green Dockers and a not quite matching polo shirt.

When they finished hugs and handshakes, Julie Waldman turned to face Susan and said, "And …?" She looked at Susan, and then from Greta to Ted.

Greta started to introduce Susan, but caught Susan's eye and both women laughed again. Susan stepped forward, offering her hand to Julie, "Hi, I'm Susan Fisher, a friend of Paul's."

Julie smiled and shook her hand, "I'm Paul's sister, Julie. Then you must be responsible for leaving him sleeping in the car?"

"Yes, that would be my fault."

Julie motioned to the young man behind her and said, "Susan, this is John Bello, my fiancé."

At the word 'fiancé' both Greta and Susan gave another chuckle with Greta putting her hand on Susan's shoulder.

Neither Greta nor Susan offered any quick explanation for the laughing, so Ted volunteered, "Your mother and Susan have some inside joke going. They won't explain, they say it is a woman thing. Maybe they will tell you."

Susan shook John's hand. She saw Julie look at her mother with a questioning expression.

Greta asked Julie, "So, is everything all finished at Dartmouth, your intersession class all done?"

Before Julie answered, Susan interrupted, "While you folks are catching up, I'll go retrieve Paul, and he'll probably want to be in here with you. He's had enough sleep for a while."

With that, Susan left to wake Paul up.

—

The big dining room table had ten chairs, and all were used when the entire family eventually sat down to the lavish meal Greta had prepared. Besides the beef roast everyone could smell, Greta's oven also disgorged fresh bread and a couple different baked dishes. There were many little dishes of condiments, vegetables, sweets and garnishes. Attuned to the kosher issue by seeing the kitchen, Susan noticed that the entire meal seemed to have been prepared without dairy products, not even butter for the home-made bread. Susan saw the harsh yellow of margarine in the 'butter' dish on the table.

After Paul had woken up and come inside, his brother Ed and wife Betsy with their children arrived. Susan had to go through another explanation, this time by Paul, of whom she was and why she was there. As the family waited for the meal to start, Susan was able to glean the details of Paul's family, and their goings on through snippets of conversation and family updates. Ed was managing a Boston branch office of whatever financial company Ted had founded and was now semi-retired from. Julia and John were both in pre-Med studies at Dartmouth, but John had just finished and was going to med school. Julie had a year left. Betsy seemed to be a full time mother, but had some sort of project for a museum she was working on in her spare time, which she said she had little of.

Ed looked very much like Paul, but shorter, not quite as handsome and a few years younger. Betsy was pretty, round-faced, a little heavy and had shiny, dark brown hair to her shoulders. To Susan's eye, Betsy was the consummate Jewish mother, and classic Jewish woman prototype. If you put a robe and headscarf on Betsy she could pose for a painting of Sarah, or Rebecca, or Esther or any of the biblical matriarchs, or maybe Tevye's daughters. And, from the bump in her belly, she was well on the way to being a perfect Jewish mother for a third time, which explained her weight. She wore a very cute 'hatching jacket,' which was clearly from a designer collection.

At last, Greta announced the meal was ready. Greta and Ted assumed positions on either end of the long table. At Greta's direction, Susan sat at Greta's left with Paul next to her. Julie and her fiancé John sat across from them. Ed sat with his toddler son, Jordan, on his father's left. Betsy sat with their kindergarten-aged daughter, Gillian, across from them. Susan noted that both children inherited their dark hair from Betsy and looked nothing like Ed.

Everyone waited as Greta sat the last food dish on the table and took her seat. Susan saw John start to take his napkin, but he had his sleeve tugged by Julie. As Greta sat down, everyone around the table, almost in unison, except for John and Susan, bowed their head and waited. John and Susan quickly followed the others.

Ted spoke out in a loud, deep voice, *"Baruch atah Adonai Eloheinu Melech Haolam, shehakol nih'yeh bidvaro."*

As Susan looked up, she saw everyone still had their head bowed and were softly saying "Amen." John made the sign of the cross, very quickly. Directly across the table, Susan was the only one at the table who could see Julie gently elbow John after he crossed himself. The young couple quickly looked at each other, with Julie's brow going down and John's brow going up. Susan could tell something interesting was in the air with this obviously non-Jewish fiancé.

The table had quickly turned into a furious melee of platter and plate passing, and requests for this and that. Susan noticed that Paul was a huge fan of mashed potatoes, which Susan noted were whipped well, but had no milk in them. She guessed they were made with margarine, not butter. And, the beef gravy was totally clear, no milk. Susan made a decision to try a little of everything that came her way.

When everybody had just started eating, Susan saw Paul look at his mother and nod. Greta got up and retrieved two bottles of dark purple wine in squarish bottles that had been placed, pre-opened, on the serving table by the wall. Greta handed one bottle to Julie who poured her wine goblet and John's. Greta poured wine in her own glass and then Susan's, before handing the bottle to Paul. Julia missed the brand of the wine, but saw a big blue Star of David on the wine bottle as it went by her. The bottles were passed up the table and even the two children got a tiny bit of wine in their glass. When the wine finally reached Ted at the far end, Paul pushed his chair back and stood, quite deliberately.

Paul held his wine glass out, as if in a toast or maybe a religious offering and said, "*Baruch atah Adonai Eloheinu Melech Haolam, borei p'ri hagafen.*"

Everyone again said, "Amen." Then all of the Waldman children and grandchildren, as well as Greta, stood in unison. Susan and John quickly mimicked this.

Then Paul continued, "To our father, Theodore Waldman, the foundation of all of our lives, on Father's Day." He paused a second and added, "And to Greta, our mother, since she didn't get to gather her brood around her this year on Mother's Day."

There was a motley collection of "To Father" and "To Mother" said around the table and everyone drank the toast. Susan drank her wine and discovered the wine was strong, but extremely sweet, almost like drinking warm grape juice concentrate. It was unlike the red wine she had tasted before.

Then Ted Waldman stood up, while everyone else sat back down. He spread his arms out to indicate the whole family and said, "I have to say that no matter what else I may have accomplished in life, fathering my children with the love of my life, Greta Alon, has been my greatest success. I am so proud of all of you."

Everybody raised their glasses and drank another sip. Ted sat down and everybody rapidly went back to the food. By the way that everyone, even the little children, seemed to know what to do and say Susan realized that family gatherings, blessings, toasts and well-wishing in the family grouping was a common occurrence in the Waldman family. Susan's own upbringing, as an only child, seemed sorely lacking. Then, thinking of her own father and mother, Susan got depressed and put these thoughts out of her mind.

Susan listened in as family news, stories, rumors about friends and plans for the summer were discussed around the table. Nothing was said to Susan, even by Paul, and Susan knew so little about anyone that there was nothing she could contribute.

At one point, Betsy, at the far corner of the table shouted over the noise at the table, to Julie on the opposite corner, saying, "Julie, I understand you two have set a day for the big event. August?"

The conversation hushed a little at this question, and everyone heard Julie's answer, "Yes, second Sunday in August. And, I'll be switching to Boston University in September to be with John when he starts med school."

"Where is the wedding going to be?" Betsy asked back.

"We are working on that. I was going to talk to Mom about that today. It is going to be here though, in Connecticut." All of the adults had stopped talking to hear this.

"So," Ted boomed, "you have decided the religious thing?" Everyone else remained quiet.

John started to answer, but Julie laid her hand on his arm. Then, she took a deep breath and answered, "We have resolved to have a Jewish ceremony, like we had said. The Catholic ceremony is not even an option, since John's priest said we had to agree that any children would be baptized and raised in the Church to have a Catholic wedding. Which I could not agree to, obviously."

Ted gave a rude "humpf!" sound at this. Then he added, "And the Rabbi?"

"Rabbi Roth at Temple Israel said he would be happy to officiate. He said that under Jewish Law the children born to me would be deemed Jewish automatically, so they don't have the problem the Catholics do. All Rabbi Roth required is that I promise to keep a Jewish home, which I, of course, could. I explained what that would entail to John and he agreed."

Ted gave another guttural sound and continued his interrogation with, "And the children, raising them, what are your plans?"

Julie looked to John and answered, "John and I have decided we don't have a problem with the children having a taste of both of their parents' cultures. We plan on observing traditions of both families as best as we can, given my promise about the Jewish home. We still have to work out what exactly that is going to be."

Ted continued, still in an overly loud voice, "When are you going to decide that?"

"Dad, it is not like we are going to start popping out babies right away. I have a year left at B.U. and then medical school, hopefully. We have plenty of time to work out the details. Paul is thirty and doesn't have children yet. I have time... *We* have time to figure this out."

"Paul isn't married. I think you need to decide your plans for raising kids before you get to that point."

Susan could hear Julie's teeth clink as she set her jaw, "Well, Dad, we have really sort of made our plans. In this day and age, John and I don't think that it will be a big problem letting children enjoy both cultures and learn about both religions. It is not like they aren't exposed to lots of different cultures and religions anyway. It's not like Jews live in a ghetto anymore. And, it is not like a little Jewish kid doesn't have to deal with the whole Santa Claus thing already. We'll be just fine. And six to eight years from now when we are ready to have kids, we'll be sure to invite everyone over to celebrate our Hanukkah-flavored Christmas or

Christmas-flavored Hanukkah with your grandchildren. Whichever way you want it." Julie punctuated this with a bite of roast beef as though to mark her decision to end the discussion.

Ted apparently had nothing more to say. And neither did anyone else. The boisterous conversations that had gone on before had stopped with the exchange between Julie and her father. This issue was obviously a longstanding sore spot for the family, and it had obviously been discussed before. Silence now fell over the table.

Susan sat silently eating with the others, but she had an idea. She spoke to the Waldman family table for the first time, "I have a little story about children growing up Jewish and growing up Christian that you folks might like to hear."

Susan felt Paul's knee touch her leg, apparently warning her she was treading on dangerous ground. She ignored him and continued, "My father was a history professor, a Jew, teaching at a Lutheran college in the little Illinois city where I grew up. That little Christian college held a Winter Festival each December and the highlight of the Winter Festival was a Christmas play and pageant. It was a really big thing around there. They recruited children from the local schools to play the parts in the Christmas play and concert which they performed in a beautiful chapel, Ascension Chapel, there on the college campus. When I was like in fifth grade, my school was asked to provide the little choir of angels to stand on the side and sing a Hallelujah song for the Christmas pageant. I had to bring home a permission slip to participate in the Christmas play and my father, the Jewish professor, signed it without blinking. Since I was the tallest girl in my class, I got chosen by the Festival Director to be the lead angel, you know, they had each angel in line a little shorter than the next. So, the tallest girl got to be the lead angel.

"On the day of the Festival, the Advent Festival I think they called it, I was all decked out in my long white robe with a tin foil hallow above my head and sparkly glitter in my hair. My father took me and he was introducing me to the College's Lutheran pastor, who was a friend and co-worker of his at the college. We were under a covered archway in front of the church. While I was telling my father and the pastor about what my part in the play would be, up comes the principal of our school, Mrs. McGruder, who knew both my father and the pastor. She said something along the lines of how she was surprised to see me as an angel because she hadn't thought my father would approve of me being in a Christmas event, since I was Jewish. All that I heard was that the principal said I shouldn't be an angel because I was Jewish. I guess my eyes got 'so' round and I was obviously ready to cry.

"At that point, my father comes to my rescue and tells Mrs. McGruder this, 'You know, Mrs. McGruder, I have it on pretty good biblical authority, that at the time Little Baby Jesus was born every angel in heaven was Jewish. Being Jewish was God's natural order for angels in those days.' The Lutheran pastor then jumped in to assist my father by adding 'And, Mrs. McGruder, if you think about it, every single character in our whole Christmas play was Jewish, except the Three Wise Men and they were Persian. So our little Jewish angel, Susan, here is just perfect. Maybe she's better than all the Christian children we have today who are just pretending to be Jewish for our Christmas play.'" Mrs. McGruder went away and, of course, I immediately went and told all the other kids that the Pastor and my father had told me that every angel was really a Jew and how all of them were there pretending to be Jewish, which created quite a ruckus with the other kids' parents who came to the Christmas pageant and the pastor had to explain himself to quite a few of them."

There were a few chuckles from the Waldmans.

Susan continued, "So, the end of that story is that last September when my father died they had a memorial service at that College chapel with that same Lutheran pastor and a rabbi jointly officiating the service. The pastor told that story about my father and the Jewish angels as part of the eulogy, leaving the identity of Mrs. McGruder out of the story. Then the rabbi got up and said 'I think I will defer to the Pastor's opinion about the denomination of God's angels, but I think we can all agree that God's angels have one more Jewish visitor in heaven with the passing of … Professor Jeffrey Fisher." Susan's voice cracked on the last sentence and she felt warm tears almost come out.

There was a murmur of approval around the table for the story. Greta put her hand on Susan's. Julie caught Susan's eye, smiled and mouthed a silent 'thank you."

Then, little Gillian Waldman asked her father, across the table, in a voice everyone could hear, "Daddy, is that true? Are all angels Jewish?"

In the laughter and chatter around the table that followed Gillian's question, Susan could not hear what Ed Waldman told his daughter, but Susan was kind of proud that another little girl had partaken of the idea.

Susan's story did as she hoped. The conversations and clatter of dishes arose around the table again. Julie and Greta started talking about the wedding.

Susan leaned over to speak to Paul in a hushed voice. "While they are on the subjects of weddings, I have a favor to ask of you."

"A favor on the subject of weddings?" Paul whispered back skeptically, "But, whatever, name it?"

"My cousin is getting married two weeks from today. Big Jewish wedding bash out in the Southampton. And the bride has told me it would be best if I came with a date... ."

Paul thought for a moment, and then said, "Of course, I'd be happy to. Out in the Hamptons, huh? Long drive. Or train ride."

"Yeh, and Ariel said the dinner that night will last late. I already reserved a couple rooms to stay that night after the wedding dinner. Is that asking too much? Can you get off from the hospital?" Susan looked sheepish.

"They owe me some time off, I'm always filling in for other docs. And it's not asking too much at all. I was going to suggest staying over. I've been to wedding shindigs out in the Hamptons and getting back the same night can be brutal. Especially so if you party hearty."

"I really appreciate it. These are like my closest relatives now. The whole New York clan. And I really wanted to get to meet everyone in a better venue than my aunt's wake."

Paul started to whisper to Susan, "I rea... ." But, he was cut off by his mother speaking to Susan and him.

"You two sitting there with your heads together, whispering, look positively conspiratorial." Greta said.

Susan answered, "Just making sure I have an escort to my cousin's wedding two weeks from now."

Greta smiled, "And maybe he should make reservations with you for two months from now. Looks like he is going to need a wedding date for a wedding right here, at the house." Greta said excitedly.

Susan first looked to Julie who was smiling broadly, and then to Paul who held out his hand to Susan palm up as though passing on his mother's offer. Susan smiled.

"I'd be happy to return the favor." Susan realized she was going to have to study up on Jewish weddings really soon.

The family conversation renewed its fervor, with much of it centered on the wedding, Julie and John's move to Boston and how the move would put Julie nearer to Ed and Betsy. At one point the conversation turned to how Julie and John had met, as though it was not obvious for two pre-Med students at Dartmouth. John turned the 'meeting your spouse' question back on Greta.

"Greta, how did you and Ted meet?" John asked.

Although the Waldman children knew the story well, the whole family listened as Greta told John much the same story of her meeting Ted at the kibbutz in northern Israel that she had told Susan earlier in the kitchen with a little embellishment, but she added, "And Ted, would you believe that Susan here spent two summers in Israel at an archaeological dig just over the hill from the kibbutz in Nahariya where we met?"

Ted said, "Oh, really?"

But, Paul interjected, "Wait, how do you know all this about Susan? How long was I sleeping in the car?"

Greta wagged her finger at her son and said, "Ted, if I know more about your pretty landlady and soccer teammate than you do, it would seem to be your problem. Susan and I becoming best buds. In fact, we are considering co-writing a screenplay. You really need to work on your communications skills and try to keep up a bit better."

Susan and Greta laughed again. The others smiled, but did not laugh, as only Greta and Susan were in on the screenplay joke.

—

Paul turned the Mercedes onto the Merritt Parkway westbound onramp. He drove for a moment, flipped on the headlights in the dusk light, and then Paul looked over to Susan.

He asked, "So what do you think of the Waldman family?"

Susan waited a moment and answered, "As an only child and recently orphaned at that, I guess I would have to say I am jealous."

"Really?"

"Yeh, the blessings on the food and the wine and the whole meal were, like, choreographed out of a family togetherness handbook. And, the only discordant note was because of an obviously stressful religious conflict with an incoming spouse. But, Julie was pretty stalwart in defending herself. The whole family eventually accepted her position and celebrated her upcoming nuptial plans. Your family is marvelous. Nothing less."

"Wow. I would never have seen it as that." Paul said, changing lanes on the Parkway.

"'Oh, little things mean a lot, appreciate what you got, if you give all what you have, it's forever we'll last.'" Susan semi-sang.

"And she can do Boyz II Men to make her point."

"Yeh, I get positively lyrical when I am tired. It has been a long day. Long week. Longer month. Really long year." Susan yawned.

After a few moments, Susan looked over and asked Paul, "So, Paul, tell me about your friend, the lady pediatrician, that you went to NYU with."

—

Chapter Nineteen

Again, the iPhone woke Susan up. Since she had nothing scheduled for Monday morning, Susan had not set her iPhone alarm. But, it was sounding, not with an alarm, but a call. Susan pulled her head out from under the pillow to the bright light of mid-morning. She found the iPhone and answered, "H-h-hello?"

"From the sound of your voice, you slept in." Paul's voice sounded annoyingly chipper.

"Uh, yeh. What time is it?"

"Nine-ish," Paul answered quickly, so she did not have to look at the iPhone screen.

Susan was awake now, slid her legs out of bed, and sat on the edge.

"So, you have a good rest?" Paul asked.

"Yeh, I was bushed. You?'

"Well, as you saw yesterday. I am a pretty good sleeper."

"Yes, I saw. But, you went about twenty-six or seven hours on maybe three hours sleep. What's on your schedule today?" Susan asked.

"Mostly chores," Paul said. "I need to go down to the clinic and sign some things, and interview a potential employee. And I need to remember to pick up my good suit from the cleaners. I have a hot date tonight. I've got to remember to call this new gal, Susy, and tell her I need to pick her up just after six, instead of seven."

"Why?"

"Cuz I called this morning and had to take an early dinner reservation to get into this place I wanted to go. Nice restaurant, Uptown. Not sure why Monday night was a problem to get a reservation. But, whatever. "

"And what kind of clothes are you expecting this hot date to wear tonight?"

"Oh, maybe something fancy, it is a nice place, and I have a couple different ideas for after dinner. What she wears depends on whether Susy wants to impress on a first date."

"If I see this Susy chick around, I'll let her know." Susan said.

"Okay, and how about you? What's your schedule?"

"Oh, I have a huge long list of errands and chores. Yesterday was my first day back from Illinois, but instead of getting my act together, I wound up spending the day gallivanting across New England."

Paul chuckled, "Sounds like you need to work on time management."

"Yeh, it's on my chore list, somewhere down below 'find a fancy dress to wear uptown.'"

"Well, if you need help with your chore list, give me a call. I guess I owe you. See ya tonight."

"Bye." Susan poked the iPhone off. Fancy dress? Susan decided it was time to check out the depths of the designer dress repository in the second bedroom closet. Susan had some things of her own that would be passable to wear for tonight, but she wanted her appearance tonight to be unforgettable, so if Rachel's classic fashion warehouse did not have something awe-inspiring, and wearable, Susan might have to change her plans to watch the next video today and go shopping instead.

—

It was possible to have some serious mental reservations about wearing hand-me-downs from your dead aunt. It was not like Susan had any money shortage to buy her own stuff these days. But, when the dead aunt was a millionairess with good style sense, hand-me-downs were something to be considered. Susan had not really made up her mind on this, but things like the unworn Prada pumps she had found were likely to sway her decision. Susan had not really gone through the main walk-in closet in detail yet, so she started her search for something to impress Paul there.

Clicking the light on in the closet, Susan recognized that sorting out what should be kept and thrown from this massive assortment would be a multi-day affair. But, today, her sole focus was to see if there was anything appropriate and eye-popping for her 'Uptown' dress for Paul.

Dresses and coordinated outfits were hung at the far left of the closet. As Susan had noticed before, the dresses farthest left seemed to be most often worn and often in a size 10, the things that seemed less frequently worn were more often than not 8's. Rachel had apparently gained some weight in recent years. Susan went through the dress rack as though she were shopping for a bargain in the store. She saw many things that probably would be donated, the larger 'business suit' type things that might work at age sixty but not at age twenty. In the less used size 8 dresses, there were many very nice dresses which Susan could actually see herself wearing, for the right occasion. There were some very sharp looking items, some still with tags. But, Susan saw nothing with the knock his socks off quality she was hunting today. From what Susan had seen in her quick search of the second bedroom closet, that closet held the special occasion dresses and haute couture items, whereas this main closet had more of the everyday and business clothes. Susan switched off the closet light and headed to the other bedroom.

Susan opened the closet door in the second bedroom and pulled the chain coming down for the ceiling light. The closet was perhaps eight by eight feet and had racks on the three interior walls. Her first brief view of this closet on her trip through with Carlos had not done justice to this collection. The red Balenciaga still attracted attention by its color and central location, but the dated red long formal was not what Susan needed today. On either side of the Balenciaga were dozens of dresses, of every color and style.

As Susan stood looking around, she was surprised by an electronic clicking behind her and a follow-on whirr of machinery. She turned and found the click came from a control panel on the wall inside the closet door showing temperature and humidity readouts, settings and controls. The machinery sound was a large white, grated box on the floor in the corner, now spewing cool, dry air on Susan's legs. Rachel had this closet outfitted with a high-tech climate control system to protect the expensive clothes. Susan's entrance had triggered the closet to try and compensate for the humid, mid-June air Susan had brought in with her. Susan was impressed.

On the far right side of the closet were several fur coats and various wraps and coats, to go with the dresses. On the floor and on the shelf above the dresses were many boxes, some with descriptions of contents or numbers on the outside. Susan decided the only thing to do was go through each dress. She started on the left, above the humidity control machine.

Some items were formal, full-length gowns like the Balenciaga. The more elaborate, formal gowns seemed to be the oldest. Some were definitely dated by their style or color. There were a few Disco Era haute couture dresses that were almost laughable in their gaudiness and bold colors. Nevertheless, sprinkled amongst these were dozens of more recent gowns, dresses, and even pantsuits that could, for all Susan could see, be from recent year designer collections. There were also some older dresses whose classic style defied the years. Some dresses were in dry cleaning bags, some were still in their store label plastic bags and many were just hanging, often still with their tags.

As Susan went through the closet's contents, when she found a likely candidate, she took it out to lay it on the queen size bed in the bedroom. As she put six, seven and then eight elegant evening dresses on the bed, it was clear that Susan did not have to go to a store to find something to impress Paul.

When she finished her run through the closet, Susan went out and looked at her choices on the bed. The window light was fairly bright, but Susan turned on the bedroom lights to make her choice.

One of her choices was an absolutely stunning, blue Jean Paul Gaultier outfit in a dry cleaning bag with a mixture of satin color streams in its skirt area and decorative embroidery on the revealing bodice. It was indeed stunning, but clearly a bit over the top for anything other than a dress ball or private party, even though you could not call it a gown. Susan hung Jean Paul's creation back in the closet. Her other seven choices covered the color spectrum, all medium to short lengths. She went back and forth amongst the remaining choices. Any of these would do for tonight.

At last, Susan picked up a golden Versace. It was knee length and its cloth was a shimmering mix of both dark and light gold strands. It did not really have any sequins or the like, but the lighter gold strands shimmered like they were sequins. Susan swung the closet door fully open and held the dress in front of her, looking into the full length mirror on the inside of the closet door. The shimmering gold Versace was the winner of the 'Uptown' dress contest. Susan discovered she had no aversion to hand-me-downs of this caliber.

She laid the dress back on the bed and went to hang the losing dresses back up. She came out and inspected the Versace closer. It was one of the dresses that still had tags. The price was expensive enough that Susan suspected it was fairly recent. She really did not have a sense for fashion trends, except in a general sense. But, this dress somewhat transcended trends with its simple, sleek, glamorous look. Susan realized its body-hugging style would be perfect for her figure and the body-hugging was accentuated by the shimmering cloth. The larger tag, under the arm, had a Post-It note attached to it that read "Shoes in Box 14." Susan went back into the closet.

Box 14 was a large white box on the floor. Inside were several loose pairs of shoes and a couple shoe boxes inside the larger box. She saw the black and gold Versace box. She took it out to the bed, pulling the light chain as she left the closet.

The Versace pumps were, indeed, a perfect match for the golden dress. The variegated sheen and gold colors of the shoes was in perfect synch with the dress. Unfortunately, the size 9½ pumps were a full three-inch heel. Susan had seen on the trip to Connecticut that with medium heels she was exactly Paul's height. With full height heels she would be a bit above his height.

Too bad! This was clearly the correct Uptown dress, and these shoes were what needed to be worn with it. Paul would have to deal with a tall woman at his side.

Susan flipped off the light and then took the dress and shoes to her bedroom. As she thought about the golden dress and what accessories to wear with it, she had a thought. She went into the main walk-in closet and opened up the shoe rack doors to reveal the compartment behind it. She smiled to herself, her memory was correct. There, hanging from one of the hooks, was an antique styled gold mesh handbag. The clasp was a cluster of rhinestones. It was perfect for tonight.

—

With the possible trip to get a dress out of the way, Susan had been able to sit down to view another of Rachel's videos before lunch.

The video started with the same setting in the dining room, but Rachel's look and demeanor had changed. She still wore the wig, but now her face was gaunt and her voice was not as strong. She looked much closer to the final video in the hospital room. Rachel wore a red terry cloth bathrobe, without any make-up.

"Susy, I hope you are getting along well with all I have left for you to do. Things have changed since I did the last video. My doctors have told me the chemo is not working and they are concerned it is just making things worse by weakening my body more than it is fighting the cancer. I was told that is always a possibility. So, we have discontinued the chemo and are hoping I can recover some of my strength to hold out as long as possible. It seems I may not make the six to eight months they predicted back in March. It is early May now. I had hoped to hang on long enough to perhaps change my mind and invite you here for the summer, so I could speak to you in person. That may not be possible."

Rachel took a drink from a water glass on the table. "It has been a couple weeks since I did that last video. I have not been very strong, and I even had a little stay in the hospital, for tests. The tests disclosed nothing good.

"I believe I told you in the last video that I would be talking in this next disk about my life in the '80's and about the other apartment across the lobby that was the scene for some of my shenanigans back then. My roller coaster years, I think I called them. I am going to have to apologize for not doing all that right now. I really don't think I have the strength to do the emotions that go with some of those life stories. But, those years are the exciting times that I first did my video journals about when I thought my life was worthy of retelling to the public. If you want to know the details of my flirtation with Broadway celebrities, my relationship with a wonderful and beautiful, but tragic, man who eventually succumbed to AIDS, in the early days of that contagion... and my own near miss in not knowing how to control my own life and the pressures and addictions life can deal out, then you can go through the journals of all that in the boxes over in the corner here, and my diaries. It was a totally different life than what I lived with my dear Isaac, and a different life from what I have lived in recent years. I have been fortunate enough to have lived several intermingled lives, I guess.

"For this unfortunately short video, I want to just do the practical things. I hope I will recover my strength enough to follow this up with another video. We'll see on that. For now I just want to tell you that I have left you a chore across the hall. You are the perfect person for me to leave this chore to. You see, throughout my life I have made a point of using my Isaac's money to support my friends in the art world and to indulge my own love of art. Were I a better organized person, I would have kept better track of things, cataloged it all and perhaps arranged for my art collection to be of some greater value to the world. But, as it is, I leave you with a mishmash of collected works in two or three rooms across the hall. Actually, I guess it is four rooms. There are artists with well-known names and not so well known. Sometimes I supported my friends by buying up their collections out of pity. Sometimes out of reverence for unrecognized talent. On occasion, I simply used my wealth to lavish on myself some fairly well known works of art. I have told you about my favorites that I have hung in my own apartment, but you should know there are similar or even more important works to be found in my in inelegant art storehouse that I leave to you. I always told myself I would see to it that this collection was catalogued, but alas, procrastination won out. I am out of time. I think if you ask the attorneys, they can direct you as to how can either enjoy this art in your own collection or see to it that others partake of this wonderful art. I suspect you will do the later.

"I really do not have a rhyme nor reason to how things are stored over there. You will find a bit of everything in those nooks and crannies. When I took a walk through that apartment in March in preparation of doing these videos for you, I realized how much work I had left undone.

"What I do have, to help in that process a bit, is one of the boxes over by the windows here in the dining room that contains everything I have been able to gather together on the acquisition, source and identity of the art I have collected. What I have not done is remove the documentation that is attached to many of the artworks across the hall. It did not make much sense to remove a receipt or provenance document attached to a painting and get it mixed up in this box here. And, you are going to have to use your expertise in art to figure some of this out. But, I think you will have fun, err, I hope that.

"Susy, go through my hoard with care, there are some gems over there. There are also some art tools that I never had the skills to make good account of. Perhaps you have an interest. If not, please see to it that they get to someone or somewhere where they will be of use.

"So, as I said, I will try to give you another, more personal video giving a better accounting of those years, if my health allows. For now, let me just say that I am entrusting the joy of my life to your care and guidance. Please be a better art historian and connoisseur than I was. Clean up my mess and uncover the diamonds in my rough."

Rachel took a deep breath, "Until next time… No, I like until we meet again better. More hopeful."

Rachel gave a weak smile and wearily reached to turn the video recording off.

—

"I can't get over how great you look tonight. You're beautiful and that dress… Well…."

Susan laughed lightly, "Yes, Paul. I understand, you like."

"I guess I've already said that a couple times, huh?"

"Don't stop though. It was my intention to impress. I just had no idea how successful I would be."

The taxi pulled up to the curb, and Paul paid the cabbie over the back seat. Paul got out reaching back to take Susan's hand and help her from the cab.

As Paul closed the door behind her, Susan looked around them and saw where they were. "We're going to Rothmann's?" she asked.

"Yes, my favorite restaurant. I thought you could satiate your carnivore tendencies here. Why, something wrong?" Paul took Susan hand and walked toward the door.

"No, nothing wrong." Susan said, amazed that in a city with hundreds of restaurants, two of her first three trips out had wound up at the same restaurant. First with Devorah and now Paul. However, she did not want to mention that to Paul. She would let him think his choice of restaurant was special.

There were several couples waiting in the restaurant lobby. At the maître d's podium Paul announced, "Waldman, we have reservations."

The girl with the menus said, "Yes, I see, Waldman, your table is… ."

"Miss Fisher! It's nice to see you again." A man in a black waistcoat with a name tag declaring him to be the manager interrupted and came over to take Susan's hand. "My, you look stunning tonight. Versace, no?"

Susan nodded.

The manager continued, "You know, I passed your message on to the people who have contact with the Rothmann's. Haven't heard back from them yet. And this is?"

The manager turned to Paul. Susan announced, "Paul Waldman."

The manager took Paul's hand and said, "Paul Waldman. You've been in before, right?"

"Yes, many times." Paul looked over at Susan, who did not meet his gaze.

The manager turned to the girl with the menus, "And where do we have Miss Fisher and this gentleman tonight?"

The girl looked at her clipboard, "Uh, F-5."

The manager shook his head, "No, that will never do. We cannot have a member of the Rothmann family sitting in the back corner. We still have the special reserved spot at A-2 open. Put them there."

As the girl moved to show them the way, the manager said, smiling broadly, "I hope you enjoy your dinner, Miss Fisher, let me know if there is anything you need."

The girl led them down the restaurant's main aisle which was flanked by walnut and brass barriers, then turned around the barrier and led them back out to the very front of the restaurant to a group of three tables, slightly elevated above the main floor and in full view of the windows and main door. One of the tables was occupied by four elegantly dressed people who Susan thought she recognized. Celebrities? Another A-list table was empty even though other customers were still waiting at the front door.

The hostess placed their menus down and pulled the chair out for Susan. Paul and Susan took their seats.

Folding her napkin on her lap, Susan looked at Paul and smiled nervously. "I guess you'd like an explanation?"

Paul answered a bit sarcastically, "No, why should I need an explanation. I try to impress a woman who is new to New York by taking her to my favorite restaurant that I have been coming to for years and… when we get there, not only has she been there before and didn't let on, but the manager knows her on a first name basis, far better than he knows me and acknowledges my 'out of town' lady as a member of the family that owns the restaurant. No explanation needed."

"That isn't quite right, about the family," Susan said softly. "The Rothmanns don't own the restaurant any more. They sold it to Burt Bacharach back in the '80's. He sold it to a company that owns it now. But, when my attorney and I came here week ago Friday, I mentioned that my grandparents were named Rothmann, and Gene, that's the manager, explained all of this, took my email and promised to ask someone if my Grandpa was related to the Rothmanns who founded the restaurant. Really, the only two sit down restaurants, other than the hotel, that I have been to in New York is this one and that place you took me in the village." Susan realized after she said that that she had forgotten the lunch with Devorah.

Paul smiled at Susan, "Okay, I was really just… ." He was interrupted by heavy-set women in a shiny coral colored gown who walked up to the table.

"Susan," the woman said.

Susan looked up and said in surprise, "Mrs. Mueller?"

Susan stood up. Betty Mueller reached to take her hand. Paul stood to politely acknowledge the older woman's presence. Susan quickly did introductions, "Mrs. Mueller, may I present Doctor Paul Waldman, Paul, this is Mrs. uhh, Betty Mueller, a friend of my Aunt Rachel."

Susan was amazed she had remembered the woman's first name.

"Doctor Waldman." Mrs. Mueller acknowledged Paul without a handshake and turned back to Susan.

"Susan, I'm sorry to barge in on you like this, but I can explain." Betty Mueller took a deep breath and pressed her lips together. "My husband and I were here to have an early dinner before going to the *Les Miserables* concert performance tonight at the Radio City Music Hall. You are probably familiar with it. It is an anniversary performance, they have various cast members from the stage performances over the years and the movie. They have a week of concerts, just music, no acting or costumes. It is an anniversary celebration of the whole show. Anyway, we were planning on going, but something personal came up, and we need to cancel. However, show time is in a little over an hour. We were just getting ready to call people we know to try to get someone to take our tickets. Then, I saw you walk by and wondered if you might be interested. They are great tickets, orchestra seating. It has been sold out for weeks, quite an event. I realize you may have your own plans though. If you are interested…."

Susan looked to Paul. Paul smiled, "Well, that is fortuitous. One of the options I was going to present to Susan for tonight was trying to get tickets to the *Les Mis* concert. I have a call in to a ticket brokering service, also known as scalpers, to try and find tickets for us."

"Well, cancel that, here you are." Betty Mueller handed a small white envelope to Susan.

"We can't just take them, let us… ." Paul started to protest.

"Sir, no, I am very happy that my dear friend's niece will be able to use them. I hope you enjoy. I really have to be going now." Betty Mueller took Susan's hand again. "And Susan, I still want to talk to you about the other matter. Doctor Waldman, nice to meet you."

And with that, Mrs. Mueller turned abruptly and left, apparently in a hurry.

Susan and Paul sat back down and looked at each other.

Paul raised his eyebrows, "I really wish I could have paid her back for those tickets. The scalpers were quoting big bucks for even mezzanine seats, those orchestra seats are really costly."

Susan shook her head, "No, she would have been insulted if you had tried any harder than you did. My understanding is that the Muellers are among the richest of the rich. The cost was probably not their concern."

As Susan was saying this, she saw Mrs. Mueller and an older bald-headed man in a formal suit and bow tie walking slowly toward the front door of the restaurant. The man, obviously Betty's husband, was walking slowly, slightly stooped over, and was using the walnut and brass partition to keep his balance. Mrs. Mueller had her arm around the man's back, as if to assist him in walking. Mrs. Mueller stared straight ahead, avoiding looking over toward where Susan and Paul sat near the entrance.

Susan whispered to Paul, "Paul, without moving your head around, look over to the entrance."

Paul followed directions and said, "He is in pain. Maybe I should check on him."

Susan quickly answered, "No. Very physician-like of you, but no. You need to leave him his dignity. Let him escape from here and go get help. The Muellers are not the type who want to show any vulnerability amongst their peers, or especially the bourgeoisie."

"Maybe so. You know her through your aunt?" Paul looked at Susan.

"I met her at the Emanu-El synagogue. That's where my aunt went."

Susan opened the little envelope and looked at the tickets. "Oohh, you are right about the price. Is Radio City far from here?" She handed the tickets to Paul.

"No, not at all. This is 54th, it's on 51st and one block over. That is one reason why I chose to come here, in case I got the call on tickets. That may also explain why this place was busy on a Monday. Many shows are dark on Mondays. Which is why I was not certain where we would go tonight after this."

The waitress came and took their food and drink orders.

After the waitress left, Paul said to Susan, "So, you don't keep kosher, I had thought you did."

Susan sat blinking a couple times at Paul. She waited moment before speaking, "Well, no, I don't 'keep kosher.' I was pretty clear in our conversation on the way back from Connecticut that I was raised in a pretty secular environment, not religious at all. Why did you assume I was religious enough to keep kosher? And… what did I do to betray my dastardly secret? I didn't order pork, or dairy with my steak. And I ordered fries, no sour cream or butter on a baked potato."

Paul shrugged, "Why did I assume? At our first lunch you refused to eat the cheesecake with the pastrami, carefully choosing the fruit salad. And then you said you were going to wait until supper to eat the cheesecake. That seemed to me like a girl who was trying to keep kosher, not mix her *fleish* and her *milch*, and even wait the right time to keep from mixing them in her tummy. And lots of Jews who aren't particularly religious try to stick to kosher. My parents attend a Reform temple which doesn't dictate kosher, but my folks have always kept Kosher at home, Mom brought it with her from Israel. I'm not particularly religious, but I try to keep kosher, but from a standpoint of a modern healthy lifestyle, as well as keeping with tradition. I was raised kosher, and I'm a physician who sees how crappy Americans eat these days."

Susan smiled at Paul when he mentioned the cheesecake. "Paul, I didn't eat your cheesecake because I was already burping from the champagne, and the cheesecake and the bubbles would have done me in with the burps. And I kept your cheesecake for supper because my apartment was empty. I really didn't have anything else there to eat for supper, except my yogurt and pretzels. But, I still need to hear what I did tonight to display my non-kosherness."

"You ordered shrimp cocktail for your appetizer."

"Oh, really? Shrimp is *verboten* too? How so?" Susan raised her eyebrows as she spoke.

"Fish that don't have both scales and fins are not kosher. That includes shrimp, clams, oysters, scallops...."

"Wow, I really don't get these rules. I am going to have to study up if I am not going to insult you or my aunt and uncle."

Paul shook his head, "It is not a matter of insult. Keeping kosher is a personal choice, unless you're orthodox or really strict conservative, where it is an immitigable rule of living a worthy life. You respect the rules when you are in someone's home. And if you know a guest keeps kosher, you try to accommodate them with what you serve. Most Jews who try to keep kosher realize they can only really do so at home. Rothmann's here and most other restaurants aren't kosher, so you would lead a really restrictive life if you didn't eat at non-kosher places, but you can still try to order things that fit the kosher tradition."

"Any other things, like shrimp, I need to worry about?" Susan asked.

"There are dozens of *kashrut* rules. I don't even try to keep all of them. Most Jews these days don't. Maybe we can discuss this some other time. A nice, non-kosher restaurant just before dinner is not a good place to go over *kashrut*. Some of the gory details aren't very appetizing."

"Understand, what would you like to talk about?"

The waitress came before Paul could answer, bringing his deep-fried onion flower and Susan's shrimp cocktail.

After he ate his first onion piece, Paul said to Susan, "So, you met Mrs. Mueller at Temple Emanu-El. How'd that come about?"

Susan chewed a spicy shrimp. After swallowing it with a sip of water, she said, "The rabbi there called my attorney right after the funeral and said they were going to mention Aunt Rachel at the service Friday before last. They wanted me to come. We went and met Mrs. Mueller at the uhh…, *Oneg* thingy. You know, the refreshments."

Paul laughed, "Yes, the *Oneg* Thingy. I'm quite familiar with that Jewish tradition. And this attorney of yours, the one who brought you to Rothmann's and to the Temple. What is he like?"

Susan looked up from her shrimp at Paul, "Oh *him*, my attorney, huh? My attorney is a snappy dresser, about five feet seven, maybe 34-24-34, wears 'his' dark chestnut hair in a shoulder length bob cut. 'He' confided in me the pressures 'he' feels between making law firm partner, and 'his' yearning to be a mother."

"Ah, I see, I did a little stereotyping there, right?"

"A little."

The waitress arrived with their steaks.

—

Paul took Susan's hand as they exited the Radio City Music Hall under the famous marquee. There was already a long line of people waiting for the taxi queue on that block.

Paul pulled Susan to the left, "Let's go down a block. We don't have to wait in line here to get a cab."

As they walked south on Avenue of the Americas, Paul asked Susan, "So, who is your favorite character in *Les Miserables*?"

Susan shook her head, "It is not even a close call, Éponine, definitely."

"Hmm, why?"

Susan answered, "Éponine, to me, is the character that displays the greatest love of any character. Well, I guess I need to qualify that as romantic love, to differentiate from the great spiritual love of Jean Valjean or the Bishop. Éponine discovers and declares that she loves Marius totally, unselfishly and unrequitedly. Cosette and Marius are supposedly the great love story, but their love, that is, falling head over heels for someone you see as a pretty face in the crowd, is not love, its lust." Susan waited as they crossed the crosswalk on the side street and continued. "Marius' supposed love of Cosette doesn't even stand strong enough to get him to think of her first instead of going off with his buddies to risk his life on the barricade. And he isn't really sure of her love, he sings about whether she will even care if he dies. On the other hand Éponine unselfishly helps Marius find her competition, Cosette, for his happiness, and against her own interest. Éponine risks danger by thwarting her father and his gang to protect the girl who Marius loves. She risks her life to stand shoulder to shoulder with Marius under fire on the barricades, while Cosette is preparing to run off to England. And, in the end Éponine's true love of Marius is only consummated by her death in his arms during the battle. Éponine is the true romantic heroine of Les Miserables, Cosette is just an immature girl who shares Marius' infatuation, obeys her Papá's commands to leave Paris, even though that will mean never seeing Marius again. Cosette is just a pretty ingénue; Éponine is a tragic romantic heroine we can admire."

"Wow, no equivocation from Susan on that." Paul said, waving to a cab heading north on the Avenue.

"And you? Your favorite *Les Mis* character?" Susan asked.

Paul indicated she needed to wait as they climbed into the cab and Paul gave the cabby directions home.

As they settled in the back seat of the taxi, Paul continued, "That's tough. I think I agree with you about Éponine, but to give a different answer, I guess I would have to avoid the canned answers of Valjean or Fantine to say my favorite character is the Bishop. Every good, noble, brave and romantic act or event in the whole story is totally derivative of the Bishop's loving forgiveness of Valjean that set the whole story in motion. The Bishop forgave the supposedly worthless street person and criminal who had betrayed his trust, and the Bishop taught Valjean the gift of love that sustained him throughout the years. It is the Bishop's gift of knowing love to Valjean that Javert cannot understand and which causes him to doubt the purpose of his own life. It is the Bishop's gift of love that provided every blessing the entire cast discovered they had in the end."

"You're right, of course." Susan said. "Victor Hugo's whole purpose in the story was to exemplify the greatness of the human soul. Did you know that even though Hugo's book was fiction, he had real people that he was writing about for every principle character. There was a real Bishop of Digne and Hugo, himself, had occasion to rescue a prostitute on the streets. Even, Valjean was a real person, but by a different name, he was a wealthy, pardoned ex-con and philanthropist who actually saved one of his factory workers from a cart accident, just like Valjean. And that real 'Valjean' guy helped Hugo with his notes on the story."

"You seem to know a lot about *Les Mis*," Paul said.

"It was a favorite book of my mother, the English teacher. She spoke French, by the way. But, I didn't care too much for the book, too lengthy with unnecessary stuff attached at odd places. And, last year I took a class on French history and the professor used Hugo's novel as his framework to talk about France between Napolean and the Second Republic. And that professor used a lesson plan that was actually prepared by my father. The French History class had always been my father's before this last year, and I had heard him talk about it at home. He and my mother had a pretty good dialog about it on a couple occasions."

Paul asked, "Did you ever see the stage musical?"

"Nope, just read the book and saw the movie. I loved it, the movie that is, one of my all-time favorites. I bought the DVD, the one with all the bonus stuff. You see the stage version?"

"Yes, Dad got tickets for the whole family, on Broadway. I was like fifteen at the time. But, I got a lot more out of it when the movie came out. I actually felt the tears ready to come out toward the end. I love that triumphal march, 'Do you hear the people sing?'"

Susan reached up with her hand and mimed marking two tally marks in the air.

"What was that for?" Paul asked.

"I was marking your passing marks on two areas of your grade sheet," Susan said matter-of-factly.

"I'm getting graded?"

Susan acted like she could not believe Paul had said that, "Of course, many men don't realize they are constantly being graded by the women in their lives. Mother, sister, girlfriend, wife, the women always keep close score on how their menfolk are doing. You silly men usually just give women a pass/fail score, except for your silly ten point scale for women's looks. And men don't realize that how you handle your ten point scale gets graded by us, too. We realize you may not consider your woman a Perfect 10, but you'd better make her feel like you do. And if a woman thinks a man is scoring another woman while in her presence, he gets a deduction for that. We women keep careful grades, on everything."

"So, with this grading, do we men ever graduate?" Paul asked.

Susan shook her head, "Ehh, not really. Oh, you might think you do when you finally get the woman to agree to marry you, but really marriage is just like graduate school, the woman still grades the man, but the grading scale is harder."

"So, what were my *two* checkmarks for?"

"The first one was for having a good soul and tears for a great heart-tug movie. The second was for the honesty and non-macho-ness of admitting to the tears when you didn't have to." After a moment of silence, Susan asked, "So who did you take to see *Les Miserables*, the movie?"

Paul paused and answered, "I don't really remember."

Susan marked another check mark in the air.

"And that was for…?" Paul asked.

"Being smart enough to not talk about a previous date."

There was another pause in the conversation, after which Paul said, "By the way, you are definitely a 10."

Susan mimed two more checkmarks in the air.

"Again… I got *two* marks for that?"

Susan nodded, "Yes, one for what I think was a sincere '10' score and one more for being a quick learner."

"I think I am understanding the system a bit better," Paul said as he shifted in his seat and ended up slightly closer to Susan.

"This music concert was nice, but I'd like to watch the movie again. Maybe we could watch the DVD together, sometime." Susan suggested.

"Good idea. My place or yours?" Paul asked.

"Yours, so I can see where you live," Susan answered.

"I've never really got to see your place, except the front hall." Paul shifted in his seat again and looked outside. "We're home."

"Well, at the risk of you assuming a lascivious meaning to my offer, I wouldn't mind you coming up now. The cleaning crew fixed it all up, and I'm pretty proud of the place now. I'd like to show it off. Wanna come up?"

Paul paused for a moment, "You know, I really ought to have a snappy comeback to the way you couched your offer, but I think I'll just say 'Yes.'"

Paul paid for the taxi. He opened the outside lobby door. Susan opened the door back to her elevator. They did not speak as the elevator went up.

In the sixth floor lobby, Susan said, "I've been thinking of having the regular elevators turned back on up here. It was a pain in the butt getting the cleaning crew, and carpet and drapery guys up here, having to go down to the lobby to get them. My aunt apparently liked the privacy, but I find it unhandy."

"I can see that."

Susan pushed the alarm code for her apartment. Paul politely looked away as she did.

The chandelier went on automatically as they entered the foyer.

Susan walked toward the dining room, Paul followed. As she walked, Susan put her hands out wide, "Well, here it is, home sweet home." Susan flipped the dining room light on and put her gold mesh purse on the table.

"My dining room, which I have doubling as my computer work center and admin office right now." She walked toward the sitting room door.

"This place is huge… and beautiful," Paul said.

"And the sitting room, for want of a better, more modern name for it." Susan said as she turned the lights on for a moment and then off. She poked her head around the corner of the sitting room door to check on phone messages. There were none. Susan would have to think about getting rid of Rachel's old land line.

Susan headed out across the foyer with Paul following and stopped to think. "How should we go about this? Let's go the back way around. Save the best for last."

Susan flipped the light switches in the foyer that turned on the light in the hallways and headed to the kitchen door. Her sidestep to the light switch caused Paul to head for the hallway, but Susan motioned for him to follow her into the kitchen door.

In the kitchen the lights turned on by themselves. "My kitchen," Susan said as she walked into the middle of the kitchen.

Paul turned around, looking around him, "Wow. The girl who eats shrimp cocktail and claims to not understand kosher rules has herself what appears to be a world class kosher kitchen. Impressive. Look at that grill, you could use this to run a restaurant."

"Yeh. What can I say?" Susan headed for a door in the rear of the kitchen. She pointed to another door. "That's the pantry and this here, is… the maid's quarters."

As they walked through the little bedroom, Paul said, "Your maid seems to be off tonight."

Susan smiled and said, "One of my recently updated life's goals is to achieve a lifestyle which justifies the maid's quarters being occupied."

Susan exited into the back hallway and crossed over to the family room. She hunted around with her hand for the light, "The family room."

Paul followed her in and looked around, and then almost ran forward to look at the poster of the Los Angeles Dodger baseball player. He put his hands on each side of the poster and leaned forward so his nose almost touched the glass.

"That's an original signature!" Paul announced. "You have a signed Sandy Koufax poster!"

"Yeh, I guess. Who is Sandy Koufax? I mean, I know he is a baseball player."

Paul scoffed at Susan, "Not just a baseball player, but probably the greatest Jewish athlete to ever live. Well, maybe one of the top two." Paul wiggled his hand as if judging between equals.

"Who is the other one?" Susan asked.

"Well, obviously Mark Spitz. As a Jewish doctor who was on a swim team, I guess I should side with Spitz, but Koufax is really the King."

"I take it Spitz was a swimming Jewish doctor." Susan guessed.

"Oh, my God, you are such a babe sometimes, Susan Fisher."

"No need to be insulting."

"Not meant as an insult, I just have a lot to teach you."

"Yes, you can be my guru of Jewish sports trivia."

Paul decided to change the subject and patted the corner of the TV set below Sandy Koufax, "Don't take this comment wrong, too, but you seem to have a state-of-the-art 1970s-era console TV and stereo. I bet it has a turntable in it. Huh?"

Susan nodded, "Yes, museum quality. Aunt Rachel lived here as a widow for, like, three decades, nobody to use the family room, I guess. The wide screen plasma TV and home theatre are in the master bedroom. If we watch the *Les Miserables* DVD here it will have to be in bed."

"Nothing lascivious about that offer. Not at all." Paul raised an eyebrow.

Susan blushed, motioned for Paul to follow her and continued down the hall. She showed Paul the back rooms from their doorways. She entered the little corner bedroom with the stained glass window. "When I was a little girl, my mother and I came here for a visit." After leaving the lights on for a few seconds, Susan turned the lights off and added, "About the only thing I can remember is lying in this bed watching the city lights reflect in the stained glass. It is a good childhood memory."

Paul nodded as they watched the outside reflections in the glass for a moment.

In the hall, as Susan passed the hall bathroom, she announced it, and Paul replied, "Would you mind if I made a pit stop? Long concert."

"Of course not, I'll wait in here." Susan pointed to the big guest bedroom.

In the bedroom, Susan quickly closed the closet door that she had left open when she had chosen her dress; no reason to advertise her high fashion stash. The humidity machine sounded like it was working full blast because of the open door. Susan heard the toilet flush from across the hall.

Paul came in and Susan simply announced, "Guest bedroom."

"I say again, this place is huge." Paul said.

Susan just raised her eyebrows and nodded.

Instead of going into the master bedroom, Susan turned the hall corner and reached in to turn on the study's light switch. She said to Paul over her shoulder, "After seeing the man-cave your father has in Connecticut, my guess is that you'll appreciate this."

Paul followed Susan into the study. As he walked in, Paul gave an appreciative "Ahh."

Paul walked across the room toward the desk, looked around at the walls full of books and up toward the mural on the ceiling, and he sat in the big desk chair. "This was your uncle's?"

Susan nodded, "My uncle Isaac Metzger. But, he last sat in that chair, what, thirty-something years ago. Aunt Rachel kept it just like he left it."

Paul shook his head up and down. "Okay, that's it. I am hereby giving notice on the lease to the second floor place. I'm moving out of my whole apartment and into this room. What kind of rent can you give me?"

Susan smiled and said, "And, like you said, I should have a snappy comeback to that line, but instead I will just say 'next.'"

Susan waited by the light switch as Paul got up, inspected a brandy bottle on the liquor cabinet table and slowly looked around as he followed her out.

In the living room, Susan turned on the light, and Paul looked around. He indicated the portraits on the opposite ends of the room, "That's... ."

"My uncle and aunt, Isaac and Rachel Metzger, circa 1976, I'm guessing."

Paul walked over and stood looking at Rachel's portrait. "You know, you are really her clone. A beautiful clone."

Susan huffed and said, "Thank you and congratulations, you have now joined every person I have met in New York who knew Rachel in declaring that. It's nice, I guess, to have that connection with her."

"You could have done a lot worse in the family genes department. They make a very regal couple. What's next?"

Susan turned to the door and waited for him to go out, before turning off the living room light. He was waiting in the hall by the door they had passed by on the way to the study.

"And this?" he asked.

"The only thing left." Susan went in and turned on the light.

"Ah, your home theater room," Paul announced as he came in.

Susan smiled.

"You know, there are airplane hangars smaller than this bedroom," Paul said.

"Yeh, the walk-in closet over there," she pointed, "is bigger than living and dining rooms together in my folks' house in Moline. Isaac and Rachel didn't do things small."

Paul walked to the corner and peeked in the bathroom, "Nice bath."

Paul walked over and stood next to Susan, "This is, indeed, awesome, I can see why you wanted to show it off." They stood in silence for a moment, and then he added, "What did you have in mind next?"

Susan looked into Paul's eyes and said, "Well, as the hostess, I guess it is my job to come up with entertainment." She paused, then reached out to hold on to his tie as though she were inspecting it, saying, "Would you be interested in finding another bottle of Bollinger and watching that DVD? Or… we could skip the DVD."

—

Chapter Twenty

Susan felt Paul move in the bed as she awoke, his back was to her. The morning light was coming in the windows, Susan guessed it was somewhere after seven o'clock.

Paul turned to her and said, "I need to get ready. I have more interviews at the clinic, and I have to be at the hospital by noon today. You have somewhere to go, too, right? We got pretty hot and sweaty last night. Can I use your shower?"

"Of course," Susan ran her finger down Paul's body from Adam's apple to navel, and then patted him on the chest as if giving him leave to go.

Paul rolled over closer to Susan and gave her a long kiss. Susan opened her eyes after the kiss, stretched her hand up and marked another checkmark in the air. They both smiled.

Paul collected his clothes from the floor and the corner of the bed. He trotted into the bathroom. Susan watched his naked jaunt, unembarrassed. Susan sat on the edge of the bed. Looking at the floor by the nightstand, Susan saw Paul had missed the trashcan and with fingertips she gingerly put the used condom into the trash can.

Susan realized all of the towels in the bath were used, so she quickly ran down the back hall to the linen closet and came back with two fluffy black towels. She felt a bit naughty running around the apartment without clothes. Naughty was not quite the right word, maybe spritely was closer.

Back in the bathroom, Paul had the shower going. Susan followed him into the bathroom, quietly. She saw that Paul had his eyes closed and hair shampooed. He had the multiple shower nozzles on the exuberant splattering pulse setting. He probably could not see nor hear her. She placed the towels on the sink and went to the big shower enclosure.

The magnetic catch on the big glass panel door proved difficult to open without sound, but she did, carefully. Paul had his head tilted back under the shower nozzle rinsing shampoo when she put her hands on his shoulders. He startled a bit at her touch, but quickly recovered. His manhood acknowledged her presence next to him. Paul finished rinsing the shampoo.

Susan leaned forward so they were pressed together, navel to navel. She could feel the target of her attention stiffly folded between their bodies. Susan held tight to Paul's shoulders and bent her right knee while lifting that leg sideways. She went up on her left tiptoe, sliding her wet-slick body upward against him. Her target slid along her wet right thigh, and then flopped under her leg. She came down from her tip toe and on top of her target, while she lowered her right leg back down, encompassing him between her legs.

"Ah, that is quite a move there, takes long legs to do that." Paul said in a breathy whisper.

"That is a modification of a ballet move I learned in my tweener years dance class, before I got so tall that ballet was eliminated from my repertoire of possible career choices. A choreographer would call that ballet step a *rond de jambe avec baton*," Susan whispered, eye to eye, as she pressed her hips against his and moved slowly up and down on her tiptoes.

"*Bâton*, huh? That would be my contribution?" Paul asked.

"Yes, *le bâton d'homme* is a critical part of this ballet move."

"And, have you practiced this move often?"

"Only in my head, this is the first dress rehearsal. It seems to have worked just as choreographed though. Your *bâton* is a quick learner to a new dance move."

"Yes, my *bâton* has some moves of its own."

"That also is critical part of the choreography I had in mind. Do you have time to finish this dance number before you go?"

"Certainly."

—

Susan had followed Devorah's advice by wearing the blue silk Anne Taylor suit. She realized it was a much better choice for a meeting in law offices than the sweater dress she had first worn to the Wassermann, Ephraim & Moore offices. So much had happened since then. It was surreal to think that it was only two weeks ago. She was still a bit giddy about the evening and morning she had spent with Paul. As she rode up the elevator, Susan recognized why everyone -- the Johnsons, Professor Moresby, Greg Harkness and Heidi -- were all shocked at how quickly Susan's decision to move to New York had come. As she now reflected on the events, Susan had a sense of unease that maybe she had been reckless in moving so quickly. Not that she was uncomfortable with what had occurred with Paul, it was just that the entirety of how her life had changed was unsettling. And, wonderful.

Susan crossed the expanse of green carpet and announced herself to the receptionist, "Susan Fisher, I have a ten o'clock appointment with Peter Ephraim."

"Yes, Miss Fisher, they are waiting for you. Do you know the way?"

Susan wanted to ask 'who' was waiting for her, but resisted, "Yes, I have been there before. But, you said they are waiting, I'm not late am I?"

"Oh no. Ms. Hennesey came at Nine-thirty. I guess they had something to do to get ready for you. I'll let them know you are coming," the receptionist smiled and pushed a telephone button.

Susan headed down the main hallway. She had no idea who Ms. Hennessey was. Peter Ephraim's secretary was waiting at his door and opened it for Susan.

Peter Ephraim was seated behind his desk. A woman was sitting in one of his side chairs. Peter got up as Susan crossed the expanse of carpet. He met Susan and moved to give her a cheek kiss. Susan was surprised, but returned the buss. She recognized there was a different social dialectic going on with Peter this visit.

Peter turned to the woman, who stood as Peter introduced them, offering her hand to Susan.

"Susan, may I present Melinda Hennessey. Ms. Hennessy, my client Susan Fisher. Please ladies, have a seat." Peter spoke as he returned to his desk chair. Susan recognized that Peter had not explained who Melinda was, as he had in saying Susan was his client.

Susan was still intrigued at how Peter could sit in his chair behind the desk and still be at about the same height as when he was standing. She had to peak behind his desk sometime. Susan sat next to Melinda Hennessey. She noted the woman was probably mid-30s, in a gray business suit with medium length, curly dishwater blonde hair and very light make-up on her broad, but somewhat plain Nordic features.

Peter started, "Susan, Ms. Hennessey and I met on this before you got here to work out the details of what we are going to discuss with you. I am going to take the first shot at it, and then turn it over to Ms. Hennessey to fill in details and correct my mistakes. Melinda works for the Columbia University Office of Charitable Giving. She specializes, among other things, in funding scholarship programs for Columbia via gifts of alumni and friends of the University. Did I get that right?"

Melinda Hennessey nodded that he had. Susan looked at Melinda, being careful not to show in her facial expression any of the intrigue she felt at the woman's employer.

Peter shifted some papers on his desk and said, "I was concerned when you let me know that the death of your aunt and the turmoil of these unfortunate events would require you to interrupt your college work in Illinois and move to New York. You told me your concerns that the timing of your loss would interfere in being able to get into a college without waiting a full year to do a regular transfer application process. I racked my brain for some solution to suggest.

Then, I remembered something Ms. Hennessey had told me about several years ago. At the time, she explained how the normal admission rules and timelines had exemptions the University put in place to allow for the full utilization of scholarship funds in the event there might be a scholarship or a grant that could only be used by certain persons. But, those persons weren't an exact fit within the normal admission rules and deadlines."

Peter raised a finger as though he had forgotten something, "Let me backtrack to explain that Ms. Hennessey and I work together on several different matters, all involving bequests and gifts by my various clients to the Columbia Charitable Giving Program, including your uncle's and aunt's trust. So, back to my explanation… Ms. Hennessey, back then, explained this policy to me using the following example – Suppose an athletic coach at Columbia had a scholarship that could only go to an athlete in a particular sport, or with certain specific criteria. For some reason the athlete who had been previously offered that scholarship decided to not accept the scholarship, maybe to attend elsewhere. Now, the coach has an unfilled scholarship to fill a need on an athletic team and the NCAA or other rules for athletic scholarships only allow so many scholarships to be given in a particular year, and if they did not award a scholarship that year they might be over their scholarship usage quota for the next year. Unless they have an existing student or applicant who meets the exact criteria or needs of the team, they have a problem. Or, I understand besides this example there are other ways the University might be caught in a 'use it or lose it' situation regarding scholarship funds and grants. So in order to cover this situation and make sure that there were no scholarships and grants lost due to lack of a proper recipient, the University, like most other colleges, I understand, has an exemption-- a confidential, unpublished exemption-- to allow the scholarship programs to recommend waivers for otherwise qualified scholarship recipients who do not meet some admissions factor, be it timing, complete qualifications or some other admissions check-off or prerequisite. Back to the example, this might be an athlete who the coach knows can meet the admissions criteria and the athletic needs of the University, but might not have applied before the deadline, because they did not know the scholarship would be available.

"But, this policy is not only for athletic scholarships; to be fair and impartial, the University allows any established scholarship program to recommend waivers, not just the sports programs. For example, if the military ROTC unit has an available federal scholarship slot for a university, the university will accomodate the ROTC by making an admission slot available to a qualified applicant even outside of the normal admissions process.

"So, a few years back, Melinda and I worked together on a situation in which a wonderful candidate for admission at Columbia had a situation in which her visa status as a non-US resident had prevented them from completing the admission process on time. But, the visa matter was resolved, albeit too late for the normal admission deadlines. Ms. Hennessey contacted me, as the trustee of a trust that had an established scholarship program, to see if there was any possibility of funding an additional spot in that year's scholarship grant so that the University could justify an exemption for this student the University wanted to admit, but which they needed a proper exemption for, so as to be fully compliant with their own rules. We successfully funded the additional scholarship funds. That student was admitted and has now just finished her degree. I know that because she sent the trust a letter thanking us for her opportunity. She is moving on to graduate work."

Peter leaned forward in his chair and continued, "So, thinking about your situation, I realized that we had a longstanding scholarship program at Columbia, funded by the Robert and Lenora Tabor Foundation, one of my clients, which funds scholarships for descendants of Jewish military veterans, with a preference for Jewish veterans who were alumni of Columbia."

Peter stopped, smiled and held out his hand toward Susan, "Of course, you are not only the granddaughter of a retired Navy officer who was a Jewish rabbi, but your Jewish father was also an Army officer and, to top it off, he was a Ph.D. recipient from Columbia. And, it happens, the Tabor Foundation had excess, unused funds available to fund a scholarship. So, with that rather long winded introduction, let me turn to Melinda who can finish."

Susan turned to Melinda Hennessey, who began, "Well, Mr. Ephraim gave me your information and his recommendation that we look into the matter for an exemption determination. Last week, I went to the Admissions people I work with. They started to set up an admissions office file in their computer system. Come to find out, you had already done your online application at CommonApp.org listing Columbia as one of your college choices, your registrar at Augustana had already posted your transcript with CommonApp.org, which transcript had stellar grades, by the way, and your electronic file from Augustana even had a superb recommendation from the History Department Chair at Augustana. You were a busy girl last week, and successfully so. The documents available electronically to our Admissions people were such that it was clear that you would be qualified for transfer student status at Columbia, but for the fact that you missed our March transfer application deadline. But, a late application is one of the possible exemptions that can be given to a qualified scholarship recipient, as Peter explained."

Melinda gestured with her hands out and up, indicating a problem solved. "So, Friday, I called Peter, told him. He asked if I could come today give you the good news. It will take a few more days for the University to generate the paperwork, but you can consider yourself a junior at Columbia next fall. The only thing I was not able to do, was get an approval for your major. You will be admitted as an undecided major. Major status needs specific approval from the department, with no waiver possible. But, with your grades, the admissions counselor said that would be a mere formality for you to be approved by the department in either Visual Arts or History, or as you are probably aware, Columbia University actually has a separate Department of Art History and Archaeology, with art history being your major at your last college. Then, to make sure I had closed the loop on that aspect, I checked with the Department of Art History and Archaeology on their requirements. I spoke with the assistant department chair, Professor Wickes. When I told him the situation, he asked about your father, whose alumni information I had from the scholarship qualification. And, low and behold, Professor Wickes knew your father. Wickes had actually taken a class from him when your father taught as a graduate student at Columbia in the '70's. So, it sounds like you are a shoo-in for departmental approval of an art history major, when you get to that point. Congratulations Susan, you are a Columbia University student."

Susan looked back and forth from Melinda to Peter. "I guess all I can say is 'Wow!' I had worried about this and wondered what I was going to do. I am just very impressed at how a problem I viewed as insurmountable was handled in what, a week? I can't thank the two of you enough."

Melinda checked her watch and spoke, "Well, I am very happy we could put this this together. I am glad Peter was able to remember our little situation a few years ago and use it to your advantage now. I guess that is what a good attorney is paid to do, figure out ways to make things work for his clients. In this case, he has done a service not only to his client, but I think, to Columbia as well. Now, I'm sorry, but I need to run. I have another meeting to get to at 11 o'clock."

Melinda stood and offered her hand to Susan, "Welcome to Columbia, you'll love it."

Peter had come around the desk to where the women stood and shook hands with Melinda. Melinda said, "Peter, we'll be in touch."

"Yes, we will," Peter answered, as though there might be more he needed to resolve with this woman.

Peter indicated Susan should sit back down as they waited for Melinda to exit the room. Peter sat next to her, rather than going back behind the desk.

Susan spoke first, "Very impressive, Mr. Ephraim. I am beginning to understand your concept of client services and truly appreciate what you did here. And, I assume my Rachel Metzger Trust needs to make a donation to the

Robert and Lenora Tabor Foundation. Right?"

Peter smiled and pointed an accusatory finger at Susan, "Young lady, you are catching on to things quite fast. And …"

Susan cut him off, "And let me guess, besides the scholarship funds the Trust also needs to fulfill a new gift to Columbia's Charitable Giving Program?"

Peter laughed out loud, "God, you are good. Maybe we need for you to scrap the Art History crap and get you into Pre-Law. Susan Fisher, you are a natural at understanding the system."

"Peter, it didn't take much for me to figure this out. Remember I grew up in academia, and its endowed chairs, stipends and grants; and institutional giving being the lifeblood of colleges. And, I therefore know that Melinda Hennessey's job is not to run interference for rich, Jewish girls who want to go to college, her job is to rake in funds for Columbia, and she gets paid based not on my level of happiness, but on her bottom line donations record. Right?"

All Peter did was continue smiling.

"So, Peter, how much did my admission cost?"

"Susan, lawyers have a maxim that says, don't ask a question you may not want to know the answer to. Let's just say your trust won't even feel it. It is entirely deductible as a charitable contribution and will, in large part, act as an offset to profits that would need to be taxed otherwise. That is the core principle that keeps people like Melinda Hennessey employed. It is what keeps places like Columbia University in business. You would be surprised how incredibly valuable a good tax deduction or charitable contribution can be. Or a good contact list."

Susan nodded, "Yes, last night one of Rachel's charity efforts and social contacts paid off with a couple of tickets to a marvelous, hard-to-get-tickets concert."

"Tickets? What'd you see?"

"The anniversary concert presentation of *Les Miserables* at Radio City. Last night was opening night of six nights where they have different cast members from the various stage presentations over the years and the movie performing the music only, not the acting. They change who does it each night this week. I heard people there say they liked it better than the current stage version. We loved it." Susan spoke before thinking about the obvious question for Peter.

"We?"

Susan thought for a moment, and then said, "Yes, I took one of my tenants to the concert. Don't worry, Peter. He is a nice Jewish doctor. And you don't need to investigate him, I'm sure Laszlo Kiss already has his credit report in the tenant files."

"Okay, I'll check." Peter said with a serious face.

"Wait, you're kidding right?" Susan looked worried.

After a moment, Peter smiled and said, "Yes, Susan I'm kidding. My job is to protect you, but I realize there is little I can do to do traffic control around a beautiful, young woman living in New York City. Father figures have been trying to do that, unsuccessfully, since the Garden of Eden. If things get serious, let me know, and we can talk. But, just as I was impressed by your understanding of the Columbia deal, I am also impressed that you scored a date with a Jewish doctor so quickly. Less than two weeks. They are considered prime targets. No?"

Susan frowned, "Yes, I guess that is the stereotype for the typical Jewish American Princess. Not me."

"Ah, I see," Paul said.

Peter's look now changed, causing Susan to be concerned that she had said something wrong about Jewish American Princesses.

"Susan, I need to change subjects now. I think I just gave you about as good news as I could. Now, I need to talk about some not so good news."

Peter was obviously thinking about what to say, but realized that his delay in speaking had alarmed Susan. He started, "I don't want you to be unduly concerned, but part of my job is to let my clients know about any bumps in the road that are encountered. There has been a development regarding your aunt's estate. As your attorneys, we need to let you know that one branch of the Metzger family is considering a challenge to your inheritance, well, part of your inheritance. We do not think this will have any significant negative result for you, other than the obvious ill will and discord that will result."

Susan's brow furrowed.

Peter shifted in the chair and said, "At Aaron and Myra's house you met Sarah Birney, Rachel's step-daughter, right?"

"Yes. She didn't say much and left early, I think."

"And, her husband Mark?" Peter asked.

"I don't recall him. But, I remember Jack Birney, her son, and Jack's wife," Susan answered.

"Yes, I don't recall seeing Mark there either. Maybe that has something to do with this.

"Our firm has been contacted by an attorney representing the Birneys, Sarah and Mark, and this attorney has informed us that they may be challenging your interest in the Metzger trusts. He has asked for copies of various documents on behalf of his clients. He has given us a basic understanding of what he is basing his challenge on. But, we need to let you know, right off, that this is only a challenge of the earlier trusts, those established by Morris and Isaac, and not the latter trust your Aunt Rachel set up to handle her own assets. That trust of Rachel's is bullet-proof as to Sarah Metzger Birney's claims. Your mother, and then you, have always been the named beneficiaries of that trust, since Rachel set it up in the late '70's."

Peter continued, "I apologize in advance if this explanation is confusing. What this attorney says is that he is considering challenging is the provisions in Morris's trust, and Isaac's trust and will that gave Rachel a indivisible half share of her husband's property, splitting that property off from the remainder of the trust so that, upon her death, the trust assets did not go back into the trust, such that the surviving children of her husband would get a share of that remainder upon their stepmother's death.

"But, you see, we, at Wassermann, Ephraim and Moore think this attorney is inexperienced in this type of matter. And, he does not realize that this trust provision was intentional, not the drafting mistake he thinks, or hopes, occurred. The original trust was established by my father for Morris, and it was pretty much copied for Isaac, and Aaron, to follow a Jewish Halakha law that a wife can have an independent interest in the property of her husband, independent of the rights of her husband's children. There is a corresponding option in normal Anglo-American inheritance law, but in many trusts, the wife's interest in an ongoing testamentary trust of her husband reverts to the trust, if she is not alive upon the vesting of the trust, which takes place, based upon a very ancient English common law legal principal, twenty-one years after the last heir alive when the original grantor died, unless the trust says it goes earlier.

"In our case that would be on the 21st birthday of the last heir born of either the last heir of Aaron or Isaac for Morris' trust, or the last child of Isaac and Rachel, or Sarah, or Joseph for Isaac's trust or will. So, we still have a ways to go, since Aaron's, Sarah's, and Joseph's children are still having kids. These trusts were established to prolong the tax savings benefits to the heirs as far out in time as possible, but also to give the wives their own share independent of the share their husband's children get. Hannah Metzger was the first person to benefit from this provision. She still holds an undivided interest in one half of Morris' original trust. And Hannah's own trust and will control where that property goes, not Morris's trust. Hannah Metzger is one of the wealthiest little ol' grandmas around."

Peter took a breath and said, "I know this is enough to glaze your eyes over, but I needed to explain it, so this next part makes sense. For Sarah Birney's attorney to be successful, he would have to also challenge Hannah's independent right to Morris's trust, and Myra's independent right to Aaron's trust, because those two spouses stand in the same shoes vis-à-vis their husband's trust language as Rachel does to Isaac's trust. The only Metzger who would be in the same spot as Sarah Birney is Joseph Metzger, Sarah's brother. And Joseph has been contacted and wants no part of Sarah's scheme; he fully supports you, his aunt Myra, and his grandmother Hannah. It seems you have apparently endeared yourself to Joe and his lady."

Peter looked into Susan's eyes, "Susan this has been a long-winded, but necessary explanation that our firm does not believe Sarah Birney's attorney is correct, and we believe he will fail. But, you should know that even if he did succeed you would still be getting a very sizable trust directly from Rachel. But, there are two other factors that trump the legal language, and that is why we think Sarah will not risk actually filing suit over her attorney's challenge idea. First, in each of the trusts and in Isaac's will there is what we call poison pill language, which serves to disinherit any heir that unsuccessfully challenges the trusts. We think that when Sarah has that provision explained to her she will not risk the possibility of losing what she already has. And, second, right now, Sarah stands in line to get a proportional share of her ninety-three year old grandmother's trust, a tidy sum. She will be told, by way of a back-channel message, that she might be removed from her place at her Grandmother's trough, if she goes against the rest of the family by attacking your inheritance."

Susan shook her head as though she were clearing cobwebs from her brain, "Do you know why she did this? I guess the money is good enough reason."

Peter nodded, "Yes, the money. But, you really need to know Sarah's back story to understand why that is important. Sarah is the oldest of the Metzger grandchildren. On her father's death in 1978, she and her brother shared one half of their father's trust, or one quarter of the total for each of them. Rachel got the other half. Two years later, at age 21, Sarah assumed her place as co-trustee of that trust and a year or so after that, she married Mark Birney, who fancied himself quite the businessman and stock trader. Sarah and Mark started taking a bigger hand in the management of the trust, as was her right as co-trustee, but many of his business exploits with his wife's trust funds were not consistent with sound trust management practices. In many cases he, Mark, pushed to have Sarah's funds removed from assets the other Metzger trusts were invested in. He wanted funds for stock trading, and venture capital investment, and wanted out of the real estate that was the bulwark of the Metzger family's wealth. For example, you know the building across the street from you, on 10th Avenue, he demanded a cash out of Sarah's interest. So, today, that building is owned by you and Aaron and Joe, not Sarah. That sort of thing continued until the '90's when his stock deals became such that our firm could no longer continue to allow a trust we were co-trustee of to be so foolhardy. My father gave Sarah an ultimatum, it was our services as trustee versus her husband's business acumen. She stuck with her husband, and we moved her trust out of Metzger Companies and her legal representation went to another law firm. The Birney's have since switched to different firms twice. We still have a few real estate assets, which were not so easy to extract her interest from that the Metzger Companies' team manages, but that is the exception, since our firm is no longer trustee.

"And, you have only to look at the track record of stock investments over the last several years, especially after the big market collapse, to guess at what has become of much of Sarah Metzger Birney's wealth. So, Sarah Birney started out with *a fourth* of Isaac's assets and that wealth has diminished as a result of poor investment handling. They are by no means destitute or in great need, but I am sure that your Aunt Rachel's *one half interest* that has also grown substantially in the last thirty-plus years is looking pretty good to Sarah Birney right now."

Susan nodded.

"Susan," Peter looked in her eyes again. "Perhaps now you understand why we, as Rachel's advisors, felt so strongly that you, as the outsider, needed to fit into the Metzger family mold as well as possible. You, as Rachel's heir, are receiving twice as much of Isaac Metzger's wealth than his own two children did. Sarah Metzger is now balking at that, but we think that is all it is, a balk. The other Metzgers are on your side, thank goodness. If you had not endeared yourself to them, we could have had one battle royal right now. As the attorney who would have been caught in the middle of the warring factions, I need to thank you for being a charming young lady who Aaron, Myra, Joe and Hannah have been proud to accept as a surrogate niece, cousin and granddaughter of the Metzger family."

"I understand. I really did not get it when you first spoke to me and Devorah was trying to give me my Jewish funeral lessons." Susan gave a small smile.

"Well, you did well. And, I wouldn't worry too much about this. My father, David and I all think the trusts are sound and inviolate. This will pass, but right now things are a bit awkward in Metzger land." Peter stood. "Now, I think you probably need to go find a Columbia University catalog and get to work planning your education."

Susan stood and gave her attorney a hug.

—

The secretary nook outside Devorah's office was empty. Susan wondered if Devorah had a secretary. Susan knocked.

"Come in." Devorah shouted from inside.

Susan entered. Devorah had her back to the door, typing on the computer on her credenza.

"Hello."

Devorah briefly turned her head, before continuing to type. "Susy, have a seat, I need to get this done. I'll be right with you. How'd it go with Peter? Wassup?"

Susan sat in one of Devorah's white chairs, saying, "Well, I guess the details are confidential, but your boss apparently has the capability of buying my way into Columbia University."

At this, Devorah turned around. "What?"

"I guess it is not as bad as that sounded. Peter knew the strings to pull and the exemptions to claim. He managed to grease the skids just enough for me to get into Columbia as a transfer this fall, nearly five months after the application cut-off. And, apparently on a scholarship."

"That's Peter." Devorah turned back to her work. "Congratulations."

Devorah stopped typing and hit a couple of keys decisively. She turned and poked a speed dial button on her phone. "Mary, I'm done. It is saved. Print the file cardamone_pleading_0619.docx. After I sign, fax file it with the Surrogate's Court in Queens and to the lender's counsel. I'll need a two copies and the original to take with me to Queens." She hung up.

Devorah took a deep breath and looked at Susan. "Sorry, gotta run to Queens for a motion hearing right after lunch, otherwise we could have lunch. You owe me a story about potato peeling in Connecticut, if I remember correctly. Who you peeling potatoes for?"

Susan pointed to the computer behind Devorah, "Can I show you quick? Open your browser."

Devorah turned, selected the internet browser program, and then got up to allow Susan to sit down. Devorah watched over Susan's shoulder as Susan went to the NY Presbyterian hospital website, selected the 'About Us' link, and then narrowed her request down to the trauma surgery department. A list of doctors' names appeared and then a formal portrait of Paul M. Waldman, M.D. with his short biographical blurb came up for Devorah to review.

Devorah looked and read, "Okay, I see cute, sandy-haired surgeon who went to Princeton and NYU. Explain the potatoes. You peeled this hunk's potatoes for him?" Devorah asked as she started to gather her things in her portfolio.

"Actually, I peeled his mother's potatoes. But, he ate them. He is quite fond of whipped potatoes." Susan paused for effect.

"Details! Quick!"

Before Susan could answer, there was a sound at the door. A pretty, young redhead walked in without waiting and handed Devorah a stack of papers. Mary, the redhead nodded to Susan, having met her on Susan's initial visit.

Devorah looked quickly over the papers, grabbed a pen, signed one paper that had a Post-It on it, giving the papers back to the Mary, directing, "Okay, copy and fax this. I'll pick up my copies to take with me from your desk. You're free to go to lunch after the faxes. I won't be back in after Court. I have to go to Great Neck and see my folks. Taking advantage of being half way there in Queens. Thanks, Mary."

Devorah turned back to her desk and said to Susan, "More details, quick ones. I gotta run."

"Paul is a tenant in my building, lives there and owns the community clinic on the first floor. We met on my first weekend, had lunch. Sunday morning I played on his Soccer team, found out he needed to be at home in Connecticut for Father's Day, but he was too tired to drive. I drive him home, meet his parent's, *yadda yadda*, I think is your way of explaining that kind of stuff. Then, last night we went out, he took me to Rothmann's. While we were there, we were given free tickets by Mrs. Mueller, you remember Mrs. Mueller, of 'Our Crowd' fame. Paul and I used her tickets and went to the *Les Mis* concert at Radio City. Later we went back to my place, and… and got to know one another. Intentional euphemism there, but if you tell Peter, or anyone, I will kill you."

Devorah put her hands on her hips, and then turned to her desk and fingered a desk calendar. "You are a mover, Miss Fisher, tomorrow is your … fourteenth day in town, and already you have scored big time, schmoozed a society maven and seem to be a natural at this supposedly unfamiliar turf. But, your story opened up lots of questions, need more facts later. Soccer? Mrs. Mueller? And this guy's a cute doctor no less!"

"Yeh, Peter seemed impressed by the doctor part, too."

Devorah raised her eyebrows, surprised, "So, you told Peter?"

Susan wiggled her flat hand in the air and said, "Sort of, I avoided the part that required a euphemism to explain what went on last night… and again this morning. Peter thinks I was impressed by the *Les Mis* concert."

"Ah, wise girl." Devorah picked up her bag. "Sorry gotta run. I'll take a rain check on a BFF's required further details. But, you have to answer the most important question… ."

"Which is?" Susan asked.

"Does your cute doctor have a buddy?" Devorah smiled coyly.

Susan smiled, "Actually yes. I met him at the soccer game. Eric, he is thirtyish, black hair, pretty tall, handsome and he is a surgeon, too, Paul's partner in the walk-in clinic. Single – Jewish -- partner."

Susan was still sitting at Devorah's computer. As she spoke, she spun back around, hit the back button on the browser, chose a different doctor's name and Eric Schwartz's picture and bio blurb appeared. Devorah looked at it quickly.

Devorah reached and patted Susan jokingly on the head, "Good girl. Call me. Let's go, I'm gonna be late to court."

Susan followed Devorah out of her office.

—

Chapter Twenty-One

12:19 EDT

From: susy@susyfisher.com

To: Devorah Feldshuh <dfeldshuh@wassermannephraim.com>

Cc: Devorah Feldshuh <devorah@feldshuh.com>

Subj: Wedding ???s

Devorah,

You were so rushed this morning, I did not have time to ask you what I came in for. Unfortunately, or maybe fortunately, it is once again fashion advice, not legal advice, so I sent this to both office and personal emails.

Ariel Metzger invited me to come to her wedding in Southampton the end of this month. I wondered if you have any advice for me; fashion, social or otherwise. Never been to Jewish wedding before, and if Jewish funerals are any comparison, I may be a fish out of water.

My guess is a Metzger daughter wedding is going to be a fashion forward type event, and I understand the basic of 'don't wear white' and 'don't try to outshine the bride,' but do you have any other advice. Dr. Paul Waldman will be escorting me and he says he is experienced in Jewish weddings in the Hamptons, but I could use whatever heads-up advice you can give me.

Are you going?

Hope you had a good visit with your folks.

Susy

—

When she got back from the lawyers' office, Susan decided to take action about the elevator situation. She found the round key Laszlo had mentioned that fit the passenger elevators and Susan crossed the sixth floor lobby. There was a single, black Down button, and a circular key hole above it. She inserted the round key and turned it. Nothing happened, visible or audio. But, when she pushed the Down button, she heard the elevator machinery inside the elevator shaft engage. In a few seconds, one of the passenger elevators opened for her. She ran back in her apartment to get her other building and apartment keys, so she would not be stranded if she went to another floor and could not get back up. When she got back to the elevators, it was closed, but opened immediately at her touch of the button. She pushed the second floor button. She had never seen any other floor except first and sixth.

The second floor lobby was much the same as the sixth, except in its dark tan and beige decor. There were four apartment doors on the second floor. She saw the one she was looking for. Apartment 2-C was the rear apartment on the 10th Avenue side of the building. Paul's apartment was straight below the back hallway section of Susan's apartment, but four floors below. If Paul's bedroom was the window room, he would sleep directly below the little pink bedroom she had slept in as a child.

Susan got out of the elevator and waited for the door to close. When it closed, she pushed the Up button. The elevator opened. She pushed 6th Floor and was rewarded by a ride to her floor. She did another ride all the way to the first floor and back to insure that the passenger elevators were now working to the sixth floor. They were. That was easy; she was ready for the delivery guys to deliver the first shipment of her household goods from Moline, which had arrived at the law firm address. More chores to do for Susan.

—

SMS Text: Paul, BTW, the Ubermenschen have arranged for the two regular elevators between 1st, 2nd and 6th floor to work now. Just thought you might like to know.☺ Susy

—

It was Susan's first visit to the other 6th floor apartment since coming with Carlos the first day. She had concentrated on the main apartment until now, but with Rachel's last video, she could not ignore this place any longer. Forewarned by Rachel of the complexity of the mess, Susan entered the foyer of Apartment 6A with her notebook and pencil to take notes on what she found.

Susan remembered this apartment was slightly smaller than the other, more than half to maybe two-thirds the size. She decided to take a quick tour before looking at things in detail.

The foyer was smaller, the floor was just the wood parquet, no rug and the light that came on when she flipped the switch was simply a large multi-bulb ceiling fixture, not the elaborate chandelier of the other place. The reason for the foyer being smaller was obvious; the area where the sitting room was in her apartment was a full-sized living room here, and the space for the elevators was taken from this apartment. This room had another stained glass window, like her dining room, but without any curtains. There were old-fashioned furniture pieces, a couch, chairs and TV pushed back to the walls and there were several of the stacks of paintings along the walls in this living room. The fireplace in this living room had a fake-wood gas burning insert. There was also a life-size, bronze neo-classical statue of a partially nude woman, under a cotton bed sheet shroud, in the corner of the living room.

Susan noticed that the atmosphere in this apartment was different than in hers. It was colder and the air seemed somehow different. When she checked the thermostat on the hallway wall, Susan saw that there was a second control next to the thermostat. It was a digital humidity control panel, just like in the *haute couture* closet in her second bedroom. Rachel had this entire apartment environmentally controlled, obviously for her paintings she stored here.

Susan's quick tour of the apartment showed its differences from hers. The dining room was smaller, having lost some space to the larger front living room. There was no dining room furniture, just the rows of paintings and stacks of boxes. The master bedroom occupied the remainder of the street side of the building directly above where the clinic was on the ground floor, nearly as large as hers and it had a bare king-size bed and basic bedroom furniture, circa 1975. The bedroom was decorated in garish, floral print wallpaper and brightly colored drapes that might have been stylish fifty years ago, *a la* Carnaby Street or Flower Power era. This bedroom did have the large stained glass window like the living room and several of the rooms in Susan's apartment. This was the only room in the apartment that did not have rows of paintings piled against the walls. Everything in the bedroom was coated in a thick coat of dust. The attached bathroom was totally old-fashioned. There were some clothes in the closet; the one item Susan looked closely at was a woman's leather jumpsuit, Catwoman style. There was a pair of thigh high black leather riding boots on the floor below the jumpsuit. Some of the other clothes seemed to be similar costume-like items, perhaps from Halloweens gone by. Kinky Halloweens gone by. The anomalous, esoteric nature of Aunt Rachel continued to be apparent.

The kitchen here was smaller and only had one set of appliances, almost antique and long unused. There were a couple large easels, a potter's wheel, kiln and clay mixing and extruding equipment sitting around the kitchen. A large assortment of art supplies covered the center kitchen island. There was a small, table-top radial arm saw and framing square on the kitchen counter near a bin full of many styles of frame-making stock. The kitchen had been transformed into an artist's workshop. There was no maid's quarters for this kitchen, and the pantry had semi-antique cans of turpentine, bottles of paint, liquid clay and gesso, and numerous ceramic molds and tools on its shelves.

This apartment had two other bedrooms, mostly without furniture, only the numerous stacks of paintings. One bedroom did have a desk with an ancient, white IBM computer and boxy monitor on it. Next to the desk was a huge old printer unit the size that could do art prints. There were two rolls of wide art paper next to the printer; one was watercolor paper, the other was a canvas weave material. The clear plastic cover on the printer was badly yellowed and cracked when Susan pulled it up to view the printer. There was a neutral gray backdrop on the wall nearby and a camera tripod, *sans* camera, sat in front of the backdrop, along with two floodlights. Susan guessed this was an art reproduction set-up circa 1990, or slightly older than Susan herself.

The laundry room was empty except for cleaning materials near the sink, and there was no equivalent of the sewing and utility rooms like her apartment. There was another smaller bathroom and a front hallway storage room, which had many boxes in it and a rear clothes bar with more old clothes. Here, the stairway to the roof had metal plates screwed between the door and doorframe making it impossible to go up or allow entrance from above without unbolting the plates. This precaution and the double heavy duty deadbolts on the front door with a security alarm that matched her place showed this place was meant to be secure.

Her quick tour finished, Susan set to work, starting in the front room. She carefully cataloged each item she found, wrote the artist's name, noted receipts and provenance certificates when they were attached to the paintings and made notes of mysteries when she found them. There were many mysteries.

—

SMS Text: Susy, I guess the news about elevators means I'm invited back again, huh? I love your shower enclosure. Working late tonight, had a Code Yellow to triage construction accident in Bronx. Paul

—

Susan had only barely begun the art cataloging task when she had to go back to her apartment to be there for the arrival of the Illinois shipment at 3:30. As she entered her foyer she saw a flashing red reflected sparkle in the crystal of the light fixture in the sitting room. She entered the sitting room and peaked around the corner. The red light on Rachel's land line answering machine was blinking. She pushed Play.

"Susy, it's Aaron. I don't know if you're answering this phone number. It was a bit strange hearing Rachel's answer message. I think Ariel said she has your cell number, I should get it from her. I wanted to check on how you are doing. I understand you have been busy these last few weeks. I was happy to hear you have decided to move in over there. It has been rather hectic here, too, what with the wedding plans. We are out in Southampton, otherwise I would have called to 'do lunch' or something. I look forward to seeing you at the wedding.

"At risk of this being too long for your answering machine, I want to tell you not to worry about this thing with Sarah. Peter told me he talked to you. It is unfortunate my niece brought this up. I think it will be worked out, and I apologize for any distress it brings you. Call me if you would like to talk. See you at the wedding." Beep!

Yes, Susan had forgot to re-record a new message for the answering machine. She checked the buttons and did so now.

Susan realized she had missed having contact with Aaron, Myra and the others. They were her only family now, and her whole life was being built on the periphery of theirs. However, except for Ariel's visit she had no contact with them since the night of the funeral. Oh, and the boots Joe Metzger sent to Susan. Not ever having had extended family, Susan really did not know what level of contact people had between cousins, and with aunts and uncles. If her previous contact with Rachel was any judge, well….

When the delivery men arrived, Susan was able to buzz them into the downstairs lobby, and they came up themselves on the passenger elevators. Susan's change to the elevator set-up was vindicated.

Susan decided to put all of the Illinois shipment in the old family TV room. By the time the men had brought everything up, Susan had another sizable pile to sort through. Between this, Rachel's closet, the boxes in the dining room, the two storage rooms and the huge art menagerie, Susan had an enormous amount of work to do. She started by trying to find her personal items and clothes amongst the many boxes from Illinois.

—

18:29 EDT

From: Devorah Feldshuh <devorah@feldshuh.com>

To: Susan Fisher <susy@susyfisher.com>

Subj: Re: Wedding ???s

CONFIDENTIAL For Your Eyes Only ☺

Susy,

Visit with parents went as expected, unfortunately. Mother actually reminded me I am approaching age 30. Hint, hint. To her I have been approaching 30 since age 21.

No, I am not attending Ariel's wedding. Law firm associates are not on Myra Metzger's radar, as you saw at the cemetery. I expect Peter, his father and possibly David will be there.

Jewish weddings are really beautiful. They have more custom and ceremony than the funeral, but nicer, and as a guest you don't need to know much, just watch, smile a lot and make sure the old guy behind you in the line dance is not too drunk. There are several good books on Jewish weddings, if you want details. Clothing wise, I would recommend two fancy summer dresses, one for the ceremony and one for dinner, but only if you have time to change. Often it is all just one big event. You are correct that your outfit needs to be nice, but not overly attention gathering. I recommend you wear something that covers your shoulders and goes to knees, or almost. If you can find a matching hat, that is also preferable. We have some time to talk, call me. Oh, are you staying overnight? Recommend it, the Hamptons are a long return trip after late dinner party.

If Paul has experience, he can give you a play by play. Lots of what goes on in a Jewish wedding is the same as other weddings, but some things like breaking the glasses, group dancing and signing the ketubah are unique. You'll have fun. Take copious notes ☺! You never know…

Also, given the current squabble amongst Metzger clan, I would recommend you avoid the Birneys and not discuss the inheritance issue with anyone. Peter can advise you better than I on that.

We'll talk.

Devorah

Sent from my Samsung Galaxy S7

—

"Hello." Susan answered. She had seen Paul's ID on the iPhone screen.

"Good evening. Did you have a good day?' Paul asked.

Susan thought for a moment. "Yes, actually a truly monumental day. I guess you might even say life changing. And you?"

"Wow, life changing. That is tough to match. Mine was horrible. Still here cleaning up from the accident victims. They had a crane and scaffolding give way in the Bronx, and we had several victims. Every trauma center in New York got a few. Not good. What was your life changing event?"

Susan paused, "Well, I wasn't planning on telling you by phone, hoped to see you. I got word I am going to be admitted to Columbia as a transfer Junior this fall. I don't have to wait for the next academic year."

"You said you missed the deadline. How'd you wrangle that?" Paul inquired.

"Well, part networking, my father got his doctorate from Columbia, but it's mostly my attorney knew who to talk to and which skid to grease. I know that sounds crude, but it is really not that bad."

"Is this the same attorney that you mentioned before?"

Susan laughed, "No different attorney, I have a full team a'them. This was the head honcho with the serious connection list, he is the other attorney's boss."

"Well, congratulations. Columbia ought to keep you busy. Uh, what I was calling about is, I need to meet with Eric and the others about the clinic tomorrow evening after work. But, I would like to maybe get together with you after I get off Thursday evening, say around nine, they have a Jazz Night at the Bistro downstairs. We could catch something to eat and the late set of pretty good music. How's that sound?" Paul asked.

"Sure. I can do that. Gotta wait two days to see you again, huh?"

"This noon to eight shift kinda takes away a lot of options, unless you wanna do breakfast, "Paul suggested.

"I can do breakfast. You tell me when you want to get up. You come up here and I'll feed you. I need to inaugurate my kitchen. I think there is a lonesome Belgian waffle machine on the shelf. That sound good?"

"Sounds good. I didn't mean you had to make breakfast, but that's great. How about eight thirty?"

"OK eight thirty it is, see ya."

"Okay, bye."

Chapter Twenty-Two

07:54 AM EDT

To: Susy@SusyFisher.com

From: David Tannenbaum <dtannenbaum@wassermannephraim.com>

Subj: Driver's License Address

Dear Susy:

In answer to the question you left with Joyce yesterday, you can use the client service address here instead of your actual residence address to get a NY Driver's License. A lot of celebrities and people with security issues use attorneys' and agents' NY office addresses for DL purposes. You will need two proofs of residence when you apply. I have prepared a NY DMV certificate of residence as your "landlord" and a copy of a "lease" document you can prove your residence address with. We actually have a sign posted on the door on the fourteenth floor telling police and others who come to the physical address how to reach us to get in contact with you. You will also need the new Social Security card we ordered for you (Joyce has it in your file) and your Illinois license. I do not think you have to take a test, if your out-of-state license is current. You will have to re-apply next October to get a license that does not show UNDER 21. Please let me know if you want to pick up the certificate, lease and Social Security card here or have it delivered to you. Joyce tells me you have some correspondence from Columbia waiting, too.

David

—

"So, our second breakfast in a row. I hope you didn't take it wrong when I suggested we go out this morning, your waffles and berries were scrumptious yesterday. I just thought you might like someone else to cook this morning." Paul held the lobby door open for Susan to exit.

"No offense could possibly be taken. And I hope I'm not being too clingy to suggest we do breakfast again today. I don't want to be too presumptuous; I realize you had a life before I showed up on scene."

Paul took Susan's hand as they walked toward 10th. "The only wrongful presumption you are making is that I actually had a personal life to intrude upon. Between the hospital and the clinic, about the only outside activity I had was the soccer team, and that isn't exactly prime socialization. I don't think I can count Worlds of Warcraft as social contact."

Susan looked at Paul, "You do Warcraft?"

"Yeh, once in a while. I picked it up as a resident. A bunch of us used it to unwind. You know 'and now for something completely different.' Nothing like a little sword slashing melee to get your mind off a rough night at the ER. You ever do Warcraft?"

"I did last summer. Me and my BFF Heidi joined a horde together. One of her beaus talked her into it. He liked the idea of getting Heidi into a Valkyrie outfit, even if online. I had to swear off it for the school year last fall, too addicting and time sucking. Never got back into it. And Heidi switched boyfriends. Good thing, this year was pretty intense. Let me guess, you're a Physician in Warcraft."

Paul shook his head. "Nope, Enchanter. You?"

"I was a Jewelcrafter, but pretty good with a sword. You ever do Second Life?"

"Couple times, didn't see much point in it, compared to the action of Warcraft. You do Second Life?"

"Yeh, I like to create stuff in world, can't do that with Warcraft."

"Maybe we can go online together sometime."

"Maybe, but the real world is pretty busy right now." Susan shifted her purse on her shoulder.

"What are your plans for today?" Paul led Susan over to the cross walk, to cross to the café on the opposite corner.

"I have more of my constant sorting, just added my whole Illinois stash to Aunt Rachel's pile. And I want to figure out the subway, so I can take it up and wander around the Columbia campus. And, on the way back I need to stop by my attorneys in Mid-Town, I guess the Columbia paperwork came in. And, after that, I have to hit the DMV office."

Paul opened the café door for Susan, "If you want, you can come with me, I take the subway right past Columbia on the way to the hospital."

"Really, I still have no idea, in my head, about how this city is laid out. Without my Maps app I would be totally lost. I'd appreciate a 'local' showing me the subway routine."

Paul pulled out a chair for Susan and said, "Then that's the plan, I'll show you the ropes on the subway this morning. And, I guess we are still on for nine tonight at the Bistro."

—

As they had arranged, Paul was waiting for her in the lobby for their evening together, when the elevator doors opened.

"Again, Wow! You are sort of an enigma, Susan Fisher." Paul spread his arms wide in a gesture of admiration.

Susan stepped up to him and said, "Enigma? How so?"

Paul kissed her, carefully, "I drop you off at your subway stop this morning, and you are a college girl in jeans and tank top. You reappear tonight and you are some sultry, Left Bank dame obviously able to eat men alive."

"I accept the compliment. This is my best shot at the proper costume to listen to jazz at a New York bistro." Paul obviously liked her slinky black jersey dress and dark-eyed make-up.

"Yes, I think you nailed the costume and, uh, all the rest. Even the perfume. Very nice."

The trip to the Bistro was quick, just around the block to the far corner of their building. Susan could hear the music as they turned the corner. At first, Susan wondered why she had never heard the music before, just six floors up, but then she realized she had never been in this apartment on a Thursday night.

At the entrance, they were met by a man with a goatee in black turtle-neck and gray, herringbone sport coat. "Doctor Waldman, you're back, it has been a while. And you brought a guest."

"Yes, Jerry, and an important guest. Susan, can I present Jerry Merrick. This is his club. And Jerry may I present Susan Fisher, your new landlady."

"Ah, then tenants' rumor control is true. Miss Fisher, I am sorry to hear of Mrs. Metzger's passing. She was a regular here for years, but we hadn't seen her recently. Welcome to our Bistro. Let's get you a place."

Susan noticed Jerry quickly raced through his condolences so she did not have to respond. He was respectful, but kept her mood upbeat. A good host.

Jerry led them across the large main room. A five piece band was performing, but not jazz, more of a big band era and Broadway medley. The room was crowded. However, Susan's eyes had not adjusted to the dim light yet, and it was difficult to see any details of the clientele. They were seated in a small round table to the side of, but with a full view of the stage.

"Will you be eating, or just drinks tonight?"

"Food, definitely food." Paul answered.

Jerry smiled and left two menus with them. "Someone will be right over to take your order."

Susan looked at the menu, "Any recommendations?"

"Yes, following your Left Bank vixen theme for the night, I've had the Ratatouille entrée, and it is pretty good, if your carnivore nature can be contained. And get the Caesar salad. They give you a good bread selection to go with the veggies."

"Hmmm."

The music stopped and the audience gave an enthusiastic round of applause.

"Thank you ladies and gentleman, and whoever else is out there, we are never quite sure on Thursdays. We are going to take a break, and when we come back, we'll have our favorite torch singer, the lovely Carla Monteith, with us. Thank you."

A waitress in a purple turtleneck and pencil skirt took their order. Susan followed Paul's advice, but he ordered a veggie pizza.

"Veggie, huh?" Susan asked.

"Yeh, I try to follow the advice I hand out to patients. The cheese on a most pizzas is bad enough, but the typical meat toppings for pizza are pure cholesterol and a real free radical cocktail."

"And not kosher at all, I get it. Explain free radical."

Paul launched into a complete explanation of free radicals, including a complete set of health impacts, premature aging, etc. He finally stopped talking when he saw Susan smiling at him.

"You're smiling at me, but I'm talking about unsmiley stuff."

Susan smiled, "I was just marveling how a couple of magic words turn on the bedside manner and in-depth scientific explanation mode. I got to see Doctor Waldman there and not Paul."

"Sorry."

"No, don't apologize. I was smiling, when I stop smiling is when you apologize." Susan touched Paul's hand on her way to grab a breadstick from the basket.

"I'll try to remember that—when Susy stops smiling, Paul needs to apologize." Paul intertwined his fingers and looked at Susan, "So how'd your trip to the campus go? And the rest of your day."

"Good day, actually. Got all my errands done. Found the basic, important places at Columbia. Big place, makes Augustana seem really dinky. I hit my attorneys'office and did some paperwork. Next, I went shopping for a dress for the wedding. And, I'm officially a New Yorker now, got my driver's license and voter registration done."

"What party?" Paul asked.

Susan answered with obvious sarcasm, "Uuhh, tough question there, considering I'm the daughter of a couple of secular, academic Jews, and I just inherited the estate of a former New York ACLU board member. How about you?"

"Well, using your standards, I'm a fairly well-to-do Jewish business owner and the son of a hedge fund founder. My mother is a veteran of the Israeli Defense Force. That would make me a…." Paul paused to make his point.

Susan thought for a minute, shook her head, and said, "Nice try at camouflage there, Paul, but you are also a knowledgeable, open-minded physician, Princeton grad, Worlds of Warcraft devotee. You recognize Boyz II Men lyrics when I quote them. You spout New Age philosophy. Plus, you get choked up at 19th Century French revolutionary anthems. Not a whole lot of Fox News fan in your résumé."

"Touché for the Left Bank gal."

The waitress brought their drinks and the bread basket.

Susan buttered her slice of rye and noticed that Paul ate his muffin without butter.

Her eyes had adjusted to the light, and Susan looked around at the other people in the Bistro. Almost every table was occupied with two people. Mostly hetero, but a few boy-boy and girl-girl couples. Susan wondered why she assumed these pairings were 'couples' instead of simply pairs of friends. She guessed it was because this was a couples kind of place and not a place to go to pick someone up. So, the few pair of guys were probably a couple instead of prey seeker and his wingman.

After a long silence, Paul asked. "Where is Susy?"

"Uh, what?" Susan replied.

"Susy is very quiet and staring at people. I wondered where her head was at."

Susan pursed her lips and gave a little nod, "Susy was looking around at all the tables and noting how most of them are couples. I used to play a people game with my father of looking at people and trying to guess their story from just their looks. Just now I was looking at all the couples, both hetero and apparently gay, and I was wondering what had made them a couple. What had drawn them together? Then, I thought about you and me. Just now, both of us described ourselves when we mentioned political affiliations and we both used 'Jew" or

'Jewish' in our self-description. And, here we are, coupled up like everyone else in this place and I wondered how much of a factor 'Jewish' was in that. I was wondering if I had been a Southern Baptist, or even a religious non-entity, whether that would have changed your attempt to get to know me. Same for me."

"But, I didn't know you were Jewish when I came back to offer you my Welcome Wagon lunch." Paul countered.

"No, you had a hunch from my last name, and God knows, maybe my looks, and you went out of your way to let me know the food was from a kosher deli and gave me the option of eating kosher with what you bought. I am guessing that was you thinking 'just in case she is Jewish.'"

Paul shook his head, "Not really, Fisher could easily be Anglo and looks-wise you could just as easily be that Southern Baptist, as a Jewess. You don't look nor act very Jewish and neither do I, at least not much."

"So, you are rejecting the idea that we are together here amongst the Bistro's assembled couples because we are both Jewish. You are the guy whose Jewish father is in a tizzy over his future Catholic son-in-law. What would Ted Waldman have to say about that Southern Baptist babe, especially when it seems Jewish law says Jewish bloodline comes from the mother."

Paul laughed. "Yeh, there is that. But, what about you? You said yourself when we first met that there is not very much Jewish about you. Do you think you accepted my offer to come up for lunch because you Googled me and saw some online data tidbits that told you I was Jewish. Are you here with me tonight because I'm Jewish? And why does that matter to you?"

Susan answered, "I guess that is the question. I got psychoanalyzed by a friend once who said I had a deep psychological need to belong to a group, like everybody does, and I was missing something by my parents not associating me with my Jewish heritage. He said I had a deep, dark hole in my soul where I was expecting God to be and I had an urge to fill it."

"Aha, Sartre. Is that urge a bad thing? You said your mother was the daughter of a Conservative rabbi. Is it surprising that the rabbi's granddaughter is sitting here with a good Jewish boy from Connecticut?"

Susan shook her head, "No, I guess it is not surprising. But, I am still having trouble fitting into the skin of a rabbi's granddaughter. That persona for me magically appeared in the last few weeks. And, it is just that being here with this handsome Jewish doctor in the jazz bistro in New York City is a long way from the redneck farm boys and mechanics I knew in the Mid-West, and whom the Girl from Moline would have had the chance to couple with at some country-western saloon there. It is a long, long way from 4th Street in Moline to 10th Avenue in Manhattan."

Paul put his hand on Susan's arm. "Well, I can't really picture Professor Fisher's beautiful and erudite daughter 'coupling' with a red-neck mechanic, but … Welcome to the Big Apple, Susy Fisher, we are glad to have you. But…but, are you questioning how you feel yourself, or are you questioning what is going on around you? Is it how you feel that is bothering you, or are you afraid events are coming too fast. I know this has all been coming at you fast and that you lost your close loved ones this last year, but the changes that have happened these last weeks all seem to have been pretty fortuitous."

"Yeh, I can't complain much about the property, the university opportunity, my new home, certainly not meeting you and actually sitting here tonight. I think your first question is right, it is how I feel myself. I always had a good idea of who I was and where I wanted to go. But, right now I'm not sure who I want to be anymore, or actually who I am. You know, when you type an online search into Wikipedia on some well-known person or concept where there are multiple different topics that might be what you are looking for? Like searching for 'Mary' or the last name 'Jones.' You know? Wikipedia gives you a page they call the Disambiguation Page where they list all the different possible identities for Mary or Jones, and they give you a chance to remove the ambiguity in whom you are looking for by making a choice."

Susan took a sip of water and continued, "I feel like I need to find one of those disambiguation pages for me, Susan Fisher; am I the middle class Illinois girl, am I the rabbi's granddaughter, am I the artist or the art historian, am I the rich girl in New York, am I the historian's daughter, am I the Metzger heiress, am I the doctor's girlfriend? Sure, I am really all of them, but I am having trouble picking which of these are the important me at the core. And yes, I can't complain much, I guess I am just trying to grasp a comfort level on some massive changes."

Paul nodded, "Okay, so what is the decision you have to make about yourself that you are being pressured on? What ambiguous thing about you is it that you need to clarify to feel better? Your inheritance and your wealth seem to be self-executing; you have good people handling all the details for you. In addition, the rabbi's granddaughter is not being pressured to do anything. And, you seem to be picking up that angle fairly fast. Fate has handed you the family losses you have suffered, but nothing changes your heritage nor the person you are because of where you came from. Our relationship? I think we are both happy with where we are and don't need to rush things. Your studies, I thought Columbia gave you an open book for picking your major. If you want to stick with art you can, if not try something else. It's not like you are having pressure paying tuition for a couple extra semesters."

Susan shook her head, "You're probably wonder why I'm whining, when

I have every blessing I could hope for."

"Not at all. I think I really understand. Change is scary. Radical life changing change is really scary. Just don't let things push you any way you don't want. Only you can decide which link on Susy Fisher's disambiguation page gets clicked next."

—

Susan finished going through the day's mail. It was more of the same junk mail for Rachel that could mostly be ignored. However, a few items of the mail forwarding from Moline were starting to come to the apartment address. Susan sorted and disposed of the junk, and then came back to the table to decide what was next. For one thing, Susan decided she needed to get organized, and move the mail sorting and computer use from the dining room to somewhere else. After all, she had an actual study and she even had a computer table in the corner of her bedroom. She had merely fallen into Rachel's groove of using the dining room for paperwork and computer. Susan would change that to her own routine, but did not know what that was yet.

With the wedding coming up the Sunday after next, Susan reread the invitation Ariel had delivered to get some idea of what she needed for a gift. She had already Googled the subject and had found out that Jewish weddings typically did not have gift tables like Susan had seen at the few weddings she had attended in the Quad Cities. Instead, Susan had learned you send a gift to the bride's parents' home or to the address given for the couple in the announcement.

Susan had purchased two new dresses for the wedding, one from Bergdorf's, one from Saks. One was heavier, and one very frilly and light. Both were pastel, summery dresses, and she would decide which to wear when she saw the weather in Southampton when they got there. She had confirmed with Paul that he was clear to come with her, and the hotel was set.

The beautiful, engraved invitation said the veiling was at "Half past Three," the ceremony was at "Four O'clock" with "Dinner and Merriment at Six O'clock" and gave the address of the Metzger home in Southampton. She noticed the date was given with both the June date and in the Hebrew month of Tamuz. Susan's Maps app had shown the Metzger house was fairly close to her hotel. Dress was "Summer formal." Then, on the back of the card Susan saw, "Please visit us online for gift information and registry" with an internet address, and then a note that gifts could also be shipped to the Metzger parents' address in Southampton.

The online web page had a charming picture of the couple, Edward Rothschild and Ariel Metzger, barefoot and in casual clothes, holding hands as they friskily walked along a beautiful beachfront. The wedding invitation was repeated, except there was no street address online. There was a brief biography page for the bride and groom, which Susan read, noting that details of their lives were scarce, as might be expected online. Eddie worked in venture capital for his father's firm on Wall Street and was a Princeton grad, like Paul, Susan noted, and Ariel only had her college work at NYU listed. There were three wedding registry links, which Susan also clicked on. Two were typical wedding item registries, Bloomingdale's and a wedding specialty place Susan did not recognize, and one was a charity site where a donation to a choice of charity groups could be made in the name of the couple. Susan smiled at these links, knowing that neither Metzger nor Rothschild needed help buying china service or linens. The charity donation made more sense, but that seemed rather gauche.

Susan clicked back to the main wedding announcement page. Susan sat looking at the picture of Ariel and Eddie frolicking in the sand. Ariel's long blonde hair was swept by the sea breeze, and Eddie held her hand.

Susan was turned off by simply signing up for a registry item, and she had no idea what an appropriate donation to the charity was. As she stared at the photograph, in thought, Susan recalled how Aaron and others had mentioned how everyone remembered the wonderful gifts Aunt Rachel had always given at birthdays, weddings and bar mitzvahs. Susan wondered what special, memorable gift Rachel would have given to these two young lovers walking on the beach. Then, almost as if the proverbial light bulb had gone on above her head, Susan had an idea -- a truly unique gift, for this wealthy couple who really did not need a traditional wedding gift. Susan stood up from the dining room table and grabbed the big key ring from other end of the table.

Susan crossed the sixth floor lobby, poked the security code and opened the double deadbolts on Apartment 6-A. She turned on the entranceway light and went directly to one of the large stacks of paintings leaning against the old couch in the living room. The front of the stack was another Edward Cucuel painting like the one of the girl picking peaches she liked in her sitting room, but this was a pastoral scene. But, this was not her goal, Susan remembered a painting in this stack of 20th century painters that was exactly what she needed. Several paintings back she found what she was looking for. She pulled the heavy gilded frame from the stack and moved to the lighted foyer.

As Susan held the painting out at arms' length and turned it up to the light, her head slowly bobbed in acknowledgement. It was about two by three feet, portrait orientation. Susan had marveled at this painting when she first found it in the stack, but now it seemed almost miraculously perfect for what she needed. The painting was by Monfort Stebbins, a well-known painter who had dabbled in a bit of revivalist Pre-Raphaelite painting early in his career, but had made his name in realistic and quasi-realistic romantic and fantasy scenes in the 1950's through the 1970's. A couple of his celebrity fantasy portraits, that he had done under contract with a movie studio, were classics. His work was fairly well-known, and Susan had a good idea of its value, a value that would be appreciated, even by the likes of a young couple with Rothschild and Metzger resources at their disposal. But, the real value, the poetic value if you will, was the subject matter of the painting. Here, like the photo on Ariel and Eddie's website, was a young couple on a beach, hand in hand. But, Ariel's jeans and t-shirt were replaced by a wispy, white dress for this painting's ingénue, her dress flowing in the sea-breeze. The young man in this painting was clothed only in a pair of short pants. This couple could easily be Ariel and Eddie, by their looks, but unlike the frolicking photo on the wedding website, this couple was dreamily wandering away from the viewer on a foggy shore, the entire painting highly detailed in shades of blue, gray and beige. The sense of depth out into the foggy horizon along the shore was amazing. Susan checked the back of the painting, and there was a certificate of provenance from the gallery on Park Avenue where the painting had been purchased. The certificate was dated back in 1978. If Susan, or Rachel, had commissioned the painting as a gift for the Metzger-Rothschild couple, it could not have been more perfect. But, this famous painter was long dead, and his view of the loving couple on the beach was truly fortuitous. Susan had her gift for the bride and groom.

Now, all she had to do was figure out how to ship a valuable painting to the address on the wedding announcement. The internet website where Susan had researched "Jewish wedding gifts" was quite clear, you sent the gift ahead and did not bring it to the wedding.

As she locked up the other apartment, Susan was somewhat in awe of her own feelings – she was unfazed about giving away such a beautiful and valuable painting, and she found herself amazingly satisfied at being able to give her newfound cousin-in-law something so special as a wedding gift. Susan imagined this act would have her Aunt Rachel's approval. Susan decided to visit the art gallery on the first floor of her building to see if they had any ideas for shipping a valuable painting out to Long Island in a little over a week's time.

—

Chapter Twenty-Three

2:36 PM CDT

From: Jesse.Morgenthau@MorgenthauMolineRealty.com

To: David Tannenbaum dtannenbaum@wassermannephraim.com

Cc: Susan Fisher <Susy@SusyFisher.com>

Re: Fisher Property

Attachments: Purchase_Offer.pdf, Grant_Deed.doc

Mr. Tannenbaum,

As instructed by Susan Fisher, we are forwarding for your attention a scan of a purchase offer we have received on Ms. Fisher's home in Moline, IL. The offer came in today, on a Sunday Open House. This is a full price, unconditional offer as per Ms. Fisher's property listing contract with our firm. The purchasers are pre-qualified for a VA loan and they are anxious to move into the property. Buyers are a nice couple with two children. Husband is an officer newly assigned to the US Army Arsenal here. All that is needed is Ms. Fisher's signature on the acceptance page of the Purchase Offer and notarized signature on the grant deed enclosed and we can get escrow opened on this. We expect a short escrow, less than thirty days. Please email us a scan of the offer acceptance and express mail the notarized grant deed.

By the way, we got word from the estate auction company that the auction of the household goods was completed. They say they will be forwarding the proceeds check to your office, less their commissions, in a few days. They will also send a full accounting of the sale.

Please give Susan our regards and best wishes for her move to New York. If either you or she have any questions, please contact me.

Sincerely, Jesse Morgenthau

Managing Broker

Morgenthau Moline Realty

—

The courtesy van from the hotel dropped Susan and Paul off near the driveway of the Metzger compound in Southampton. There were many cars parked on nearby streets and a couple of attendants were doing a valet service to park wedding guests' cars on the huge lawn.

"Good idea you had, to park at the Inn. Quite a crowd." Susan commented. She saw Paul stretching his back as he got out of the van. "You going to be all right, that was quite a flip you took this morning, and you didn't even get the goal."

"I'll be fine. But, this is going to be a long day. If we'd had anybody to fill in, we should have foregone today's soccer game."

Paul took Susan's hand, and they walked down the long asphalt driveway toward the white mansion across the lawn. It was a warm afternoon, and they could smell the ocean in the light southerly breeze on their faces. Several other groups of guests walked with them.

"This is quite a place your Uncle and Aunt have. Looks like they have a huge tent out back," Paul commented.

Susan smiled at Paul and said, "Yeh, the house is almost as big as your folks' place."

Paul retorted, "My parents' place isn't on the beach in the Hamptons. And, you said this is just their summer place."

"Remind me to show you a picture of the little plebian cottage I grew up in, to put things in perspective," Susan said.

"And your point is…?"

Susan did not reply.

"Paul?" a high-pitched woman's voice asked from behind them.

Both Paul and Susan turned to see a woman separate from the man she was walking with behind them in the driveway and nearly run toward Paul. As the woman ran towards them, Susan could see she was a pretty blonde of medium height wearing a pink shirtwaist dress that did little to conceal that she was quite pregnant. As she ran up, she threw her arms up around Paul's neck and gave him a hug and kiss on the cheek.

"Candace!" Paul exclaimed.

By the time Candace let loose of her hug of Paul, the man with her had caught up to them. The man had a rather surprised look on his face, as did Paul.

"I didn't know you knew Eddie. I thought he got to Princeton a couple years after you." Candace said.

"Eddie, the groom? No, I don't know him. I'm here with Susan, she is a cousin of the bride." Paul turned to indicate Susan. "Susan, may I present Candace Swain, she's a, uh, friend of mine from Princeton days. Candy, this is Susan Fisher."

Candy offered her hand to Susan, and they quickly shook hands, while Candy corrected, "Not Swain anymore. Mrs. Candace Hart, now. This is my husband William Hart. Bill, this is Paul Waldman."

William Hart gave a knowing smile and said, "Ah, the notorious Paul Waldman. I've heard all about you." He offered his hand to Paul. They shook.

Paul ignored this comment and looked down at Candy's rotund belly. "And, you're…?"

"Yes. Due in August. We just found out it is a boy." Candy could not conceal her joy at her impending motherhood. In fact, Susan noticed Candy was effusive with emotion. High strung and bouncy barely described Candy's persona. Her personality was in synch with her fluffy blonde curls and doll-like face.

Paul congratulated the couple on the expected baby, and then asked, "So, you are friends with Eddie Rothschild?"

Bill Hart answered, "I work with him at his father's investment bank. But, actually I met Candy through Eddie. She, of course, knew Eddie from Princeton." As he said this, Bill Hart made a motion that they should continue up the driveway toward the house. While they walked, Bill Hart asked Paul, "So, Paul, what do you do?"

"I'm a trauma surgeon, at New York Presbyterian." Paul replied.

Bill did not say anything, but Susan saw a look on Hart's face that said 'of course… he's a doctor.' There was some background between Candy and Paul that Susan wanted to find out about. Bill Hart was clearly telegraphing that he had just met his wife's ex-boyfriend. Notorious?

"And, Susan, you're Ariel's cousin?" Candy asked.

"Yes, that's what we call it, an extended family thing, my aunt was her aunt by marriage." Susan answered. Candy had to think about this for a moment and nodded her head.

They reached a checkpoint in the driveway where two attendants in blue sport coats were checking that everyone who got close to the house had invitations or were on a list? Bill and Candace Hart were on the list, and so were Susan Fisher and Guest.

After he checked them in and crossed their name from a list, the attendant handed both Bill Hart and Paul a gold trimmed white yarmulke from a box full of yarmulkes at his feet, and he recited his spiel, "Lady's facilities are available in the main house. Gentlemen have portable facilities behind the garage, near the greenhouse. There are also portable facilities and washrooms behind the white tent. The reading of the *Ketubah* and bride's veiling will take place in the small blue tent at Three thirty." He looked at this watch, "Which is in just a few minutes. The huppah and seating are on the back lawn near the shore, and the ceremony begins at Four o-clock. *Yichud* will be in the blue tent immediately after the ceremony, please keep a respectful distance from the blue tent for that. Dinner and festivities are in the big white tent at Six. Your seating assignments are marked on both the lawn seating for the ceremony and at the tables for dinner. There will be ushers with seating charts around to help you find your seats. Enjoy yourselves."

After they walked on, Candy stopped short and said, "Bill, I really need to find those lady's facilities." She patted her belly as if to explain her reasons. "Susan, you need to join me?"

Susan shook her head 'no.'

Bill Hart took over, he said, "Well, nice to meet you folks, maybe we can talk later." He quickly put his hand on his wife's shoulder and steered her toward the house.

Candy gave them a little wave over her shoulder. "Bye bye, see you later."

"Well, that was charming." Susan said in a hushed voice as the Hart's departed, "By the way, I love your little hat. You realize you are going to have to explain about the 'notorious Paul Waldman' comment and exactly who Candy is."

"So, I figured," Paul said as he took Susan's hand and headed around the house for the blue tent.

Susan stopped Paul for a moment and with the back of her hand wiped a smudge of Candy's pink lipstick from Paul's cheek.

"So, I need details on this *ketubah* and bride's veiling ritual. I understand the veil, but not a formal veiling event. That's something special for Jewish weddings I'm not familiar with." Susan said as pulled Paul onward.

"I suspect there will be a lot of that for you today. I'll do my best to explain things."

The blue tent and the larger white tent were essentially circus tents. There was a small placard near the blue tent listing the events company in Sag Harbor who supplied the tent. The blue tent had its canvas wall rolled up when they got there so the crowd that was standing around could see the inside. There was a table of refreshments on one end of the tent with a pair of overstuffed blue satin couches sitting close by. Susan could see a bottle of champagne on ice was sitting on the refreshment table. The refreshment table and couches were cordoned off with a ring of stanchions and a white rope with Do Not Disturb signs and a young woman in waiter's blue uniform guarding the table. On the other end of the blue tent was a plain wooden table. A few people were standing inside the tent, but most everybody circled around the tent, kept out by a team of ushers in blue sport coats.

As Paul and Susan stood waiting with the others, Peter Ephraim and his wife and Joseph Metzger with Sandra Will saw Susan and came over to say hello. To each, Susan introduced Paul as 'Dr. Paul Waldman, my friend." After they left Susan gave Paul a better description of exactly who these people were.

Eventually, the crowd gave a murmur as two parties of people walked out from the main house. First, came the Metzgers. Aaron had Ariel's arm. Ariel's dress was a shimmering long gown of embroidered silk. She had a long veil flowing behind her head from her tiara, but her face was not veiled. Myra and Hannah followed. Two young women Susan assumed were bridesmaids from their matching gowns followed the mother and grandmother. Susan recognized Amee Metzger as one of the bridesmaids. The other close relatives of Aaron and Myra followed them. They came and stood near the bare table in the tent. Susan saw that the fat rabbi from Rachel's funeral was now standing by the table, too, holding something in his hands. The rabbi was wearing a fedora.

Next, the other group from the house arrived. Susan could recognize Eddie Rothschild in front walking jauntily with another young man. An older couple followed them and several other people behind that. Susan assumed this was the Rothschild parents following their son and the best man. The Rothschild couple were both tall and dark haired like their son. They walked to the table in the tent and stood facing the Metzger family. The bride and groom faced each other near the table.

Susan was not close enough to hear what was being said, but after a moment Eddie stepped forward and carefully drew Ariel's veil from behind her tiara and down over her face. They turned and faced the old rabbi, across the table from him.

The rabbi stepped forward and Susan saw that the object the rabbi had been holding was a paper scroll, which he unrolled now. In a strong, deep voice the rabbi read from the scroll. What he read was in a foreign language, but it did not seem to be Hebrew. To Susan's ear what the rabbi read almost sounded like Arabic. Paul saw Susan's questioning look and leaned over to whisper in her ear.

"He's reading the *ketubah*, marriage contract, it is written in Aramaic," Paul explained. Susan gave Paul a quizzical look, as though a marriage contract in Aramaic, instead of Hebrew or English, did not make any sense.

After the rabbi finished reading, the best man and one of the bridesmaids, not Amee, stepped forward and said something to Eddie and Ariel, who both nodded and replied. Then the rabbi pushed a golden writing pen across the table. The best man took a pen and signed the scroll. He gave the pen to the bridesmaid.

As she signed the scroll, a violinist started playing a folksong-like Jewish melody that Susan thought she recognized from somewhere; from a movie? Several ushers started to untie and roll down the canvas sides of the blue tent. When they were done, the ushers moved through the crowd urging everyone away from the blue tent and toward the seating area.

The crowd of maybe two hundred people moved and started to take their seats. With the help of an usher, Paul escorted Susan to their seats in the fourth row on the right side, on the center aisle. Susan could see that in the front of the seats was an elaborate four posted awning covered in satin draperies and blue and purple flowers.

As they sat down, Paul leaned toward Susan and said, "The square structure is called the huppah, it is the symbol of the house of love the new couple will be building together." Susan nodded.

Susan saw a musical ensemble of twelve to fifteen musicians forming in chairs to the right of the huppah. As more and more of the crowd took their seats, the ensemble started playing a medley of romantic and classical music, interspersed with Hebrew folk melodies.

More and more of the crowd found their seats. Susan recognized some of them from Rachel's funeral. Susan saw several Metzgers and the Birney family members sit in the first two rows on the right. David Tannenbaum came up and touched Susan on the shoulder. She introduced him to Paul, and David introduced a pretty, dark haired woman to Susan as his fiancée. Susan could not help but notice the huge diamond on the ring finger of the fiancée. They sat several rows behind Susan.

Eventually, the seats filled, and everyone got situated. Susan had purchased a new shoulder strap purse to match her peach colored dress. She sat her purse in her lap. Paul reached over and took her hand in his.

The rabbi now walked up to the huppah from the side and took his place behind the huppah. Susan could see the ragged fringe of his prayer shawl under his black silk suit. Another man, similarly dressed, but with a yarmulke instead of fedora, followed him with a woman in a long, blue gown at his side. She wore a prayer shawl also. They stood beside the rabbi.

Paul whispered in Susan's ear, "Good, they have a female cantor, too. They make the wedding blessings much prettier."

When the rabbi took his place he looked over to the musical director, who waived his baton in the air to signal with finality. The musicians stopped playing the current song in mid-stanza, and went silent. They shifted music pages and started playing a folk tune that Susan thought she recognized. The song had violins, cornets and clarinets playing a cheerful, but somehow melancholy tune.

Susan leaned to Paul and asked, "Where do I know that from?"

Paul whispered to her, "It is the Wedding Procession song from the musical *Fiddler on the Roof.*"

Susan nodded.

Shortly after the song began, Susan saw Bubba Hannah walk past her up the main aisle. One of her grandsons escorted Bubba Hanna to the front row on the right side. An elderly, gray-haired couple in expensive clothes followed her and sat in the front row on the left side.

As the procession music played on, the other bridesmaid, not Amee, was escorted on the arm of a young man Susan did not recognize. The escort led this bridesmaid to her place near the right post of the huppah. The escort departed to the side. Susan realized that the bride's side of the wedding seemed to be on the right, as opposed to the opposite in weddings she had attended before.

Next came the best man all by himself, who stood by the left post. He was followed by Eddie Rothschild, with his father to his left and his mother to his right. Mr. and Mrs. Rothschild took their position on the left side of the huppah facing inward. Eddie went and stood in the center of the huppah, facing down the aisle.

Amee Metzger was escorted by another male escort. She stood near the other bridesmaid by the right post. Then, Myra and Aaron came up the aisle on either side of Ariel. Myra's long gown of blue beads and lace was stunning, but not more than that of the bride. Ariel's white gown was simply the most beautiful wedding gown Susan could imagine. A flicker of rhinestones accentuated the embroidered silk that hugged the curves of her body.

As they were well past her, Susan whispered to Paul, "No 'Here Comes the Bride' at Jewish weddings?"

Paul cupped his hand around his mouth as he very softly answered, in Susan's ear, "Richard Wagner was a brazen anti-Semite and he was Hitler's favorite composer, so Wagner's wedding march is rare at Jewish weddings. Same for Mendelssohn, he was born a Jew, but converted to Catholicism, so you won't hear Mendelssohn's Midsummer's Night wedding march much either."

Susan gave a tiny nod.

The three Metzgers stopped in front of the huppah. Eddie came out to take Ariel's hand from Aaron's. Ariel handed her bouquet to Amee. Aaron smiled at his mother sitting in the front row as he and Myra took their place on far right side of the huppah.

As the processional music ended, Eddie led Ariel under the huppah, turning to face her, hand in hand. Ariel had her back to the audience, facing the groom and the rabbi.

Eddie took two steps back from Ariel, standing in the very middle of the huppah. Myra and Mrs. Rothschild now walked over to each side of the bride, taking hold of her arms. As the two mothers started to guide Ariel walking around Eddie in a circle, the female cantor started to sing a light, chanting, almost playful song in Hebrew. The mothers and the bride circled Eddie seven times, with a new chant or song from the female cantor each round. By the end of the seventh circling, it seemed that Ariel's step was more of a playful skip in time to the cantor's song. Her mother and soon-to-be mother-in-law seemed to follow her gait.

Susan smiled and let out a little puff of air as a restrained laugh. Paul looked over to here in question. Susan gave a little shake of her head that it was nothing, but pressing her lips together to try and thwart a smile. Ahead of them, the circling of the bride and the mothers ended.

The mothers left Ariel facing Eddie and went back to the side of their husbands. Ariel took Eddie's hand and they turned to face the rabbi and the cantors. The rabbi took a large silver cup from a little table beside him, and held it aloft in front of the bride and groom. The male cantor then sang, *"Baruch atah Adonai Eloheinu Melech Haolam, borei p'ri hagafen."* Susan recognized this as the blessing Paul had given the wine at his family's dinner table in Connecticut.

Then, the female cantor gave a much longer blessing in Hebrew. After this blessing was finished, the rabbi handed the cup to Eddie. Amee stepped forward and helped Ariel lift her veil back over her tiara. Eddie put the wine cup to her lips and she took a sip. Ariel took the cup and gave Eddie a sip. Ariel carried the cup over to the Rothschilds, giving each of them a sip. Next, she gave the cup back to Eddie who did the same for Aaron and Myra Metzger. Eddie then gave the cup back to the rabbi, and took his place beside Ariel. Susan recognized the merger of families motif to this.

The male cantor now sang something in Hebrew.

Next, the rabbi said something to Eddie and Ariel that Susan could not quite hear. Eddie and Ariel stood to face each other. The best man stepped up and handed a ring to Eddie.

Eddie spoke out in a loud voice, *"Haray aht m'kudeshet li b'taba'at zu k'dat Moshe v Yisrael."* He followed this in English, "By this ring you are consecrated as my wife in accordance with the traditions of Moses and Israel." Eddie lifted Ariel's right hand and put the ring on her pointing finger.

Susan looked quickly at Paul and pantomimed her question for him with her hands in her lap, motioning putting a ring on her right pointing finger. Paul nodded and leaned to her ear, again whispering, "Just for now, it is the finger she would use to read the *ketubah*, they'll move it to the wedding ring finger later."

Next, Amee opened a little satchel she had tied to her wrist and extracted another ring, which she handed to Ariel. Ariel took Eddie's hand and said to Eddie, "*Ani l'dodi, ve dodi li.* I am my beloved's and my beloved is mine." She pushed the ring on his finger.

The rabbi handed the *ketubah* scroll he had read from earlier to Ariel, who handed it back to Amee.

Now, with the couple still facing each other, Eddie reached into his pocket and took out a white card. Holding the card in his left hand, he held Ariel's right hand in his. He read, "Ariel, I Eddie, promise to dedicate my life to your happiness, to honor the commitment we make this day in all things I may do in my lifetime, to do all that I can to make you proud and to protect you and our family."

Then he handed the paper the Ariel who read, "And I Ariel, promise you Eddie, that I will be at your side for our lifetime, delighting in your achievements and dedicating my life to your happiness, standing with you in all things."

Eddie and Ariel then turned to face the rabbi and cantors. The rabbi and the cantors took turns reciting or singing seven different prayers, in both English and Hebrew. The cantors would sing the blessing in Hebrew, and the rabbi would translate into English.

The rabbi gave the groom the cup of wine, and Eddie and Ariel each took another sip.

Finally, the rabbi stepped forward and in a loud voice declared, "By the authority vested in me by the State of New York and in accordance with the traditions of Moses and Israel, I declare you to be husband and wife."

The rabbi went to the table and picked up a white velvet bag. He handed it to Eddie. Eddie opened the bag and showed the crystal goblet inside to Ariel and the audience. Eddie put the glass back in the bag and put it on the ground. With a firm stomp on the bag, Eddie broke the crystal in a tinkling of broken glass that all could hear.

The audience stood and everyone shouted, "Mazel tov" and "Siman tov u masel tov," as Eddie leaned forward to kiss Ariel.

As the Mazel Tov shouts died down, Paul leaned, once again, to whisper in Susan's ear, "The symbol of the breaking glass is symbolic that like the irrevocability of the broken glass, so, too, is the marriage irrevocable. Another interpretation is that it is symbolic of the breaking of the hymen after the wedding. Again, it being irrevocable."

To the music of a Hebrew folk tune, Eddie and Ariel, by themselves, now headed happily down the aisle, smiling and waving to friends and family in the audience. Susan turned and watched as the couple walked down the aisle, and over to the blue tent. Two ushers closed the door of the blue tent and stood guard at the entrance.

Paul was watching from behind Susan's back. He put his head near her ear and said, "The tent is for the bride and groom to be in seclusion, called the *Yichud*. In olden days it was when the marriage was consummated. But now, it is just ten or fifteen minutes for the bride and groom to be together, relax and maybe have a glass of champagne, and get a snack to break their fast they should have been doing before the wedding."

Susan turned her head so that she was face to face with Paul, "Are we sure they aren't consummating?" She whispered with a risqué smile.

Paul raised his eyebrows, "Could be. Under Jewish law, I think it is actually Ariel's right to demand it. In the old, old days, by tradition, then the groom's mother would have the right to see a soiled white cloth to prove that the hymen had been broken, if her virginity had been promised in the *ketubah*. Many a barnyard animal was poked with a needle to produce bloody white kerchiefs for the bride to hide under her dress to give to skeptical, meddlesome in-laws."

Now, Susan raised her eyebrows, "Hmmm. I'm glad that tradition died out. What next?"

"Well, pretty much everybody meanders, finds the ladies' and men's room, meets and greets everybody else, until the dinner and party." Paul looked at his watch. "We've got a half hour."

"Ladies' room it is."

—

Paul was waiting for Susan by the pool when she came out of the main house.

"Beautiful house. The main bathroom is all Carrera marble," Susan said. "Unfortunately, nothing brings out the savage in otherwise civilized women as a long line for the potty."

Paul smiled, "The men's Porta-Potties were first class, too. They were the finest green fiberglass available."

Susan came and stood by Paul as he stared at the pool. "What are you standing here contemplating?"

Paul pointed to the smaller square pool he was standing near. "I was contemplating this lap pool. Totally state of the art. I'd kill for one of these."

"Lap pool? I thought it was a spa. How do you swim laps? Its only ten or twelve feet long?" Susan asked.

"It's a continuous flow pool. You get in, and it flows the water past you so you can swim as long and fast as you want in one direction. Watch this," Paul said as he took a few steps and pushed a stainless steel footpad on the edge of the pool.

Machinery in a low cabinet behind a row of deck chairs whirred to life, underwater ports opened up and after a bit of turbulence, the water in the pool flowed rapidly, but very smoothly from right to left. Paul kicked the footpad again, and the water increased speed. Paul kicked it again and it stopped.

"These were just coming in when I was on the Princeton swim team. We went to Cornell for a meet, and they had a couple of these in their clubhouse. We were so jealous. They were pretty expensive. The technology to make it flow without turbulence is something special."

"Well, if you are a good boy, maybe Uncle Aaron will invite us out here for a weekend, and you can use it. Speaking of Uncle Aaron, there are lots of people I probably need to say hello to."

"Yeh, the receiving line should be forming in the white tent." Paul took Susan's hand. They walked toward the big tent. As she walked across the manicured turf, Susan was glad she had worn the flats instead of the heels.

The receiving line had, indeed, formed at the door to the tent. It consisted of Aaron, Bubba Hannah, Myra, their daughter and her new husband, followed by the groom's mother and father and two older couples who Susan assumed were the Rothschild grandparents.

At the thought of this set of Rothschild grandparents, Susan wondered about the absence of Myra's parents, as only Hannah was there to represent Metzger family grandparents. Susan realized she knew next to nothing about Myra or her background.

Quite a few people were already in the tent, and there was a line formed to meet the receiving line. They got in line with Susan ahead of Paul.

Aaron was still talking to the old couple ahead of her when she got to him, so he had not seen her until she stepped in front of him. When he saw her, Aaron smiled and hugged Susan. He held onto her arms and looked at her. "My, you are lovely tonight."

Susan smile and said, "Thank you, Uncle Aaron, may I present my friend, Doctor Paul Waldman. Paul, My uncle Aaron Metzger."

The men shook hands. Susan did not hear what they had to say as Bubba Hannah had grabbed her in a bear hug and a rapid stream of words. "Susannah, Susannah, where have you been? And you are so beautiful tonight. We need to see more of you. But, I guess we have been out here all month. You do need to come by to see us. And, who is this you have brought?"

Susan introduced Paul. "Bubba Hannah, this is Doctor Paul Waldman. Paul, this is…"

"Doctor Paul Waldman, are you a real doctor or a dentist or professor or something?" Hannah asked.

Paul smiled and said, "A real doctor, I'm a surgeon."

Susan cut back in, "This is Hannah Metzger, Ariel's grandmother."

As they tried to step sideways to Myra, Hannah gave a quick nod and wink to Susan, showing that she approved of Susan's escort.

As Susan stepped in front of Myra, she saw Myra was smiling at Hannah. Susan got a gentler hug and double cheek touch from Myra. "I'm glad you could make it, Susan. I should have tried to meet for lunch or had you over, but things have been pretty hectic with the wedding preps."

"I can believe that. Everything is wonderful. And your gown is stunning."

"Thank you, Susan. When we get a chance, I'd like to talk to you. Maybe after we eat."

"Sure, whenever you are free."

Myra nodded.

Susan got another hug from Ariel. Before Susan could introduce Paul to Ariel, Ariel was introducing Susan to Eddie. Susan shook his hand and then said, "Ariel, Eddie, let me introduce Doctor Paul Waldman. Eddie, Paul is a fellow Princeton alum."

Paul shook hands with Ariel and Eddie, and congratulated Eddie on the marriage.

Sharon Rothschild was probably in her fifties, high cheekbones, long thin nose and patrician features. She wore a light silver gray gown that was serene and elegant. Her black-gray hair was in an up-do with several diamond hairpins. Susan introduced herself to Mrs. Rothschild, who introduced herself by saying, "I'm Sharon Rothschild. And if I am not incorrect, you are Ariel's cousin. Right?"

Susan was a bit shocked that the groom's mother had heard of her. "Yes, actually cousin-in-law is the best description."

Susan introduced Paul, as before. But, after a short hand shake with Paul, Sharon Rothschild turned back to Susan.

"Yes, Susan, I was hoping to meet you. When we were looking over the wedding gifts with my son and Ariel, I couldn't help but notice your gift to them. It was marvelous. I'm not sure if you know, but my avocation is helping run a gallery in Tribeca. Sort of a hobby. When I saw the painting you gave them, I contacted my partner and asked him to research it. It has quite a provenance. An original, verified Monfort Stebbins, one that has not been noted in provenance journals since entering a private collection in the 1970's. Other Monfort Stebbins paintings are in the Guggenheim, the National Gallery and the Getty."

Susan was painfully aware the extended conversation with Sharon Rothschild was bringing the receiving line to a halt. "Yes, I love that painting. When I saw the photography of Ariel and Eddie on the beach on their website, I knew I had to give that painting to them. I think it was meant to be in their home. The couple in the painting are Ariel and Eddie, to me."

"I thought exactly the same thing when I saw it. Susan, I have to tell you, even though the Rothschilds and Metzgers have attempted to show our joy at this marriage with the best gifts we could, I have to say that if prizes were awarded for the most perfect and, indeed, precious gift, that that prize would surely go to your painting."

Since their conversation had brought the receiving line to a standstill, Eddie was listening in to his mother and leaned over to say to Susan, "And Ariel has already told me your painting goes in the foyer of our condo."

Susan looked over to Eddie and saw Ariel standing behind him nodding her head enthusiastically. Everybody within earshot had listened to Sharon Rothschild. Susan was almost blushing at the attention and said, "Well I'm glad everybody liked my idea. Like I said, it seemed like it was meant to be."

"Yes. They appreciated your idea, and your generosity." Mrs. Rothschild smiled and gave Susan a formal kiss on the cheek.

Susan smiled back, said, "I'm happy they can enjoy it." She quickly turned and introduced herself to Mr. Rothschild and Eddie's four grandparents.

As they walked away from the receiving line, Paul took Susan's hand again and said to her, "If I understand what just happened, Susan Fisher just wowed a matron of one of high society's premier families with her 'generosity' and gift giving style."

Susan shrugged. "Apparently."

"So, what was this painting you gave them?"

"Just something I had laying around."

"Right. And how much is this painting worth, that it impresses a Rothschild?"

Susan looked at Paul and with a kind of sheepish rise of her eyebrows, she said, "I'm not totally sure, but my guess is it is worth almost in the range of your annual salary at the hospital." Susan saw a momentary flash of expression from Paul. Disbelief, or awe? Then, Susan waved to an usher with a clipboard to find their seats.

—

The huge tent was quite a place. The floor was a grid of interlocking wood panels that had been placed over the underlying turf. The center area was an open space, apparently for dancing. Well over a dozen huge, round dinner tables were spaced around the room. A long, head table stretched along the far tent wall, slightly elevated. All of the tables were decorated with more of the blue and purple flowers, like the huppah. The two center tent poles had rings of lights to illuminate the whole area inside the tent. A latticework of sparkling streamers and dark banners above the lights gave the impression of a starry night sky. The rear wall of the tent, on either side of the entrance had two open bars and two buffet tables crowded with food. Susan had seen two large supply trucks and the washroom facilities trailers behind the tent as they walked up. There was a bandstand for the orchestra to the far right, but recorded music was softly playing as they entered.

The usher took Susan and Paul to their table., which was in the row next to the head table two tables away from the orchestra. When they got to their table, half of the twelve chairs were already full. Introductions were made. Susan realized their table was a mix of both Metzger and Rothschild friends and miscellaneous family members, but nobody she knew before this. One young woman who was wearing a nice, but fairly plain, blue dress did not identify herself as to which side of the wedding she represented. Susan saw that after introductions, this young woman made a few quick notes in a small spiral notebook, and then pulled out a cellphone and typed something with her thumbs. Did they invite reporters to weddings?

Their table and the others soon filled, with each new addition bringing more introductions. Finally, the orchestra started to take their seats. The main family members moved toward the head table. Everyone else took their seats. The crowd quieted. Susan saw Aaron stand and signal to the orchestra conductor. The orchestra started to play a cheerful Jewish folk melody.

When the melody was done, Eddie and Ariel came down from their spots at the head table and stood by a banquet table between the head table and the dance floor. The banquet table had several huge, long loaves of golden brown bread and a stack of silver platters. Eddie lifted a piece of bread cut from the middle of the loaf in his hands. A photographer took a picture. Together, Eddie and Ariel recited, "*Baruch ata Adonai, Elohenyu Melech Ha-olam, hamotzi lechem min ha-retz.*" The bride and groom seemed to have a wireless microphone, as their voices were amplified on the tent's sound system.

After the blessing, the orchestra started playing another tune. Ariel took one of the silver platters, on which Eddie put a portion of bread on it. Ariel and Eddie delivered the bread to their parents and grandparents at the head table. The head table stood as the bride and groom delivered the bread. Then, Ariel and Eddie proceeded to deliver other portions of bread to each dinner table in the room. At each table the guests stood to offer a quick greeting and congratulation to the couple. The bride and groom delivered to every table, even gave a platter to the orchestra members, the ushers and waiters who gathered by the entrance. The photographer followed the couple around the room, taking pictures at each table.

When they were finished, Ariel and Eddie took their seats in the middle of the head table. After a pause, Myra stood and showed everyone she had a small pamphlet in her hand. When Myra stood many people in the room reached forward for a pamphlet that was at every place setting. Susan opened her pamphlet. Myra spoke, again using a wireless microphone over the tent's speaker system.

The front of the pamphlet was a copy of the wedding announcement. Most of the pamphlet was a series of seven different prayers or blessings, in English. Susan saw that some lines showed they were to be said by "The Women." Some were just for one speaker.

Myra, in a loud, calm voice, recited Psalm 126;

"When God returned us to Zion from exile, we thought we were dreaming.

"Then our mouths filled with laughter and cheers were on our tongue.

"The other nations saw and said, "The Lord has done great things for them.

"The Lord has done great things for us, and we were very glad.

"Return us again to freedom, Adonai, like stream, long dry, to the Negev returning.

"Those who sow in tears will reap in joy.

"The farmer wants to weep when he buries the precious seed,

"But, singing he comes back with his arms filled with grain."

When she finished, Myra handed the microphone to Sharon Rothschild who arose. She read the next blessing from the pamphlet. It was one where the women in the audience were supposed to supply the chorus for the blessing. Susan joined in the reading the women's lines.

Sharon said, "Friends, Let us give thanks!"

The women read, "May the name of God be praised now and forever."

Sharon said, "With your consent, then, let us praise God from whom our abundance is taken."

Then the women said, "Praise God from whose abundance we have eaten and by whose goodness we live."

Sharon Rothschild finished with, "Praise God, praise God!"

Then, one by one, five more women from the head table, including Bubba

Hannah, read various blessings from the pamphlet, a couple of which had more recitations from the assembled women. Susan noted with interest that Sarah Birney did one of the blessings. When the last of the seven blessings was read, the orchestra started to play softly. The waiters rushed to deliver dinner plates, pitchers and bottles of drink and more bread to every table. The dinner was underway.

Each dinner plate had two small entrees, chicken and beef, each of gourmet quality. Garnish and relish plates were delivered, filed with pickles, jams, jellies and fruits. Susan noticed the bread and pastry plates had chilled margarine balls, and little tubs of whipped margarine and honey, not butter. Several bottles of champagne and a selection of wines were delivered by cart to each table.

Susan leaned over to Paul and whispered, "When the blessing promised 'abundance,' they were not kidding."

Paul smiled clinked his wine glass to Susan's.

After the guests finished the main course, the waiters brought bowls of non-dairy fruit iced glasé and little plates of warm chocolate filled cakes, followed by fresh champagne bottles. As the guests started their dessert, Aaron stood and the orchestra went silent. Aaron started a round of typical toasts, blessings and stories from people at the head table for the bride and groom. At the end of the toasts, Eddie arose with Ariel and whispered something in Ariel's ear. Then, they drank champagne with their arms intertwined.

When they sat their champagne glasses down, Eddie took Ariel's hand and led her to the dance floor. The orchestra started a waltz that Susan recognized as being by Edvard Grieg. After Eddie and Ariel had waltzed around the dance floor for a couple of circuits, they were joined by Aaron and Myra, and the Rothschild parents. As the Grieg waltz ended, a Liszt waltz began, and more guest couples joined them on the dance floor. The photographer took photos of the couples on the dance floor. Susan noticed the young woman she had thought might be a reporter had gotten up from their table, kept talking to the photographer and seemed to be directing him as to whom he should photograph.

Paul took Susan's hand and indicated they should join in the dancing. On the dance floor Paul held Susan close. They moved off in time to the airy, Liszt waltz.

Susan put her mouth to Paul's ear and said, "Wow, you are a good dancer."

Paul smiled and said, "One of the side benefits of a private school education in Connecticut. Our gym teachers also taught ballroom dancing."

Susan took her hand from Paul's shoulder and marked another tally score for him in the air between them.

As the couples' dances ended, it was replaced by a Jewish folk tune with cornet, clarinet and accordion. The dancing turned into a line dance, Susan tugged Paul's arm to leave the dance floor.

"Not interested in participating in the ethnic dances?" Paul asked.

"Not necessarily. I just have no idea what is going on and need to watch for a while."

They sat at their table. Paul poured another glass of champagne for each of them. Susan saw that the young woman with the notebook was now moving from table to table, meeting people and taking notes.

Susan heard the tinkling tone from her iPhone in her purse. It was not a call, but the unique tone you get when someone has tagged you on Facebook. Curious, Susan pulled the iPhone from her purse. She quickly saw that a Facebook page called 'Metzger-Rothschild Wedding' had tagged her and Paul in a photo of them dancing. The young woman in the blue dress was a hired blogger, documenting the wedding in real time. Susan clicked comment on her iPhone, so that the picture of her and Paul would go to her personal timeline and Twitter account. Susan noticed several other people at the tables also had cellphones in hand, posting, tweeting and texting. She showed Paul the photo.

As she watched the dancing, Susan saw a couple walking towards her. It was Jack Birney and his wife Marjorie.

As they walked up, Susan stood and Paul did, too. Jack and Marjorie both gave Susan a quick kiss and hug.

Jack said, "Susannah, it is good to see you again. I was hoping to get a chance to see you tonight."

Susan smiled and said, "Jack and Marjorie, can I introduce you to Doctor Paul Waldman. Paul, this is Jack Birney, my Aunt Rachel's grandson and Marjorie Birney, his wife."

The other three all shook hands.

Jack said to Susan, "Are you getting all settled in? I understand you decided to move from Chicago to New York."

Susan had given up correcting the Susannah and Chicago references, so she just said, "Yes, getting settled. Lots to do."

Jack continued with, "And, I'm glad to hear that the problem with my mother was resolved."

Susan blinked and said, "Oh really, I hadn't heard that it was, uh, resolved."

"Oh, yes. Marjorie and I tried to tell Mother that that attorney of hers was all screwed up with the probate advice he was giving. But, Dad thought this attorney was giving good advice. He told us we are both criminal law attorneys, so what do we know about trusts and estates. However, it seems it was all resolved without the need for attorneys. Aunt Myra called Mother and told her she was calling on behalf of Bubba Hannah. Myra let Mother know that Hannah and Myra were not happy with Mother challenging the trust clause that gave not only Rachel and you your inheritance, but is also the same thing that gives Hannah and Myra their wives' share of the Metzger family goodies. The Metzger matriarchs spoke and Mother listened."

"Ah, I see. I wasn't really in the loop as to what exactly was going on there." Susan thought a little white lie would help here.

Marjorie cut in and said, "Well, we just wanted to stop and say 'Hi.' And let you know we are happy the family waters are now calmed down. Nice to meet you, Paul. We need to run and find out what mischief our two boys have gotten into."

After another round of handshakes and cheek touches, the Birneys walked away. Paul and Susan sat back down.

Paul said, "Okay, three questions. Susannah? Chicago? And, if I may ask, what the rest of that was all about?"

Susan explained the Metzger family's problem with knowing her name and hometown, and then, looking around to see if anyone was in listening distance, she explained, "Jack's mother is really my Aunt Rachel's step-daughter, not real daughter. Joe Metzger and Sarah Birney's mother died when they were kids. Rachel inherited half of her husband Isaac's estate, and her two step-kids each got half of the other half. Isaac had already inherited a quarter of the original Metzger estate. His estate was actually bigger than the original estate, because Isaac was a better dealmaker. But, Rachel's estate was set up to go completely to her sister, that's my mother, and when they both died it all came to me, as my mother's and aunt's only heir. This was all based on some common language in all of the family trusts and will documents. So, when I inherited half of her father's estate, Sarah Metzger Birney, Jack's mother was all bent out of shape and made sounds like she would challenge that arrangement. But, Hannah and Myra, that's the bride's mother and grandmother, my Aunt Rachel's mother-in-law and sister-in-law, have the same kind of position in the family estates as my Aunt Rachel did. And, they didn't like their niece and granddaughter rocking the Metzger wives' boat. And they told her so."

Paul thought for a minute and asked, "But, if it might mean half of her father's estate, why, other than family affinity, did Sarah care what her grandmother and aunt thought?"

Susan waited for a moment while someone passed close to them, "Ah, the real reason comes out. Bubba Hannah is the widow of the original Metzger millionaire dealmaker, Morris Metzger, and under the same kind of clause in his estate, Hannah got half of everything he had. All of her children and grandchildren and spouses, that's Aaron, Rachel's husband Isaac, Myra, Sarah, her brother Joseph, and all the rest only got quarters and eighths and sixteenths of the original fortune which old Bubba Hannah got half of. Hannah is now ninety-three, fairly healthy, but getting on, and if Sarah keeps her Bubba Hannah happy, she is guaranteed to get exactly the same share of the family fortune from her Grammy as she would have gotten by her risky attack on my share, risky since all the attorneys except her husband's said she would probably lose anyway. But, if she gets Grammy mad at her and she loses her fight with me and my attorneys, well.... Understand?"

Paul thought for a moment and asked, "So what does the bride, Ariel, or this guy Jack get from the family fortune?"

Now Susan thought, "I don't think they get anything directly until their parents die or decide to give it to them, and then they get a share of what their parents had left, split with their siblings. Maybe a sixteenth or thirty-second."

"But, you, Susannah of Chicago, the non-blueblood interloper, manage to plop yourself down in the middle of the Metzger family and inherit… what?... an eighth of the whole family estate, immediately?"

"Actually, I think it is a half of Isaac's estate and an eighth of Morris's, I guess.

"Still, you had the *chutzpah* to walk into the Metzger tent tonight, with only me as your bodyguard. Brave girl!"

Susan shook her head, "It's not that bad, everybody but Sarah, even her own brother, Joseph, you met him, were on my side. But, I guess you can see why I don't really mind giving Ariel one painting, when I've got hundreds more where that came from."

Paul shook his head, as if to clear it, and stared at Susan, "You have hundreds more where that came from? A painting that costs what I make in a year?"

"Well, they probably aren't all that valuable. I haven't figured that out yet. But, I do have lots of them. Actually, I haven't counted them yet. I should do that." Susan looked at Paul, who was staring at her, open mouthed. She reached up and with her peach-lacquered fingernail pushed up under his chin, closing his mouth. She leaned toward him and kissed him. "Let's go dance, I'm ready now. That dance is called the hora, right?" Susan stood up and led Paul toward the current line dance.

—

As the orchestra finished the music for the second group dance Susan and Paul had been part of, Amee Metzger stood up in the center of the head table. A young man with her turned on the wireless microphone and handed it to her.

"Hello, everybody. Can you all hear me?" Everyone shouted 'yes,' and she continued. "Okay, I don't want to throw a wet blanket on the party, it will be going on for hours. But, I have been asked to remind everybody who took the train out here that this is Sunday and the train has a reduced schedule. The last westbound train from Southampton leaves in about forty-five minutes. We have the two passenger vans waiting in the driveway to get you to the station. If you don't make this train, the next one will be the red-eye commuter train at one-thirty tomorrow morning. Ugghh! And the vans will be running all evening to take you folks who stayed over to your hotels. We want to remind you that if you've been drinking and you drove here that you should take the vans to your hotel. Your car will be just fine parked where it is. Don't drink and drive. If you need the train, head to the driveway. But, for now, party on! Maestro?" Amee waved the microphone toward the orchestra.

The orchestra now played its version of a classic rock song, trying to change things up a bit.

Paul looked at Susan who shook her head. "I've had enough for now. Maybe we can take a walk and clear the champagne cobwebs?"

As Paul led Susan toward the tent door, their paths intersected with Aaron and Myra.

Aaron spoke in an overly loud voice, his champagne intake showing itself, "Susy, are you having a good time?"

"Oh, certainly. The arrangements you have made are nothing short of awesome," Susan said.

"They should be, I started making plans for this night twenty-two years ago." Myra laughed and touched Susan's arm as she spoke. "I saw you two were tripping the light fantastic fairly well on the dance floor. Where'd you meet?"

"Paul is one of my tenants in the building."

"And, Paul… Susan said you were a doctor?" Myra asked.

"Yes, a surgeon, at Presbyterian."

"Oh yes, I remember Bubba Hannah asking that now." Myra said with a nod and a smile.

"Myra, I understand I have you to thank for ending the problem with Sarah." Susan said.

Aaron seemed surprised, looking at his wife and saying, "Oh, really?"

Myra raised her eyebrows at Aaron and patted him on the shoulder, "Yes, dear. Your mother asked me to have a heart-to-heart talk with your niece. It seems the lawyers had blown the whole thing out of proportion, and we Metzger womenfolk have things well in hand."

Aaron looked from Myra to Susan, who gave a little shrug, saying, "Yes, Jack says everything is fine now."

"Well, that is nice to know. I haven't seen Sarah and Mark since the opening toasts," Aaron commented.

Myra said, "They probably left early. You know, Mark is doing the whole A.A. thing. I saw he used a water glass for the toasts."

"Ahh," Aaron nodded knowingly.

"And did you two stay over?" Myra asked Paul and Susan.

"Yes, they had a cancellation at the Southampton Inn. I was able to get a couple rooms. Luckily, everything else was booked up."

"Yes, you didn't really get much notice, did you? And summer in the Hamptons is busy. First graduation parties, and all the weddings and all the festivals they hold. We booked this tent in April, and this was the only weekend in June they had left." Myra said. "Well, you two have fun. We have to go say goodbye to the train riders."

"Say, is there a way to walk on the beach?" Susan asked.

Aaron answered, "Yes, you can take the pathway that leads from the hedge behind the huppah through the dunes. But, if you want a romantic stroll on the beach, I'd recommend waiting about an hour. We had an almost full moon last night, and it should be coming up just after sunset."

Susan smiled at the 'romantic' comment and said, "Thanks, we'll do that," as the Metzgers walked off.

—

Chapter Twenty-Four

Twitter by @SusyFisher: @ArielRothschild impressive already changed ur Twit acct & ur wedding is beautiful as are you. Have Fun on #Honeymoon ! @AmeeMetzger bridesmaid luvly 2

—

Two young men were already loading the audience chairs on a stake truck when Susan and Paul walked out to the huppah. Susan went to stand under the huppah in the darkening light of dusk.

Paul tested the sturdiness of the huppah, first, and then leaned his shoulder against a huppah pillar to watch Susan standing in the middle of the huppah.

"So, what did you think of the wedding?" Paul asked.

Susan turned to face Paul, "It was beautiful. Anything this elaborately staged would be beautiful, but the ceremony, the traditions and all the little things seemed so perfect. Of course, the religious part of it all and the Hebrew was a beyond my grasp. The beauty and the pageantry were really special. After a while, all of it seemed so perfect and natural."

"The rabbi's granddaughter gives her approval then, huh?" Paul smiled. "Did you get even a little bit of Sartre's deep, dark hole filled?"

Susan looked at Paul, "I'm not sure I can say that. I did seem to synch with what was going on. I thought about my grandparents and all the ancestors, who created the pageantry. Then, I had to think about my mother who rejected all this."

Paul stepped forward to take Susan's hand, "Well, talking about the pageantry and the ancestors, you are moving from Sartre to Joseph Campbell. You familiar with Joseph Campbell?"

They started walking from the huppah to the break in the hedge behind it and down a path. Susan answered, "Name is familiar, but that is a pretty common name. Who's Joseph Campbell?"

"He's the pre-eminent psychologist who talked about all this. There is a whole Center for Depth Psychology based upon his works out in California. His philosophy of myth and religious belief being the reflection of the human psyche is an advancement of the simple deep, dark hole concept Sartre voiced. George

Lucas used Joseph Campbell's teaching as the basis for the Star Wars concept of there being an overarching 'Force" that guides mankind and the universe that transcends simple religion, but is reached by a human seeking it by immersion in the myth or religious pageantry. The whole Jedi thing Lucas invented was based on Campbell's theorems. Campbell would liken that same thing to all religious tradition, ceremony and what you call pageantry."

Susan just hmmed at this and motioned for Paul to explain more. They walked down a macadam path through the beach dunes. The sun was setting into the deep red of the low horizon over the far off city to the west. The full moon could be seen just rising over the ocean to the East.

"Actually, if you follow what Joseph Campbell spoke of, it makes a pretty good explanation of the difference between Reform Judaism, like you saw at your Aunt Rachel's synagogue and the more strict religious or God based principles of the Conservative Jews or the full-on Orthodox. The Reform Jew, like Rachel or my parents, believe that keeping the traditions. They believe following those traditions is important for the individual to stay focused on who they are and to achieve a oneness with the whole essence of what it means to be Jewish. Whereas the more orthodox view would say we must do these things because God himself commands it. Of course, there is a little of that in the Reform viewpoint, too. I know you've seen *Fiddler on the Roof.* This thing that I am talking about is the whole concept behind the 'Traditions' song Tevye sings and which he bases his life on. It is what his whole family has to come to terms with when their old way of life gets torn apart at the end of *Fiddler.* Tevye's 'traditions' was the same thing Joseph Campbell called the God Metaphor. Tevye dealt with the real world and the acts of his family, Campbell dealt with the psychological reasons we humans like the traditions Tevye yearned for."

Paul continued "And another thing that Campbell would note from this wedding today was the mythological Earth Mother aspects of this ancient ceremony that have lasted down through time. Most people would say traditional Judaism is a very male dominated religion, but today you saw the two mothers and the bride circling the groom and the womenfolk issuing the seven blessings to the couple at the dinner. Campbell would love the Earth Goddess motif in all that."

Now Susan added, "Yeh, you heard me laugh in the middle of that. I saw the three women circling round and round the groom, and I couldn't help thinking of a pack of wolves circling their prey."

"Yes, I heard you snicker. And I'm sure Campbell would appreciate your wolfpack analogy, but I am not sure the Rothschild and Metzger matriarchs would."

Susan added, "Probably not."

They stood on a wooden deck built just above the high-tide mark and waited for the moon to rise more.

Susan spoke next, "I noticed that both you and Devorah, that is the female attorney, when asked about your religion both answered in terms of your parents. When Devorah was explaining the difference between the Jewish sects, I asked her which she was and her answer was that her father was a Conservative rabbi. Just now, you said 'a Reform Jew, like Rachel or my parents' and not 'a Reform Jew, like me.' Why do you guys do that?"

Paul smiled, "Well, isn't that exactly what you are doing and having trouble coming to terms with? Your religion, or lack thereof, is based upon what your parent's raised you with. Of course, we all build on that as we go through life, but we all start with what our parents give us."

Darkness advanced quickly. The dark red to the west deepened and the fat Moon rose quickly in the East.

"So, can you see yourself having a wedding like the one they had today?" Paul asked.

Susan took a minute to answer, "That was a very well-worded question. You avoided the innate touchiness of a man asking a woman about wedding plans without venturing into dangerous waters"

"Acknowledged. Consider it a scouting mission."

"Yeh, I could really see myself up there. Probably not as elaborate as this shindig, but along these lines. I guess it is my inheritance as the rabbi's granddaughter, irrespective of what my parents intervened with. Is this kind of wedding what your folks will have for Julie and John?"

"Yes, my guess it will be right along these lines. Maybe more in English and the signing of the *ketubah* and *yichud* won't be so prominent. But, yeh, just about like this."

"*Yichud*, that's the consummation thingy, right?" Susan asked.

Paul laughed, "Yes, the consummation thingy. Actually, what they did in the tent was probably more like this…."

Paul reached for Susan's arm and pulled her toward him. They kissed. Then, they stood arm in arm with Susan's head on Paul's shoulder until the moon was fully up and the beach flies forced them back up through the dunes to the wedding party.

—

Chapter Twenty-Five

With the Metzger wedding behind her and the uncertainties of what the coming year had in store for her out of the way, Susan set about to get life in order. She moved Rachel's stack of memorabilia boxes from the dining room to the study and worked at reducing the pile of boxes from Illinois in the family room. Slowly, she sorted through Rachel's clothing and possessions. Susan found herself keeping more of them than she would have thought. Still, the pickup guys from the Dress for Success charity were becoming weekly regulars. Susan liked the idea of Rachel's business suits and old shoes, plus all of the old men's clothing, going to people who needed them to improve their lives.

The paperwork from Columbia she submitted resulted in a series of emails giving instructions for online registration for fall classes and various offices she needed to contact. Susan went round and round in her head over what she should take. She had been fairly certain of her college goals at Augustana, but getting put in an undecided major at Columbia opened up possibilities for her and that indecision meshed with her own internal doubts. It seemed like a perfect opportunity to reassess what she wanted to do. In the end, Susan registered for an upper division specialty course in Renaissance Art History, but several other miscellaneous courses to test the waters in other subject areas.

Susan took her morning coffee and bagel into the study. She was not sure why, but the study had become her haven of choice to read and sort. Rachel had obviously chosen the dining room for this and perhaps it was Susan's urge to go her own way that caused her to move her chore area into the study. The study seemed to have been unused for decades. Susan assumed this was Rachel's way to preserve 'My Isaac's Room." However, after a little inspection of the study, it seemed to Susan that perhaps Isaac Metzger had not used the study all that much, at least not for study. Susan had checked out the books. It seemed to her that many of them were bought in bulk and placed on the shelves back in the '70's as more of a decorator item than a storehouse of intellectual pursuits. There were many Great Books and dozens of standard works, as well as '60's and '70's era bestsellers that did not seem to have ever had their backs cracked open. Several of these decades old 'new' books were duplicates. It was like Isaac had told a decorator what he wanted in the room, and this contractor had installed the books as they would the owner's choice of wallpaper. The big desk chair seemed barely used, as compared to the oft-used leather sofas and side chairs in the study. Susan surmised that Isaac Metzger had used his study for a place to meet, bargain and discuss, rather than a place of reading and contemplation. The well-worn liquor cabinet and the cigar humidor that had bare wood on the lid, where Isaac had opened it a thousand times back in the '70's, confirmed this suspicion.

Susan had thrown out the ancient cigars and put the humidor in the storage room. She reminded herself to ask Paul to help her check out the liquor as she suspected the crystal decanters had held their product unused for nearly forty years. Some of the commercial liquor bottles in the cabinet were so old they did not have bar codes on them.

It was the day before the 4th of July. Paul had told her he was working a double shift to free himself up on the holiday, so they could go down to Battery Park for the fireworks in the evening. So, Susan had the day free to herself. She quickly went through the mail. There was nothing of interest, except for her New York Driver's license, forwarded down from the law offices.

Susan checked emails and her usual online destinations. Nothing of interest on Facebook, Twitter or Tumblr. Susan found an online map of where Battery Park was, and while she was at it, she read about its history. As she sat looking at the laptop on the huge desk, she had an idea that had occurred to her before. It seemed to her that this big desk needed a big, modern computer display on it. Like the ones she had seen in the law offices. Susan had looked at the computer on the corner table in her bedroom, but it had turned out to be an older Windows all-in-one computer. Susan knew how to use Windows, but preferred an Apple. Susan decided to consider buying a big new Apple for this desktop.

She Googled apple-desktop-store-Manhattan-NY, and she got a list of several stores. Apple itself seemed to have a couple big corporate stores, but Susan decided to go to big B&H store up by Macy's on 34th since they advertised they also had televisions and video equipment and Susan had thought of replacing the old console TV in the family room, so there was someplace to comfortably watch television in this apartment besides her bedroom.

Susan closed the laptop, took her new driver's license with her and went to change clothes for a day of shopping. Even though she had pretty much free rein to shop with the credit cards from the trust, Susan knew the money from the Moline house sale would be coming in within a week or so, so she had her own money to shop with. She was not sure why that mattered to her, but it did.

—

10:14 IST-Z+2

From: dgoldfarb@his.biu.ac.il

To: susy@susyfisher.com

Subj: Archibald Project

Miss Fisher,

The Israeli Antiquities Authority forwarded your email inquiry to me. I was sorry to hear of your father's passing. But, it is nice to hear from the young lady who scrambled through the dusty orchards with us those two summers.

Yes, the excavation of the Crusader fort your father worked on has been concluded for the time being. Your father's expertise in that era's politics was essential in identifying the ruins south of Nahariya as a ducal property of Duke Archibald assigned to the Knights Hospitaller for protection of the road between Jerusalem and Tyre. Further excavation of the site has been put on hiatus due to funding constraints, as is the case with many archaeological sites in a country as rich in antiquities as Israel. Unfortunately, the Crusader period is not a priority given the wealth in older Hebrew archaeological sites in our country.

I have asked my assistant to find the final report on the Shivaei Zion site that was prepared the year after your father's last visit to send to you, so that you can see your father's contribution.

Best wishes, and if you have occasion to come back to Israel, please look me up.

Sincerely,

Dan Goldfarb

Dept of Social Sciences,

Bar-Ilan University

Tel Aviv, Israel

—

The B&H store was big; it occupied the entire end of the block just south of 34th street, a few blocks west of the big Macy's. She entered and asked a young man at the information podium where she could find Apple desktop computers. As he directed her to the back of the store, Susan noticed the young man had sidelocks just like Jerry Berg at the law firm and wore a yarmulke. As Susan walked through the store, she noticed that virtually every male worker was obviously a Jew. There were middle-aged men with obvious Jewish looks. There were many more salesmen with sidelocks. A couple of the older men even wore prayer shawls under their B&H employee vests. Susan had unknowingly happened across the technology store equivalent of her all-Jewish law firm. It took Susan a moment to consider this. High tech computer, video and photo equipment did not seem to be a Jewish thing. But, then, why not? This place seemed to be a Disneyland for techies. It was packed with equipment of every possible kind and it was packed with customers.

Susan eventually wandered back to the area with a huge Apple logo on the wall. After taking a number to get time with a salesman, Susan wandered amongst the Apple merchandise and waited.

Her number was called. Susan found herself face to face with a totally bald fiftyish man who introduced himself as "Mort Grinberg, Deary, how can I be of service."

Susan smiled and noticed he did not offer his hand in introduction. He wore a blue yarmulke and he happened to be one of the men with a prayer shawl on. "I'm Susy Fisher and I'm looking for an Apple desktop computer, big screen, touchscreen if I can."

"Sorry, Susy, Apple doesn't really do touchscreens on desktops, at least not what I could recommend. We can jury-rig a Mac Pro to work for you, but we don't recommend it until Apple comes out with it themselves. That should be soon. Let me show you what I recommend. And, if you want a touchscreen we can add an iPad to the package for you. Or we could set you up with a touch sensitive WACOM input tablet. I find the hand-held touchscreen much handier than reaching across a desk to touch a monitor."

He led her to a counter with several iMac all-in-one models. Mort gave Susy a quick interrogation as to her needs, price range, who else would be using it, what kind of network connection, and what she would be doing with the computer. At last, they settled on a 27 inch iMac with just about every embellishment it could have. He seemed impressed that Susan did not seem to be concerned with price.

After adding a nice color printer, the typical software and the iPad to the package, Mort asked, "Will you be taking this with you or would you like it delivered? We can have a crew make sure it is installed, networked and get it up and running for you, too. Usually same day, in the local area."

"That would be nice, delivered and installed. Can I take the iPad with me?" Susan liked this service.

"Yes, we can split the order, take the iPad home now. Do you live alone? Will there be someone else there?" Mort asked.

"Why would you need to know that?" Susan asked, sounding concerned at this kind of question.

Mort smiled, "Because right now most of our installation crew are Orthodox, and they don't like to go into a woman's home, especially a young Jewish girl like you, by themselves. We send one of our women employees with them, if a female customer lives alone."

Susan smiled and said, "Okay, I understand. I live alone. But, how did you know I was Jewish?"

Mort Grinberg chuckled at her. "Miss Fisher, I have been a most careful student of Jewish girls for most of my fifty-eight years. I can tell a nice Jewish girl from a *shiksa* half a block away. A Jewish girl has a grace, beauty and bearing that most *shiksa* cannot hold a candle to. Let's go enter your order and you can pay at the front counter."

"Wait, I needed a TV and home theatre set-up, too," Susan added.

"Let me enter the computer stuff. I can get you over to video next.""

Susan followed Mort to the computer console. She assumed Mort had just guessed at her ethnicity from her name, but he had sure made her feel good that she had the grace, beauty and bearing of a Jewish girl. Susan realized she had just been the recipient of a flirt, or a reasonable facsimile thereof, from a fifty-eight year old Orthodox Jew. And, this Jewish electronics store had some interesting ethics rules that you did not find at a Best Buy.

—

10:14 EDT

From: esmiley@mgt.cerberuscapital.com

To: susy@susyfisher.com

Subj: Super Store Proposal

Ms. Fisher,

Our office was forwarded your email sent to Jewel Stores Marketing Dept. As you may know, Cerberus Capital Management is the corporate parent company of the Jewel/Osco retail brands.

We read your question and proposal regarding a New York Jewel Super Store with some interest. While it is far too soon to say much more, let me tell you that your conceptual proposal is not inconsistent with directions that we anticipate Jewel Stores to be going in coming years.

With that in mind, we have several questions that need to be answered before we can fully evaluate what you are suggesting. If you are interested in further discussions, please contact me and perhaps we can get together here in New York.

Sincerely,

Eleanor Smiley

Assistant for New Business – AB Investments

Cerberus Capital Management, Inc.

New York, NY

—

The first email Susan got when she entered her email account into the iPad was the one from Cerberus. In the rush of the wedding, Susan had almost forgotten the emails she had sent out when she got back from Moline and could find nothing in her area of Manhattan that could hold a candle to the supermarkets back in Illinois. She was surprised she had received an answer and wondered what might come of this.

—

11:54 EDT

From: susy@susyfisher.com

To: Laszlo Kiss <lkiss@metzgercompanies.com>

Cc: Devorah Feldshuh <dfeldshuh@wassermannephraim.com>

Subj: An Idea

Laszlo,

I had an opportunity to discuss with someone important, the building on the corner of 10th across from my place, the one you said was having tenant and cash flow problems. I think I may have happened across a way the Metzger Companies might be able to make a good profit regarding that building.

Can you get the current tenant roster and the remaining time and terms of the existing tenants?

Also, I know it is old, but does Metzger still have the blueprints for that building. Also, it would be nice to get the current zoning and land use approvals for that building.

Please gather that info up and when you get it, we can set up an appointment to get together, and I can explain what is going on.

Sincerely,

Susy

—

They actually had an iPad app to do provenance on an art collection, digitize the painting's photo and create a database of the art collection.

Susan had decided that whatever she decided about her further studies of art, her Aunt Rachel deserved to have Susan finish cataloging the art collection and coming up with some plan to have the collection do something for the world besides gathering dust in the other apartment.

Susan set as her goals for the rest of the summer. First, to get the apartment sorted, modernized, and organized enough to base her future in it. Second, she wanted to do at least a bit of work watching the life story journal videos that Rachel had done years ago about her life after Isaac's death, and see what was in the diaries of Susan's mother. Third, she also had to finish the art collection work before the semester at Columbia started. To do that there were certain standard art provenance works she really needed to have. She could get them online, but Susan found a big bookstore in the East Village of Manhattan that had a specialty collection in art provenance. Susan decided that after the 4th of July holiday was over she would find her way across Manhattan and check out this bookstore.

—

Chapter Twenty-Six

"Hello, Susy!" Paul said as he saw the caller ID on his cell screen.

"No, this is not Susy. Is this Dr. Paul Waldman?"

"Yes. Who is this? You are calling me on Susan Fisher's cell phone."

"Yes, Dr. Waldman. This is Rita Collinson, I'm the admitting nurse at the Bellevue ER, maybe you remember, we worked together when you did your residency. Miss Fisher asked me to call you. She can't talk right now. In fact, we just barely understood we should call you. Luckily, you were on redial."

"What happened?" Paul asked.

There was a pause as the nurse thought of what to say.

"She was brought in by ambulance. She was attacked on the street. Apparently, three or four gang members roughed her up pretty bad. They knocked her out and kicked her when she was on the ground. She had a partially dislocated jaw and two broken ribs. We had to suture both her earlobe where the ripped her earrings off, and the inside of her cheek where they kicked her face and her teeth almost came through the cheek. We are admitting her for observation as she may have some internal bleeding from the kicking."

"God!"

"A police patrol saw the end of the attack and chased the perps, caught one. They recovered Miss Fisher's purse and the earrings from the one they caught. The one they caught is here in the ER, too, under police guard. She got hit by a taxi while running from the cops."

"She?" Paul asked incredulously.

"Yeh, female gang member. Pretty rough cookie. Miss Fisher was lucky it wasn't worse."

"Okay, tell Susy I'll be right there. Well, it is quite a ways, I'm at Presbyterian, but I'll leave right now."

"Anybody else we should call?" Nurse Collinson asked.

"She has an aunt and uncle, the Metzgers, here in town. I don't know how to reach them. And Susy is pretty close to her attorney. I think her name is Devorah Feldman, or something."

The nurse replied, "Just a sec, let me check… Yeh, that's Devorah Feldshuh.

I have her number here in her phone, I'll call her next."

"Okay, tell Susy I'm on my way." Paul clicked the phone off.

—

The hospital orderlies ran out to meet the van with the Columbia/ Presbyterian Hospital markings that pulled up to the emergency room doors at Bellevue Hospital, thinking it was an incoming patient. Instead, they saw a man in a doctor's lab coat hop out of the passenger seat, thank the driver, wave the orderlies off and run past them into the building.

Doctor Paul Waldman ran through the automatic doors and directly to the crowded main counter in the ER. He went up to a young woman with a surgical mask pulled down under her chin who sat at a computer console.

"I need to know where patient Susan Fisher is," Paul told the young woman.

The young woman blinked at the Crown emblem of Columbia Presbyterian Hospital on Paul's lab coat.

Paul looked closely at her name tag. "Nurse Jeffries, I'm Doctor Paul Waldman. I have full Bellevue/NYU privileges. Rita Collinson called me in, I need to know where a patient last name Fisher, first name Susan is."

The nurse did not say anything, but gave a slight dip of her head in response. She typed on her console.

Nurse Jeffries read the screen and nodded. "Here. Fisher, Susan. Received by Ambulance. Admitted at 1847 hours, multiple trauma, possible internal injuries, admitted for observation. She is either waiting to go up or is already up on Fifteen East. Doctor Opalescu attending. If she is still here, she'd be waiting for transport in the main triage room, it's down...."

"I know where triage is, thanks." Paul said, heading down the hallway to the right.

Another nurse in the ER triage room knew about Susan and was able to give Paul a room number on the fifteenth floor.

Paul had not been back here much since, but during his residency and his specialization, he had spent long hours on Bellevue's fifteenth floor, Trauma and Critical Care Surgery. As the elevator doors opened, he headed directly for the room.

As he approached, Paul could see the door to Susan's room was wide open. As he turned into the room, Paul saw there was no bed in the nearest patient space and the other bed was empty. As he started to turn toward the nurse's station, he heard a voice from inside the room.

"Paul?" a woman's voice asked.

Paul stepped into the room and saw a woman standing up from the armchair in the far corner of the room. The hospital room only had the dim recessed lighting on, so Paul could not see the woman well. She seemed to be a young woman, in a business suit.

"Doctor Waldman, I'm Devorah Feldshuh, I'm… ," the woman said reaching out the offer her hand.

"I know, Susy has told me about you," Paul interrupted her.

"And, me, you." Devorah said.

"Where is she?" Paul asked.

"Right when we got up here, two orderlies came to take her for an MRI. They seemed upset she had come up here without the MRI. They said I had to wait here. She's been gone for ten or fifteen minutes." Devorah stood next to Paul at the door.

"How is she?" Paul asked.

Devorah gave a slight grimace, "She looks pretty bad. When I got to the ER, they had an ice pack tied around her head, on the right side, with gauze. Her eye and lips seemed really swollen. Some bandages on her ears. When they moved her from the ER gurney to the hospital bed, she really screamed from the pain. I guess her ribs are broken. I have her dress here, from the ER, in a bag, and it is all bloody."

"I heard the girl they arrested for doing it was in the ER, too." Paul said.

"Girl?" Devorah blurted out.

"Yes, the admitting nurse said she was a gang member, one of three or four who attacked Susan." Just as he said this, Devorah looked over his shoulder, Paul felt movement behind him and turned to see a hospital bed being rolled down the hall toward them.

As the orderlies moving the bed slowed to turn into Susan's room, Devorah moved from the doorway inside the room out of the way, and Paul stepped out into the hall.

They rolled Susan into the room headfirst and Paul was able to see her as she passed. She had her eyes closed, but one eye seemed swollen shut, and as Devorah had said, Susan's lips and the right side of her face were swollen and starting to bruise pretty badly. There was a gauze bandage on her left ear. Susan's hair was stuffed into a turquoise hair net cap. The ice pack that had been mentioned was gone.

Paul followed the bed into the room, but stood back as the orderlies attached the monitor wires and oxygen tube from Susan's bed to the wall, and hung her drip bag and a urine collection bag on the intravenous stand in the room. The display readouts of pulse and blood oxygenation on the wall display panel flickered to life. The orderlies looked at Paul. The heavy set female orderly nearest to him did a double take at the logo on his lab coat and his nametag.

When the orderly on his side stepped to the foot of the bed to straighten the bed against the wall, Paul stepped forward, bent down and spoke, "Susan?"

"The radiologist ordered her sedated to get her into the MRI tray. She was really screaming from the pain, I guess from her ribs and hip. He gave her Amidate, so she should come out of it real fast. Are you the attending?" the female orderly asked.

"No, Dr. Opalescu is. I'm a… a personal friend." Paul said.

"Well then, we better let the station know she's back." The orderlies left the room.

Devorah now stepped forward, facing Paul on the other side of the bed. "Susy told me a lot about you. I had hoped to meet you under better circumstances." Devorah said to Paul.

"Yeh, this has been a wild month for Susy. Hasn't it?" Paul spoke as he reached for Susan's left hand. He checked it for injury before cupping her hand in his.

Devorah glanced behind Paul, as a man's voice spoke, "Paul?"

Paul turned to see a doctor at the door and a nurse entered the room behind him. Paul recognized the doctor and let go of Susan's hand to offer his hand to the doctor, "Mike, I heard you were her attending."

"I thought you were an Uptown Doc these days. Why are you slumming downtown? Is this a …"

"Yeh, personal." Paul finished Mike's sentence.

Doctor Michael Opalescu went around the bed. Devorah backed out of the way. Paul got out of the way of the nurse who stepped to the bed to pull the chain for the light over the bed. She took Susan's vital signs and copied readings from the wall display onto a tablet computer.

Doctor Opalescu was checking the side of Susan's head and opened her eyes with his thumb and forefinger to check response to his penlight.

The nurse read from the tablet, "Radiology had to remove the ice pack to do a jaw and face x-ray. We are still within ninety minutes, so should I put another ice-pack on?"

Opalescu told her, "Yes." The nurse handed him the tablet and left. He read through the information on the computer tablet. Then, he turned to ask Devorah, "And you are?"

"Her attorney, and close friend," Devorah admitted.

"Wow, I'd better watch myself, this patient brings her own trauma surgeon and attorney with her to the ER. Paul, would you close the door?"

The doctor kept reading the tablet, looked at Susan's face, neck and head again and then put the tablet at his side, as if waiting for something.

Opalescu saw Devorah staring at him, obviously wondering what he was waiting for. He told her, "I need the nurse in the room to do the next part of the exam."

The nurse came back in the room with a couple of blue plastic icepacks, a small IV bag and a handful of other items. She put them on the bed and hung the IV bag just above the auto-drip controller on the IV stand.

Opalescu sat the tablet on the table, folded the blanket on top of Susan's belly and carefully started to pull her gown up from under her on the right side of her body.

"May I?" Paul asked, as he stepped around the bed.

Opalescu shrugged. Devorah backed away, but kept within full view as best she could.

Paul helped pull the hospital gown that opened in the back from under Susan's legs. When this was folded up, atop her belly, the doctors could see two crescent shaped dark red marks on her hip and side midriff. They were clearly the marks of a toe of a shoe. Each crescent was surrounded by a large purple bruise. The bruise on her rib cage was a deep reddish purple.

"Write-up says three hard foot impacts to right side of face, ribs and hip. Bruising to back of the head from blunt impact. Possible concussion. Ribs R11 and R12 have medial breaks, well positioned." As Opalescu mentioned the ribs, he carefully touched them, noting the movement near the breaks. Susan let out a moan. "Ah, she's coming back."

They tucked the gown back under her.

The nurse asked the doctor, "What morphine setting should we start at?"

"She's coming out now, so use 120 until she stabilizes. Put a note in Orders that she can go up to 150, if she requests additional." Opalescu said, to Paul's nodded agreement. The nurse connected a tube to the IV and poked a setting onto the control panel on the box on the IV stand. Before she started the ice pack, the nurse adjusted the oxygen tube under Susan's nose.

"Just ice the jaw and cheek. I don't think the ribs and hip will benefit from it." Opalescu said, looking sideways to see if Paul agreed.

"ER surgeon put sutures inside the right cheek and left earlobe," Opalescu said to Paul. "Left earlobe was split out from the piercing hole. The other ear was damaged, but not ripped out. They put in temporary studs to prevent heal over of the piercings."

"Damn," Paul cursed. He looked up to see the dark mark and bruising on Susan's cheek and jaw.

"What happened to her ears?" Devorah asked from the end of the bed.

Paul answered, "Police said the gang tried to take her earrings. Police caught the one who took 'em. She's in ER, too, from getting hit by a taxi in her escape try."

"She?" Opalescu and the nurse asked at the same time."

"My reaction, too. Apparently, a female gang member pulled the earrings off and took her purse. I guess it wouldn't be ethical for me to go down and visit the gal that did this," Paul joked.

Opalescu took in a deep breath, "No, that would be board of review inducing, but it might be satisfying to check records and see what kind of shape the perp is in right now."

"I didn't hear that," Devorah said.

"Hear what?" Paul asked.

The nurse finished wrapping gauze around Susan's head, chin and the ice pack, and taped it off.

"Well, we're done for now. I assume you'll be staying in here. Let the station know when she's alert. We have the standard questions to ask her." Opalescu turned to leave. Paul stepped out of his way.

When the nurse finished checking the IV machine, she turned to follow the doctor out. Paul resumed his place on the left side of Susan's bed. Devorah came back up to the other.

"I guess it is sexist to say it is surprising this was done by a woman. But, you know?" Devorah said.

"Yeh, well, they said there was three or four. Maybe the woman was the grabber, you know the 'bagman' or woman, and the ones who did this were male. It takes a pretty strong kick to break two ribs and dislocate a jaw. But, then, I've seen this little lady here kick a mean soccer ball," Paul said.

They stood next to Susan's bed in silence for a while. Devorah fiddled with the pastel blue cotton blanket, smoothing it tight under Susan's arm and, carefully, along her side. Paul had hold of Susan's left hand again.

After a while, Paul looked over to Devorah, "So, I know you are an attorney, but what exactly do you do?"

Devorah looked over, "That requires a multipart answer. Our firm specializes in commercial law and probate and trust matters, but we have the typical transactional and litigation work to support our specialty. My boss is the trustee for Susan's trust and the rest of her relatives. For Susan, he has assigned me as a sort of guardian angel to get her situated in the new lifestyle we foisted upon her when her aunt died. You know, troubleshooter and question answerer. Also, we became pretty good friends in the process. For other clients, I do mainly transactional work, real estate deals and business formation, plus some court appearances for probate cases and miscellaneous law and motions."

Paul nodded. "She told me about the funeral and her trip to the synagogue with you."

Devorah smiled, "And she told me about the soccer games and your fondness for whipped potatoes."

Paul did not seem to understand the potato reference at first, but finally gave a small smile.

"And the wedding," Devorah added.

"Yeh, she was pretty wide-eyed at her first Jewish wedding. Like a kid at Disneyland."

"We'll make a New York Jewish princess out of this corn-fed Illinois girl yet, huh?" At the sound of Devorah's voice Susan stirred, shifted her shoulders and head.

Susan's eyes fluttered. She tried to reach up to her head. Finally, she squinted at the bright light. Paul pulled the light chain to turn the direct lighting of and the reflected ceiling lighting on.

"There, that better?" Paul asked.

"Wh… Wha…?" Susan half moaned, half spoke, through barely open lips.. The gauze strip under her chin prevented her from speaking.

"Susy, don't try to talk, you can't right now." Paul held onto her left hand still. "Calm down. Can you understand me? Calm down, and I'll try to explain what happened to you."

Susan's eyes now focused on Paul. She tried to turn and look around her. "I… I…."

Paul put his hand on her forehead. "Shhh! Lay still. You can't talk. You have an ice pack on your jaw and some stitches in your cheek."

Mention of stitches in her cheek excited her. She tried to sit up.

"Susy, stop! Lay still. The stitches are inside your mouth, you face is fine."

Paul reached up with his free hand and stroked Susan's forehead. "You're pretty banged up and you are going to be really sore, but you'll be fine. No serious injuries."

Susan frowned at this. "Hurs!" her swollen lips tried to say.

"Yes, I know it hurts. You are on morphine for the pain. Susy! Do you understand what happened?"

Susan frowned again, and then said, "Sohta," and tried to move her head, causing her to jump in pain and cry out.

"Sorry, my fault, I shouldn't have asked you a question. Just lay still and I'll explain." Paul moved so he was above her, looking down. "All right, you sort of understand, huh? You are in Bellevue Hospital. Devorah is here with us. You were attacked by a gang on the street. They kicked you hard and injured your jaw, and ribs and hip. Two ribs are broken. Your jaw was dislocated, but it is OK now. You can feel the ice pack on your jaw and face. Your jaw and ribs probably really hurt. When they kicked your jaw, it cut the inside of your cheek on your teeth. They had to stitch that, so you can probably feel the stitches with your tongue, and your cheek and lips might still be numb from that procedure, like at the dentist. I looked at your face. There is no external damage, no facial cuts, just a bad bruise. They did an MRI to see if there is any other damage inside. That's just a precaution. You are going to be fine."

Susan rolled her eyes up at this.

"Devorah, can you go tell the nurse's station that Susan is awake and responsive, but in pain and has difficulty talking," Paul asked.

"Okay." Devorah leaned over the bed to be in Susan's line of vision near Paul, and gave Susan a smile and little wave.

Paul looked in Susan's eyes again and said, "Okay, Susy, you relax, maybe close your eyes. I'm gonna stay with you. The nurse will be in soon, and you'll probably have some more tests done. You're going to be just fine."

Susan rolled her eyes again at this, and said, "Ah luf New Yorg," followed by a very guttural, thick-tongued "Nodt!" Then, she did close her eyes, while squeezing Paul's hand.

———

Susan awoke during the night to find a nurse and a doctor standing over her. The nurse was getting ready to take another blood sample and change the urine bag. The doctor was unrolling the gauze from around her head.

"Ah, you're awake. I'm taking the cold pack off. It's not cold anymore and you don't need it." The doctor said in a quiet voice.

When he pulled the cold pack off, Susan reached up with her right hand and touched her face, feeling her chin and the tubing under her nose.

"Careful there. Your jaw and cheek are going to be really sore for a while. You'll probably have trouble opening your mouth more than a little bit." The doctor sat the cold pack on the serving table.

"A little prick here," the nurse said as she started the blood draw from Susan's left arm.

"Paul?" Susan asked.

The doctor answered, "Doctor Waldman is asleep in the chair in the corner. He's been here all night."

The nurse left the room and another woman in a lab coat stepped to Susan's left side.

"Susan, this is Doctor Ehrenreich. She'll be taking over now. I'm going off duty. I wanted to tell you that we got your scan results and everything inside you is fine. No sign of internal damage. And your urine tests have cleared up, no blood at all in the last one. We think you just had a little bruising to the kidney from the kick to the ribs and it has gone away. If everything remains the same until morning, we should be able to release you, maybe mid-morning."

Susan lifted her hand to touch the right side of her face. She flinched a bit when she touched her cheek and jaw.

"Yeh, you are going to be sore for some time. Your ribs will take many weeks to heal." The doctor turned to look behind him. "Looks like Paul has woken up."

Paul came over to stand next to Doctor Opalescu. "Paul, let me introduce you to Doctor Pamela Ehrenreich. She's coming on duty. Pam, Paul Waldman is a colleague, a trauma surgeon from Presby. We did our residency together here. Paul, I was telling Susan it looks like blood in urine is gone and MRI was fine. And no bone damage in jaw or cheek. We can release her into your good hands in the morning."

Doctor Ehrenreich touched Susan's hand and said, "How's the pain? Are you getting enough pain meds?"

"I think I'm all right. Kinda buzzed 'n groggy 'n sore, but pain is a lot better than before. And, I can talk better, my tongue was huge and my lips numb before." Susan's eyes moved from one doctor to the other, and her speech was a bit unclear, since she was careful to not move her head and kept her jaw almost closed, even while talking.

Doctor Ehrenreich spoke again, "Okay, we'll leave you with Doctor Waldman now. Get some sleep. You can buzz, if you need anything. If you need more pain med, you can click this button here and the machine will give you a bit more. If you need more than that, tell us." She showed Susan where the morphine clicker was attached to the bed rail.

As the other doctors left, Paul moved closer to Susan and took her hand.

"How do I wook?" Susan asked, moving her lips as though they were beign uncooperative.

"You look a lot better than you did when I got here. And you are talking a whole lot better." Paul gave a little smile.

"Not an answer."

"That's all you are going to get."

"That bad?"

"Actually, your left profile is great. Right side is pretty bruised. But, you should see the other gal."

"What?" Susan asked.

"The gal who the police arrested who did this to you. She face planted onto the hood of a taxi and broke her left femur running from the cops."

"They caught her, huh?"

"Yes, but its best to not talk or think about that now."

Susan was touching her face again. She grimaced when she put her finger near her ear.

"Devorah was here. Right?" Susan asked.

"Yes, she went home. Before she left she got a call from your Uncle. He is going to visit you in the morning." Paul pushed her hair cap up out of her eyes.

"God, don't want anybody to see me like this."

"You can't expect him to not visit you. Can you? We'll get you home tomorrow. And you'll be back on your feet in a few weeks."

"And back on the plane to safety in Moline."

"You really wouldn't do that to me would you?" Paul raised his eyebrows.

Susan looked at him a long time. "I guess not." She tried to smile, but stopped and put her hand to her chin. "It hurts to smile."

"Oh really? Well, a priest and a rabbi walked into a bar…."

Susan slapped his hand.

"There's a good sign. You're on the mend and getting feisty again."

Susan 'grrred' at Paul.

"Get some sleep now. Big day for you tomorrow. I'll be here, you need anything, just growl."

—

"I can't! … hurts to open my mouth, an'I sure can't shew," Susan protested with her jaw almost closed.

"You have to have something for breakfast, It's just Jello, you don't have to chew. Want me to cut it flat you can suck in without opening your jaw." Paul motioned with the spoon.

"No, I guess, just give me more of the drink." Susan spoke without opening her mouth.

Paul let out a breath and handed Susan the can of Ensure again, positioning the straw to point at her mouth.

Susan took the can in her left hand and reached out to touch Paul's face with her right. "Your beard is growing out. You look like an anti-hero in the movies. Have you ever grown it out?"

Paul shook his head, "I tried in college, but my beard had holes in the cheeks, really uneven."

"I have holes in my cheeks, too."

"Your cheeks are fine."

"You should feel it from this side. It's all prickly, the stitches." Susan held the can out for Paul to take. "Do you think I can get into the bathroom? I need to get in there."

"Sure, you can move, it is just going to hurt. The twist when you sit up and swing your legs will be worst. Let me go get a nurse to help. Sit tight."

Paul took the can and set it so she could reach and left to get the nurse, leaving the door open.

He came back in with the nurse.

"I understand you want to try getting into the throne room, huh?" an elderly nurse asked.

"Yeh, if I can."

"Well, lets start by getting the catheter out. The doctor's orders say we are done with urine tests, and you are ready for discharge. Doctor Waldman, you can step outside." The nurse shooed Paul out and closed the door.

When she finished deflating and removing the catheter, the nurse opened the door and Paul returned.

The nurse lowered the railing of the bed on the left side.

"I thought I would get out on the right side, I'm closer," Susan suggested.

The nurse shook her head. "Whatever way you want. But, it is your right hip that's injured, you don't want to be spinning and rolling over on the bruise."

Susan thought for a minute and then admitted, "You're right, err, correct, to the left is best."

Paul and the nurse managed to lift Susan to a sitting position. They helped turn her legs out and over the edge of the bed. Susan set her teeth and grimaced, but did not cry out.

"Gosh, that hurts," she said as she was sitting on the edge of the bed, breathing deeply.

"What's worst, hip or ribs?" Paul asked.

"Right now ribs, but I just thought about sitting on the toilet with this sore butt."

The nurse unhooked the wires and tube to the wall and Paul pulled Susan's IV stand along with them. They were able to lift Susan to her feet with only a small whimper from Susan. She walked with one of them on each side, grimacing each time the weight went on her right leg.

In the bathroom Susan said, "I can make it from here. I can use the bars."

"Nope, hospital would have my head, if I let a patient who can barely move try to seat herself in here, and you fell down." The nurse again shooed Paul away of the bathroom and closed the door.

Paul heard a yelp from Susan, but the nurse came out and said over her shoulder to Susan, "Call me when you are done."

As they were waiting for Susan the nurse asked Paul, "You did your residency here, right?"

"Yes, and my specialization. You looked familiar, too." Paul leaned back on the bed.

"So, she's your, ah..." the nurse asked.

"Yes, my landlady."

"Huh?"

"She is my landlady, but we are working on branching into new areas." Paul said with a smile.

"She doesn't seem the typical landlady type," the nurse smiled, too.

"I can hear you, you know," Susan announced from the bathroom.

In a few moments, they heard the toilet flush and then bathroom doorknob click.

"I told you to let me know when you're ready." The nurse ran to the door and helped Susan exit the bathroom.

"Oh, nurse, I'm ready!" Susan sing-songed with clinched teeth.

The nurse looked at Paul, "Is she always this feisty."

"Yeh, pretty much always. She had an hour or two last evening when she lost her edge, but this is pretty much what you get with her."

When Susan had limped halfway to the bed, she heard a familiar woman's voice from the door, "Oh, my dear!"

Susan looked up to see Myra and Aaron at the hospital room door. From their perspective, they could only see the bruised right side of her face and bandaged ear. Both her aunt and uncle stepped toward her and seemed ready to hug Susan, but the nurse and Paul's presence on either side of Susan prevented that. Instead, they watched as Paul and the nursed maneuvered Susan back onto the bed. As she lay back, Susan gritted her teeth and closed her eyes. When they were done, Aaron and Myra came to Susan's side. The nurse left, and Paul went on the other side of the bed.

"Oh, Susy. I just can't believe this. How are you?" Myra asked.

"Well, you saw, just now. Not moving very well. Oh, Paul can explain." Susan turned to Paul and closed her eyes, apparently in pain again from the flop back on the bed.

Paul nodded, "Well, she has two broken ribs, some really bad bruising, a few stitches and her jaw doesn't work very well, it was dislocated. But, that's the worst of it. No internal injuries. She's going to be really sore for some time. It takes six to eight weeks for ribs to heel. She's on pretty strong pain medication and will be for a long time. You have to really kill the pain from broken ribs so the patient feels free to breathe deeply and not get lung complications, like pneumonia."

Aaron asked, "This happened last evening?"

Paul answered for Susan, "About five-thirty, as I understand."

"And this happened near your building?" Aaron looked from Paul to Susan.

Susan answered, looking up at Aaron, "No over on the East side. I was trying to get from the big bookstore to the cross-town bus to go home. I guess I went into the wrong place. A gang jumped me."

"They didn't... I mean... there wasn't...?" Myra had trouble phrasing her question.

Paul explained what he knew of the attack, sparing Susan from having to do so again.

"And how long will she be in here?" Aaron inquired.

"Her doctor signed the discharge order. She can go home this morning. They are processing it now."

"But, she doesn't seem ready to go home, she can barely move."

"I'll be fine, I want out of here. I don't do 'patient' very well." Susan asserted.

"Oh, I forgot, here!" Myra handed Susan a bundle she had been carrying under her arm. Then thinking again, she decided to unbag it herself and hand it to Susan. She gave Susan a fluffy, white velour robe and matching satin nightgown. "The gowns and robes they give you in the hospital are so horrible, when I heard you were in the hospital I thought you might want this."

Susan reached up and took the robe, hugging it to her chest. "Thank you, but how did you find a place to buy this, so early in the morning?"

Myra smiled, "Let's just say my contact list has a few store managers' cell phones on it. A good contact list is essential in this town."

At this, Aaron seemed to think of something and said, "Excuse me, I need to make a call." He stepped outside the door into the hall.

A new nurse came in and announced, "So, Miss Fisher, are you ready to go home?"

"Yes." Susan nodded.

"Well, if you folks could excuse me for a few minutes, I need to unhook Miss Fisher's attachments and get her ready. Is this what you're wearing home?" the nurse said, patting the new robe and gown.

"I guess so, my dress I was wearing is all bloody."

Paul and Myra left the room. Outside, they saw Aaron talking on his cell phone.

"…and I appreciate you handling this. Bill it to my account, not hers. And don't spare any expense, get good people. And get them over there this morning, ASAP." Aaron was finishing up his call. "Thanks, David, we'll be in touch."

When he hung up, Myra asked him, "What was that?"

Aaron answered, "I called Tannenbaum to set up some help for Susan at home. She'll have a girl there round the clock and a visiting nurse check in on her several times a day. You can give the nurse directions, right Paul?"

"Yes, thanks, that's a good idea. I was thinking of having my nurse from the clinic downstairs in our building go up, but if you've already made arrangements, that would be fine."

"Oh, you run that clinic there, downstairs?" Aaron asked. "I thought you were at Presbyterian."

"Both, my partners and I run the clinic, side business," Aaron explained.

Aaron gave Paul a look, as though he really appreciated the concept of Paul running a side business.

Myra put her hand on Paul's arm, "So, Paul, is she really all right. Or were you just saying that in front of her."

"No, everything I said is right. No major injury, other than the broken ribs and partially dislocated jaw. She is really gonna be sore for weeks. But, I am concerned about her reaction to it all. She was talking like she was afraid to live in New York." Paul looked back and forth between Myra and Aaron.

"And well she might be, every New Yorker knows there are places to avoid and times you just don't go places, especially a young woman alone," Myra added.

Aaron shook his head and said, "Yes, and I partially blame myself. We're her closest family, and because of the wedding and all, we sort of ignored her move to New York. I should have paid more attention to her. I wouldn't let my own daughter walk home alone, or to a bus after business hours in the East Village, I should have made sure Susan was aware of things like that."

Paul's cell phone rang. He answered and listened. "Yes, thanks. We're actually ready for you now. Come up to fifteenth floor, I'll meet you at the elevator. I'll be riding with you."

Paul hung up and explained to Aaron and Myra. "I arranged for an ambu-cab to pick us up. She is too sore to get in and out of a taxi. They'll bring a wheelchair right up here. She won't have to stand up 'til she gets to the apartment."

"So, Paul, you spent the night here, huh? You're looking a little bedraggled yourself," Myra noted.

Paul fingered his day old beard and said, "Yes, I got someone to cover me for last night and today. My colleagues all owed me paybacks. There are only three of us single docs on our service, and we are always covering for the husbands, fathers and mothers who have school recitals, bar mitzvahs, sick kids and the like."

"Well, I'm glad you were here for her." Aaron clapped a hand on Paul's shoulder as he spoke.

—

Chapter Twenty-Seven

Paul brought two extra pillows from the guest bedroom to Susan's bedroom to help prop Susan up in her bed. The tall, black woman in the visiting nurse uniform was standing by Susan and the young Puerto Rican woman in the same black uniform as Aaron and Myra's maids stood back, not knowing what to do.

Paul placed the pillows and asked, "You sure you want to be up this high?"

Susan was still talking through a partially open mouth, "Yes this is fine."

The visiting nurse said, "Okay, if that is all you need now, I'll be off. I will be back by at around Four o'clock. The night shift nurse will be here this evening. However, you said you would be here today. Right, Doc?"

"Yes, I'll be here." Paul moved back so the nurse could leave the bedside.

"Okay, Hon, you take care. You got my card and our service phone number." She patted Susan's hand as she left.

After the nurse left, the house cleaner asked, "Anything I can do? Would you like some tea or something?"

Susan nodded, "That would be nice."

Paul lifted his hand, "Ah, hate to be a wet blanket, but if she has tea, you need to put some ice in the cup to cool it after you brew it. She has stitches inside her mouth and shouldn't have anything too hot on the stitches."

The maid looked to Susan, who lifted her hands palms up as though she had no choice.

"Cream, sugar?" the maid asked.

"Both. That is if the good doctor doesn't object to that." She raised her eyebrows at Paul.

Paul waved the maid to go with a smile.

Paul sat on the bed next to Susan and stroked his hand up her forehead pushing hair out of her face. "How you feeling?"

"It's been hurting a lot more since I left the hospital." Susan gingerly moved herself in the bed.

"That's the effect of going off the morphine drip. They gave you one kind of pain pill to get you home, and keep you relatively awake and capable of walking. But, these little beauties we just gave you should kick-in in ten minutes, and you'll be delightfully loopy and not feeling much pain at all. Pretty much blitzed." He picked up two pill bottles from the nightstand. "The pain medication you take for broken ribs has to be really effective, so you're not afraid to breathe deeply. That's why we don't tape broken ribs anymore, it causes trouble from restricting deep breathing. I'll put these bottles in the bathroom cabinet."

"Wait, I can't get them in there," Susan protested.

Paul shook his head, "We never leave narcotic medications within reach of a patient who is in pain. They can overmedicate."

"Oh."

"You can take the pain pills every three hours. I will tell the maid when she can give them to you. If you need her and she's out front, you can use your cell, call the land line number on this Post-it note. She can hear the phone ring out front. But, today I'll be here." Paul moved Susan's iPhone over to the edge of the nightstand nearest her, where he stuck the Post-it.

"There's two bottles. What was the other one you gave me?"

"It is a short term sleep med. You woke up early at the hospital when they did the last blood test early this morning, you could use a nap. You'll be out soon."

"Hey, I don't want to be sleeping. Not when you took the day off to be with me." Susan's brow furrowed.

"Don't worry, I won't molest you while you're out."

"Oh, drat, now you've spoiled that fantasy!"

—

"Miss Fisher?" the maid poked her head in the bedroom door.

"Yes, Maricella, I'm awake." Susan turned her head, carefully, toward the door. "You can call me Susan, not Miss Fisher. What do you need?"

"The police detectives are back again." Maricella sounded nervous.

"Police detectives?" Susan questioned.

"Yes, they came yesterday when you were asleep, and Doctor Waldman asked them to come back. I think they are the ones working on your attack, er, your case."

Susan straightened up in bed, "Gosh, I don't want to see them in bed. Help me up. I'll walk into the living room."

Maricella stood by the bed as Susan carefully moved her legs over the edge of the bed. Susan winced in pain as she moved. Maricella moved the fuzzy slippers over near Susan's feet and offered Susan her hands to pull herself up. As she stood, Susan eyes went wide. She held her breath as the pain showed on her face. Finally standing and in the slippers, Susan put on the white robe and tied it closed. She slowly walked out of the bedroom into the hall. At the far end of the long hallway, Susan could see two men standing in the foyer. The living room door was open, as usual these days. With Maricella's help Susan sat in the armchair by the windows that faced the door.

"Okay, go ask them to come in," Susan directed.

After a short wait, the two police detectives came in. They were both middle-aged white men in nondescript sportcoats and poorly knotted ties. One of them carried a black leather portfolio. Maricella came in with them.

"Do you need me here?" the maid asked.

Susan shook her head.

The officer with the portfolio showed his badge on his belt and spoke, "Good afternoon Miss Fisher, I'm Detective Reynolds, and this is Detective Cosgrave, sorry to intrude. How are you doing?"

"Fairly well, all considered. I am not moving very well. Sorry I wasn't awake when you came yesterday."

"That's okay. Doctor Waldman was able to tell us some of what we need. How do you manage to get a doctor to do housecalls in this day and age?" Reynolds asked.

Susan smiled, "Well, he lives in this building, and he's a close friend. He's back at the hospital today. Please have a seat."

Reynolds sat in the other chair and turned to face Susan. Cosgrave sat on the edge of the couch .

Reynolds opened his notebook. "Ah, figured that he was a close friend from the way he talked about you. If you don't mind, could you briefly recount for us what happened?"

Susan went over the attack again and what her condition was.

When she finished Reynolds nodded and asked, "I understand you got your purse back from the patrol officers at the ER, right?"

"Yes,"

"We try to do that on things like purses and wallets when we manage to get hold of them, but we do have something else for you today. We kept the earrings the beat cops got from the perp, and if you can identify them and sign a receipt accepting them, we can give those to you. We have documented them for evidence. Are these them?" Reynolds stood and handed Susan a plastic bag labeled 'Evidence –NYPD' on it.

Susan took the bag and peered closely at them. "Yes, that's them. It looks like some of my blood is still on them."

Reynolds nodded, "Yes, I see the bandages on your ears. Please sign here." He handed her a pen and an evidence receipt form. Reynolds gave her his notebook to write on. "We never did find anything of the books that were stolen. The other crooks that got away probably still have them, or ditched them."

Susan smiled, "Well, I can't see that a gang member will have much use for books about 20th Century art provenance. So, you haven't found any of the gang other than the one?"

Reynolds sat back down. "No, but the gal who ran and got hit by the car is out of Bellevue, and in women's lock-up over at the Singer Center. She's in a leg cast. The judge denied bail. If she wants to cut a deal on her charges, she's gonna have to give us some information on her gang and accomplices. But, that's a tough spot for her. It's dangerous to rat on a gang."

"Have you seen her?" Susan asked.

"We haven't seen her yet, just heard about the cast from the report, but we do have her booking photo. We need you to ID it." Reynolds pulled a 4x5 inch photo from his notebook and showed Susan.

Susan looked at the unattractive photo of a broad-faced, young woman with no make-up, unkempt hair and bruises around her nose. "Yes, that is the girl who jumped out in front of me. I thought we had to do a line-up or something to identify her."

Detective Cosgrave took the opportunity to jump into the conversation, "Sometimes we need that if there's doubt as to ID. However, here the patrolman chased her right from where you were to where she got hit by the taxi. No doubt about her ID. Your ID of her photo was just confirmation."

"What's going to happen to her?" Susan handed the photo back to Reynolds.

Cosgrave again answered, "If she cooperates, it will go better on her. If not, these are hefty charges, class B felonies, gang involvement and serious injury, she could get several years."

Reynolds closed his notebook and said, "Well, that's about all we have for you. Here's my card, if you think of anything else or if we can help you with anything, call me. Hope you are feeling better."

Susan took the card and said "Thank you."

"We'll show ourselves out," Cosgrave said.

"If you see Maricella out front, could you send her back here?" Susan smiled as she spoke.

The detectives nodded. After they left, Susan peered at her earrings again and sighed. She put the detective's card in the bag with the earrings and closed it. Then Susan put her hands on the arms of the chair and decided she would get back to the bedroom by herself.

—

"Do I really have to go downstairs? Can't you do it here?" Susan protested. "And, I thought stitches these days were dissolvable, or absorbable, or something, and they come out by themselves. Why do I have to have these snipped."

Paul crossed his arms and looked at Susan, "First off, I'm not doing it. I asked Eric to come in, and while I am quite happy to give you in-home service, I am not going to ask a colleague to do that. We need to go down to the clinic.

"Second, some stitches are absorbable. The ones in your ears should be falling out any time. You can tell when they are ready to fall out when they start itching instead of hurting. But, for whatever reason, the ER surgeon decided you needed full strength, non-absorbable stitches in your mouth. I wasn't there. He had his reasons and decided to do regular silk stitches. Could be the depth of the laceration, maybe conditions in the mouth, maybe the swelling he was dealing with then. His decision. But, it has been well over a week now, plenty of time for a mouth cut to heal."

"Why can't you do it?" Susan asked.

"It's just the principle, an ethical thing. You don't do a procedure, even something as simple as stitch removal, on a close friend or family member. It's one thing for me to be here and hold your hand and give you instructions on taking care of yourself; it is another to go inside that pretty little mouth and start snipping away and maybe hurting you."

"It's gonna hurt?"

"Not really, you only have ten stitches. You've been through far worse this last week or so. If you want, I can poke you in your broken ribs while Eric's taking out the stitches, you won't even notice a little pain from the snip in your mouth. Actually, he'll probably spray some Lidocaine in your mouth to numb the area before he snips." Paul waited a minute and then smiled. "Hurry, he'll be at the clinic at Five."

"Well, let me get dressed and fixed up a bit. I'm not gonna let your buddy Eric see me like this."

"Fine, but hurry, and no lipstick," Paul ordered.

Susan started to protest, but stopped and said, "Oh, yeh, I guess not."

—

"Are you sure you can't make it?" Devorah asked. "This whole concept was your idea."

Susan started to shake her head before realizing she was on the phone. "No, I'm not ready for a taxi ride yet. The thought of bouncing around with one of your maniacal New York cabbies driving through traffic with these ribs isn't something I need. You and Laszlo are who is needed for the meeting with Cerberus and Jewel. The deal making and technical stuff about the building do not need me. The Jewel store people liked my idea, now you and Laszlo get to see if you can put a deal together. I still think it is a great idea to put a superstore in here. They seem to agree. Just do it!"

"How are you really doing? Things looking up a little? Maybe I can make it down to pop in on you after this," Devorah suggested.

"Good idea, it would be great to see you in person and not just on the phone. I'm doing a lot better. The purple and yellow splotches on my face have faded enough for me to be able to cover almost all of it up with a healthy coat of Covergirl and mineral powder. I can almost open my jaw full again. My ribs still hurt like hell, but getting better. The worst part is I have gotten totally spoiled with Maricella around, that's the maid Aaron hired for me, and with Paul being here so often. I'm tempted to try some sort of relapse to keep the status quo going."

"Well, you know, you can really afford to keep the maid service. And I'm guessing you are well on the way to making Paul's drop-ins more or less permanent. But, I'm glad you are doing better. I really freaked out when I came in that emergency room and saw you there."

Susan huffed, "I was kind of freaked out, too."

"Well, I'll do my best today. Maybe Isaac Metzger will do a guardian angel thing for us on this superstore deal."

"I'm sure you'll make both Isaac and Grandpa Morris proud," Susan assured Devorah.

"We'll see. I'll try to stop by and report on how it goes. Bye."

—

As Susan had instructed, Maricella used the two-wheel dolly from the utility room to move the old red metal trunk from the family room to the study. Now that she was feeling a bit better, Susan had resolved to try and get at least one of the tasks she had set for herself done before classes at Columbia started, in spite of the setback of her injuries. She was going to compare her mother's old journals she had found in the Moline garage with the box of Fisher family memorabilia from Rachel.

"Where do you want this?" Maricella asked.

Susan was standing next to the big desk. "Let's move the lamp and set it on the end table. That way I can go through it without having to bend over or stretch. I'm feeling better, but don't want to exacerbate anything by lifting. Yeh, right here."

Next, Susan moved the other table lamp back and said, "And, could you set that box over by the wall labeled 'Fisher' on this other end table? Here."

"Thanks."

Maricella asked, "Anything else?"

"No, not for now," Susan answered.

Maricella delayed leaving and turned to Susan, "Miss Fisher, err, Susan, I wanted to remind you that your uncle told my service you needed me for about six weeks. And my classes at NYU start the last week of August. So, I, uh…."

Susan nodded. "I understand. All good things come to an end. I'll miss having you around. You've been great. But, I'm feeling better and I have to start my own classes the first week of September. Do you work at all during the school year?"

"Yes, but nothing like this full-time, live in work. This was a great way to work for my summer. I usually do fill-in for weekend parties and stuff."

"Well, maybe we can work something out for you during the year to come in here. This place is huge, and I can use some help around here. Where do you live during the year?"

Maricella shrugged, "I have been living with my folks, but that is all the way out in the Bronx."

"Maybe we can work something out to do a room and board for a little help around here. This is a lot closer to NYU than the Bronx, right? Would you be interested?"

"Uh, well, I guess that might work."

Susan smiled, "Well, let's think about it. It might work for both of us."

Maricella nodded, "Yeh, let me think about it."

As Maricella left, Susan opened the red trunk. She had put a strip of duct tape over the lock hole to keep it from relocking on her. She took out the tray and started to stack her mother's journals in date order on the corner of the desk. Next, she sorted the stacks of letters and papers from Rachel's 'Fisher' box. It was going to be a lot of reading.

—

Susan peeked through the view port on the front door. As she suspected, it was Paul. She opened the door.

"Ah, Susy, you're up and around. Good to see." Paul kissed her, but did not immediately come in.

"Come on in. What are you waiting for?" Susan asked.

"I was hoping Maricella would open the door. I wanted to surprise you with something."

"Maricella has the afternoon off, she had to register for fall classes at NYU. Surprise me with what?" Susan asked. Then, cocking her ear toward the door she added, "What's that sound?"

"Your surprise," Paul bent to pick something up outside the door. He stood up and presented Susan with a fluffy off-white kitten with a brown nose and feet.

"Ohmigosh!" Susan said as she grabbed the kitten and hugged it to her neck. "So fluffy."

Paul bent again picked up a box from outside the door. Susan backed away so he could come in.

"She's lovely. But, why? Is it a he or she?" Susan fired questions at Paul.

Paul sat his box on the floor by the kitchen door and said, "He's a he. And he's a prescription cat. It is a well-known fact that having a pet to care for is great therapy for getting a person back on their feet. So, I heard you tell me a while back that you wanted a cat when you were growing up, but your father had an allergy, and you lived in a small house. So, I decided to prescribe a therapy kitten for you."

"What's in the box?"

"Selection of food, a catbox and filler. The lady I got him from potty trains them before she gives them out, so patients don't have to worry about teaching them or cleaning up messes." Paul bent and showed Susan a can of cat food."

Susan was holding the cat out at arm's length. "What big blue eyes he has."

"Yeh, he's a purebred, Himalayan. It's like a long haired Siamese. He's about twelve or thirteen weeks old. Not a tiny kitten, just old enough to be potty trained."

"So, this lady actually raises cats to be therapy kittens?"

"Yeh, so it seems, hand raises them so they're really loving when they get to the patients. I got her name from the physical therapy department at the hospital. And, I thought you might put his box in the guest bathroom."

"Sure, let's bring it and show him around." Susan headed off down the main hallway.

Paul grabbed the plastic tray and bag of cat litter from the box, and followed her. Walking behind her up the hall, Paul could see she still favored the right leg. "So, you're Okay with this, right?"

Susan looked back over her shoulder, "Of course, wonderful idea. And, who am I to argue with doctor's orders."

—

Twitter by @SusyFisher: Pic of my new kitty cat named Valjean. Thanks to @PaulWaldmanMD ! http://SusyFisher.com/valjean.html.

—

Susan sat on the leather couch in the study. The table lamp lit her reading. Even though it was mid-day, the darkened skylight above her blocked most of the sunlight. She was reading the last of the journals, the one right before her birth. It revealed little she did not already know, except for how she had been named Susan Rachel, instead of Susannah Rachel, like her aunt. It seems her father had agreed with her mother that if the baby was a girl they would name it after Aunt Rachel. However, her father was mindful of sticking a young girl with a moniker that would not be fitting of a professional when she was an adult. He had not liked giving her the name Susannah, as he thought it sort of old fashioned and biblical. But, the main reason was that the name Susannah was too connected to the old Stephen Foster song. Her liberal history professor father thought *Oh! Susannah* was politically incorrect as a nonsensical, black-face minstrel song and one in which the original lyrics used the word 'nigger.' So, Susan's naming had been shortened by mutual agreement of her parents to just Susan Rachel Fisher.

As Susan closed this last journal, Valjean took the opportunity to move from his resting place beside her on the couch to nose under her arm and insert himself on her lap. He instantly purred as she stroked the long fluff on the sides of his neck. Susan set the journal aside and jostled Valjean. She laid her head back and thought about the highlights of what she had learned of her parents from the journals and correspondence.

Her mother had greatly varied in the contents of the journals. At times, they were replete with introspection and candid comments, at others they skipped months without an entry at all. In the holiday 1984 entry, Rebecca Fisher had given a detailed description of the sexy, fantasy outfit she had bought at the Hollywood Lace store in the Moline mall to wear for Jeff for their New Year's Eve together. She was downright meticulous with her report of the results she had gotten from Jeff with the black vinyl outfit. On another occasion, Rebecca Fisher confessed her concern that as she hit thirty-five, she was mindful that her husband spent his days in close contact with dozens of college age co-eds. Her entry admitted that Jeff had never given her cause for concern, but that could not stop the thoughts from arising. Then, probably the most heartfelt emotion that the journals had shown was the sheer joy expressed when Rebecca Fisher, in her forties, had found out she was pregnant and looked like she could take the baby to term. Rebecca Fisher was ecstatic that Susan was coming into their lives.

Susan sat Valjean back on the couch and turned off the lamp. She needed to double-check her preparations for the trip to the Columbia campus tomorrow to scout out the locations of her upcoming class schedule.

—

Chapter Twenty-Eight

Susan felt good to be out and around. Except for a few short trips with Paul, Susan had not been anywhere outside of the apartment in what, four or five weeks? She definitely felt better, but she took a taxi from Chelsea to the law firm offices in Midtown, instead of the bus or subway. Her time laid up had definitely set her back on acclimatization to New York.

She was right on time and went directly to the sixteenth floor for David Tannenbaum's office. At his door, Joyce, his stoic secretary, motioned her to go in, "They're waiting for you."

Susan thought, "They?"

In David's office, Susan saw Peter Ephraim was sitting in one of the side chairs by the desk. David was behind the desk. Both of them stood as she came in.

"Wow, I get two of you, what service." Susan announced.

Peter replied, "Well, I heard you'd asked to see David, I thought it would be good to see you, since no one here except Devorah has seen you since, since… what do we call it?"

Susan smiled and interrupted him, "Yeh, I've had the same question when I've had to describe it to people. Mugging sounds so crude, but probably the correct word. Attack sounds like a heart condition. You can probably come up with some cool euphemisms for what happened. But….." Susan took the chair next to Peter, sitting slowly.

David asked, "Would it help to sit over on the couch, it's softer."

Susan shook her head and said, "No, the straight chair is actually best. On a soft couch you flop down and have to struggle to get up. But, really, I am almost healed. Just being careful about how I move. Don't want to reinjure the ribs now that they've almost healed."

"Well, you are looking good. I must say," Peter said.

"Thanks, but some of that is the miracle of make-up. There is still a bit of yucky bruising, especially on the hip. Apparently they broke some blood vessel in the hip, and it really deep bruised the whole area."

"But, other than the physical injuries, how are you doing?" Peter asked. "Your spirit and head space back to normal?"

Susan smiled, "Pretty much. It will be a long time before I go to the East Village or anyplace new without a full security detail. I think I will be satisfied with buying my books online from now on. But, I'm Okay."

"So, you said you had a question you needed to ask about the trust?" David asked.

Peter added, "Is this something you need me for or…?" He started to get up.

"Well, I actually could use you here, because depending on the answers I get from David, I guess I'll need to ask you, as Trustee, for an approval."

Peter sat back down, raising his hand to tell Susan to proceed.

Susan looked back and forth between Peter and David, folding her hands in her lap on her purse. "You remember back early on I sent you an email asking about the process of paying estate taxes on personal property? David sent me an email that said you had used some estimate Rachel had given you to file an estimate of the taxes on the personal property?"

Both attorneys nodded.

"OK. Well I have some questions I want to ask about that. I have done a little research just to know what to ask you. I think this is really somewhat important."

Susan shifted her weight in the seat with a slight frown as she moved and continued. "Peter, you told me how many of your wealthy clients have charitable foundations they use to reduce taxation, and aid in their ability to transfer the wealth to do good things and to worthy causes. Right?"

"Yes."

"That is part of what I need to ask about. Am I correct that, if you inherit something really valuable and you transfer it to a charity, instead of taking it for your own property, you can avoid taxes because the charitable deduction offsets the profit you got from getting the inheritance? Right?"

Both attorneys started to answer, but David motioned his deferral to Peter who answered, "Well, that isn't the correct wording for that, but your concept is correct. That is the reason for creating a charitable foundation, to avoid taxation on the assets."

"Okay, now to my real question. Suppose a person got a really valuable inheritance and the estimate that was given to pay the taxes on the inheritance was not quite right. If they transferred that inheritance directly into a charitable foundation then the value of the inheritance, I think they called it the basis of the property transferred, … wouldn't that go directly into the tax exempt charity and wipe out any underestimation of estate taxes to the person who inherited it?"

Peter and David looked at each other, then Peter answered, "Pretty much so, you would have to structure it right, but, yes, you can avoid an underestimation of estate tax by transfer of the corpus to an exempt entity."

Now David spoke, "Susan, am I hearing that you think we have underestimated what Rachel gave you?"

Susan gave a nervous smile, "When Peter was talking to me about getting into Columbia and I asked him what his greasing of the skids cost, he told me you attorneys have a rule that there are times when you don't want to ask a question you might not want the answer to. This might be that for you. But, maybe not." She smiled again and looked between the two men.

She continued, "Actually, I am not sure of all this, since I haven't actually asked you what value you had for the estimate of Rachel's personal property. But, I have my suspicions, as I'll explain." Susan took a breath and continued. "Let me give you an example. When Ariel Metzger was married, I chose one of the paintings Rachel had stored in the other apartment to give to them as a wedding gift. It was a lovely painting by a good, well-known artist and looked like the two of them cavorting on a beach. It was just one of many paintings, many dozens actually, and I thought it was a wonderful gift. Then, at the wedding, Mrs. Rothschild, who you may know is an art gallery partner, made such a deal over this painting I had given Ariel and Eddie, saying how precious and wonderful this gift of a painting was. I had known it was valuable and suspected its value, but her reaction and a little bit of research after the fact confirmed that my gift to the bride and groom had been well into the six figure range."

Susan stopped to see the reaction of the attorneys. She continued, "Yes, and what I needed to ask you about is whether you agree that I need to get one of those foundations set up to deal with the artwork Rachel left me. I have done an initial survey by myself. Rachel said on the video she wanted me to do that. But, this has gone totally beyond my abilities. From what Rachel told me on the video, I am not sure even she realized the extent of what she had collected over the years. She started collecting in the '70's, so even the starting prices she paid have appreciated a lot over forty years. Some of her purchases were obviously fairly well thought out and fortuitous. Not everything is really valuable, some are really weird pieces. Rachel must have taken pity on some of the old artists, but there is enough of the elite paintings, Cucuels and Stebbinses, like the one I gave them, and a couple original Merritts, to make me doubt that you attorneys could possibly have had an accurate estimate, and not have set up the foundation on your own volition to protect it all from the estate taxes."

Peter asked, "How many of these do you have?"

Susan gave a nervous grimace, "I did a little database on my computer for the paintings I found stacked in the other apartment, plus what Rachel had inside my apartment. I have just under two hundred data entries. Plus, there is a large statue in the corner of the living room over there that appears to my eye to be an Augustus Saint Gaudens studio proof bronze, really precious."

Both Peter and David raised their eyebrows.

"I am really not good at estimating value, no experience there, but comparing just some of this with similar items I found on auction sites on the internet, I'm guessing we have many millions of dollars of art in that old apartment, maybe tens of millions. What I wanted to suggest is that we do three things; set up a Rachel and Isaac Metzger Foundation to take title to all the art, hire a real art appraisal firm, not a college girl, to do the survey, and probably get another level of security on that place, maybe video surveillance, because that vacant apartment is an art heist waiting to happen."

Peter locked his expressionless stare on Susan for a short moment. Then, he turned to David and gave an expression and a gesture toward Susan like he was saying 'See what I told you?'

"What? What was that about?" Susan asked.

Peter smiled, "Susan, after I finished talking with you about getting into Columbia, I commented to David about how well you had done figuring out exactly how the angles were worked in pulling off something like that deal. Remember, I told you how you might want to give up on this art history stuff. You'd make a good lawyer. Well, now, once again, you have showed your mettle, coming to give us a suggestion of how we attorneys should have done things in the first place. We probably should not have accepted Rachel's estimate, but we had no reason to doubt her. You have done well coming to us. We'll get right on it."

Now Susan raised her eyebrows, "So, now that I have come clean, are you going to tell me what the personal property estimate for the estate was?"

David now winced. "Of course we'll tell you if you insist, but maybe you don't want to ask that until we get it put into the foundation. Just a suggestion."

Peter nodded with a coy smile.

Susan shrugged, "Well, if you gentlemen are squeamish about telling me the estimate you used because of what I've told you about Rachel's artwork stash, I don't suppose you want me to tell you about the jewelry and coin collection, huh?"

—

Twitter by @SusyFisher: Beautiful August day, but did not know Connecticut got this hot. Up here with @PaulWaldmanMD

Twitter by @SusyFisher: Wonderful, beautiful wedding for Julie Waldman and John Bello -- Be Happy! @JulieWaldman_

Facebook - Susy Fisher: Susy likes Temple Israel of Westport, CT

—

19:37 CDT

From:Heidi@Heidi.ws

To:Susy@SusyFisher.com

Subj: Greg Harkness

Susy,

I got a Friend Suggestion from FaceBook for a guy on your Friends List, Greg Harkness. I friended him and we started to talk and … we went out last Saturday. Wonderful guy, really smart. He says you guys dated once. Any pointers you have for me? I'm interested.

New semester starts in a couple weeks at Augustana, I miss you not being here this year. How you doing? You did not tell me much about what happened to you last month. Call me.

Heidi

—

Paul had explained that she could take the closest subway station to their building, two blocks over and two blocks up on 8th street, but that was the A Train and you had to change to the No.1 subway at Times Square or Columbus Circle. Or, you could just walk another block over and catch the No.1 on 7th Street.

After the mugging, Susan was still hesitant to walk too far, but her first morning heading to Columbia campus was bright and sunny. She decided to walk the extra block and avoid the transfer.

She had already been up to the campus for a couple of orientation and book buying trips. Now, on the Tuesday after Labor Day, she headed for 7th street with her book bag over her shoulder. She had a wonderful day yesterday with Paul taking her to a Mets Game with the big Labor Day crowd. Unfortunately, he had to start work at the hospital at midnight, so he was not around this morning. Other than that, it was a wonderful morning for Susan's first day as a Columbia student.

—

Twitter by @SusyFisher: Awesome Yom Kippur at Emanu-El Temple in NYC. Attended with @PaulWaldmanMD and @DevorahFeldshuh Very inspiring!

—

The courtroom was about half full when Susan and Devorah entered. Devorah put her finger to her lips to tell Susan to keep quiet and pointed her to some open seats in the third row. Devorah pulled a business card from her leather portfolio and continued on through the swinging gates in the bannister that separated the court audience from the judge and attorney area. Susan sat where she was told, with her purse and the paper bag she had brought with her on her lap.

Court was already in session with an attorney standing next to a prisoner in orange coveralls at the right hand attorney's table listening to the judge on the podium. The judge was reading something. Another attorney sat at the left hand table. There were several more prisoners sitting in the jury box with a uniformed bailiff hovering near them. Several people, men and women, dressed like attorneys sat in a row of chairs just on the other side of the bannister. A court reporter sat near the judge speaking into a cone shaped mask over her mouth. Another uniformed bailiff and a clerk sat in desks on the far right. The judge was a gray haired man of portly stature with Ben Franklin glasses on his nose. He was precisely what Susan would picture a judge to look like, scholarly and very serious. This judge was a virtual clone of the old law partner, Benjamin Ephraim, Peter's father, except maybe a little larger in stature, as his bulky frame sat rather tall behind the judge's rostrum.

Devorah quietly walked behind the defense attorney and her client, nodded to the seated bailiff and handed her card to the Clerk. She bent forward to whisper something to the clerk. On her way back, Devorah stopped and also whispered to the attorney sitting at the table on the left.

Devorah sat next to Susan with her portfolio on her lap with hands folded, as though they had quite a wait. Susan watched as the Judge and attorneys discussed a myriad of different topics, court hearing schedules, trial dates, plea bargains, and probation reports. Occasionally, one prisoner would sit down in the jury box and the clerk would call another, who would go to the right hand table. Sometimes the attorneys switched off with another one coming forward. A couple of times the defendant came forward from the audience, apparently having been released on bail instead being in custody. One of those defendants who came out of the audience had charges dismissed by the judge and hugged his attorney, before coming back to the audience area and hugging family members.

Finally, the clerk announced, "The People of the State of New York versus Carmen Beatriz Amador, case number F16 51860087."

At this, Devorah touched her elbow to Susan's arm. A prisoner stood up in the jury box. Susan could see it was a young woman of medium height and a slightly heavy figure whose bosom stressed the orange jail jumpsuit. The young woman wore heavy black framed glasses, no make-up and had a broad and not quite plain, but almost pretty, face. From her name, Susan knew the girl was Hispanic, but her features showed her to have a good part regular Caucasian heritage and maybe some black, from her full lips. Susan had not seen this girl in person since that day on the street, which memory was a blur. She did not look very much like the ugly booking photo the police detective had shown Susan.

Two defense attorneys had switched seats. Susan saw the inmate nod to the new attorney, a young woman, as she walked up to her. The defendant also looked to several people seated directly in front of Susan and Devorah, smiling. The people, obviously Carmen Amador's family, became animated, wishing the girl luck. An old woman clasped her hands together as though saying she was praying for her. Then, as Carmen Amador looked to her family, she saw Susan sitting behind them and her facial expression changed. Fear? Dread? Remorse? Hatred? Susan could not read that expression.

As defendant Carmen Beatriz Amador took her seat beside her attorney, Susan could see a tattoo on the side of her neck. A large dark tattoo in unreadable gothic letters reached almost to her ear on the right side of her neck.

The attorneys announced their names to the Judge and the judge asked if the prosecution was ready.

The attorney at the left hand table stood and spoke, "Your Honor, this case comes on for entry of plea, probation report, victim's statement and sentencing. The people have reached agreement with Defense on entry of the plea and an indeterminate sentence. The draft Plea Agreement should be in the court's file. Originally Defendant Carmen Amador was charged with Gang Assault in the First Degree in violation of Section 120.07, a class B felony, Robbery in the First Degree in violation of Section 160.15, a class B Felony. We have prepared the papers for a plea to Robbery in the Third Degree, in violation of Section 160.05, a class D felony and Assault in the Second Degree, in violation of Section 120.05 a class D Felony. The People's reasoning for thi…"

The judge interrupted the district attorney and said, "I see from the court file that this was clearly a gang related assault and there was serious bodily injury, yet the People are agreeing to wiping the gang enhancement and bodily injury. This Court has to question that."

"You Honor, we understand the Court's concern. May I ask the Court's indulgence in this until the Probation Report and the Victim's Statement are available to Your Honor."

"Very Well, proceed," the judge ordered, clearly unhappy.

The district attorney called a probation officer, who came up from the audience. This heavy set, middle-aged, black woman had papers she handed to each attorney and the bailiff before she sat in the witness box. The bailiff gave one paper to the clerk and another to the judge.

The probation officer was sworn in and read her report to the court. She started with her review of the crime, the assault on Susan. Then, she gave some background information on the Defendant, Carmen Amador. Carmen's mother was deceased, her father was unknown. She had been raised by her grandmother and aunt, along with four siblings and cousins. She had finished high school, but had never held a job for more than a few months. She was twenty years old and had apparently been involved with a lower East Side gang since high school. She had no criminal convictions, but there was apparently a juvenile record that was sealed and off limits for consideration by this court.

At the end of her report, the probation officer said, "So, in light of the proposed plea bargain and especially in light of the fact that the gang connections remain a pressure for any young person in a situation like the Defendant's here, Probation recommends incarceration in the women's gang member rehabilitation program at the Bedford Hills Correctional Facility for a period of one year with a further two years of supervised probation."

The family members got noisy in objection to this recommendation and the judge banged his gavel. "We'll have none of that. Order in the Court."

When things got quiet, the judge asked, "Do counsel have anything for Probation."

Both attorneys shook their heads. The probation officer got up and sat back in the audience.

The district attorney stood and said, "The People call Susan Rachel Fisher, for purposes of her making her Victim's Statement. Normally, this would only be done for sentencing, but we ask the court's indulgence to hear from Miss Fisher, so she can address the issue of the plea bargain and sentencing, as well. That has been requested by the Victim's counsel, Miss Feldshuh, who is present in court."

Devorah stood up at mention of her name and nodded to the Judge.

The judge asked, "Does defense have any objections?"

The young female public defender representing Carmen Amador shrugged her shoulders and shook her head. Devorah stood, leading the way for Susan through the swinging bannister gate that separated the audience from the main court area. Devorah stood near the speaker's podium between counsel table and motioned Susan to the witness stand. As Susan passed, Devorah whispered to her, "You'll be fine."

Carmen Amador's family was surprised that their relative's victim had been sitting right behind them. They turned to look at her as Susan stood and walked forward.

On her way to the witness box, Susan stopped in front of the floor-standing easel that had roadway markings and magnetic cars for witnesses to describe traffic cases for the court. As Devorah had told her, Susan opened her paper bag, took out a cream colored dress on a hanger and hooked it up on top of the easel. Everyone in the court could see blood spatters on the shoulders of the dress and a larger splotch of dark red on the chest area. There was a murmur in the court. Susan sat in the witness chair. The court clerk asked her to swear to tell the truth and give her full name. Susan did.

The district attorney spoke next, "Miss Fisher, thank you for coming today, I understand from your attorney you have a prepared statement for the court. Please proceed."

Susan took a deep breath and nodded, "Let me apologize in advance, I'm pretty nervous. This isn't easy to talk about, and I have never done anything like this before."

The judge cut in, peering down at Susan from above, "Don't worry, just take your time. And you should know, you can just address your comments to me, don't talk to the attorneys or the defendant. Nothing to be nervous about."

Susan smiled weakly and nodded. She unfolded a piece of paper she took from her bag. "First, let me explain what happened. Last July, it was a nice warm day, late afternoon, or early evening. I was walking on the street on my way back from a bookstore. I had bought several books at a big bookstore on the East Side and was taking what I thought was a shortcut to catch the crosstown bus over to my apartment in Chelsea. I had never been to that area before, but thought I knew where I was going. I guess I was wrong. I have been told by others there are just some places a young woman doesn't walk after business hours in New York. I had apparently found one of them.

"I don't remember much about the assault. It started with the defendant, Carmen Amador, sort of jumping out in front of me. I really don't know where she came from. She just sort of appeared, blocking my way down the sidewalk. I don't think she said anything, but from behind I heard someone say "whatcha doing, pretty lady.' Before I could turn to the voice, a guy's voice, someone hit me in the head from behind. I was stunned, I fell, but was not totally out. I felt someone try pulling my purse and shopping bag from my hands. When I resisted, I got kicked hard, in the ribs. I found out later that kick broke two ribs. Then, someone kicked me, really hard, on the side of my head or face. That was it, I blacked out. I sort of came to in the ambulance, but I really wasn't aware of anything until I awoke in the hospital emergency room.

"I found out in the emergency room that I was beaten up pretty bad. The muggers had ripped my earrings from my ears, tearing my earlobe right through on the right side and damaging to other ear, too. The kick to my head had dislocated my jaw and hit me so hard that my teeth almost came through my cheek. I was bruised from several other kicks and the blow to my head caused a concussion. You can see the dress I wore, hanging here, has the blood on the shoulders from my ripped ears and my mouth and lips were bleeding all down the front. You can also see the black toe prints where I was kicked in the abdomen and in the hip.

"I am told a police car came around the corner just then, while they were kicking me. I guess I could have been worse. One officer stopped to help me and another chased the people who attacked me. That other officer managed to chase the defendant and catch her when she ran in front of a taxi and got hit. She tried to ditch my purse on that run and the officer picked it up. And when they searched the defendant, the police found my bloody earrings in her pocket. I am told that is why she decided to plea bargain, since there was no doubt she was involved in the robbery and assault. The police never did find my bag of books that was stolen."

Susan stopped for a moment. She took a small red velvet box and an envelope from her paper bag and set them on the railing of the witness box. She continued, "These are those earrings, in this box. They are pretty expensive, diamonds. Some people might say it was foolhardy to wear something like on a walk like I was taking, in that area. Maybe. Who knows?" Susan looked up at the judge and shrugged. He gave a fatherly nod.

"I do know it took me weeks to recover. I could barely move from the pain, of the broken ribs and my jaw that wouldn't open up. Oh, and I forgot to say the kick also bruised my kidney, caused bleeding inside. I wasn't able to do much for those weeks. I pretty much just sat around, watched TV, surfed the internet, played with a kitten I was given to help my rehab. That kind of stuff.

"But, part of the television watching I did was to watch my favorite DVD. The musical *Les Miserables*. My boyfriend came over and watched it with me. I love that story. Are you familiar with *Les Miserables*?" Susan looked up at the judge.

The judge nodded and gave a smile, as though he knew where Susan was going, "Yes, of course, a wonderful story."

"Well, watching that movie again, at that time, while recovering from this crime, gave me a epiphany. I realized that I had absolutely no understanding of why this crime would have occurred. I have no idea at all of what could make another young women, Miss Amador, who is almost exactly my age, participate in such a violent attack. Sure, I understand poverty and the greed that can drive people. But, I cannot hope to understand what is in the mind of Carmen Amador. Although I have lost both of my parents this last year, I had their love and direction for my childhood and formative years. She did not have that. And today, I have every blessing that life can offer me, my health, considerable wealth, I am studying at a great school, I should have a promising future. I have every blessing imaginable. So, I cannot possibly understand what it might be like to never have known a father, like Miss Amador. To not have her mother and to be raised by a grandmother and aunt in what I am told by the probation officer were very difficult conditions for Miss Amador. I cannot understand what it must be like to have so few options in life that running with a street gang seems like a good choice. So, I would have a very hard time judging Carmen Amador's actions based upon anything in my own understanding or experience. I do not envy Your Honor's job.

"But, then I watched my favorite movie, *Les Miserables*. Now I don't for a moment think that I can display the kind of selfless love the Bishop displayed in giving Jean Valjean another chance after he had robbed him. But, I can try. If I find it impossible to understand the violence that I was a victim of, then why should I try to understand, rather than accept and forgive. The whole purpose of an inspirational message is to inspire the recipient to greater things. In that movie, the message was that the Bishop was blessed with the gift of love and understanding as soon as he displayed his forgiveness, he did not have to wait decades like Valjean did to understand the gifts of love, forgiveness and hope. And on the other side, there are those Inspector Javerts in life, for whom the only thing that matters is the letter of the law, not the spirit.

"So, with that said, Your Honor, could you ask the bailiff to come over here?"

The judge said "Bailiff," and motioned for the bailiff to come over.

Susan handed the bailiff the earring box and envelope to the bailiff. She said, "Please give these to the Defendant."

The bailiff looked quickly to the judge, who nodded. The bailiff sat the box and envelope on the table in front of the defense attorney and her client, who stared wide-eyed at Susan.

Susan continued, "Your Honor, those earrings were what the defendant took from me. I cannot bring myself to wear them again, so I am offering them to Carmen Amador, in hopes that she may find some value in that which she stole. And in the envelope is my equivalent of the Bishop's candlesticks, which he added to Valjean's pile of loot after the theft was reported to him. In the envelope is a letter of credit prepared by my attorney. It is drawn up to be presented to my bank along with an invoice for payment for one year's tuition to any school the defendant wishes to enroll in, whether a junior college, university, trade school, it doesn't matter. I will pay for that year of education. So, just like Valjean used the sale of the Bishop's valuables to build a future for himself and the little girl he raised. So, too, Carmen Amador can use the diamonds and letter of credit to build her future.

"You see, your honor, right now the crime that was committed is a horrible act of violence, and a bitter and painful memory for me. And, right now that crime has the potential of driving a nail in the coffin of Carmen Amador being able to have a fruitful and happy life. While a gang rehabilitation program at New York state prison may be better than a life of crime, it certainly is not better than an education and a future of hope. If I am successful in what I am trying to do here, then the violent act I was a victim of becomes, for me, an act of love and hope. And for Carmen Amador, it will hopefully be the act that changes her life.

Susan studied the paper she was reading from and looked up at the judge again, "But, Your Honor, I need your help to do this. By agreeing to the plea bargain for lesser offenses, this court can make my hopes for a *Les Miserables* event possible. You see, the original charges are Class B felonies, which require mandatory prison time, in most cases. But, the district attorney has agreed to drop the charges to Class D felonies, which give this court some leeway. Probation is recommending a year's sentence to a gang rehab facility, but you do not have to follow that recommendation. With Class D felonies, Your Honor can defer sentencing, and then you can award probation only. So, what I am asking the court to do is act under…" Susan looked down at her paper, "Section 380.30 to defer sentencing on the plea bargain you accept today. Defer sentencing for twelve months, you can under that law. Then, make a condition of the deferred sentencing that the Defendant enroll in an educational program to be paid for by my letter of credit and that she find employment. And, you should require the defendant to have no contact or communication with any gang member for the period of the deferred sentencing and any probationary period that comes after that. If the defendant does not comply, you have the power to throw the proverbial book at her when she comes before you again. If Your Honor will do what I ask here, then two young women will be able to erase a horrible event from their lives and replace it with an act of kindness and love. Please consider this."

Susan looked up at the judge and he looked back at her for a long moment. The judge drew in a deep breath and turned to the attorneys, "Do counsel have any questions of the witness?"

The district attorney stood and started to say something, but looked at the judge who gave a tiny shake of his head, and the prosecutor took the judge's hint and sat down. Neither attorney had any questions for Susan.

The judge turned to Susan, "Miss Fisher, you are excused. Thank you for the effort you have made here today."

Susan got up and walked across the courtroom, taking her dress with her, putting back in the bag. Devorah turned from the podium, nodded to the Judge and held the bannister gate for Susan. As she passed Carmen, the two looked into each other's eyes, but said nothing and showed no expression. The Amador family all looked sideways at Susan when she went to take her seat on the row behind them. The old grandmother looked up into Susan's eyes, but she neither said anything nor showed any emotion. Susan saw her eyes were wet with tears.

As they sat, Devorah leaned over to Susan and whispered, "Good job. Let's see what he does."

The courtroom was silent as the judge sat silently. He thumbed through the pages in the court file.

At length, the judge said, "Well, this is quite a quandary. A few minutes ago I was chiding the prosecution for dumping the gang enhancements and dropping the serious charges, and now I have the victim asking me to defer sentencing entirely."

He paused again, "But, whatever I decide, we have some paperwork to get out of the way. Does the prosecution have a final plea bargain prepared?"

"Yes, Your Honor, I have already given it to the defense."

The defense attorney stood and handed a form to the bailiff, who handed it to the clerk. The Clerk looked it over briefly and handed it to the judge. The defense attorney pulled Carmen's elbow, getting her to stand.

The judge read through the form, flipping pages. He faced the defendant and asked, "Carmen Amador, is this your signature on the plea form?"

"Yes, yes it is," Carmen said very nervously.

"And do you understand that with this plea, you are admitting to the crimes listed and are waiving any right of appeal on these charges?"

"Yes."

"And do you understand that it is within this court's power to sentence you to incarceration in the state prison for a period up to the maximum bargained for punishment on the form, which is an indeterminate sentence?'

"Yes, Your Honor, I understand that."

"And is it your testimony… Wait, the defendant has not been sworn. Clerk?"

The clerk stood and asked the defendant to identify herself, raise her hand and to swear to tell truth. She did.

"Now, Miss Amador, is it your testimony to this court that there is a factual basis for your entry of a guilty plea to these charges. That you in fact did commit these crimes and if we went to trial that you believe you would be found guilty of these crimes?"

"Yes, judge."

The judge again waited a long time before continuing, "Then, Carmen Beatriz Amador, this court accepts your plea and finds that you are, in fact, guilty of the crimes of Robbery in the Third Degree, in violation of Section 160.05 and Assault in the Second Degree, in violation of Section 120.05 of the New York State Penal Code."

The judge paused one more time, then opened a large blue book from a rack of books beside him and turned to a page in the book. Then he said, "And, this court finds pursuant to Section 380.30 that this is the first felony conviction of the defendant and the court believes that prompt institutional confinement is not necessary to preserve the safety and security of society, that the individual may benefit from the rehabilitative opportunities presented by the deferral of sentencing, that absent such a rehabilitative opportunity there is a likelihood that the court would impose an indeterminate sentence of imprisonment, and that upon satisfactory completion of the period of deferral the court would be more likely to impose a sentence other than an indeterminate sentence of imprisonment under article seventy of the penal law. Sentencing is hereby deferred for the period of twelve months. During the period of deferred sentencing the defendant shall report bi-weekly to the probation officer assigned to her, at least one such report every two months shall be in person. She shall have no contact with any criminal gang member or convicted felon. She will comply with standard probation instructions as to lifestyle that will be explained to her upon her release from custody. She will find gainful employment and she will take advantage of opportunities presented to her to obtain an education, and shall enroll in a formal educational program to advance her station in life."

The judge looked up from the law book and stared at the Carmen Amador, "Miss Amador, there is one last condition on your deferred sentencing. I am not sure you, as yet, fully understand to the importance or the true nature of what Miss Fisher did for you here today, or why. But, I want you to understand, so I am adding as a condition of deferred sentencing that you view the motion picture *Les Miserables* and perhaps even read the original book, so you can understand what Victor Hugo's view of humanity and Miss Fisher's hope should mean to a criminal who gets a second chance to make her life work. Let us hope life will imitate art.

"Also Miss Amador, this court is putting a lot of faith in the hope that your victim's forgiving nature is not unfounded. You should recognize that this is your sole opportunity to avoid a prison sentence. I suggest you make the best of it."

The judge turned his desk calendar to look at the back side. "Defendant is ordered released on her own recognizance, pending further hearing of the court. Sentencing review date shall be set for October 3rd of next year in this department. Probation is directed to make quarterly reports to the court on the Defendant's progress in her education and other matters they deem appropriate with a full report for the sentencing hearing. Miss Amador, you will be released after the Corrections and Probation people process you out. The Court will recess for fifteen minutes."

—

Chapter Twenty-Nine

"Susan. I have bad news and good news about our date tonight." Paul said.

Susan rolled her eyes up, and then spoke into her iPhone, "Okay, I'll bite. Good news first."

"I'm not cancelling our date."

"Okay, sounds good, and the bad news."

"I'm gonna have to postpone the starting time until 9:00."

"You're still at the hospital?" Susan asked.

"No, I am six floors below you, in the clinic. Our duty physician called me on my cell just before I got home. He said his daughter is going into labor out in Queens, with his first grandkid, and he needed to be out there. I am stuck filling in at the clinic until closing."

"So, I guess I'll see you at 9:00 then?"

"Well, what I was thinking is this. It is just after 6:00 now. It is really slow here. You have never gotten the tour of our little operation down here. Instead of starting our date at 7:00, you can come down here, maybe bring me a sandwich to tide me over, I'll give you the grand tour and introduce you to my evening staff. I'll let you play with my stethoscope, and I can entertain you until I get off at 9:00."

"How romantic!" Susan said, pausing a moment, "No, really, sounds interesting. I'll see you at 7:00."

—

"So, not much action tonight, huh?" Susan asked. She sat in the armchair in the corner of the duty physicians' office at the clinic.

Paul was seated behind the desk, "It's like that here. Sometimes nothing at all, sometimes utter chaos. But, weekday evenings are usually slow, until flu season kicks in. That's why I asked you down, to keep me company. I could probably go up to my apartment and wait for a call down, but there is a medical standard that if you advertise certain services for specified hours you need to have a physician on site. The rules aren't clear whether my apartment on the second floor is 'on-site,' so I usually stick around down here until closing. Anyway, if somebody walks in the front door with a spurting wound, you don't want the nurse to have to call upstairs for a doctor. Actually, Eric and I rarely get evening fill-ins, the usual need for a temp fill-in is to cover the busy daytime hours."

Renee, the nurse, stuck her head in the office door and said, "Whoopee, we have a patient. I just took details. 40-year-old white male, heavy set. No temp, elevated BP. Workplace injury, today. He hurt his leg at work, late afternoon, went home and put ice packs on it. It got worse. Now he is here, severe pain when he moves his knee, some edema and minor hematoma around the patella. It is covered by Worker's Comp, he has his union med card and employee ID. You're up, Doc!"

Renee, a short, pixie-haired blonde, reached in through the door and handed Paul a medical chart. She smiled over at Susan and left. As Paul opened the chart, Susan could see there was only one page in the folder. Paul read it quickly, and then stood.

"I'll wait for you here." Susan sat back in her chair, reaching for a New Yorker magazine from a side table.

Paul, at first, nodded, and then stopped to think and turned to Susan, "You want to come watch me work my medical magic?"

"Is that even allowed?" Susan asked.

"It's not the usual, but this isn't anything confidential," Paul said as he reached for a lab coat on a hat tree in the corner. He unclipped an ID tag from the lab coat. "Besides, I know the boss around here, and he won't mind." He smiled and handed Susan the lab coat. "Wear the coat, stand in the corner, look concerned, but just watch. If I need you to leave, I'll let you know."

Susan shrugged and donned the lab coat. "He not only wants me to play doctor, but I can do dress-up, too. And it's still a week until Halloween."

She followed Paul down the hall and into an examining room. A man was sitting on the blue vinyl exam table with one khaki pants leg rolled above the knee. A slightly rotund woman in a cotton print housedress and winter coat stood next to him. The woman clutched her purse to her chest. She had her free arm on the man's shoulder.

"Good evening, Mister, ahh, Ravenich," Paul had to refer to the medical folder to get the name, "I'm Doctor Paul Waldman." Paul offered his hand to the patient. They shook.

Susan took a spot standing in the far corner of the exam room, between the trash can and a red sharps container attached to the wall. The woman looked at Susan and smiled weakly. Susan returned the smile.

"Are you Mrs. Ravenich?" Paul asked the woman.

"Yes, doctor." was the woman's answer, in a thick Eastern European accent with the first "o" in "doctor" coming out as a long vowel.

Paul pulled a round, rolling stool over in front of the man and sat down.

He opened the file folder.

"So, I understand you hurt your leg at work. Tell me what happened."

The man nodded, cleared his throat and began, in a thick accent that matched his wife's, "We ver finishing up for ze day. Doink concrete work on a building that is, ahh, going up on twenty-eight street. We remove forms from yesterday's work. We always remove last… previous day forms each night so we have them ready for another pour next morning. We use crowbars and pry bars to knock the forms off of dried concrete. We had one that would not come. I use a pry bar. Two guys helping me, pull hard… and then it, all of sudden…Uff!… come off and two of us we go flying. I stop from falling down into stairwell, but I landed on yust one leg. This one." He touched his leg.

"So, all of your weight came down on one leg? Did it hurt then? And where did you, or do you, feel pain."

"It hurt bad… immediate…, immediate-ly. Right here," He put his fingers on his knee, near where Susan could see a bruise. "But, was quitting time and pain went away, sort of. In this job, construction, you get little hurts and bumps all the time, is part of job. At quitting time, we all want to go home, I not want to act like a pus…" He stopped talking and his eyes flicked quickly at his wife and then Susan.

Paul interrupted, "And then, at home?"

"Vell, on the bus home it gets vorse. By ze time I come off bus, it hurt to go down steps. By time I get home, it really hurt."

"I put ze ice pack on it," his wife volunteered.

"Let me look. Tell me when it hurts. Let your foot hang loose. Don't tense up." Paul indicated what he meant by 'tense' with his hands tightening.

Paul rolled his chair to the side and started to touch the knee, moving it slightly and pushing his fingers in around the kneecap. The man grimaced at his touch in one spot. Paul grasped the man's knee with his left hand, with this forefinger curled around the kneecap and started to lift the man's ankle up in an arch with his other hand. After a few inches of lift, Mr. Ravenich screamed out and clutched the edge of the exam table.

Paul stopped and moved the leg back down slowly. He asked the man, "Was that pain right here?" Paul touched under the man's kneecap.

"Yes, right there."

Paul nodded his head and pursed his lips.

"Vat is it, doctor." The man asked

"It will take some x-rays to be sure, but you seem to have had a pretty bad tear inside your knee. Let me explain."

Paul checked the chart again, setting it on the table. He looked into the man's eyes and said, "Okay, Pavel, your knee is not a joint like other places in your body like your hip or your fingers, where there is a real joint that hold things together and allows the bending." Then, Paul moved back and lifted his forearms level with the floor, making a fist with both hands. "In your leg, your knee, there are two big bones, the tibia," he wiggled his left arm, "and the fibula." He wiggled his right arm. "The tibia and the fibula meet at your knee, but they just meet like this," he butted his two fists together, "and they bend like this. Just moving against each other. They are connected by several tendons and lots of different muscles, but no real joint, just a thin pad of slippery cartilage, called the … the, ahh…."

Seeing Paul was having trouble was having trouble remembering the word to tell the Raveniches, Susan forgot Paul's instructions to her and volunteered, "Meniscus?"

Paul's eyes shot over to Susan. She saw his deeply furrowed brow, glaring at her. She was worried he was mad at her impertinence of speaking out. But, then, as suddenly as he had glared, Paul gave a quick smile and turned back to look at Pavel Ravenich, saying, "Yes, the meniscus, it sits right across the top of, and attached to, the tibia and acts like a bearing, a lubricating pad, between the two big bones. I think what you did with the quick, lunging jump with all your weight on it, was to twist the meniscus, maybe tear it and push it out of the place it is supposed to be. I actually think I can feel the cartilage over here on the inside edge under the kneecap. I should not be able to feel the edge of it there."

Mrs. Ravenich asked, "So, what do you do? Is serious?"

Paul nodded, "Well, yes it is a serious problem, but one that can be fixed. When you see a football player hurting his knee on the football field, it is often something like this. An orthopedic surgeon can go in and get it put back in place and stable. It can be fixed fairly easily."

"Surgery?" Pavel asked.

"Yes, almost certainly surgery, but we have new techniques, arthroscopic surgery, where we can make a 'tiny' little hole and do everything with a tiny little video camera without much cutting, er, the surgery like you are probably used to thinking of."

"What do ve do? You can do that?" Mrs. Ravenich asked.

"Well, I could, and have, done that surgery. But, up at Presbyterian Hospital. Not here. That is not something we can do here, at this clinic. And, that really isn't my specialty. You need to be seen by an orthopedic surgery specialist. Soon. The sooner you get this dealt with the easier it is to fix. If you let it go, it doesn't heal as fast or as well. Every time you bend your leg you risk making it worse. I need to get you to a hospital with an orthopod tonight. Since it is clear you have damage to the meniscus, it doesn't even make sense for me to x-ray it, the ER will just do it again for themselves. They will probably do a scan of it, since the cartilage tear may not show fully on an x-ray. We need to immobilize your leg, so you can't keep bending it and then get you to a surgical hospital. Do you have a car?"

Both people shook their head 'no.'

"Just as well, it is hard to get into a car, or a taxi, with your leg straight. I am going to carefully straighten your leg out, causing as little pain as I can and splint it out straight. That will keep you from hurting it worse. I'll give you something for the pain. This injury is covered by Worker's Comp from your employer, so the insurance company will cover the cost of medical transport service to get you to the nearest hospital, I recommend NYU on the East Side for this kind of thing tonight. We'll get you fixed up and transported over to NYU Langone.

"Mrs. Ravenich, I think you should wait in the waiting room now, while my nurse and I immobilize the leg. You should go to the hospital with your husband, if you can. And, you should call home and tell anybody that you need to that you will be away awhile tonight, over at NYU. Understand?"

She did.

Paul stood and put his hand on the man's shoulder, "Pavel, you relax, we'll get you fixed up."

Paul picked up the chart, turned and with a curled finger motioned for Susan to follow him.

They walked down the hallway and around a corner toward Paul's office. After turning the corner Paul stopped suddenly and turned back to Susan, very close, almost nose to nose with her.

Paul gave a little smile and said, "So, Doctor Fisher, 'Meniscus' huh?"

Susan gave a sheepish smile, and replied, "Yeh, it's his meniscus."

"And you know about a meniscus because?"

"I learned it in my human anatomy class at Columbia. We started at the bottom, this week we get up to the hips. It's very interesting."

After a moment, Paul smiled again. "Okay, Doctor, thank you for the memory assist. You can go read your magazine now, while Renee and I cause Pavel to scream a little when we put his splint on."

He looked at his watch. "We have about forty-five minutes left tonight. Then we can go get something to eat, and you can explain why an art history major is taking a human anatomy class."

He leaned forward and gave Susan a quick kiss on the tip of her nose. He stepped around her and went back towards the exam room.

—

Twitter from @PaulWaldmanMD: Happy Birthday and Happy Halloween @SusyFisher The black Catwoman suit was out of sight

—

Chapter Thirty

"Wow, why are you all dressed up this morning? Not your usual college student outfit." Paul held the lobby door open for Susan, as they left to go to the Metro Café for their breakfast together.

Susan had on a knee-length black wool dress coat. Paul had his hospital logo blue parka and a stocking cap on.

"Yeh, taking a morning off from classes. Gotta meet with the lawyers and hopefully make some money." Susan buttoned up her coat collar to keep out the cold air and gave her hand to Paul as they walked.

"Okay, I didn't know you were involved in that business kind of thing." Paul said. "I do have something I wanted to run by you. It is kind of an imposition, so don't hold back, if I'm asking too much. Betsy called from Boston. She and Ed had an idea for our folks' anniversary coming up. Looking at the calendar we seem to have a five-way coming together of events that we think we may be able to take advantage. Our parents' 30th wedding anniversary happens to fall, this year, on the fifth day of Hanukah. You probably know that my birthday is two days before that. Betsy checked your Columbia University class schedule and the Boston University schedule for Julie and John have classes ending the day before that. All of you have finals the week after that. Since the fifth day of Hanukah is the feast day we thought it would be cool to do a three-fer with anniversary, birthday and Hanukah feast all at once with all of us together and on a day when all of you students are free from classes."

"Sounds like a good idea. What's the imposition on me?" Susan asked.

"Well, we don't want to all descend on the folks' house for this. We want their anniversary to be a real holiday for them. So, that means either we all go up to Boston, or everyone comes to New York. And, I wanted you to be involved in the celebration, this year, too. You know, to see how we did Hanukah in the Waldman clan. We could do the out-of-town visits in a hotel, but it would be better to do this in someone's home. Ed and Betsy don't have any open bedrooms with the new baby. Julie and John live in married student housing at B.U. But, I have a guest bedroom…."

Susan interrupted. "And, I have three open bedrooms?"

"Yeh, hence the imposition, foisting my relatives on you…." Paul sounded hesitant.

Susan smiled broadly, "Paul, you don't even have to ask. I would be thrilled to have them. And, we can have the feast at my place, too."

Paul shook his head. "No, we can do that at my place. Betsy says she will handle that end of this."

"No, Paul. Your little kitchen is barely adequate to handle a male bachelor pad and your dining table only has four chairs for, what… ," Susan counted people on her fingers, "… eleven people counting the baby. No, if Betsy wants to handle the cooking fine, but she does it in my huge kitchen with me as co-pilot. And, I'm guessing your mother will be doing mentor duties for both of us."

"If you insist." Paul gave a little smile.

"That will be something new for me. I've never hosted anything like that. This only child orphan will have a house full of family for the holidays. Sounds fun." Susan walked a bit more before adding, "So, This is your 29th birthday… what do you want for your birthday?"

—

"I think I have seen that outfit before, but you've done something with the blouse," Devorah commented with a smile, as she gave Susan a quick hug. Everybody else in the Wassermann, Ephraim & Moore main conference room were introducing themselves to one another and taking their seats at the long, mahogany table.

Susan laughed and fingered the collar of the Donna Karan jacket. "Yes, your rip fixed up fine. I decided it is still my best 'serious business' outfit."

Susan wore the same outfit with black jacket, skirt and cummerbund she had worn to Aunt Rachel's funeral, except the dark blouse was replaced with a blazing crimson silk blouse. She had matching ruby earrings and make-up complimentary to the crimson splash of her blouse.

Susan and Devorah circumnavigated the big table, skirting the large cube shape at the front of the room that was shrouded in a blue cloth covering. Susan folded her outer coat on a chair by the wall and took her seat near the head of the table on the window side, Devorah next to her.

As Devorah shifted her portfolio in front of her, she asked Susan, "You ready for this?"

"Not me, you! All I have to do is introduce people, you have to pull this together."

Susan saw Aaron Metzger enter the room. He headed for her. They hugged warmly, and Aaron asked, "Where do I sit?"

"Here, right next to Devorah," Susan pointed.

As Aaron was pulling out his chair, Peter Ephraim walked up. They shook hands. Peter pulled out a chair next to Aaron, but remained standing and watched people mingling around the room. He checked his watch, reached for an empty water glass in the middle of the table and rang it loudly with a ding of his fountain pen. People turned to sit down. All of the main table seats were filled and some of those chairs along the wall were taken by what looked like younger staff people.

"Excuse me, everyone. We are just about on time. If you could take your seats…." Peter announced.

When everyone had been seated he continued, "Ladies and gentlemen. I am Peter Ephraim, managing partner of the Firm of Wassermann, Ephraim and Moore. I am also the primary Trustee for and Executive Vice-President of the Metzger companies. But, this is not my show today. I'll turn the floor over to one of my favorite clients, Miss Susan Fisher, who is responsible for putting this meeting together. Susan?"

Susan smiled, stood up and moved around to the head of the table, next to the blue cube. She had a yellow legal tablet in her hands. Jeremy Berg rushed from his seat along the wall and moved a podium from the corner over to the head of the table for Susan to use.

Susan began, "Good Morning everyone, I hope all of you had a great Thanksgiving holiday and stayed warm in this horrible, snowy weather we're having. I think I have met almost everyone here and most of you should know what our purpose is here today. But, I wanted to start out with my view of how we got here, and in so doing, I'll have a chance to introduce the people here today in the order that they came into the story with me.

"As many of you know, I recently inherited my Aunt Rachel Metzger's interest in some of the properties owned and managed by the Metzger Companies. In the winding up of her estate, I met the attorneys of Wassermann Ephraim," She motioned to her left, "Mr. Peter Ephraim, who you have heard from. Mr. David Tannenbaum, David?" Tannenbaum stood up at the far end of the table and gave a wave to the group, "Mr. Tannenbaum is our trusts' business affairs attorney. And Miss Devorah Feldshuh, who is my personal counsel and the chief legal architect of the project you are here to discuss. Devorah?"

Devorah looked around the table, raised her hand and nodded, but did not stand.

"I also need to introduce the two other primary owners of the property we are here to talk about. My uncle, Aaron Metzger and my Aunt Rachel's step-son, Joseph Metzger." Susan waited for Aaron and Joe, farther down the table, to stand and nod to everyone.

Susan checked her legal pad and continued, "I would also like to introduce Mr. Marvin Gluba of the Cerberus Capital Management /Jewel Stores. I know you have quite a few of your team here today. I'll let you introduce them when you make your presentation. Oh, and the other key member of our team here is Mr. Laszlo Kiss, real property manager for the Metzger Companies, who has played a key role in bringing everyone together on this. Laszlo?"

Laszlo Kiss was next to Joseph and he stood up. Susan could see he felt out of place in a suit in a boardroom.

"OK. Let me tell you how this idea came about." Susan flipped to a new page.

"My aunt owned a building on lower 10th Street. It was where she had lived for forty years. When she passed away, I inherited it from her. When Laszlo Kiss took me down there to show me around, he happened to also explain the background of another neighboring property, a five-story building across the street, which was owned by several of the Metzger family trusts and managed by Laszlo. He explained how that building, a big hulking ex-factory converted to commercial/residential mixed-use, was nearing the end of the useful life of the original leasehold estates and financing arrangements set up in the '70's and would soon need either a cash infusion or new ownership to bring it back to commercial usefulness. That building was getting a bit long in the tooth, had an undesirable tenant base and was in bad need of new life. I thought nothing more of that at the time, but did think about that building every time I left my new home across the street, viewing the vacancy signs, since I decided to live in my Aunt's apartment. My bedroom window, living room window, and dining room window, all face that building, too.

"When I set up housekeeping in that building across the street, I found myself living in Chelsea, one of the most elite and expensive residential neighborhoods in New York. And in a city with the greatest consumer shopping Meccas on Earth, I soon found a serious problem with the Chelsea neighborhood. I could not find what I considered to be a decent supermarket to shop for groceries. There were a myriad of small grocery stores, specialty shops, mom and pop stores and even a couple big chain store locations, but even those big chains were semi-specialty stores, that is, health foods, organic and 'New Age' product lines. I could find nothing like the great shopping I remembered from back home.

"You see, I grew up in the medium-sized, Midwestern metroplex called the Quad Cities. Moline and Rock Island, Illinois, and Davenport and Bettendorf, Iowa, the Quad Cities, on either bank of the Mississippi River. After living in my new home in New York for a while, I had occasion to go back home to wind up my affairs in the Quad Cities. Back there, within a short distance of my old family home in Moline, were a half dozen large, full service supermarkets, Safeway, Hy-Vee, Aldi, a Wal-Mart superstore and several others, and I found that there was a new Jewel-Osco Superstore opened just across the street from the field where I used to play soccer when I was a girl. That Jewel-Osco Superstore was a sight for sore eyes for this girl who was tired of not being able find a store in New York that had a jumbo-sized potato chips, or a wide selection of choices for basic foods. I stood in the wonderful Jewel-Osco Superstore in Moline, Illinois, in front of a yogurt and dairy case with hundreds of different products wondering why New Yorkers did not have such places. Manhattan may have the huge Macy's on 34th Street and consumer goods strips like Park Avenue that the whole world envies, but it did not have anything with the shopping selection that a Jewel-Osco the size of two football fields that little Moline, Illinois had. I went through that big Jewel-Osco and found that I could choose from a choice of five different kinds of this, a half dozen different styles of that -- I could get any variety, of virtually any consumer product I could imagine, at a really decent price, and then get checked out in one of fifteen check-out counters, with no waiting. Mighty New York had nothing to match the convenience and selection of that hick Midwestern city.

"Coming back to New York, I took the taxi from the airport and found myself on the corner in front of my new home, looking at the huge building across the street that was such a headache for the Metzger Companies, and according to Laszlo, needed a new tenant. I absent-mindedly thought 'Why couldn't they put a Jewel Superstore there. That would be so convenient and these New Yorkers would go ga-ga over it.'"

Susan smiled, put her tablet down and put her hands over her head, indicating she was holding something round, "Imagine the light bulb flashing above my head. Here I was the part owner of a huge building in the one of the most elite neighborhoods of the greatest city on Earth, and I could not figure out why they could not put in a superstore like a thousand smaller towns across America have. I knew New York, at least my home section of Manhattan, had nothing quite like it. I knew we needed a new anchor tenant for our building. Why not?" Susan raised her hands in a big dramatic shrug.

"So, I searched the internet for Jewel and found they were owned by Cerberus Capital Management, right here in New York. I sent some email inquiries to the email addresses I found online that seemed to be pertinent. And, Ssshhhhh! I also sent a few emails to Jewel's competition, Wal-Mart, Kroger and the like. I suggested that there was a need for this type of store and that I happened to own a prime property to put it on. Imagine my delight when I got an email back from one of Mr. Gluba's project managers at Cerberus Capital Management and a phone call asking for more information. I got that information from Mr. Kiss, our property manager, and Miss Feldshuh, our attorney, and the process that led to this meeting today was off and running.

"Now, I will turn the floor over to Mr. Gluba and let him tell everyone what they hope to do with my little idea. Mr. Gluba?"

Marvin Gluba was a stocky, balding man in his fifties. He wore a carefully tailored gray suit, red tie and thick glasses. He nodded to Susan and began speaking, "Thank you Miss Fisher. It was indeed a fortuitous email you sent my staff. You see, it had only been two weeks before that when our corporate executive board had approved a business plan to move into the Eastern Seaboard with the Jewel Superstore Concept. Cerberus Capital Management is a major investment firm has a broad mix of business entities and investment partnerships, including different retail chains under our corporate umbrella, all across the country, California to New England. For those of you not familiar with Cerberus Capital Management or Jewel Stores, we have put a folder with our corporate information at each place at the table. We are headquartered in New York and have a different geographic focus than Jewel's previous owners, Supervalu, with their Minnesota headquarters. Jewel is, of course, one of our flagship chains and a broadly recognized, historic retail brand, Jewel Tea Company, established over a century ago in Chicago. You may have heard of the 'Jewel Tea Man' who was an iconic door-to-door salesman in early 20th Century America. But, after Cerberus' recent acquisition of several retail store brands from Supervalu, we realized this retail mix did not have any significant presence in the major metropolitan Eastern Markets. We, from a total different perspective than Miss Fisher, had made the same conclusion about the potential of the New York and other Eastern cities' marketplaces. We were in the process of reassigning managers to the new project when one of our marketing people happened on Miss Fisher's email proposal.

"To explain why we were so intrigued at Miss Fisher's proposal, I want to show you a couple of graphics we used at that executive board meeting, discussing our entry into the big Eastern markets." Gluba picked up a controller and turned on the big display screen. An outline map of Manhattan in gray surrounded by blue New York Harbor and East River appeared. "You see, to explain what we were going to try, we used the island of Manhattan as our example to our top executives and investment partners. To this basic geographic map, we added some carefully studied demographic data."

He clicked the controller and Manhattan changed color, into a pattern of cubes and rectangles in red and pink. "This is our graphic of the population density of Manhattan, the highest concentrations of people per square mile are the deepest, bright red, lesser density shading off to grayish pink. Then we overlaid this information with demographic data on the mean household income of the residents, that is, the buying power of those residents." As he spoke the reds morphed and many areas brightened.

"So, here is the map of the best places in Manhattan in regards to potential purchasing power of the most populace. We didn't use either just density or buying power, because for groceries, even the poorest people are good customers, and a wealthy populace gets just as hungry as the poorer, they just buy different priced food to satiate themselves. But, *all* groups love great selection and good prices."

Gluba changed pages of his notes, and continued, "To these market data we needed to add our competition. Not the mom and pop, and smaller stores that are every few blocks in New York, but the major food retailers who would fill the niche we intended to fill. We found that the major nationwide players just were not in the market, as Miss Fisher herself determined. So, if you add the few Food Emporiums, Fairway Markets, plus some others and even the Whole Foods, which are really a niche seller as Miss Fisher correctly deduced, but with big stores …" He clicked the controller and bright white dots appeared in random areas of Manhattan, overlaying the red pattern.

Gluba continued, "So, with this very simple graphic, you can clearly see where the Manhattan buying public is at and where the big stores are at. And, everyone in this room can see the glaring holes in this graphic." He picked up a laser pointer and flashed it on the screen, "Here, here, here and all along here. There appeared to be huge markets, in many parts of the city, which were not being served by high volume grocers. So imagine our interest when this woman from New York contacted us immediately after that and suggested she had a property she wanted to suggest for a superstore site, right here." Gluba clicked the controller again and a yellow "X" appeared on the lower left side of the map in the middle of the strongest red color, and far away from the nearest white competition dot.

"Susan Fisher's gut instinct had confirmed what it had taken our crack team of Wharton MBAs weeks to figure out…" he paused while the snickers died down, "– the Chelsea/Garment District area of Manhattan needs a superstore. And, this is what we intend to do about it … Rudy?"

A young man sitting in the chairs against the wall ran up to the big six foot square cube on the table in the front of the room and pulled the blue shroud off of the cube. It revealed an architectural model of the "problem building," but with several prominent changes, a new façade on the lower two floors and around the top floor, large 'Jewel' marquees running vertically on each corner, and 'Jewel Superstore' spelled out horizontally on both of the faces the people could see.

Gluba gestured to the building and said, "Behold the proposed Jewel Superstore on lower 10th in Manhattan."

Gluba waited for the murmurs to die down and continued. "The best part of this is that thanks to a remodeling idea of Metzger Companies' Mr. Laszlo

Kiss and with the skills of our design team from PRK Nickerson of Trenton, New Jersey," He gestured to some people sitting in the middle of his side of the table. "... we are going to be able to utilize the existing structure, but with a major remodel, instead of the new construction we assumed we would have to do in an urban area. That will cut eighteen months and tens of millions of dollars off of the effort to open our first new store. Now, let me turn to the experts, first the design team, then the marketing and operations team, and finally, the attorneys and finance people, who are going to package this as a business entity."

—

Devorah flipped the pages of her legal pad closed to indicate her explanation of financing and legal structure of the new partnership was drawing closed. "So, while I may have given some of you more than you wanted to hear about real estate investment trusts and limited partnerships, let's just conclude that with these arrangements we have proposed you will have a well-financed, dynamically capable ownership structure for fifty years to come. Jewel will have the real property base to enter the New York market in very short order, and the built-in financing they need for the capital outlay without the need for further investment from their corporate parent company. The owners of the building will have a nearly guaranteed income easily commensurate with the value of the property they are contributing and as far as I can tell, it is a win-win situation for everybody, including the grocery buying residents of Chelsea, of whom I am one. If anyone has any further questions, I am sure each of the presenters you have heard from will be willing to answer those questions while we partake of the refreshments available at the back of the room."

As everyone stood up, Marvin Gluba jumped up, raising his arms and, in a loud voice, said, "Whoa, whoa, just a minute. Before we break, our Jewel Stores Development Team at Cerberus Capital Management has one more proposal to make." Everyone quieted to listen to him.

He was facing Peter Ephraim across the table and he said, "Mr. Ephraim, I want to say how impressed and appreciative Cerberus Capital Management and Jewel Stores is with the efficient and trouble free manner the negotiations, financing and transactional preparations for this project have been. To get this done in a few short months is amazing. Therefore, we wanted to suggest to Wassermann, Ephraim and Moore, if you can get the Metzger families' waiver of any apparent conflicts in representation, for Miss Feldshuh and your people at this firm to represent Jewel Stores in our acquisition process and development of the other Jewel Superstores we intend to put in the New York area in the next few years. Who knows, maybe the Metzger Companies have another diamond in the rough we can work together on, and whether or not that works out, we want Miss Feldshuh to put together a package like this for those future efforts."

Peter Ephraim smiled broadly and raised his eyebrows at Devorah who seemed shocked and at Aaron and Susan, standing on either side of her, who were congratulating her.

Peter said, "Well, if that pat on the back from Aaron Metzger is any prelude to a conflict waiver from the Metzger trusts, I think our firm and Miss Feldshuh would be most happy to represent a major corporation like yours."

—

Chapter Thirty-One

"You sure the living room wouldn't be better than here in the family room?" Susan asked Paul as they surveyed the room. "We'll have to move all the boxes and stuff."

Paul walked over to the boxes by the back wall. He spied the three framed documents sitting on top of the open 'Rothmann' box. He looked down at the top frame. "You've got your grandparents' *ketubah*?"

"Yes, Aunt Rachel left all of that for me." Susan watched as Paul picked up the old *ketubah* and studied it.

"Would you mind if I took a picture of this? It's beautiful, all the gold leaf and highlighting." Paul asked.

"Feel free."

Paul took out his smart phone and selected the camera app. He adjusted the frame to try and get the glare off of it. "Susy, can you hold it like this… so the glass doesn't glare?"

Susan did as he asked. Then she asked, "Why do you need a photo of this?"

Paul gave a little smile, "Oh, it's a really classy example of a nicely decorated *ketubah*."

Susan smiled back, "Yeh, I'd guess you never know when you might need a marriage contract handy, just in case. Huh?"

Paul did not answer, but took several shots from different angles. He sat the frame back with the others and said, "I think this room is the best for the family events. Your living room is so formal. You've got the new television in here and the old couches aren't that bad. The wood floor is a great place to spin the *dreidel* with Gillian and Jordan. Where do you want me to move the boxes?"

"I've never had a *dreidel*. Heard of 'em, but never had one." Susan shrugged.

"My goodness, what a deprived childhood! No *dreidel*. You did have a *menorah* though, right?"

"I've got two *menorahs*. Rachel left me a beautiful, big, golden one."

"Let's see."

———

Julie Waldman Bello stepped through the kitchen door and announced to Susan and Betsy Waldman, "Table is all set. Baby is awake. Crowd is hungry. What is next for me?"

"Green beans need to be drained in the colander and potatoes mashed and whipped. And the formula bottle is ready on the stove." Betsy answered.

"I'll feed the baby," announced Julie.

"Huh, uh, I already called that." Susan protested.

"Come on girls let's not fight. He eats every three hours, there's plenty of opportunity for all," Betsy chided the other two.

Susan quickly grabbed the bottle from the pan of water on the smaller stove and stepped around Julie with her tongue stuck out in jest. Julie reluctantly took the lid off the pressure cooker full of potatoes.

—

Greta Waldman looked into Susan's family room where her husband, their two sons and son-in-law were watching her grandchildren play a river rafting game on the new Xbox Paul had purchased. When Paul looked up, Greta motioned to him, crooking her finger for him to follow her.

Outside she told him, "Follow me, you gotta see this. It's precious. Keep quiet."

As they walked down the hallway into Susan's foyer, Greta walked quietly and to the far left side, as though she were keeping out of someone's sight. Near the dining room door she put her finger to her lips, and pointed for Paul to carefully peek around the corner of the sitting room door.

In the far end of the sitting room, on the plush, red chaise lounge, Susan was reclining on her side, her head on the pillowed end of the chaise with Betsy and Ed's new baby cradled in her left arm, feeding the baby with a bottle. Susan had a beatific smile on her face and she seemed to be singing a song very softly to the baby. Paul pulled his head back from the peeking and nodded to his mother with a grin. They quietly retreated away from the sitting room.

As they walked back down the hallway, Greta told her son, "Paul, you do realize that she is a keeper. Right?"

"Yes, Mother, that thought had occurred to me."

—

Susan sat back in her chair and looked around at the Waldman family surrounding the dining room table. The dinner had been a marvelous success. Everyone was completely satiated with the food. It was obvious that they all felt the afterglow of the wine. The blessings, the conversation and the memories shared around the table during the meal had been wonderful to listen to. The retrospective Ted and Greta gave their children with their stories of the past thirty years was easily as informative as the narrative Susan had gotten from Aunt Rachel's videos.

During dinner, little Gillian had been given the task to light the fifth candle on Rachel's big golden menorah on the table by the stained glass window in the dining room.

The conversation around the table had come back to the present and everyone was exchanging current events with one another.

"So, Betsy, I understand you're trying to get back to work at the art museum?" Julie asked her sister-in-law.

"Oh, nothing full time, just helping out with the new expansion. The university has received a new grant, and it has been a wonderful shot in the arm. They are trying to get the new wing decorated and with a full complement of pieces for the opening in March."

Susan's interest was piqued by this and she asked, "What kind of new pieces are you looking for?"

Betsy finished her sip of wine and answered, "The new wing is meant as an American wing. The museum already was a great classical collection and lots of ethnic art. This will be paintings and sculpture from exclusively American artists, focused on the 20th Century. We are hunting for opportunities to collect and exhibit the great uniquely American painters like John Singer Sargent, Wyeth, Hopper, Remington, Cucuel, and Stebbins…"

"Stebbins isn't that…," Paul interrupted, asking his question of Susan.

Susan quickly held up her hand, quieting Paul, and she looked at Betsy, "Betsy, let me get this right, you are trying to find paintings by Cucuel, Stebbins and the like to exhibit in a new wing of your university's museum?"

"Yes, why?" Betsy looked quizzically at Susan.

Susan gave a smug smile and said, "Betsy, if you finished you're your dinner, I think you need to come see something."

"Can I come, too?" Paul asked.

"Oh, yes, any of you can come. But, I think Betsy is going to enjoy this the most."

Susan went to where her purse was hanging on a hook inside the kitchen door. She pulled her key ring from her purse. The entire Waldman family except Julie, who stayed with the baby, followed Susan out her front door and across the hall.

Susan stood in front of the door to Apartment 6-A and turned sideways. She pushed Paul back away from the door with the back on her hand, "Paul, you need to step back, so they can see me."

Susan turned to look up at the video camera Peter Ephraim had ordered installed on the wall above the apartment door. She pushed a button on the black box by the door and smiled toward the camera. In a moment they heard a deep voice, "Security desk, how can I help you?"

"This is Susan Fisher, my code word is Chocolate Éclair, I am entering with, uh, eight guests."

After a short pause they heard, "Good evening, Miss Fisher, you are clear to enter, let us know when you are done."

"Thank you," Susan said as she put her key into the first deadbolt lock.

"Okay, I'm sufficiently impressed," Paul stated.

Susan smiled, "Just wait."

Susan turned on the light in the entranceway and picked up a clipboard on the folding table that had been put there when the art appraisal contractors has done their work in September and October. She flipped through the pages of the clipboard until she found what she was looking for and she turned to Betsy, "Betsy, shall we start with Stebbins, he's my favorite."

Susan turned on the overhead light in what had once been the living room. It now had several metal racks with paintings carefully arranged and numbered. She went to the third rack from the left, checked numbers and selected a Stebbins painting of a famous movie star. "Paul could you take this one out and hold it up for us to see?"

Paul did as instructed.

"That's one of his silver screen period. It's original?" Betsy asked. Her eyes were wide.

Susan huffed at this, and then quickly added, "Sorry, didn't mean to be rude, but yes, everything here is original."

"And, you have more Stebbinses?" Betsy asked.

"Yes, and a few Cucuels, too. And one Remington. Plus many more of that ilk. And, if those are the kind of thing you are interested in, this place is a treasure house."

"And, these are yours?" Betsy semi-blubbered.

"Well, no, they belong to a foundation," was Susan's answer.

Betsy asked, "And, how would I get…, or how could we get some of these to exhibit in Boston?"

"You'd have to talk to the foundation."

"How do I do that? I'm really interested." Betsy's excitement showed on her face.

Susan stepped back, did a quick Pirouette spin that sent her skirt billowing out. She pantomimed putting on a different hat._She offered her hand to Betsy to shake, "Yes, Mrs. Waldman, how can the Foundation help you."

"God, Susy, you are a smart-ass sometimes," Paul exclaimed.

Susan winked at Paul, "I try. It keeps life interesting."

—

Chapter Thirty-Two

Twitter by @SusyFisher: Here comes the Bride! Heidi @PoodyTat Hapsburg (soon-to-be Harkness) looks ethereal on her wedding day

—

Paul Waldman parked the rental car in the parking lot. He took another look at the aerial photo map of the Augustana College campus that Susan had emailed to his cellphone. The college campus was just as he had pictured it on this sunny, mid-winter Saturday afternoon. It had lots of trees and ivy-covered brick buildings -- a classic college campus that reminded him a bit of his years at Princeton, but on a smaller scale. However, the thigh-high piles of plowed snow alongside the sidewalks and roadways were something he had never seen in coastal New Jersey. But, in spite of the piled snow, the bright sun made the day fairly warm and some of the snow was melting. Paul really did not need the overcoat Susan had warned him to wear for the trip.

He followed the signs directing him to Ascension Chapel, walking up the pathway and saw the campus chapel. It was not the quaint, little chapel he had envisioned. It was an impressive church. Paul saw a cluster of men standing to one side of a covered archway leading to the chapel, two of them wore formal blue military uniforms. He pulled out his cellphone and pushed the redial button.

It took longer than normal for Susan to answer. When Susan answered he simply said, "I'm here. By the arches."

"Okay, I'll be right out," Susan said.

After a moment's wait, Paul saw Susan coming out of a door to the chapel. She was resplendent in a floor-length blue and white bridesmaid's dress. She threw her arms around Paul and kissed him.

He returned her kiss and hug, and then pulled her out to arm's length, saying, "I thought there was a rule that the guests at a wedding shouldn't try to overshadow the bride. You look positively awesome. The bride has to be jealous."

Susan shook her head, "Ah, no. You couldn't be more wrong. Heidi looks like a golden-haired fairytale princess today. She cannot possibly be jealous of anybody. Glad you made it. Just in time. Any problems?"

"No, your little airport isn't exactly difficult to navigate and how could they possibly need a six lane freeway with so little traffic. But, I wish I could have come out with you."

Susan again shook her head, "No, this is fine. You would really have been in the way. Heidi and I, and her Mom and sister have been doing bridesy, women's stuff these last three days. Getting me into this dress and things."

Paul looked around and said, "So, this is the scene of the infamous 'All the Angels are Jewish' story,"

Susan smiled, "Yes, right where we are standing. Here, let me introduce you to the groom. You can talk to him, and then go find your seat. We'll be going in about ten minutes."

Susan waived to the cluster of men by the archway and shouted, "Greg, Greg!"

One of the men in military uniform came over to them.

Susan said, "Greg, meet Dr. Paul Waldman, my guy, Paul meet Greg Harkness, the male romantic lead for our little event today."

The men shook hands.

"I'll let you two get to know each other. I need to get back inside," Susan said, as she nervously checked her watch.

Paul looked at the diamond Rolex on Susan's wrist and said, "You're wearing a watch? I've never seen you wear a watch before."

Susan patted her satin-encased midriff with both hands and said, "No place to stick my iPhone to keep time with in an outfit like this, 'cept maybe in my garter and that would be tough to retrieve. Sorry, gotta run." Susan lifted her dress hem and scurried into the church, disappearing inside.

Paul turned to Greg, "So, I know Heidi was Susan's best friend, since school days. Did you know Susan, too? Before?"

Greg nodded, "It is kind of hard not to know people on a little campus like Augustana. I had one class with Susan, her last year. I took a class from her father, before he passed away. In fact, I was in his class when he had his stroke. And, Susan and I had a date once upon a time, just one. I think we mutually understood that we did not have the right mix to ever make a romance work. We both had too much Yang and not enough Yin, or vice versa. You know, opposites attract. Plus, Susy had her sights set farther afield than I did. But, I can see why Susan and Heidi get along so well, they are pretty Yin versus Yang themselves. I actually met Heidi as a friends' recommendation from Susan's Facebook page. And now, Heidi has managed to Yin herself into all the voids my Yang leaves open. That's why I am happy to meet you, to see who Susan thinks will Yin her Yang, so to speak."

Paul smiled at this. "Speaking of voids, you wouldn't happen to be the one who told Susan about Sartre's deep, dark hole in the soul, would you?"

Gregg said, "Yes, that would be me. She seemed to be struggling with religion and with her parents' death, she wasn't sure how to deal with how she fit into things. How's she doing with all that?"

"She seems to be getting a handle on things. But, she isn't really good with talking about how she's feeling deep inside." He indicated Greg's military uniform, "Army Lieutenant. Susy didn't mention that you're in the military?"

Greg nodded, "Iowa National Guard now, just got my commission in December. But, I was active duty, enlisted back a few years ago, in Afghanistan. My best man served with me there, actually my boss, I worked for him as his Chaplain's assistant. Heidi thought it would be cool to have us in our dress blues, instead of tuxedoes. And, what the bride wants is all that matters on a day like this."

Paul nodded his agreement.

A middle-aged woman in blue satin religious vestments calling to Greg from the church doors interrupted them. Both men looked toward her.

Greg said, "Well, it's time. My mother is officiating today, and I'd better follow orders. Nice meeting you."

Paul followed Greg Harkness, his best man and Reverend Ingrid Harkness into Ascension Chapel.

—

The Ramada Inn room in Moline had two queen beds in it, but only one had been slept in. Paul lay spread-eagled under the sheet listening to Susan finish in the bathroom.

Susan came out and set her make-up bag on the dresser. She carefully moved the water glass in which the bridal bouquet she had caught the day before was sitting.

"After I caught Heidi's bouquet yesterday, Greg came over and whispered something in your ear. Would you mind telling me what he said?" Susan asked.

"There is no big secret. He was pretty much telling me the obvious." Paul replied. "I think his exact words were 'You're toast, Doctor Waldman.'"

Susan laughed, "Yes, Heidi's toss kind of sealed your fate."

As Susan carefully folded her bridesmaid's dress into her red Louis Vuitton bag, she said to Paul, "You need to get up now, we have to be going."

"The plane doesn't leave until ten o'clock. It won't take that long to get breakfast," Paul protested, as he nevertheless started to get out of bed.

"Besides breakfast, I have one more errand I need to run before I leave town. Get moving!" Susan ordered.

—

Seeing where Susan told him to turn, Paul finally understood the nature of Susan's last errand. He followed Susan's direction and pulled their rental car onto the frontage road. He could see the two gray headstones with the Star of David on them, close to the road.

Paul got out and ran around to open Susan's door for her. Instead of following Paul to the graves, Susan opened the back door and retrieved something from the back seat.

As Paul waited for Susan to catch up to him, he saw that she had the bridal bouquet in her hand. They walked through the melting snow on the ground and stood by the graves of Jeffrey and Rebecca Fisher.

"I wish I could have known them," Paul said.

"Me, too." Then Susan added, "I read somewhere that Jews don't usually put flowers on graves, I never knew that and really don't understand why, but I wanted to bring this here." She held up the bouquet.

"Only one bouquet. You could put it in between them," Paul suggested.

Susan shook her head, "Oh, no, I already thought of that. This is a bridal bouquet. It goes to Mom." And she bent and carefully fanned the brilliantly colored bouquet out against the gray of her mother's headstone.

After a moment's pause, Paul asked Susan, "Would it be all right if I said something? Here, over their graves?"

Susan thought and answered, "Please." She stepped back from the grave and over to stand beside Paul, taking hold of his arm.

"I certainly can't say the whole thing, but once upon a time I had to memorize the Kaddish and I can remember the end," Paul said as he bowed his head, as did Susan.

"Y'hei sh'lama raba min sh'maya v'chayim aleinu v'al kol Yis'ra'eil. Oseh shalom bim'romav hu ya'aseh shalom aleinu v'al kol Yis'ra'eil."

Paul paused a moment, and then they both added, "Amen," in unison.

When Susan finally released her grip on Paul's arm, he turned and looked at her. He reached up and carefully wiped a tear from her cheek.

Susan lifted her wrist to look at Aunt Rachel's watch.

"Time to go?" Paul asked.

Susan nodded, "Yes, time to head back home to New York."

—

Chapter Thirty-Three

As class concluded, Susan opened the canvas satchel she used as her book bag and stuck the Hebrew grammar text into the bag next to the other books she had used for classes that morning. Her second semester at Columbia was definitely different, curriculum wise, than she would have thought last summer. Now, in the spring term, this Hebrew class was really the only true liberal arts class she was taking, which was a total turnaround from her studies at Augustana. She was comfortable with this change.

Paul was waiting for Susan outside of Fayerweather Hall after she finished the early afternoon Hebrew language class. She had her fluffy white down parka over her ivory cable knit sweater and jeans. She zipped it up to her neck in the cold January air. She could see Paul had her out-dressed with a gray overcoat over a dark suit and tie.

"What is with your clothes? You are just coming from the hospital, aren't you? You never wear a suit."

"I had to sit on a board of review for one of the residents. The hospital wants you to look the part," Paul lied.

"Are you going to tell me where we are going? You are never secretive like this. Mysterious text messages, 'Meet me in front of Fayerweather at 2 o'clock. I want to take you 'someplace special.' And now, you are dressed like you are going to court or a funeral."

Susan thought she saw Paul smile at this.

"If I told you, it wouldn't be a surprise." Paul said, as he took her hand and led her across the main courtyard of Columbia, past the library.

Seeing where they were headed, Susan asked, "So, we're taking the subway?"

"Yup," was all he answered.

Susan took Paul's hand and followed his lead across Columbia's campus over to the Broadway intersection toward the No.1 Train subway stop. Susan shifted her book bag on her shoulder. Paul looked over at her and held out his hand.

"Let me carry that for you," he said.

Susan looked at Paul and smiled. "It's been a long time since some boy offered to carry my books for me." She pantomimed another tally mark for Paul in the air as she handed him the bag.

"God. What all you got in here?" Paul hefted the canvas haversack in the air to check its weight, and then set in on the sidewalk. He flipped the flap open and checked the books.

"Hebrew, yeh. But, what's with Organic Chemistry and Statistics. Whoa! Cell and Molecular Biology? What the hell happened to our Art History major?" Paul flipped the bag flap closed and looked at Susan.

"Who says I am an Art History major?" Susan raised her eyebrows.

"You did. You told me about the great Renaissance class you took last semester. And, you've got the piles of your art provenance stuff piled in your apartment." Paul moved the book bag to his shoulder and took Susan's hand again, continuing on past the domed Library.

"I didn't say I was an Art History major here at Columbia. That was my major when I was at Augustana. I told you they admitted me as an undecided major. I had to request acceptance by the department. You just assumed I had done that. You never really asked me about that."

"Well, I assumed you would have mentioned anything else. What are you going to major in? You never really talked to me about that." Paul sounded annoyed.

Susan said, "Don't give me that tone. I tried many times to talk to you about this. I told you in our very first conversation on the roof about how I had started to wonder after my parents died whether art and history was something I wanted to spend my life doing. We just never got all the way into the conversation to talk about what I thought about for an alternative. Anyway, I did tell you about this before. Remember when I visited you at the clinic and I was able to suggest 'meniscus' for you when you forgot the word? Huh?"

"Yeh, what? You took a human anatomy course. I assumed that was for your art studies, you know, anatomy for figure study."

"Well, last semester I also took a Biology for Science majors course and a course in Psychology. I told you about the Psychology class, too. I asked you for help on the terms. And, I got A's across the board," Susan bragged.

"Yes, you mentioned the good grades you got. And, everybody can take Psychology. So, where is all this leading?" Paul turned down the sidewalk to the south.

"You should be able to see it. What do Cellular Biology, Statistics, Psychology, Organic Chemistry and the Physics elective I took back at Augustana sound like to you?"

Paul stopped and turned to face Susan on the sidewalk. "They sound like the pre-requisite list for taking the MCAT."

Susan batted her eyelashes at Paul.

"You're prepping for medical school entrance exams?"

Susan smiled, "My academic advisor says that I have all my general studies requirements in the transfer credits I brought from Augustana. If I stick to a full schedule I can finish the upper division stuff for Pre-Med in the next year. And, my grades are great, easily good enough. The academic advisor gave me the go-ahead and the assistant dean of the College approved my major change to Pre-Med, so I could get into the advanced upper division classes I need."

"You switched to a Pre-Med major and didn't even talk it over with me?"

"I thought you'd be happy. And, that I could surprise you."

"Well, I guess I am happy. It's just such a change. I never saw you as a Pre-Med type." Paul turned to start walking again.

"Why not a…, a…, Pre-Med type. Not smart enough? Not cut out for it? Not what?" Now, Susan sounded annoyed.

"Of course you're smart enough. Easily so. I just never thought you had an interest. It seems so new for you. Where'd that come from anyway?" Paul stopped at the intersection to wait for the light to cross over to the subway station.

As they walked across, Susan spoke and animated her words with her free hand, pointing and gesturing towards Paul, "Well, dear sweet medical doctor, that shouldn't be too hard to figure out either. I've had a pretty bad year of it this last year. My father died of a stroke, my mother died of cancer in a really horrible way, my aunt, that's my last remaining blood relative, by the way, she died of cancer, and then I got the shit kicked out of me last summer and had to be put back together again. Each of those events was centered on what a medical doctor either did, tried to do or couldn't do. And then, I met this guy in New York. He knocks my socks off, like totally. He talks to me about his work, explains what he does to reassemble broken bodies and shattered lives, and he tells me all about what is needed to live healthy. He nurses me back from my horrible injuries. He takes me to his clinic and shows me how he can heal people. This guy that I find myself totally in love with has dedicated his life to being the best doctor he can be. So, if I am able, and I think I am, then maybe I should dedicate my life to the same thing. Especially, since it seems we are thinking and planning about living our lives together. Paul, jump in here and tell me if I'm wrong."

They reached the opposite curb and headed for the green globes marking the stairway down to the subway.

"Why didn't we go down the stairs across the street? I always do." Susan asked, pointing behind them.

"Because that stairway takes you down to the northbound platform. I don't like to walk through all the tunnels under the street to get to southbound." Paul continued, "Susan, medical school is a hell of a lot of work, and you really don't need that, do you? It is not like you need a job to survive. With your inheritance, you could never have to work a day in your life." Paul glanced over at Susan who met his glance.

Susan explained, "Yeh, of course, I thought of that. I have thought of it a hundred times since this whole inheritance thing fell in my lap. But, just because I became independently wealthy doesn't mean I have to give up on having a life's work that is fulfilling and uses my abilities to its maximum. Lots of wealthy people have pursued careers when they didn't have to. All of the Kennedys and the Rockefellers didn't have to spend their lives in public service. There are lots of other examples. I want to do something important with my life, and not be just some, some… rich bimbo with a platinum credit card and a seat on some charity board."

They each pulled out their MetroPass and went through the turnstile to the subway platform. Paul grabbed Susan's hand again and led her out of the crowd of people, over to the dirty, ceramic tile-covered wall of the tunnel. He turned to give Susan a kiss, "I think it is a wonderful idea, don't know why I never thought of it. I was just surprised when you dropped a planned career change on me out of the blue. You'll make a wonderful doctor. It will take some planning though, we can't have a pregnant medical resident running around, although there is some precedent. But, we can work it out."

"You are already making plans about getting me pregnant?" Susan asked.

"The thought had crossed my mind. And, don't deny you haven't thought on that. I saw you holding Betsy's new baby for her. You looked positively jealous, as well as perfect in the role. Mom pointed it out to me, we peaked at you while you were feeding the baby in your little corner room."

Susan gave a little, embarrassed roll of her eyes. "I can wait. If Julie can do it, I can do it," Susan stated firmly. "You're really not going to tell me where we're going?"

Paul shook his head. They heard the southbound No. 1 Line start to rumble in. They hurried to the platform.

—

Susan was totally turned around when Paul switched from the No. 1 Train to the Q Train at Times Square Station. In her few months as a New York resident, Susan had never had need nor opportunity to ride the Q Train subway. She had a vague recollection of someone saying the "Q" stood for Queens. Her only trips to Queens had been for Rachel's burial and in taxis to catch the flights at La Guardia Airport. Where was Paul going?

Susan had some general idea of where they were when Paul got off at a stop for the Q Train labeled 'Lexington Avenue." They had not gone all the way to Queens, but Susan had no idea where exactly they were until they came up the exit stairway. She saw the building across the street.

"We're going to Bloomingdale's? What for?" Susan asked.

Paul actually laughed aloud at her. "No, not hardly, but nice try."

Paul took her hand again and led her around the corner, and up Lexington Avenue north.

Paul walked Susan determinedly north on Lexington. He looked at his watch and picked up the pace. Susan was glad she was in tennis shoes, and that she had a warm jacket.

Several blocks north Susan was looking at the crosswalk ahead of them, when Paul pulled her arm and took a turn down a side street. The street seemed to look vaguely familiar, but so did almost all of New York's streets. It was only when Paul stopped mid-block and straightened his tie that Susan looked around and realized she knew where she was.

"Uncle Aaron's house?" Susan gasped.

"It took you long enough." Paul took her hand again and led her up the steps.

"What? Why? Paul!" Susan said to Paul as he ignored her.

As before when she was on this porch, the door opened before they had a chance to knock. A black-uniformed maid opened the door and said, "They are expecting you. In the living room."

"Aaron and Myra?" Susan asked Paul.

Paul motioned for Susan to go in first and said, "You'll see soon enough. Just be quiet and go with the flow. Trust me."

The maid held out her arm to take their coats. Paul also gave her the book bag. The maid led Susan and Paul across the foyer to the living room. Myra met them in the foyer. Susan noticed a slight dip of Myra's eyebrows as she looked down Susan's jeans.

Myra shook Paul's hand briefly, gave Susan a hug and a kiss on the cheek, then she leaned in to whisper to Susan, "You should keep quiet and let the men speak until they ask for you. You understand?"

"Uh, Okay," was all Susan could think of to say. Her brow wrinkled in confusion.

When Susan saw who awaited them in the living room, her hand went up to her mouth. She gave an audible gasp as she, at last, realized what was happening. Everyone in the room looked at her -- Peter Ephraim and the fat, old rabbi from

Aunt Rachel's funeral --whose name Susan could not remember-- sat with Aaron Metzger on the left hand couch. Bubba Hannah sat on the right, on the other couch that had been moved to face the first. The three men in the room stood up as Susan and Paul entered.

Susan said, "Paul?"

Paul gave a little smile, and then he walked in to shake hands with Peter, the rabbi and Aaron. Susan now realized she should have understood what was going on as soon as she saw the Metzger house. Between the couches was a coffee table that had several cups with saucers and a black fedora on it.

After shaking hands with Paul, Peter walked over quickly and took Susan's hand in a lengthy grasp that really was not a handshake at all. He just looked into her eyes and smiled, before he went back to his seat. Aaron also smiled, but he was busy directing Paul to a single chair placed at the far end of the two couches. The rabbi just seemed to stare at Susan, or maybe that was her imagination. She saw the rabbi look down at her jeans.

Before Aaron could come over to Susan, Myra took Susan's arm and led her to the couch past Bubba Hannah. As Susan came close to her, Hannah struggled to her feet using the arm of the couch, reaching up for an assist in rising from Susan. When she was up, Hannah gave Susan a strong hug, the kind that Susan had learned to expect from Hannah. When she saw Susan start to speak to her, Hannah gave Susan a single finger to the lips signal to keep quiet. Susan looked at Hannah's clothes and realized that everyone in the room was dressed rather formally, except her. She felt silly in her jeans, Reeboks and fluffy sweater.

Myra turned to sit next to Hannah and motioned to Susan to sit on the end, nearest Paul. When the three women sat down, the men followed.

Aaron said to Paul, "I assume from Susan's reaction and her wardrobe that coming here today for this was a surprise to her."

Paul smiled, "Yes, I thought she would love a wonderful surprise like this."

"But, you have discussed this *Ketubah* with her?" Aaron asked in a firm tone. Aaron held out his hand to the rabbi, who gave him what looked like a rolled up parchment, encircled by a large, engraved silver ring.

Paul nodded, "Oh, yes. In fact, she wrote it. I had the preamble part translated from draft wedding vows she wrote and gave to me. And most of the traditional commitment part is taken directly from the *Ketubah* of Susan's grandparents, the Rothmanns, which Susan provided me." Paul smiled at Susan.

Aaron unrolled the scroll and dropped the heavy silver ring on the coffee table. The ring started to spin and wobble in a noisy death spiral on the table. Aaron quickly swatted it to a stop. He looked at the scroll for a moment, and then looked toward Paul.

Aaron said, "I understand that this has been approved by Rabbi Roth of Temple Israel, in Connecticut. He advised you and signed his approval of this?"

"Yes," Paul answered.

Aaron handed the scroll to Paul, who quickly pulled the scroll out flat.

"Paul Moishe Waldman, do you propose this as your *Ketubah* with Susan Rachel Fisher."

Paul looked over to Susan and said, "Yes."

Now Peter Ephraim spoke up, "And Paul, you understand that the clause I told you to add to the vows, this *Ketubah*, requires a separate prenuptial agreement to be signed in which you renounce any claim against Susan's assets or inheritance for a period of fifteen years, and after that such claim being conditioned upon living issue being born of the marriage?"

Susan raised her eyebrows at Peter's words. She looked quickly at Paul.

Paul stared at Peter and answered, "I agree to whatever Susan's family and advisors require. I have no claim on her assets and require nothing reciprocal in return from her." It sounded to Susan like Paul had been coached by Peter on this line, he recited it too mechanically. Paul handed the scroll back to Aaron.

Aaron pressed his lips together in an expression that further dimpled the cleft in his chin and gave a slow nod. He looked to the rabbi and Peter, who both nodded. Then, Aaron partially rose and handed the parchment across the coffee table to Susan. He asked, "Susan Rachel Fisher, is this *Ketubah* satisfactory to you?"

Susan unrolled the parchment. The entire elaborately decorated and gold embossed page was written in delicately hand-lettered Hebrew script, although Susan understood it was really in Aramaic. Looking at this document, Susan realized it was a true work of art, and probably very expensive in this day and age. It was easily the artistic equal of the *Ketubah* of her grandparents. The only thing Susan could remotely discern from the page were the two names written in Romanesque calligraphy at the very top, hers and Paul's, and with her second semester knowledge of the Hebrew alphabet, she could make out their names underneath each Roman lettered name. She saw several blank signature lines on the bottom, with a signature line with some hand printed Hebrew at the very bottom, along with a similar another blank next to it.

Susan thought for a minute and said, "I don't need a pre-nuptial with Paul, but I defer to the advice of my counsel and uncle that they think it is important, since Paul also agrees. If this is a true translation of the vows I drafted and my grandparents' marriage contract that I gave to Paul for his review, then this *Ki…* *Ketubah* is satisfactory."

Susan handed the scroll back. Aaron took it and handed it to the rabbi.

"I certify this *Ketubah* is in compliance with *Halakha*," the rabbi declared. The rabbi took out a fountain pen from his coat pocket and wrote in Hebrew on the scroll, near the other Hebrew signature, and handed it to Aaron.

Aaron blew on the wet ink, and then rolled the scroll tightly, inserted it back in the silver ring saying, "Then I give my approval to this *Ketubah* as the patriarch of Susan's family. I think we are done for today. We can wait for Susan to discuss this with Paul's mother and Myra, and schedule a wedding date when we can get this *Ketubah* signed and witnessed."

Aaron stood up, followed by everyone else.

Susan's heart was pounding. She wanted to embrace Paul, but saw that Aaron immediately took Paul's hand. The rabbi and Peter were waiting to shake Paul's hand also. Susan felt a hand on her arm. She turned to find that Hannah had pushed past Myra and was ready to give Susan another smothering hug. During the hug Susan heard the rabbi tell Paul, "Mazeltov!"

After the hug from Hannah, it was Myra's turn to hug Susan.

The Rabbi already had his hat on to leave after congratulating Paul. The rabbi shook hands with the Peter, Aaron, Hannah, and Myra. But, when Susan stepped forward and raised her hand, the rabbi quickly tipped his hat to Susan, and turned to leave, in a rush. Hannah escorted him to the other room. After the rabbi turned away, Susan turned to Myra raising her hands, palms up, in a question of what was wrong with the rabbi.

Myra repressed a laugh at Susan, "Oh, my dear. You are '*niddah.*' Rabbi Berenson is very much an old school Conservative rabbi, he practices *shomer negiah* like the Orthodox do, and won't touch an unmarried woman, even to shake her hand." Myra then added, "I can explain sometime. Or, better yet, you can ask Paul to explain. That is his job now."

Peter Ephraim came to Susan, took her hand, but pulled her toward him and down a bit, so the short attorney could reach to kiss her cheek. "A good choice, Susan. I think this will save me some counseling work. I hope you don't mind me helping Paul keep his secret. We'll talk soon. It looks like Paul has something to say to you."

Peter turned, and Myra and Aaron walked him to the front door, leaving Susan and Paul alone in the Metzger living room.

Paul stepped around the coffee table and reached for Susan, saying, "My betrothed," and drew her into his arms.

Susan kissed him, but then pushed herself back away from his body a bit, saying, "Yes, this was a good surprise, but you realize there will be retribution for dragging me into this room, for something this momentous, in blue jeans and tennis shoes. I do not know where, and I do not know when, but I will have my revenge. And, you are complicit in this somewhat sexist summit today, in which the little lady is told to keep quiet until the menfolk give her permission to speak." She glared at Paul with a stern gaze for a moment, before a smile curled at the edge of her lips.

Paul replied, "Well, the main purpose of this 'summit' under Jewish law is to promise the 'little lady' a deal she can live with, for a lifetime. But…Yes, I am guilty as charged and I will accept my punishment. But, be gentle, I had good intentions."

Paul and Susan kissed again. Then, Susan looked into Paul's eyes, reached her right hand up where he could see it and marked one check mark in the air.

—

Chapter Thirty-Four

Mrs. Susan Fisher Waldman

c/o Wassermann, Ephraim and Moore, P.C.

Mail Stop 4614-26

New York, NY 10019-4614

Dear Mrs. Waldman:

My probation officer got me your address and suggested I write this letter in preparation for my probation report to the Judge. She is helping me with this letter.

I see you are married now. Congrats, hope you are happy.

I want to start out by thanking you again for your act of kindness and forgiveness in court that day. It really did change my life. I did not know how to react to you asking the judge to show me mercy when I had caused you such pain and injury. I followed your advice, and the judge's order, and watched *Les Miserables*. I understand now what you did and I cannot offer enough thanks for your doing that.

You know that I used your letter of credit to pay for a chef's course at a culinary academy. But, I want to let you know I have completed the course. I have always liked to cook and I seem to be a natural at it, like my Grandma. I have now been employed for several months at Amontillado's Restaurant in the Financial District. I was recently promoted to reserve Sous-Chef, so things are going well for me.

I also wanted to let you know that I sold the earrings you gave me, as you suggested that I do. Like you, I had no wish to wear them and I was able to put the money to good use. My probation officer and my advisor at the culinary school both told me that if I wanted to get a good job in food service, I needed to get rid of the gang tattoos. So, I used the money from selling your earrings to pay for tattoo removal at a dermatologist who works with the Probation Department. I know you do not expect to be paid back for the earrings, but I would like to offer that.

I am engaged to Alan Saltzmann, the Maître-D' at Amontillado's. He is quite a bit older than me, but treats me like a princess, which is a new thing in my life. I was honest with him about my past and I told him the story of what you did for me. I bought the DVD, so he watched the *Les Miserables* movie with me.

I had dinner last Sunday with my family and fiancé. I told them I was writing this letter to you. My grandma told me to tell you she often lights candles at the cathedral and gives thanks to the Savior for the act of forgiveness you gave me. I know you are not Catholic and may not understand that, but my fiancé is Jewish and he says I should just tell you that what you did was a really fine mitzvah. One last thing, my fiancé, Alan, and I decided that when we get married and have children, we will name our daughter Susan after the wonderful woman who changed her mother's life. If you ever want to stop by Amontillado's, please let the Maître D' know who you are and I will prepare the best meal you ever ate.

Forever Grateful,
Carmen Amador

—

The End

About the Author

Kevin E. Ready

Kevin Ready studied Government and Politics at the University of Maryland Univestiy College in Berlin, Germany and received his Juris Doctor degree from the University of Denver. He had four decades of experience as a US Navy officer, US Army officer and government attorney. He has twice been a major party candidate for US Congress. Kevin E. Ready lives in the Santa Barbara, California with his wife, Olga and children. He is the author and editor of several books.

—

Visit Kevin's website at   http://www.KevinReady.net
Kevin produces a blog on Politics and the Law at
http://www.LawfulPolitics.com

Other Books by Kevin E. Ready:

The Big One (1997)

Gaia Weeps - The Crisis of Global Warming (1998)

The Holy Koran - Modern English Translation (editor) (2014)

Credit Sense: How to Borrow Money and Manage Debt (1989)

<u>and with **Cap Parlier:**</u>

TWA 800 - Accident or Incident? (1998)

all the Angels were Jewish

by

Kevin E. Ready

Published by

Saint Gaudens Press

Wichita, Kansas — Santa Barbara, California

http://www.SaintGaudensPress.com

**Saint Gaudens, Saint Gaudens Press
and the Winged Liberty colophon
are trademarks of Saint Gaudens Press**
Copyright © 2014 Sarah Sarnoff
All rights reserved.
eBook ISBN: 978-0-943039-31-2
Print edition ISBN: 978-0-943039-20-6
Printed in the United States of America

SAINT
GAUDENS